BENEATH BLA[CK]
~ III ~

Under Black Skies

Clare Sager

Copyright © 2021 by Clare Sager

All rights reserved.

No part of this book may be reproduced in any form or by any electronic or mechanical means, including information storage and retrieval systems, without written permission from the author, except for the use of brief quotations in a book review.

To everyone who's ever blamed themselves for someone else's decisions, someone else's actions.

IMPATIENCE

Despite the sea breeze, the air was already thick with heat and sweat. The low morning sun forced Vice to shield her eyes as she left the quarterdeck's cabins. Even the cries and clatter of work were quieter than usual, as if the weather had dulled everyone's energy, leaving only lacklustre shanties ghosting the air.

A cheer broke the muffled quiet. Then laughter… clapping… a gruff shout.

Vice stalked towards the noise. Men and women had grouped together, backs to her.

Crowding wasn't so unusual—with Munroe's Navy crew still aboard, space was at even more of a premium than normal. But to see a couple of dozen pirates *and* Navy sailors gathered…

Trouble—had to be.

"Come on," someone shouted.

"Hit him!"

She groaned. This would be the fourth fight she'd broken up in as many days. Surprise, surprise, the Royal Navy mixed with pirates about as well as oil with water.

"Not this again." Rolling her eyes, she pushed through the crowd. "Out of the way, you bloodthirsty—"

A flash of white hair. *Knigh*. Her body coiled, ready to spring forward.

She blinked, stopping short. He and Aedan wore brown leather practice gloves. Not a fight, just sparring.

Something in her chest remained tight, her heart thrumming against it.

The pair circled, eyes locked together. Their bare torsos gleamed with sweat, highlighting each ripple of movement, each tensed sinew, each shift in stance.

Not sparing her a glance, Knigh passed, broad shoulders squared. The shadows of his muscles merged into the dark lines tattooed over his upper back—the moon and stars of the Blackwood family crest.

Aedan's frown deepened, leaving a look intense for a man normally so carefree. As he moved, she caught glimpses of the twin swallows inked across his chest in blue and black.

Two men both over six feet tall, muscular, skilled fighters—no wonder they'd drawn an audience.

A jab, a dodge. Vice twitched as if she were in the ring, as if her actions would keep Knigh from Aedan's strikes.

A right hook, the slap of leather on flesh, a whoosh of air forced from lungs.

She rocked on the balls of her feet and had to catch herself before she ran forward and pulled Knigh away to safety.

Sparring, not danger.

Aedan backed off a step and waited for Knigh to catch his breath.

Although that strike must've been hard, it was only a moment before Knigh looked up, teeth flashing in a fierce grin.

Uh-oh, Aedan was in trouble now. Vice swallowed, the sweet taste of victory already on her tongue.

Knigh sprung at him, jabbed for his belly, but at the last instant he pulled the blow.

Aedan had already taken the bait, defence low and ready for a strike that never came.

That left his cheek open as Knigh connected, the punch so fast Vice would've missed it if she'd blinked.

But watching this fight, blinking was out of the question. Her heart thundered, and the grunt that came from Aedan was as bright in her bones as if it were her own victory.

Hands fisted at her side, she exhaled, long and low, trying to expel some of the energy that had her twitching and tensing over a fight that wasn't hers.

They circled again, bringing Knigh almost in arm's reach. Tanned... tall... hair a little scruffy in contrast with the close-trimmed beard emphasising the angle of his jaw and the perfect lines of his cheekbones...

Wild Hunt take her if he wasn't good to look at.

And that was the problem—she was looking at him too much. Far, far too much for *just friends*.

She straightened, clearing her throat. She had things to do —primarily *not* loitering to stare at Knigh Blackwood.

Get a grip. She pressed through the crowd, heading fore again.

She'd just checked on Barnacle in the captain's cabin, which, thanks to the presence of two crews, she was sharing with Perry. Unsurprisingly, the little grey cat was in the sea chest she'd claimed as they'd fled the sinking *Respair*. Her cushion had survived. Its declaration of *non obsequiorum—we do not submit*—somewhat at odds with her position lying with half-shut eyes.

All four kittens were tucked against her, a row of wriggling fluffy bodies. They let out the occasional mew or squeak as they fought over the best spot. Vice, Knigh, and Perry had named the kittens now. The girl who looked like a miniature version of Barnacle was Flotsam. Her sister was a pale silvery tabby, and they'd called her Jetsam. The two boys were Anchor and Cable, the former all black and the latter a dark smoky tabby like their father.

Barnacle had accepted the fuss and chin scratches and hadn't so much as miaowed as Vice grumbled at the delay to their plans. Saba and Perry had been less understanding of, as Perry put it, her *bloody impatience*.

Five nights ago, as they'd sailed away from the *Sovereign*, Knigh had shown her the shape of Hewanorra's twin mountains in the jagged edge of Drake's poetry. And she'd been itching to get there ever since.

If not for this diversion to Redland, they'd already *be* in Hewanorra. She'd be uncovering the next clue to Drake's treasure this very second.

But they'd agreed to leave Munroe and his crew in a safe place. And Ichirouganaim fit the bill.

She nodded to Wynn and Effie as she passed. The sisters waved, then went back to inspecting the port cannons's gunlocks and side arms.

Called Redland by most Albionic folk, Ichirouganaim was also Saba's homeland. Munroe and his men would have no concerns about food, water, or survival, and Saba's mother would welcome them. Once the *Venatrix* and its new pirate crew were far away, she'd get a message to the Royal Navy saying their crew were there and in need of assistance.

At least Hewanorra was only a day's sail from—

"Vee," Knigh's voice carried over the deck, "hold on!"

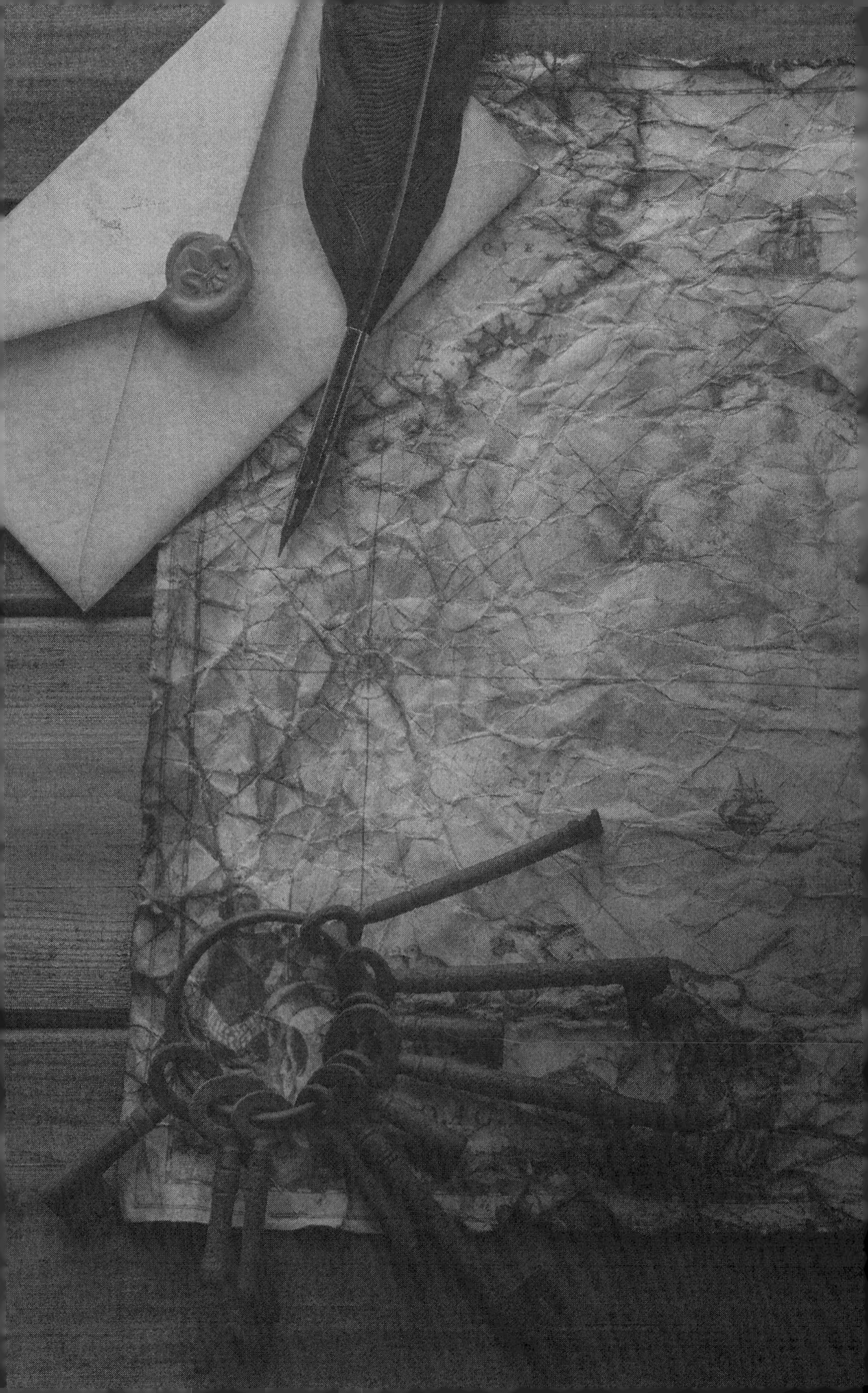

JUST FRIENDS

Vice's stomach fluttered. Ridiculous thing—it didn't seem to understand they were just friends.

Steeling herself, she slowed and let him catch up. Still shirtless.

Bollocks.

Her heart beat harder, faster, a distant thudding in her ears.

"I have a proposal for you." His smile dazzled in the low morning sun as he dropped into step beside her. "Good gods, it's hot." He squeezed a soaking towel over himself, sending water trickling down the taut lines of his shoulders and chest. A low sigh escaped his lips, and he wrung the towel out over his head, plastering his hair around his face in a way that simply *begged* her to smooth it back.

Stop staring.

Grimacing, she scrubbed her eyes to hide the expression

and shield herself from him. Double-bollocks. She *had* been staring. *Hard.*

She clenched her hands against the want—the want to grab his arm and make him face her. The want to slide up over that chest and into his thick hair, to try to squash that white streak that refused to be tamed.

In short, the desperate want for Knigh Blackwood.

Gods damn it.

This was ridiculous. *She* was ridiculous.

She'd been with plenty of attractive lovers—Aedan was handsome and drew looks wherever he went. And although dark-haired, intense FitzRoy was his opposite in almost every way, he won his fair share of admiring glances. So why the hells did the mere proximity of Knigh Blackwood have this power over her?

As further excuse to avoid looking at him, she checked over her shoulder. The crowd had dispersed, and Aedan stood alone, wiping himself down. *He* was still shirtless and gleaming, and yet she didn't itch to grab him. There was something wrong with her.

In control of herself again, she cleared her throat and chanced raising an eyebrow at Knigh. "You two really bonded while I was gone."

"*Because* you were gone, and we were both losing our minds over it." He shook his head, grin fading below a brief frown as he looked aft. "Though I must confess I'm puzzled, considering he was ready to shoot me when we returned from Albion and then I almost…"

Cut his arm off on the Sovereign.

She inclined her head, wincing. That was her fault. And the sudden change that came over him tied a knot in her gut.

Instead of sinking into gloom, Knigh exhaled, and the corner of his mouth lifted. "But I'm trying not to question it too much. I'm just glad to have a friend on board."

Somehow, *his* relief eased *her* belly. "Don't you mean *another* friend?" She cocked her head and flashed him a smile. "You've got Me, Perry, Aedan, Barnacle..."

His mouth twisted, but amusement sparked in his narrowed eyes. "We're having to count the cat now?"

"Hey, she's a very discerning cat."

He scoffed, fingers scraping against the trimmed beard at his jaw. "This is true."

"But seriously—you also saved Aedan's life that day, and you've more than proved yourself to the crew. You came after me"—her stomach flipped to say it, so close to his words *I'll always come for you*—"even though that meant attacking the Navy's flagship *and* her division. And you saved them all when the *Respair* sank."

"*You* saved—"

"There wouldn't have been anyone *to* save, if you hadn't evacuated so quickly. Just accept it, Knigh"—she grinned up at him—"you're one of us now."

"*One of us.*" He said it like it was a cause for wonder—his mouth softening, no longer sardonic. His gaze roved over her face as though he might find the hint of a lie there.

Maybe he believed it at last. Maybe he felt like he belonged here.

Maybe he'd want to stay, even once they had Drake's treasure.

With a single nod, she wiped the grin from her face, aiming for something more earnest. Maybe, just *maybe*, despite all the horrible things she'd said and done to him, she could make him feel better and not only worse.

Gods only knew if her expression *was* earnest, but as they moved fore, his grey eyes were still on her—on her mouth, specifically.

Her heart pounded against her ribs, loud in her ears.

Perhaps she wasn't the only one who felt this *thing* that still hung between them.

But it was out of the question. Off limits.

They were *friends*. Not so long ago that had seemed impossible, and it had been a tough battle to get here. But here they were.

No way was she going to ruin that.

When they'd discussed taking Munroe and his crew to Redland, he'd asked, "What about getting back to the Navy?"

But she'd heard the unsaid words in his question: *What about getting back to the Navy, like I cannot?* And they were a dagger in her gut.

So she cocked her head, the picture of light-heartedness, certainly not affected by his presence or intensity. Not in the slightest. "You have a proposal?"

"Oh, er, yes." He shuddered as if ridding himself of confusion—or perhaps of that moment that had stretched out between them.

Ahead, the low, green mass of Redland rose from the glittering sea. The breeze ruffled her hair, briny and fresh, tinged with distant smoke. They'd dock within half an hour, and it would take maybe an hour to drop off Munroe and his crew.

Then they could finally set sail for Hewanorra.

They stopped at the bow—she with a smile, he with a preoccupied frown.

His knuckles turned white as he gripped the rail and leant back against it. "The thing is, I can't spar with Aedan all the time."

"Aedan?" She frowned back towards where they'd been sparring, but there was no sign of their blond friend. What did this have to do with—?

"And this is how whittling went." He held out a lumpy piece of sun-bleached wood. Jagged lines scored their way across the surface, splinters jutting out.

She squinted at the... *thing*. What *was* that?

Face screwed up, he turned it over. "I'm not sure I have Saba's knack for it."

"I wouldn't say that." She tensed her cheeks, attempting an encouraging smile. "It's... it's..."

It was a shape. And it was wood. That was all she had. She willed something recognisable to appear.

An elongated blob with splintery gouges and twisting woodworm holes.

She swallowed. "It's... nice?"

"Don't patronise me." His fingers folded over the *thing* and he shoved it in his pocket. "It's meant to be a whale shark—you know, like at the reef?"

"Oh? Oh. Oh!" She forced her mouth into a bright smile,

rather than the confused grimace she'd given the alleged 'whale shark.' "Well, it's—erm—kind of—"

A low chuckle rumbled through him and raised his eyebrows at her. "Seriously, Vee, don't worry. I've already given up my whittling ambitions—I'll leave that to Saba. Too many splinters, anyway. And frustration is the exact opposite of what I was aiming for."

"So, sparring. Whittling. I must be missing something, because I'm not connecting the dots."

"Ah, yes." His hands opened and closed into loose fists. "Perry said I needed a distraction for my hands and my mind. An activity to focus on and keep me calm."

A pang hit Vice in the chest. Small but definitely sharp, like one of those splinters from his whittling. He was still talking to Perry about the reasons behind his anger—the darkness that made him lose control sometimes.

Since Vice had returned to the crew, she and Knigh had spent every night chatting over rum after the others had drifted to their bunks, catching up on their time apart. He'd told her how talking to Perry was helping make sense of the feelings that plagued him—feelings about his father in particular.

Talking to Perry. Not to her.

And why should he have come to her? Yes, they were friends, but as she'd just said, she wasn't his *only* friend.

If that pang was jealousy, it was stupid. Whoever helped Knigh with his anger, it could only be a good thing. It wasn't like she had any claim over him.

She coughed, as if she could get rid of the troublesome splinter. "An activity?"

"Well." He eyed her sidelong. "I was hoping you'd let me help decipher the Copper Drake. Perry mentioned it was going slowly."

"More like Perry said I'd been moaning about it being utterly glacial."

He cleared his throat, but the twitch at the edge of his mouth betrayed that he was covering a laugh. "The words *grousing* and *bellyaching* might've been uttered. I didn't have the heart to point out the irony that *she* was complaining about *you* complaining."

She chuckled, using it as an excuse to look away from him and delay answering. Working together on the clues would make it quicker.

But it also meant her and him together in a little cabin. Alone. All the time in the world to drink up those little expressions of his—the ones she'd seen echoed on his brother George's face back on the *Sovereign*. Far too much time with the constant warmth of cinnamon, soap, and worn leather in the air.

She caught it now, just lightly, before the breeze swept away all but briny air. It made her suck in a sharp breath, but that only drove the scent of him deeper until she was swimming in it, drowning in it, sweet and spiced and clean.

It would be unbearable. Impossible.

But he was the only other person in the crew who spoke Latium, so it wasn't as though she had a lot of options.

They said 'familiarity breeds contempt.' Maybe time cooped up together was exactly what she needed to get rid of any lingering feelings for him.

"The help would be…"

Ahead, in the open bay, three black-sailed ships cut through the glittering water, not yet at dock. Something about them had stilled the words in her throat. Something was wrong.

A second later, she realised. Black sails. *Full* sails, like voids against the brightly painted buildings beyond.

The ships weren't prepared for docking.

It twitched in her belly.

Still leaning against the rail, Knigh glanced over his shoulder and stiffened. "What's wrong?"

Whose ships were they? And why were they sailing through the bay rather than slowing ready to dock? "Can you see a flag?" She craned to glimpse one.

Now standing to attention, the alertness practically rolled off him. "There." He bent close and pointed.

On the nearest ship—a black flag with a white spear piercing a crimson heart. Whose flag was that? A new captain, perhaps, allying with more experienced crews.

"They're all flying the same," he muttered. "Anyone you—?"

Cannons boomed.

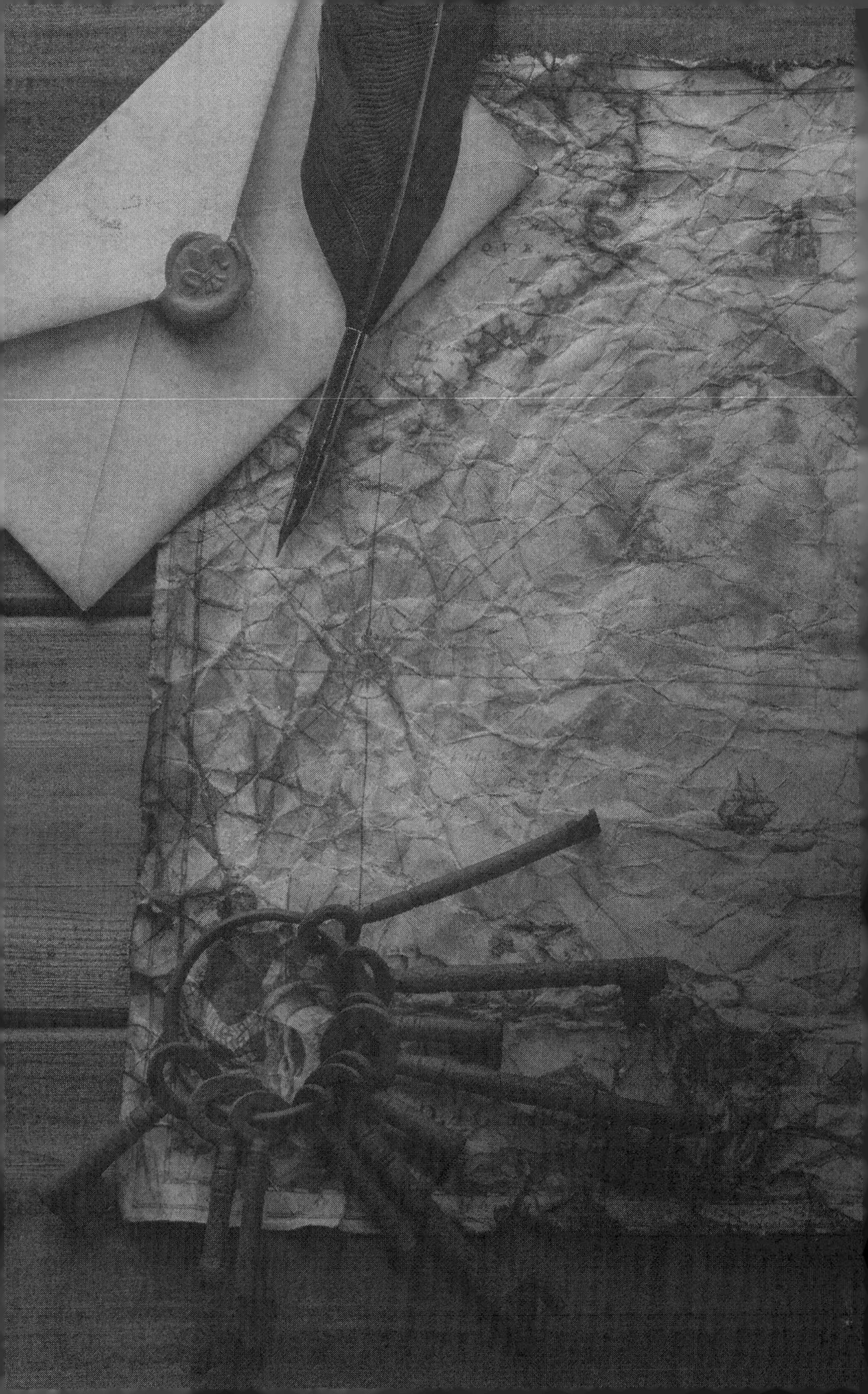

GUESTS

Hurrying through the quiet streets, Knigh scowled at the ships in the bay. Black sails, black flags. But this was a friendly town—why would pirates attack?

Vee had set the currents against the attacking ships, shoving them out to sea for now. But the sounds of gunfire and steel said they'd already made landfall, undoubtedly seeking to loot anything of value they could find.

Knigh, Vee, and dozens of the crew had landed on the southern side of the bay. Munroe had wasted no time in declaring he and his men would join the battle, too—after all, it was the Royal Navy's duty to stop pirates.

Just like it had once been Knigh's.

Somehow, here he was, a pirate himself, and yet still fighting that fight.

He shook his head and ran towards those telltale sounds.

In every direction, doors and shutters were closed. At one upstairs window, a trio of small faces appeared and watched them pass, dark eyes round. Children.

Knigh's chest tightened. A moment later, a woman's face appeared above them. Her mouth dropped open as she spotted him. Brows shooting together, she dragged the children away, leaving only a darkened window.

The best he could do for them was end the attack. He drew his first pistol. From ahead came shouts and the clash of blades.

Vee threw him a glance, her guns ready too, brows low and determined. She inclined her head in a grim nod.

On the other side of her, Saba stared ahead as they jogged closer to the sounds of battle. He and other Albionic folk were just guests on Arawaké's islands, but this was her family. Her homeland. The town where she'd been born and raised. Those battle cries were the shouts of people she knew, men and women she'd grown up with.

If it were his family under threat, his friends, his home, he wouldn't be able to hold off the fury, the terror. He'd berserk. No question.

"Round this corner." Vee huffed as she loped ahead, long legs eating up the distance towards the ring of steel on steel. "Any luck, we'll catch them by surprise."

"Aye, bad luck for them," Saba growled.

Lips tight, Knigh tried to give a reassuring smile as he patted her shoulder. But reassurance wasn't much use right now, was it? All he could do was fight.

He cocked his pistol, already loaded, and sped after Vee.

Heart pounding and ready for battle, he drew level just as they turned.

A group of men in red and white battle-dress stood over two fallen comrades, blades raised in defence. Around them, almost two dozen pirates pressed in, their brown and faded black clothes drab in comparison. Their cutlasses, though—they shone as they beat against the islanders' swords and axes.

"Let's even the odds, shall we?" Vee slowed and levelled her pistols.

"Let's." Knigh matched her, drawing his second gun while he aligned the sights of the first.

A blond man's teeth flashed bright as he hacked at a stocky defender.

Exhale, squeeze the trigger, then the *crack* of gunfire and a plume of acrid smoke.

The blond pirate's head snapped to one side. His cutlass stopped in mid-air. A smear of red appeared at his temple, then he staggered to his knees.

Two more shots sounded an instant later from Vee, and two more pirates fell.

With his other pistol level, Knigh took another stride. His blood ran hot and fast. Attacking other ships that were armed and ready for battle was one thing, but these pirates had attacked a town full of civilians. Families. Farmers. Craftsfolk.

Jaw clenched, he took aim with his second pistol and fired again. Another attacker hit the stone-slabbed road, mouth and eyes open.

With the slapping feet of their team behind, Vee fired once more as they closed the distance. Then there was only the sour stink of sweat, the metallic tang of blood, and the grunt and clash of battle.

He shoved and sliced as they caught the attackers from behind. They were still reacting to the gunfire, still registering that it was *against* them and not their own forces closing in to take down this knot of resistance.

More fool them.

His nose twitched as he ran a woman through before she could cut into a defender.

To his right, Saba and Aedan fought the enemy with sword and axe, Saba shouting in fury with every strike. The island's men fought with grim determination, their broad blades hacking through limbs now the enemy pirates were flanked.

Knigh's heart hammered with each strike, and his muscles burned hot and bright. He sliced and slashed, parried and twisted from a thrusting blade.

At his side, Vee fought just as fiercely, her face bloodied, though she was uninjured.

She was safe. She was well.

The heat in his veins eased.

She feinted, distracting the sharp-chinned man who'd managed to evade every one of Knigh's strikes. The man's blade flicked to catch Vee's false-strike, but she'd already turned her sabre to slash his thigh. He grunted, face screwing up as he looked down at the line of crimson.

A distraction. An opening.

Knigh lunged.

This time, Knigh's blade pierced the air until it hit the resistance of flesh and muscle.

The sharp-chinned man gaped like a fish brought onto land, and a trickle of blood ran down that pointed chin of his, catching in the stubble.

He'd come to kill and take. He'd come where there were children and fisherfolk and artists—peaceful civilians—and he'd have cut through any of them to get to gold or silver or whatever madness he'd come for.

Now he slid off Knigh's blade and slumped to a street that was slick with his own blood.

A well-earned fate.

Only a few attackers remained standing and they were hard-pressed by islanders and *Venatrix* crew alike.

Knigh caught his breath, nose wrinkling an instant later.

Blood and sweat and death, yes, but also... *smoke?*

Not the sulphurous stink of gunpowder, but the homely winter scent of wood smoke. Except this wasn't Albion on a chilly December evening.

"Fire," Vee gasped. Her eyes were on the north.

Knigh followed her line of sight towards the heart of the town. Dark lines of smoke rose against the setting sun.

His heart dropped. "Hells and damnation."

"Those bastards," Saba growled between ragged breaths as the woman before her fell. "They're torching the town."

Fire meant indiscriminate destruction. More cowardice. "Vee, can you—?"

But when he turned, she wasn't at his side.

Movement flickered ahead—Vee running down the street. He took a step after her but stopped, huffing. With her gone, the rest of the team needed a leader.

Saba turned from where she was speaking to one of the men defending the town—tall and slim, he was the youngest amongst them, close to their age. "Go, we'll be fine." Brows drawn together, she nodded towards the smoke. "We'll head for the fires, see if we can help."

He pursed his lips and glanced from Saba to Vee's retreating form. She'd almost gone from sight. "Stay safe." He clapped Aedan on the shoulder before running after Vee.

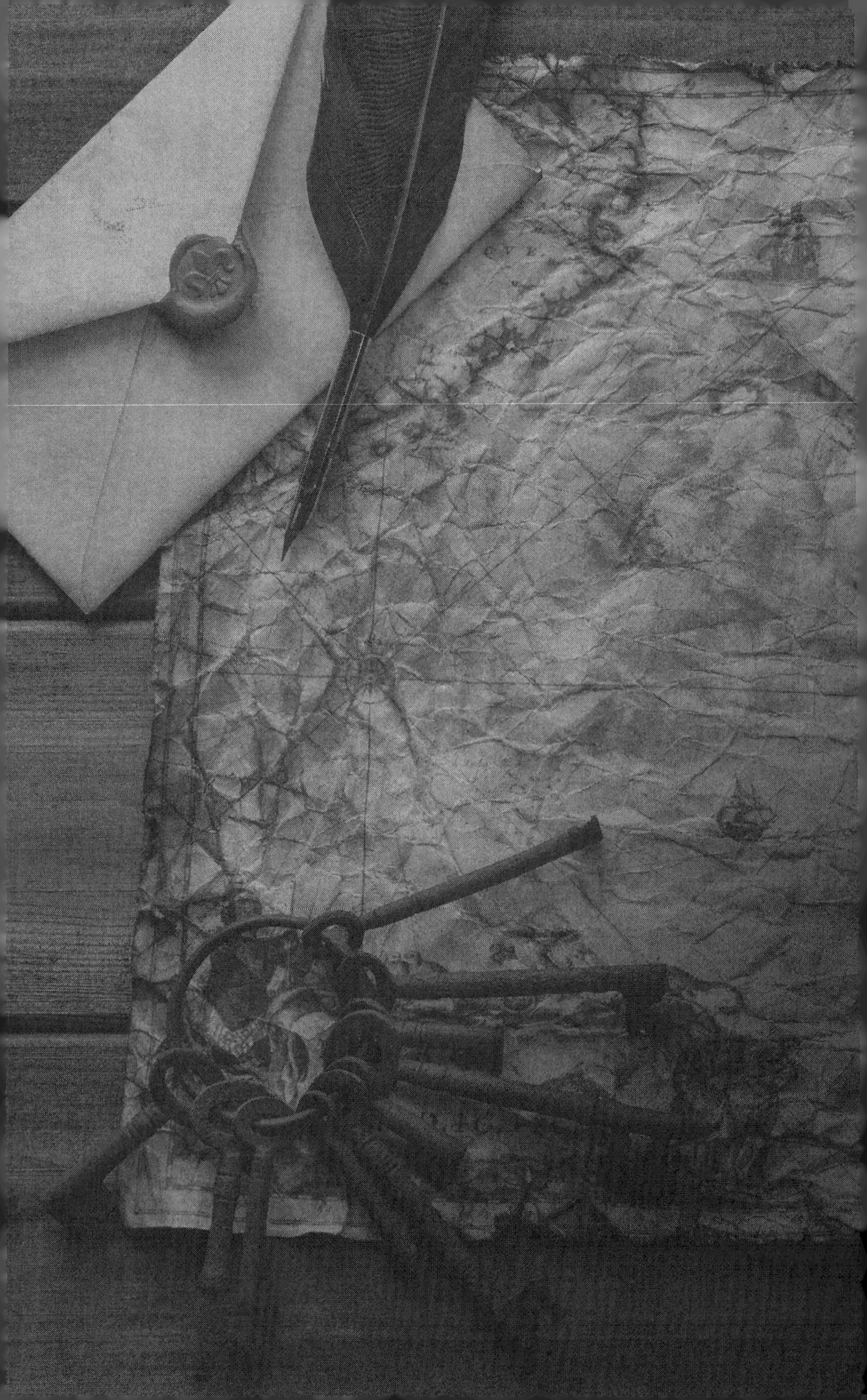

RAIN

Vice charged through Redland's streets. The thickening smell of smoke spurred her on, making her legs and arms pump. Her shirt clung to her in the sticky heat.

A thread of her awareness always pulled towards the sea. As she ran, she let it have its way, drifting across the bay, pulling water into the air, forming puffs of light clouds.

High ground. She needed high ground. If she could see the town properly, she'd make those clouds heavy and thick and let them rain over the fires.

One corner, then another. She kept her eyes fixed on the yellow Sun Tower a few roads away. Taller than the surrounding structures, it would be the perfect spot for working her gift.

Shots and the clash of blades echoed from streets she passed and every instinct pushed her that way. Having sabre and pistol sheathed felt so wrong when battle raged, but if she stopped to help the skirmishes, the fires would rage unchecked.

Scowling, she forced her feet to keep sprinting as she approached more islanders and attackers. The tower was only one street away now. In the distance, the plumes of smoke had grown thicker.

Knuckles tight, she drew her sabre. She couldn't stop, but she could still help. She veered to the left, panting air that grew more acrid by the minute.

Both sides were too absorbed in battle to notice her closing in. A young man amongst the defenders grimaced as he parried attacks from two pirates. They jostled backwards and forwards—if she got too close, she risked getting caught up in the fight and being too late to prevent the fires from doing more damage.

Tucked low, she ran along the attackers' line, two feet behind them. Her blade closed the gap, jerking in her grip as it slashed the backs of their legs.

Cries of pain and surprise and the thud of two enemy pirates falling sounded in her wake.

Maybe she shouldn't smile, but she'd helped, and that eased her guilt at having to run past the fight.

Around another corner, then she reached the square tower's base. Its painted stucco walls stretched up seven storeys—the yellow and gold glorious on any other day. The open sides of its top floor would give a clear view of the town.

Pausing, she wiped off her blade and returned it to its scabbard. With a grunt, she shouldered open the door, then ran up the stone staircase winding around its interior walls. A couple of minutes later, she emerged in the open air, lungs and muscles burning. Leaning on one of the square pillars holding up the roof, she caught her breath.

From up here, the entire town spread out before her. To the north-east, tiered temples and the council hall rose above the low-level houses and workshops. Amongst them spiralled dark streaks of smoke.

Beyond, forest licked at the town's edges—encroaching pockets of trees preserved along most streets. The green shade amongst the stone and stucco structures could've been sacred groves in Albion, except these were mahogany and frangipani rather than oak and ash.

To the west, white sails bobbed at anchor, mostly smaller merchant and fishing vessels. The sea glittered between the shifting canvas.

Black sails approached from the north-west, where the attacking pirates pushed into the current she'd set against them. The *Venatrix* cut across the bay, sailing out to meet them. Alone.

But that was Perry's job, and she had Clovis on the wheel and cannons ready to fire.

Vice's work was here. She centred herself over her feet, hands resting on the rough stone pillar, and let more of her awareness ride out over the bay, joining the part of herself that was already there.

With her help, the air siphoned more moisture from the sea. Fluffy white clouds thickened and grew and darkened. A sudden wind brought them inland.

Squinting, she followed the largest plume of smoke to its

base—near the market square. Bollocks. Timber stalls would be ripe fuel. More plumes snaked above areas that were predominantly stone built. The fire at the market had to be her priority.

She ushered her clouds in place with localised gusts of wind until they merged with the black line of smoke.

Then she let go.

A deluge, thick and drenching, crashed onto rooftops and paving. The electrical scent of petrichor filled the air, even from here, and more smoke billowed from the marketplace fire.

She nodded to herself. That cloud was in the right spot.

More moisture, more clouds, now crowding the sky over the bay.

Hand pressing against the pillar, she tried to pry the clouds apart, but they slipped between her fingers and spilled together like drops of mercury.

Come on.

Her arms ached—she needed to know where the fires were, so this wasn't a time to use the wellspring. She had no sense of place on land like she did at sea, where she'd used her awareness to locate the kraken in the water. Here, if she closed her eyes, her magic would be blind.

She scraped and scratched at the clouds, but they refused to be divided into neat parcels for her to push in place. If she spread one large cloud over all the fires, it would be too thin, too weak to deliver enough rain to drown the flames. The wellspring would allow her to gather plenty of water to snuff out the fire, but…

Back to square one.

Damn it.

Her first cloud had grown wispy, and it felt sluggish, like it was running out of rain. But a thin trail of smoke still drifted up, so she herded this new cloud to join it. Rain sheeted down once more.

Siphoning more water from the sea, she blinked. Wait, it *felt* sluggish. She couldn't feel the land, but she *could* feel her clouds. If she marked the locations of the fires with a wispy cloud, it wouldn't be enough to put them out, *but* it would let her navigate while she dived into the wellspring.

She nodded to herself, grinning. That was it.

With a deep breath, she splayed her fingers, stretching her cloud thin until it stretched over the three plumes of smoke. The one near the marketplace only smoked a weak grey trail now, but the rain had stopped and with dry fuel it might still roar back to life.

Not on my watch.

Her cloud, despite its light, hazy appearance, covered all the fires.

She closed her eyes and dived deep.

Darkness surrounded her, stretching on for what might've been infinity. But here, lightning crackled. Something inside, right at the centre of herself, sparked in answer, bright and humming.

Inhale. Exhale. She was still *out there* as well as *in here*.

And her haze of cloud stretched over a town somewhere out there, its fuzzy form right on the edge of her awareness.

She thrust her hands into the pulsing, crackling power, and it rocked through her.

Every hair on her body stood to attention, the sensation powerful enough that it registered through her separation from the physical world.

Water. Sea. Rain. That's what she'd come here to do.

With one hand, she held the cloud formation in place and with the other, she pulled on her sea.

It gave up its moisture willingly, each minuscule mote glittering in her awareness as it rose into the air and joined others, becoming cloud.

No more wispiness—this was thick and dark and heavy with rain.

So heavy, it was a weight on her shoulders. So thick, if she walked through it, it would've left beads of water on her face and hair.

She let it fall.

Water in, water out. Like breathing.

A century might've passed with her standing there, drawing moisture from the sea to the sky, only to fall again.

Had it been long enough?

Inhale. Exhale.

Fingertips and palm on the rough stone. Feet planted firmly. Here. Now.

A breeze wafted stray hairs onto her face, cooling the sweat on her brow and through her shirt.

No longer siphoning water from the sea, she let what was already in the clouds rain down and peeked out.

The sky spun, the tower's pillar lurched drunkenly. The stone scuffed her skin as she caught herself.

Eyes closed, just for a moment, then the world was right

again.

She blinked away the last of the dizziness and surveyed the town. Her clouds were just pale and white and fluffy now, only releasing a light drizzle.

And beneath them?

No more smoke.

She sagged against the pillar. It was done. And after that much rain, the attackers would be hard-pressed to start any more fires.

She turned towards the bay, lips pursed, when a *crack* tore the air.

The breath caught in her throat. Gunfire. Close.

There had been no fights on the streets below the tower when she'd arrived, but how much time had passed since then?

She craned over the edge and glimpsed flashing steel at the tower's base.

Flashing steel wielded by a man with a wild white streak in his hair.

Knigh, flanked by two enemy pirates. Another lay at his feet.

Her heart leapt to her throat. What the hells was he...?

He must've followed when she'd broken away from the group.

Outnumbered and alone, he could so easily berserk. She couldn't have that on her hands.

"Gods damn it, Knigh," she huffed, voice shaking as she loaded her pistol.

Movement further up the street. Another three pirates, not from her crew, but coming this way.

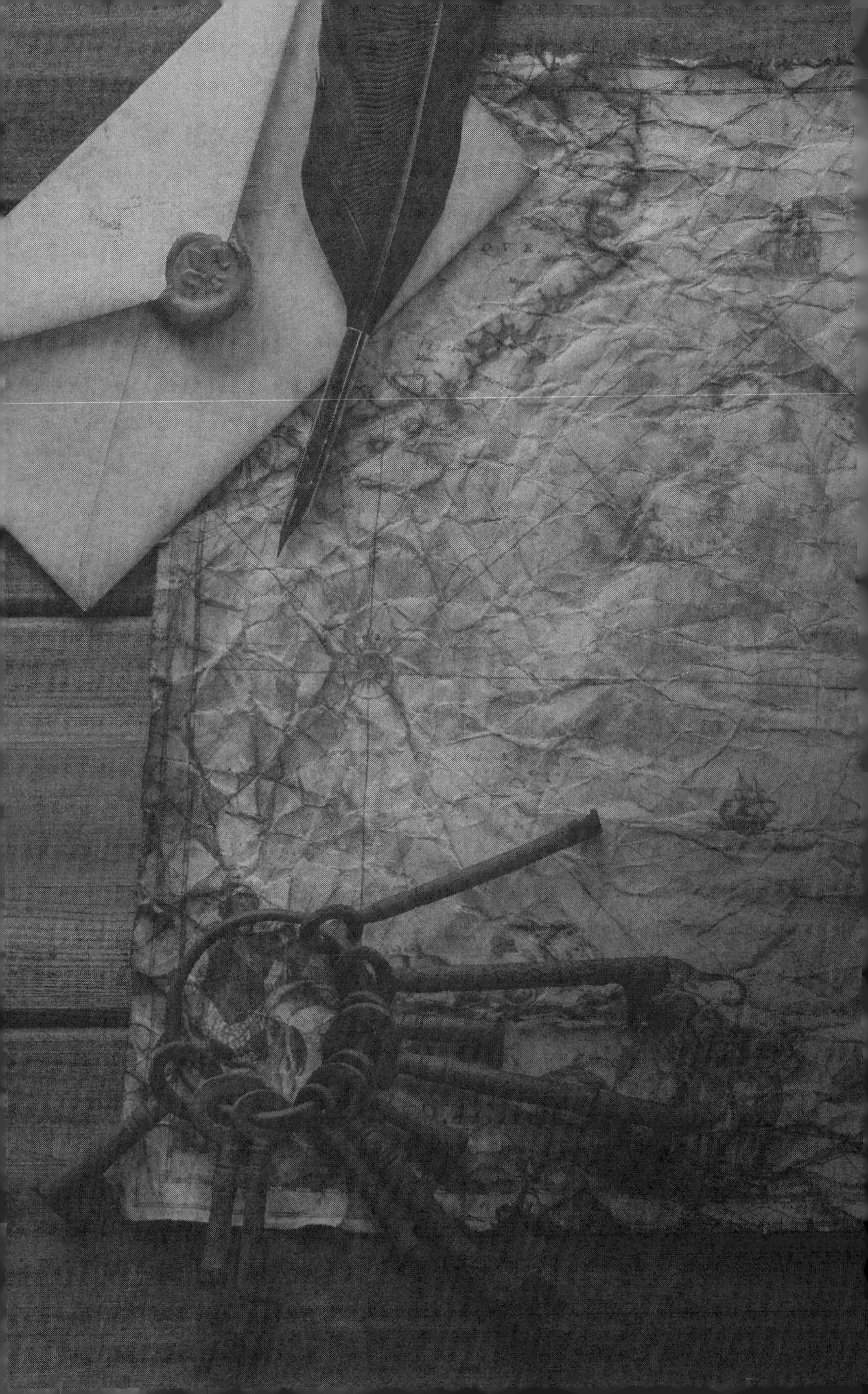

CORNERED

Hack. Slash. Parry.

Knigh's arms burned. Sweat tickled his brow and threatened to drip into his eyes. In his ears, the roar of blood.

The red-haired man to his right snarled, sunburnt skin on his nose wrinkling and cracking. Grunting, he cut down with a powerful but clumsy overhand strike.

Clumsy it might've been, but it required his attention to catch all the same. Jerking his head left, he kept Red and his blond friend in the periphery of his vision.

He'd followed Vee here. Realising she was planning to use her gift to bring rain, he'd lingered at the base of the tower to guard her. Perhaps the attackers had spotted her at the top of the tower, working her gift, or maybe they'd seen him hunched in the doorway and wondered what he might be guarding.

Either way, the trio, Red, Blond, and Brown, had appeared

and attacked. He'd taken Brown quickly, but rather than scaring away the others, it had only made them more determined, as if they wanted to make their comrade's loss worthwhile.

Blond circled further left, attempting a flanking manoeuvre.

Eyes narrowed, Knigh pivoted and took a step away, placing the tower at his back just as he parried another hit from Red. The clang of steel echoed off the walls of the shops opposite, making it sound like a full skirmish rather than only three men.

But there was no time to think of that as his sabre twisted again, barely throwing a thrust from Blond off course.

He darted and sliced a thin line in Blond's shoulder with the dagger in his left hand. But it was only a shallow cut, because Red was already pressing with a series of slashes that jolted through Knigh's sabre and bones.

He grimaced, and the motion sent a trickle of sweat snaking into his eye, stinging.

Shouts came from somewhere down the street. Not voices he recognised. Reinforcements for Red and Blond.

Damnation.

His heart surged, driving the roaring in his ears louder and louder.

... You let us down...

Soft but insistent. In his head.

... and then you left...

His blades flashed, catching the sun breaking through the clouds. Fast. Faster.

Hack. Slash. Parry.

Again.

... You lied...

He kicked Blond's knee, a guttural growl coming out with the strike.

... You ruined us...

No. Stop.

He blinked, taking a jolting step back.

Those thoughts would only lead to berserking.

Breathe. In. Out.

Parry. Parry. Parry.

Lords, it would be easy to sink into that pattern. Thinking of Father summoned hurt and anger that sparked in his muscles and pushed him harder than anything else. But he had to take his thoughts elsewhere...

Sparring with Aedan. Trying to carve that damn wood. Cheese and bread for breakfast. They were safe thoughts.

He nodded as he parried yet again. *I am in control.*

But he wasn't in control of this fight anymore. He couldn't only defend—at some point he'd fail, and then he'd be dead.

Vee's in her gift and I'm her only line of defence... Vee dead... Because of me.

Not safe thoughts.

Perry had suggested keeping his attention on here and now, rather than disappearing into his mind.

One breath. Two. Three.

He couldn't lose this fight, and berserking *had* helped him survive worse odds than this. Perhaps...

But—no—he couldn't give in. He *wouldn't*.

His chest tightened, air entering as desperate rasps. His eyes stung.

Four. Five. Six.

Embrace the rage and survive. Cling onto control and...

In. Out. Seven.

"I will not lose myself," he muttered between gritted teeth.

Red's eyes widened, and he threw a glance at Blond, who only returned a frown of confusion.

Maybe they thought him mad.

Maybe he was.

But they still attacked. One strike, two, three. Clang, clang, clang. His hands buzzed from the reverberation.

Four. Five. Six.

Was he counting hits or breaths?

"Bugg—"

A *crack* tore the air. He was already ducking as the gunshot echoed through the street. Blond and Red's friends must've got in range.

Knigh panted. Gods only knew how many breaths that was. But... wait, he wasn't hurting. They'd missed. Or had the pain just not started yet?

He wiped the sweat from his eyes and brow.

Red and Blond were still. Why hadn't they pressed their advantage?

Then Blond made an odd, choking sound and stumbled back. Red stared, mouth open.

Of course. Their comrades had missed him and hit one of their own. Knigh let out a soft laugh.

But there was no time to dwell on this stroke of luck. He

sprang at Red, blade meeting resistance all too quickly, and ran him through.

The man staggered back, slipping off the sabre and falling to the ground.

Another *crack* echoed.

The man at the head of the approaching pack missed a step, then sprawled across the ground, his run sending him sliding across the paving.

The shot came from above. He glanced up and there she was—Vee peered over the top of the tower, face pale. She nodded, features set in grim lines, then disappeared.

Rolling his shoulders, Knigh spread his feet and waited for the group to reach him. But instead of continuing this way, they turned down another road, footsteps growing quieter.

He huffed, and the roaring in his ears faded. Not such an easy target now he wasn't alone. As he cleaned his sabre and dagger on Red's shirt, he scanned the street. No sign of anyone else.

By the time he straightened and sheathed his blades, Vee came jogging from the tower. Uninjured, though her eyebrows knotted in a glower.

"Are you...?" She examined him, jaw muscles rippling.

"A couple of scratches. Not even worth my time to heal. You look—"

"I'm fine." She waved him off. As she exhaled harshly, she threw her hands down at her sides and started along the same road as the attacking pirates. "What the bloody hells did you come here for?"

He blinked, striding after her. "What did I...?" It was obvious, wasn't it? He'd followed her, he'd defended her. And from the way she acted, she was *annoyed* at the fact. "I came after you."

"I didn't need you to." She folded her arms. "You could've got yourself killed."

"And you could have got *yourself* killed." He huffed, somewhere between laughter and anger. "Why didn't you ask me to come with you? We could've made a plan *together*, brought Aedan along."

She blinked, jaw going slack. "Ask you to..." Frowning, she shook her head. "I... I didn't think to." They jogged on a few more paces, the frown on her brow more thoughtful than annoyed now. "Besides, I couldn't put you in danger like that." A tremor laced her words.

He arched an eyebrow at her, but she only looked ahead, not at him. "But you were happy to dive into it yourself?"

"What happens to me doesn't matter."

"What happens..." he spluttered. Was that what she thought? Was that the truth behind her recklessness? He'd always believed it was simply that life was short and she half-expected to die tomorrow, but this? Feet anchored to the ground, he grabbed her arm and whirled her to a halt a foot away. He stooped, making her meet his gaze, even though her eyes were dark and stormy. "It matters to me."

A frown flickered between her brows as she stared back at him. "You shouldn't..." She gave a small shake of her head. Something about the gesture so vulnerable it lanced through him. Her arm twisted in his grasp, but she didn't pull away—instead she caught his shirt between her fingertips and gave a half-hearted tug. "You shouldn't."

Shouldn't what? Shouldn't care? Shouldn't stand so close that he could smell battle and rain on her? Shouldn't—?

Footsteps from behind—perhaps half a dozen, running.

Drawing weapons, he and Vee spun on their heels. Adrenaline rippled through him and his muscles thrummed, ready for the next fight.

Moments later, six pirates—not *Venatrix* crew—burst into sight from the intersection he and Vee had just crossed. As he angled his blade ready for defence, the strangers didn't spare the two of them a second glance and raced across the road.

"We haven't got time for this," Vee muttered.

Every time she let herself be vulnerable, there had to be some interruption, some reason why *not now,* and the moment was lost. But he nodded. "Agreed."

They ran after the enemy pirates, alert in case it was a trap, ready to stop any attack they might try on the townsfolk. But the pirates seemed intent on running as quickly as they could —taking a straight course until they hit a stretch of sandy beach beside the docks, then turning right.

The sand sank beneath Knigh's feet, making his calves burn as he ran. In thin gaps between the fleeing figures, he caught glimpses of low, dark shapes. "Their boats," he panted. One was already in the water, rowing hard. "They're retreating."

Vee surveyed the backs and shoulders and the shirts grimy with blood, sweat, and dirt. She nodded, triumph glinting in her eyes.

From inland, more feet pounding, accompanied by cries.

The red and white battle gear of the islanders flashed into view. They shouted, weapons raised, chasing off their attackers.

As the pirates scrambled for the nearest boat, Knigh and Vee slowed, letting the islanders harry the launching boats with shrill battle cries and strikes from the flats of their blades.

Hands on his knees, he caught his breath, the air sweet in his lungs.

"You're out of practice, Navy Boy," Vee puffed from a similar position beside him. She flashed a grin.

"You can talk," he huffed. *"Barely."*

She chuckled and straightened, chest still heaving. "Too much time on those clues, pushing pens. Extra duties aloft for both of us, I think."

He groaned, muscles sore at the thought, but the sound was lost in a great cheer as the last boat pushed off into the water. The attackers rowed frantically out to their ships, the *Venatrix* firing once in their wake as she returned to dock with a cracked yard her only visible damage.

Saba appeared between Knigh and Vee. She clapped them on the backs, nodding. "It's done. The battle's over." Her shoulders sagged as she tore her attention from the retreating enemy. "We did it."

Vee squeezed Saba's hand. "The town's safe."

Saba's smile turned stiff in a way that made him glance at Vee in question. But Vee was intent on her friend.

"There'll be a feast tonight," Saba said. "Mother will want us there, you know." At the word *Mother*, her eyes shuttered more.

"Blackwood," Lizzy called from further up the beach.

No time to ask what had dimmed Saba's usual brightness. Knigh nodded to her and Vee, then hurried towards Lizzy. They might have won this battle and tonight there would be a celebration, but right now, he had wounds to mend and lives to save.

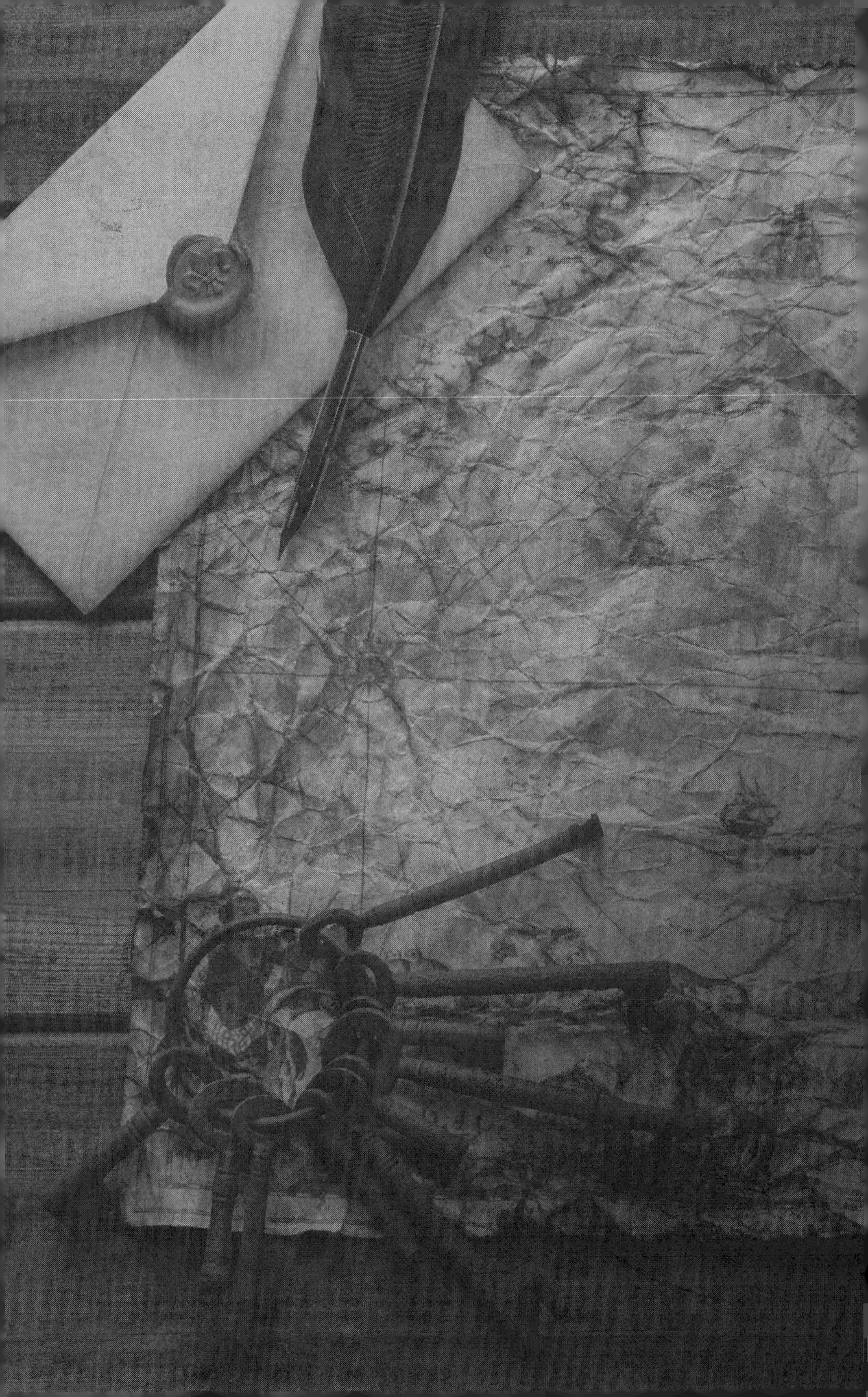

COME BUY

Another night's delay stuck here, rather than setting sail for Hewanorra. The island was so tantalisingly close, too, just a day's travel west. Vice sighed. She could've declined the offer from Saba's mother to stay for the feast, but she couldn't argue with Perry—the *Venatrix* needed repairs and the crew wouldn't want to turn down the chance to eat, drink, and be merry.

Patience, Perry had said before waving her off to enjoy the town with Saba. Vice had grumbled about how if the treasure grew legs and wandered off before they reached it, there'd be hells to pay.

But here she was in the marketplace.

It was as lively as Vice remembered, with towers and tiered temples on all sides reflecting the chatter and cries of "Come buy. Come buy!" The priestesses had performed rituals for the dead, which she'd kept clear of, respecting their privacy. But now that was done, it was like they'd drawn a line under the matter, and the square bustled with local women wearing bright beads and feathers in their hair and at their necks, as busy as usual.

Stalls groaned under the weight of goods. Fish of so many varieties that every time Vice came, she spotted at least one she didn't know. Fruit and vegetables in a similarly dizzying variety. Exquisitely carved wooden goods of every rich shade of brown imaginable. Worked metal from iron tools whose presence tickled the back of her neck to steel weapons, and jewellery of silver, copper, and bright, beautiful *guanín*.

But it wasn't Drake's treasure. She sighed again.

Saba looked past the huge mango to Vice. "Now, I *know* you're not huffing at the quality of wares." Her dark eyes narrowed. "You want after that clue."

Vice only pursed her lips in response. Was she so predictable?

"What difference does it make if we leave tomorrow at first light, like Perry promised, rather than *right now?*" Saba cocked her head, and held out the fruit. "Smell that."

Not much difference to a centuries old clue, true, though what relevance the mango had to the matter was anyone's guess. "Fine, I'll humour you." Vice took the mango, its heft in line with the fact it was as big as her head. Its sunny yellow-blushed-crimson made her smile, despite her frustration. And when she held it to her nose and inhaled, the heady sweetness threatened to overwhelm her, drawing a soft moan from her.

Saba grinned and paid the shopkeeper, a wiry, middle-aged

man who smiled and bowed his head. "See?" She took the fruit from Vice and secured it in a bag over her shoulder. "If we hadn't stayed, you'd never have got to experience that. If it smells this good, just *imagine* what it tastes like." She waggled her dark eyebrows and patted the bag.

Mouth watering, Vice chuckled and waved at the shopkeeper before they carried on along the stalls. "Fair point. Even if it only tastes half as good, I'll still be impressed."

"Trust me. I'll prep it for you later, but I'm claiming the seed."

"Another one for the collection?" Vice asked as they passed a stall selling leather goods, the rich, earthy smell enough to banish the mango's sweetness. It tugged on a memory—large, strong hands on her thighs, grey eyes, a teasing smile.

Gods damn it. A memory of *Knigh*.

Cheeks hot, she coughed and scrubbed a hand over her face, as if that would scrub away the memory. One she was *not* supposed to be lingering on.

Friends. *Just* friends.

Saba gave her a long look, eyebrows rising. Vice stared back and fought to keep her expression neutral, like Knigh's blank mask.

She must've been successful enough, because Saba looked away, lifting one shoulder. "I'll give it to my sister for safekeeping for now. She'll plant it, get it started for me." Pausing, she ran a hand over a red leather bag that gleamed in the late afternoon sun. "Then I'll come back for the pot and take it to its new home. It'll be several years before it bears fruit, but for this variety, it's worth it."

Its new home. The plot of land Saba would one day buy where she'd build a home and studio and start a smallholding to support herself. A long way off yet, but it still twisted in Vice's belly.

Everyone leaves. They leave or let you down or die. As if she needed a reminder from that dark corner of her mind. *Saba's no different.*

Vice sucked in a long breath. Saba wasn't going anywhere yet. She pushed a smile in place, in spite of the discomfort. That home was what Saba wanted from life; Vice couldn't begrudge her it, even if it meant…

"So it'll already have fruit by the time you collect it," she said, voice full of false brightness as she feigned interest in a table of coin purses on the leatherworker's stall. "Will it still be transportable at that size? Ah, no matter"—she shrugged—"I'm sure we'll fit it on the Venatrix for you."

Saba chuckled. "It won't have grown *that* big in a year."

Vice froze, the hairs on the back of her neck straining to attention. She must've misheard. *Must* have. "A year?" She prodded at the purses, unable to stand looking at Saba while she waited for the answer.

"Well, roughly. I mean, you think we're close to"—Saba cleared her throat and came closer, voice lowering—"that *haul*, right?"

The treasure. Vice frowned at Saba, but the smile she found on her friend's face—bright, hopeful, excited—tied that twist inside her belly into a knot. "Gods willing."

Saba's eyes shone as her smile grew. "Perfect. With all the

seeds I've collected over the years and the money I've saved, that will give me the last of what I need to get set up."

"So"—Vice shook her head, throat suddenly tight—"so you mean... But..."

Head cocking, Saba's smile faded to a small frown. "A studio. A *home*. Somewhere to raise children where they're free to be themselves, not"—frown deepening, she glanced at a trio of women walking past with bags of shopping—"not bound by rules because they're boys or girls. It's what I've been working for all these years. You know this."

The knot squeezed tighter. Vice grabbed one of the coin purses and pretended to examine it. "I—I know. I just thought you meant far, *far* in the future. More like a decade than... a year." Those last two words rasped her throat, sharp as broken glass, stinging as salt.

"Aye, this haul brings it closer, but even without that, I'd have saved enough within the next few years. This just means I'll have quality tools, the best stock to get started, and a nicer house."

There it was. She did mean it. She was...

Saba's leaving. Those four syllables tolled in her heart.

Sa-ba's lea-ving.

Ba-dum, da-DUM.

It hurt. And it was heavy. And it made her eyes sore.

But it's what she wants.

Arm stiff like some mechanical marionette, Vice put down the coin purse. A smile creaked in place, pulled by cogs and pulleys. *I'm fine. I don't need her. I don't need anyone*.

"Great." She met Saba's gaze. "That's great."

"You'll be able to visit, you know." One side of Saba's mouth rose in a lopsided smile. "In fact, you'd better, or else."

Vice rolled her eyes. "Hey, is that…?" Beyond Saba, a curved wooden something peeked out from another stall.

Thank the gods, a distraction. Anything was better than talking about this.

If they didn't speak about it, she could pretend Saba wasn't going anywhere for a long, *long* time.

Neck craned, she stalked closer to the stall, which seemed to sell an array of used items from books to clothing. Strings and a neck came into view. "It *is*." A guitar.

Smiling—this one not forced—she picked it up, running her fingers over the strings as Saba appeared at her side. "I haven't seen one of these since…"

The *Covadonga*. When they first took the ship, there had been a guitar on board. And the night they'd celebrated, Knigh had played it. That was also the night they'd first kissed, first slept together, first given in to what had sparked between them for months.

Warmth flooded through her. He'd looked so relaxed as he'd played, toes tapping, staring into the fire.

"The bonfire when Blackwood played." Saba plucked a string, the note coming out as a discordant *twang*. "What happened to that one?"

Vice stilled the trembling string. There had to be a knack to making it sound as beautiful as Knigh did, or perhaps it just needed tuning. "I don't know. It was probably still on *The Morrigan* when… when everything happened."

Saba stiffened, eyebrows rising. "I see."

Vice cleared her throat and turned the instrument. She didn't know guitars; they were more common on the continent than in Albion, so gods only knew what she should look for to ascertain its quality. It didn't appear damaged—no cracks or chips. The wood was smooth and well-lacquered, decorated with a small flourish of inlaid scrollwork at the widest part of the body.

It was a similar size to the one from the *Covadonga*, so it would fit well in Knigh's hands. "I haven't seen him play since..." *Since I told him I killed Avice Ferrers.* But Saba didn't know about that whole mess and no way was Vice going to broadcast or revisit it.

"Hmm, yes, I remember—he stopped playing before I went to the *Covadonga*." Saba surveyed the instrument, a thoughtful frown creasing her brow.

Following her line of sight, Vice traced the strings, letting them bite into her fingertips.

The firelight on his hair; his fingers flying across the strings. The sweet burn of palm wine. Vice shivered at the memory of several nights merging where he'd played and she'd danced, lost in his music. Alone, they'd enjoyed each other, but with the rest of the crew, they pretended—the only touch was his smouldering gaze upon her as she moved to his rhythm, both of them making secret promises for later.

But that was then. Before he'd crushed her with betrayal, and she'd smashed him with her cruelty to push him away. Yet here they still were, bound by Drake's treasure.

His voice did things to her insides that were damn unfair,

but that aside, his playing was still wonderful and seemed to bring a calm over him.

And Perry had said distracting his hands might help with his anger...

Perhaps it could be an apology—she owed him one after snapping earlier. After all, he'd only taken that risk because of her.

The horror of seeing him at the base of the tower, alone and outnumbered, had seized her, near maddened her, a taste of what it must be like for him to berserk. She'd already been responsible for Evered's death. And every night since returning, she'd dreamt of Evans disappearing in that trap and Mercia silencing his cries for help. Last night the two had merged in a horrible replay where Evans fell, but the sound was of a body on deck.

If Knigh had...

She shuddered. It didn't matter if anything happened to her—as far as anyone was concerned, Avice Ferrers was long-dead. She'd already failed Mama. But Knigh's family needed him if they were to ever escape Mercia's clutches. The treasure would free them from—

"It's a shame, really." Saba sighed. "I hate seeing such skilled fingers go to waste."

Vice blinked, looking up from the guitar—she must've been staring.

Saba had made a comment about him being good with his hands the night he'd first played. Definitely a double entendre—the smirk on the edge of her lips confirmed it.

Where normally Vice would've laughed, she frowned at the

uneasy sensation unfurling in her gut.

"Saba!"

They both started and turned to find one of Saba's sisters waving from the end of the lane.

Shoulders sinking, Saba groaned and waved her sister away. "Time to prepare for the feast."

"Come on," Vice put the guitar down, noting where the stall was. She would buy it for Knigh, but doing that in front of Saba would only raise questions she didn't want to answer. She offered Saba her elbow. "It won't be *that* bad."

Lips pursed, Saba looped her arm through Vice's. "It's all right for you," she muttered. "Mother loves everything you do. Hells, I think she loves you more than she does me."

Vice's heart fell. It had been so long since they'd come to Redland, she'd almost forgotten how hard it could be for Saba. "No, she doesn't." They started towards the seafront and the large tiered house Saba's mother lived in as the head of the council. "She just doesn't have expectations of me."

"Expectations *I* fail to live up to." Saba stared ahead, expression sullen.

Vice pulled Saba's chin, forcing her to make eye contact, the fakery of her earlier smile disappeared. "Expectations that are unfair. You hear me?"

The frown didn't fade from Saba's face. Her lips tightened. Thinking about it, maybe, but unsure.

Vice squeezed her hand. "And that's why you're going to start your smallholding and live *your* way and teach your children to be true to themselves."

The smile was genuine, but the twist in her gut remained.

Saba's shoulders lowered, the tension fading. "Thank you." As they walked, she tiptoed and kissed Vice's cheek.

"Besides"—Vice flashed a grin and winked—"if it *is* that bad, you can just drink yourself into oblivion."

Laughing, Saba butted into her. "I'll drink to that."

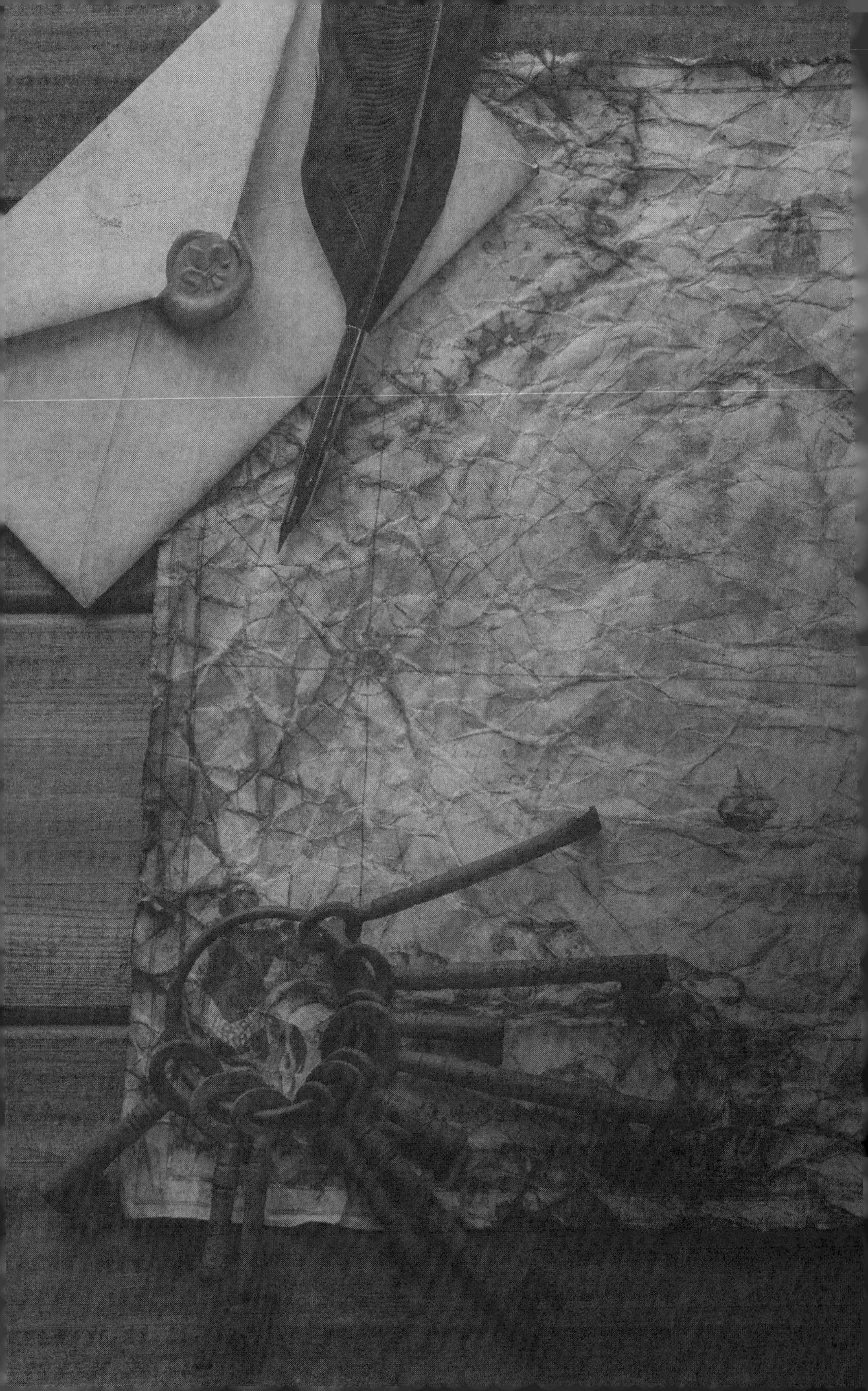

RISKY BUSINESS

Sweet and strong—this was clearly where Saba had learned to make palm wine. His eyes watered as the drink went down, burning. Knigh shook his head at a young lad approaching with another pitcher of the stuff.

No more. Gods. Please.

For the feast, they'd set up long tables in this large paved square near the waterfront. Thanks to Vice's reassurance that no further rain would come, they hadn't erected the leafy awnings and overhead an ink-black sky stretched on and on, stars reaching from horizon to horizon.

Now the feasting was over, apparently it was time for drinking.

Lots and lots of drinking.

Aedan and Saba's voices rose over the general clamour. It sounded like they were setting up a game with her younger siblings and several of the crew.

Munroe stood on the edge of the group, knuckles white on a drink, silent, eyes constantly flicking to Saba. Poor fellow. He was so obviously torn between duty and the desire to make the most of his last hours with Saba, it made Knigh smile.

Were all men who captained the *Venatrix* destined to face that conundrum—naval duty or an alluring pirate?

Perhaps he'd best flee the scene in case his presence made Munroe even more uncomfortable. It had become clear when they'd fled the *Sovereign* and her escort Munroe still looked at Knigh like he was his superior officer.

Knigh snaked away through the crowd, which grew more raucous by the minute. If Munroe thought that, he was a fool—Knigh was well and truly a pirate now.

"Huh." He blinked, then smiled. That thought was no longer the same weight it had been just weeks ago.

Chin up, he scanned the odd assortment of people who'd gathered for the feast. The *Venatrix's* pirates, her former naval crew, and dozens of islanders, all scattered to talk. Clovis and his partner Erec led a game involving pins and a ball. A growing group danced around the musicians who'd just started playing.

At the far end of the square, several older men and women gathered in deep conversation, Saba's mother, Shoko, amongst them. Somehow it had slipped Saba's mind to tell him that her mother was the head of the island's council and much-respected in Arawaké.

Yet Saba roamed the seas as a pirate—now *that* was a question to tuck away for later.

Curious as he was, he hadn't dared ask during the feast when he'd been honoured with a place near the head of the table with Shoko, Perry, and Vee, opposite the other council members.

For all her importance, she'd laughed when Knigh and Munroe had attempted to bow to her, and had smiled and chatted freely over dinner. Trade was good, and the Arawakéan Union was in a state of relative peace. Importing silks from Shénzhōu and dyeing them with local logwood was a profitable business, especially as purple was *the* colour for fine ladies on the mainland and Europa this year.

The only time she'd frowned, the expression strikingly like Saba's, was when she mentioned the recent spate of pirate attacks on the islands. He and Vee had shared puzzled looks at the news. Since pirate hunters from Europa had arrived in the area, pirates had largely stopped sacking towns, because it attracted the harshest punishments. It had stopped before Knigh's time, but he'd served with men who'd seen whole flotillas of pirate hunters gathered to track a single ship foolish enough to attack Arawakéan interests.

He scowled and swirled his palm wine in its wooden cup. Despite the danger, those fools had come and attacked Redland. They hadn't looked starving and desperate or—

A shriek came from the crowd gathered around Saba and Aedan, and Shoko glanced up from her conversation. Her mouth drew in a flat line before she looked away again.

Knigh had noticed tensions between Saba and Shoko, though the council leader had welcomed him with genuine warmth. As for Vee, Shoko had engulfed her in a hug, exclaiming at how shiny her hair was, asking if she was using the oil she'd gifted her.

The only sign of approval she'd given Saba was when she'd presented a lizard carving to her pregnant sister—the same one he'd spotted her whittling on the *Respair*. Saba explained she'd dreamt it would be the child's animal, so she'd sculpted the beautiful little statuette like a kind of talisman. Her sister had been thrilled, grabbing her for a hug around the large bump that suggested the child would make an appearance soon. Shoko had merely nodded once.

Knigh took a long gulp of his drink. It hit him, sweet and strong. *Right*. This wasn't normal wine or even grog. He blinked at his cup and shook his head. Lords, he had to be careful with this stuff.

Speaking of which...

He knew that shape at the edge of the square. Silhouetted against the stars and their reflections upon the sea, a tall woman leant on the rail, nursing a drink.

And, knowing Vee, she was also nursing her agitation that they hadn't set sail for Hewanorra yet.

He sidled over. "Stewing over the fact we're still here, rather than off treasure hunting?"

She let out a breath that might've been a laugh—it was hard to tell her expression with the light flickering and flashing off the water. Eyebrows raised as she turned to him, she gave a half-smile. "Am I so easily read?"

He chuckled, mirroring her stance. "No, I just know you."

She stilled, eyes narrowed upon him in a way that made him want to fidget. Only the years of training kept him from shifting. "Huh." She looked away at last, with another half-laugh, half-exhale. "Maybe you do."

The sea breeze loosed hair around her face as she took a long draught from her cup, and his fingers itched to push it away.

Gods damn it, around her, his body wasn't entirely his own. Each part of him pulled towards her like he was a compass point and she was north. Did that make her his course? His guiding point?

He glared at the cup in his hand. This stuff was too strong, making him think ridiculous things.

But he didn't know what to say, so he took another sip—anything to distract himself from her, if only for a moment.

"It isn't just that," she said at last, and he had to backtrack over the conversation to catch her meaning.

"Not just the delay?" He raised his eyebrows. "Then what in the world could be keeping *you* from drinking and dancing?"

She held up her cup. "Still drinking."

"True, but you've had that same drink in your hand for half an hour."

"Been watching, have you?" There was something challenging in the spark of her eyes and the smirk twitching at the side of her mouth. Something teasing, just like the scent of her on the breeze. They'd been given the chance to bathe after the fight, and she must've taken it, because she didn't smell of sweat and blood, and there was a citrus zing to her usual vanilla and petrichor scent, as though she wore lime oil in her hair.

This was risky. Being alone with Vee always was, but flirting with her…

His heart took up a faster beat, almost at the speed of the reeling music that led the dancers in a wild spin.

"Perhaps," he murmured.

She leant closer, the movement so slight she might not even have realised she was doing it. Her look grew intense, searching, as if asking a question.

Whatever that question was, he wanted to say *yes*. A hundred times, yes.

But... he wasn't meant to be flirting with her; he was meant to be asking what was wrong. He'd offered himself to her the day they'd escaped the kraken, and she'd chosen friendship. With what he was capable of, with what he'd done to Aedan, he couldn't blame her. He'd been a fool to even ask.

Pulling back, he cleared his throat. "Sorry, I was asking... what's the other thing that's keeping you from dancing into the small hours?"

"Ah." Her expression sank with her shoulders. "It's Saba." She explained how Saba was planning to use her share of treasure to buy a plot of land and make the home she'd dreamed of for years. "I always knew she planned to grow crops and livestock and, eventually, a family, I just"—she shook her head, frown deepening—"I thought it was just that, *eventually*. Not for years and years yet. But the sooner we get Drake's treasure, the sooner she goes."

Well. Genuine—what was it? Disappointment... sadness? Not even softened with a joke or false cheer, as if she didn't care. He blinked at her, the downturned lines of every angle of her body and face, the inward knot she'd become.

"And you'll miss her," he said at last. Seeing her so upset

and admitting to the source made him cut away every sharp edge in himself, any hint of mockery or tease. He kept his voice as soft as the touch he wanted to trace over her shoulder. Perhaps it would coax her. At least it might be a comfort. But... no.

He swallowed, exhaled, then squeezed his cup. "I'm sure you'll be able to visit her. In fact, I'm positive she wouldn't have it any other way."

She turned to face the water again, bending over the rail, face cast in shadow and flickering sea-light. "Mmm."

"You can't expect her to be a pirate forever." It wasn't an easy life. Certainly not a safe one. "I know some love life at sea"—like him, like Vee—"but it sounds like it's only a means to an end for her."

"A means to an end. A new life." Vee sighed, collapsing further in on herself, though he'd have sworn that wasn't possible, not for her. "Everyone leaves," she muttered, so quietly, it might've been to herself rather than him. "They leave, they die, or they let you down. I know that. I *know*."

His heart shrivelled. *Oh, Vee*. He fastened both hands around the cup to keep them from her.

"Just..." Her voice came out strangled. "So soon?" She drained her drink, smacking her lips after. As if the alcohol buoyed her, she straightened. "And—and I want her to be happy"—she gestured with the cup—"but I didn't think I had to prepare for it yet."

He gave in and squeezed her shoulder, warm and firm in a way that tightened his gut. He was on the edge of danger touching her, but he couldn't take it back, not when it made her look up at him, eyebrows raised, a hopeful light in her eyes.

With an encouraging nod, he smiled. "You can make the most of her while she's still here."

Vee's brows drew together, a softer echo of the determined expression she wore in battle. Her shoulders rose and fell as she took a deep breath. "True."

"And, you know"—he cocked his head, a grin tugging at his mouth—"I have a feeling there are still plenty of adventures to be had on the way to Drake's treasure. You don't think just because we have the cipher and a location that the rest will be easy, do you?"

She chuckled. "I suppose not. After all, where would be the fun in that?"

"Where indeed?"

She covered his hand with her own—he hadn't even realised he'd left it on her shoulder, it was so natural to be near her and thus touching her. Her laugh faded to a smile, and she nodded once. "Thank you, Knigh. For cheering me up and not letting me mope alone."

"As if I cou—"

A squeal came from the dancers, making him and Vee jolt apart. Saba towered over the group, standing on Aedan's shoulders, laughing, a jug balanced on one shoulder. From the fact he and she were drenched, she'd originally been balancing two jugs.

But the musicians didn't miss a beat, their infectious tune keeping the rest of the dancers moving. It even had Knigh's fingers tapping on his thigh.

"This is what happens when you leave them unattended," Vee said, grinning. She glanced from Saba and Aedan to him, to his fingers. "You know… Hold on—I'll be right back." She hurried towards Shoko's large home at the end of the square, where they had rooms. "Don't go anywhere," she called over her shoulder before disappearing.

Knigh shook his head after her—what *was* she up to? He drained his drink and this time let the lad doing his circuit refill his cup, as well as the empty one Vee had left behind.

A few minutes later, she returned, holding something barely concealed behind her back. She gestured for him to put the drinks down, and he balanced them on the rail.

"I'm sorry for snapping at you earlier," she said. "I really didn't think of asking for help, and I was so horrified when I saw you alone and outnumbered…" She shook her head, expression brightening. "Well, what I'm trying to say is… This is a peace offering." She pulled out the bulky object.

Gleaming, lacquered wood, taut strings, and a long neck. "A guitar."

Nodding, she held it out to him.

He paused, fingertips a few inches away. It had been months since he'd seen one. He hadn't had the stomach to play the guitar they'd found on the *Covadonga* after he'd made that final decision to arrest Vee, not when its music had led to that first time they'd slept together. Truth be told, that night at the bonfire, he'd played for her and her alone. And once he'd made that terrible decision, it didn't feel right to touch the damn thing.

But here was another. An elegantly beautiful specimen, perfectly proportioned, lightly decorated. And gifted from Vee.

"You…" He shook his head, glancing up at her. His fingertips strayed to the dagger earring he'd bought her months and months ago. It sat in his breast pocket, pressing into his chest. "You didn't need to."

"No, but I wanted to." She nodded and raised it. "Go on, it's yours. And you have to accept, because I can't return it."

"This must've cost a pretty penny." But his grip closed around it and he took its familiar weight in his hands. "You shouldn't waste your money on me."

"I'm a pirate, I—"

"Wait, you didn't steal—?"

"No!" She laughed. "All legal and above board. I just mean that"—she shrugged, a little sorrow touching her smile—"I don't have a farmstead to save up for like Saba."

"Sorry," he muttered, cheeks burning. Perhaps it wasn't unfair to think a pirate might've stolen something expensive like a guitar, but it was embarrassing to have jumped to that conclusion about her. He looked away, grateful to have the guitar to focus on. He gave an experimental pluck of each string and grimaced at the off-pitch twangs. "Lords, needs tuning."

"There," Vee said, "I knew it would work."

When he looked up, she was beaming. He'd rarely seen such a broad smile on her outside the moment of victory in battle. It made her eyes sparkle in the dim torchlight, and the whole expression warmed a place in his chest that had been cold and dark for a long while.

Risky, Blackwood. Risky.

He paid a great deal more attention than was necessary to tuning the highest string. *"Knew it would work?* You were already forgiven by the time we'd chased those stragglers to their boats."

"No, not that. Perry's advice. I thought it could be something to distract your hands."

"I can think of better ways to distract my hands." It burst out of him before he really thought about it. He huffed a laugh and glanced up at her.

And that was the mistake.

Because her gaze was like a strike to the face. Her eyebrows were raised, her lips parted. Maybe she'd been about to reply, but thought better of it.

Just like *he* should've thought better of making that joke. Except, damn it, it wasn't really a joke, was it?

She was a place he could very easily and very happily lose himself in. The dangerous thing was, she was far, far more than just a distraction.

Still wearing that same expression, she stared at him. The only movement was her hair in the breeze and the long, slow rise and fall of her chest. He knew that rhythm well—he'd rested his head just there, above the swell of her breasts, below the line of her collarbone as he'd drifted off into a blissful sleep.

Suddenly the guitar blocking his body from hers felt alarmingly fragile, like he was a knight with nothing but a paper shield.

Beyond risky. This was downright dangerous.

Because they were *friends*. She'd forgiven him for betraying her, yes, but that forgiveness was new—young and fragile.

Peace between them had taken so much to achieve and it had been damn painful at times. To get to this place where they'd forgiven each other was worth it. Perhaps after going through so much, it could lead elsewhere.

But.

There had to be a *but,* and this one was weighty, holding him in place.

Although she'd forgiven him enough to be friends, that didn't mean she trusted him to let him closer, to be more.

After handing her over to the Navy, he was lucky to have her forgiveness. Asking for anything else would be too much.

No matter how much he wanted it.

And back at Yule, when they'd tried to be *just bodies,* as she called it—well, that had gone horrifically. It had nearly broken them both. So although that flirtatious joke was the sort of thing he would've said to her when they were lovers on *The Morrigan*—what an innocent time that seemed now—he couldn't flirt with danger like that anymore.

He closed his eyes and backed off one step. No, two—*two* would be safer.

They were two of the hardest steps he'd ever taken in his life, but if it meant they could remain friends, it would be worth it.

"Sorry," he muttered, shaking his head. "I—I'm sorry, I just... bad joke..." He cleared his throat, swallowed again. "Thank you so much, Vee." He smiled at her, but it was stiff on his cheeks, and her brows drew together in a deep valley. "It's a wonderful gift. I'm going to put it somewhere safe."

She blinked and took a long breath, as if waking. "Of course." She inclined her head, and he fled.

"Idiot," he muttered, swinging the guitar in one hand as he strode away as quickly as he could without breaking into a run. "Bloody palm wine—never touching that stuff again." He hurried to the *Venatrix*, safely away from her. He would stay there tonight, far away from Vee and her room in Shoko's house.

"Knigh Blackwood," he muttered, "you need to leave that Pirate Queen well alone."

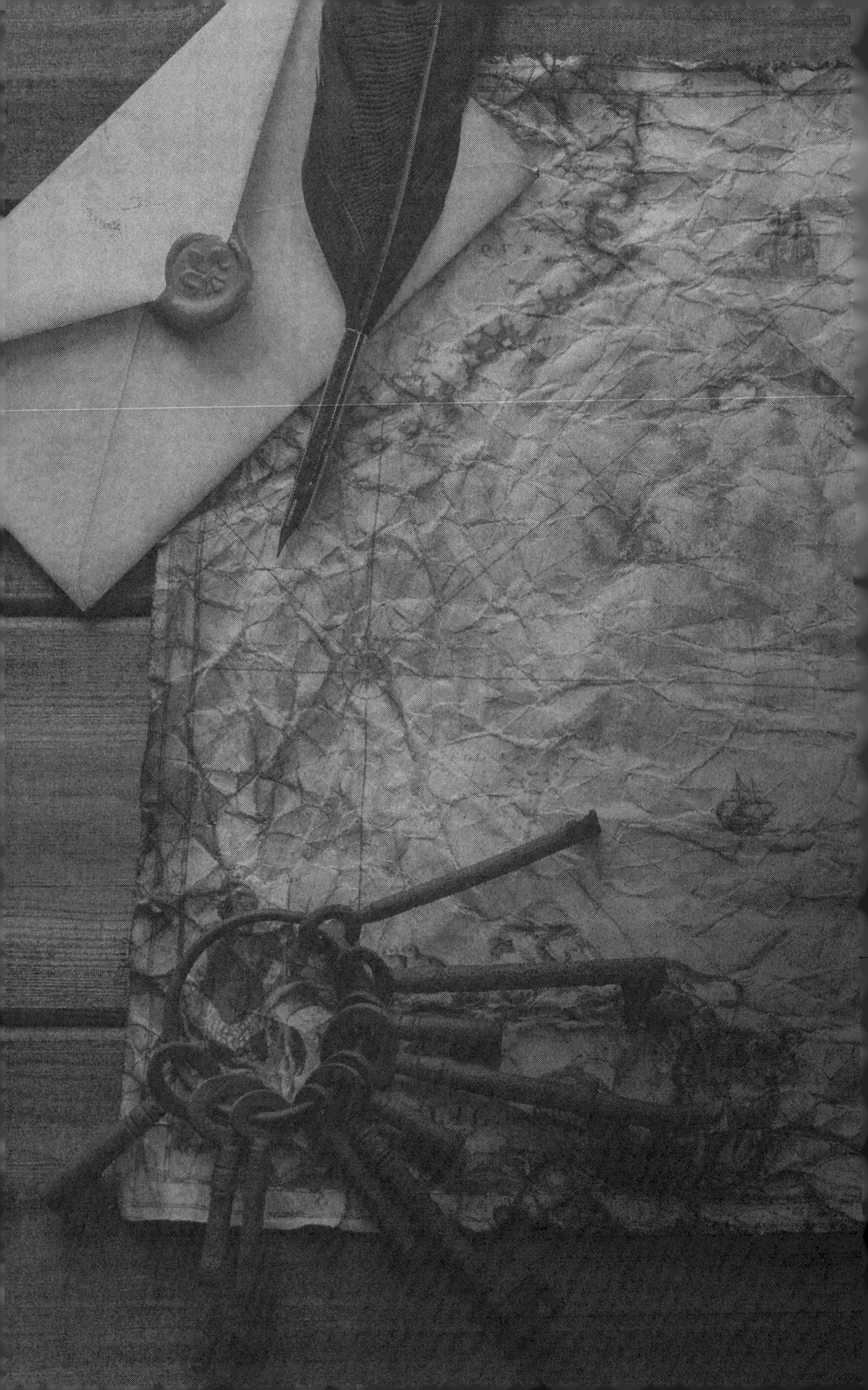

ABSOLUTELY FINE

Fiddling with the drake pin at her collar, Vice watched Knigh's broad shoulders retreat through the crowd. It was probably a bad idea to picture the clean, sinuous lines of his tattoo across his back, but she did it anyway.

What had that been? Flirtation? A joke? *An offer?*

No, just a witty remark. The way he'd apologised and backed off was a clear sign he hadn't meant anything by it. He'd seen that she'd read too much into it, though. It was simply idle flirtation, like she'd always had with Aedan, Fitz, Lizzy, Saba...

She only *wanted* it to be more.

Which was a stupid want.

If she followed it and Knigh also wanted her, there was the risk he'd hurt her or he'd leave or, perhaps worst of all, that she'd hurt him. After all, hadn't she already shown immense skill in that area on the *Swallow* and the *Respair?*

More likely, he didn't want her after seeing her sickly body back in Portsmouth. It had been a grotesque sight, and she wouldn't have blamed him for it. Yule, yes, that happened, but they'd been drunk and desperate and in the middle of an ocean. It didn't count.

Plus, there was the matter of the uniform. Being on the *Venatrix*, on what had once been his ship, a corner of her mind kept whispering Munroe's words: *the Navy was the making of him*. Knigh's uniform had been his identity.

And he'd lost that. Because of her.

If she couldn't stop thinking of it, it had to be on his mind, too.

And if she, the notorious Lady Vice who never felt guilty about anything, felt guilty about what she'd cost him, how must *he* feel about it?

At best, he resented her. At worst—well, that didn't bear thinking about.

So, no. Not an offer, or meaningful flirtation, only a poorly conceived joke.

"Just friends," she hissed at herself and tore her gaze away. She grabbed both cups he'd left on the rail. Both full. *Good.*

She gulped one down, barely tasting the sweetness. She'd suggested Saba drink herself into oblivion if it helped her deal with her mother… well, maybe she should take her own advice.

With that cup empty, she scanned the crowd and couldn't spot him anymore. Thankfully. Her eyes had a traitorous way of seeking him out whenever possible. He was nice to look at— more than *nice*—but…

She huffed. Her head was fuzzy, but she clearly hadn't

drunk enough to forget Knigh. Yet. Eyes shut against the burn at the back of her throat, she quaffed the other cup.

When she looked again, the world swam as though underwater. *Better.*

Then she registered the familiar dark-haired figure at her side, offering another cup. "Saba! Good work." She took the drink and grinned at her friend, whose eyes were bright even in the dim light here at the edge of the celebrations.

"Friends look after each other." She tapped her cup to Vice's and took a sip while Vice gulped hers. "So." Her eyes narrowed. "What's the deal with you and Blackwood?"

Vice shook her head, clearing her throat. "We don't have a deal."

Saba smirked. "Maybe I should've asked before I gave you the drink. What I mean is, I thought you two were friends, but then I saw you give him that guitar." Her gaze drilled into Vice. She didn't need to ask, it was all there in her expression and the spaces between her words.

Are you and him together?

"Oh, you think..." Vice scoffed and shook her head. "You're asking whether we're shagging. That—the guitar was just a gift between friends." She touched the feathered earrings tickling her neck. "Like you gave me these."

Excellent argument, Vice. Well done.

She nodded at herself, though it made the ground tilt. *Getting there.* Definitely heading in the right direction to forget all about Knigh and stupid jokes about distracting his hands. Distracting them with her body. That's what he'd meant.

Yes, yes, it's very obvious what he meant. You're meant to be forgetting about that.

So sensible. Like Perry.

But Saba's eyes were still narrowed.

"And," Vice said, unfurling one finger from her cup to point at Saba, "*and* Perry said he needed a distraction from his anger—something to do with his hands. So, guitar." She gave an exaggerated shrug.

Chuckling, Saba shook her head. "Obviously." She took a sip of her drink and leant on the rail, looking out over the sea. "So you won't mind if I get with him, then?"

Every inch of Vice, inside and out, froze. She couldn't even breathe.

Her heart might've stopped.

"I mean," Saba went on, "if you're not going to make use of him, I will. You don't mind, do you?" She threw Vice a glance, dark eyebrows arched.

Gods. She had to move. She had to do something—staring like this was stupid. Sucking in a breath, she blinked, but every movement was mechanical. She swallowed and turned, stiff and clumsy. She pushed out a laugh. It sounded like something from one of those terrible stage shows they put on in Nassau. With a sip of her drink, she bought herself time to make her voice work.

Was it really any surprise that Saba would be interested in Knigh? He was ridiculously charismatic, funny in that dry way of his, deliciously flirtatious when he actually relaxed. He was capable, smart, kind…

Reliable. Gorgeous. Fierce. Stronger than he gave himself credit for.

Her chest ached.

Of course Saba would want him. Who wouldn't?

It wasn't like Vice's pairings usually meant more than physical pleasure. Why would Saba think this one any different? As far as she knew, he and Vice had slept together a few times last year, all the way back on *The Morrigan*. Only Perry knew the full extent of their relationship and the mess on board the *Swallow* and the *Respair*.

And it wasn't like she had any claim over him, was it?

Just friends.

"Course not," Vice croaked. It was fine. *Fine.*

Saba exhaled, perhaps with surprise or relief, then sipped her drink. Nodding, she looked back out over the dark ocean. "It would be a shame to let him go to waste. Besides, I'm pretty sure he's keen."

"You're one of my favourite people," Vice blurted, burning eyes fixed on a point in the distance where the stars disappeared, signalling that the sky met the sea on a night-shrouded horizon. "Of course he…" But bitterness flooded her mouth, stopping her from finishing the sentence.

She'd had too much to drink. And that weird moment of flirtation from Knigh had thrown her off course. She took deep lungfuls of sea air and a small sip of palm wine, so the sweetness would wash away that bitter taste.

When she could trust her voice, she nodded. "Must admit I'm surprised. I thought you and Munroe…"

"He's… lovely, aye. But he's staying here when we go

tomorrow, isn't he?" Saba sighed. "Not much more to be done there. Though he's taught me Navy and *former* Navy men aren't so bad. You could've told me they were so *eager*. Must be all that time on a ship full of men."

Vice clung to her cup like it was the lifeline that had kept her tethered to the *Swallow* in that Yule storm.

No, she'd been wrong. She hadn't drunk *enough*. More—much, *much* more would numb her, make her forget Knigh, and stop any thoughts about Saba enjoying his *eagerness*.

She drained the cup, eyes stinging. It was just the alcohol. That was all.

"Thanks, Vice," Saba said, finally turning from the sea with a bright smile. "I knew you'd be fine with it. Lizzy reckoned not, but"—she shrugged—"what does she know?" In a wave of sweet frangipani perfume, she kissed Vice on the cheek. "I'm going for a dance. Join me?"

"I—um, in a bit. I need to..." Vice upended her empty cup.

With a knowing nod, Saba backed away. "In a bit," she said and stalked away.

Limbs not quite her own, Vice made for the opposite end of the square. She scanned the crowd for Knigh or one of the boys serving more palm wine; the plan being to avoid the former and grab a full jug from the latter.

It was fine that Saba wanted Knigh. Fine.

And it was fine that she'd given her blessing. Absolutely fine.

She and Knigh were nothing more than friends for good reasons. *Great* reasons. She needed to remember that.

Would getting them tattooed somewhere be too extreme?

No—no, she wouldn't need the reminder forever. Soon she'd be over this pathetic yearning to be close to Knigh, and she'd have no problem being his friend. It was all that business on the *Venatrix's* deck after the kraken had fled, that was all. Opening her eyes from her gift and finding him there. The fact he'd come for her. Again.

It was like something from a story, and she'd always been a sucker for a good story. Anyone would get caught up in a moment like that. She was only suffering its afterglow. It would fade soon.

It *would*.

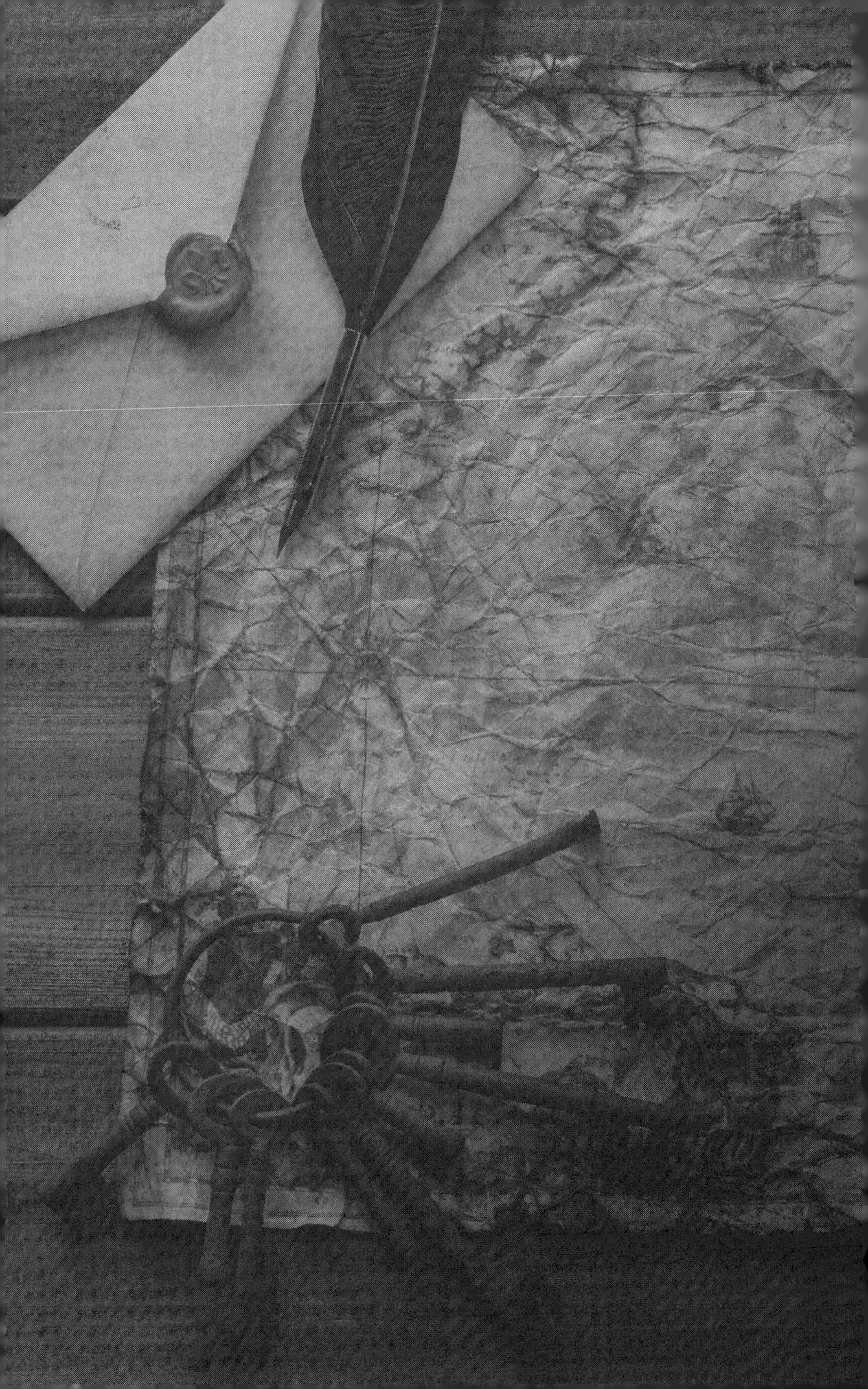

EPSILON TAU GAMMA TAU

psilon. Tau. Gamma. Tau. Vice blinked at the Copper Drake and what she'd once believed nonsensical Ancient Hellenic. As they appeared on the page, they made no sense—the same ten letters repeated in different combinations. But now she had the cipher key.

Who'd have imagined it would be as simple as a grid? Five along the top, five more down the side—the ten letters that appeared again and again in the Copper Drake. In the centre, the Latium alphabet.

	A	B	Γ	Δ	E
Ϙ	A	B	C	D	E
Ρ	F	G	H	I/J	K
Σ	L	M	N	O	P
T	Q	R	S	T	U
Y	V	W	X	Y	Z

Each pair of Hellenic letters gave a location on the grid, indicating just one Latium letter. No wonder she hadn't been able to make sense of it.

She traced her finger across to *epsilon*, down to *tau*, giving the answer—*U*. She noted that. Next, across to *gamma* and down to *tau* again. *S*.

She rubbed her eyes and sat back. "*Vicus*. That's quartz." Frowning, she cocked her head at Knigh, sitting at the other end of the table in Perry's cabin.

"Quartz." With a nod, he dipped his pen in the inkwell and added that to his Albionic translation.

At the foot of Perry's bed came soft squeaks and mewls as Barnacle rose and stretched, apparently annoying the kittens. They were taking wobbly steps around their nest, but hadn't yet ventured out of the sea chest.

"Patience, little goblins," she called over to them, "your mama will be back soon."

Patience? Lords, that's what Perry had said to her about a million times over the past twenty-four hours.

The *Venatrix* left Redland yesterday at first light, wishing goodbye to Shoko and the council, as well as Munroe and his crew. They swept the area, checking the attackers weren't hiding nearby, waiting for the*m* to leave. Only then had they *finally* set sail for Hewanorra—the island identified in what had once been FitzRoy's clue.

To think, she'd once been excited at holding the very writing and words of Drake. *Ha!* That had dissolved somewhat with the drudgery of translation and the headaches like this one throbbing in her temples.

When she looked up, a glass of water swam into view. Knigh pressed it into her hand, a sympathetic smile on his mouth. "Headache?"

She grumbled and raised the drink in a mock toast. *"Again."* She gave a sardonic smirk. At least she had help now—the translation was going quicker with two pairs of hands.

As she drank, Knigh looked from the Latium she'd written to the nonsense in the Copper Drake. "So you'd have been able to read this, if it was actually Ancient Hellenic?"

"Mmm-hmm." She nodded and took another sip. It was odd, since she'd thought Drake had only spoken Albionic and a smattering of Hesperian. But here was his book written using two other languages—or their alphabets at least.

"And you speak Latium, Hesperian, and Frankish, too, correct?"

"They were some of the only lessons I was really interested in." She shrugged, flashing a grin—all those poor governesses they'd paraded through the house as one-by-one they left. "The governesses were just relieved to find something I enjoyed."

He narrowed his eyes at her in the way that suggested she was a puzzle he was trying to work out. "Why languages?"

She sat back in the chair and stretched, neck cracking. She let out another groan as it loosened. "I think the silly little girl I was..." Cringing, she looked at the ceiling to avoid him.

Avice Ferrers really *had* been a silly girl, a naïve dreamer with stories in her head. Vice wasn't that girl—hadn't been for a long while. Avice had wanted impossible things, had got lost in her foolish ideas. And she'd dragged Evered into it all.

"I was convinced that I'd need them in my adventures around the globe." She shook her head at him, cheeks hot at her childish foolishness. "Stupid, eh?"

"Not that foolish. After all"—his eyebrows rose—"that's what you're using them for now, isn't it?"

She blinked, frowned, but there was no hint of mockery in his expression.

This didn't *feel* like an adventure—it just felt like life. But then, was what she did *so* different from the stories she'd stayed up reading by candlelight?

True, life didn't exactly look how Avice had pictured. But maybe she hadn't been entirely foolish. She'd made a new life for herself. She'd made this happen, and *this* was much closer to those dreams than to her old life locked up in a country estate by Papa. She'd escaped. She'd survived.

Vice took a long breath and frowned. "I'd never thought of it like that."

He tilted his head, a small smile curving his lips.

Tap-tap at the door.

"Yes?"

Perry poked her head in, glanced from Vice to Knigh and back again. "We're almost there."

Vice was on her feet before she'd even finished the sentence, grinning. She shook Knigh's shoulder.

But he only straightened, apparently immune to the excitement buzzing through her muscles. "Let's see if this really does lead us to the next clue or just a dead end."

A dead end? The idea hadn't even crossed her mind. "We haven't put in this much work for it to all be for nothing." She nodded at the table full of notes and met his gaze. "I won't *let* it be for nothing."

With an exhale, his stiff shoulders eased, and he threw her a small smile. "Then I pity the dead end that tries to block your way."

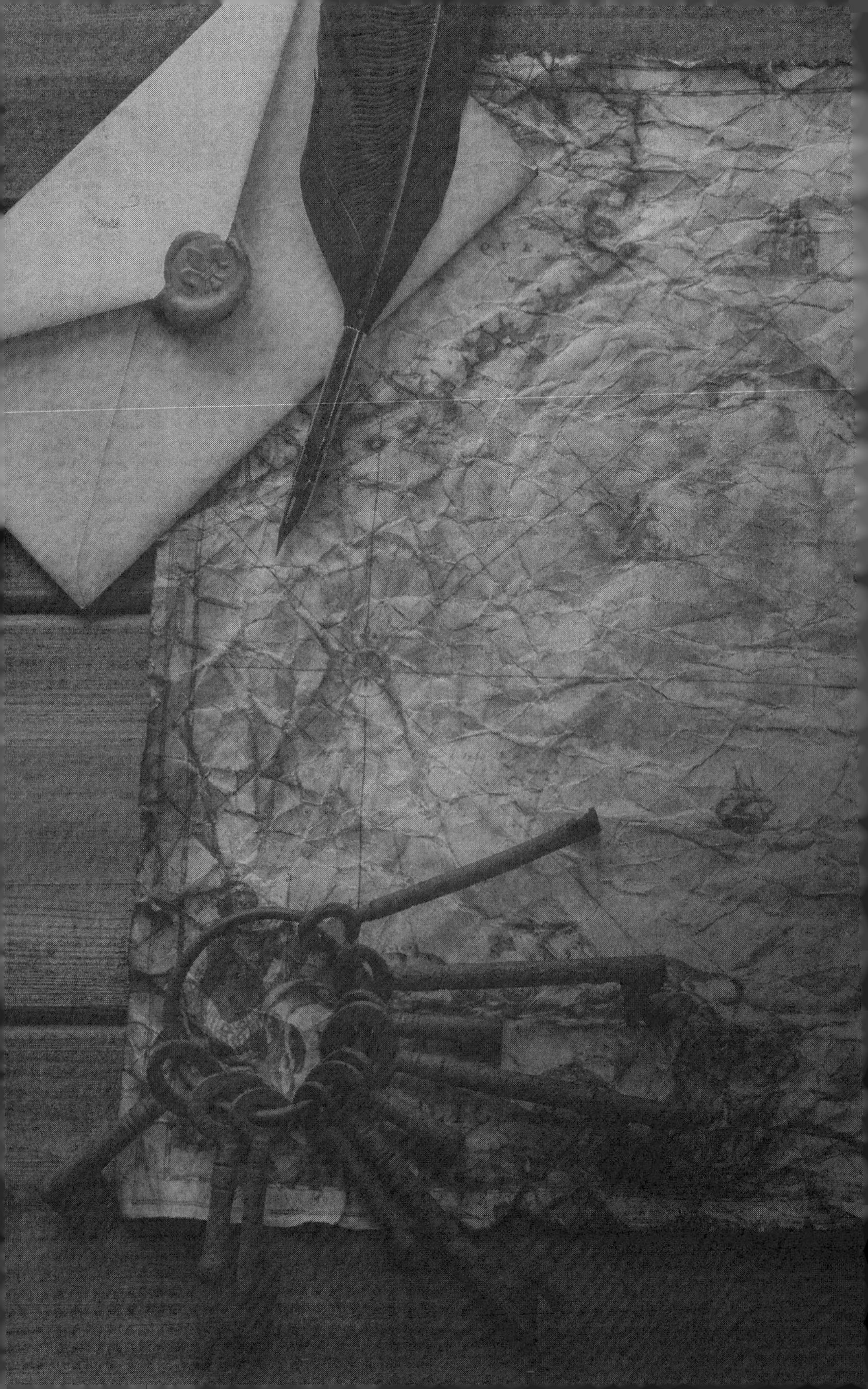

POLARIS

Spotted dolphins leapt alongside the ship as they approached Hewanorra. Vice shook her head at the jagged line formed by the edge of Drake's poetry on the page fluttering in her hand. Ahead, the island's peaks rose against the sky—a perfect match. How hadn't she realised?

Leaning against the bow, wind blasting her hair, she couldn't help but smile at Knigh as he stood close to her side and squinted at the mountains. Thank the gods *he'd* recognised the shape.

His long fingers gripped the other side of the page as he traced the longest river, then pointed it out on the hillside ahead. A line scored in the dense green growth.

"The text says there's a cave here." Vice tapped the spot where a tributary fed into that main river, thankfully near the mountain's base.

Knigh's teeth flashed—her excitement had infected him at

last. It throbbed in her chest, leapt through her veins, as high and joyous as the gleaming dolphins jumping from wave to wave just a dozen feet away.

Perhaps this life *was* an adventure, like he'd said.

They anchored in the bay north of the twin mountains and rowed for shore with their usual boarding party, while others went ashore for hunting, foraging, or simply to enjoy the island. Lizzy stayed with the foragers, planning to gather medicinal plants for her poultices and teas.

They'd packed food and water, as well as rope, shovels, lanterns, a compass, and various other pieces of equipment they guessed might be useful. Vice carried the Copper Drake together with their notes in a bag slung across her body. For all they had the book and its clues, its contents were still vague. Plus, the work of deciphering and translating it was so slow, she'd barely made it a tenth of the way through. Working with Knigh yesterday and today had gone much quicker, though—thank the gods.

Parts had to be coded, speaking about colours and animals, while other passages seemed to recount someone's observations—more like a logbook or journal. Descriptions of flora and fauna, as well as the local cultures as they were a couple of hundred years ago. Saba's eyes had widened when she'd shown her, and Vice had promised to make a copy.

Other sections contained the images and diagrams she had pored over long before she'd found the cipher, except now she could read the surrounding captions and notes. Or at least she *would*, once she translated those passages.

"Patience," she muttered, mimicking Perry's voice.

Their clothes clung to their bodies by the time they reached the river and they were all grateful to splash cool water on themselves before continuing along its bank.

Vice forged ahead, wiping her brow—the tickle might've been sweat or a fly or a drip from the broad leaves above. The air was thick with humidity, as if clouds clung low to the land, and it filled every breath with moisture.

"The book says we'll reach the tributary soon." Knigh's voice made her jump. She'd pushed on in silence for so long, she'd almost forgotten she wasn't alone. "The cave entrance should be behind a boulder or rocky outcrop near that fork."

Snorting, she glanced over her shoulder at him. "Don't think I didn't notice you saying *should*. Still doubting?"

"*You?* Never." One eyebrow raised, he nodded towards her bag. "A ciphered text written two centuries ago? *Perhaps.*"

But he had no need to doubt—they found the tributary five minutes later, and after fanning out to search, Saba discovered the narrow entrance to a cave behind a pair of boulders that looked exactly like a sketch from the book.

"What do you know?" Vice said, holding out the page. "This old book just *might* be useful after all." She grinned at Knigh, who rolled his eyes, but softened the gesture with a half-smile.

"After you." He gestured inside.

"Such a gentleman!" With a wink, she passed.

The entrance was around a dozen feet across. Compared to the dense forest outside, the cave was even darker, despite cracks in the ceiling. The air was drier, too, as though the trees trapped the moisture below their branches.

Knigh stuck to Vice's side, adjusting the rope over his

shoulder before lighting his lantern. As they circled, he pointed out small, regular scratches on the walls that suggested human visitors or habitation.

The last time she'd been in a cave with Knigh, things had heated up rather quickly. She dared a glance at him, but he was intent on scanning their surroundings.

With another lantern, Saba and Aedan joined their exploration. Wynn and Effie lingered near the entrance, glancing outside.

Ahead, a passage led deeper. To one side, the charred remnants of a fire littered a patch of scorched ground. The cracks would help draw smoke up and out, acting like a natural chimney—perhaps people had lived here long ago or someone caught in a storm had taken shelter here last month. The burnt wood gave no clues of its age.

Once they'd finished a circuit of the cave, Knigh made a thoughtful sound. "Wonder if there are any glow-worms in here."

Vice shot him a look, but he only looked at the ceiling, all innocence. *Innocent, my arse.* She gave a soft laugh. Was it a comfort that his mind had gone in the same direction? Or just plain dangerous?

Aedan lifted his lamp and peered down the passageway. "Guessing it's this way."

She shook away thoughts of Knigh and glow-worms, busying herself with pulling out the translated notebook. "What gave it away?"

"I have a sixth sense for these things." He flashed her an

over-wide grin. "With any luck, the rest of the route will be so obvious."

"I wouldn't count on it," Knigh muttered.

"Well, I hope it's not too far." Saba glanced back to the entrance. "I don't want to miss out on the hot springs."

"Hot springs?"

Leafing through her notes, Vice nodded. *"Glorious* hot springs." Two of the best features of the island—thick, warm volcanic mud that was said to ease any ailment, and hot pools to wash in afterwards. It made for a blissful combination. She waved off Saba's grumbles. "They'll be better this evening when the air's cooler."

"Glorious? Sounds like something that would be on the Navy's forbidden list." With a sardonic smile, Knigh produced a piece of chalk from his bag and nodded to Vice. "Lead the way."

"Just remember what I said about traps." If only she'd given Evans that warning...

Logically, the book should warn them if there were any traps, but... The clack of stone, a puff of dust, Evans' whimpers of pain... She shuddered.

Focus, Vice.

Swallowing, she squared her shoulders. What *is*, not what might be.

She'd already found the section of the Copper Drake relating to this location—it even had a narrow stub of paper showing where a page had been torn out. So she and Knight had focused their translation efforts on the relevant pages.

One passage described the flight of a bird following various stars as it migrated, but when they'd shown it to Saba, she'd explained that this species didn't migrate. Plus, it was a creature of the day, not the night—it wouldn't even be able to *see* any stars. That left the possibility it was a set of coded directions.

Polaris. North.

Mintaka rising. East.

Mintaka setting. West.

Crux. That had to be for the southern constellation.

She frowned from the translated page to Knigh, stomach twisting. "It seems straightforward, but..." She shook her head, brow tight in a frown. "I... I don't want to get it wrong." Not with such a high cost, like the one Evans had paid.

A gentle smile curved his lips, and he nodded. "You won't. I'm sure this is right. And we're marking the route with chalk, so we can get out quickly. We'll be fine." His steady gaze stilled the churning in her stomach.

If it wasn't a set of directions, what else could it be? And it was on the page after the drawing of the boulder that had helped them find the cave. It *had* to be this.

With Knigh at her side, holding the lamp high, she strode into the darkness.

The passage allowed them to travel side-by-side, though the craggy walls almost brushed their shoulders. A pull on her shins belied the apparently level floor—the path took a slight decline.

After a few minutes, they reached an intersection and Knigh leant close, his warmth welcome in the chilly cave. Book in one hand, compass in the other, she angled, letting them catch the light.

... towards the rising star.

"East." She nodded at the passage they should take.

Knigh chalked an arrow on the floor, pointing back the way they'd come, and they started down the branch.

All the way, Vice scanned the ceiling, the floor, the walls, but there was no sign of any carving or symbols or hidden doors, as there had been on the storm-shrouded island she'd visited with Mercia. The craggy walls and stalactites suggested this was nothing more than a natural cave network. And there had been no such warnings in the Copper Drake.

Maybe they didn't need to worry about any traps here. She managed a tight smile.

The passage widened, but Aedan, Saba, Wynn, and Effie kept a few paces behind her and Knigh, chatting in soft tones that echoed off the walls. She and Knigh paused at each intersection, conferring on the book's instructions and the route before deciding which way to go.

The tunnel snaked and turned at places, then ran straight for what might've been a hundred feet—it was hard to tell. But the way always led down.

Time, too, was difficult to gauge. It felt like they'd been walking through the dark, following the Copper Drake's directions, for almost an hour when they rounded a corner and stopped short. Loose stones clicked underfoot and ahead the lamp flickered yellow light and deepest shadow upon a pile of rock and dust.

"Bugger," Vice hissed, glaring at the blockage. She checked the book—no mention of an obstacle here. "A cave-in? Or have we gone the wrong way?"

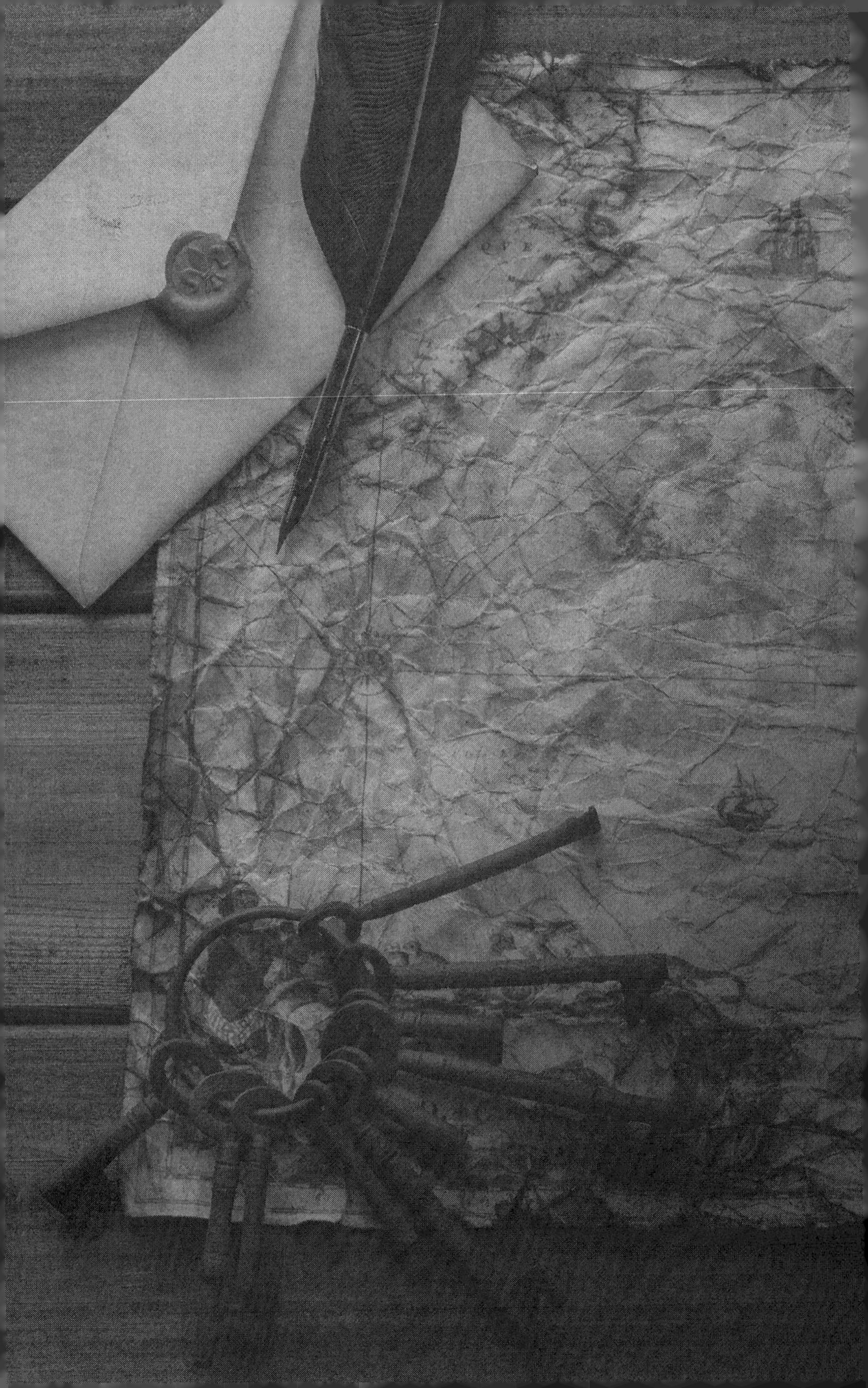

CAVE-IN

Lips pursed, Knigh shook his head. "No, we've definitely followed the directions exactly. It's uneven, no sign of tool marks—this looks natural." He lifted the lamp, examining the blockage.

The others caught up, their chatter fading once they spotted the problem.

"There has to be a way through," Vice muttered. They'd come this far and whatever the next step towards Drake's treasure was, they'd discover it here. This was the only way.

She shoved the book in her bag and clambered up the rocks. The ceiling was only ten feet up—perhaps there was a gap to crawl through. Her years of experience on the shrouds and before that in the trees of her family's estate were little use here. No matter how sure a foothold seemed, the rock could suddenly tumble down, and scree slid as soon as she put her weight on it. Jagged stone tore at her hands, despite the sailor's calluses.

But she gritted her teeth and tried the next foothold and the next. She let the damn rock scrape her skin until eventually, puffing, she reached the ceiling.

Catching her breath, she motioned for Knigh to lower his lantern so her eyes could grow accustomed to the darkness and let her fae sight take over.

The shadow resolved into shapes. All rock and dust. She crawled to the right, around a huge boulder only partially visible in the tunnel—the rest disappeared above, making the back of her neck prickle with the thought of it falling the rest of the way and squashing her. *It's been here for years. It isn't going anywhere.*

On the other side of that boulder, she found a narrow gap between it and the rocks beneath.

"Perhaps..." She crawled in, the scree sharp on her hands and knees. After a few feet, the way narrowed, forcing her to elbows and thighs, almost flat on her belly. But the gap continued, and as she shimmied past the boulder, it turned left and opened up into the tunnel beyond.

She huffed a laugh and started the harder task of crawling backwards. A few minutes later, she smiled down at her friends from the top of the cave-in. "It's tight, but there's a way through"—she nodded at Knigh and Aedan—"big enough for you two."

With a sharp nod, Saba started up the cave-in. "Let's go, then." She used the secure footholds Vice pointed out.

Vice took Aedan's lamp so Saba could see on the other side. "Ready?"

A sheen of sweat on her brow, Saba nodded.

Vice showed her the way around the boulder, and let her go ahead before passing the lamp through the gap. The clack of stones signalled Saba scrabbling down the other side.

Heart in her throat, Vice called through, "You all right?"

"Aye, all's well." The light shifted in the gap, casting the stones into shadow again. "Tunnel's just the same on this side. Can't see any more cave-ins."

"We'll be with you in a minute. Just wait there." Vice wriggled out and dusted off her hands, a trickle of sweat making its way down her neck and back. Hard work, but so far, so good.

"Who's next?"

The four remaining had knotted together in a low conversation. Wynn and Effie stood shoulder-to-shoulder, heads bowed. Aedan had his hand on Effie's shoulder, bending so he was closer to their height. Knigh glanced up at Vice, expression almost blank, but a tightness around his mouth gave him away.

"What's wrong?" she called down.

Effie shook Aedan off and stomped back, shaking her head. "I can't." She squeezed her eyes shut, Aedan and Knigh's lamps painting the lines between her eyebrows with shadow. "I can't!"

Vice cocked her head at Wynn in question. What had her sister so afraid?

Wynn slid an arm around Effie, making a low, soothing

noise. Lips pinched, she grimaced up at Vice. "It's the small space, she—"

"And the rock," Effie groaned, covering her face. "The weight of all that rock. I can feel it—it's suffocating—it's—"

"Hush, now." Wynn pulled Effie against her and stroked her back as she shook in silent sobs.

Vice nodded and gave what she hoped was a reassuring smile. "It's fine. Don't worry, Effie," she said, coaxing. "Wynn, take a lamp and go back. You can follow the marks Knigh left, right?"

Shoulders squared, Wynn nodded. "I'll find the way."

"Keep her safe."

"Always." With an arm around her sister, she took the lamp in her other hand. She nodded again at Vice before turning and ushering Effie back the way they'd come.

Once they were out of sight, Vice talked Aedan, then Knigh through the narrow gap. Their broad shoulders made for a tight squeeze around the boulder, but Vice helped brace their legs from behind and Saba pulled their arms. After a few minutes, both got through safely, soon followed by Vice.

They stood there, dusty with scraped hands, but *safe*. And Wynn and Effie were safe, too. They'd follow the chalk arrows pointing their way out.

Vice gave a tight smile as she pulled out the translated notebook. It was as Saba said—the tunnel continued exactly as it had the other side of the cave-in, except with just two lamps, the way seemed that much darker.

"Onward."

They continued for what might have been five minutes or

fifteen. Saba and Aedan, chatting, fell back with one lamp, but Knigh kept close to her side with the other.

"... they did *not!*" Saba's giggles echoed.

"I'm telling you—three men at once," Aedan replied with a chuckle, lowering his voice. "And I bet she..."

Vice stifled a laugh.

"So," Knigh murmured, voice velvety in the dim light, "now we're friends, am I allowed to ask you about...?" He gestured vaguely.

She raised an eyebrow at him. "You're going to have to be more specific."

"I mean the past"—he shot her a sidelong look—"but I don't know how to start without ending up with your dagger in my gullet."

"I'd never put my dagger in your gullet, Knigh." She gave him a sugary smile. "I'd cut off your tongue, remember?"

He chuckled. "Of course! With *my* own dagger. Silly me."

Smirking, she cocked her head. But if anyone had earned the chance to ask questions, it was him. "What did you want to know?"

"Everything?"

"*Oof.* Everything is *a lot*, Knigh." A lot more than she was ready for, too. She paused at an intersection and consulted the book and compass. "Maybe start at the beginning?" She shrugged. "Seems as good a place as any."

"Fine." He padded on a few steps in silence and Vice thought perhaps he'd decided against it. "Did I really make such a poor impression when we were children?"

"*A poor impression?*" Was he joking? He only looked ahead,

sharp eyes flicking across their path, up the walls. Good to see he was taking her warning about traps seriously.

"Knigh, you drove me nuts."

"What?" He stared at her, eyes wide.

"You were *so* arrogant. You really thought you were better than me—than *anyone*." She raised her hands and grinned at him. "Don't get me wrong, you're different now, but the boy you were? You hardly spoke to me and you *obviously* thought yourself far above taking a dip in our lake."

He barked a laugh, shaking his head. "Bloody hells, Vee, I wasn't quiet because I thought myself better than you." He resumed scanning the way ahead. "I found you *intimidating*."

"Intimidating?" She scoffed. "I was two years younger than you—a little girl, when you were about to go away to naval college."

"Yes, but you were already beautiful"—he shot her a glance, brows lowered, all earnest and intense—"and even then you had that spark of... of... free abandon that you burn with now."

That damn look of his made her shift away, pretending to check the next page in the book. Too intense. Too much.

And his words? She shivered. That little girl had been a damp smoulder, almost put out by Papa. She exhaled through her nose. "You didn't see me around my father much, did you?"

A beat of silence, then he made a sound low in his throat. "No, I suppose not. After Mother and Father presented me to your family, we were always sent away. I... you were quiet, though."

So ironic that Knigh had been intimidated by the very thing

Papa had tried to extinguish. "My father didn't much like that 'free abandon' you found so intimidating."

"I'm sure he was only concerned about society and what—"

"That time I swam across the lake without you..." She tried to apologise for interrupting with a glance, but she couldn't tear her eyes away from the gloom ahead. Something in her chest was knotted too tight. "After you left, I got the birch. I know that's not so unusual." Her sister, Kat, had been rapped across the knuckles a few times. "But... I could barely move for a week." She shook her head. "Every time I sat down, I cried."

His boot scuffed on the floor, and the lamplight bobbed. In her peripheral vision, he watched her rather than the route ahead. That was bad enough—the shock, the pity... He had to be imagining that weak, sad little girl growing to the shape of her cramped cage.

"Vee," he breathed at last. "I—I'm so sorry. I never expected—"

"You see why I don't like to talk about it? About... back then." She lifted one side of her mouth, as if that might make it all a joke.

"I... yes. It does make sense." He exhaled, then touched her shoulder. His warmth seeped into her, gentling her smirk into a soft smile. "I see why you wouldn't want to marry someone that man had chosen." He snorted, hand dropping, leaving her cold. "Especially when he was such an arrogant cad."

She shouldered him, playful. "That wasn't the *only* reason. As you said—*society*. The lady of the manor, prim and proper, popping out babies one after another." Just saying it was enough to make her gag. "I would never have survived that life, no matter who I married." She frowned into the darkness ahead. "It was that life I was really running away from, not you. And poor, foolish Evered just got caught up in it."

"I'm sure he was only too happy to follow you anywhere," Knigh said, voice soft.

"No." The guilt was bitter on her tongue. "He was happy with that world. He was safe in it. It gave him everything he wanted. I... I think he only followed because of my fae charm. I didn't realise then... what I..." She shook her head.

What I was.

The night she'd eloped with Evered, Mama had told her how she'd begged the fair folk for help to have a second child and a fae lord had granted her wish, fathering her baby. But Avice hadn't *believed* such a wild story. It was beyond implausible. Being the daughter of some mysterious fae lord had felt like a ridiculous impossibility.

Even though she'd burned her hand on an iron padlock, she'd tried to explain it away. Heat. Or an allergic reaction. Or... Or...

Not that she could be fae-blooded. Never that.

If she'd known, might she have acted differently? Would she have questioned Evered's willingness to go along with her plans to run away to sea, realising it was fae charm? Would she have let him be?

Or would she have dragged him along anyway—anything to avoid being alone?

"Well," Knigh said softly into the silence she'd left in her wake, "for the record, I liked it when we were sent to play together. I *liked* young Avice Ferrers, though I agree—that wasn't the world for her. She was too bright, too alive, too passionate. Though, I also remember a softness in her..." The skin around his eyes crinkled as he looked into the distance, as though he could squint through the darkness and into the past. "Around your mother, especially."

Mama. She held her breath to stave off the ache building in her chest. A box she'd kept closed for years threatened to burst open.

I'll send for you. I promise.

Three years later, she still hadn't. Maybe with Drake's treasure she could unbreak that promise.

"And there was this one older lady amongst the servants," Knigh continued. "She brought it out, too."

The passage narrowed, forcing them into single file—lifting the lantern, Knigh went ahead. At least it meant he couldn't look at her.

Throat thick, Vice nodded. "Nanny Alder."

He snapped his fingers. "That's the one. As for the lake... If I may defend myself from charges of excessive pride, it wasn't that I thought myself above you or your family grounds or didn't want to spend the afternoon with you. It was far simpler than that"—he turned his back to her, watching the path ahead—"I couldn't swim."

She stopped in her tracks, blinking. "You couldn't—but—"

"Of course," he went on, flashing her a dazzling smile over his shoulder, "I made sure I learned as soon as I—"

Then he wasn't there.

Grinding rock. A crash somewhere below.

She stood, staring. Knigh wasn't there. No light, no lamp, no smile.

No Knigh.

Blood roared in her ears. No Knigh.

Like... like before. Evans and his blond hair, smiling as he exclaimed at the opening door. The clack of stone and hiss of dust. Her rushing pulse.

Another young man, blond-haired too, at the end of a rope at the start of a grand adventure. Swinging. Boarding.

Falling.

The thud of a body smacking into the deck.

Every trace of warmth she'd ever felt fled her body. But that icy coldness brought her back to herself—to here and now. She sucked in wheezing breaths, blinking as if she'd surfaced from a too-deep dive.

Evans and Evered... they were then—days ago for one, years for the other. This, now...

Ahead, where Knigh had been moments earlier, there was nothing but a gaping, dark hole.

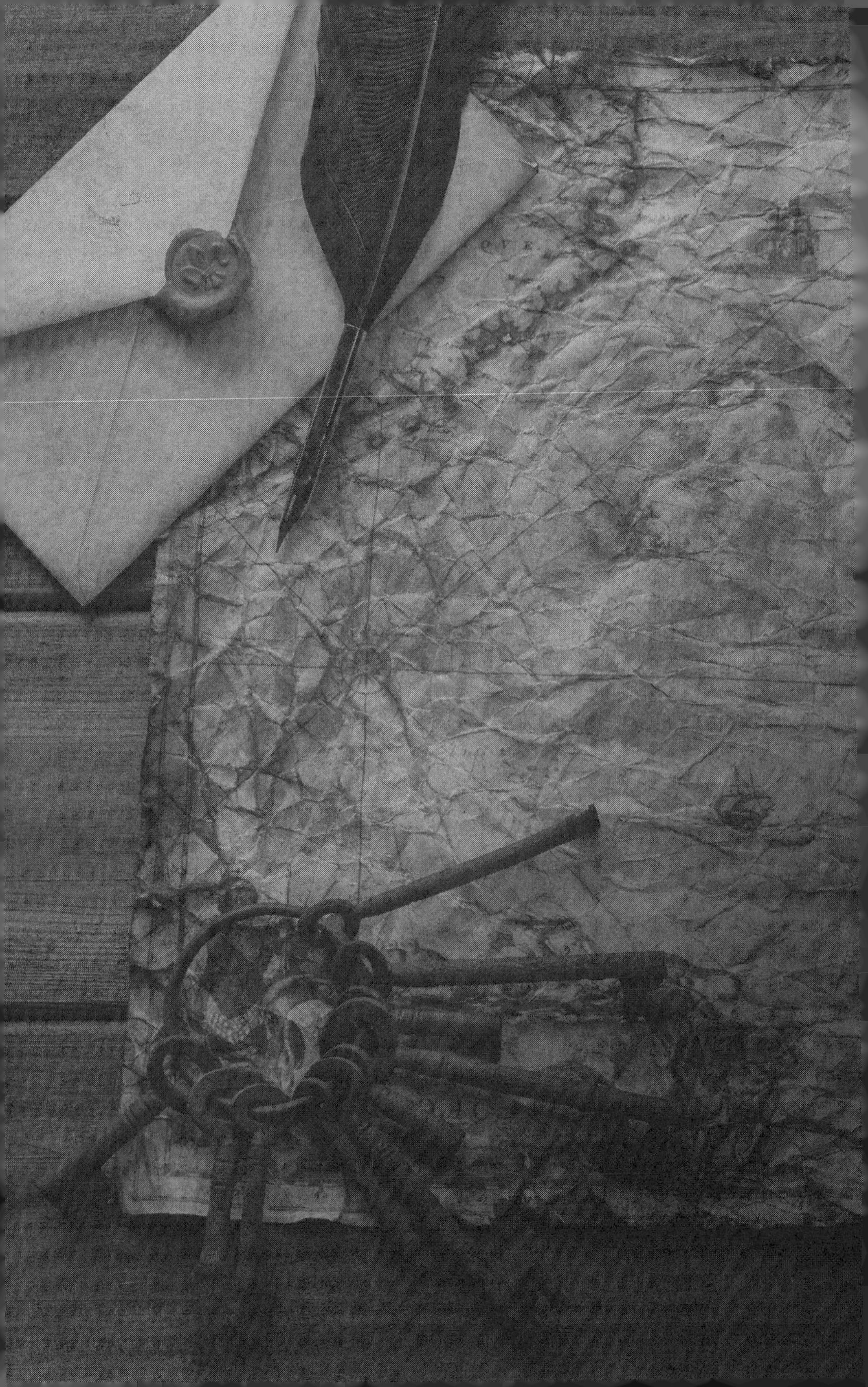

DAMNATION & DARKNESS

The ground vanished. Air and dust and nothingness beneath his feet.

His heart jolted.

Falling. He was falling.

The world was thick, slow treacle, but—no, that was wrong, a trick of the mind. He was plummeting down—had to be. And if he fell too long and landed on the stone that had been beneath his feet, he'd be pulverised.

Damnation.

He dropped the lamp and grabbed—for anything. But there was only the void.

And darkness.

Only a second or two had passed since the ground dropping, but perhaps he was already dead.

Except air whipped around his face and stone rumbled below.

Not dead yet.

He reached out and... *something* grazed his fingertips, tearing the skin. Pain streaked through him.

Pain meant it was solid.

Against all instinct, he reached towards the source of that pain. He could heal himself later. Right now, he had to survive.

He grabbed, but there was only sheer stone, jagged and cruel, taunting him with its solidity and lack of handholds.

He grabbed, but it only tore his fingers.

His chest tightened, like he'd been crushed beneath the falling stone. But he hadn't—not yet. There was still a chance. He sucked in air, heaving against the threatening panic. There had to be an outcrop, a handhold, a way...

He grabbed.

Cold, but solid. Sharp, slicing his fingers, but *solid!*

The air blasted out of him as he crashed into the rock face, right arm wrenching as it stopped his fall.

Hold damn fingers, hold.

They did.

A dozen points of pain flared on his body, bright because they meant he was alive.

Half-groaning, half-panting dust-flecked-breaths, he reached up with his other hand. Another hold—that's what he needed.

Right hand fixed in a death-grip, he groped in the darkness with his left. It skidded over the rough stone, searching for an indentation—anything that would give his fingers the slightest purchase.

Just as his fingertips curved over a lip of rock, there was a tinkle of broken glass and light flared below.

Now he had a two-handed grip, it only took a moment to find cracks to poke his toes into. He huffed and peered down—the rock that had seemed so solid beneath his feet moments ago was nothing more than boulders and rubble. The remains of his lamp burned in a pool of oil, billowing black smoke.

Water lapped at the fallen rock—perhaps an underground stream or the encroaching sea. Too much dust clogged his nose to tell if there was a briny smell. But as his heart steadied, there came a rush and sigh from below. The sea, then. And it had eroded a cavern below their tunnel, leading to the cave-in.

Shadows and light shifted above, and Vee's face appeared at the edge of the precipice. Hands over her mouth, she stared. When she saw him, she let out a low moan, eyes closing for a second.

Had she thought…?

Of course she had. *He'd* thought it—it had seemed inevitable. But here he was, still breathing.

Fingers tight on the handholds, he exhaled a shaky laugh and rested his forehead against the craggy rock. Still alive. He laughed a little harder—he didn't sound far from madness. Maybe he wasn't.

But Lords and Ladies, *somehow*, he was still alive.

Aedan and Saba appeared, squashed at Vee's side. "We'll get you out," Aedan called. "Think he's losing his mind down there," he muttered, but the sound bounced off the walls.

Vee had the rope from Aedan's shoulder and was feeding the looped end down the ravine, every inch of her face tight, attention fixed on her work. Moments later, it was looped around Knigh's back and under his armpits, and its familiar roughness scoured his hands.

The others pulled, and he walked his way up the sheer rock. One step over the other, until Vee's hands closed over his and she hauled him over the edge.

Blessed solid ground. He sucked in a deep breath, clear of dust, and blew it out again, letting the tension ebb with it.

He was alive, and he was safe. His fingers would take a minute to heal with his gift, but they were little more than scratches.

"Well." He brushed dust from his chest, forcing out a shaky laugh. "That—"

The air burst from his lungs as Vee flung her arms around him and squeezed. She might shout at him next, as she had in Redland, but at least he was alive to hear it.

He managed to ease from her grip and patted her back. "I didn't know you cared." He said it with a chuckle, but, damn, that idea was warm and bright, like the first sunny day after Albion's winter. He let his hands plane down her back—just for a moment before she would inevitably shake him off and back away.

Except she didn't.

She had her face buried against his shoulder, and was that...? Gods, she *was*—she was *shaking*.

Laughter gone, he blinked at Aedan and Saba as if they might have an answer for her reaction, but they only stared, faces crinkled, then shared an odd look.

After a few seconds, the trembling through Vee's body

eased and her rib cage expanded in a long breath, pressing against him. Another thing he was alive for, and he wasn't meant to enjoy it—*just friends*—but...

He closed his eyes and tightened his hold on her. Just a second longer. Two seconds... Gods, she felt good—solid and soft, warm, strong, alive, alive, *alive*. Like he somehow still was.

But they were in a cave on an island, looking for Drake's treasure. They couldn't stay like this all day. "Vee?" he murmured.

"I thought..." She released him and pulled away. "But, no spikes." She shook her head and refused to meet his eye. Two clean lines ran through the dust on her cheeks.

She'd been crying.

He'd barely registered it with a lurch in his belly before he was reaching for her again. But she turned and busied herself coiling the rope. Instead, he closed his hand around the little abalone shell that still sat in his pocket.

No spikes. She'd told them about the young lad—Evans—who'd served on the *Sovereign*. About how he'd been kind to her while she was captive. About how he'd died in a trap.

No wonder she'd looked so horrified when she'd peered over the edge. His heart squeezed, and he had to grip the strap of his bag, even though it sharpened the pain in his torn fingers, to keep from trying to touch her again.

Their silence extended, the air somehow thicker and heavier now there was only one lamp. When Knigh forced a laugh to lighten the mood, Saba only gave him a slight smile. Aedan didn't move. He only stared at Vee, brows knotted, nostrils flaring.

No wonder the silence was so heavy. Was Aedan *bothered* by the fact Vee had been so worried? It didn't mean anything— she'd have been just as afraid for him or for Saba.

But there was that look Aedan had given her when they'd reunited in Nassau, and the way he'd reacted when she'd disappeared... He and Aedan were friends now, but Vee and their feelings for her were a gaping hole in their friendship— one they both skirted.

Aedan was in love with her—*had* to be. How did she feel about him, though? And was it any of Knigh's business?

Grimacing, he cleared his throat. "Well, let's be careful, eh?" He smiled stiffly at Saba. "We should link ourselves together, like mountaineers do."

"Good idea." Vee finally turned to face them, holding out her rope.

She consulted her notebook while Knigh healed his fingertips in a flare of warmth and golden light, then secured the rope around everyone's waists. He was careful to avoid touching Vee. It made for awkward manoeuvring, but that way lay temptation. And with their past and Aedan's involvement, this particular temptation could only be messy.

He nodded to himself, tying off the rope around his middle. *Friends.*

This tunnel continued ahead. Thankfully, a narrow ledge led around the cave-in. Beyond that—he frowned and squinted —not solid blackness, like behind them, but...

"There's light up ahead." Just dim lines of rocky walls, but brighter than earlier. Daylight seeping in from outside?

Vee blinked and peered into the distance. "I thought that was just my vision in the dark, but…"

"No"—Saba shook her head—"he's right. I see it too."

Knigh tugged the knot tight and started for the ledge. "Maybe that's our destination."

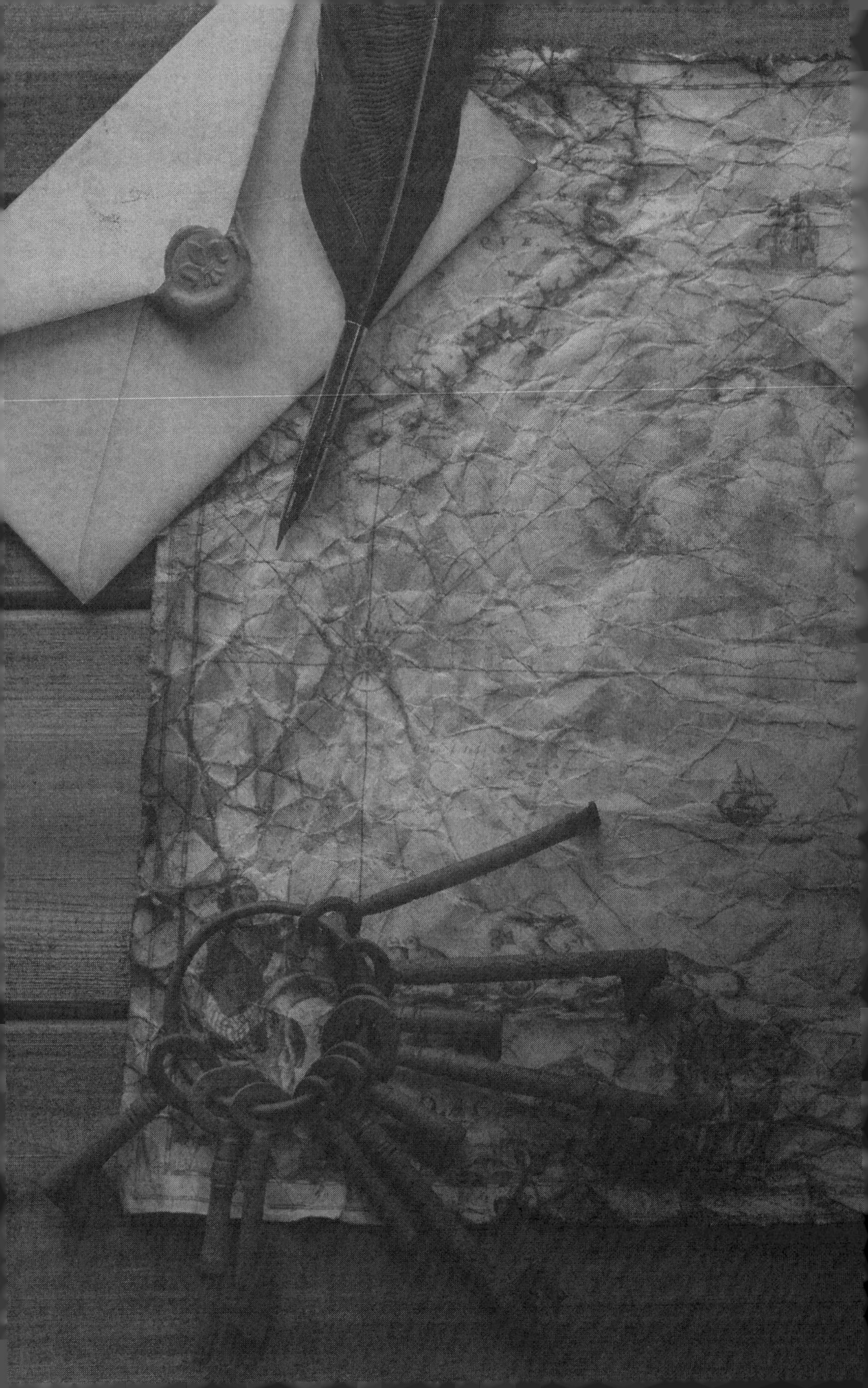

VICUS

Sure enough, once they'd inched along the ledge and past the open maw that had nearly killed him, the passage grew steadily brighter, and with it, Vee's mood.

Knigh bit back a smile. Her excitement was infectious, practically buzzing through the air as she strode at his side, attention fixed ahead, lips slightly parted. He could hardly blame her. The treasure, when they found it, would change lives. For his family alone, it would mean no more reliance on George's relationship with Mercia.

They turned, and the tunnel opened into a cavern filled with sunlight. Eyes closed, he exhaled and let it bathe his face. Glorious sunlight.

Once his sight had adjusted, he turned on the spot. Jagged stalactites clung to an arching ceiling. The air was damp rather than dusty, as it had been further back. The cave walls stretched in a rough circle about forty feet across, except for ahead, where they tapered to a narrow crack that opened to the outside world. Beyond, the rush of waves suggested they weren't far above sea level. Several smooth boulders littered the floor, with the largest at the centre—a flat, waist-height rock forming a kind of natural table around the size and shape of an altar at a temple or sacred grove back home.

Brows drawn together, Vee stalked through the cavern. Her bright eyes—currently a clear, sharp turquoise—roved across it all.

Saba untied her tether and ventured further in. "Look," she called, peering ahead, "the floor drops away."

As he started after Saba, Knigh gestured for Aedan to douse his lamp. It was the only one they had left, and it would be best not to waste the oil while they had daylight. Journeying back through the tunnels in the dark? He shuddered.

Around two-thirds of the way in, past the flat rocks, the floor ended in a drop as sheer as the one he'd clung to minutes ago. Below, the sea undercut the rock they stood on, probably connecting with the cave he'd almost fallen into. Maybe this cavern wouldn't exist in another century or two.

Aedan peered over the edge and shook his head. Eyebrows raised, he turned. "What are we looking for exactly?"

"Anything that looks manmade or otherwise unnatural." Vee's face screwed up, and she lifted one shoulder. "I was kind of expecting it to be obvious once we got here, but..."

Bright smile undimmed, Saba toed the pebbles scattered by a boulder. "Maybe it's just hidden under all this. Aedan, help me search through this crap."

Aedan and Saba crouched, and with the click and clack of stone, they raked through the debris. While Vee ran her hands over the boulders, peering at the surface, Knigh worked his way along the walls.

Craggy and irregular, the same darkest grey stone as the rest of the cave network—nothing stood out. He continued until he reached the sheer drop. No hidden doors or man-made holes. Across the cavern, the other wall was the same.

"Oh!" On the other side of the altar-stone, Saba knelt up, eyes wide. "I found a crystal!" She held up her hand, showing off a long, thin shape that glinted in the sunlight.

Vee paused from her examination, back suddenly erect. "Any symbols on it? Or writing?" He didn't need to see her face to know the expectation rising in her—it was clear in the brightness of her voice, the breathlessness. "Or is it carved in a shape? Or..."

"Just natural, I think, but..."

"Oh." Vee's shoulders slumped, and she bent over the altar-stone again. "Good find," she muttered.

Saba exhaled, a line forming between her brows. "Wonder what I can sell it for." With a shrug, she stowed it in her bag.

From hunched shoulders to bowed neck, even from behind, every part of Vee spoke of frustration.

It made Knigh's own shoulders tighter. She was too invested in the treasure—since their reunion, she'd done little but work on the Copper Drake's deciphering and translation.

He clenched his hands. If Perry were here, she'd go over and stroke Vee's back, offering a smile and some words of wisdom. But every time he and Vee touched, it shook through him, stirring a storm of emotions—care, want, comfort, desire, a drive to protect... All of it far too strong for *just friends*. And every touch chiselled away his self-control.

He had to honour her decision. No matter how hard it was.

At the altar-stone, a jolt tensed along Vee's back and legs. In an instant, he was at her side. "What is it?"

She scrubbed her shirt cuff over the smooth rock, smearing away dust and dirt. A straight edge emerged—too straight to be accidental.

He bit his lip, pressing his hands into the cool rock as he strained closer. A bright thread of excitement weaved its way through him, lighting up his veins.

As she wiped, the line reached a corner—a right angle—and another line and another, finally revealing a carved rectangle barely an eighth of an inch deep.

She glanced at him, eyes on fire, a faint smile of disbelief on her mouth. Mouth dry, he couldn't say anything back, but he nodded, and as one they scrubbed their hands and sleeves over the rest of the altar-stone in a frenzy of movement.

Maybe there was more. Perhaps it would be a puzzle or spell out another code or... or...

There! Several inches from the rectangle, a tiny, perfect circle—more a dot, really. Scouring the heel of his hand against the worn-smooth stone, he bent closer. Another dot surfaced from the dirt, and another and another. "What's this?"

Six dots arranged in a perfect circle. That was no accident either.

But what did it *mean?*

Vee had her cuff balled up, frantically wiping at an area inside the rectangle. "What is...?"

The carved shape of a key. Just small, inside the bounds of that indented rectangle.

A symbol.

It spiked in his veins, his heart, as bright and thrilling as any storm. *This* was something they could use, something they could decode. It had to *mean*—

"Bastard!"

He jolted at Vee's outburst, but apparently it wasn't at him, because her gaze followed the lines of the rectangle. "What's wrong?"

She ran her finger over the key, glaring as if it had done her a great wrong. "Bloody bastard!" She pounded her fist into the altar-stone with each word.

Even staring didn't change it—still just a small key carved into stone. What about it had her so worked up? "Vee?"

Her shoulders sank. "I've seen this symbol before," she muttered, nostrils flaring. *"And* this shape..." She traced the rectangle. "Gods damn it all—we need Mercia's map."

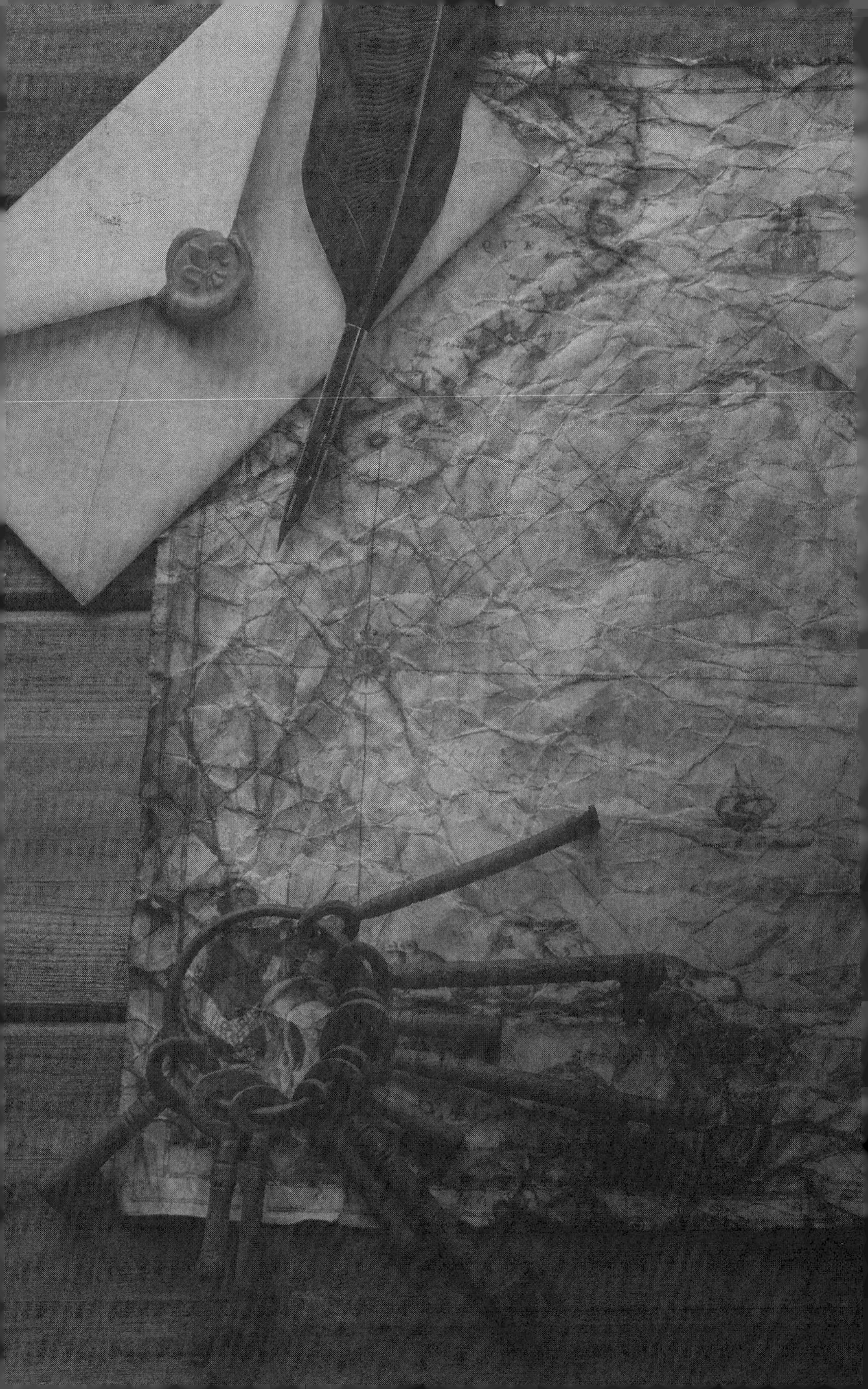

MISSING PARTS

At the name, Knigh flinched. *Mercia.* Was that man destined to dog his every step in life? He regained his composure and blinked from her to the key. "You mean, the map would fit in that space?"

Her eyes closed as she nodded, shoulders sinking. "The key was the only symbol on it, showing the island with the cipher key." Grunting, she thumped the stone surface again. "I should've known we'd need it. I should've taken it while I had the chance!"

Except guards had followed her at all times, and Mercia had been very protective over his map. "From the way you described it," he said softly, "you *didn't* have a chance."

She grumbled. "I didn't *make* a chance. With just the key on it, I assumed it was only useful to find that location. If I'd realised…"

"Vee," he sighed, leaning against the altar-stone. But she

remained staring at the enigmatic little symbol, jaw rippling as she ground her teeth. "Vee," he said again, voice lower as he brushed his little finger against hers.

She scowled up at him.

"You're a sea witch, not a psychic. You couldn't have known we'd need that map. Now we know its importance, we can work out a way to get it. For now"—he raised his eyebrows and gave a coaxing smile—"we can use a dummy piece of paper, draw on the rectangle and key, then make a note of whatever this location tells us."

She blinked as if playing through his suggestion, then nodded. "That's... actually a really good idea." She fished in her bag. "Let's see what the Copper Drake can tell us about what to do."

Using the rock as a table, they bent over the Copper Drake and the notebooks containing the Latium and the Albionic versions. He flicked through the Copper Drake while she placed a sheet of paper over the rectangle and traced the edges and the key. The tension in her ebbed, easing through her shoulders and ending that rippling clench of her jaw.

Small mercies. There was something disturbing, *unnatural* about seeing Vee so on edge.

He found the page with the sketched boulders from near the cave entrance. Next were the bird directions. "It must be around here." He placed the book on the altar-stone and turned the page.

Vee pressed beside him so she could see the book clearly, too. "Maybe this part." She traced her fingers down another coded passage.

Thankfully, it was a section they'd already translated. Heads together, they turned the two notebooks to the right pages and read out both the Latium and Albionic versions, in case anything changed in translation.

When the sun meets his lover at day's end, follow the purple path.

There was no purple in the cave and no path but the tunnel they'd entered through. Vee's screwed up expression suggested it made as much sense to her as it did to him.

"Let's break it down," he said, voice reassuring even in his own ear. *"When the sun meets his lover at day's end."* The answer had to be there, but... He shook his head.

Lips pursed, Vee scanned both versions.

"Sunset," Saba called, voice sing-song.

Knigh blinked at Vee. Vee blinked at him. They both frowned, following Saba's voice.

A dark silhouette, she stood at the edge of the precipice, hands on her hips, back to them. When she turned, she grinned.

"Sunset. It must be." She raised her hands like it was obvious. "The sun is the masculine; his lover is the earth. He spends his days gazing at her longingly, and when he sets, he finally gets to touch her, sinking into her embrace, and snuffing out the light." She arched an eyebrow suggestively. "Because, you know, the best things happen in the dark. Plus"—she jerked her chin over her shoulder—"that's due west. I'd bet my entire seed collection that the setting sun shines through that crack and reveals... I don't know, *something*." She looked expectantly from him to Vee and back again.

"Huh."

"I'll be damned." Vee stared. "You're right."

Knigh snorted—they'd been too absorbed in the books to realise what was staring them in the face. "So, we just wait until sunset?"

Vee closed the book and shrugged. "I suppose so."

So they waited. They chatted and ate rations from their bags—fruit, dried meat, and crispy flatbreads made from yuca. For the first time since they'd entered the cave, Vee relaxed, leaning back on her elbows, head thrown back, rather than hunching over the Copper Drake and its translations.

When the light in the cave shifted to a brighter gold, Knigh nodded. "It's time."

Vee was on her feet, hurrying back to the altar-stone. So much for relaxing. Knigh bit back a sigh and followed. Saba padded after.

The shadows inside the cave were sharper now, longer as the sun hit the crack directly. Aedan readied himself to light the lamp so they wouldn't be stuck in the dark.

Light blazed through the fissure to fall directly on the stone table and Vee behind it, turning her into a creature of pure sunshine. Her skin gleamed, her hair shone, and for a moment Knigh couldn't breathe.

But then she frowned.

Clue. Puzzle. Treasure. Right. He blinked and followed her line of sight.

Light came through the crack, yes, but it was a wide band on the floor, the table, and the wall behind. There was no pin-pointing beam and no hint of purple.

Vee spun and moved out of the light to look at the back wall, shaking her head. "I don't..." She craned over the altarstone, examining it again. "There must be something we're missing. Something..." Disbelief etched itself across her face so deeply it made his heart ache. "Maybe a lens or a mirror or... or..."

Knigh bit his lip. The paper waited in the rectangle, Vee's pencil resting on it—so expectant, so sure they'd find an answer here today.

What if there *had* once been a lens or mirror, but the delicate glass had broken in the two hundred years since Drake had been here? Or a freak wave or storm could've come through that crack and washed it away. A curious bird might've stolen something small and shiny...

"Look, then." Vee's voice shook. She crouched and scrabbled through the pebbles and scree on the floor. "Come on, look!"

Lips pursed, Saba blinked at Vee. The crease between her brows could've been frustration or helplessness. "We looked earlier." The concern softening her voice—it was helplessness. She was worried for her friend and her fixation on the treasure, but there was nothing she could do about it. "There was only that crystal."

The light of the setting sun inched across the floor as, through the crack, almost half its disc disappeared into the sea.

Tick-tock.

Knigh squared his shoulders and straightened. "We're running out of sunset." He nodded at Saba and Aedan, every inch the confident captain. What a lie!

Nonetheless, they spread out around the stone table and searched. Rocky rubble clacked as Knigh swept it aside. The sound echoed as the others did the same. He frowned so intently, it made his brow ache. Any glint or glimmer…

"There must be something," Vee muttered. "The Copper Drake wouldn't lead us here… The purple path… That bloody key…"

She was right—all the clues had pointed them here at sunset. At the *rapidly disappearing* sunset. Maybe there *was* something they were missing. The flat rock. The rectangle with its key. Those six dots. None of this was accidental.

Six dots. What were they for?

Six. Something stirred in his memory, something thousands of miles away. "Six… Hexagon." What if they weren't arranged in a circle, but a hexagon? And in the book this morning… "*Vicus.* Quartz."

That was the distant memory tugging on his attention. Aunt Tilda's orangery, all the way back in Albion. It housed an indifferent collection of ferns and other plants left from her parents, but she'd always been far more interested in her own mineral collection. The orangery's glass walls showed off their glittering facets perfectly, she always said, and the place did indeed gleam with purple, green, orange, and blue, and a dozen more shades reflecting and refracting off and through the different rocks.

Many times as a boy, he'd examined the collection, reading the labels, holding gemstones up to the light. Scratching clear, fractured gypsum with a fingernail. Marvelling as moonstone gleamed in iridescent shades of blue to green to gold. He'd loved how labradorite was similar, but dark, like the aurora he saw on his first tour of duty in the frozen north.

He knew their colours, their hardness, their shapes...

"Quartz crystals naturally form in hexagonal prisms." Breathless, he sprung upright. "Saba, that crystal you found. Show me."

Saba shot to her feet. Still crouched, Vee had gone quiet and only stared as Saba rifled through her bag.

Knigh bit the inside of his cheek. *Please, gods, let it be whole.* Quartz wasn't as delicate as glass, no, but it could still break.

Saba pulled out a canvas-wrapped package, half a foot long and a couple of inches wide. She placed it on his outstretched hand and when he unwrapped it...

A perfect prism of clear quartz shone in the dying light, throwing light on his palm—red, orange, yellow, green, blue, indigo, violet.

"Purple," Vee whispered. "The refraction!"

Knigh grinned, nodding, chest too tight to reply. He bent over the stone table and placed the flat bottom of the prism so each corner rested on a dot.

He met Vee's gaze over it, and they both gave the barest nod. A perfect fit.

At Vee's side, Saba gasped, and Aedan slapped her on the shoulder.

The broad line from the setting sun inched across the stone table. But there was still enough to hit the prism and split into a glorious rainbow that spread across the spot where Mercia's map should've been.

"The purple path." Hand trembling, Vee grabbed the pencil and traced the line of violet light.

A thrill ran through Knigh's veins and across his skin, bright and buzzing like the lightning she controlled. "That must be our next course." Once they plotted it on Mercia's map, it would lead them somewhere. *Follow the purple path.*

Beaming, Vee held out the paper for him to see.

It was only a line, but he couldn't help grinning back. That infectious enthusiasm in action again. His fingers itched to pull her into a hug, but before he could decide whether it was something *just friends* did, Saba grabbed Vee from behind and kissed her cheek. "You did it!"

Vee chuckled. "I haven't done anything yet. But... *we* are another step closer."

"Closer than anyone else has got in two hundred years." Aedan slung an arm around Knigh's shoulders. "Thanks to this one."

Knigh patted Aedan on the back. *His friend.* Not a subordinate for him to command. Not another officer to look upon as an equal, an ally, a brother-in-arms, but not quite a *friend*. Beyond the sparking excitement, something else warm and bright bloomed in his chest. He took a moment to simply enjoy it.

"Thanks to Vee's translation and tracing of the cipher, more like." He nodded to her. Her face was the only part of her left in sunlight, and the cave air grew cool on his skin. "Let's light that lamp and get back to Perry to tell her the good news. I'd wager Saba's seed collection that Drake's treasure will be ours before the year's out."

Laughing, they gathered their bags and equipment.

Not immune to the giddiness, it took him a couple of attempts to light the lamp, his hands were shaking so much.

Lords and Ladies, he hadn't even believed in Drake's treasure two months ago, but between the Copper Drake, the scrap of paper that had led them here, the cipher key, and the sheer force of Vee's conviction... he'd be a fool not to believe.

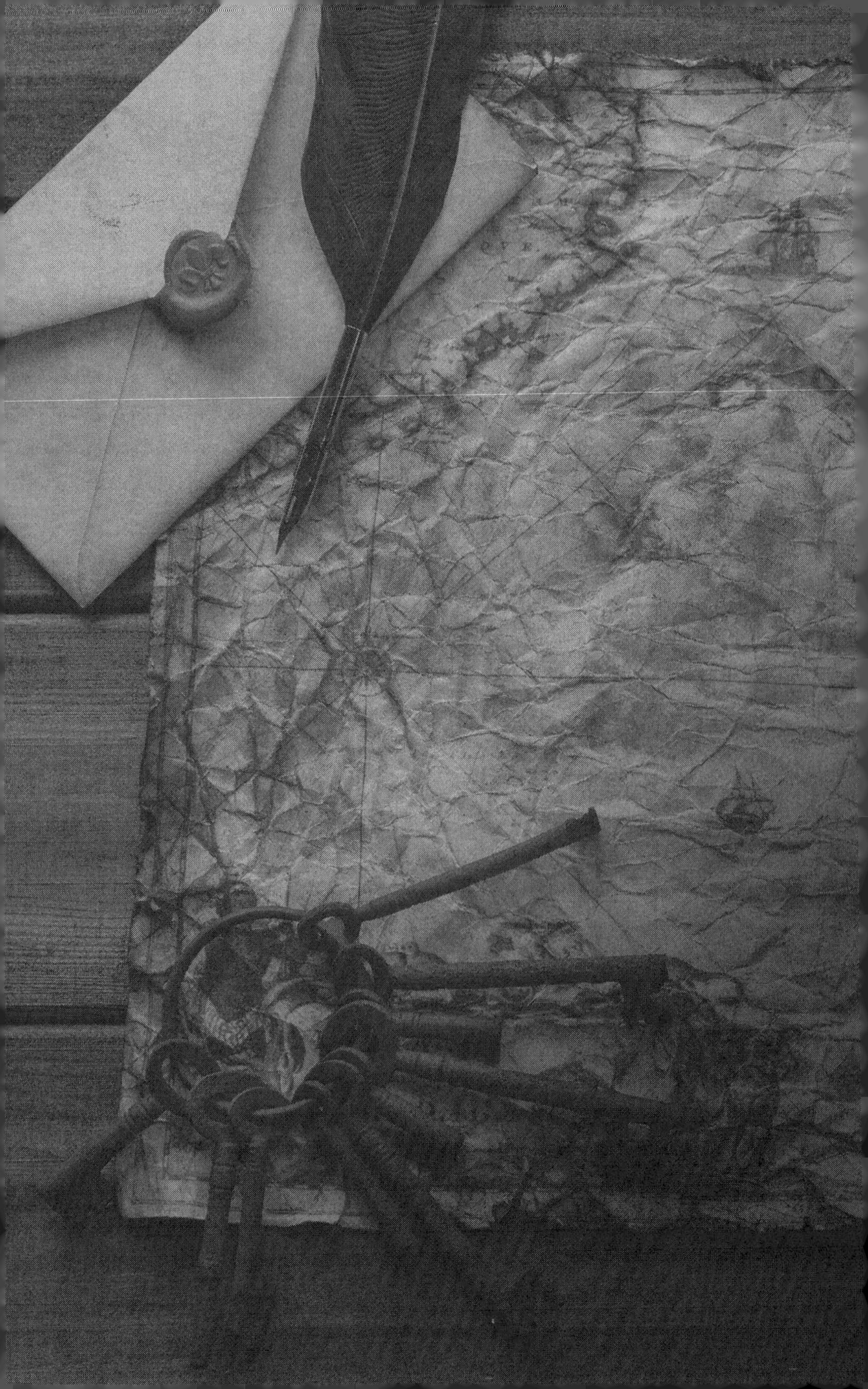

TRUTH OR DARE

Night creatures chirruped and whooped in the dark forest, but aside from the occasional rustle in the undergrowth, none came near their lanterns and torches. Saba, Aedan, Wynn, Effie, Perry, Lizzy, and Knigh chatted amongst themselves, apparently enjoying the nighttime walk.

Out in front, Vice twitched aside a broad leaf that strayed over the path. She tugged at the bag over her shoulder and trudged on uphill.

Another night's delay.

Their lantern had lasted long enough to see them through the tunnels and back to the beach where the crew had set up camp. But rather than setting sail, Perry had insisted they stay until morning. Those who'd gone out hunting during the day were still preparing their kills, and plenty of the crew had enjoyed a drink or two. So, captain's orders were to relax.

Vice's shoulders were anything but relaxed.

They needed Mercia's map. The sooner the better. But getting it meant going near His Royal Slyness.

She couldn't do that to Knigh again. Not after he berserked on the *Sovereign*. Whatever plan she came up with to get that map would have to keep Knigh safe. Problem was, as they'd seen in Redland, he wasn't the sort to stand back while others went into danger and he was remarkably prone to coming after her. In Portsmouth. On the *Sovereign*—twice.

Warmth seeped through her tense muscles, even as she ground her teeth.

I'll always come for you.

And that's exactly what worried her.

Damn Knigh Blackwood—she'd never had cause to worry about things before he'd come along. Now, here she was fretting for his safety in body, mind, and soul. What if—

"We might not have the map," Knigh's voice, low and private, cut through her thoughts, and she jumped to find him at her side. The side of his mouth twitched, perhaps at the fact he'd surprised her. "But we've still made progress." He threw her a glance, eyebrows raised. *"You've* made progress—on a two-century-old mystery, no less. That's impressive."

"We translated it together. And you were the one who—"

"But I wouldn't have been there if not for your"—he paused and gestured, as if the right word was somewhere in the damp evening air—"determination. But right now, we don't need your determination—we need that relaxed Vee whose laugh is so bloody infectious it even gets me."

Maybe he had a point. "Hmm." A smile inched in place.

After all, winning a full, *real* laugh from Knigh always felt like an achievement.

He cleared his throat softly, gaze flicking away. "*I need that Vee.*"

Mouth dropping open, she blinked. She'd been expecting a speech about how she should be glad of their progress, but...

"It's time to celebrate what we've achieved," he went on, "how far we've come. And I hear that this hike through the forest is going to end somewhere quite spectacular, although none of you will tell me exactly what it is." He scoffed and shook his head. "But I don't need a spectacular place. You are remarkably skilled at prising open my control and helping me just... *be*. Like when you got me to dance after the Grays' ball. I was about ready to murder someone that night, but you... you saved me. You had me laughing and, of all things, *frolicking*. I don't think I've ever frolicked. I'm not a spring lamb, for goodness' sake!"

She snorted at the image. But something rose in her chest, like a rising tide lifting a boat. He'd been tense that night, true, but *saved?* Just the other day, she'd thought her primary skill where he was concerned lay in hurting him. Here he was saying he needed her, she'd saved him.

"And yet you..." He looked at her sidelong, grey eyes golden in the lamplight. "Somehow, you have that effect on me. And after today's scrape with death, I could do with laughing and... well, maybe not *frolicking* but certainly enjoying myself."

"My word," she murmured with a half-smirk, "Knigh Blackwood might be about to say the word 'fun'. Someone alert the press!"

"Oh yes," he said, deadpan, "because I'm not known for loosening up—I see what you did there. That's *very* funny." The look he gave her, one eyebrow arched, underlined his sarcasm. *"But,"* he said, nudging her with his elbow, "it's equally alien seeing you with your shoulders tensed up around your ears."

"Touché."

Ahead, the forest cleared, giving way to smooth stone and steam. Knigh's lamplight gleamed off a smooth grey-black pool. Past that, clear water trickled into the steaming hot spring.

Vice breathed in the warm, moist air and exhaled with a groan, shoulders loosening in anticipation. Maybe setting off tomorrow wasn't such a terrible idea.

"A mud bath?" Knigh drew level with her and peered at the dark water. "You want me to wallow in mud like a pig?"

Laughing, she dumped her bag on a clean stone as the others joined them in the clearing. Trust Knigh to see it that way. "I thought you said you wanted to relax."

He backed away from the muddy water, the edge of a scowl on his tense brow. "This wasn't what I had in mind."

Aedan had already stripped off his shirt and used it to slap at Knigh. "Suit yourself, but you're missing out." Grinning, he shucked off his breeches and tossed them with the rest of his belongings. He slid into the mud, letting out a groan.

"Aye," Lizzy added, slipping in after him, "the volcano makes it warm, see. 'Tis lovely after a hard day's work."

Everyone else was already undressed and making their way in, but Knigh hung back, watching with a sceptical twist to his mouth.

Once Vice had finished stripping, she slid into the liquid mud. Slick and warm, she couldn't help but sigh and that tension in her shoulders that Knigh had pointed out dropped away. She found a seat on a submerged rock and leant back. Maybe he'd been right: relaxation and celebration—that's what they needed tonight.

Saba dipped her fingers in the mud and drew a stripe down the centre of her face and a crescent moon on each cheek. Smiling, she came to each of them and painted their faces in black lines and dots. She always ended the ritual in the same way—a nod, then a kiss on the brow before moving to the next person.

When she came to Vice, with two fingers she followed the lines of her cheekbones, then dabbed a dot on her chin.

When Saba pressed her lips to Vice's brow, something about the gesture formed a lump in Vice's throat. Once Saba moved to the next person, she closed her stinging eyes and took a shaking breath. In the gibbet cage, on the *Sovereign*, even on the *Swallow,* when she and Knigh had been in the same place but not talking and certainly not friends... *this* was what she'd missed.

"You all right?" Perry murmured, her expression as soft as her voice. She held out one of the rum bottles they'd brought along.

Vice swallowed back the lump and took the bottle. "I am now. Have I told you how much I—?"

"Come on, Blackwood," Saba called from her spot opposite Vice. "It's your turn. You wouldn't want bad luck, would you?"

Frowning, Knigh shot Vice a glance as if to ask what Saba meant. Bad luck because he wasn't painted with mud? Not something Vice had heard before, but that didn't mean it wasn't true. Then again, maybe Saba was just trying to persuade him to join in. With a half smile, she shrugged back, then took a sip of rum, its toasted sugar sweetness coating her tongue.

"Blackwood," Wynn and Effie chanted. "Blackwood. Blackwood."

Laughing, Vice took up the call and within seconds, the entire group had joined in, calling his name over and over and—

"Fine," he shouted over them, flinging his hands in the air and ending the chant. "Fine!" He rolled his eyes and stomped to the rocks where they'd left their clothes. He peeled off his shirt, the taut flesh of his chest gleaming in the lamplight.

Vice's breath caught and her fingers tensed around the bottle, but it made a poor replacement for that taut flesh, the firm muscles, the ripple of—

Wild Hunt, stop!

Biting her lip, she tore her attention from Knigh before he got to his breeches.

Just friends. Just friends. Just friends.

Friends didn't letch at friends. And doing that with him and all their history and the temptation she found impossible to resist, even when she'd been angry and hurt—it was a recipe for assured disaster.

At her side, Perry resolutely stared up at the star-specked sky. Wynn, Effie, and Lizzy stole glances and giggled while Aedan rolled his eyes. Saba, though—her gaze lingered on Knigh, a small smile on her lips.

That was fine. Totally fine. Or at least she'd told Saba it was. If Saba wanted him, she could...

Vice took a gulp of rum, then another, still refusing to look at him.

"Hey, stop hogging the drink, you." Chuckling, Aedan reached across and scooped the bottle from her grasp.

From the right, a faint slosh and ripples across the grey-black surface of the pool signalled that Knigh had entered. At least that meant the liquid mud would hide most of his body now.

Vice exhaled and eased back against the rocks. She would be fine about Knigh and Saba if anything happened between them. It was just lingering desire. "That's all," she whispered to herself.

Perry touched her shoulder—small hand warm and callused and familiar in a way that brought back that ache in her throat. "You sure you're—"

"Uh-uh, Blackwood," Saba said, as he started towards the space next to Vice, "you're not finished yet." She dipped one hand in the mud and beckoned, her smile bright.

With a sigh, Knigh changed course, muttering something about *in for a penny...* "Fine, go on, then."

That left his back to Vice and clearly her eyes hadn't got the message about not letching at friends, because they followed the sinuous lines of the tattoo. Lines that met and intersected, then split again, only to join another set, etching out moon and stars and waves and rising sun. Lines her fingers knew well and ached to trace again. Lines that were so uniquely his, that spelled out his complexity, that—

Bollocks.

This wasn't just lingering desire. It was infatuation. Childish, stupid infatuation.

And it needed to stop.

"Good gods, where's the rum?" she muttered, searching for the telltale glint of glass in someone's hand.

Wearing an odd expression, part-crumpled, part-pursed-lipped, Perry sloshed across the pool and grabbed a bottle from Effie, who had it half-way to her lips, but was too busy staring at Saba and Knigh to pay attention to the rum.

"Here," Perry murmured, pressing it into Vice's hand.

One, two, three long swigs that streaked warmth down her throat. Maybe that would be enough.

Maybe a couple more, just for good measure.

At least Knigh's broad back blocked her view of Saba running her fingers over his face, cocking her head at him, looking up from below her thick, dark lashes, licking her lips while she stroked a fingertip along the hard line of his jaw and his neat beard…

No. More rum. Much, *much* more rum. Vice screwed her eyes shut and drank. Because although she couldn't see it, she could *imagine* it all too clearly.

When she looked again, Perry tugged the bottle from her hand. But it didn't matter—she was already warm and rosy.

Knigh sat opposite, next to Saba, a single stripe running across one cheek, over the bridge of his nose, and across the other cheek, like she'd underlined his eyes. It certainly served to underline his good looks, emphasising the perfect planes of his cheekbones and nose.

At least that ordeal was over.

As they chatted and drank, the rum took full hold of Vice—her limbs loosened, and her head grew a little fuzzy. She laughed louder and louder and grabbed Perry in a rough hug as they joked about how, between Vice and Knigh's work and Barnacle and the kittens, she'd all but lost her quarters. She flicked mud at Aedan for teasing her. She poured rum in Wynn and Effie's open mouths until they erupted into gurgling giggles and pushed her hand away.

This was what she'd been missing. Friendship. Pure and simple friendship. And that was what would cure her of this infatuation with Knigh.

He didn't seem the type to tend crops, but then again, he hadn't seemed the type to screw a notorious pirate and desert the Navy, had he?

Vice searched for a bottle—surely one was due here on its rounds of the group. But the nearest was firmly in Perry's grip and Saba drank from the other, watching Knigh. Vice would have to wait her turn.

She drew a long breath and lay back against the rocks. Knigh maybe wasn't a natural smallholder, but he would excel at it as he did most things. And he'd want to settle somewhere. As he'd said—piracy was a means to an end. A way to find a fortune. It wasn't a lifestyle—not for him. And not for Saba.

She would be happy for Saba and Knigh. She'd toast them at their wedding and coo after their children.

She *would*.

"You'll play, won't you, Vice?"

She blinked, shaking away thoughts of Saba and Knigh's

beautiful children with grey eyes and midnight hair. "Of course!" She pushed a grin in place, then bent her head to Perry. "What have I just agreed to?"

"Truth or dare," Perry muttered and pursed her lips. "Yours was the deciding vote, so now *I'm* playing too. *Thanks.*" She shot Vice a sidelong look—only low-grade withering on this occasion.

Vice bit back a laugh and gave a helpless shrug.

Wynn picked Perry, who chose *truth*, which was standard for her. With an impish grin, Wynn asked an innocuous question about her favourite crew member.

"I love all my children equally," Perry said with a laugh in her voice, lifting the bottle.

Groans and boos echoed across the mud bath. In response, Perry just laughed harder and blew kisses back.

Mouth quirked, Knigh raised the other rum bottle in a mock-salute. "Well-answered, Captain. Did you ever consider a career in politics?"

"Captaining you lot *is* a career in politics."

"Aye, maybe." Vice leant closer to Perry and continued in a stage whisper, "but I'm your favourite, right?"

Wynn and Effie splashed mud, forcing Vice to shield her face or end up eating the stuff.

Once the laughter died, Perry cleared her throat. "My turn to ask. I choose... hmm..." She surveyed her crew for a long while, then her head snapped to the right. "Vice," she said, one eyebrow arched in a way that said this was revenge for making her play, "truth or dare?"

Vice went to answer—

"Dare," Saba called.

"Hey," Vice chuckled. "It's my turn—my choice."

"Yes"—Saba cocked her head, grinning—"but you *always* choose *dare*. I've never seen you pick *truth*."

"Too afraid," someone muttered. It was a female voice, but so soft, she wasn't sure who'd spoken. Maybe she wasn't meant to have heard it.

Vice huffed, shaking her head. "Too afraid, am I? I'm not afraid of anything, thank you very much. Perry"—she turned and smiled—"I'll go for a truth."

Perry stroked her chin. "A truth... Erm..."

"Are you in love with Blackwood?" Aedan asked.

The words jolted through Vice like gunshots. "What?"

In spite of the warm mud and rum-fire in her belly, a chill prickled its way down her spine.

Silence consumed the clearing. Knigh stared at a point on the mud-pool's surface a foot away from his chest, face still, eyebrows raised.

Vice laughed, shaking her head. "What—that's... ridiculous."

"Ridiculous, huh?" Aedan's chin lifted. "The way you reacted earlier when you thought he'd fallen and died—"

She snorted, silencing him. "Just because I don't want him to die doesn't mean I... that I..." Her pulse throbbed in her throat and temples. She didn't know what words were meant to come next, only that there was a void in the sentence. Not knowing what to say prickled panic in her chest. "It doesn't *mean* anything."

Still, silence. She didn't dare look at Knigh, but on the edge of her vision he hadn't moved. Gods, did he think...? Would it be worse if he thought she loved him or that she didn't?

Saba took a slow sip from the rum bottle, never taking her gaze from Vice.

Lifting her chin, Vice cleared her throat. "Well, I don't believe in love, so I can't answer that question. If you're not happy with that answer, just give me a forfeit—I don't care."

"Kiss Aedan." Saba's voice was soft, but with the quietness hanging over the pool, it carried. "Or Blackwood."

Vice froze. Her heart was somewhere in her feet—no, further down, squelching in the mud under her toes.

Saba stared back, mouth flat, brows tight.

That look. This wasn't a game anymore. Was Saba asking her to prove she didn't have feelings for Knigh by choosing Aedan?

Problem was, Vice didn't want to kiss Aedan. She'd done it in the past, yes, but that was *before*. The idea of kissing him roused nothing in her. Doing it in front of Knigh? Her throat closed.

Bollocks.

As for Knigh... She wanted to kiss him too much—far, far too much. Her lips tingled as heat flared across her skin, banishing the chill from moments earlier.

Bollocks!

If she kissed him, even under the guise of a dare, they'd all see.

They'd know.

No way would she be able to hide how much she wanted him, how she burned for him. It was bloody embarrassing.

Lizzy, Wynn, and Effie looked from her to Saba to Knigh and back again, like this was one of those gods-awful plays they put on in Nassau.

But she couldn't kiss Aedan…

And here she was, back at the start. This was impossible.

No quips came to mind, no cunning plans to twist her way out of the trap and escape.

Her chest heaved, and she stared at Saba in a silent plea. *Don't make me. Don't make me. Don't make me.*

Saba could change the forfeit, add herself as a third option, or an even worse forfeit for refusing to kiss either of them. But she only stood there, dark eyes as stony and unreadable as obsidian.

"I think it's time to rinse this mud off," Perry announced to the ringing silence.

The hot spring—the next part of the mud bath. Yes. That. *That.*

Vice splashed to her feet. "It is," she muttered, making for the low rocks—her escape route.

Yes, she was running away, but the alternative…

Shaking her head, she clambered out, limbs slick and black with mud. A hush remained in her wake.

Just keep moving.

As she stalked over to the pool of steaming water, her heart throbbed so hard it made her hands tremble.

The slop of mud told her Perry followed. Which meant she'd want to try to talk about this.

Screw that.

Vice leapt into the hot pool. She tucked into a ball and let the water consume her from head to toe. Her skin tingled, the temperature near-unbearable like a good bath.

It would wash away the mud. Maybe it would wash away these stupid feelings for Knigh, too.

She hugged her knees to her chest and hoped.

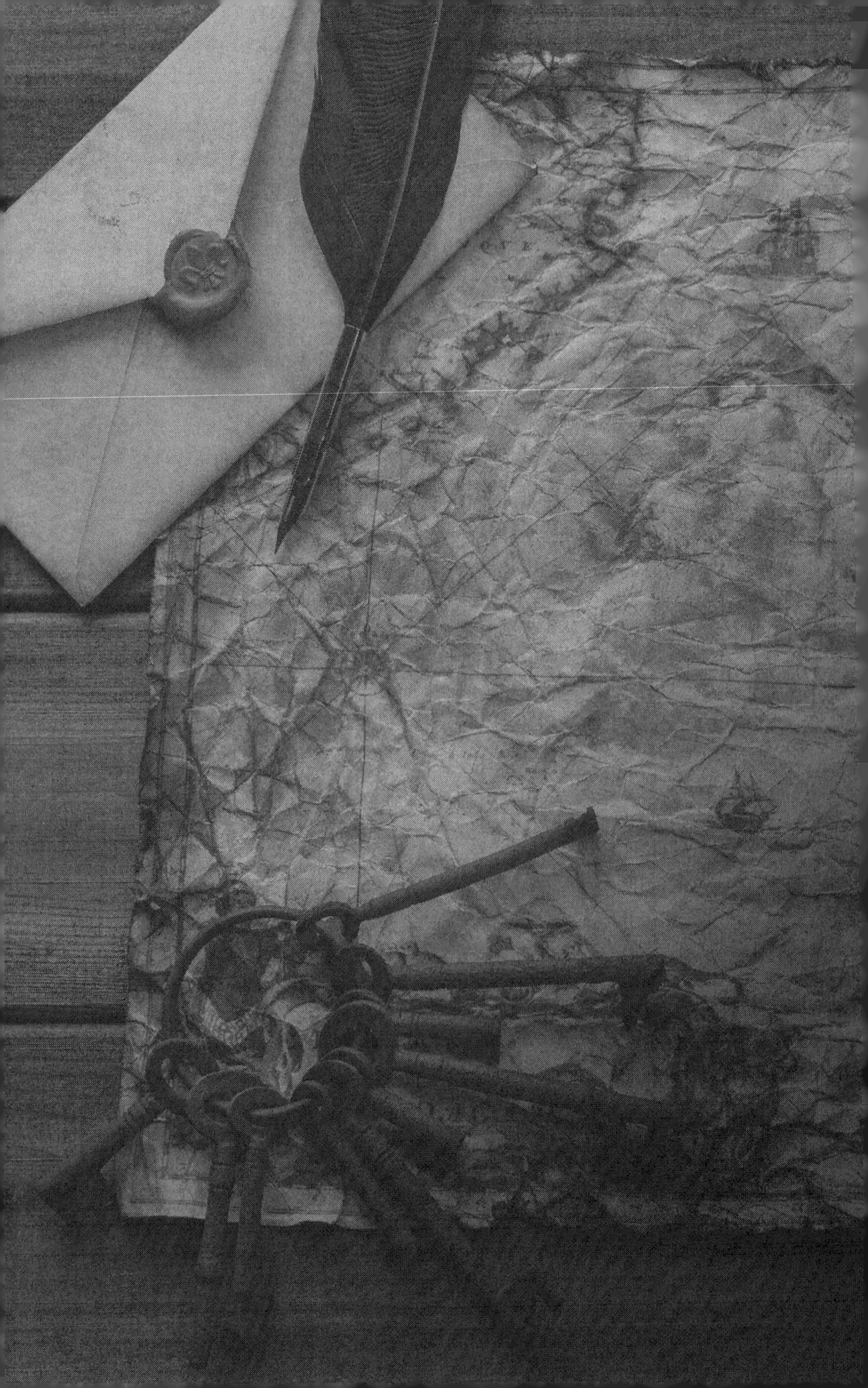

THE ROVER

T he hot water made her skin bright pink but didn't wash away thoughts of Knigh. The next best solution was to avoid him. Easier said than done. A few days later, they arrived in Kayracou, and Perry sent Vice and Knigh to dig up information on the whereabouts of Mercia—*and* his map. Much as she tried to keep the trip strictly business, they ended up chatting and joking as they looked up old contacts.

That had been yesterday, and now Vice gripped the *Venatrix's* wheel, jaw tight. Their chatter had been the only thing worth laughing about in Kayracou. With his height and charisma, Knigh wasn't exactly great at blending in, and although it was a friendly town, too many pairs of eyes had lingered on him far too long. He didn't have the knack she did for slouching and making herself smaller, less noticeable.

Thankfully, the guards had done nothing but look. Maybe

he only tugged on their memories vaguely, not registering as the naval deserter thanks to the tricorne hat covering his telltale shock of white hair.

At least Saba was back to normal, laughing and chatting, no sign of that challenge at the hot springs. It must've been a test to see if Vice really was fine with her pursuing Knigh. Which she was. Absolutely fine.

Urgh.

At her shoulder, by the helm, Knigh cleared his throat. "If you don't want me to come with you, you'll have to take it up with Perry."

To Port Royal. Right. *That* wasn't happening.

And yet he was *still* going on about it. They'd discussed this. He knew her answer. When they'd found no leads on Mercia, they'd agreed that Port Royal would be the best place to find the *Sovereign* or information on her location.

That was the only thing they'd agreed on.

Taking him, a fugitive and deserter, to the Royal Navy's stronghold?

"No," she said, voice low. "You're staying on the ship." She screwed up her face, staring ahead at the glittering sea.

"We'll see." He said it lightly, like he didn't believe her. "But unless you tie me up and leave me in my berth, I'm not sure how you're going to keep me away."

"Now *there's* an idea." Despite the wrench in her belly at the idea of Knigh anywhere near Mercia, she gave him a wicked grin. Knigh tied up was a pleasing image on so many levels.

He stilled, lips parted, eyes on her.

The wrench became a flip.

Just friends.

Clearing her throat, she jerked her attention back to the sea. Safer. Much, *much* safer than thinking about Knigh tied up.

She shifted the wheel to take better advantage of a fresh wind coming in from the east. With Kayracou in their wake, they traced an easterly course alongside Arubeira and the tiny islands scattered nearby. In a few more miles, they'd leave the island chain and turn northeast to open sea and Port Royal.

"I'm not forcing you into the lion's den." *Again.*

She'd lived in that lion's den for over a month and it wouldn't bother her to set foot in it again, but *Knigh*...

That wrench again, this time accompanied by a shudder.

She couldn't do that to him, not after last time.

"You're not forcing—"

"Sails!" The cry drifted from above. "Off the port bow."

Vice sucked in a breath, head snapping to port. Pale craggy rock rose sharply from the sea. These waters were popular with fisherfolk, but with sheer cliffs in all directions, it was impossible to land on most of the islands.

The sails that emerged from behind this islet didn't belong to any fishing vessel—they billowed black and bold compared to the almost white stone.

Pirates. She narrowed her eyes. Whoever they were, they'd been using the land to hide and get as close as possible before revealing themselves.

"Someone you know?" Knigh asked, gaze on the large brig turning and cutting a line through the water towards them.

She frowned from sail to sail, all of which were full to make best speed. Ah—there, fluttering... A white spear piercing a red heart. "No, but I know that flag."

"Damnation. I see it. Same as at Redland. But there was no brig in the attack."

Vice shifted, wrinkling her nose. Something about this was off—worse than milk left in the sun all week. It crawled over her skin until she shuddered in an attempt to shake it off.

"The *Rover*," the watch shouted.

Knigh glanced from the *Rover*, ahead, then back again. "On an intercept course," he muttered.

In a second, she'd taken in the same angles he had. "You're not wrong. Larger than us, too. And gods know how long they've been using these islands to stalk us." With a growl, she tightened her grip on the wheel and steered a touch to starboard. No use making it easy on them. "Aedan!"

He hurried over.

"Give the order to load all guns with chain," she said, "and have everyone armed. But nice and quiet—I don't want them realising we think they're anything other than friendly."

Brows lowered, Aedan watched the *Rover*, then nodded and strolled down the steps and along the ship, pausing to murmur to each crewmate he passed.

There would be a fight. It sang in her veins, thrumming like an ancient beat on drum and bone. Her muscles and gift lit up in response.

"Blackwood," Perry called as she emerged from her cabin and trotted up to the quarterdeck, "on the helm, if you please."

Perry felt it, too.

"Aye, Captain." Knigh snapped to attention.

Vice couldn't help but smile at that. You could take the man out of the Navy, but you couldn't take the Navy out of the man—not *this* man, anyway. She stood to one side and offered him the wheel.

Eyes shifting between the brig and their course dead ahead, his long fingers closed around the handles. His arms flexed with the natural shift as water pulled against the rudder, which in turn tugged on the wheel.

A true sailor, grip soft enough to let the sea have her way, just a little, keeping their sailing smooth, but not weak so the wheel could wrench from his grasp and the *Venatrix* dragged off course.

He was made for this—for ships, for the sea, for taking the wheel at her side.

Ba-dump—her heart gave a heavy beat that stole her breath.

Perry arrived at her elbow and watched the approaching ship. "Anyone we know?"

Vice flinched with a sharp inhale. *Damn, is that what I really think—that Knigh belongs at my side?*

Blinking, she shook her head. No. Infatuation.

That war song still hummed in her blood and coiled muscles, reminding her this was not the time or place.

"The *Rover*," Knigh said. "Same flag we saw at Redland."

"Hmm." Perry nodded and patted Vice on the back. "Doesn't look like they're just coming to say *hello*. Ready to evade, please. I won't start this, but let's be the ones to finish it, eh?"

"Couldn't have put it better myself, Captain." Vice inclined her head. "Maybe they think a little frigate like us is an easy target. Can't wait to prove them wrong." She placed her hand over one of Knigh's and tried to ignore the way her nerves sparked at the contact.

Focus. Inhaling, she released parts of her awareness into sea and sky as Perry went to give more of those quiet orders.

Between Vice's currents and Knigh's hold on the wheel, they kept the *Venatrix* moving on a subtly evasive course.

First, they sped just ahead of the *Rover's* broadside. So the brig turned, aiming her cannons towards the *Venatrix's* stern. At that point, Vice cut their speed until they dropped behind the *Rover's* cannon arc, never giving them the chance to fire.

"What a vexing woman," Knigh murmured, amusement edging his voice, glinting in his eyes.

"*Ha!* So I'm the only one doing this, am I?" She arched an eyebrow at him as they adjusted the *Venatrix's* course once more.

His face straightened, almost innocent, and he lifted a shoulder. "I only do as I'm bid by the wicked Pirate Queen who holds me utterly in her thrall."

"If only that—"

Cannons boomed.

Her hand tensed against his and she twitched the current; in answer, he took them sharp to starboard.

A trio of shots splashed into the water.

So the *Rover* had grown fed up of waiting to get a full broadside and instead settled for using her bow chasers. Perfect. Exactly what she'd been waiting for.

"Bringing us around," Vice called, scowling at the enemy—because that's what they were now. In three seconds, they'd have the *Rover* lined up to take *their* broadside.

Two seconds.

One.

The deck shuddered beneath her feet as their port cannons fired like thunder, launching chain shot right at the *Rover's* masts and rigging.

"Beautiful," Knigh breathed, eyes bright as they followed the arcing trajectory.

With a creaking crash, the *Rover's* foremast and a yard splintered and fell. Holes opened up on three of her remaining sails.

Vice exhaled, almost laughing in relief at such a great strike. Another broadside like that and they'd be dead in the water.

The *Venatrix's* crew cheered as the teams reloaded their cannons.

Knigh nudged her with his elbow, and when she looked up, he flashed a broad grin. "Glad I'm not your enemy anymore, that was..." He shook his head and gave a low whistle.

"I'd never have hurt the *Venatrix* that badly." Grinning, she stroked her thumb over the end of the handle they both held, the varnished wood smooth as silk.

He laughed as they shifted course, then caught her thumb under his. "Sometimes I think this ship was built for you."

He gave her a sidelong look, and her heart leapt in her chest again. Gods, he was intoxicating. Especially this new version of him, still controlled in so many ways, but with a blossoming ease that made his laughter less rare and his smile more relaxed.

Boom.

She blinked and tore her gaze from his. They were in a fight. *Concentrate, Vice.* She plunged into her gift, bending the current and wind to her will, even though it made her muscles ache almost as much as her heart did. His thumb slid off hers as he adjusted course to follow, and together they dodged another handful of shots from the *Rover*.

With a few more turns and rounds of chain shot, they took the top of the mainmast and most of her mizzen canvas.

"Clovis," she called, spotting him down on the main deck, "helm, if you would."

Knigh raised an eyebrow, still watching the *Rover*. "Why? Where are *we* going?"

"To find out why the hells they attacked us."

"They're pirates, aren't they?"

Of course that was all he saw—despite having hunted them for years, there were some areas of pirate society he really didn't understand. "You're so naval, sometimes." She nodded as Clovis arrived and took over at the wheel.

"Take us in," she told him and smiled her thanks before tugging Knigh's sleeve to get him to follow her fore.

"They're pirates, yes, but so are we." As they strode to the weapons racks, she picked out her boarding party amongst the crew—Saba's patterned headscarf and Lizzy's red locks being the easiest to spot—and beckoned them to join her. "Most pirates don't attack others"—they reached the racks and Knigh selected a rifle—"unless there's bad blood... or someone takes a truly impressive haul that they haven't fully secured."

He checked the gun, long fingers running over the lockplate with ease, each movement deliberate. "Are you telling me there *is* such a thing as honour amongst pirates?"

Slinging her fae-worked rifle over her shoulder, she chuckled. "Shocking as it—"

"Vice," Perry's shout rose over the rush of sea and crew in movement, the clatter of loading guns. A moment later she was there, a sheen of sweat on her brow. "What are you doing?"

"Preparing to board." Vice plucked the rifle's strap. "Why else would I be wearing this?"

"They're dead in the water." Perry's brows knotted together, lips pursing, dangerously close to a full-strength withering glare.

So perhaps battle wasn't the time for sarcastic remarks to her captain, just as it wasn't the time for lusting after Knigh. Fine. But she had to say *something*—Perry couldn't seriously be considering *not* boarding the Rover.

Vice cleared her throat and inclined her head. "We can't let them get away with attacking other pirates. And certainly not us—we allow that, and within weeks word's around Nassau that the *Venatrix* is a soft touch. Who won't take their chances against us, then, pirate or not?"

"Reputation, then? I might've known." Perry scowled at the *Rover*, jaw working side to side. Eventually she exhaled through her nose, shoulders falling. When she nodded at Vice, her frown had grown determined—wrathful, even. "Get over there and teach them a lesson. I want to know why they came after us in the first place. Was it just an opportunity or...? That flag..." She shook her head. "This doesn't feel like a random opportunity to me."

Huh. So Perry agreed with her. And so easily. Wonders would never cease. Vice grinned and slapped her on the shoulder. "That's exactly what I intend to find out."

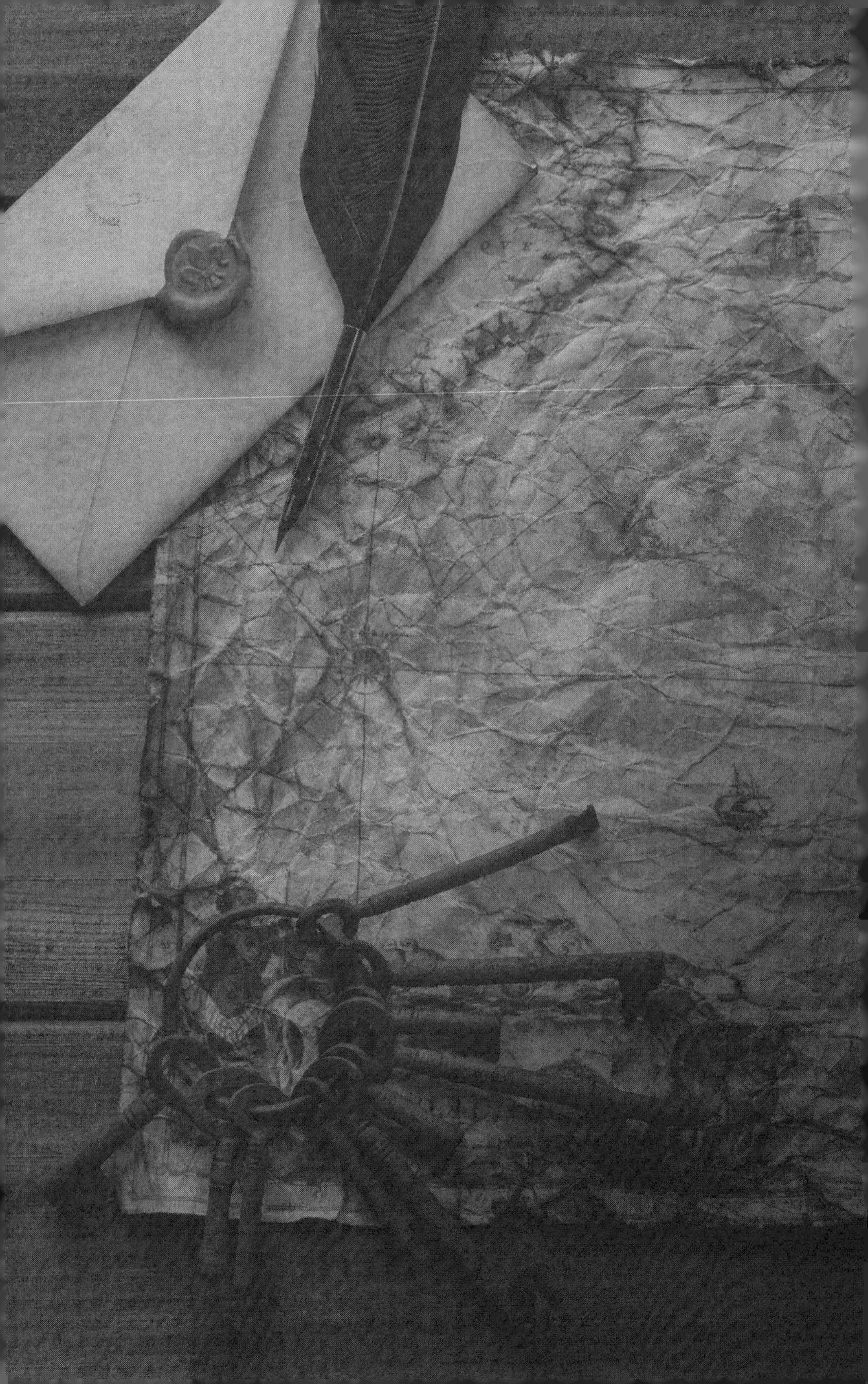

LACKEYS & TOMBSTONES

Shoulder-to-shoulder with Vee and Aedan, Knigh forged space on the *Rover* to allow more of the *Venatrix's* crew to board. His blade rang, catching strike after strike, the sound blending into the percussion of steel on steel as a full melee broke out across the deck. More and more of their crewmates poured over the ship's rail and onto the *Rover's* deck, blades between grinning teeth, pistols in hand.

His heart hammered a fierce accompaniment to the beat of battle. Every muscle coiled, stretched, sprung loose. Being so close to the possibility of death brought life and living into such sharp focus. The sweat on his brow. The heave of each breath. The gleam of sun on an axe blade.

Perry had said focus would help his anger. The here and now, not thoughts of Father.

The breeze cooling his skin. The flap of torn sails overhead. The coppery tang of blood in the air.

He was in control. He could do this—he could fight without erupting.

One blow after another, Vee angled them towards the pale, red-haired man they'd identified as captain from his ostentatious waistcoat and the knot of fighters around him.

With a clash of swords, Knigh engaged the closest, each strike ringing through his bones as Vee, Aedan, Saba, Lizzy, Wynn, and Effie took their own opponents. The captain edged behind one of his men.

"The captain, I assume?" Vee flashed a cocky grin. "What do I etch on your tombstone?"

"No tombstones at sea, lassie." He grinned right back, rolling his shoulders. "But you can address your surrender to Tew."

Half-scoffing, half-grunting, Vee punched her opponent in the nose with her sabre's knuckle-bow. He slumped to the deck, leaving no one between her and the captain. "What the hells are you playing at, attacking us like that?"

"War's war even to the *great* Lady Vice," Tew said, his borders accent lilting as he stepped into the space left. "Don't know what you did to piss off Vane so much, but it's no matter to me."

So Vane was behind this. And they flew the same flag as at Redland—he had to be behind that attack, too.

"Vane?" Vee said. "You're sailing for *him?* Lords and Ladies, that's low." She spluttered a laugh, lip pulling up in what was almost a sneer.

"Too proud for your own good. Just as he said." Tew flashed his teeth in a cheerful smile before raising his sabre.

"You've needed taking down a peg or two for a long while, lassie."

"Maybe I do"—Vee inclined her head—"but you're not the man to do it and neither is Vane. Let's parley—save your life and your crew's."

"Sorry, to disappoint ye"—he shrugged as if helpless—"but I'll stick with my reward from Vane."

A reward? For what, Vee's life?

No time to puzzle that now—Tew's blade flashed as he launched at Vee, and Knigh's muscles coiled, shouting at him to intercept.

But she could handle this herself, and Knigh's enemy took his captain's attack as a signal to surge forward. Knigh clenched his jaw and feinted high, then slammed his foot into the man's knee. With a crunch that ached in his bones in sympathy, it bent the wrong way, forcing an agonised scream from the man's mouth.

"Vane's lackey, huh?" Vee jerked her chin up. "Is that his flag, too?"

"*Our* flag," Tew sneered.

"Oh, I'm sure it's a terribly equal partnership." She dodged a blow, then countered. "You're a fool if you follow him."

"Then I'm not the only fool in these waters, and all of us are hungry for your blood, little girl."

"My blood, eh? That's the reward Vane promised you?" She clicked her tongue, so nonchalant, then a second later lunged.

Tew twisted, but she still caught his shoulder, leaving a red-edged tear in his shirt, staining the gold-braided waistcoat. He hissed in pain.

"See," she went on, recovering her stance, "it's your blood we'll have today. Vane has nothing for you—no money, no blood. Blackwood, remind me, what's a crewmate's share of nothing?"

Sowing the seed of doubt in the *Rover's* crew—even if Tew wouldn't back down, perhaps more of them would. A grin tugged at Knigh's mouth. With their combined fae charm, it just might work. Steel singing, he parried a blow from the woman to his left as she tried to get to Vee. "A great big pile of nothing."

"That's what I thought."

Tew laughed as he caught a quick swipe from Vee. "Oh, don't you be worried, lassie, he'll have plenty for me and mine once he gets that merchant he's after."

Vee snorted, blade coiling back. "A single merchant? Even if he did share it with you, it's going to be slim pickings between *two* crews and the rest who fly that pig-ugly flag."

Eyes narrowing, Tew smiled like a sabrecat having his chin rubbed. "Not once he ransoms the girl and her ma' to her brother. Navy captains earn a pretty penny and I'm sure he'll be mighty keen to get them back, safe and sound."

Cold crept over Knigh's flesh. His blade was already up, catching a blow from an opponent, but he didn't see who it was and he hadn't told his arm to move.

No, it couldn't be Is and Mother. Plenty of captains had sis—

"Especially with him being a pirate hunter—never know what the likes of Vane will do to a pirate hunter's sister, eh?"

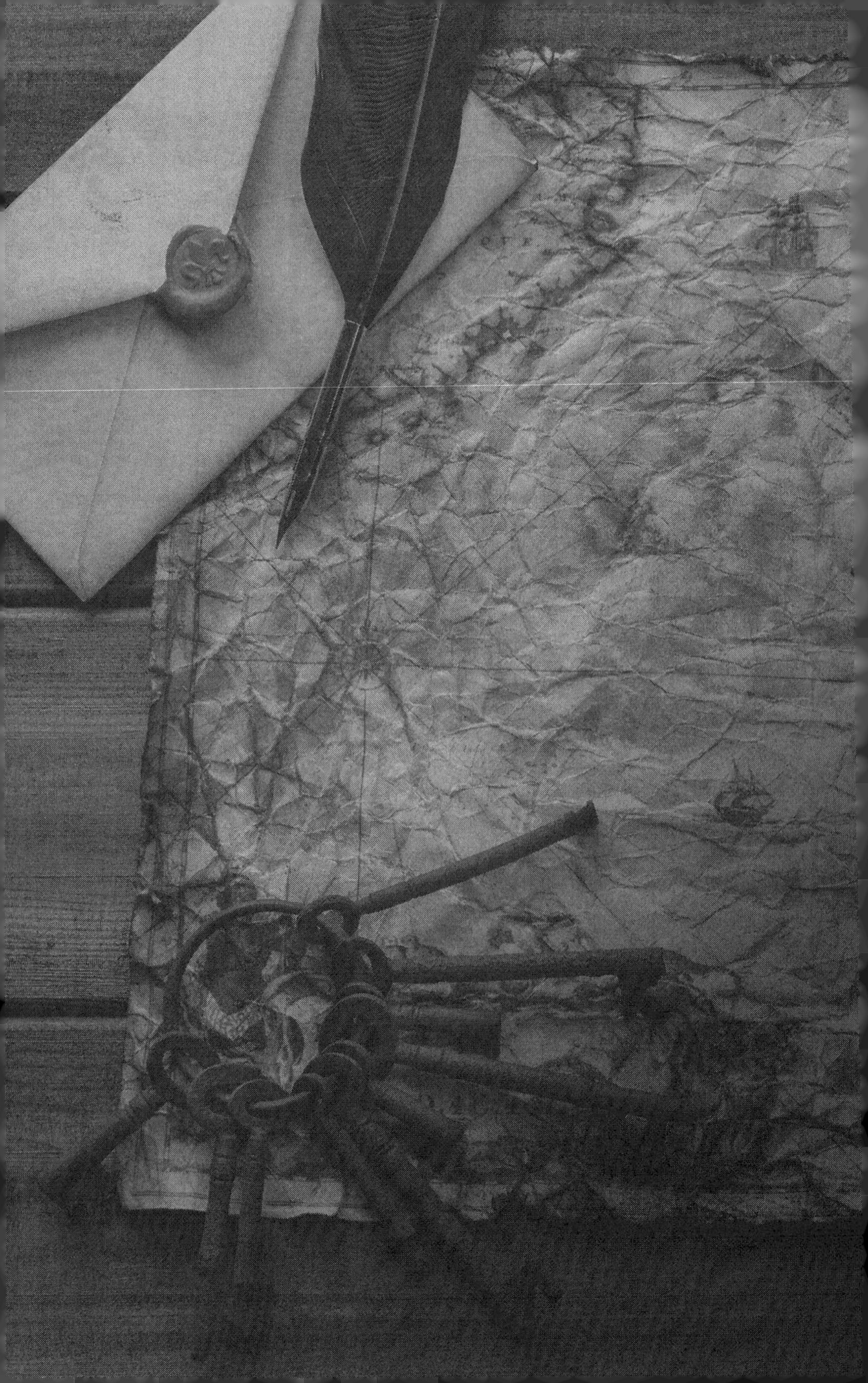

WHICH SHIP?

Every hair on Knigh's body stood on end.

The only sound left in the world was the thunder of his pulse.

A pirate hunter's sister.

Those women... They could be Is and Mother. And the merchant ship—that could be the *Swallow*. Billy had promised to deliver Knigh's letter to them personally, but the letter didn't tell them to come here. They had no reason to leave Albion. But...

But.

A pirate hunter's sister.

That thundering in his ears. The fire in his veins.

Knigh didn't tell any part of himself to move, but his muscles exploded.

In a blink, he was an inch from Tew's face, fingers closing around his wrists. The whites showed all the way around Tew's eyes and sweat trickled down his cheek. His wrist creaked under Knigh's hand as he tried to turn his blade.

Growling, Knigh released Tew's left arm, snatched his sabre away and flung it to the deck. "Which merchant ship is Vane after? What's the pirate hunter's name—the family's name?"

Nostrils flared, Tew bared his teeth. "Ha," he spat. "I'm telling you nothing."

Knigh squeezed his wrist until it groaned.

A vein bulged in the pirate captain's temple.

He kept squeezing.

A strangled sound came from low in Tew's throat, as if trying to hold it back. Good. Pain would make him talk. Had to.

"Knigh." Vee's voice was full of warning.

He blinked. Beyond his pounding pulse, no sound but sea and sail. The fight had stopped. Everyone was probably staring, but he couldn't tear himself from Tew.

"What pirate hunter?" He bit out each word. "Which ship?"

Tew puffed out between his gritted teeth, spittle hitting his lip.

A pirate hunter's sister.

Blood simmering, his fingers wrapped around Tew's throat.

"Knigh," Vee said again, "he's probably lying. Getting you angry is—"

"I'm nowhere near angry yet," he snapped, chest tight. "If I was, he wouldn't be breathing." But he eased his shaking grip on the man's worthless neck and instead seized his shirt with both hands. "I'm only going to ask one more time. *What* pirate hunter? *Which* ship?"

Silence reigned on the *Rover's* deck. Even the sea seemed quieter, as if it too strained to hear the answer.

Ragged breaths tore through Knigh's lungs, threatening to become a roar if this man didn't—

Crack.

It split the air—split Knigh's ears.

Tew's head snapped to one side. He might've made a sound, but Knigh only knew the sharp ringing that followed a too-close gunshot. He slumped in Knigh's grip, blood and gore covering his gaudy waistcoat.

"A pirate hunter's sister... *My* sister?" Knigh shook him, but he only flopped, body loose.

Dead. He was sodding dead. And he'd told them *nothing*.

Knigh's head snapped right.

On the other side of Vee, smoke hazed from Saba's pistol. She still stared at Tew, eyebrows low. "He pulled a knife." Her voice trembled. "Behind his back."

On the floor below his dangling hand, a slender stiletto lay on the deck, still rocking as if it had only just fallen.

She'd saved his life. But possibly cost Mother and Is theirs.

With a growl, he dropped Tew to the deck. "Who knows?" He raked the *Rover's* crew with a glare, their faces blurring into a meaningless sea of wide eyes. One of them had to know. "Who knows?" he bellowed, lungs burning with the words.

They backed away. There was a *clang* as someone dropped their weapon. Then another. A pair of hands rose in surrender. The rest soon followed.

He didn't give a damn about their surrender. He needed—

A touch landed on his shoulder, cool through his shirt. It

swept past his collar to his neck, such a blessed relief against his skin he could've moaned.

"Knigh," she said, voice as cool, as calm as that touch, "stand down. We'll get answers. I promise."

He'd nearly berserked, hadn't he? Only a spider silk thread away—if that had snapped, he'd have lost himself completely.

So much for focus. So much for control. What a fool.

He hadn't even considered Tew having another weapon, and yet it was achingly obvious. Of course a pirate would have a knife behind his back—he'd arrested enough of them, pulled daggers from down boots, up sleeves, between shoulder blades.

A stupid mistake. And it could've cost his life. Then where would Is and Mother be? Tew might not even have planned to use it against him. Vee was right here, easily within reach—he could've stabbed her.

His stomach wrung itself out, touching his tongue with the bitterness of what that mistake could've cost.

Hand still on his neck, Vee's thumb traced a light path into his hairline, quenching the last of the fire in his veins. "Knigh?"

He shut his eyes and nodded. "I'm sorry." For snapping when she was trying to calm him down. For nearly losing control again. For being this wildfire that she always had to put out. But his throat was too thick to say all that, his chest too tight. Instead, he nodded again. "Thank you."

Past Vee, Saba's shoulders sank, and she returned her pistol to its holster at last.

He owed her a *thank you*, too, but he didn't trust himself to say anything more.

Vee accepted the *Rover's* surrender and demanded to speak

to the first mate. But the first mate was dead and the quartermaster, too. A woman with a shaved head and umber skin came forward declaring that she was Oba and the most senior person left. None of the others argued. She stood with Knigh, Vee, and Perry as the *Venatrix's* crew collected the *Rover's* weapons and surveyed her holds.

"Only captains went to Vane's talks," Oba said, the flat set of her mouth spelling out her disapproval, "so I don't know much."

Knigh's heart dropped, but he schooled his expression to the comforting blankness he'd worn for so many years at sea. "What *do* you know?"

What pirate hunter? Which ship?

"Two women set sail from Albion—mother and daughter." She glanced at Perry and Vee. "The daughter's a woman grown"—her teeth flashed bright, bared—"the way they spoke of her, that much is obvious."

He bristled, jaw clenching so hard it was painful. But at least it was controlled. He was still here, still in charge of himself.

In the periphery of his vision, Perry shot him a look. Vee touched his back, the coolness of her hand a balm through his shirt.

Exhaling, he pulled his teeth apart and gave Vee the barest nod—acknowledgement and thanks.

She'd promised to get him answers. They might not be answers he liked, but anything was better than the empty questions circling each other. *What pirate hunter? Which ship?*

"Like Tew said," Oba went on, "Vane reckons they're the

mother and daughter of some Navy captain—a hunter." She shook her head, frowning. "Or maybe he *was* in the Navy and left—I heard different things."

Knigh's heart stopped. Vee would turn and tell him it was fine, it could describe anyone.

But she'd gone still, staring at Oba.

"What things?" Her lips barely moved.

"Someone said he was a deserter." Oba shrugged. "But you know what gossips some folk are—take anything you tell 'em and repeat it halfway across the world before they stop and wonder if it's true. Lies or not, Vane reckons he can get money out of this hunter. Believes it enough to go after his sister and mother."

A deserter. The words tolled through him. He couldn't move. That had to be him, didn't it? How many captains of the Royal Navy hunted pirates and then deserted?

Vee tugged on his shirt sleeve, pulling him closer. "Anything else? Tew mentioned a merchant ship. Do you know its—?"

"Aye, I know its name." The corner of Oba's mouth lifted as she turned from Vee to Knigh, though no amusement lit her dark eyes. "This one asked the question enough times—I was waiting for you to ask again."

His mouth dried, tongue sticking to the roof of his mouth. He strained forward. "And?"

"The *Swallow*."

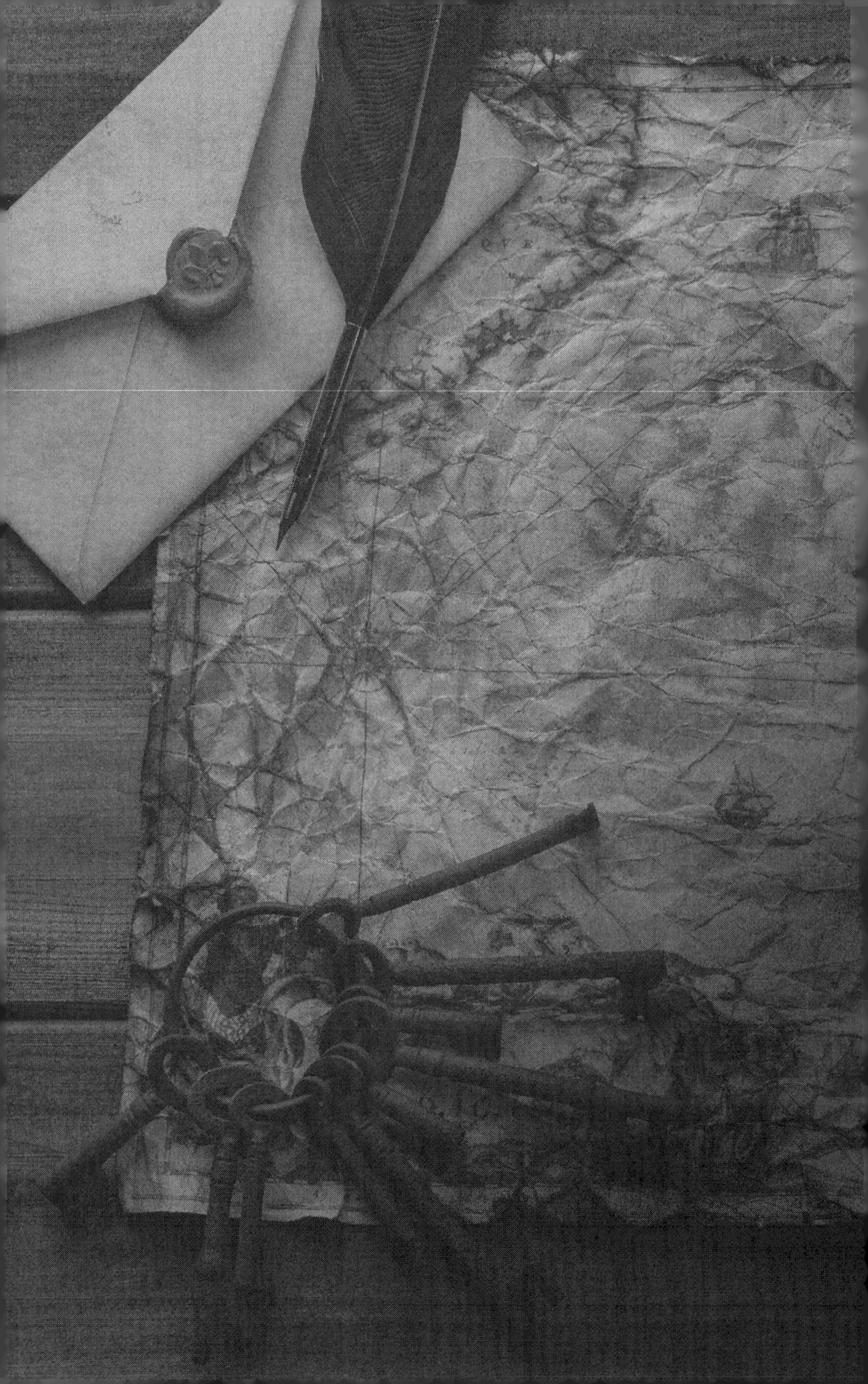

MR FERRERS

By the time they arrived in Ayïti, dark smudges ringed Knigh's eyes. Every morning, Vice had made Aedan grab him for a sparring session before she shoved lunch under his nose. After that, she pulled him into Perry's cabin to work on the Copper Drake for the afternoon, usually plopping a kitten in his lap. It was impossible not to smile as they purred and wobbled around, trying to explore every surface and interesting smell. Despite the comfort of tiny wet noses, she still kept an eye on him working. His handwriting was as impeccable as always, but his beard grew a little longer, a little more ragged with each day that passed.

They worked long hours, burning through candles and lamp oil. Sometimes Perry went and slept in Knigh's berth to let them work as late as they wished. But every morning Vice had the same reports from the night's watch—he'd been up in the small hours, pacing the deck like a caged animal.

Walking along Ayïti's docks, arm-in-arm with him, her heart ached. This was like watching him be tortured—far worse than seeing his tense struggles with self-control when they'd first met.

His beard was only neat today because she'd sat him down and trimmed it this morning—a necessary part of their disguise. He wore a smart suit in dull grey like a respectable businessman, and she'd borrowed the elements of an outfit befitting such a man's wife—plain bodice and skirts in grey-blue. With gloves hiding her padlock scar and a hat covering his white streak, their distinguishing features were out of sight. They mostly blended in with the merchants and other middling folk strolling through town or hurrying to their business.

She had pinned the wide brim of his hat up on one side, like the illustrations in her childhood books about musketeers and their swashbuckling adventures. He would've looked quite dashing if not for the shadows beneath his eyes and the bleakness in them.

He strode in gritted silence, gaze constantly flicking across their path and down side streets, lingering on the marines patrolling in packs of two or three. His arm was solid under her hand.

She squeezed and butted into him gently. "Are you all right in there?"

He blinked, threw her a quick glance, brows drawn together, before resuming his vigilance. "In where?"

"In your head. I see you watching every movement on the street. But I also see that the rest of you is in there churning over and over and over. Probably blaming yourself, if I know you." They turned right, now only a couple of streets from Billy's offices.

He exhaled through his nose. "Vane's after my family. That *is* my fault. I should never have left the Navy. I thought turning pirate would allow me to send home money and make my family safe from Mercia, not put them in more danger."

The ache in her chest yawned, hollow. More guilt at deserting. On this occasion, though, perhaps it was unnecessary.

"First of all, like Perry said, this might all be a load of bollocks. Tew could've been lying to his crew. Vane could've been lying to him. Oba could've lied to us." She winced. There were too many links in the chain to know which were false. "Or it could be a trap. For all we know, Billy might be in Albion, your family tucked up safely at home." Hence this visit to his offices—they'd have Billy's schedule and an idea of where he might be right now, as well as any letters from Knigh's family.

"Oba had too much information," he said, raised voice drawing looks from a couple they passed. "She knew—"

"Maybe," she murmured, smiling up at him and patting his arm as if they really were married. That lost the couple's attention—just an angry husband being placated by his wife. "And maybe not. Let's get this information and see what we need to do. In the meantime, you need to stop blaming yourself. *Please*. All those years of pirate hunting could've put them in the sights of a dozen disgruntled crews—leaving the Navy might have nothing to do with this."

Something inside her twisted, as if a great serpent might

live in that aching hollow. Was she trying to ease his guilt or her own? He'd only deserted the Navy because of her.

His mouth tightened, but the solid muscles in his arm eased. "Mmm." His head bowed, throwing shadow over his face from the wide brim of his hat. "Let's cut down here. I don't like how much those marines are looking at us."

Adjusting a lock of hair, she hid her glance at the trio in their red jackets. *Looking at us.* Looking at *him*, more like. Just as in Kayracou Port, Knigh was too tall, too straight-backed, too noticeable. She could draw attention when she wanted it, yes, but she knew how to turn it away as well.

"Good plan."

They ducked down a narrow lane, then another and another, before coming out opposite Billy's offices.

When they knocked, a woman opened the door and narrowed her eyes. In her forties, with that expression and her neatly braided hair touched with grey, she might've been reminiscent of a governess. But when the door opened a fraction further, it revealed a frothy day dress in duck egg blue, trimmed with flounced lace and pastel pink ruffles—a million miles from the prim, drab gowns governesses wore.

After a moment, she smiled. "Mr Ferrers?" She cocked her head as if not sure.

"Mr Ferrers?" Vice whispered. *Her* surname—or at least it had been. She was *technically* a Lyons after marrying Evered.

"First thing that came to mind when Billy brought me," he muttered. Of course, Lord Villiers or Captain Blackwood would've been incriminating. He inclined his head to the woman. "Miss Laliwa." When he pushed up the brim of his hat, her smile broadened—his face had that effect on women—on *people*.

"It *is* you. Come in, come in! I'm afraid I don't have any letters for you, but I'm expecting the *Swallow* soon—maybe she'll bring you good tidings."

Soon? Vice exchanged a look with Knigh. If the Swallow was due in Arawaké 'soon,' maybe Oba's story wasn't a total fabrication.

Inside the smart, comfortable offices, Miss Laliwa offered them tea as one of her colleagues continued working at his desk and a maid disappeared to fetch refreshments. They declined, citing business to attend to. Not entirely a lie, just that the business they needed to attend to was not getting caught by the local guards.

Once they explained the reason for their visit—checking on Billy's schedule—she pulled out a hefty book and consulted a bookmarked page. "Yes, as I thought. Mr Hopper is due in the next fortnight, sea willing."

The next fortnight. That placed him over halfway through the crossing. If he took the same route they'd sailed over Yule, he'd land at Karukera first to take on water, then come to Ayïti. And if Vane *was* after the *Swallow*, he wouldn't want to sail that far into open water, strike, then double back on himself. Why take the trouble to equip the *Maelstrom* for a longer journey when he could simply wait for his quarry to come to him?

If it were Vice, she'd strike once the *Swallow* was a day from Karukera—near enough to land that she could lie in wait with access to fresh food and water, but far enough into open water that no one was likely to spot the battle and come to help a merchant barque in distress.

Knigh nodded as if he'd done the same calculation, the set of his jaw and shoulders radiating tension.

Still, that didn't mean Knigh's family would be on board. "Do you have details of any passengers? A manifest or...?"

With an apologetic smile, the manager shook her head. "I'm afraid they wouldn't know that until leaving Portsmouth. Most people don't book in advance, you see."

"Thank you, Miss Laliwa." Vice smiled, cheeks stiff, then tugged Knigh a small distance from the manager's desk. "He won't attack until they're closer to land," she murmured. "That gives us time to get help. Maybe we can keep the Rover." They could fly Vane's stupid flag, make him think they were *his* reinforcements—that would really confuse him.

She could practically hear his teeth grinding. "But—"

"We still have two weeks before we need to—"

Three sharp raps at the door.

"Royal Navy, open up!"

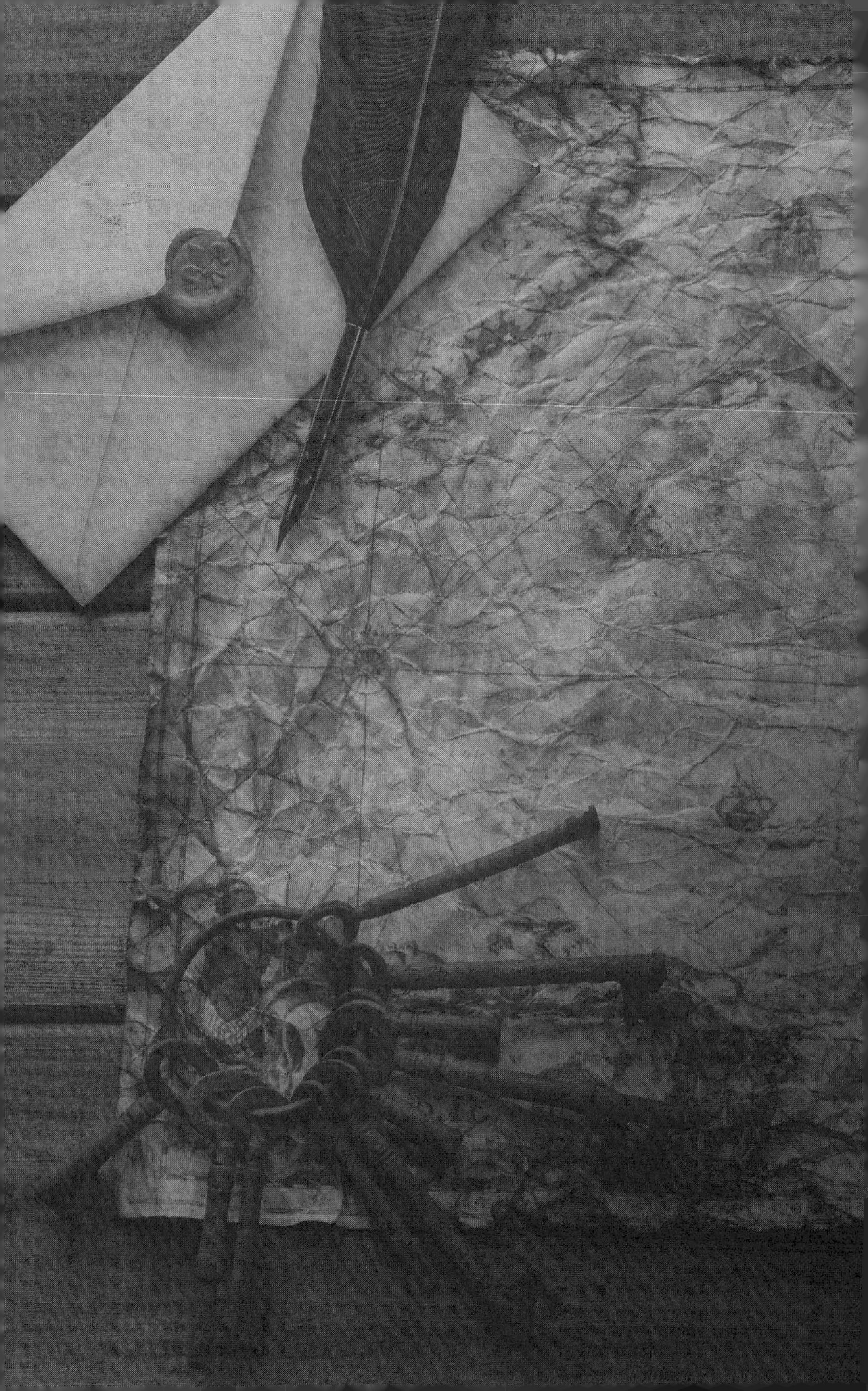

SUGAR & STEEL

ollocks.

Vice's stomach dipped. They must've recognised Knigh. She couldn't let them arrest him, and no way was this the day the Navy would catch her. They'd done it once, and she'd be damned if they were going to manage it a second time.

But they were cornered. If the offices had a back exit, no doubt more marines waited there. And any minute now, Miss Laliwa would open this door.

Knigh surveyed the room, evaluative.

But Miss Laliwa merely cleared her throat as if she'd been inconveniently interrupted while entertaining guests, and approached the entrance. "The door's locked," she called to the men outside, voice calm as she looked from Vice to Knigh. She leant closer. "I assume you'd rather avoid the uniformed gentlemen, yes?"

Vice winced. "That would be preferable."

"But we can't ask you to lie to them," Knigh said. "You'd get—"

"You're not asking." Her sly smile wouldn't have looked out of place on a pirate. "Billy said you could be trusted. No matter what. So." She gave a firm nod.

"Open up, in the name of the Queen!" They banged this time, making the door rattle on its hinges. "We have reason to believe you're in danger."

Miss Laliwa only raised her dark eyebrows a touch. "And I'd say you don't have time to argue. Mr Ferrers, be a dear and put those broad shoulders of yours to use by moving that desk in front of the door."

Vice exchanged glances with Knigh and gave a slight shrug before Knigh did as he was told. Billy clearly had a knack for picking employees. With that frothy gown, Miss Laliwa somehow coated steel with sugar.

"Maybe we can Munroe this." Vice cocked her head at Knigh as another barrage rattled the door.

"A fake threat?" He nodded, an ounce of tension dissolving from his tight features. "Good thinking."

The door jumped on its hinges—they were trying to knock the damn thing down.

"If they ask," Vice said to Miss Laliwa, drawing a pistol hidden in her skirts, "we forced you to help us." She waved it meaningfully, keeping it pointed at the ceiling.

Her eyes glinted as the corner of her mouth rose. "Oh yes. I was so terribly afraid." The glint was gone and instead she looked up at them with eyes so wide and dark, Vice almost believed her.

"Perfect."

Her colleague still sat at his desk, watching proceedings with a mildly perplexed expression, as if this was only unusual because it was happening on a Wednesday.

The maid reappeared. "I locked and barred the back door, but they're still hammering on it, miss."

Shit. How were they going to get out of this? They could up the ante on this pretence and take Miss Laliwa 'hostage' as she had with Munroe on the *Venatrix*. But a civilian hostage who presumably didn't know her way around a fight? All the stories like that had ended badly for everyone involved. Badly, bloodily, permanently.

"Now," Miss Laliwa said, calm despite the banging now coming from the back door, "go to the attic. The back windows open onto the roof. I hear it's flat enough to walk across, especially for someone with a sailor's balance." Her knowing look turned from Knigh to Vice and back again. "The roof of this block practically touches the next one."

Vice and Knigh exchanged a look. The woman worked for a shipping company in one of Arawaké's main ports. Perhaps it shouldn't be a surprise she knew a sailor when she saw one.

"Go on—what are you waiting for?"

"Thank you." Vice kicked over a chair and swept some papers on the floor. "For appearances." She nodded, starting for the back door leading to the staircase.

"And if you so much as think about following us," Knigh bellowed, throwing the door open with a bang, "you'll taste my steel." He started up the stairs and muttered, "For appearances."

The last thing Vice saw before she followed was Miss Laliwa rocking with barely suppressed giggles.

Legs pumping, they sprinted up the stairs. One flight, two… three…

By the time they reached the fourth, the attic, they were both panting, and Vice's heart hammered against her ribcage as insistently as the marines hammering at the front and back doors.

But there was no time to stop. The sooner they led trouble away from Billy's offices, the safer Miss Laliwa and his other employees would be.

And then there was the matter of escape.

"One thing at a time," she huffed as she hauled one of the back windows open.

Just as Miss Laliwa had described, it led out onto the roof, hidden from the street. In the courtyard behind, a dozen marines in red crowded around the back door, thankfully absorbed with trying to knock it down.

"Why is it whenever I need to escape, I'm wearing a bloody dress?" At least she'd put on flat shoes more suited to a middling woman's day time walk rather than the dainty heels of a fine lady. She tucked her skirts into her waistband and clambered out, Knigh close behind.

The gently pitched roof was no challenge to either of them —she'd faced far worse in a storm—but the clay tiles rocked and clicked, threatening to slide from underfoot. Grimacing, she crept as quickly as she dared. If a single tile fell, the men in the courtyard would—

Her left foot jolted from under her. "Shit," she hissed, scrabbling to stay upright.

But it wasn't that she'd slipped—

A tinkling crash echoed through the courtyard.

Below, faces turned up. "Knigh—"

"I know. Go, g—"

Crack.

Something whistled past.

They were firing. "Shit!"

Stealth and slipping tiles be damned—they ran.

The tiles clattered under their desperate steps, and more rained down on the courtyard, but a moment later, they were at the edge of this roof and it was only two feet away from the next. Vice's breaths heaved, her heart pounded, and as she leapt over, gunshots joined the cacophony in her ears.

They raced over rooftops and terraces. Heat radiated off the tiles, and blinding white light reflected from painted stucco walls. Sweat trickled down her back and dampened her gloves, but her muscles coiled and sprung and coiled again, ready to send her over one gap and the next.

Clattering steps told her Knigh was right behind. If he was here, she'd make it. Somehow. There was no logic to the thought, just belief.

Shards of tile burst from the roof two feet away, and she let out a yelp, shielding her face from the shrapnel.

"They've got someone on the rooftops," she huffed.

"Or a tower," Knigh called back.

She sprinted on, ducking behind clustered chimneys, keeping below the roofline as much as possible.

More shots, close. Crumbs of clay dusted her hair and trickled down the back of her neck.

Too close.

"We need cover." Even she couldn't deny the desperation in her voice. Her heart was in her damn throat—it was a wonder it hadn't come out with the words.

"Left," Knigh called. "The balcony."

The next building ran perpendicular to this one, and all the windows on the top storey had wide balconies with wrought iron balustrades and glazed doors. The nearest was open.

There was no time to think.

She ran, she leapt, she soared, only air beneath her feet, and for heart-wrenching seconds, she fell.

Crack.

Something struck her skirt, but she had no time, because here was the ground. She ducked, rolled, staggered to her feet, blinking at the sudden dimness. Catching herself on a—was that a dressing table? She shook her head, and the world stilled.

A dressing table, an armoire, silk drapes, a bed.

On the bed, a beautiful man and an even more beautiful woman sat entwined, their flesh bare and dusky in the low light.

A thud and explosion of movement announced Knigh's arrival. He righted himself more smoothly than she had and straightened his hat.

The couple on the bed eyed them, shared a look, then each raised an eyebrow in what might've been a question or an offer.

"Way out?" Vice panted.

"Pity," the man said.

"Wishful thinking." The woman shrugged. "But I know a getaway when I see it." She stood, not bothering to cover her nakedness. "You have money?"

Vice lifted her chin. Knigh touched her elbow, perhaps a suggestion to move on—the bedroom door was only six feet away. "Of course."

"How much?"

"Enough."

"Then our madame will help you. Leave your money on the dressing table and take clothes from the armoire. Cover your hair with a scarf. They won't recognise you."

Shouts of query echoed up from the courtyard, then footsteps. The marines hadn't seen them enter, but there was nothing to stop them from coming in here, searching.

Vice dumped the coins from her pocket as instructed. Knigh watched, flat mouth saying they didn't have time for this.

"Disguises buy us time," she muttered, "get that lot off our tails."

He sighed, but opened the armoire. A few minutes later, he'd dressed in a dark cherry red jacket and black breeches, the other side of his hat pinned up to create a bicorne.

As she changed, Vice discovered a hole in her skirts—that puff as she'd leapt had been a shot too close for comfort. In addition to a patterned headscarf, she put on an emerald green gown, the neckline so low she'd spill out if she bent over. That was probably the point.

Knigh looked her over, eyebrows twitching, before he

cleared his throat and turned for the door. "That'll distract them, all right."

The *professionals* directed them down the hall, where a back staircase led to an exit at the far end of the block. "We call it the escape route," the man told them with a wink.

When they emerged onto a side street, all was quiet, just a couple of townsfolk going about their business. They strode towards the docks, only two streets away.

Vice's feet itched to run. They might have different clothes now, but nothing could disguise Knigh's physique. Besides, the marines were on alert. Her height, even slouching, would draw attention. Knigh must've realised the same, because they sped along, around one corner, then the next.

At the end of this lane, ships swayed at anchor. Almost there.

But between them and the docks were three men in red.

"Keep your head down," she whispered to Knigh, curling her shoulders in, bowing her head to demonstrate. She didn't look to see if he obeyed, but he shifted under her hand.

Her heart sped as they walked past the marines, and she dared a glance.

A pair of blue eyes stared back.

Damn it.

Maybe if he didn't look too closely at Knigh...

She smiled, gave him a look from beneath lowered lashes, then angled toward the marine—just a touch, but enough to give him a good eyeful of cleavage.

Those blue eyes slipped lower. His lips parted.

Mission accomplished.

They were past.

She squeezed Knigh's arm, and he covered her hand in return.

It felt like ten years passed, but it must've only been minutes and then they were at the Venatrix and a few tense words had them disembarking. As she dipped into her gift and turned their course out of the harbour, Perry arrived, hands on hips. "Well?"

Face blank, every muscle tight, Knigh shook his head.

Vice squeezed his shoulder. "We're going to need help."

Perry's mouth flattened to a grim line. "To Nassau."

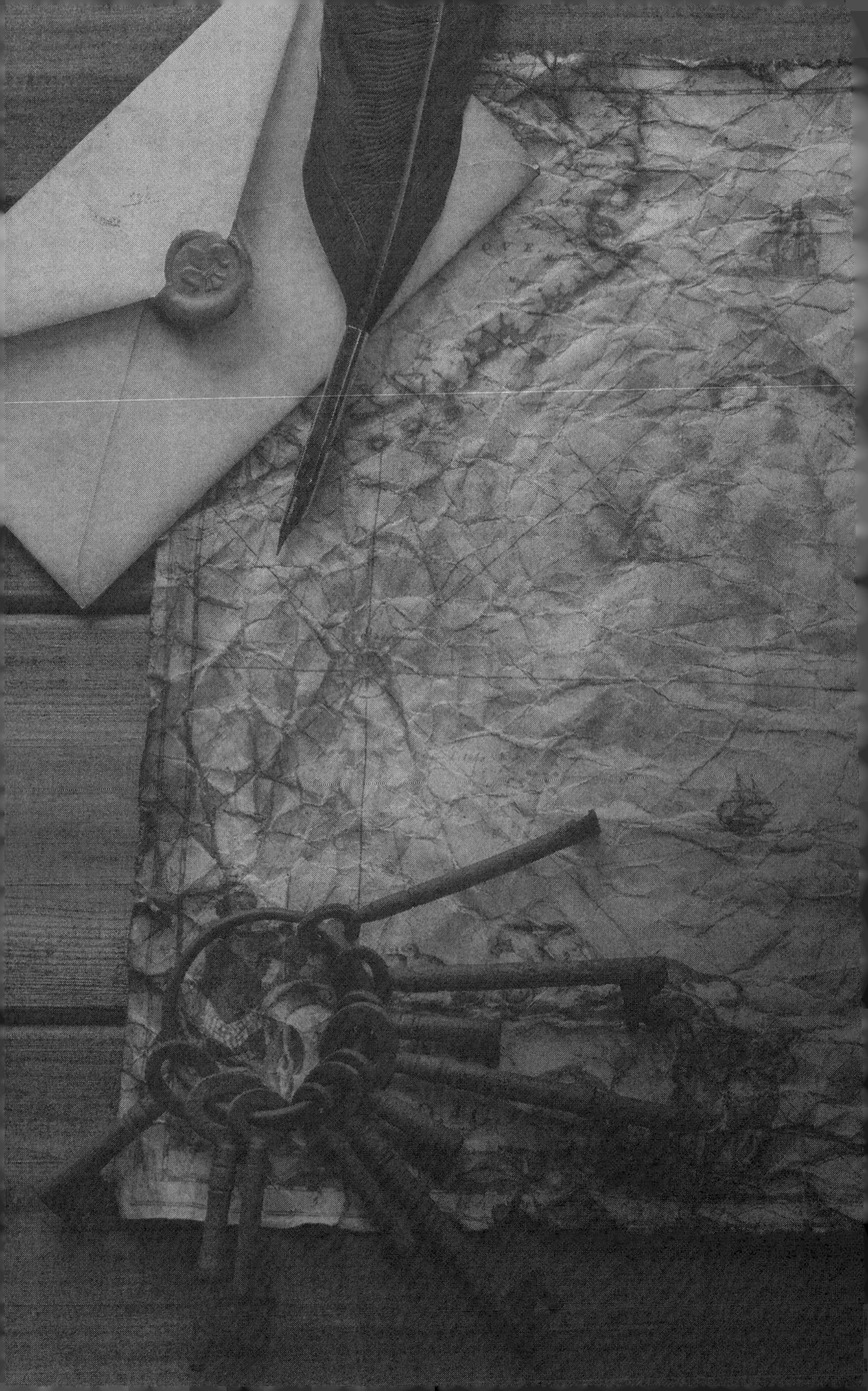

DISAPPOINTING FATHERS

When Knigh saw all the furniture pushed back against the bulkhead, he raised his eyebrows at Vee. Even Barnacle's sea chest was off to one side, the kittens asleep within. Vee had summoned him to Perry's cabin, and he'd expected to find the inkwells and notebooks set up for their work on the Copper Drake. Not this. Whatever *this* was.

She finished shoving back the table they normally worked at and exchanged looks with Perry, who stood in front of the sea chest and gave an encouraging nod.

This—the way Vee drew a long breath, so obviously unsure —it tugged on his feet, whispering *danger*. Hands gripped behind his back, he held his ground.

"Perry asked for my help with something," Vee said at last, leaning against the table where they usually worked. "And… and I think it's the best idea she's ever had."

Lords and Ladies, those two agreeing on an idea…

Danger. Run.

At least his back was to the door. "And what *is* this idea?"

Perry cleared her throat and gave another nod—this one, apparently to herself. "I've been giving your anger some thought, the source of it, in particular. I think the problem is… you have unfinished business—things you didn't say. To your father."

He twitched upright, that word lancing through him—*father*. His throat blocked and his teeth fused.

Instinct roared, *No. No. No.*

But—he held himself very still—he had spoken to Perry about it before, and to Vee a little.

He *could* breathe, he *could* talk. And doing so helped.

Instinct, sometimes, was wrong.

He unlocked his jaw. "That… *is* what I think of when I fight. It… sustains me. But"—he hung his head, a flash of blood streaking across his vision—"sometimes it's what I'm drowning in when I lose control." Billy's blood. Aedan's. By some miracle not Vee's, though it had been close. His cheeks burned as cold closed over the rest of his body.

"And your anger seems tied to the physicality of fighting," Perry murmured. "As if that's what opens the door."

He folded his arms, squeezing his biceps. Speaking to Perry about this was one thing, but having them both here at once was… He could *feel* Vee looking at him, piercing layer upon layer upon layer, and the officer and the warrior in him panicked, erected steel walls, the blank control he'd worn for so long.

But part of him—the boy who hadn't been able to swim to the island in a lake on her family's estate—wanted it.

Wanted her to see, wanted to bare his throat to her, show her the scars and the dark and see if she'd turn away.

Because she hadn't yet.

She knew about Billy. She'd seen him on the *Covadonga*, brutal and murderous. On the *Sovereign*, she'd talked him down, even as Aedan's arm had been hanging off, when she could have just run him through.

Although she didn't want to be with him, she *was* his friend. In spite of everything.

Maybe she would see the full extent of his brokenness and that would be the end of it. She'd pity or despise him, treat him with the contempt that he arguably deserved.

But perhaps she wouldn't...

There was a chance she'd still be his friend, still offer her support.

He raised his chin and finally met her eye.

She'd come closer and the late sunlight from the stern windows painted the edges of her features gold. A shallow crease sat between her brows, and in her look...

Compassion.

It pierced the bubble of worry and tension that had formed around him. Her gaze was somehow solid enough to do that and yet soft enough that he could sink into it, safe and warm like a feather mattress.

"Maybe," she murmured, "you need to *say* the words."

She really did want him to bare his throat. To say those

things in front of anyone else would be impossible, but with her, with Perry...

He shivered, part-fear, part-longing.

"And as you do so," Perry said, voice low, "you need to spar. Recreating those times you use your anger to fight, but *saying* the words, instead of only thinking them."

His feet backed off a step before he could stop them. *No.* Heart hammering, he shook his head. Definitely not. It would be suicide for his opponent.

But Vee only nodded. "Instead of bottling them up."

He scrubbed his hands over his face. Anything to block that look she was giving him that made him want so badly. "I can't. Don't you understand? If I spar with Aedan just *thinking* those things, I might come apart and—and *kill* him. He's strong and fast, yes, but he isn't..."

Fae-touched.

Fae-touched meant faster, stronger. So did fae-blooded.

Vee dipped her head, eyebrows rising.

That's why Perry asked her to help.

"Oh, no." He backed off further, bitterness flooding his mouth. "No. Absolutely not. I will *not* fight you. I won't take that risk."

"Knigh," Perry said, "it has to be Vice. She's strong enough, fast enough. She—"

"I said *no*. I won't do that to her."

Vee exhaled through her nose. "You won't be doing anything *to* me, I—"

"You'll be working together"—Perry craned into his line of sight, forcing him to meet her steady gaze as she held out the practice pads and boxing gloves—"as a team. And, never thought I'd say this about Vice, but you two make a damn fine team. Your boldness tempered by *your* attention to detail. Your determination and *your* experience. Your combined intelligence—no, let's call it what it is—*cunning...*" She blew out a low whistle. "If you two captained a ship together, I'd pity the navy who tried to withstand you. Together, you two are unstoppable and in this... I think that leviathan is just what's needed to break the blockade."

Her words burned through him. *We made a good team.* A lifetime ago, Vee had stood in a gibbet and told him that.

She wasn't wrong. Perry wasn't wrong, either. But...

He shook his head. Perry didn't understand. She was usually so sensible, but in this she'd clearly lost her mind. Vee, though...

"Perhaps it would fix it—fix *me*, but I will not risk hurting you." His eyes burned as he willed every ounce of horror into the look he bored into Vee. The fear in every moment he'd come back to himself with blood on his hands and her nearby saying his name and he'd wondered, *have I hurt her? Whose blood is this? Is it hers?* "Vee," he said, throat rasping, "I could kill you."

"You won't." She said it so easily, almost flippant. "I'm sure of it, Knigh. I trust you—you won't hurt me. And I think saying the words means you won't berserk—they'll be like a safety valve, rather than keeping it in until you explode. But even if you do, I've been able to talk you down before. I can do it again." Her eyes gleamed, and she paused, throat constricting in a swallow. "I'll do it as many times as it takes."

She *would*. She meant that. She really...

If she had faith in this plan and in him...

He shook his head again, but there was no force left in it.

"All the more reason it needs to be Vice," Perry said, voice soft like she was coaxing a flighty sabrecat.

"Please," Vee said, "let us try." Before he could argue, she cradled his cheek, touch cool, comforting, familiar. *Everything*.

He broke, breath rushing out on a sigh instead of a denial. He squeezed her hand, squared his shoulders, and nodded. "Let's try."

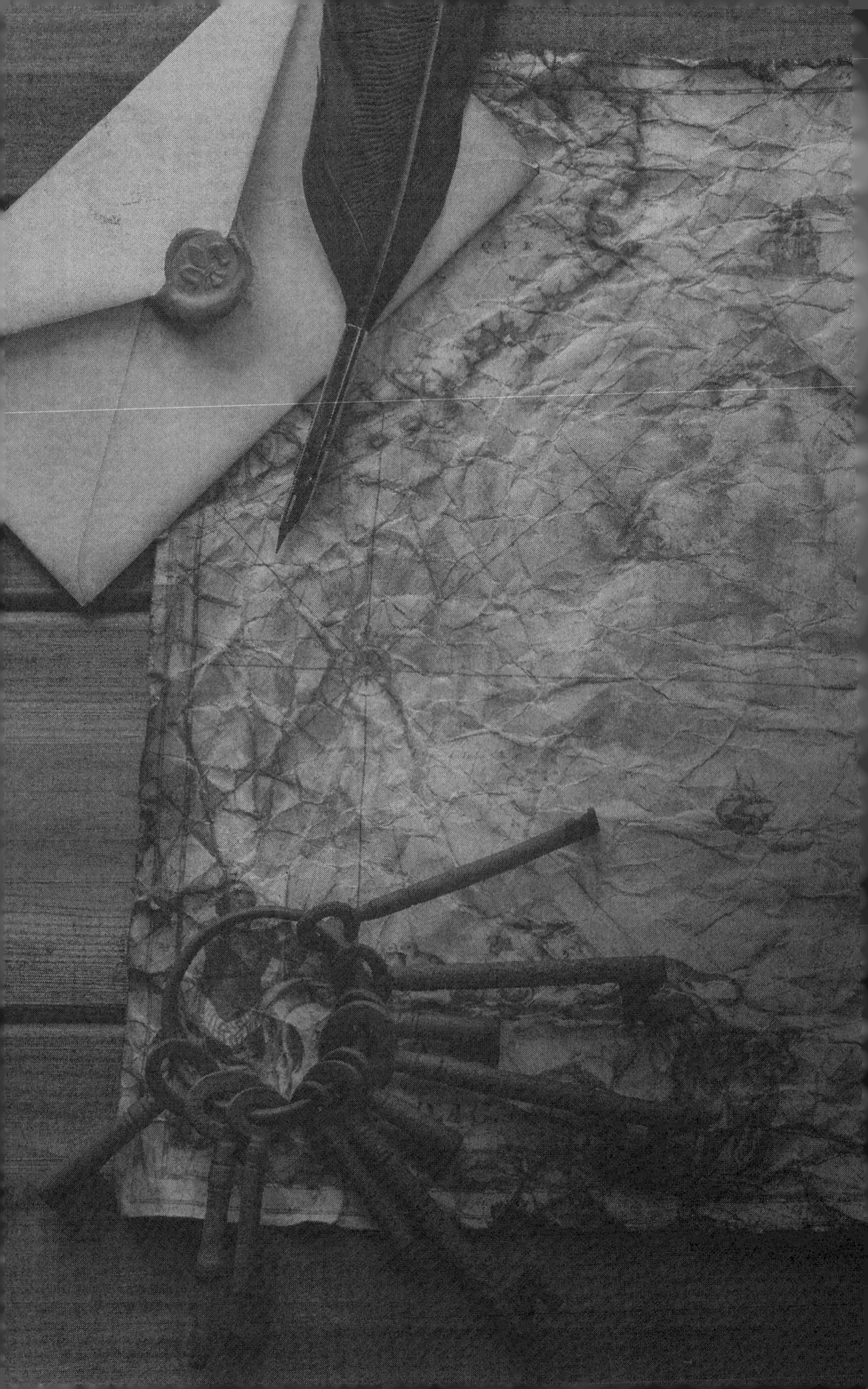

SHARED INSANITY

Knigh laced on his boxing gloves, frowning at them, at how wrong this felt. No such frown on her face—no apparent concerns whatsoever, in fact—Vee tugged the large practice mitts over her hands. She clapped them together, the slap of leather-on-leather filling Perry's cabin, and gave an appreciative nod.

In her sea chest, Barnacle had woken and sat up watching him, green eyes half-closed as though bored.

"Right, I think that's everything." Perry raised her brows at him, then Vee. "Both ready?"

Vee raised the padded mitts and jerked her chin, inviting him to begin.

Agreeing to this was one thing, but now he actually had to do it... What a terrible idea. Truly, astonishingly, unutterably terrible.

"If you start with just hitting me," she said, like this was a normal thing, "get used to that first, then you can… say what you need to say."

Surely hearing that must've made Perry realise how ridiculous this was. But she only gave a soft smile and an encouraging nod.

They were both insane. Utterly insane.

But he'd agreed to this—perhaps that meant he was, too.

He hit the pad.

Vee arched an eyebrow at the worn leather, then at him. "Seriously? Come on, Knigh, I know you. *Hit* me."

He hadn't exactly pulled the punch, but neither had he gone in as hard as he did with Aedan. Yet Vee hadn't even rocked back on her heels.

When had he decided she was some delicate flower? She'd flung herself out a window the first time they'd met in Arawaké, and even as children, she'd been strong. She was fae-blooded. She was a sailor and a pirate. She'd fought in hundreds of battles, and here she still stood.

He was being absurd.

Shaking his head, he blew that foolish idea out and struck.

She huffed, taking the blow with just enough resistance that his knuckles flexed inside his gloves. "That's it."

That wasn't so bad. This was training—just like he did with Aedan.

Breaths steady, he circled as with Aedan, and she matched his movement. He threw a few more blows, leaving time between each one for her to recover and ensure the practice mitt was raised and ready.

"Now," Perry said, voice soft, warm, "what do you think about when you use your anger to fight?"

"How he... he let us down." He clenched his teeth but made himself punch the practice pad.

"Say *you*. *You* let us down."

Vee peered over the pad as they circled. "Say it like *I'm* him."

His heart clenched. It was grotesque, just the idea of speaking to her like—

"Do it." She had her brows drawn tightly together as she did in battle. She meant it. More than that—she was *determined*.

And he'd agreed to this. She and Perry hadn't arranged it to torture him—they were trying to help. He had to be just as determined. He had to repay their trust with his own.

Heart in his throat, he licked his lips. "You... you let us down." His pulse leapt.

He threw a right hook. Vee caught it.

"Good," Perry murmured. "Keep going."

"And you lied," he said between gritted teeth, the treachery so fresh it still stung all these years later.

He swung in with a left hook.

Vee took it with ease, barely exhaling with the slap of glove on pad.

He wasn't the only one Father had let down, either. There was—"Mother and George and Is—you ruined us." That deserved a hook. *"Ruined* us." Another.

The blood roared in his ears.

Still frowning in determination, Vee nodded, took it all.

"Betrayed us." His voice cracked, but his veins sparked hot and bright. He struck.

She took a step back with that one, but raised the pads again, this time in front of her face.

"And your woman..." Father's lover—it was easier if he didn't think of her name, but... this wasn't meant to be easy, was it?

"Miss Langtry and her boy—did you stop to think what might become of her?" One strike, then another. "Did you think what the world might do to a woman alone with a child?" Another. "What they might call her? What she might have to resort to?" Another and another.

He sneered at the brown leather pad gleaming in the low sunlight that slanted through the windows. It was so easy to see Father's greying blonde hair and drink-reddened cheeks in his own indistinct reflection.

"Don't worry, though"—*whack*—"I cleared up your mess." *Whack*. "I made sure she was safe"—*whack*—"and the boy. *I* worked." *Whack*. "*I* saved." *Whack*. "*I* took care of them."

His breaths were ragged now, harsh in his lungs.

Pressure on the back of his eyes building, he hit that pad again. If only it was the man who deserved it.

"You didn't give a damn." Another hit. "You only cared about yourself." Again. "You were never the man I thought."

Gods, his eyes burned, and the world blurred. But it didn't matter—he could see well enough to smack that pad. He did it again and again and again.

"You were always selfish."

Left hook, right hook.

"I was a fool to believe in you." Jab, jab. He made a sound, half-laugh, half... something else, something choking. "Such a bloody fool."

Uppercut.

"I should've known." *What Father was.*

His knuckles ached. His head ached. His heart ached.

If he'd spotted the signs sooner or looked more closely at the ledger...

He tried to exhale, but it choked him. Gasping for air, he shook his head.

"I should've known." *What Father had done.*

If he'd secured the deeds to their lands, kept them safe, out of Father's possession...

He didn't want to hit the pad anymore. His arms hung at his side, trembling, and his face was wet.

Enough.

A blurry face peered around from behind the pad and he had to blink because it didn't look like Father.

For a second...

But, no, it was Vee shucking the pads off her hands and letting them fall to the deck. Father was dead. Long dead and not a hero.

He shook his head, a wave of tiredness washing over him, deep and heavy.

If he'd been home more, rather than chasing glory at sea...

If he'd sat the man down with a decanter of whisky, had a father-and-son talk...

If... If... If... Every unrealised possibility shook through him. He'd failed. He'd *failed*.

"Vee," he sobbed, knees buckling as she closed the space between them, "I should've known."

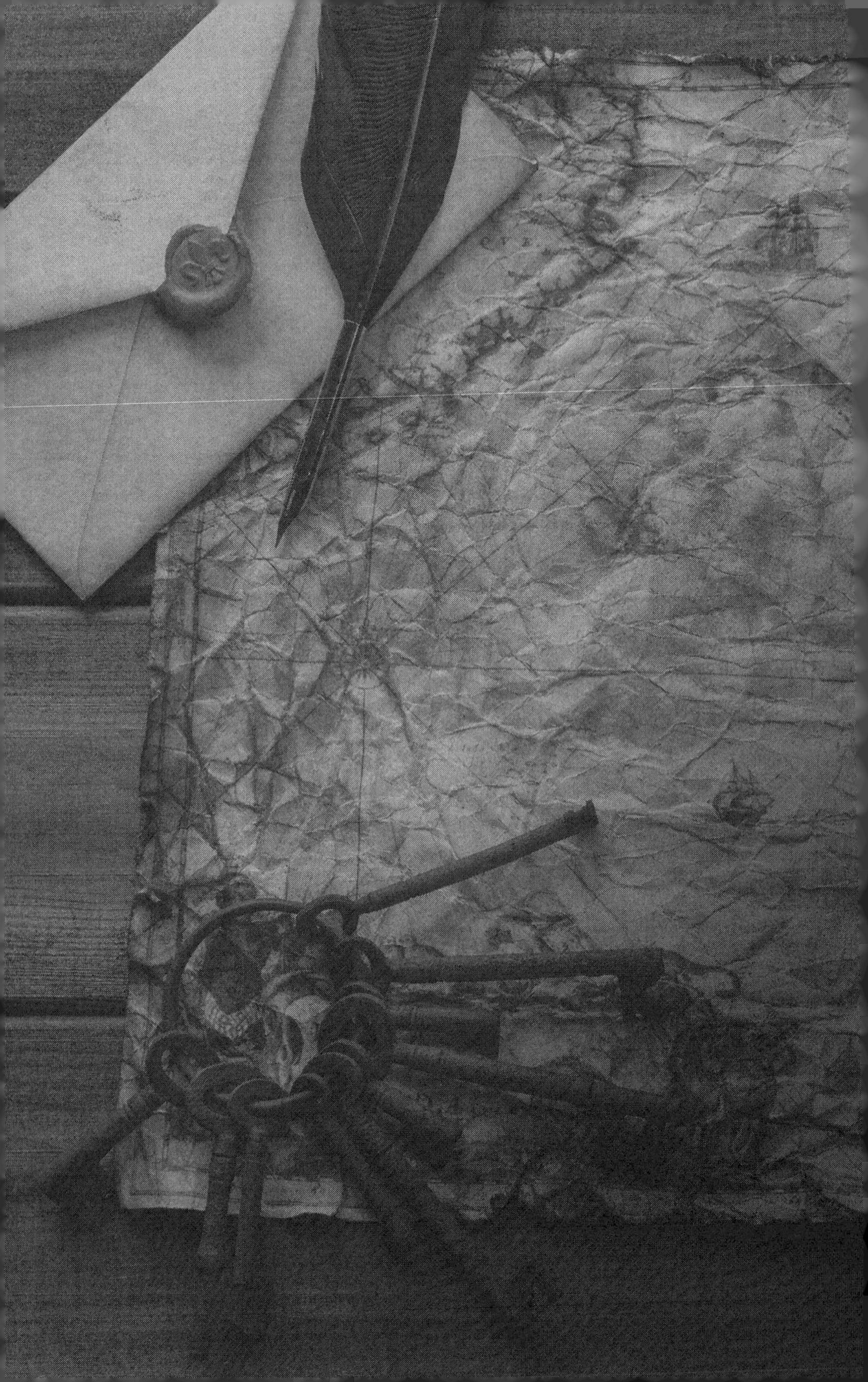

FAULT

Vice caught Knigh. After he'd been so courageous, she could at least do that. As she lowered to the floor with him, she caught Perry's eye, seeking direction. What was she meant to do?

Perry only nodded, like that was all the answer she needed.

Silently begging for more help than that, Vice sat and pulled his head into her lap. He lay on his side, curled around her, more like a child than a naval officer. Had they broken him?

Throat and chest tight, she squeezed her stinging eyes shut. All that hurt. All that pain. All those words he'd been carrying around unsaid.

And the fact he blamed himself.

Shaking her head, she gathered him close and rubbed his back as it shook with sobs. "I've got you," she whispered, rocking him gently. "You're safe." Gods knew why, but it was suddenly of vital importance that he knew he was safe right now. To cry... to talk... to *feel*... to do whatever he needed. She would hold this space for him for as long as it took.

Arms around her waist, he buried his face against her and took choking breaths. His shaking was already subsiding, though, and that in turn eased the tightness in her chest.

"I'll sleep in his berth," Perry mouthed, then ducked out, closing the door in silence.

So he could stay in here. So he didn't need to worry about getting out of her way or worry about *anything*.

See, Vice hadn't even thought of that. Perry, though? *She* knew what he needed. *She* should be the one here with him. But she'd gone. She'd bloody left poor Knigh with no one but Vice, who was so emotionally stunted she didn't have words to help in the middle of this... of this...

He blamed himself.

Lip trembling, she cradled his head, caressed his shoulder—little touches that maybe, *just maybe,* gave some small comfort. "I've got you, Knigh. You're safe." What else could she say? What else did she have for him at this moment?

After all his father had done, he blamed himself, and that crushed her—as if the rockfall in Hewanorra's cave had landed on her head.

All that work to help his family... and he still thought he'd let them down.

He had to understand he was wrong. *Surely.*

She stroked his hair, pushing it back from his wet cheeks. Something dripped off her chin and mingled with his tears. Barnacle jumped from her sea chest and padded over. She curled up behind his knees and took up a rumbling purr.

They stayed that way a long while—him locked up in whatever feelings raged through his soul like a hurricane, her whispering over and over and making nonsense soothing noises, willing her fingers to ease his hurt.

Over time, his breathing came more easily, no longer heaving like it might break him.

At last, he stilled, calmed, his ribcage expanding and contracting, slow and measured. He no longer clutched her waist, and the anguished lines of his face eased. Eyes shut, now lying on his back with Barnacle lying on his belly, he looked peaceful. Perhaps he'd fallen asleep.

That might be a mercy. He could wake in the morning and Perry would come back to help him with the wise words Vice didn't have.

Perry would be able to make him understand that nothing —*nothing* about his father's actions was his fault. He had to see that. It would be an intolerable cruelty for him to go through life bearing that man's errors as if they were his own.

He opened red-rimmed eyes and blinked up at her, a slow, small frown inching in place as he scratched Barnacle behind her ear. "You're..." He reached up, ran his thumb over Vice's cheek. One side of his mouth rose. "I understand *my* tears, but why are *you* crying?"

She scrubbed her face with her cuffs. If he felt well enough to tease her, maybe this whole exercise had helped—or at least hadn't destroyed him entirely. "It... it breaks my heart to see you like this. And, *yes*, I do have one, before you say anything." She joked, yes, but her voice faltered, close to cracking.

"I wasn't going to. I've known it for a long time."

That heart squeezed, and she dried his cheeks to distract herself because this was too serious. Too personal. "Well, don't tell everyone."

"Your secret's safe with me. Although, I have to admit, it's nice to know you care so much."

She *did*.

Damn it. This wasn't infatuation. It was... something else. Something deeper. Something dangerous. Something that made her pulse hammer like this was a battle that could cost her dearly. Something that made her want to shrug this whole conversation off and make a stupid joke.

But she owed it to him to be serious. She owed it to him to *mean* this.

"Of course I care." There, she'd said it. And although her heart drummed that warning over and over, the world didn't end. No one died. There wasn't even any bloodshed.

Maybe it was safe to go on.

"Knigh... Your father—what he did to you and your family... the hurt he left behind... I understand why you get so angry—holding that in all these years. It's something I might wish on an enemy, but you're..." She shook her head, more foolish tears trickling down her cheeks. "You haven't been my enemy in a long, long time."

He lay there, looking up at her for moments that stretched out. Then he cocked an eyebrow. "That might be the nicest thing you've ever said to me."

"Knigh, you bastard!" She gave him a shake. "I'm trying to be serious here!"

"So am I." But he straightened his face, took a few deep breaths, and let his gaze fall from her to the stern windows.

Outside, the setting sun painted the sky scorching orange and hot pink—brilliant and beautiful. It eased the ache in her heart and its panicky beat.

"All this time," he murmured at last, absently stroking Barnacle, "it wasn't him I was angry at—it was me. That I didn't protect them. That I didn't protect myself. That I trusted the wrong person. That I didn't see the truth. Such a long list of reasons to rage at myself. And I didn't even realise until now."

Was that truth a help, though? Would it heal him? Or was it just a new wound? She shivered. Please, gods, say she'd helped.

"*That's* why I kept such rigid control," he went on. "Why I was wary of allowing myself enjoyment, pleasure, *a life.*" He screwed his eyes shut. "Why I was so willing to believe the worst in you—it confirmed everything. I couldn't be trusted to know who to believe in, and I was *not* allowed happiness. I needed to be punished for my failures, not rewarded."

When the quiet ticked on, she lifted his chin. "I hope you know none of that's true."

His neck and shoulders solidified against her lap. Muscle in his jaw ticking, he frowned at her, like he was going to argue. Maybe he was just fighting to remain silent.

"All this time, you've been blaming yourself for your father's actions, but he was *your father*—and Isabel and George's—and he was meant to protect you, keep you safe. *He* failed. He failed in that and he failed you all." Her voice shook as Papa's face swam into view, a vein at his temple bulging, rage contorting his features.

Lords, was that memory still there after all these years of stamping it down?

She shook her head to rid herself of his distant spectre. "And it wasn't that he tried and failed. It wasn't one poor decision or an unlucky break. *He* wilfully chose himself, chose pleasure and excess and selfishness above you... above his responsibilities, above his family, again and again and again. And *he* hid it. *He* did all that, not you."

Knigh still wore that tight frown.

"How is any of that your fault?" She raised her eyebrows in challenge, because no way was she having him believe this about himself for a moment longer. "Tell me—tell me *how* you can be held responsible for his actions."

Exhaling, he sank into her lap. "I... I can't argue."

Good. It was a start.

In unspoken agreement, they fell silent and watched the deepening sunset turn magenta and scarlet—perfect little panes of colour at the stern windows. One by one, the kittens jumped from their sea chest with much less elegance than Barnacle had, and joined them, curling up in any warm spot—on Knigh's chest, between his neck and shoulder, tucked against her stomach.

Just as violet and indigo came creeping at the edges of the stern windows, he made a soft sound in his throat. "That was hard, Vee." He rubbed his eyes, the rest of his body limp against her and the floor. "I'm exhausted."

"I'm not surprised." She stroked his hair again—not because it was out of place, but because it was impossible *not* to. "A smooth sea never made a skilled sailor."

He snorted, features edged with the dimming light. "I can't believe you're quoting Navy idioms at me."

"It's probably your fault." She shrugged, the movement goading Flotsam into an irritated squeak. Just as imperious as her mother. "Anyway, Perry's going to stay in your berth tonight, so you can stay here, sleep, drink—whatever you want."

"Don't you want to move?" He arched his back, stretching, winning him a glare from Barnacle and more mewls from the kittens. "You must be uncomfortable sitting on the floor so long."

"My arse *is* numb. But I can stay here as long as you need." She kept her voice light, but the words did something strange to her heart, making it skip a beat.

"I... I want you to stay," he said so softly it was little more than a breath. "But," he went on, firmer, "I won't have you suffer on my account, no matter how comfortable this is." He removed all four kittens and Barnacle before rolling to his feet and offering his hand.

She let him help her up, but sweet Lords and Ladies, moving made it worse. So much worse. She rubbed her backside and hobbled to the bunk, pain shooting in where the numbness abated.

Worth it, though. To help him. She'd suffer it a million times over to help him.

She piled pillows in the corner and propped herself up, somewhere between sitting and lying, before sinking into them with a sigh.

Limbs loose, Knigh joined her, drooping eyelids and each

movement spelling out his exhaustion. He nestled his head in her lap again, and Barnacle resumed her spot on his belly. "Is this...?"

"Yes." Her hand found his hair and took up a smooth, slow stroke.

"Mm." He stirred briefly when a series of squeaks announced the kittens wanted to join them, so he helped them up two at a time. The little fluffy grey and black bodies settled into the warm nooks between her and Knigh. A few minutes later, his rhythmic breathing said he was asleep.

That was quick for him. With any luck, this had lifted a weight from his shoulders. He'd certainly spoken to her more freely than he ever had before.

"Sleep soundly, Knigh Blackwood," she murmured.

Surrounded by purring darkness, it wasn't long before sleep claimed her, too.

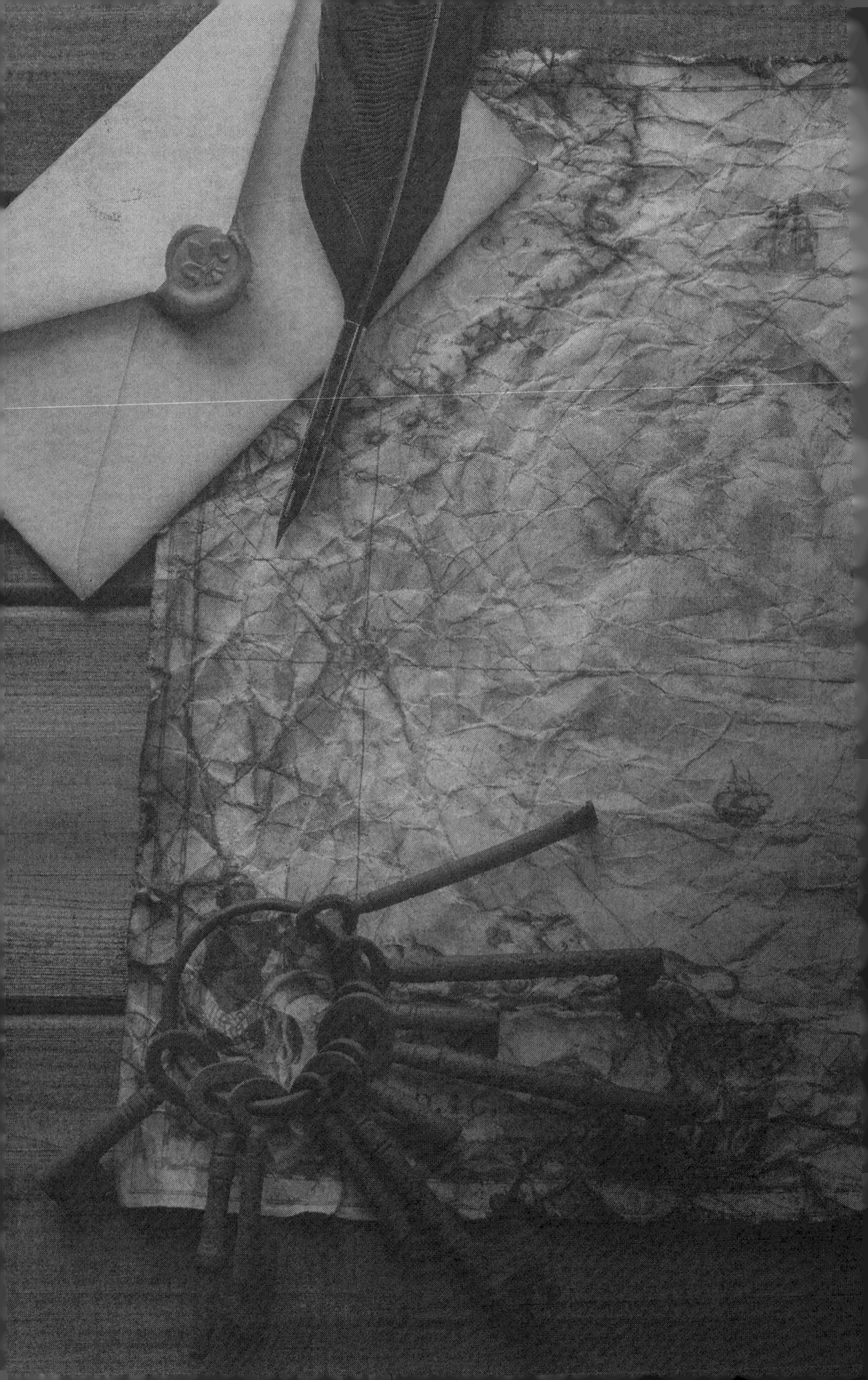

WORTH THE RISK?

Oba had told them Vane sailed with three or four other ships accompanying the Maelstrom, and the *Swallow* couldn't stand up to that alone. Even if Knigh's family weren't on board, Billy was in danger and that was enough. So when they arrived in Nassau the next day, Vice set to work recruiting help to protect the *Swallow*.

At least that was the plan. Lips pursed, Vice nudged Perry as they walked between taverns. "Do you think the others have had better luck?"

"I hope so."

"I asked what you *think*, not what you hope."

Perry adjusted her hat to keep the sun from her eyes. "Pirates don't want to attack other pirates—especially not Vane. So, no, I doubt they've done any better."

Vice groaned. "I was afraid you'd say that." So far they'd recruited one other ship. The boys from the *Firefly* would never let her down. If only the same could be said for other crews and captains. Knigh was with Aedan, and Saba had gone with Lizzy—all trying their luck.

Surely it couldn't all be the bad kind.

"Maybe Knigh's fae charm will help... As long as no one realises his old occupation."

"Wondered how long it would be before you mentioned him." Perry eyed her sidelong. "And how *are* things between the two of you?"

"*Hmpf.* That's a loaded question if ever I heard one." She scoffed, shook her head—anything to delay answering.

Last night had been... intense.

Understatement.

Her eyes had still been sore when she woke this morning, and Knigh's bloodshot. They were curled up together on Perry's bunk and had quietly gathered the discarded practice mitts and boxing gloves. At last, Knigh had taken the pads from her, set them down, and pulled her into a hug. "Thank you." That's all he'd said, and the hug had stretched on, warm and comfortable and comforting until a knock rattled the door and Lizzy called through—they were in Nassau and had work to do.

Vice cleared her throat and shrugged. "I don't know... good, I suppose? We're just friends, so..." She shrugged again. "Not going to lie, I've been tempted a few times." *More* than a few times. "I thought it was just infatuation, but..." She exhaled. This was Perry, so maybe she was safe to say it. "I've realised it isn't."

Which left the question of what it *was*.

"Infatuation?" Perry raised her eyebrows. "No, I don't think so. And you worked that out without my help."

"I did! Are you proud of me?" Vice threw her a sardonic grin. "Dealing with my own feelings—whatever next?"

"And have you *acted* on those feelings? Last night, perhaps?"

Was that why Perry had ordered the carpenters to split her cabin in two? Just before they'd left, she'd asked them to erect a new bulkhead, making her cabin smaller but creating space for Vice. She'd said it was because the ship was theirs and they could configure it in a way that worked for them. Vice had assumed she was fed up of losing the space to her and Knigh for their deciphering. But was it because she thought they needed the privacy?

Meddling wretch.

No, there was no need for privacy in Vice's life right now. *More's the pity.*

She huffed, grin replaced with a tight frown. At the end of the road, the sign of the Laughing Kraken swung in the breeze, squeaking softly. "Course not," she said, voice hoarse. "Last night wasn't the… We're just friends."

"As you keep saying. Twice in the past minute, in fact."

Bollocks. She had, hadn't she? *Just friends*. She'd been telling herself that so many times, she'd started saying it out loud. "Well, it's true. You remember what happened last time, don't you? It would be a terrible idea to be anything more."

"Are you trying to persuade me or yourself?"

Vice jerked, shooting Perry a look as her heart dipped. "Then you *don't* think it would be a terrible idea?"

For all she teased Perry for being sensible and responsible and her opposite in so many other ways, she had to listen to her when it came to feelings. As recent events had proved, this was not Vice's area of expertise.

Smiling, Perry slipped a hand through her arm. "Do you think you've changed since then? You, yourself, as well as your relationship with him."

"Oof." She ran a hand over her face, sudden tiredness dragging on her. So much had happened since they'd fallen into each other's arms in that glow-worm cave. Betrayal. Jailbreak. Sacrifice. That emotionally horrific crossing from Albion to Arawaké. So many mistakes and hurts.

Then the ill-advised boarding of the *Sovereign* and their argument after. More mistakes.

And after that... the time apart—the *much-needed* time apart. Missing him. Realising what he'd given up. The way he'd stuck with her in the face of all her attempts to push him away. It more than outweighed the betrayal.

The fact that after it all, he'd still come for her. He'd risked Mercia, the *Sovereign,* and the kraken to get her back.

And he'd done so *twice.*

Knigh had more than proved himself, more than redeemed himself.

The world spun.

She, the notorious Lady Vice, the scourge of the seas, the Pirate Queen, had been able to forgive him. Did that mean she'd changed? And she'd realised this thing she felt wasn't infatuation—that had to be a sign that she was, what? *Growing?*

Dragging in a long breath, she clutched the brim of her hat, as if that might stop the spinning and fix things in place. Perry touched her back, comforting. A reminder that there was solid ground despite the maelstrom of events, questions, feelings... uncertainty.

One thing she was sure of: she trusted him. And if last night was anything to go by, he trusted her, too. That wasn't something she could've said when they'd been together on *The Morrigan* or when they'd screwed on the *Swallow*.

Do you think you've changed since then?

With a heavy sigh, she nodded. "I bloody hope so."

Perry tugged on her arm, coaxing. "And I think we can both agree he's changed, right?"

He was battling his anger. He'd been so brave last night, so vulnerable. Her heart squeezed. The Knigh she'd known on *The Morrigan* never would've cracked himself wide open like that—never mind let her see inside.

But he'd changed in smaller ways, too. He'd started to relax —he smiled more, laughed more, joked more. Smaller ways, perhaps, but no less important, because they had to be symptoms of some bigger shift inside him. That rigid control slipped day-by-day, and gradually released the man who'd been trapped inside.

And he was spectacular.

Chest too tight to speak, she only nodded in reply.

Perry angled her head and raised her eyebrows in gentle inquisition. "Then why do you think the same thing would happen again?"

"Because he'll leave." She didn't think before she said it, it was just there, already spewing from her mouth before she realised just how true it was. Her heart tolled, heavy. "Eventually. When we find Drake's treasure, his family will be safe and he won't need to slum it with us anymore."

"Hmm." Perry's mouth shifted from side to side as if she were tasting the answer like an expensive whiskey. "I can't say whether you're right or wrong. That's down to him. But if it is true, is it not worth making the most of him—of the pair of you together—while he *is* here?" Her shoulders bobbed. "And I can't say if it is or isn't worth it—only you and he can know what it's really like between you. The question you need to ask is this: is the joy, however temporary, worth the risk of future hurt?"

Throat tight, Vice could only stare back.

That was an impossible question. One she'd never considered. If it was going to hurt, she avoided it—easy. But...

Staying away from Knigh was anything but easy.

For all its pain, last night had been... It had been *real*. Not a joke. Not play. Not flippant or foolish. Real and raw and beautiful. And he'd thanked her for it, so maybe it had helped. He'd been so happy this morning, so at ease...

"Speak of the devil," Perry murmured, tugging on her arm.

She blinked away the warm afterglow of last night and took in the way ahead. There he was, on the other side of the road, standing outside the Laughing Kraken's doors. He wasn't happy now—at least not if his folded arms and deep scowl were anything to go by.

As Perry led her closer, Vice's cheeks burned like he'd

caught her talking about him. Which was ridiculous, because firstly, he *hadn't*, and secondly, she was a little beyond *blushing*.

Mouth flat, he acknowledged them with a nod.

One thing Perry's advice had failed to take into account was Knigh's feelings for her. He might simply not be interested. She might've misread that conversation at the *Venatrix's* stern when they'd been reunited. She'd thought it an offer of something more than friendship, but he'd never said that outright. There were plenty of reasons he might not want to be with her.

Perry clapped him on the shoulder—or at least as close to his shoulder as she could reach. "What's got you so royally pissed off?"

He exhaled through his nose, eyes flicking to the tavern. If anything, his scowl deepened. "FitzRoy."

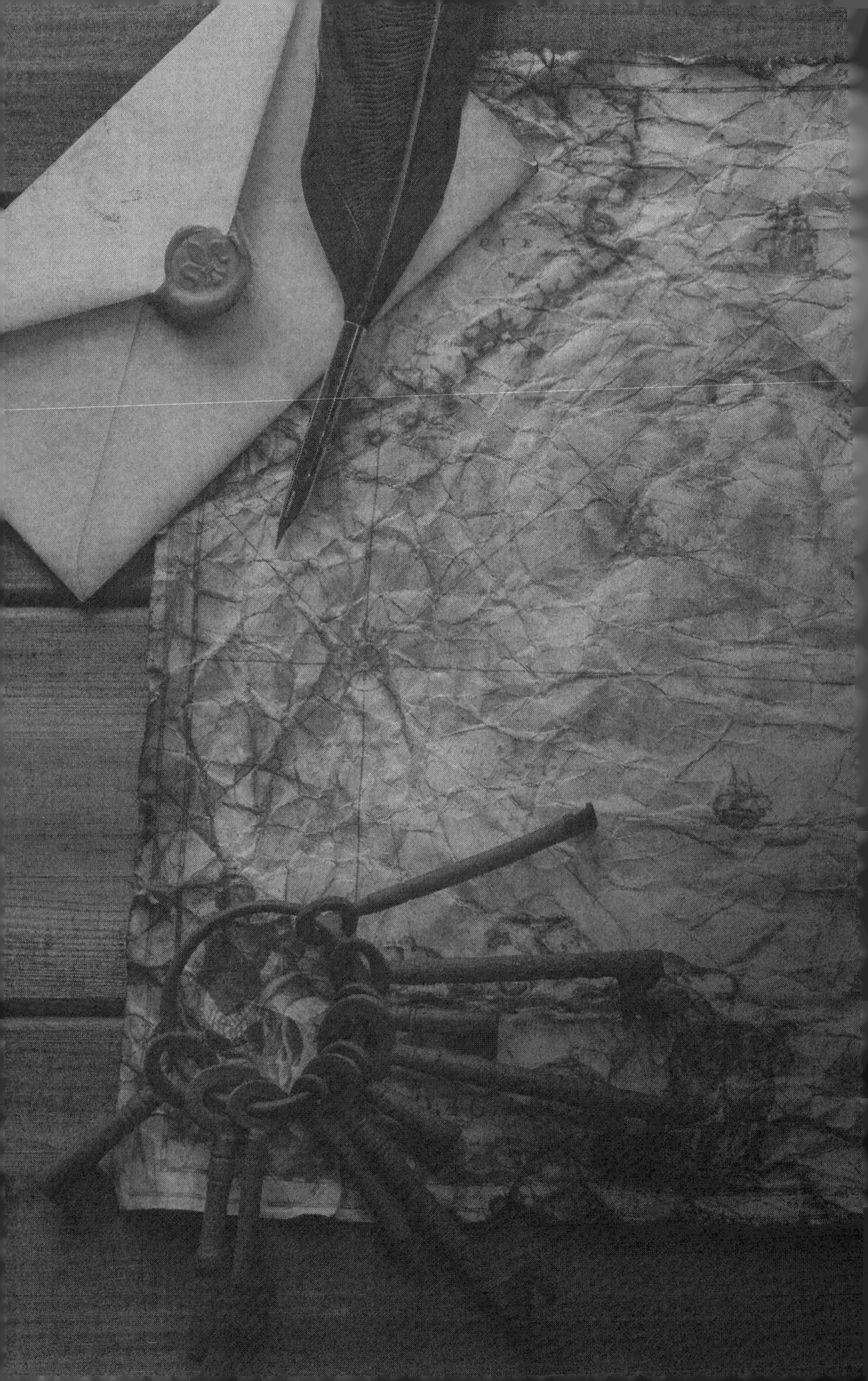

RECRUITING

It turned out Knigh and Aedan had split up to cover the taverns on this street more quickly, and Knigh had spotted FitzRoy inside. So Knigh had spun on his heel and walked straight back out.

Vice's teeth creaked as she ground them. Fitz-bloody-Roy. Except for the distant view of his ship fleeing the *Sovereign's* division, she hadn't seen him since the day they'd found her guilty in Portsmouth. The day he'd revealed his own treachery.

It was about time they talked.

Every inch of Perry's face tensed. "He might be able to help, but—"

"*Him?*" Knigh stared back.

"We have the *Venatrix* and the *Firefly*. That's it." Although she had to crane her neck to look him in the eye, Perry did so while looking every inch the captain. "We're not in any position to be choosy. Unless you've managed to recruit an entire fleet this afternoon?"

Lips pressed together until they paled, he shook his head.

"Thought not. By my reckoning, he abandoned us in the middle of that fight, so he owes us. Vice"—Perry turned to her, eyes softening—"FitzRoy has wronged you the most. It's your call."

Finally, Vice prised her teeth apart. "Vane always respected him. He might be able to broker peace." Whatever she'd done to make Vane so angry that drink-murky night had to be fixable. And if it had turned his attention towards Knigh's family, she had to fix it. Even if that meant swallowing the desire to wring FitzRoy's neck.

She raised an eyebrow at Knigh. "You said he seemed sorry for what happened in Portsmouth, right?"

"Hm." That low sound in his throat and the narrowing of his eyes said he put as much weight in FitzRoy's appearances as he did to sailors' claims to have mermaid wives. "So he hinted."

"Come on, then." As she shoved the door open, she glimpsed Perry's frown and tightening mouth.

Sat there in gold and black, raising a tankard, amusement bright in his face, though he didn't do more than smirk, Fitz was hard to miss. Around him, a crowd of men and women laughed as if he'd just told the most hilarious story they'd ever heard.

Then his hazel eyes landed on her. Even from the opposite side of the tavern, she could see him gulp a deep breath. No more amusement or cockiness remained at the corners of his sensuous mouth.

One-by-one, his companions followed his line of sight and fell silent.

The rest of the tavern quickly followed.

If so much as a drop of ale had leaked from a barrel behind the bar, she'd have heard it.

Word had spread, then.

"Vice," the owner, One-Eyed Nell, said, voice low, "you're always welcome here." She gave a tight smile, her single eye swivelling from her to Fitz and back again as if sizing up who to back. She'd be better off staying out of it. "And so is Captain FitzRoy. But"—she leant on the bar, brows lowering, making her eyepatch bob—"I don't want no trouble in my establishment. You know the rules."

Vice inclined her head before giving Fitz a once-over. "No trouble. Unless he makes it."

The most shocking thing was, she meant it. Mostly. She'd expected her muscles to coil like they did before battle, ready to spring at him and grab the front of his coat as she had in that cell below Portsmouth's courtroom. But they barely twitched, and her pulse only drummed a touch faster than normal.

Remarkably calm, all things considered.

Good. She'd kill him in a calm, collected manner. Something planned. Something painful.

She smiled.

With a flick of his hand, Fitz dismissed his companions, gaze never leaving hers. He stood, placed his drink on the table, and sauntered over, each movement deliberate, slow.

Boots shuffled on the stone floor behind her—that had to be Knigh. She put out a hand to hold him back. She needed no protection from Fitz—she wasn't bound and weaponless this time.

When he was within arm's reach, he stopped, only breaking eye contact to examine her from head to toe and back again. A faint frown creased his brow, and he gave the barest nod—she knew him well enough to read his words in that gesture. *You look well.*

Pulse faster, blood hotter, hands clenching, she glared at him. *No thanks to you.*

His chest rose and fell in a long breath.

And he kneeled.

Kneeled.

FitzRoy, *kneeling* at her feet.

She blinked, but he was still there, still on his knees. The hiss of a collected gasp sweeping through the tavern confirmed it was real.

"Vice," he said, voice thick as he shook his head and looked up at her, "I was a fool. I *am* a fool. Please forgive me."

Him, asking her forgiveness? It was ridiculous enough to make her laugh, and yet...

There was no sly flicker on his lips. His wide eyes searched hers, apparently earnest.

If he was being earnest, it was the first time in his damn life.

His brows rose. "Are you going to make me beg?"

Now *there* was an idea. "Well, you're already on your knees, so some might argue you already are. But you *could* make it official. When everyone tells the story later, I want us all to be on the same page."

"Very well," he said with a slow nod. "My greatest Vice, I beg you to forgive me."

Her mouth dropped open. He'd actually done it—and loud enough for the whole room to hear.

The fire in her veins fizzled out. Somewhere along the way, her hands had loosened, too.

Still, it wouldn't do to make it too easy on him. And she might use this to her advantage.

"I'll think about it."

Knigh stepped to her side, expression beyond incredulity as Fitz rose and dusted off his knees. "Are you joking? He left us to face the *Sovereign* and he and I... we... But you forgive him just like that?"

While I had to go through Hells. That's what he wasn't saying.

Now her blood burned. She spun and leant in so close her nose almost touched his. "Yes," she hissed, "but..." She clamped her mouth shut before she finished the sentence. *But when you did it, it hurt more.*

He almost mastered his response, but this close, she couldn't fail to spot the twitch of his eyebrows.

She heaved a sigh, quenching her anger. "Knigh," she murmured for his ears only, "I've only said I'll think about it. For him to do that in a room full of people—people who'll go back and tell their crews... he's just decimated his reputation." She let that sink in, then cocked her head, adding a sly smile. "Besides, if he thinks he has a chance of forgiveness, he'll do whatever I ask."

His shoulders sank as he exhaled. "Like helping us save my family."

She nodded and squeezed his arm before turning to Fitz. "You can start by buying me a drink."

A FEW MINUTES LATER, they occupied a rectangular table in the corner, Fitz at the head of the table to Vice's right, Perry opposite her, and Knigh rigid at her side. She'd engineered it to avoid the two men facing each other, which would only have encouraged their antagonism, though it left her feeling like a human shield. A flimsy one at that, going by Knigh's bunched muscles; they brushed her arm with every mechanical movement as he fiddled with his tankard.

A ring of empty space had formed around their group, as if the other patrons didn't trust their truce. Between Knigh's solid muscles and Perry's face that looked like she was chewing wasps, Vice couldn't blame them.

"Oh, Perry," Fitz said, a sigh edging his words, "don't look at me like that. I left to draw away the frigates, which I did, *thank* you. I knew Vice would find a way to claim the *Venatrix* and help even the odds." He raised an eyebrow at Vice, mouth lifting at the same time in that roguish smile that had got her into his bunk in the first place.

It had no effect. Not when she'd seen the full force of one of Knigh Blackwood's smiles and had—barely—lived to tell the tale.

"Although," Fitz went on, "I didn't expect you to get

someone to *give* it to you." He paused with his drink halfway to his mouth and smirked. "I still can't believe you relied on someone to give you something, rather than just taking it for yourself."

Cocking her head, she smiled sweetly. "Maybe I should've taken that approach to captaincy on *The Morrigan*. Would've saved us all a lot of trouble."

"Oh, touché."

"So you're sorry," Knigh said, leaning forward, hands pressing into the table, arm solid against hers, "but you're still an arsehole?"

Fitz finally sipped his drink, watching Knigh over the rim. The air hummed with tension. "Vice didn't always think so."

Good gods, this was getting dangerously close to a cockfight.

Under the table, she nudged her knee against Knigh's. The warmth of him and the intimacy of the gesture made her instantly regret it. *Just friends.* Her pulse spiked in a way that was more than friendly.

But this was touching with a purpose—they needed Fitz on board and Knigh needed to not piss him off. She cleared her throat and pulled her leg away. "What can I say? I've seen the light."

Exhaling, Knigh sank back into his chair.

"Much as it's lovely catching up," she went on, "we have business, and it strikes me that you owe us. Big time."

FitzRoy's eyes narrowed, and he cocked his head. "How big are we talking?"

"Vane."

"Huh." He swirled his drink, peering into the bottom of the tankard. "That *is* big. But then, I suppose you owe him a visit after he sold you to the Duke."

"I do." She squeezed her cup. Getting her hands on Vane would be sweet, but Perry would argue that getting him to stand down would be, if not sweeter, more *sensible*. And she might not share Perry's penchant for all things sensible, but she appreciated that peace meant no bloodshed.

"But we don't plan to fight," she went on, "not unless we have to. He's attacking a merchant—we merely intend to stop him. If anyone can persuade Vane, it's you." There, massage his ego a little. Not that it needed it. "And if you can't"—she shrugged—"well, I hear you have seventy-four guns. That's quite a persuasive number."

FitzRoy's drink sat on the table, forgotten. He watched her, expression thoughtful, which was a surprise. She'd have expected him to preen when she mentioned the size of his— ahem—*firepower*. "So you want me to persuade Vane to leave these merchants alone, and failing that, we force him? Why? What's the prize?" Greed lit his eyes—she'd seen it in him enough times to know.

She resisted the urge to glance at Knigh. Fitz didn't need to know this involved his family. "I owe the merchant—he brought me here from Albion after you screwed me over." A spiky little reminder of what he'd done. "Would be a beautiful bit of symmetry, you helping me rescue them from scum like Vane."

"Vane *is* an awful bore. And I'm sure my assistance would go in my favour when it comes to your forgiveness."

"I'm sure it will."

A smile dawned on his face, and he waved Nell over. "Well, I'll drink to that. You have yourself a deal."

And she had herself three ships.

Please, gods, let that be enough.

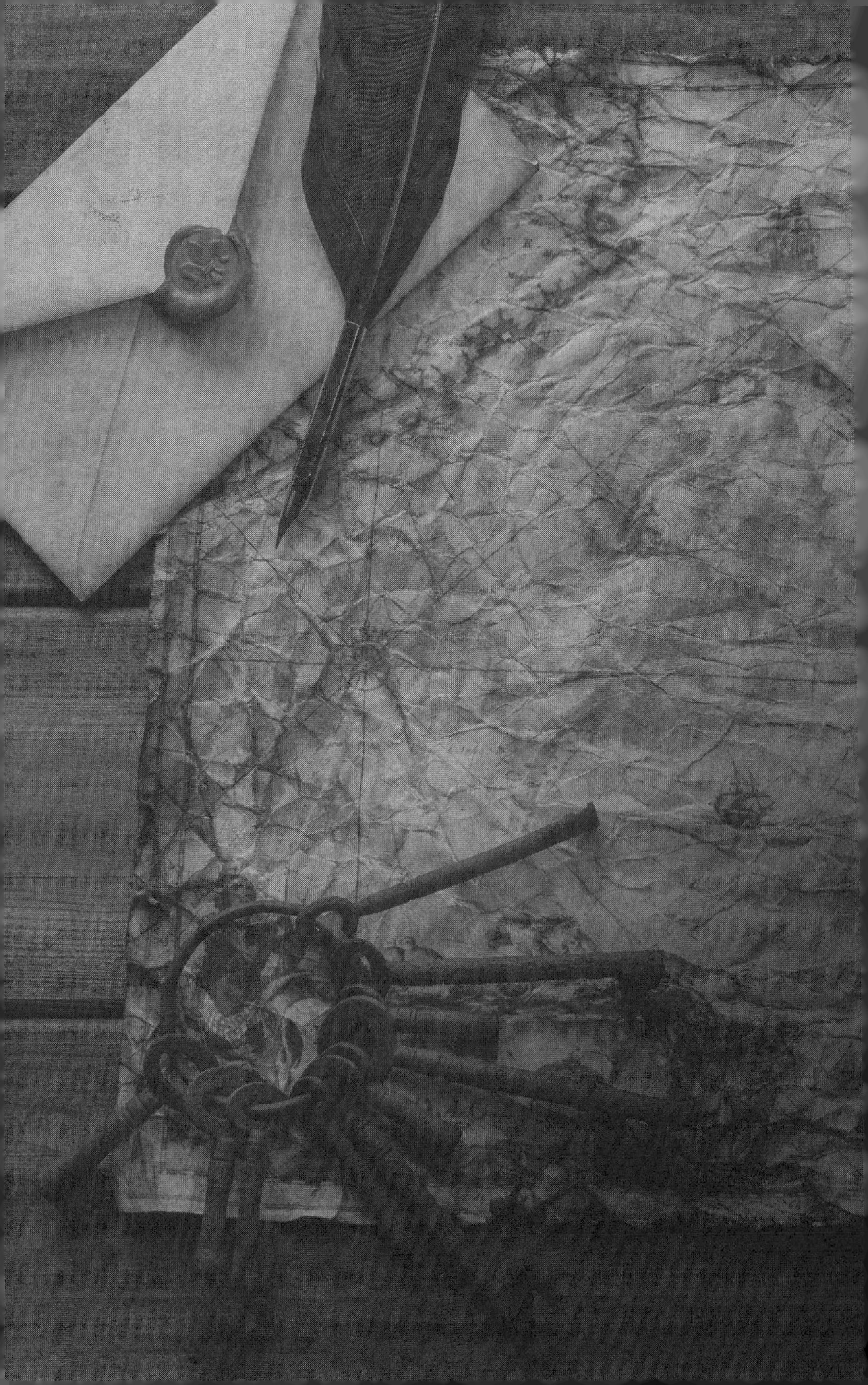

HORIZON TO HORIZON

In the ring of the spyglass, horizon. Knigh swept it to port. Horizon. To starboard. Horizon.

They'd pored over maps and charts for hours, calculating the area the *Swallow* was most likely to be. It was *here*—or within a hundred nautical miles, anyway. Unless they'd hit poor weather or were becalmed or...

Sighing, he lowered the spyglass and rubbed his eyes. His brow ached. His neck, too. His shoulders had been knotted for days. At least the breeze up here on the main top was cool, and he'd taken the watch alone, so no one could bother him with the demands of small talk.

Not that the cool or the solitude were *much* comfort. Not when he might spot Vane's black sails or the *Swallow's* white any minute.

The thought twitched through him, and he lifted the spyglass again.

Horizon, horizon, and more horizon.

They were a week from Nassau with their odd little flotilla —the *Venatrix*, the *Sea Witch*, and the *Firefly*, a neat sloop not so different from *The Morrigan*. Who knew what they'd face once they found Vane? Oba had made it sound as though he'd forged alliances left and right, forming a fleet set on… *what*, exactly? Waging war on Vee? That's what Tew had suggested before Saba had splattered his brains over his shoulder.

If Vane had a fleet doing his bidding, how many ships sailed with him? Oba seemed to think it was only a loose alliance, with most vessels operating separately, but she hadn't been in that meeting between captains.

His aching brow pulled into yet another scowl.

Vee was optimistic they'd be more than a match for the *Maelstrom* and whoever accompanied her. But of course she was—that was her.

Every morning since they'd left Nassau, she had him sparring with Aedan and her, sometimes both at once. It was just normal sparring, without the words he'd spilled to her and Perry, but it left him more at peace with each day. In the afternoons, he worked with her on the Copper Drake—they'd translated about two-thirds of the book so far.

It was strange being alone with her in such close proximity for hours and hours on end. On one hand, they worked well together and relaxed in each other's company like good friends. But he'd never seen a good friend stretch her arms in the air and felt such an overpowering urge to run his hands from her waist, over her ribs, up her arms, and trap her hands while he kissed her to within an inch of her life.

He was sure she felt it, too. More than once he'd looked up from his work to find her watching. Each time, it was like a bolt of her lightning shot through him, and they both paused, staring, for gods knew how long, heaving chests the only movement. Then one would clear their throat or shuffle their papers and look away.

Comfortable ease *and* physical tension—a strange contradiction. That was the only way to describe working with Vee.

But yesterday and today, as they'd patrolled the area in which they expected to find the *Swallow*, his pen had fallen still after less than an hour's work and his attention had drifted out the port windows. She'd squeezed his shoulder, exclaimed at the knots there, and sent him to get some air.

Both days, he'd found his way up here and relieved the watch.

He huffed at the lack of sails on the horizon.

It wasn't that he *wanted* to find the *Swallow* under attack, but this nothingness was unbearable, far worse than waiting for battle. This was waiting for an unknown.

They might find the *Swallow* and assist her to port untroubled. Mother and Is might not even be on board.

They might find Vane and parley. FitzRoy could end it without a fight, although the idea of *that man* calming a situation rather than exacerbating it was beyond laughable.

They might find the *Maelstrom* presiding over the sinking remains of the *Swallow*.

His stomach turned, setting off the writhing sensation he'd endured all yesterday afternoon and last night. Like that damn barrel of eels.

Tucking away the spyglass, he swallowed down the sour bile coating his tongue. "All will be well," he muttered, closing his eyes and raking his hands through his hair.

"It will," Vee's voice came from nowhere.

He jumped, then spotted the telltale shake of the shrouds that said someone was climbing up.

She beamed as she climbed onto the platform with practiced ease and unhooked a bag from her shoulder. "Here you go"—she held it out—"you'll feel better after some sugar. Fitz brought me a pineapple and lucky for you, I'm gracious enough to share." She tossed her head with a grin, clearly mocking herself, then offered a canteen. "And I bet you didn't bring water with you, eh?"

He hadn't, but...

FitzRoy was an arse. A total and utter arse. He'd come to the *Venatrix* this morning under the pretence of speaking to Perry about something *desperately* important. In reality, he'd spent most of the time watching Vee as she sparred with Knigh and practiced her sabre skills with Saba, Lizzy, and the sisters. The way he'd stroked his bottom lip as he'd watched her parry and lunge had irritated Knigh enough that Aedan had landed twice as many punches as usual.

Even worse, Vee hadn't told her former captain to take a running jump off the rail. In fact, she'd stopped and chatted with him as she'd wiped off her face and neck with a wet towel. She'd smiled. She'd laughed.

And Knigh had smouldered.

Teeth grinding, he took the canteen. He didn't even look at

the bag. "Tell Fitz he can keep his damn pineapple. Maybe he'll ask you to feed it to him. I bet he'd *love* to eat it off—"

"Knigh!" She frowned at him, but her eyes were wide, as though she were more shocked than angry. "What the hells?"

He blew out the breath he'd kept to finish that sentence. Rubbing his aching jaw, he flicked open the canteen. He glared at that instead of her. *I bet he'd* love *to eat it off you.* That's what he'd been about to say. *That man* probably would love it, but that didn't give Knigh the right to—

"I understand you hate Fitz," she said, "but bloody hells, Knigh. I only brought him with us to help. The more firepower we have, the better chances for Billy and your family." She huffed through her nose. "Is this even about him? Or is it because of what we might be sailing into? Your shoulders were so tight earlier..."

Knigh almost choked on his mouthful of drink. Eyes watering, he forced it down, then blinked at Vee. She was right. He hadn't even realised, but she'd seen it. "Am I that transparent?"

She gave a lopsided smile, pulling a parcel wrapped in waxed paper from the bag. "I can't take credit. Perry said that might be why you were particularly tetchy with Fitz this morning."

"I'm sorry. I shouldn't have snapped at you. FitzRoy, yes. You, no." He sighed and shook his head. "I... I have to admit, though, it's hard."

She raised her eyebrows in question.

He winced at the parcel in her hands. He wasn't proud of it, but—"It's hard to see you forgive him so easily."

She grumbled, unwrapping a wooden bowl. "He is *not* forgiven." The sweet-sharp scent of pineapple reached his nose before he even caught sight of the fruit's golden slices. As she held out the bowl, his mouth watered. "This is part of his penance, but he's not clear yet. I need to keep him sweet if we're going to deal with Vane."

He groaned and bowed his head. "I'm sorry. I'm being an arse, aren't I?"

With a finger on his chin, she made him meet her gaze. "Yes, but only a little bit. And I'd say with the current situation, it's understandable. Now shut up and eat this." Grinning, she held out a slice of pineapple.

It was a few inches from his mouth. Did she mean for him to eat from her hand or...? If he did, his lips would end up at her fingertips. Then there would be the question of what to do about the sweet juice glistening on her skin...

She must've realised the same thing, because her grin froze, then faded.

Yes, they were potentially sailing into battle. Yes, he might be about to discover his mother and sister in the middle of the ocean, wanted by a dangerous pirate. But this was a sweet and welcome distraction—just for a moment.

His shoulders and neck had already eased, replaced by a different tension that thrummed through his nerves, full of potential, like air buzzing before a storm.

A rivulet of that clear juice ran down her index finger and trembled on her knuckle, threatening to fall onto his shirt at any moment.

He could lick it off, save his shirt.

His mouth watered more.

Too much. Too dangerous. Too...

He caught it with the pad of his thumb instead. Licking his own thumb was far safer.

But the way Vee watched each movement, her lips parted, felt far from safe. It sent that delicious tension shooting low in his belly and spiked his pulse into something hot and loud.

Eyes locked with hers, he inched forward. He just wanted the pineapple, that was all. It was only that he was hungry.

He could tell himself that. And he knew it was a lie, but...

She didn't pull away. Her tongue darted out, moistening her lips as his closed on the fruit.

And he watched the flick of that pink tip running over her lips, wishing they were his.

But he had to make do with the sweet-sharp fruitiness of the pineapple overwhelming his tongue, the juice flooding his mouth. He did, though, let his lips brush her fingertips. The scrape of her nails on his sensitive flesh sent sparks through him. The sound of her breath hitching said he wasn't the only one affected.

Holding in a groan, he forced himself to sit back. It would've been easier to take her finger in his mouth and suck the juice from it—far, far easier.

But they were already playing with fire.

He knew her well enough—knew *them* and what they were together well enough to see this was moments away from clothes being torn off.

Chest heaving, cheeks flushed, she stared at him. The way the air seared through his lungs—he probably looked the same.

"Vee—"

A distant roll of thunder.

No. Not thunder.

Gunfire.

The spyglass was already back in his hand before she'd even gasped.

That had to be the *Maelstrom*. Anything else was too implausible a coincidence.

"We're too late," he muttered, "they've already found the Swallow." It tolled in his stomach, setting off the seething once more.

Horizon. Horizon. Horizon. He swept along that curved line.

"Or it could be someone else—a different battle," she said, but her voice wavered.

A dark shape broke the smooth line between sea and sky. Black sails. And alongside, white sails in a configuration he recognised—one he'd sailed on.

He passed the spyglass to Vee, expecting his hand to shake, but it didn't. "It's them." His voice sounded remarkably calm, considering the way his heart roared.

She honed in on the same spot he had. Her sinking shoulders told him the instant she saw it. "Bollocks."

More of that distant rumbling gunfire.

Squaring his shoulders, he sucked in a deep breath, even though his chest complained that it was too tight to take in so much air. He bellowed to the deck below: "Sails!"

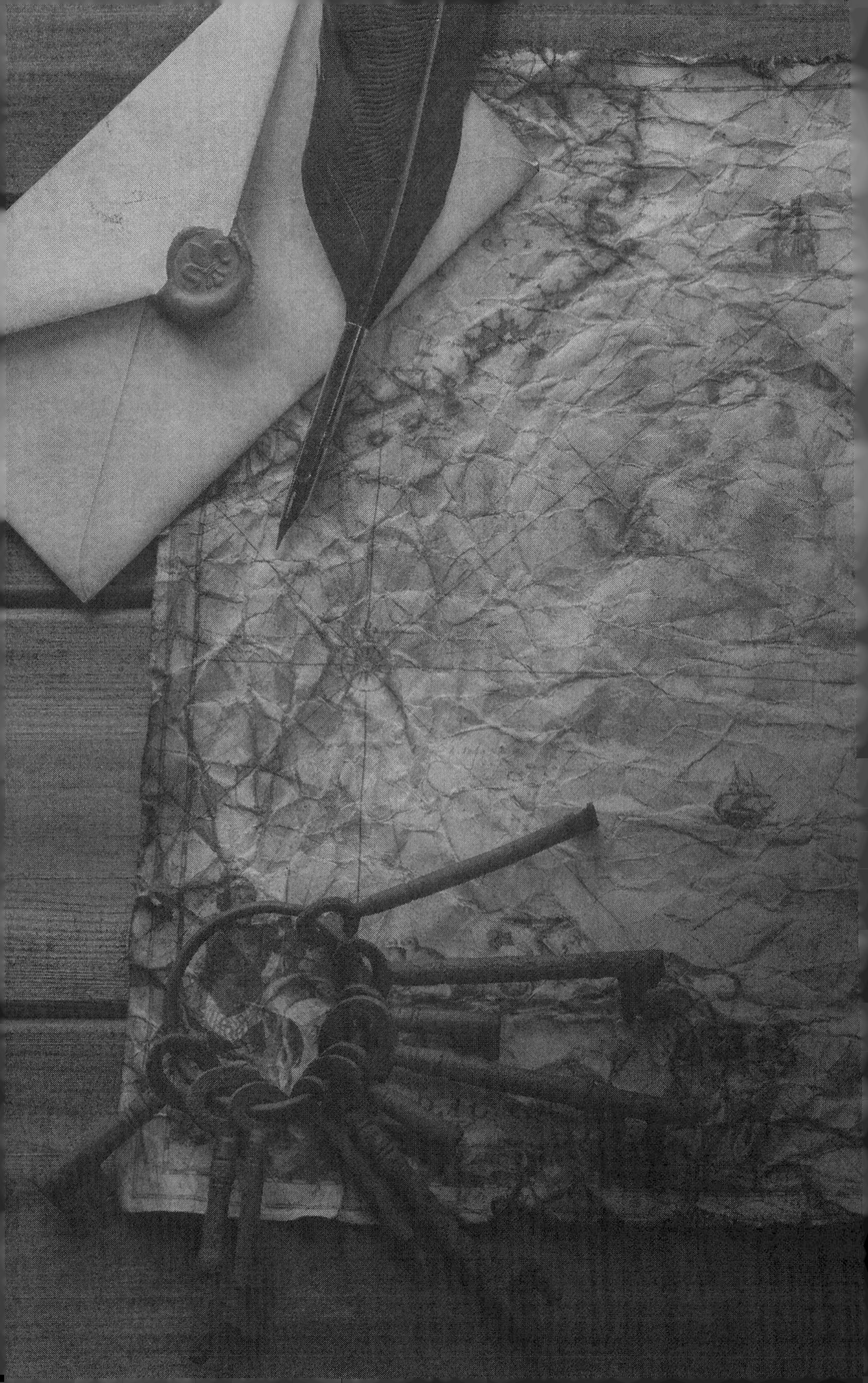

EVEN THE ODDS

The steady boom of cannons marked the time of their approach—agonising minute after minute. Heart in her throat, Vice stood at the helm with Knigh, one hand over his on the wheel, the other on his shoulder.

Every inch of him was so solid, so gritted, he might've been made of stone. His granite-grey eyes didn't leave the battle ahead.

With her gift, she sped the *Venatrix* towards the *Maelstrom* and four other black-sailed ships that harried the *Swallow*. They fired and manoeuvred, cutting through the water and foam, and Billy's crew shot back.

Knigh's anguish was a palpable force rolling off his shoulders. Each thundering shot from the *Maelstrom* and her allies trembled through him.

She'd already told him that Vane wanted to ransom his mother and sister, so his crews would aim to disable the ship, not kill. But she'd also told him Billy was smart enough to recognise he was outnumbered and so wouldn't fight back.

And yet the *Swallow* fired her meagre cannons and raced west. Her enemies swept across her course, forcing her to veer to port or starboard or else risk a collision.

Mouth dry, chest tight, Vice followed their trajectories. The *Swallow* was trying to outrun them. They were so close to land, it was a sound tactic, but the pirates had the advantage in every respect—numbers, firepower, and a starting position between the *Swallow* and Arawaké.

But the odds were about to even out.

The *Sea Witch* and the *Firefly* fanned out behind the *Venatrix*, and Vice kept dipping her awareness into their waters to pull them along so they wouldn't be left behind.

"Almost there," she whispered to Knigh and squeezed his shoulder.

Within minutes, the *Maelstrom's* companions broke away from the *Swallow*, two veering to starboard, two to port, their courses set to surround and engage the *Venatrix* and her allies.

"Here we go," Perry bellowed from the quarterdeck rail, just out of arm's reach. "Gunners, load. Ready on repairs. If we're hit, I don't want to lose an inch of speed." Her teeth flashed in a fierce grin, bright against her tanned skin. "Let's show Vane the price of betraying his own."

The crew roared.

The deck bustled as they worked with grim smiles of determination, their energy renewed by Perry's call to arms. Clovis and Erec clapped Knigh on the shoulder as they passed, but he didn't so much as twitch.

"Knigh"—she rubbed her thumb over his—"you have the *Venatrix*. I'm going to pay a visit to Vane's friends."

Eyes still on the *Maelstrom* and the *Swallow*, his face angled a few degrees to her. He gave the barest nod.

Seeing him like this had her in knots—it was like he'd regressed to the rigid man she'd first met. But saving his family—assuming they were on the *Swallow*—would bring him back.

Exhaling, she sank into the waves and the wellspring. She could strike them with lightning, but she'd seen a ship's magazine explode. A horror of red and orange and black, black smoke. The loss of life. And the pain the kraken had sent to her when she'd hit it with lightning…

It turned her stomach.

Instead, she tugged a current from its usual course, and drew power from the dark lightning cloud inside her to strengthen it. Energy crackling, she shoved her new, stronger current into the port bow of the first ship.

They'd have to scramble to ride that sudden shift in the sea. Serve them right for attacking her friend.

The wellspring throbbed under her hand, pushing as it sought to drive freely through her, like it was keen to wreck and ruin.

But she pushed back.

She let through only the power she needed. She wouldn't let this thing overwhelm her, erase her sense of self.

The sea whipped up choppy, unpredictable waves as its currents ran across the wind and she carried her current past that first ship to the next.

The other two sailed much further to port, looking to surround the *Venatrix* and her allies.

We'll see about that.

Breaking the sea's surface, she rose into the breeze and clouds, the air a little harder for her magic to grasp as always. But the wind filling the third ship's sails—she could get a grip on that.

She snuffed it out.

They slowed, only momentum carrying them forward. That was enough—it would give the *Firefly* the advantage, let them choose their angle of approach.

Next, the fourth ship—she stole their wind, and their shape in the water slowed in her awareness.

Somewhere in the distance, she exhaled. It was hard to tell how long had passed since she'd dived so deeply into her gift. But the ships weren't quite engaged yet, so it must've been minutes.

A gap remained between the paired ships… A closing gap, but maybe the *Venatrix,* out front, could cut through and reach the *Swallow*, leaving the *Sea Witch* and *Firefly* to deal with Vane's allies. They could evade, chain shot their masts and rigging.

She had a second to decide.

She pushed.

Current and wind—they ran with her, driving the little frigate on.

The first ship she'd struck with the current had regained control and righted course. Her wide lines charged through the water, turning to close the gap.

Vice closed the hand inside the wellspring into a fist and let sparking energy surge through it, through her, and into the ocean and sky.

The *Venatrix* surged in response.

That's my girl.

The energy shook through her, and she took more. It seared and crackled. It roared in her ears, against her skin. It scorched her veins and snapped in her teeth.

Something moved. Something—a hand?

"Vee?"

A gasp tore through her and she opened her eyes. The world pitched, and she staggered as sea spray cut through the daze.

"Vee?" It was Knigh, warning in his tone. He caught her with an arm around her waist.

But there was another sound, not just him.

The ship groaned. Wood creaked. Lines strained. She couldn't take it.

"Too much." Bollocks. Letting Knigh worry about her body, she split her awareness between sea and sky and pulled back. They wouldn't make it through the gap, but if she kept up that acceleration, she risked destroying the ship.

"Sorry," she said, returning to herself again now the ship was at a safe speed.

Knigh was practically holding her upright, arm still around her waist. He nodded and steered to port. "Nearly wrecked the ship, but you've bought us a clear shot."

Any other day, she'd have called that a joke coming from him, but there was no twitch at the corner of his mouth. She took a steadying breath and extricated herself from his hold, resuming her earlier stance—one hand over his on the wheel, the other gripping his shoulder. She bent the wind and current to their new course, and the *Venatrix* arced smoothly, swiftly through the water, presenting an enemy vessel, the *Seahorse*, with her broadside.

The deck trembled as they unleashed.

They raked the *Seahorse* again and again, but in the distance, the *Maelstrom* still fired on the *Swallow*.

Goosebumps rose on Knigh's arms and although he steered the *Venatrix* true, working with her currents in the sea and air, his grey eyes constantly flicked to the *Swallow*. "This is too slow," he said, voice full of grit.

"I know." She stroked his shoulder, resting her forehead on it for a moment.

Above, the *Venatrix's* sails turned as the crew heaved on lines, adjusting for the changing wind. "I've got it," she shouted, and waved for them to stop. She could adjust the wind instead, make sure they weren't taken aback.

Wait. *Taken aback.*

That was it. That would be quicker.

She exhaled a laugh and patted Knigh. "Keep me in sight of their sails." Using the wind, she couldn't sense the ships displacing seawater to help direct her magic. Eyes open, no wellspring for this one.

The *Seahorse* turned to starboard, yards turning to keep the wind behind her sails as she came around to face them with her own broadside.

Fixed on those billowing black sails, she gritted her teeth and felt for the gusting wind.

There.

She rode it, resisting the urge to grab on—it would only slip between her fingers. Instead, she tugged the wind she'd built behind the *Venatrix's* sails and diverted it towards the front of the *Seahorse's*.

Her heart thudded. Thudded. Thudded.

Her breeze was almost there...

Like a child blocking a trickle of water with their hand, she stopped the natural wind behind the *Seahorse*.

The sails fell slack.

A second later, her breeze gusted against their front and pressed them back against the masts.

Wood trembled, groaned, creaked...

Muscles aching, she pushed harder.

The creak became a great crack, as loud as thunder or cannon fire.

The *Seahorse's* foremast went first, splintering and falling like a felled tree. It struck the mainmast, which had been thrumming with tension and now cracked, sending lines whipping into the air as they broke free. The mizzenmast followed seconds later.

Huffing, Vice let go of the winds and sagged against Knigh. The *Seahorse* was dead in the water.

"That was..." He tore his gaze from the *Maelstrom* and *Swallow* and met hers, the sky's brightness touching his steel-grey with blue. One corner of his mouth lifted—just a touch—and he nodded.

"Not the end of it, though." She shook out her trembling arms before pulling a handful of nuts from her pocket.

The three remaining ships had scattered away from the *Venatrix*—one facing the *Firefly*, one the *Sea Witch*, and the other, the *Undine,* made for the *Swallow*.

She blinked past them, and her heart leapt to her throat.

The *Swallow* also sat still in the glittering water.

"The way's clear," Perry yelled. "To the *Swallow*."

"Quick as we can," Vice murmured, giving Knigh what she hoped was a reassuring smile. The way her cheeks had stiffened, though, it might've looked more like a grimace.

Munching cocoplum seeds and cashews to replenish energy as quickly as she burned through it, she pushed the *Venatrix*. Now she knew the ship's limit, she kept just this side of it.

Dead ahead, grappling lines flew from the *Maelstrom* to the merchant barque. As each one grew taut and pulled the two ships together, the sinews of Knigh's body drew tighter and tighter still.

The *Undine* drew level on the other side.

Buggeration, they were also planning to board. The *Swallow* only had a merchant crew—far fewer men than served on a warship or pirate vessel—so she didn't require that many attackers to force her surrender. Unless...

Ah. That was it. The *Undine's* captain was using the same thing she had when they'd faced the *Sovereign* and the kraken. If the *Undine* grappled the *Swallow*, the *Venatrix* and her allies couldn't risk attacking for fear of damaging the merchant ship.

Smart move. Albeit an irritating one.

Vice and Knigh brought the *Venatrix* around, aiming to

cross the *Swallow's* bow and board from there. Four ships grappled together—it was going to be chaos. Carnage.

As they approached and their crewmates readied grappling hooks and weapons, she exhaled and squeezed Knigh's shoulder. She couldn't put it off any longer. "I suppose it's a waste of my breath to suggest you stay behind and let us handle this."

He snorted and shot her a look of disbelief. It felt like the first sign of life from him in over an hour. He didn't answer, though. Maybe he thought she was joking.

When she didn't laugh, he mastered his expression into something that was almost blank—his brow too tense, his jaw too rigid for his full mask. "It is."

No surprise there. If it were Kat or Mama in this situation, she'd react in the same way.

Except Mama *did* need her help. And she'd promised it. And…

She shook away the thought, though the guilt lingered in her gut, small and dark and dense. That was an old promise, long broken, even if it seemed to haunt her more and more lately.

Right now she had this battle, this day, this family—*Knigh's* family to save.

"Fine," she said, aligning the wind and current as Knigh turned the wheel. "Then get ready."

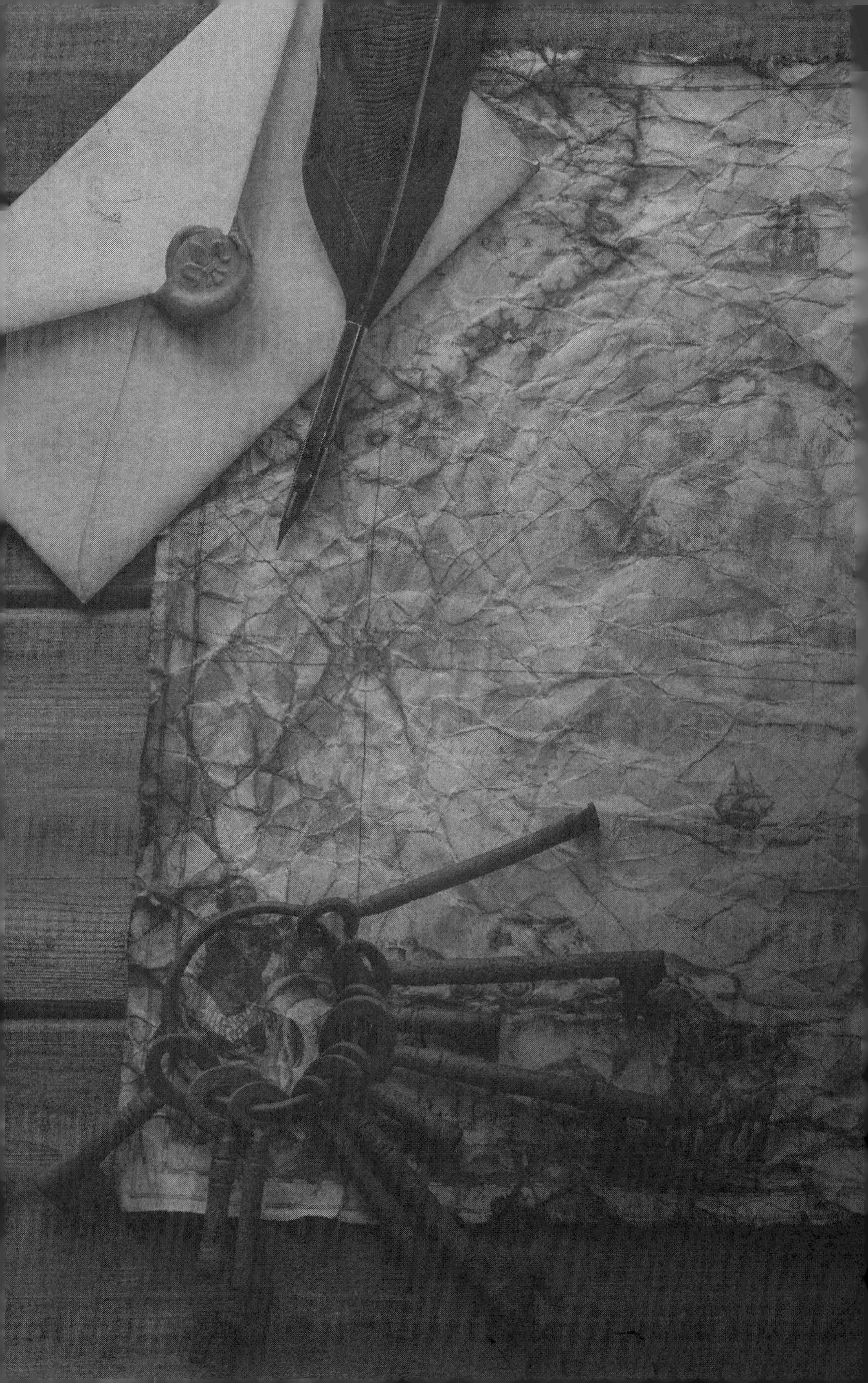

SURGE & HEAVE

Shouts, grunts, steel, and sweat. Bodies jostled left and right. Blood soaked into the sand and sawdust scattered across the deck.

Chaos. Total chaos.

No surprise—there *were* four crews on the *Swallow*, after all. Knigh gritted his teeth as he fought to keep his arms clear of the men and women pressing in, battling back and forth. Slowly, he, Vee, and their usual boarding party cut a path through the attackers.

"No sign of Vane," Vee grumbled between strikes.

And no sign of his family, either. There was still a chance they weren't here—Vane's information could've been false. Or they could be shut belowdecks, away from the fight.

Blocking a clumsy strike, he craned over his attacker's head, searching for Billy.

The clash of steel rang over and over, though it was nothing to the frantic pounding of his heart.

If they're here, please gods, let them be safe.

He lunged for his opponent, but Vee crashed into his arm, knocking his strike wide—she barely kept her feet as two men careened through the mob, smashing each other's faces with fists and sabres' knuckle-bows.

She twitched aside, missing a swipe from the man he'd been fighting—so close it made Knigh's heart seize.

But—there. A triangle of white linen, visible between Vee and the brawlers.

Knigh thrust. Steel flashed through the narrow gap she'd left and an instant later his sword point met resistance and slipped between the man's ribs.

There was time for a single breath before another took his place.

But he too fell, and the next one and the next, until they reached the forecastle's aft edge. Vee kicked a man down the stairs, buying Knigh time to scan the decks from this high ground.

More blood. More bodies. More chaos.

Aft, on the quarterdeck—yes, he knew that dark hair, that cock of the head. Billy. Just above the doors to his cabin, he fought two of Vane's men, catching their blades and slashing back.

If he was sticking near his cabin, did that mean Is and Mother were inside?

"Vee," Knigh rasped, still blocking and slicing as enemies tried to retake the forecastle.

She must've followed his line of sight, because she grabbed his shoulder, a moment's gentle comfort on this jostling deck. "I see him."

Billy and his crew had cleared the quarterdeck of invaders and now he stood at the rail looking fore. Even from here, Knigh could see his chest heaving. Not wasting time, he clamped a pistol between his left arm and his belly and reloaded.

He scanned his ship's decks, a frown inching into place, as if he was only now taking in the number of people on board and the fact that pirates were fighting other pirates.

When his gaze landed on Knigh, his mouth dropped open.

Knigh shoved his current adversary overboard, then nodded to his friend, raising his eyebrows in question.

Shaking his head and wearing a smile of disbelief, Billy mouthed something that looked like *What the hells are you doing here?* As he loaded his next pistol, he raised his chin. "Your sister and—"

"I know." If Billy was mentioning Is, that meant she was on board. And if she was, then so was Mother. The knowledge weighed in his belly and tightened his throat, but maybe it was better than all this time not knowing.

But *why?* Why had they come here? Why risk the crossing? Why leave home? More unknowns.

He ached to ask where they were, but that would only draw Vane's attention. Instead, he cocked his head—with a little luck Billy would understand.

Sliding the pistol's ramrod to its home below the barrel,

Billy glanced left and right. With the gun still clamped against his body, he patted his hand on the rail three times.

There was no reason for him to pause like that unless it was a message. Mother and Is were in his cabin. Had to be.

An invisible line tethering him to that door, Knigh pressed aft.

Vee, Aedan, Saba, Wynn, and Effie slashed and sliced, keeping pace with his advance. He had to reach his family, had to make sure they were safe. There were no other options.

But a whole deck stood between him and that door, packed with pirates, some friends, most enemies.

His sabre rang with a strike he hadn't even told his arm to block. He must've returned it, because fresh blood sprayed his hand a moment later. And he must've looked at his opponents to see their attacks, but that door, Albionic oak with a brass handle, was the only thing that existed.

He pushed and pushed and pushed.

In the distance, a pair of blond men—not *Venatrix* crew—blocked his view. Broad backs to him, they yanked on the handle.

"No." His pulse spiked, fast and heavy, as another parry clanged through his arm.

The men shared a look, their bumped noses perfectly matched—brothers, perhaps. They stepped back. Giving up?

As one, they charged and shouldered into the door.

"No!" He intended to shout it, but the only sound was a pounding in his head, which might've been his heart or the men trying to knock down that door.

He barged, he sliced, he barely saw the blades coming at him, but he parried them anyway.

You let them down, but I won't.

There might've been pain in his thigh, but it paled against the stab of each heartbeat in his chest. And even if it was a cut, he could heal it later.

He had to get to them.

I won't fail. Not again.

His arms burned, so he kicked.

I can't...

I won't...

I won't.

A growl grated at the back of his throat as he pushed himself on and on and on.

"Knigh." A grip on his shoulder, cool and strong. "Knigh? You said you'd always come for me." She gave him a shake, as though trying to wake him up. "Well, right now, I need you to *stay* with me."

What did she mean? He blinked at her.

Blood and bodies at his feet—Vane's men. He'd done that. There were others at her feet, too.

I need you to stay with me.

She looked up at him, eyes wide and dark.

If he'd carried on...

"You're still here." She gave him another shake. "You didn't go anywhere."

But *almost.*

All that work, all that pain, breaking himself open and

showing her... and he'd still started down a path that would've ended with him out of control.

And on the same ship as...

"Mother. Is." If they saw him like that—witnessed what he was... A shudder jolted through his entire body.

"Look." Vee jerked her chin aft, half a smile playing on her lips.

Twenty feet away, those blond brothers pulled back, ready to shoulder the door again.

A shot cracked.

Billy.

He stood above them, still on the quarterdeck.

One brother slumped and before he'd hit the deck, Billy leapt over the rail, sabre drawn. As he landed, he slashed down on the other's shoulder, opening a seam of red.

Never had a man's death been cause of so much relief. Knigh exhaled, stomach unclenching so suddenly it spasmed like he was going to be sick.

Squeezing his shoulder, Vee lifted her sabre and caught a strike from one of the pirates crowded before them, who'd decided she was distracted. More approached, some backed off into the mob.

With a deep breath, he took his place at her side, blade ready.

As he caught a strike, reposted, and watched for the next, a dismayed cry rose from further aft, and the crowd's attention drifted to starboard.

The rail, then the sea, then an oak hull. Above, billowing

canvas. The *Maelstrom* had broken off from the *Swallow* and was sailing away. Vane must've retreated.

"Bollocks," Vee hissed. "No." She reached out, a familiar crease between her brow.

Knigh's ears popped as the wind changed direction.

A flash of steel. Her opponent batted her sabre to one side and coiled back, ready to thrust.

No thought, only action, Knigh lunged.

Pain streaked across his shoulder, but the shriek of bone against the blade in his hand said he'd struck true.

"Shit." Vee swept in, brow creased in anguish, nostrils flaring as she parried another woman's strike. "I'm sorry." She reached out for him now, the wind forgotten, hand stopping just shy of his arm.

"I'm fine." He gave a nod of reassurance. It was a scratch. He'd heal it later. And he could understand the urge not to let Vane escape, even if using her gift in a fight wasn't the best idea she'd ever had.

"No," she huffed, counter-attacking, "I—"

"Enough!" The bellow blasted across the deck. "Parley." A woman's voice, not one he knew. "*Undine*, surrender weapons."

Stillness, save for the sea and a hundred sets of lungs heaving.

The nearest enemies straightened, movements slow and steady. A moment later, their weapons hit the deck, and they raised their hands.

Those nearest parted, and a tall woman with braided hair approached. Her eyebrows met in a frown as determined as the one Vee wore. "The famous Lady Vice," she said, and dipped her chin. "Glad it's you"—she held out her wrists—"always said I'd never surrender to any man."

Vee sheathed her sabre and exhaled a laugh. "My captain will be pleased to hear it."

There was movement from fore, and Perry appeared on the other side of Vee. Mouth set in a grim line, she nodded. "We accept your surrender, Captain...?"

The woman shot a look at Perry, brows rising. "Kisi."

Perry said something more, but although the battle had stopped, blood still thundered in Knigh's ears and his gaze had drifted aft. The door to Billy's cabin was still shut. Mother and Is could come out at any moment and then they'd see him all bloody and sweaty, still buzzing with deadly energy. His throat closed.

They'd *see*. They'd take one look at him and they would *know*. What he was. What he'd done.

Something pressed into his arm—Vee's elbow. His pulse eased a fraction as she flicked him a sidelong glance. "So glad you see the sense in bargaining. We offer your people's safety and your ship."

Kisi arched a brow—and well she might. She was lucky to keep her vessel after this defeat. "In exchange for?"

"Information."

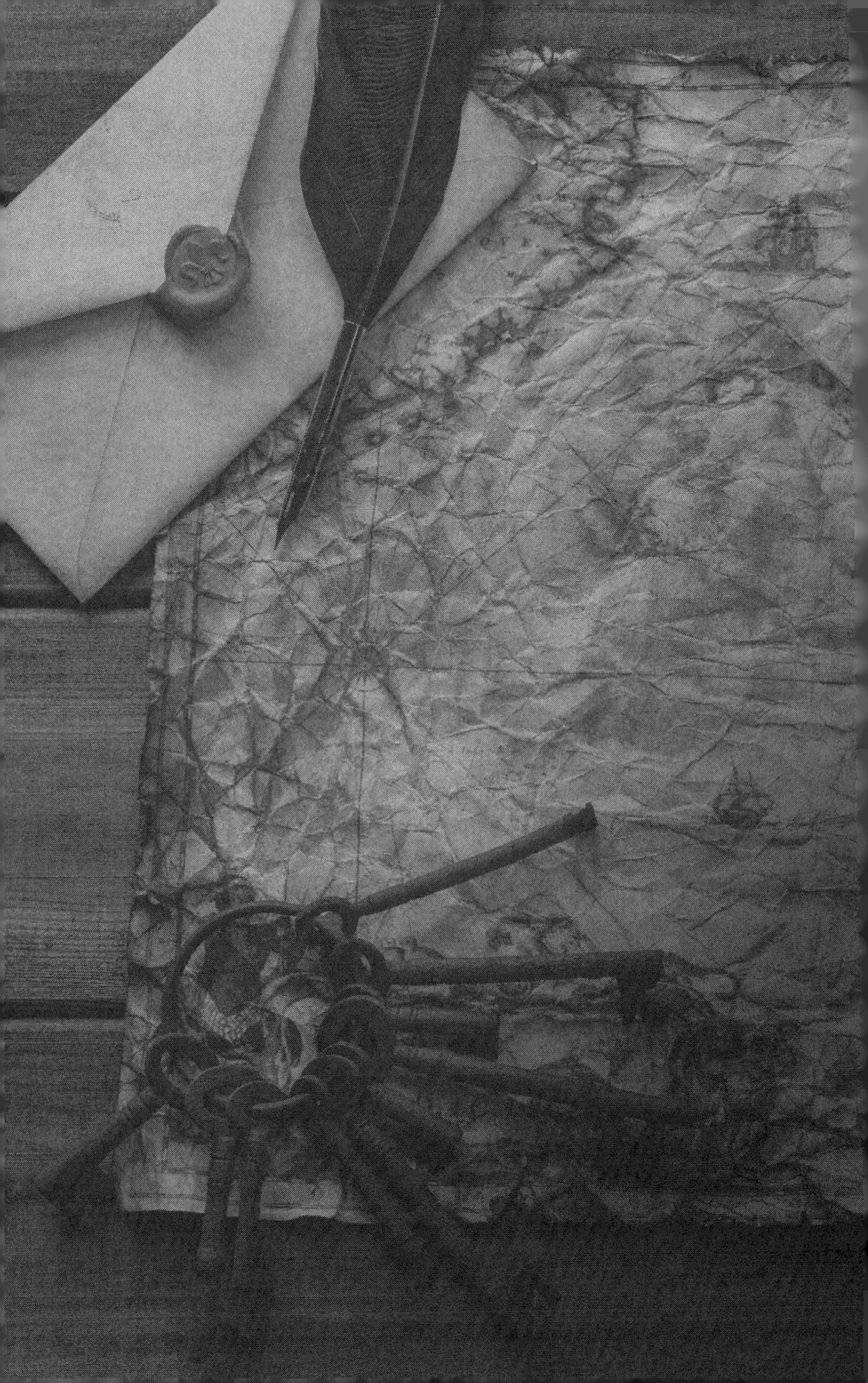

LORD & LADY

"Vane wants an alliance with the Duke of Mercia." Kisi's brows rose like she found the information surprising, even though she was the one reporting it.

Vice narrowed her eyes. "Of *course* he does." Hadn't he ransomed her to His Royal Slyness? He must've made a pretty penny from that deal. And if anyone had more to spare, it was Mercia.

"And he wanted to use my family to get it." Knigh's voice was almost under control, but she caught the gravel scraping along its hull. He'd been fixated on reaching his mother and sister earlier, but he hadn't given in to the rage. He'd been frightened for them, but he hadn't lost himself. And that gravel in his voice was the aftermath.

The *Venatrix's* crew worked with the *Swallow's* clearing up after the fight. After a brief greeting, where Knigh had thanked him, Billy had gone to his cabin to check on Knigh's family.

She'd reassured him they had this under control and had suggested he go with Billy, but he'd declined, planting his feet beside her.

She frowned at him sidelong. Why had he stayed? His breathing was a steady rise and fall now. Maybe that was it—he needed time to calm down after the fight.

Meanwhile, Vane's other allies had fled when they'd seen him doing the same, and the *Sea Witch* and *Firefly* pursued them now, harrying their retreat so they wouldn't loop back and attack again.

Perry folded her arms and lifted her chin, looking up at Kisi in that way she had—the one where she didn't seem to face a much taller person. "What else do you know?"

"Well, Vane doesn't like you *at all*." Kisi jerked her chin at Vice. "He's declared his own personal war on you."

Vice arched an eyebrow. "A war that you joined." She was the captain, she'd chosen to ally with Vane.

Kisi made a soft sound in her throat, like she was clearing it. "That my predecessor joined. I took over last month after his untimely demise."

"What happened?"

"*I* happened." The skin around her eyes crinkled the barest touch—Vice probably wouldn't have noticed it if she hadn't spent so much time deciphering Knigh's ghosted expressions. *I dare you to question me,* it said.

It didn't matter that she'd killed the former captain. "And yet you stayed with Vane."

"For now. He promised... a lot. I needed to see whether he'd follow through with it." She pursed her lips. "Nothing personal, but I couldn't deny my crew their share."

"Vane makes a lot of bold claims. You should've known he couldn't follow through."

Kisi cocked her head. "Aye, he talks a pretty patter. That braggart's been boasting to anyone who'll listen that he's got the Pirate Queen's sabre. Flaunts it like a trophy."

Vice's nostrils flared. *My sabre.* Evered's—the one she'd lost when Vane had taken her in Nassau. "The prick."

"That's what I thought. But gold's gold even if it does come from a prick."

"Ahem." Perry leant in. "Can we get back on track?"

Easy to say when *she* wasn't the one Vane and his fleet had declared a war against. But Vice stood back and let her ask her questions.

It turned out Vane's fleet numbered some dozen ships, maybe more. Vice winced. That many? No wonder the captains she'd spoken to in Nassau had refused to help, even the ones she counted as friends. Who wanted a dozen ships after them?

Kisi confirmed that Vane only kept between three and five vessels with him at any one time—the others scoured the seas searching for Vice, taking prizes to share, or completing other tasks for him.

Such as discovering Mercia's whereabouts in order to make the offer of alliance.

Vice shared a glance with Knigh.

"He's docked at Ayay. Has been for a while—refitting his ships. Reinforcing the hulls, new cannons—*more* cannons. The lot."

"Port Ayay?" Knigh leant in, head cocked. "Not Port Royal? You're sure?"

Kisi's chin jutted out as she gave Knigh a fiery look. "I said what I said."

Nodding, apparently unruffled by her ire, Knigh made a soft, thoughtful sound, but said nothing further.

They spoke to Kisi a little longer, but none of her information was as interesting or useful as that gem. Mercia was in Ayay, which meant his map was there. And Port Ayay wasn't a naval dockyard, so it would be much easier to take.

When Perry dismissed them, Knigh pushed up his sleeves and strode to where Lizzy had gathered the injured and coordinated their treatment. Not to his family.

"Hey"—Vice hurried after and grabbed his elbow—"aren't you going to check in on your mother and sister? They could be injured."

He stiffened, but didn't stop. "Billy would have told me."

True. "Fine. But you haven't seen them in months, not since you..." She waved her hands vaguely, which was easier than saying *quit the Navy and became an outlaw*. "All the way here you were desperate to ensure their safety, and yet now you're mere yards from them, you haven't so much as said hello."

His neck corded, but he gave no reply and stopped to check on the first person Lizzy pointed towards—one of the older men from the *Swallow* who held a wound on his head.

Teeth grinding, she waited until he'd used his gift to heal the cut and shared a nod with his patient. The old sailor saluted, blue eyes bright. When they landed on Vice, they widened, and his mouth dropped open. "Wait... My Lord? My Lady?"

Ah, so he'd recognised them.

Vice flashed him a stiff grin and nodded. "Good to see you... Old Tom, wasn't it?"

"Aye, madam."

After more pleasantries and shocked exclamations from the old sailor, they broke away.

"What's the matter with you?" she hissed at Knigh the instant they were alone.

"There's nothing wrong with me." He frowned at her like it was an absurd suggestion. "That's why I'm the one doing the healing."

"I mean, your family, Knigh. Why won't you—?"

"Because I nearly berserked," he snapped, arms going rigid. A moment later, he shook his head, nostrils flaring. "You had to call me back to myself. After all that work... I'm still broken."

The frustration left with the air rushing out her mouth, leaving her heart aching in his wake. "Oh, Knigh. You... you were miles from losing control. Like Perry said, it's going to take time. You've made progress, but you can't expect all that pain, all those years to be forgotten overnight."

But he only stared out over the open ocean that rolled dark grey with white peaks.

She touched his shoulder and when that didn't work, she whispered, "Please?"

Maybe it was shock at her asking, or maybe it was the softness of her tone, but he turned his steely eyes to her. Steely was the right word—hard on himself, the sharp tip inward-pointing. How had she missed it? It wasn't only the corded neck, but the lines bracketing his mouth, the tension thinning it... This had been troubling him since the fight.

"You were so fixed on that door, you left yourself open. That's why I told you I needed you with me—there were too many for me to look after both of us."

His eyebrows twitched. "Vee, I..." His fingertips grazed down her arm, from shoulder to elbow, and she couldn't help but shiver. But he said nothing more.

"Look," she murmured, "this was your first—"

Attention darting past her, he twitched upright and the blank mask slid in place.

When she turned, she found Billy approaching, two ladies in fine gowns at his side. Although the elder's chestnut brown hair was streaked grey now and her skin had grown pale, Vice twitched in recognition. Knigh's mother, Lady Villiers. Every sinew tensed, and something bubbled in her throat. She'd met Avice Ferrers. With all the focus on finding and rescuing his family, Vice hadn't even considered that Lady Villiers *knew* her.

That was over a decade ago. You were a child last time she saw you.

She tore her attention from the black-clad dowager. At her side, Isabel was a beacon of honey-blonde hair in the grimy aftermath of battle. She was as beautiful as her brother—her bone structure a more refined, feminine version of Knigh's. Her large blue eyes fixed on Knigh, and that beautiful face broke into a broad smile as she launched forward and flung her arms around him.

"Knighton! How on earth are you here?"

Despite her warm hug, he remained at attention, solid, staring ahead.

"I should've known," she went on, "that even in the middle of the ocean you'd find us."

In silence, he patted her shoulder before extricating himself. A small frown flickered above Isabel's smile as she took her mother's arm.

No wonder—Knigh's behaviour was...

"Mother." He nodded, stiff as an automaton. "I am glad to see you are both safe. I believe the final preparations are now complete for us to set sail. We will assist you in reaching an island where we will help repair the *Swallow* more fully."

Hearing him speak with such ridiculous formality tightened her throat. She wasn't the only one who found it strange, wrong: the lines between Is's brows deepened as her lips pursed. His mother's face remained still, albeit a little tense, like any studied lady, but her hands clenched around each other.

Out of their sight, Vice slid a hand to his back, a reminder. *You didn't berserk. You've nothing to be ashamed of.* But his muscles didn't ease as they so often did under her touch.

"For now," Knigh went on, apparently oblivious to their reactions, "I have duties to attend to on the *Venatrix*." He bowed his head, turned on his heel, and strode away.

Frowning, Billy opened his mouth as if he was going to call after him, but only closed it and gave Vice a questioning look.

Soon Isabel and Lady Villiers were doing the same.

Oh right. Now she was left here with someone who knew

her—*her* as Avice Ferrers, not Vice the pirate. Her throat tightened.

As she stared now, did she get a sense of familiarity?

The hairs on the back of Vice's neck stood on end. *Get out. Now.*

She cleared her throat, gave what was meant to be a smile, and bobbed in something that was more than a nod, but wasn't quite a bow.

Then she turned and fled.

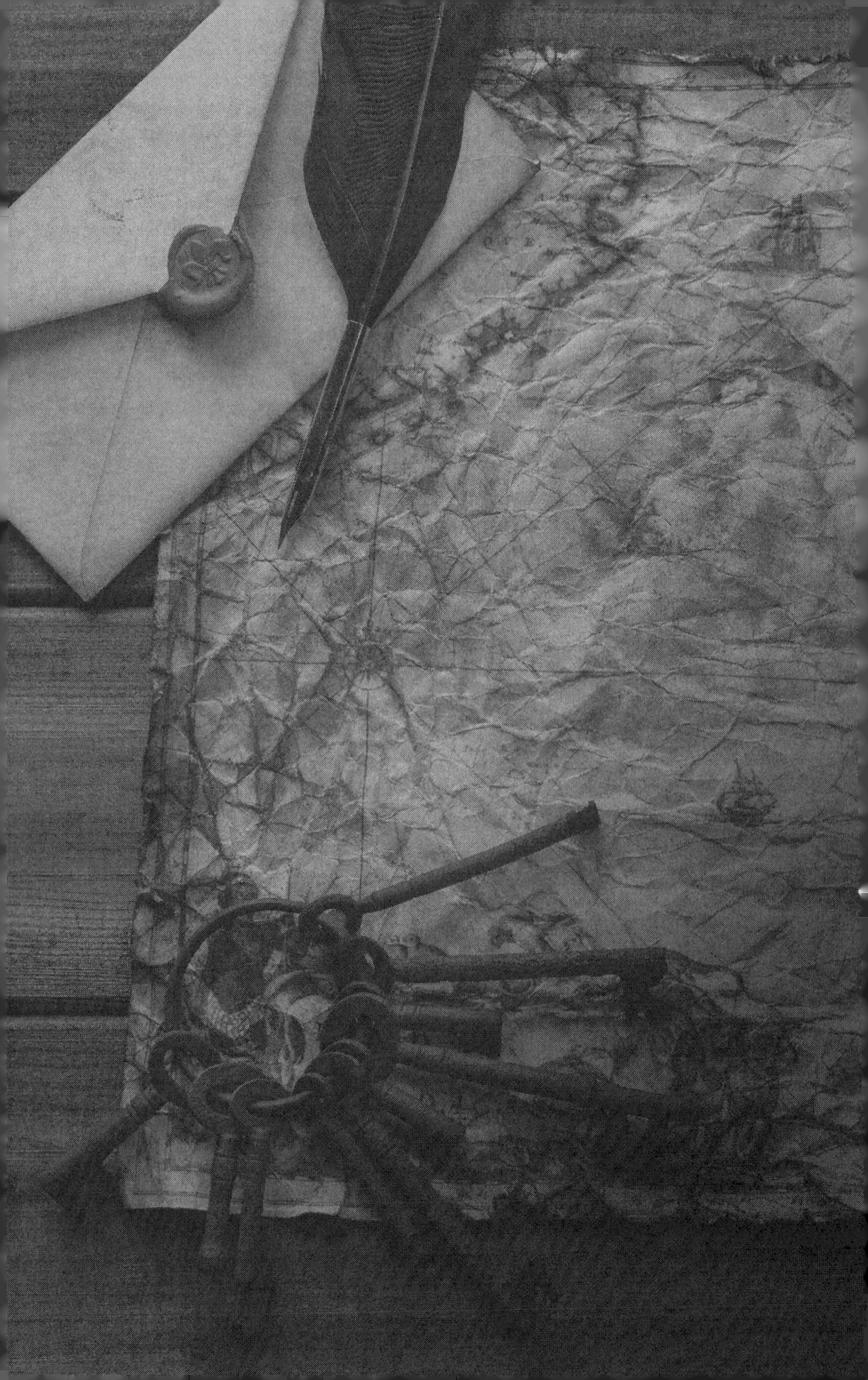

NO MORE DISTRACTIONS

They sailed southwest for some hours, with Vee towing the damaged *Swallow* using her gift. At last, land rose ahead. Knigh kept himself busy healing his crewmates and, after, helping with repairs, but that impossibly green island with its arc of improbably white beach signalled time running out.

No more distractions, he had to face Mother and Is.

The *Swallow* trailed them, with the *Sea Witch* and *Firefly* fanned out behind.

Had Billy seen? Had Is been peeking through a crack in the door and *knew* what he'd almost...?

Progress.

That's what Vee had called it. She was so sure, just like when she'd insisted Father's actions weren't his responsibility. His failure to realise...

I hope you know none of that's true.

He exhaled, coiling the trailing end of line they'd replaced in the mizzen shrouds. The rough rope in his hands, the twist of his wrist as he turned it to ensure it would lie flat, familiar, meditative, calming. A balm for his troubled mind.

Still, there shouldn't have been any need for Vee to keep an eye on him.

It's going to take time.

Perry had said it first, but it was Vee's voice chiming in his head. Again.

It was alarmingly easy to summon her voice. Or her face, for that matter... or hands... or that moment on the main top with the pineapple.

It was getting harder and harder to pretend being her friend was enough. It wasn't just that he wanted to touch her, to hold her, to do wonderful, wicked things to her. He wanted to sleep at her side, to whisper secrets in her ear and listen to hers, to share himself, his life... everything.

The rope creaked in his tightening grip. He'd offered; she'd said no. And he couldn't blame her.

"Let me guess, you're torturing yourself?" She was behind him, but he could *hear* the arched eyebrow in her voice and the way she softened it with a half-smile.

How did she know? Head down, he swallowed and tied off the line.

She appeared at his side and leant against the shrouds, one hand reaching up and gripping a line. It pulled her body long and lean, putting him in mind of Barnacle lying in the sun after clearing the hold of rats—a well-earned stretch after hard work.

"I told you, Knigh, you did well in that fight."

She thought he was... He stifled a laugh. Well, at least she *hadn't* developed the ability to read his mind. Thank the gods. Though the way he'd trailed that look down her body and back up, she probably didn't need to.

No, she meant his berserking, and of course that was lurking just below everything. Taking a spare length of rope, he cleared his throat. "I'm sorry I snapped at you earlier. And, don't get me wrong—I'm grateful you watch out for me, but..." Shaking his head, he exhaled through his nose, trying to blow away this thing haunting him as he busied his hands coiling. "You shouldn't have to. I thought I was done with it and it with me, but no... I'm still carrying that spectre, that threat, that *danger* to everyone around me. I was so, so close..."

A crease between her brows, she watched him a long while, even as he ran out of rope to coil. "See, I was thinking about that. You say you came close to losing control and, because you're Knigh Blackwood"—one side of her mouth twitched, not mocking, but fond, perhaps—"that's a failure and a reason for you to be hard on yourself. But I see it somewhat differently."

She looked at the coil of line that had fallen still in his hands before leaning in and taking it. She pulled on the end until she had a clear length to tie off. "Your family were in mortal danger in what's possibly the most chaotic battle I've ever seen." As she spoke, she wrapped the line's end around the coil, eyes fixed on him. They'd lightened now, matching the shallower, brighter waters around the island. "Sounds like a recipe for losing control." She cocked her head, hands still tying off the end of rope. "But all it took was a few words from me and you were fine. That's a huge improvement, Knigh—*huge*. You should be proud of yourself."

Her smile made warmth spread through his chest, his limbs, right to the tips of his fingers and toes. Proud of himself? That was a new idea.

"I..." Her voice dropped in pitch. But she didn't go on. Instead, she held out the coiled rope, tied in a perfect gasket coil hitch.

Just like he'd suggested back on *The Morrigan*. He stared at it, blinked, blinked again, off balance from her words and the fact she'd remembered and executed it so perfectly.

He should've lost control earlier, but didn't—that's how she saw it. And he should be *proud of himself* for it.

Her hand closed over the back of his, wrapping his fingers around the coil before she let go. *"I'm* proud of you."

She...

His chest was not only warm, but full as well—so full, it was a wonder he could breathe. But he did, and above, the sun shone, and in his face, the wind blew, touching his nostrils with sea salt and vanilla.

He *hadn't* lost control. He *hadn't* killed in cold blood. He *hadn't* turned into a monster. Perhaps she was right.

When he looked up, she was already slipping away across the crowded deck.

By the time they anchored in the calm bay and rowed to its sandy shore, he was ready to face his family.

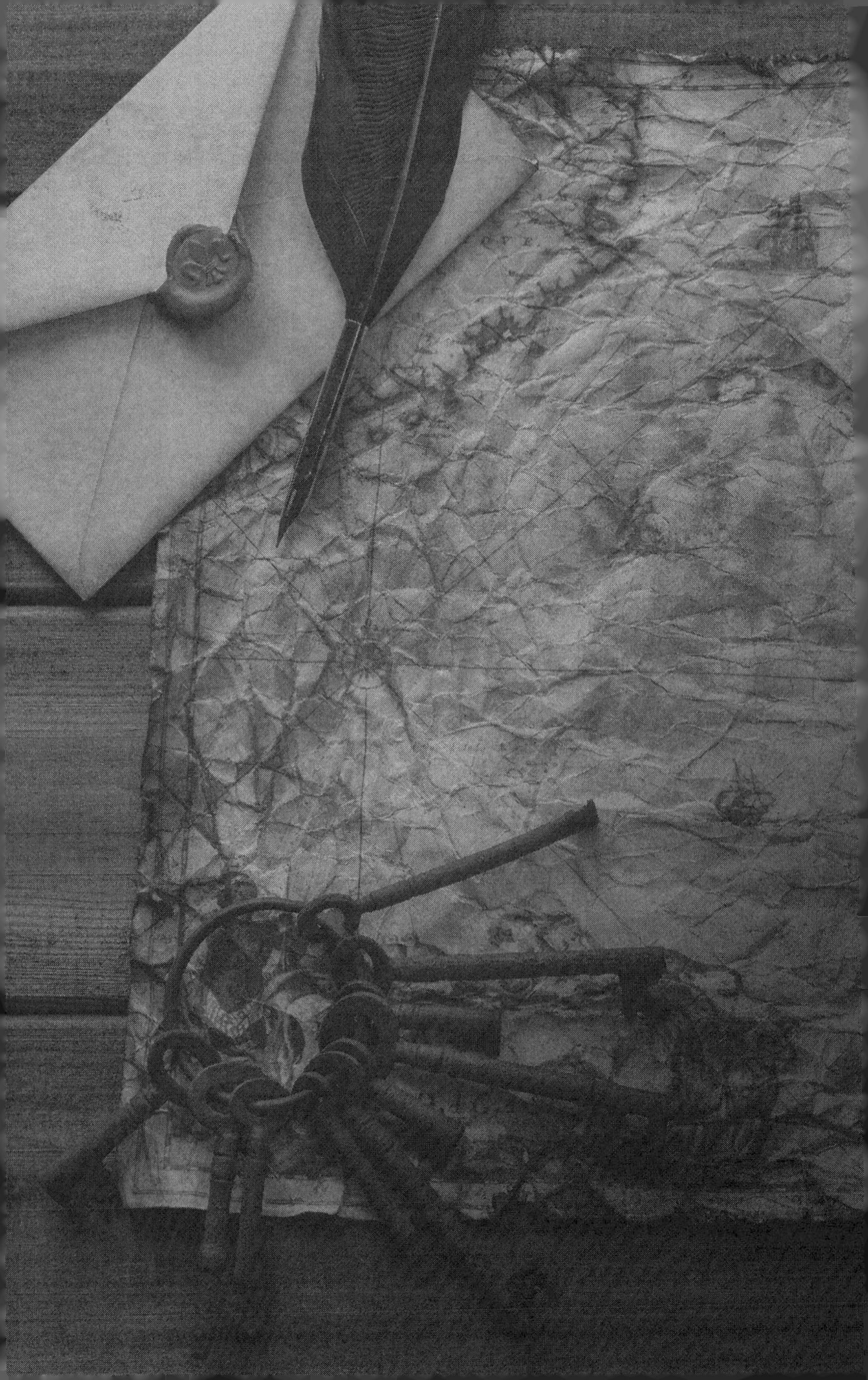

CATCHING UP

He reached Is first and swept her into a hug without so much as a word. She was sunshine, even here in such a bright, bright place.

"*There* you are," she said against his chest, narrow shoulders easing in his embrace.

He stood back with an apologetic smile before gathering Mother into his arms. Still too thin, but her hold around his waist squeezed, strong.

When he pulled away, Billy held out his hand to shake, but he'd earned far more than that, and Knigh used that handshake to pull him into a bear hug. "Thank you," he breathed, "for keeping them safe." It wasn't enough, but what possibly could be?

As he emerged, throat aching and tight, Perry and Vee still hovered nearby, the latter toeing the sand.

He made introductions, which were all very polite, if a little awkward, especially with the way Is looked from Vee to him and raised her eyebrows. She knew—she *knew*. She'd seen it written in his face, his actions, his brooding all the way back in Albion. Once she'd received his letter, she must've pieced together that the reason he'd helped the notorious Lady Vice escape ultimately boiled down to his feelings for her, even if she didn't know the particulars.

It was a relief then, when Billy laughed and shook his head, giving Vee a once-over. "You really *are* Lady Vice, aren't you?"

Snorting, she lifted her hands, palms up. "I thought you worked that out back on the *Swallow?*"

"Yes, but I didn't…" He shut his eyes, exhaled. "Knowing it and *seeing* it are two very different things."

Billy's men had finished setting up a canvas shelter between four palm trees, and under it, a rug, a table, and comfortable chairs from his cabin. When the group drifted towards it, Perry excused herself, and Vee made to follow, but Perry waved at her to stay. With a smile that looked like it was through gritted teeth, Vee joined them in the shade.

Mother, Is, and Billy sat, but Knigh had worked his way through tiredness from the fight and the use of his gift, and now a low buzz of energy hummed through his muscles. He leant on the corner of the table, while Vee circled the assembled chairs and took a spot leaning against one of the palms that supported the shelter. Is peered over her shoulder at Vee before raising her eyebrows at Knigh.

He angled his head, mouth flattening, silently telling her *not now*.

Not when he had *so many* questions.

"What are you doing in Arawaké?" He frowned from Is to Mother and glanced at Billy. "What happened? Don't you know it's not safe?" Exhaling, he rubbed the bridge of his nose as a dull headache formed. "I don't have a suitable home for you." The *Venatrix* was his home—nothing like the comfortable townhouse they'd rented in Lunden.

Is bristled upright. Mother's lips pressed together and she glanced at Is. No answers.

They'd flung themselves across the oceans and just *hoped* for the best? Good gods, how was he going to get them home? Perhaps Billy would take them on his return trip, that way they'd only be in Arawaké for a few weeks. Shoulders tightening the more he thought about it, he huffed. "What the hells were you thinking? You know what—what I *am* now. How could you possibly imagine this was an appropriate place for you compared to..." Shaking his head, he gestured east—towards Albion where they belonged.

Here he'd been the naval officer and was now the outlaw pirate. This was not the place for him to be the Viscount or a brother or son. He could do all these things in Arawaké because his family were so far removed from it all. They were safe—from what he did and what he was... berserking and all.

But they'd been mere yards from it today. Even if he hadn't berserked, he'd killed. There had been blood on his blade, on his hands, and on the clothes he'd taken off before leaving the *Venatrix* to come to this spotlessly white beach.

He wasn't *ashamed*, exactly, but a wide ocean had always separate these parts of his life and now here they were—Mother's grey eyes unreadable, Isabel's fixed on him. In judgement perhaps.

Let her judge. Let Mother, too. He squared his shoulders. He'd done the right thing—saving Vee, turning his back on a Navy that elevated someone like Mercia to one of their highest ranks. He'd killed for his country, and he'd killed to save their lives.

"Well? I don't ask these questions for my own amusement. You're lucky you didn't get killed on the journey, let alone in battle."

"Blackwood," Billy said, leaning forward with a frown, "I don't think you're being—"

Is silenced him with a touch, her pale fingers on his sleeve that ended so abruptly. "Are you quite finished, Knigh?" Lips tightening, she cocked her head at him. "Only the way you were going on, I thought perhaps this was merely a monologue to soothe your own nerves rather than an actual enquiry."

When had the sky blue of her eyes grown so steely? No, that wasn't right. They weren't as hard and grey as steel like his own—even in the canvas shade, hers still gleamed blue and bright.

No, her eyes were as hard and glinting as sapphires.

Past Is, Vee shifted and folded her arms, and when his flicked gaze to her, she lifted one shoulder and the corner of her mouth as if to say, *She has a point.*

Fine. Perhaps he *had* berated them with an onslaught of questions. He clamped his teeth around his tongue and gestured for her to go ahead. *This had better be good...*

"I rather lost track of all your questions in that tirade, but I think the general idea is that you wish you know why we're here." She took a quick breath and sighed it out, gaze drifting past him to the sweeping beach where the various pirate crews were landing their boats. Her mouth tightened again, but she went on, "We didn't undertake this journey lightly, Knigh. We had little choice." Her voice was softer now. "His Royal Highness the Duke of Mercia saw to that."

Heart roaring, Knigh stiffened and beyond Is, Vee did the same. "What did he do?" He bit each word out, barely able to get it past his tight throat.

Mercia must've stayed in Albion a while after Vee's trial. Knigh had assumed he'd been too distracted by his sister's coronation and too keen to keep George's good opinion to dare do anything to his family. But, no, nothing was beyond him.

If he'd hurt them…

Knigh gripped the edge of the table, knuckles groaning.

"It started not long after you left, when we went to Lunden," Is said, sharing a glance with Mother. "Although with hindsight, I can see its threads snaking back further, before you visited, so subtle I hadn't even realised at the time." Again, that tightening of her mouth. Had she realised she still had her hand on Billy's arm? "Small things at first, little reminders of his presence, of his power—of his *control*. I thought it was a kindness when he sent me an invitation for a ball. But then a box arrived containing a gown and instructions to wear it to the event."

A movement behind Is—Vee straightened, the muscles of her jaw rippling. She met his gaze, smouldering with ill-concealed anger. She'd told him how, during her time on the

Sovereign, Mercia had only supplied her with pretty gowns, however many times she'd asked for breeches and shirts.

She'd used that same word—*control.*

He dipped his chin, pressing his lips together and hoping she understood. Forcing his features to relax and smooth, he exhaled. "And did you wear it?"

"Of course I didn't." The corner of Is's mouth twisted. "It was an insult to the family—it said we couldn't afford one good enough for his soirée. And I already had something made at one of the best ateliers in the city—something perfectly suited to such an occasion. Despite that, when I arrived, I was turned away. Not a coincidence, I think."

Knigh ground his teeth. "No, not a coincidence." Is had spent so much time around astute Aunt Tilda, the sharp-eyed woman had rubbed off on her. Still, there were worse people to be influenced by. Despite the tension in his muscles, pride kindled in his chest.

"There were more things like that," she said with a sigh. "Securing me invitations to events at the very highest echelons of society—the most exclusive parties and balls. But there would always be some caveat, like lending me a diamond and pearl necklace from the royal collection and demanding I wear it."

Vee had been uncharacteristically quiet up until this point, but now she exhaled with a growl in her throat. "Stamping you as *his* property."

Eyebrows lifting, Is blinked—perhaps she'd forgotten about Vee's presence. Slowly, deliberately, she turned and gave Vee a look he couldn't see, but it made Vee incline her head with a grim smile and settle back against her palm tree trunk. "Exactly that," Is said, turning back to him, "and most publicly done."

Billy's jaw went solid, his brows drawing together—the glower so out of place on his usually cheerful face, it sent a shiver down Knigh's back.

"I thought nothing of it, at first," Mother finally said, voice low, "but then we received your letter and..." Voice guttering out as suddenly as it had begun, she frowned and knotted her fingers together in her lap.

His letter, that Billy had delivered. "Enter you," Knigh said, eyeing his friend.

Billy met his gaze and his throat bobbed in a slow swallow as he slid his arm out from under Is's hand. "Enter me." He nodded, shot Is a glance, then gave Knigh a stiff smile.

"I already felt unsafe," she said, folding one hand over the other so neatly it was as if it had never been on Billy's arm. "But when B—Captain Hopper arrived with your message, I knew my instincts, my fears were right—perhaps inadequate." Blonde eyebrows drawn together, she shook her head at him. "If you were warning us about him and had braved committing it to writing, I knew it had to be bad. Worse than you stated, even. I felt sick. I didn't know what to do." As she shook her head again, her eyes wavered and that sharp sapphire showed a crack.

He went to go to her, and Billy leant on his armrest, closer to Is, but she raised her hand and lifted her chin, holding them at bay.

"So I did nothing. What could *I* do against a prince?" She

scoffed, the sound bitter and dark, ill-suiting her. "Even after he'd left the country, it continued to escalate, until one day I spotted a man outside and realised he'd been there the previous day."

The cold hit him like a lungful of snow-flecked air. "He was watching the house."

When she met his gaze and nodded, she did not waver. "I believe so. It continued for a week. Not always the same man, but always *someone*. Even when we went shopping or promenading in the park." She reached over and placed her palm over Mother's clasped hands. "One night, I saw them outside as we rode home from a ball." Her chest heaved in a deep breath. "I wrote to Captain Hopper that very night."

"Good," Knigh found himself saying. It was true. Billy could be trusted and what Mercia had done... All that gradual escalation, where had it been leading? He shuddered.

"I thought we'd be taken," Mother said, voice cracking in a way that fractured Knigh's heart.

He went to her and crouched, covering her and Is's hands with both of his. "You weren't. But Is did well." He fixed his gaze on his sister, all his earlier irritation gone. "I'm sorry for my barrage. I should've known you'd never have done this without good reason. You made the right decision."

Her lip wavered, but she nodded and almost smiled. "Thank you. And thank you, too, Captain Hopper, you've delivered us to my brother as you promised." When she looked at him, she really did smile, radiant despite the teary gleam in her eyes.

For a long moment, Billy did nothing but stare back at her.

He might not have been breathing—his chest didn't move. Then he blinked and inhaled as if remembering how, before shaking his head with a self-conscious smile. "I—uh, yes... When I returned to Albion, after leaving you and..." He flicked a glance over his shoulder at Vee, pausing there as if still unable to believe who and what she was. "And Miss Vi—"

"Just Vice," Knigh muttered, leaning closer to Billy. "She doesn't like Miss Vice—gets a bit... stabby." He gave Vee a small smile, raising one eyebrow. For the first time since they'd gathered here, her shoulders eased and she gave him a conspiratorial wink, a smirk flickering at the edge of her mouth.

"I see." Frowning, Billy glanced between them again. His head tilted in an unspoken question, and Knigh schooled his expression to neutrality. Best not to think about what that question was exactly.

As if realising he would get no answer, Billy raised a shoulder and went on, "As I was saying—I left you and Vice in Nassau, returned to Albion, and received Lady Isabel's letter, informing me she and Lady Villiers were in danger and needed to escape the country." He nodded to Mother with a comforting smile—the kind that came so easily to him. "I sent back the fastest messenger I could find, while I turned around the *Swallow's* cargo quicker than ever before. By the time the ladies arrived in Portsmouth, we were ready to set sail.

"And a good thing too." Brows lowering, his expression darkened. "Within minutes of us disembarking, men in fine, black clothes raced along the docks. Is—you, uh"—cheeks flushing, he glanced at her—"Lady Isabel said she'd seen riders following the coach as they entered the city. I'm sure they were pursuing your family, Blackwood."

Strangers in black. He'd wager every penny he'd ever possessed that they were Mercia's men—the type he kept out of recognisable livery to do exactly this sort of work. He gritted his teeth and nodded to Billy, then to Is, squeezing her and Mother's hands. "Thank the gods for your sharp eyes, sister."

Perhaps it was because the story was finished or maybe just the fact they were safe, the family reunited, but everyone's shoulders lowered at last and the tense lines of their faces eased. All but Vee, that was. She still leant against the trunk of that palm tree, arms folded.

Oblivious, Is began telling the story of their crossing, marvelling at the smooth running of the *Swallow* and the wide expanse of the ocean.

Beyond their canvas shelter, the crews made camp, the *Swallow's* men keeping a distance from the *Venatrix*, *Sea Witch*, and *Firefly's* tents. Knigh couldn't blame them—on a different day, with a different captain, they would've been prey for pirates rather than allies.

As they worked and Knigh caught up with Mother and Is, the sky flared into evening orange and gold and the hot coral pink he loved so much. Billy excused himself—he still had a crew to run, after all. Vee had already slipped away. She'd kept her distance and her silence for much of the conversation, so stiff it sat wrong in Knigh's bones. Perhaps it was foolish, but that day at Aunt Tilda's when he'd told Is about Vee, he'd wanted them to meet so she could see and understand. A corner of him had even thought perhaps they could be friends.

Instead, Vee was the quietest he'd ever seen her. What had her so uncomfortable?

Then again, *was* it such a bad thing? Mother and Is had already seen too much of Knigh Blackwood the pirate as opposed to Captain, the Viscount Villiers, and Vee was the epitome of what he'd become. She was the difference between Arawaké and Albion writ large. A woman on a ship—impossible back home. A woman who was a pirate and famed as such —a million miles from the perfect lady Albion had expected Avice Ferrers to become.

His heart tolled, heavy in his chest.

That was it.

That was what running away from their betrothal had bought her—the possibility of a different life, one *she* got to choose. He'd known it, yes, but seeing Is sip tea from a porcelain cup here on the white sand... Well, as Billy had said—knowing it and *seeing* it were two very different things.

And now he saw it. Vee would never have survived a life sipping tea and folding her hands neatly. Her body as his wife Lady Villiers would've still moved, she'd have still eaten and attended parties and balls, but that bright spark in her that he'd always admired—it would've died, snuffed out by such an oppressive society.

Wouldn't he have done the same, living the life of a lord without adventure or the sea?

"Grub's up," someone bellowed from the fires they'd set further along the beach.

He blinked, shaking off the thoughts that had pulled him far away. Is and Mother looked at him, the angles of their eyebrows hopeful. Indeed, the scent of roasting meat made his mouth water, too, so he excused himself with a promise to bring back dinner.

By the fires, he bumped into Vee and Aedan both eating off broad banana leaves as they all did when ashore. As they chatted, he reached for leaves to serve Mother and Is.

"Hmm, no"—Vee frowned at her wild turkey and yuca and passed it to him—"you're going to need plates for the ladies Villiers. Back in a second." She grinned at him—all ease again—and stalked away.

Eyebrows raised, Aedan peered past him towards the canvas and palm tree shelter. "And she's your *sister*." He shook his head in disbelief, his mouth set in a lopsided smile.

A rakish smile.

Oh, no, no, no. Knigh cleared his throat, bringing Aedan's attention back to himself. "Yes, Aedan. She's my *sister*. And I'm telling you to back off."

Aedan lifted his hand defensively, the other cradling his food. "Hey, I thought you respected women, including their decisions. If your sister were to *decide*—"

Knigh laughed and shook his head. "Oh, my friend, you misunderstand. I say back off not as *her brother*, but as *your friend*. She would run rings around you." He'd heard enough stories of Aunt Tilda's youth and Is was heading in the same direction. He wasn't about to put his friend through that when what he really wanted, really suited was someone straight forward.

Mouth open, Aedan peered past him again, eyes widening. "So Knigh Blackwood isn't the only member of his family with a few surprises up their sleeve." He shrugged and took a mouthful of roasted yuca.

"Apparently not." Knigh glanced back at his sister. It had been smart of her to get them out of Albion, and Arawaké *was* the only other place they had ties to, even if it did mean the two sides of his life colliding in such an excruciating way.

"Message received and understood. Your sister is safe from me—or should I say, *I'm* safe from her?"

Knigh scoffed as Vee appeared waving a pair of plates. There was a chance Aedan was too late to approach Is, anyway. Those shared looks. Her hand on Billy's arm, lingering. The way she'd almost said *Billy*, and he'd said *Is* rather than Lady Isabel. Was there something between them? Or merely mutual admiration?

The next time he caught Is alone, he would have to do some digging about their voyage and what she'd left out.

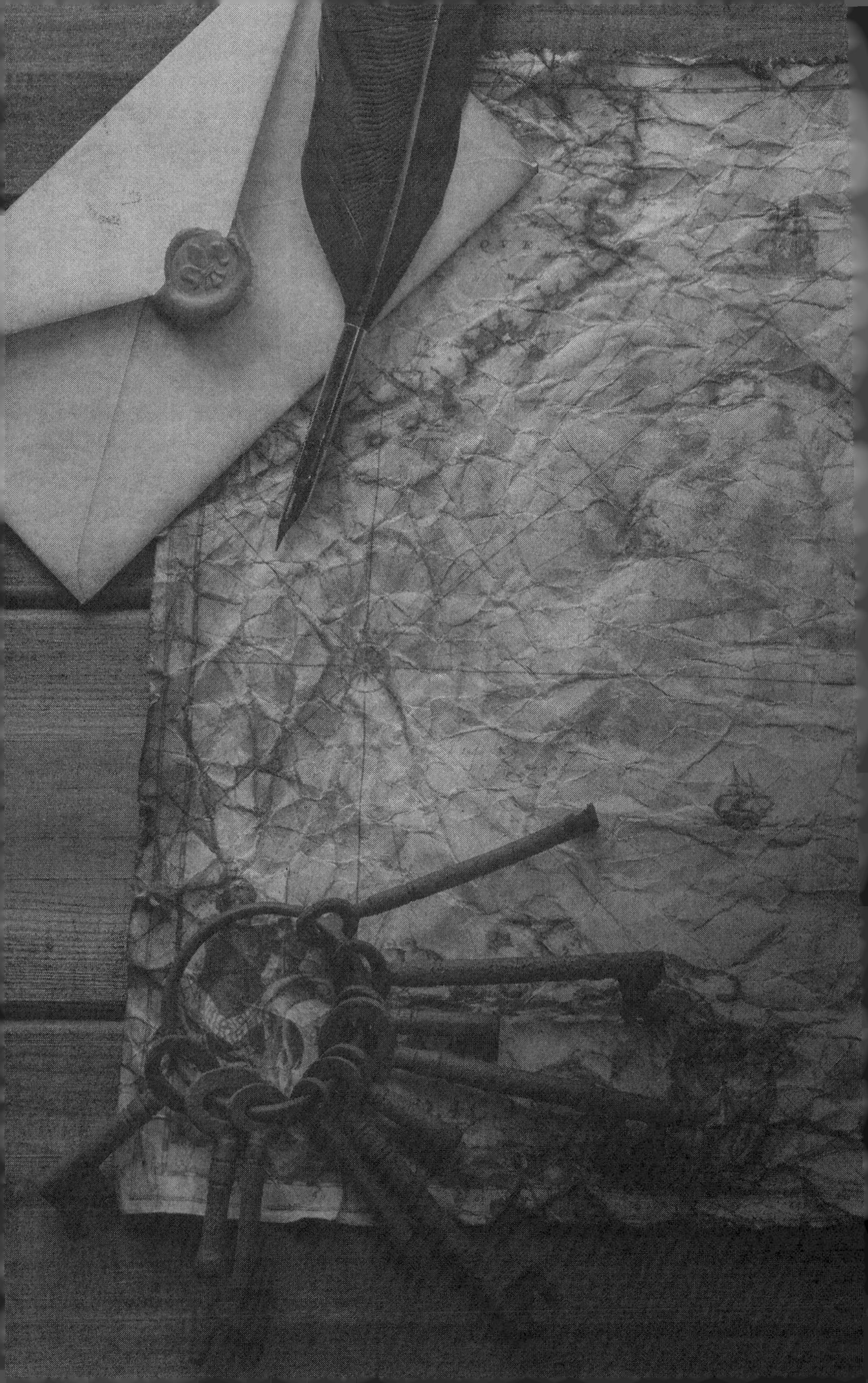

PLANS & CHARTS

Hammering, sawing, chatter—activity hummed through the camp. Four ships needed repairs, the *Swallow* most of all, and four crews needed food and water. The *Firefly's* crew had hunted a boar that morning and the thing had been roasting all day. The smell of juicy meat was driving Vice slowly mad.

As were these charts.

Inside Perry's tent, which had become a kind of command centre with one side open to a cool breeze and that mouthwatering smell, Vice leant over the table. She frowned at the chart showing Ayay. Saba and Perry stood either side of her, hands on hips. Barnacle sat in her sea chest in the corner, eyes half-closed, while the kittens played in an enclosure Vice had built to ensure they couldn't get lost.

The sun had only just started glittering on the water when

she'd emerged from her tent this morning. She'd slept well, but the instant her eyes had opened, she'd sat up, alert. Now Knigh's family and the *Swallow* were safe... Now they knew Mercia's location...

Now they could finally go after his map.

"At least he isn't in the Navy's stronghold," Saba said. "It won't be nearly as well guarded as Port Royal."

"Thank goodness for small mercies," Perry said with more than an edge of sarcasm.

Vice straightened, rolling her aching shoulders—too much time bent over maps and charts and the Copper Drake. "We still can't just waltz on in and take it."

"Can't we?" Saba cocked her head, one eyebrow raised. "If they're not expecting it and the *Sovereign* is dry-docked for her refit, the *Venatrix* could attack as a distraction, while our boarding party does indeed *waltz on in and take it.*"

Like sabotaging the *Venatrix* to prevent Knigh giving chase, it *was* the sort of thing she'd do.

But her gut tightened with dread. *No.* This time, it wasn't an option.

"And if she isn't dry-docked and is still operational?" It was a cowardly excuse, avoiding the truth that she would *not* take Knigh so close to Mercia again. She certainly wouldn't lead him onto that ship. Any plan they came up with had to keep Knigh's scarred soul safe from that man and their bloody past.

Saba exhaled, pursing her lips and looking back over the chart. "Fair point."

"Not to mention the fact we have no idea where in Port Ayay the map will be. Mercia always kept it locked in his desk, but if he's relocated during the works, he could be staying anywhere in town."

"Anywhere *fancy*." Saba's mouth quirked as she eyed Vice sidelong.

"Fair point." She threw Perry a questioning look. Maybe she had a better idea, an answer that would work.

Frowning, Perry's mouth twisted as she bent over the chart and ran a small hand over Ayay's outline. Eventually, she shook her head.

Shoulders sinking, Vice folded her arms. "It's no use—we need more information. The position of the *Sovereign*, where Mercia's staying, what their guard arrangements are like."

"Sounds... boring." Saba flashed a grin and backed off a step from the chart. She bent and stroked the kittens, then shared a glance with Perry, who inclined her head the barest touch. "I'm going to..." Her hand swept towards that open side of the tent. "Go and see to that thing."

Vice laughed and waved as she sidled out. Any excuse to escape this planning. She couldn't blame her—they'd been at this for over an hour, going over the scant information they had. Even Knigh had avoided it—apart from a brief glimpse across camp this morning, she'd seen no sign of him all day.

"We're going to have to recon, then work out a plan. If we land here"—she lapped the north side of the island, away from the port—"they won't see the Venatrix's sails from the town. It's only seven miles or so. I'll cross on foot—"

"You and *your team* will." Perry arched one eyebrow. But she wasn't rejecting the idea entirely.

"Of course." Vice pressed her lips flat, nodding sagely as if that had been her plan all along. "We'll sneak in, disguised if necessary, and get the lay of the land. *Then* we'll plan the final approach."

"Well." Perry huffed the word out, hands landing on her hips again as she said it. The corner of her mouth raised in a way that might've been amusement or... something else. "I never thought I'd see the day, but... that's a relatively sensible plan."

"You're rubbing off on me."

"I knew it would happen eventually." After a moment, Perry's eyes narrowed and the quirk sank from her mouth. "But you don't normally let a lack of information stop you. And much as I'd love to take credit for this more considered approach, I've been trying to rub off on you for over three years now, and this is the greatest concession you've made to being sensible in all that time. What's the real reason?"

Vice frowned at the chart. It was much safer than Perry's penetrating gaze. And she'd been concerned about *Saba* seeing too much. Should've known Perry was the dangerous one—danger in a small package.

"It's Knigh," she said softly. "I need to keep him safe—or as safe as I can. We all risk our bodies in a fight, on the sea. That's part of the job, but..." She shook her head, brow tight. "Not his heart, his mind. I'll gladly lead him in battle, that's what he signed up for—we all did. But I led him poorly when we boarded the *Sovereign* and that was because of a lack of information and my own single-mindedness." Her chest clenched, a clamp around her heart. She'd had an inkling that he'd served on that ship, but she hadn't asked—she'd let her determination lead. And it had led her to stomp all over him. She swallowed, throat thick. "I can't do that to him again. I can't risk *him* again."

Silence inside the tent, even the kittens had fallen quiet. The only noises were those encroaching from outside. The sea, the breeze... the hammers and saws had fallen silent—a break for food and water, perhaps.

Vice swallowed again, pulling her arms tighter across herself. Would Perry just *say something?* Maybe she thought Vice had said enough for both of them—too much, even.

At last, a long inhale crept into the quiet and Vice's head snapped to her, ready to seize on whatever words were about to come. Her green eyes were soft, shining, her mouth open, ready to speak.

"Vice!" Not Perry—a shout from outside.

They whirled towards the open side of the tent.

A crowd approached across the sand, mostly *Venatrix* crew, Knigh and Saba at the front, but Billy and his men numbered among them, and Fitz's dark hair gleamed in the sun, too. Regardless of which ship they served, every face sat in solemn lines.

"This all looks very serious."

Perry only raised her brows.

There had to be some disagreement. Maybe a fight, like when they'd shared the *Venatrix* with Munroe's crew. Or maybe Fitz had decided he wanted payment after all and thought Billy should make it.

When they stopped outside the tent, Vice frowned from Knigh to Saba and back again. They said nothing and they gave no hint of the issue with a subtle nod or flash of the eyebrows.

"What's wrong?"

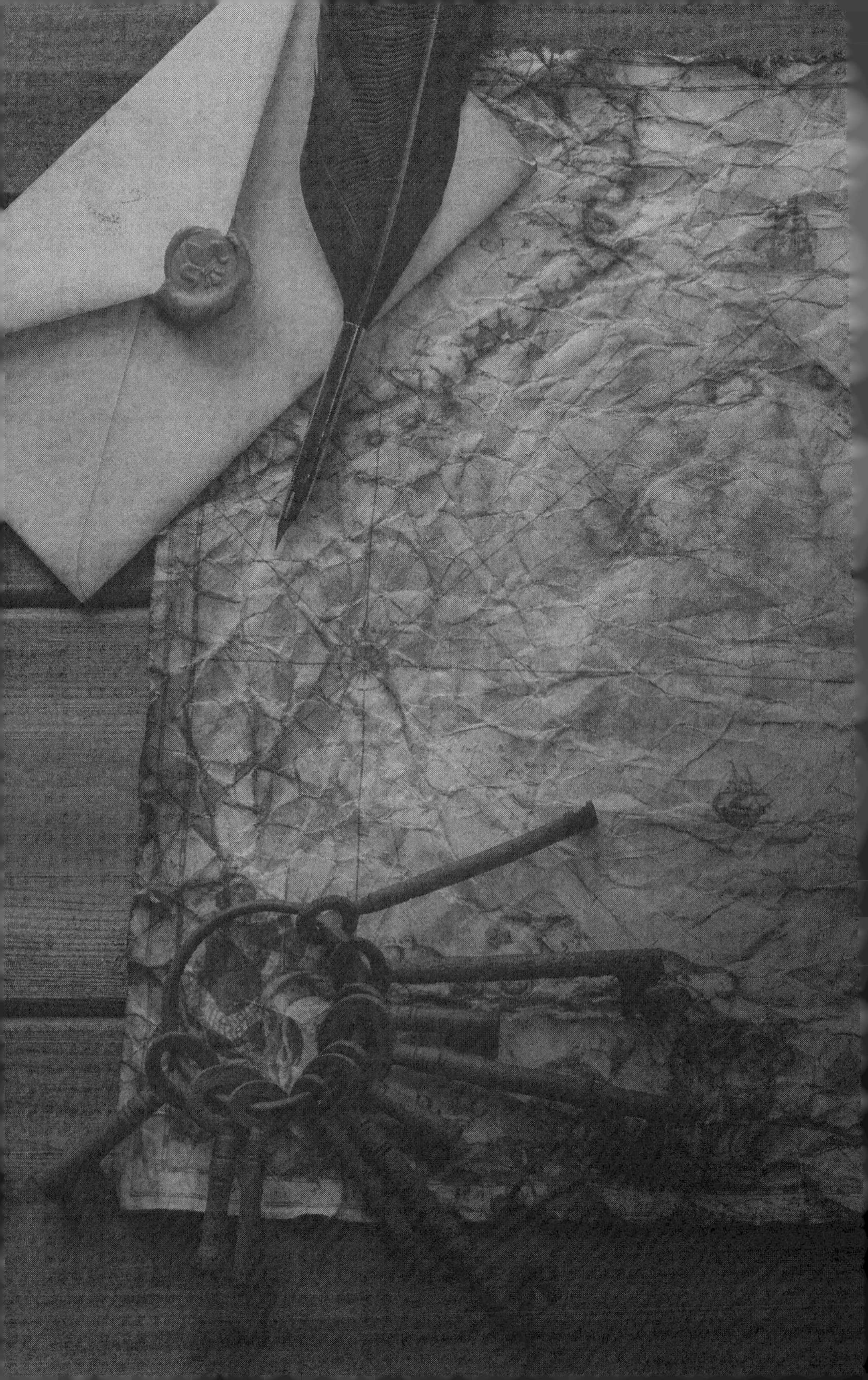

TROUBLE

Knigh shook his head and let out a sigh. Saba pursed her lips, a crease between her brows.

Damn, had to be serious. Vice lifted her chin and placed her hands on her hips, ready.

"It's no good," Knigh said and shared a glance with Saba.

Saba's shoulders rose and fell as she gave a heavy breath. "You can't hide away in here all day, obsessing over maps and charts." She eyed the table.

"Not when it's your *birthday*." One side of Knigh's mouth rose, part-amused, part-teasing.

"My..." She squinted. Was it really the—?

"Happy birthday," Wynn and Effie cried, faces breaking into bright smiles as they leapt forward and grabbed her into one big hug between them.

Had to be, then. She squeezed them back with a bemused laugh. She'd been so absorbed with Mercia's map and Knigh's family before that, she hadn't realised they were approaching her birthday. But her friends had remembered and that could only mean one thing—a party. And with three pirate crews, a massive, *messy* party.

Oh, this was going to be *good*.

When she looked over Wynn's shoulder at Perry, her captain only grinned with no hint of surprise. Of course she'd been in on the whole thing.

A fiddle appeared, then a drum. The music began, with more instruments joining in. They were still almost drowned out by shouts of *happy birthday*. Half the crowd broke away to dance and clap and laugh, while others swarmed in to crush her with hugs or slap her on the shoulder. The *Swallow's* crew tended toward the latter, still giving her the same disbelieving smiles Billy had worn yesterday.

Saba hugged her next, then pressed something small and smooth into her hand—a palm-sized carving of Barnacle, curled up tight. "So she's with you always."

Made by Saba. For her. Vice's chest was too tight to speak at first, especially with the stinging threat at the back of her eyes.

Before she could master herself and say thank you, Saba winked and said, "I know." With a nod, she disappeared into the crowd, muttering something about palm wine.

Perry stepped forward and cleared her throat. "To keep you safe when I'm not around to keep you sensible," she said before producing from behind her back a shining sabre in a black leather scabbard. The hilt gleamed, steel along one side, leather bound along the other, with a simple, elegant knuckle-bow sweeping back to form the guard.

Exhaling the tightness in her chest, Vice shook her head and closed her fingers over that hilt. Evered's sword, now in Vane's possession, had always been a touch too long and wide in the grip, made for his father during his Navy days. But this? This was... "Perfect," she breathed. Her hand sat snugly between the curved pommel and the crossguard. "Perry, thank you." This time, she was the one dragging Perry in for a hug. *"Thank you."*

"You are more than welcome, my friend." Perry patted her back. "Just as long as you don't hug me to death."

"Too late." With a grin, Vice growled and lifted Perry clean off the ground, straining her neck and shoulders as if she were squeezing tighter and tighter.

Eventually, she released her, and Perry made a show of clutching her chest before backing away to allow Clovis and Erec to wish her happy birthday.

Even Fitz slinked forward and tilted his head. "Any excuse for a party," he muttered, but it was a smile on his mouth, not a mocking smirk.

"Of course." She arched an eyebrow at him. "It's not that you're sentimental or missing me or anything."

"Never." He grinned and sank into a bow—*all* mocking—before grabbing a bottle of rum from someone and stalking away into the crowd.

"Still a prick, I see." Knigh's voice, right behind her.

She whirled on her heels. "I didn't..." She could only finish that with an exhale—he stood barely more than a foot away, eyes narrowed on FitzRoy's disappearing form. When his gaze turned to her, it still carried that intensity, but it shifted from enmity as a smile claimed his lips.

She swallowed, heart beating a little too fast. "So you and Saba organised this, I'm guessing."

He lifted a shoulder. "With some help from Aedan, Wynn, Effie, and Lizzy. The usual suspects. And Perry's done a good job keeping you distracted all day. Though I think Aedan's still working on the palm wine."

"And Saba trusted him with that? Lords, it's going to be *strong.*" No wonder she'd been muttering about it as she'd left.

His brows rose. "Even stronger than usual?"

"Oh, my dear Blackwood, you have no idea."

Wincing, he cocked his head. "Well, I suppose it *is* a notorious pirate's birthday party. I'd better give you this before I'm too drunk to remember." He held out a small brown paper parcel, no more than two inches long and just over half an inch wide.

"You got me a present?" She blinked up at him, not ready to take it yet. Not when her heart was pounding against the inside of her ribcage. Foolish thing—it was only a gift.

He gave a half-smile. "It *is* your birthday. It's customary."

"But..." *You've done enough. You've given enough.* She shook her head, blinking that away. "You didn't have to."

"No. But I wanted to." He lifted the parcel. "Are you going to open it? Because I always find it incredibly awkward when the giver opens the present on behalf of the receiver. *Please* don't make me do that." The pleading look he gave her, eyes wide—it was tempting to have him open it.

She grinned up at him and the flicker of his brows said he could see that temptation in her expression. With a snort, she took the little package. "I'm not that cruel. But note that I was tempted and resisted."

"*Such* kindness."

"What can I say? I'm the very soul of benevolence."

"Just open the damn present before I regret giving it to you."

Laughing, she tore away the paper and...

Silver gleamed in a tiny point, barely more than an inch, and black jet twinkled in the afternoon sun, arranged in a tiny hilt complete with crossguard. A dagger, exquisite and near complete except for a short section between the guard and blade where only a thin bar linked the two pieces.

"It's an earring," Knigh murmured, head bowed over her hand and the tiny dagger sitting on it. "The blade pulls off, forming the back."

"Ah, and this is the post." She tapped her nail on the bar—exactly the width of an earring wire. "Knigh, it's..." *Beautiful.* More than she deserved. More than he should've spent on her.

"Well, there was an element of self-preservation in the choice." He gave her a lopsided smile. "When you eventually try to cut out my tongue with my own dagger, I'm hoping you use this one. That way I—and my tongue—might stand a chance."

She laughed, and the earring's jewels glittered with the movement. "I can't make any promises, but that's some good forward planning." Shaking her head, she exhaled the rest of the laughter. "Knigh. Thank you. This is... You give such wonderful gifts. This, the Copper Drake..."

Heartbeat still heavy, she blinked up at him. Only her hand

with that earring on it stood between them. How was she meant to convey what it meant that he'd chosen such thoughtful gifts?

Kiss him. Some corner of her whispered it. *Go on, kiss him.*

As if he'd heard it, his gaze trailed to her mouth. His chest rose and fell. And who knew if there was even a party going on around them, because all she could hear was her heart and their breaths—too deep, too drawn-out, like this moment.

Just friends. Just friends. Just friends.

He'd have bought a gift for anyone on their birthday. This wasn't...

But he wouldn't have had that moment yesterday on the main top with just anyone, would he? Her fingertips tingled with the ghost of that touch—his lips on her flesh, taking the pineapple piece she'd offered.

He dragged in a sharp breath, attention snapping away from her mouth. "Shall I—I could..." He gestured to the earring, blinking and shaking his head. "Shall I put that in for you, since you have no mirror?"

Throat far, far too tight, she barely managed to swallow. Words would've been impossible. So she nodded, and he took the earring, fingertips grazing her palm. She pulled her hair back from her ear and neck, each tickling lock of it on her skin suddenly a pinpoint of bright awareness. Fighting to keep steady, she angled her head to give him better access.

He pulled the blade off the little dagger, unsheathing the earring's post.

Another man, a different kind of man, might've done this with trembling hands. But not Knigh. Not Mr Control. He did everything with such precision and this was no exception as he ran a finger along her earlobe, lifting it, making her shiver.

Though as she watched him out the corner of her eye, his lips parted as if the concentration was enough to distract him from that one facet of control. The edge of his hand rested on the side of her neck, tickling the sensitive spot right below her ear. She had to bite her tongue to keep from making a noise, but that touch—*every* point of contact from him on her neck and her ear lanced through her, tightening her thighs and low in her belly.

A moment's pressure then he pushed the earring into her pierced lobe. More touches as he felt for the back, and like a teenage girl in her first season in society, her knees trembled.

"Hmm." He frowned and ducked closer. His every exhale fanned her neck, raising goosebumps on her flesh as he pushed back her hair.

She gasped. She tried to stop it, but that movement of her hair sent a tracery of sensation—of *pleasure* across her scalp and it was... too much. *He* was too much, with his perfect gifts and forbidden touch and his strength and vulnerability and teasing smile and warm body and nobility and insistence on putting right his wrongs and... and...

"There," he murmured, and she felt the hot breath of that word on her neck, so vivid and vital that he might as well have been kissing her there. "All done." He straightened, smiling, but when his gaze went from her earring to her face, he stilled and his lips parted again. He licked them as his gaze fell to her mouth.

It was only because she'd frozen herself in place that she

didn't jump on him then and there. Even so, her muscles thrummed with the tense need to do so.

"It suits you," he said, voice low and private, rumbling through the inches between them.

She couldn't move. If she did...

Well, it would end in something not appropriate for *just friends*.

And there was still that question Perry had raised: *is the joy, however temporary, worth the risk of future hurt?*

She had no answer. Hurt was something she knew well. When Evered had died, for all his failings, it had been a sledgehammer to her body, her heart, her life. One minute he was alive and bright and her lifeline, the next he was dead. That had been debilitating enough.

And here was Knigh, a million times the man Evered had been. Was that worth the risk?

The hurt would be huge. Devastating. The joy...

That would be just as devastating.

So they stared at each other, breaths that bit too deep, too long, her heartbeat too fast.

"Vice," Aedan's voice, close and loud, broke the spell.

She backed off, hand on her tense belly as Knigh also took a step away.

"You need your birthday drink!" Grinning, Aedan thrust a large pewter tankard at her. It was full to the brim with palm wine.

"Lords and Ladies"—she blinked at the tankard—"are you trying to kill me? I haven't eaten yet!"

He laughed, too loud, eyes bright—he must've already been

at the palm wine as he made it. "It's your birthday! Eat, drink, and be merry!" He jerked his chin up the beach where the fires were. "Erec's got you sorted for food—what do you think he's been up to all day? Hog roast!"

Her mouth watered. No wonder the smell had been so torturous all day—Erec made an incredible whole hog roast. "Oh, gods, Knigh, you have to try—"

But when she turned, he wasn't there.

She huffed, shoulders sinking as her hand strayed to the smooth metal of her new earring.

The earring. It was perfect. Silver, not gold. Subtle black jet rather than bright, flashy jewels. It couldn't have been more different from the gaudy stuff Fitz used to give her. He'd always chosen things that were expensive and *looked* expensive, like she was a display of his wealth and success. It had always been about gilding her, about making her more beautiful in his eyes… about *him*.

But this? This was personal to her and Knigh and all the times she's told him she would cut off his tongue with his own dagger. A blade—it stood for fighting, for physical strength, for protection, and a dagger specifically? That was the last weapon left—the one tucked down a boot or up a sleeve that just might snatch victory from defeat.

It was about not giving up.

Her heart pounded in a chest that felt full of… of *something*.

But the source of this warmth suffusing her had disappeared into the crowd. She would have to find him later to thank him again. To explore what exactly she was feeling. So for now, she just smiled and lifted her tankard. "Well, if I've got to drink *all* this, I'm going to need to line my belly."

"All this? That's just the first drink. Come on, then." Aedan offered his elbow and they strode into the crowd, the music swallowing them up.

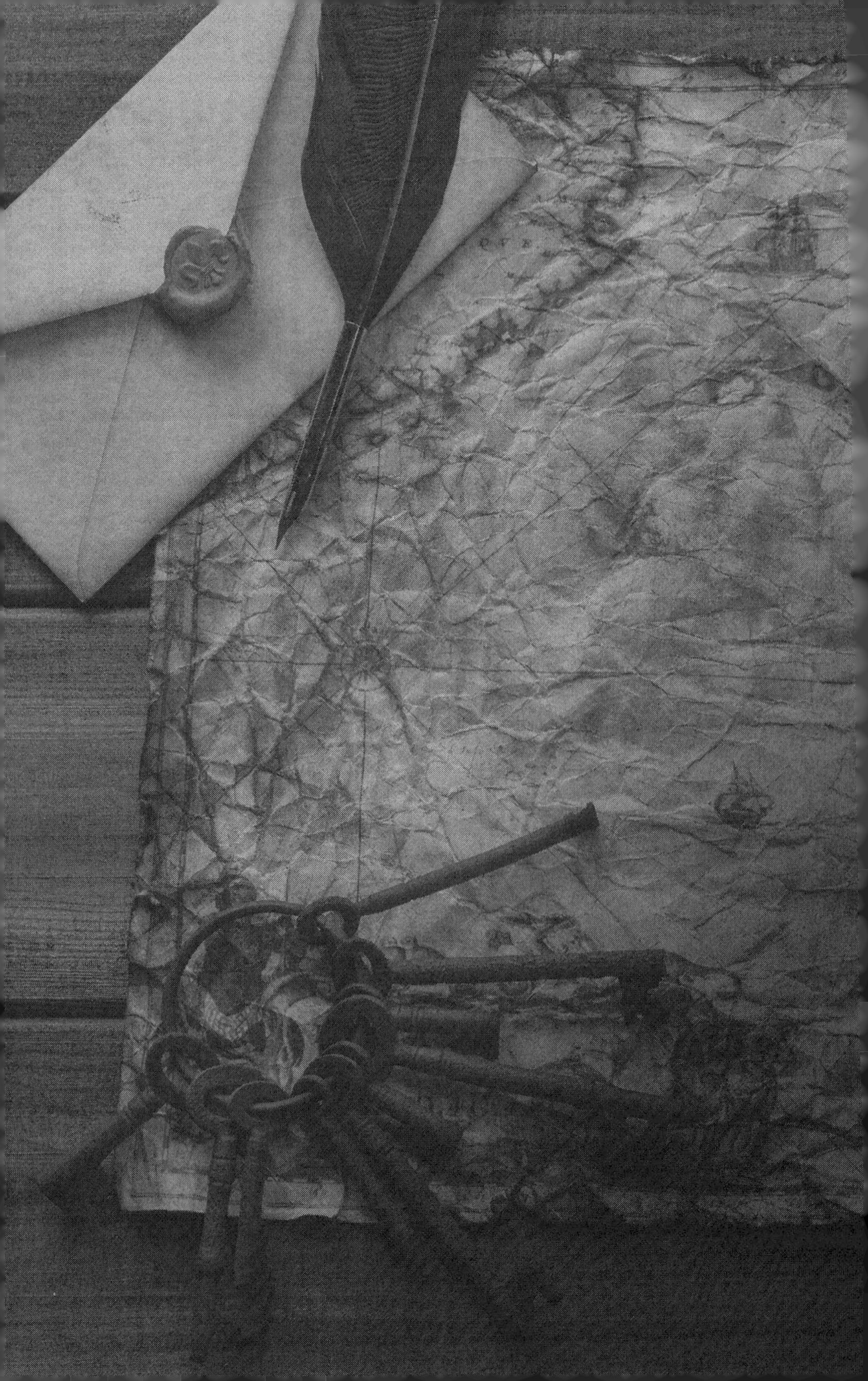

PROPOSITIONS

She ate, she drank, she danced, and hours later, she staggered out of the throng to cool off.

And stop her head spinning. She'd managed to avoid having her tankard topped up too many times, so she was only a little drunk, but add in the giddy, breathless dancing, and, yes, the world tipped, off-kilter.

She walked a crooked line to a fallen log and plonked onto it, somewhere between panting and laughing.

Above, the sky was dark now, speckled with more stars than she could count, and the sea blew its breeze across the beach and over her hot face. Eyes closed, she inhaled, exhaled, the air sweet with palm wine and salty with sea air and sweat. Smoke tickled her nose and merged with the frangipani growing along the tree line—the smoke toned down the scent that she normally found sickly-sweet.

When she opened her eyes, she smiled—the world was

steady and her chest was full and warm again. Her friends danced and laughed and drank, and even if Fitz was right and it was any excuse for a party, that was just a sign that he didn't understand. It didn't matter whether or not this was for her, it mattered that she was here with people she cared about.

As she lifted her cup to her lips, the smile froze. She blinked.

Near the largest bonfire, two people stood silhouetted. One tall, well-muscled, male—a figure she'd know anywhere. The other, smaller, fit and lean with a glorious mass of wavy hair.

Knigh and Saba.

All that warmth she'd so enjoyed? Now it burned in her gut, threatening to bring back her drink for another appearance.

They stood facing each other, and from the angle of their heads, they were talking. Saba bent towards him like a plant leaning towards the sun. Knigh stood upright, but there was little space between them. He gestured with his cup, maybe cocking his head, and Saba threw her head back, laughing. Knigh lifted his drink to his mouth and she could picture the pleased smile he gave before sipping—it was a gesture she knew well. Part of his arsenal of dry humour.

Once Saba had stopped laughing, she angled towards him again, reaching out. That dark silhouette of her hand crossed the bonfire, until there was no flame left between it and him. She was touching him. *Touching his chest.*

Vice couldn't help the soft noise that came from her throat. She had no claim over Knigh, and yes, she'd given Saba her blessing to pursue him, but...

It *hurt.*

Worse than when she'd been shot, it pierced her chest and twisted, stealing her breath like the coldest winter day.

Eyes stinging, she leapt to her feet. She'd given her blessing, but that didn't mean she had to watch. She turned and—

"Aedan!" She caught herself on his shoulder, inches away from walking straight into him. "Sorry, I..."

"Easy there, I've got you." A hand at her elbow, he grinned, teeth bright, torchlight kissing the smooth planes of his face, gilding the strong line of his jaw. "Thought you might want company, sitting over here on your own." The shadows and light flickered and shifted as he frowned. "In fact, I'm pretty sure that's not allowed on your birthday."

She must've done something right in life to deserve such good friends. And Saba was one of them. She had to be happy for her. One hand on her hip, she lifted her glass with the other and grinned back at him. "Come to save me from myself, have you?"

"And from sobriety." He held out a bottle and cup, both in one hand. His other hand remained on her elbow.

"Is that more palm wine?"

"Lords, no. Not after all these hours—can you imagine how strong it is now? I don't have a death wish. Just rum." He flicked the cork out the bottle and offered it to her, eyebrows raised in question.

Maybe it would help her forget. She drained the last of the palm wine, fiery and sweet, then held out her tankard. "Don't fill it."

"Mmm-hmm." With a sceptical twist of his mouth, he poured and poured and poured... But he did stop short of filling it all the way. "There, see, I can do as I'm told sometimes."

"Aye, you're ever such a well-behaved crewmate." She chuckled and took a sip of the rum, its sweetness different from the palm wine, richer like caramelised sugar, and spiced with vanilla, nutmeg, and cinnamon. He'd brought her the good stuff. "I'll be sure to let Perry know you're ready to obey orders at any given moment, even when drunk."

"Maybe not Perry's—not right this second." The way he murmured it, voice dropping, a crease forming between his brows silenced her. "But yours..." His hand had remained on her elbow and now he traced circles across her skin, right on the edge of her rolled-up sleeves. "I'll do whatever you tell me to, right now... tonight..."

The hairs on the back of her neck sprung to attention. He was... His darkened eyes, that velvet tone to his voice with its lilt of flirtation... Except this wasn't just idle flirtation. This was a proposition—or at least, it sounded like one to her drunken ears. "What are you saying, Aedan?"

"We never did pick up where we left off after FitzRoy tried to kill me"—he cocked his head and a rakish smile eased into place—"but he isn't captain anymore and I don't think Perry will try to splatter my brains all over the hold."

She snorted a small laugh, part at his phrasing, part surprise at this, which was definitely a proposition now. "No, we didn't." It felt like a safe reply—one that would buy her time to work though her surprise and this situation.

She'd thought they were just friends, but... Maybe he

wanted to be friends who screwed. Aedan was someone she could have *just bodies* with.

"I know things happened between you and Blackwood, but..." He shrugged. "Well, that was a while ago now and I saw him and Saba looking cosy. She wouldn't do that without your say-so"—he licked his lips—"so I figure you've moved on."

Her eyes burned when he said it. She kept still—any movement might give away just how much the idea of Knigh and Saba was a spear through her gut.

"So," he murmured, "I thought the birthday girl might like some fun for the night, someone who'll do exactly as he's told over"—he bent closer—"and over"—closer—"and over again." Barely two inches separated their lips and he closed that scant distance.

Vice blinked, backing away before his mouth touched hers, like her fluttering eyelids had woken her up.

Because she *hadn't* moved on.

And she couldn't have *just bodies* with Aedan. As handsome as he was, as skilled as he'd been that one time they'd had sex, as close as he was standing now with the promise of a warm body and pleasure, she wasn't interested.

There was only one person she had any interest in. And even if that person got with Saba, that didn't mean she wanted anyone else.

Aedan frowned, mouth open as he stared at her.

She shook her head, holding her hand up. "Sorry, Aedan, I... No."

"Why not? Sorry"—he winced—"that's an arsehole question. I just mean, I thought you'd want a bit of fun."

Why not? By the bonfire, they still stood there. Knigh had backed away, arms crossed, drink held between his body and hers. Saba's shoulders were rounded. Had he backed off after that flirtatious touch?

"What?" Aedan scoffed. "Because of Blackwood?" He must've followed her eyeline. "You still want him? After everything he did?"

She bit her lip. The conversation between Knigh and Saba was less animated now, and he'd looked away. A moment later, he backed off, they waved awkwardly at each other, and he walked from the bonfire's glow.

For her birthday, she could have Aedan's warm, firm body, with no risk of pain, no strings attached.

Or she could, maybe, have Knigh. She could lose herself in him, taste him, touch him, make love to him tonight and for however many other nights they had before he left. She could whisper to him in the dark, wrap her arms around him and enjoy the feel of his around her, listen to that steady heartbeat and fall asleep to its steadfast rhythm.

If she took the chance, asked him, offered herself to him—not *just bodies* but all of herself... That moment earlier with the earring and yesterday with the pineapple—he'd surely say yes.

Is the joy, however temporary, worth the risk of future hurt?

She could have that temporary joy and make the most out of every damn moment, and it would be worth each spark of stabbing pain that came after, and the lonely ache after that.

"You still want him?" It sounded less like a question this time.

"Heh," she exhaled. "Yes, turns out I do."

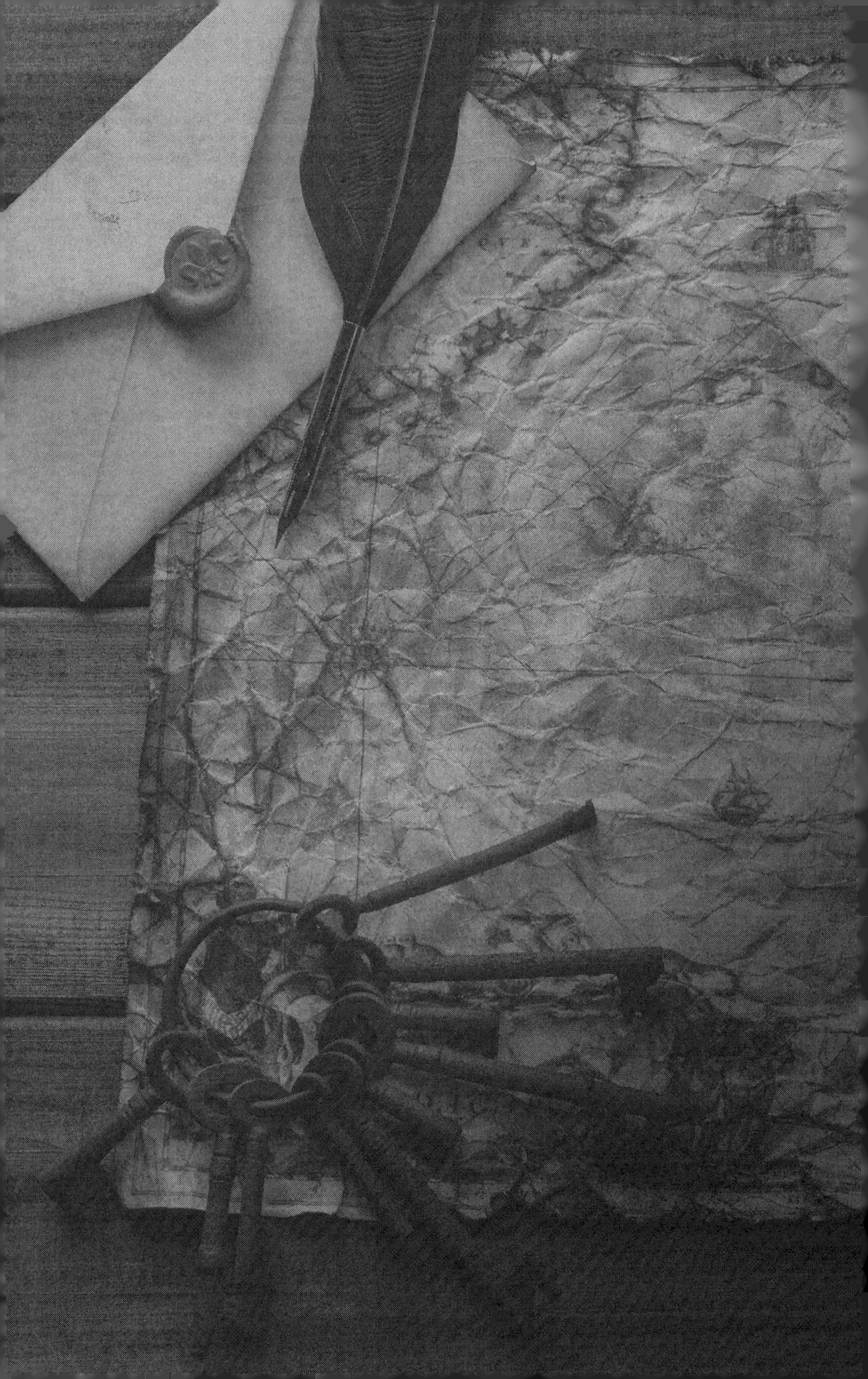

TOGETHER

It didn't take her long to find a bottle of rum and then Knigh. He stood near one of the larger bonfires, watching the dancers, firelight flickering in his eyes making them more gold than steel.

She approached, and with any luck her expression looked relaxed and didn't give away the twitch of terror in her belly at the fact she wanted him—not just his body, but *him*.

All of him.

Every hair on the nape of her neck stood on end, but she took a steadying breath as she crossed the sand. The drums and fiddles and flutes pounded and snaked their music through the air and around the dancers, growing louder and louder the closer she got.

"Knigh." She slid into place next to him and nudged his elbow.

He turned from the twisting, stomping dancers and smiled like he was pleased to see her.

That was a good start, and it eased her tense shoulders. This was Knigh, this was—*they* were easy. Or at least they were when they were talking. It was the other stuff—the betrayal and cruelty that tended to be hard. But they were past that, right?

She blinked, face heating—she was staring at him and now his smile had turned bemused. He cocked his head as if asking *why* she was staring at him. Clearing her throat, she raised the rum bottle in offer.

Smile still a little puzzled, he held out his cup and she filled it. The rum trickled in, looking like liquid flame as it reflected the bonfire. It gave her a good excuse to look away from him, gather herself. She needed to say something more than just his name.

"Are you having a good time?"

He squinted and ducked closer and might've said, "Pardon?"

The music, too loud. The drums thundered too close. Or was that her heartbeat adding to it, making the volume seem louder?

This was a good excuse to get him to herself and it might buy her time to work out what to say, exactly.

She went on tiptoe, steadying herself on his broad shoulder, and near-shouted in his ear, "Do you want to go somewhere quieter?"

"Good idea," he mouthed and gestured for her to lead the way.

Further along the curving beach they found a smaller bonfire—the last one in the row—with only a few dark figures on the edges of its light. Much better. She stopped in a spot far from the others and swept her tankard. "Does this meet with ser's approval?"

"Well, I can actually hear you now, so…" He raised his cup and grinned.

Her heart leapt. His smile could kill at twenty paces, beautiful and, right now, bright and untinged by sarcasm or that brooding darkness that sometimes shadowed him. It had done so less often since they'd sparred and he'd 'spoken' to his father, but she'd caught it lingering on the edge of his expressions a couple of times.

She swallowed and reminded her lungs that they needed to take in air as goosebumps chased up her arms. Her tankard clinked against his cup. "Cheers."

His smile softened, less dazzling without his teeth showing, but still capable of blasting a hole right through her hull. "Happy birthday, Vee."

Those goosebumps redoubled at the sound of that nickname on his tongue. The name only he used. She sipped, holding his eye over the pewter rim of her tankard. He returned the look, the gesture.

"I realised something earlier." She took another gulp of her drink for courage.

Because she, Lady Vice the notorious Pirate Queen of a dozen exaggerated stories, was *afraid*.

Admitting this. That she wanted him. That it was more than just bodies. That…

It was far more terrifying than any battle. Perhaps even more frightening than waiting for her own execution in that iron cage.

He watched her, eyes crinkled in that way they did when he was trying to work out the knot she'd tied herself into. The knot she'd designed to be inscrutable and impossible to untie. But now she had to loosen it for him—she *wanted* to loosen for him.

Only her tongue had grown thick and heavy. Words weren't...

Another gulp of fiery rum.

"So." She cleared her throat as her voice came out in a rasp, seared by that strong liquor. She plucked his cup from his hand and nestled it into the sand with her own, then faced him, nothing between them but the smoky sea air and a few layers of clothing.

"You realised you didn't want to give me that rum after all?" He arched an eyebrow at their abandoned drinks, but the look faded when he met her gaze as though he could see the fear, the uncertainty, the battle roiling in her eyes.

"I realised"—she edged closer, just a few inches between them now, his warmth bridging that gap with ease—"that I didn't thank you properly for the Copper Drake." It was easier to phrase this as a transaction, safer, less vulnerable, though her pulse still hammered.

His head tilted the slightest amount and he opened his mouth as if he might speak. If he did, she'd lose momentum.

"I didn't..." She swallowed and took his hands in hers. As warm as ever—something about that settled her racing heartbeat, just a touch. He stilled, lips slightly parted. "We were in such a strange place then. Not—not geographically, I mean, but…"

Wild Hunt, she was tripping over her words left and right. Elegant this was not. But with a little luck he'd understand what the hells she was trying to say in her own broken way.

"And I never showed you how much I appreciated it." She ran her fingertips up his forearms, the hairs rising under her touch as if lightning threaded static through the air. "I thought"—she reached his elbows where his rolled-up shirt sleeves sat and continued, the linen doing little to block his warmth—"it was past time I rectify that."

All he did was watch her. But, gods, how he *watched*. His wide pupils turned his eyes dark and glinting. His chest heaved as it had when he'd given her the earring earlier and her mind had told her to kiss him.

At last, she was about to listen to it.

She swallowed, breathing ragged as though she were running or fighting rather than simply standing on a beach facing him.

As her touch planed over his biceps to his shoulders, she caught every tremble of simmering tension running through his muscles. So like the moment she'd looked up at him in the glow-worm cave, right before they'd finally kissed. It said, now, as then, he was fighting to keep still.

Maybe it was that it had been so long since she'd allowed herself to touch him like this, every recent contact had been restrained to the boundaries of *just friends*—albeit they'd pushed those boundaries a couple of times… Maybe it was that… But her legs shook, knees as weak as all those stupid arguments she'd made about why they shouldn't be anything more than friends.

The pure pleasure of touching him, even this simple caress of his shoulders, the joy of his company—it was worth every ounce of the inevitable pain that would come when he left. How had she ever doubted it?

She exhaled what was almost a laugh as her thumbs ran along his collarbones. When she reached that hollow in the centre, just below his throat, his breath caught.

It was a sound so sweet she could've listened to it forever.

His lust-darkened eyes turned to her lips as he blinked lazily, stoking the warmth in her to heat. His head dipped, just a little, but she knew the motion and that it preceded a kiss.

Maybe she'd kiss him here and then they'd find somewhere even quieter—her tent or the forest would work. It didn't matter where, so long as it was him—*them* together, at last.

Hands skimming the sides of his neck, her fingertips tickled the edge of his hairline. That gloriously thick hair, so untameable, as if it was always a hint that he was not a man made for control.

That thought broke something inside. A dam or a rope—she couldn't have said what, but a shiver streaked through her.

"Knigh," she murmured, simply to taste his name as she rose on tiptoes and tilted her head to reach his lips.

With a sharp inhale, he caught her wrists, pulled them away, and edged back, all so quickly, she stumbled forward.

"Vee, what…?" He blinked and shook his head as if waking.

Whatever easing her heartbeat had done from his

comforting warmth disappeared as it now smashed against her ribs. "I thought it was obvious what... what I was... what we were..."

His brows pulled together as he stared at her. The distant music, the sighing waves, and her own frantic pulse marked far too much time passing before he finally shook his head again. Solid. Emphatic.

"Vee." That nickname had never sounded so devastating from his lips. He looked away, dropping her wrists. "I—I'm sorry, I don't..." *Another* shake of his head. "If I gave the impression that I wanted... then I'm sorry. But you're drunk and"—he met her eye—"I don't want *just bodies* with you." His jaw flexed, then he turned and stalked away.

She opened her mouth to argue but...

But her tongue had gone thick and slow and stupid again. What was she meant to say? How could she argue?

He'd said no.

He'd rejected her.

But you're drunk and I don't want just bodies with you.

So simple. So emphatic. Like that shake of his head.

She blinked, eyes burning with pressure and salt.

Except...

Yes, she was drunk, but she wasn't *that* drunk. She still knew what she was doing. She still...

She'd wanted him yesterday and the day before and the day before that without so much as a drop of alcohol in her body.

And she didn't—this wasn't meant to be *just bodies*.

Gods damn it—damn *her*. She scrubbed her face. Why had she ever used that phrase with him?

Maybe it's for the best. That dark corner of herself whispered it, cruel and cowering.

Just as well he'd said no. The alternative…

The possibility she could've had what she wanted, albeit temporarily—that was too frightening to consider.

With a sigh, she sank into the sand and grabbed her tankard and his cup. She drained one then the other, the rum's fire little more than a trickle of warmth compared to her burning cheeks.

But… No, that dark corner was wrong. *She* had already decided—yes, it was frightening, yes, there was a risk, and yes, there would be pain, but she had decided the cost was worth it. She'd made her decision.

It was the decision to live as she had the night she'd comforted him in Perry's cabin when he'd slept with his head in her lap. It was the decision to live with a moment's joy and endure the painful aftermath.

It was the decision to *live*.

She'd already chosen it and if that cowardly corner of herself regretted it, well that was too bad.

Problem was, she'd let him walk away thinking she'd intended for this to only be sex, not more, not… whatever it might be between them.

And why *wouldn't* he think that? After all, she'd presented it as a transaction—merely an expression of gratitude for his well-chosen gifts.

"Wild Hunt take me for a bloody fool." Her fist thumped into the ground, the sand muffling the blow.

She'd tried to seduce him instead of voicing what she

wanted, what she *felt*.

That wasn't her forte, but had knots always been her forte? Had the workings of line and sail been Lady Avice's forte when she'd first set foot on a ship?

She'd learned. She'd done the hard work, built the calluses on her fingers and hands, studied the way rigging braced yard and mast and canvas.

Maybe talking about her feelings was much more scary, much more vulnerable—much, much more dangerous as her constricting heart reminded her. But maybe it was something that could be learned, all the same.

After all, keeping them locked up was what had led to them spewing out in ugly ways, like when Knigh had got too close and she'd run to FitzRoy, or the cruel things she'd said to him on the *Swallow*.

But if she spoke about her feelings, they wouldn't explode and destroy everything like a cannon bursting its barrel.

Leaping to her feet, the world spun as though the sudden movement caused those last two drinks to kick in. She clutched her head against the tilting spin and scoured the bonfires, the groups of people talking, the dancers.

She needed to find Knigh and she needed to explain. But he was lost in the crowd and the darkness.

And she—she *was* drunk now, the world or her head fuzzy and spinning... But she would explain when she was sober and he couldn't blame it on alcohol.

For now, she had a birthday and a starry night to dance away... and perhaps even a little hope.

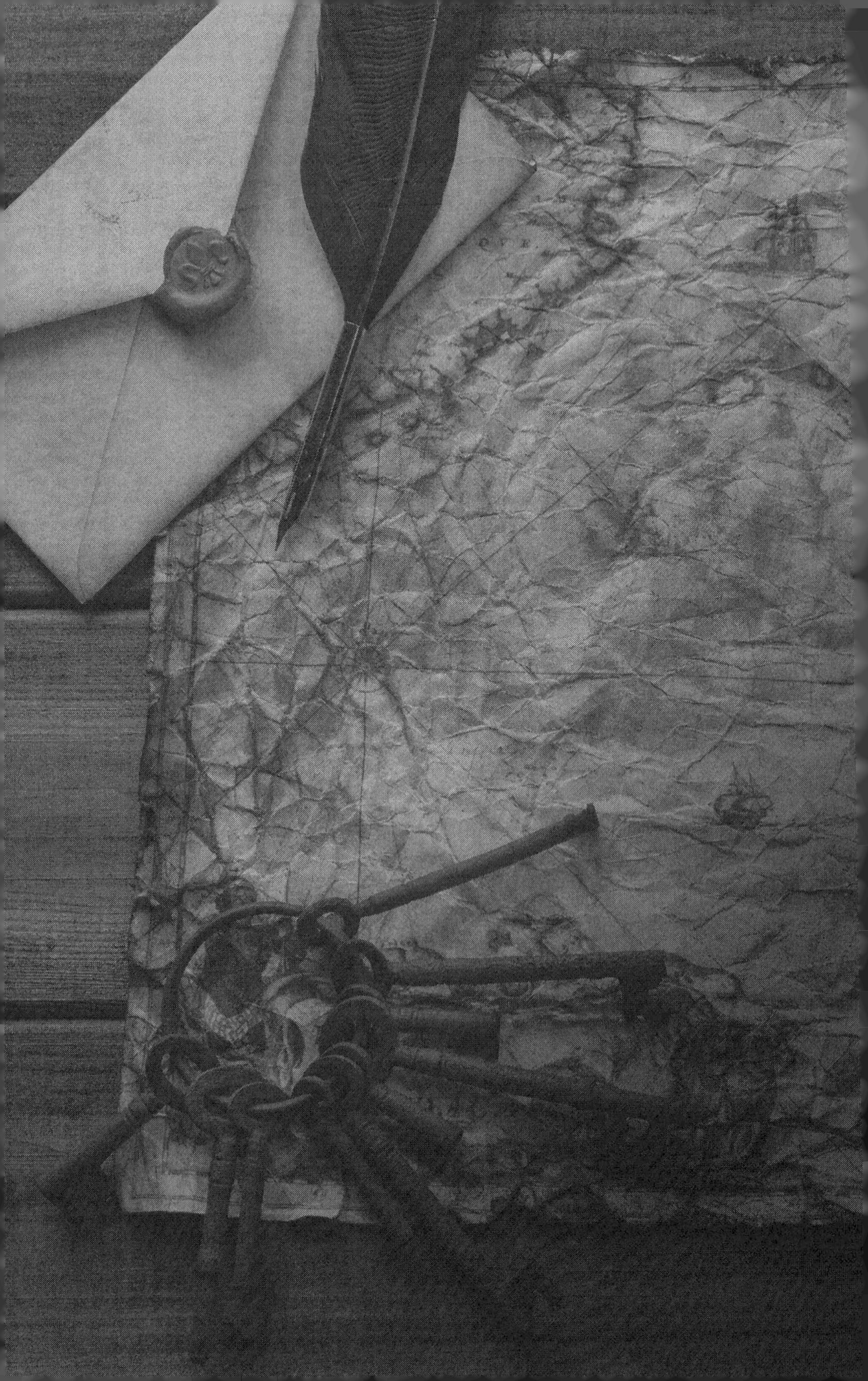

A RUN THROUGH THE FOREST

Blood thrumming, Knigh strode for the furthest edge of the camp and didn't look back. He needed to get as far as possible from Vee. And temptation.

If only she'd wanted more than *just bodies*.

He'd offered himself to her, that first night they were reunited on the *Venatrix*, in a tentative way that asked without asking. *Do you want me? Will you have me?* He'd made it clear without saying that he wanted her. But she only wanted friendship.

He'd thought it was because of his berserking. Who'd want to be with him after seeing what he'd done to Aedan? After they'd sparred though, and she'd been so kind and fierce at once, skewering his beliefs about his father, it was clear she didn't judge him for that.

But this?

For a moment, he'd been so hopeful. Earlier, when he'd

given her that earring at long last and had seen how it affected her, when she'd let him put it in her ear. That had been hope. Possibility.

Except, turned out it was only the possibility of something purely physical, more like torture than pleasure.

Still, the temptation tingled on his skin, twitched low in his belly, seared through his veins, given free rein by the alcohol. He could've said yes. He could've told himself it was something to enjoy, even if only a physical something.

Huffing a sigh and turning his face to the cool breeze coming off the sea, he stopped and closed his eyes. His hand drifted to his pocket and the pad of his thumb tucked into the little cup of that abalone shell she'd given him when they'd dived the wreck. Such a small thing and yet...

He'd only made it to the next bonfire, less than fifty yards away. He could turn back, give in.

She could've denied it. He'd said *just bodies* with the hope she'd say it wasn't only that. But the way she'd stared back...

Groaning, he raked his hands through his hair. No. It was better this way, even if it did leave his chest hollow and aching.

After a few minutes, he circled back to the party, smiling and nodding at friends and crewmates, at members of Billy's crew who still watched him with puzzled frowns. How had the Viscount Villiers, a captain of the Royal Navy, ended up a pirate? The question was written across their faces.

Ahead, golden hair gleamed in the firelight. Is tilted her head and narrowed her eyes, a cool smile on her mouth. One of the young men from the *Firefly* stood a little too close, bending into her space.

A frown tightening on his brow, Knigh adjusted his course in that direction. But before he reached them, Is said something, lifted her chin and raised her eyebrows, and the young man's shoulders caved in and he backed away.

By the time Knigh drew level with Is, the young man was nowhere to be seen.

At his questioning look, she lifted one shoulder in a ladylike shrug. "Trying his luck. Turns out it was the bad kind."

"Poor fellow." Just as he'd told Aedan—his sister didn't need him looking out for her. Speaking of which... "Now I have you alone"—he cleared his throat—"do I need to be aware of anything else about your crossing of the ocean?"

She looked up at him, blue eyes wide. Oh, Lords, it was a look that could've won her anything she wanted, except those apparently innocent eyes glinted too brightly in the firelight, and her cheeks darkened a shade or two.

He cocked his head. "Anything involving a certain *merchant captain*, perhaps?"

Brows lowering, she huffed out through her nose, realising she'd been caught. She looked away and scanned the crews around them, like this was a ball and she knew precisely who to be seen with and who to avoid. "You noticed that, then?"

"I did." He kept his tone neutral, but she must've felt his gaze on her, because she finally returned it.

The corners of her mouth rose, shy like she was still a girl rather than the knowing young woman she'd been a mere moment ago. "Wasn't he dashing, Knigh? The way he..." She waved her hand in what might've been an approximation of swordplay, the gesture so unstudied, so unladylike, he couldn't help but smile.

"He *is* Navy-trained. You know we served togeth—"

"Of course." She gave a dismissive flick of her hand, once more the lady holding court at a ball. "And I suppose he's your friend, isn't he?" She sighed, lips finishing in a little pout. "Are you going to stomp in and play the big brother and tell me I can't—?"

He raised his hands in defence. *Never tell me that I can't.* Vee had told him that and he owed his sister the same respect. "That wasn't why I brought it up. I merely wish to know *if* something is happening and if so, what?" He captured the hand she'd flicked and gave a gentle squeeze. "You're my sister and I care for you, but I don't own you and I don't pretend to."

It was only when her delicate shoulders settled that he realised she'd been holding them squared. But she eyed him sidelong and gave a little smirk. "Quite right, too." She kissed his hand and gave an impish wink. "I believe your friend likes me." She dipped her chin and watched the dancers cavorting near the bonfire once more. "And I like him. Very much, in fact. But"—she frowned, lips pursing—"I'm not sure what Mother would say, considering our relative stations."

There was that, but—

"Besides," she went on, "*if* Billy wished to make me an offer, the situation is complicated now, isn't it? Do I need your permission or would it be George's now you're...?" Her fingers unfurled, indicating him and the collected crews of three pirate ships in that one, small movement.

"Now I'm a pirate." He pushed a smile in place. "You are

allowed to say it, you know." Lords, telling his sister to call him a pirate—his two worlds really had collided.

"Now you're... a pirate." She giggled and covered her mouth. "It sounds so... improbable. And yet, here we are." She flashed him a glinting look, lifting her chin. "My brother the pirate. I'm still proud of you, you know."

His chest stilled, suddenly too full to take in air.

I'm still proud of you, you know.

Despite deserting. Despite becoming the very thing he'd hunted and despised.

It meant more than passing his lieutenant's exam so young, more than earning those epaulettes that had declared him a captain, and certainly more than becoming Viscount Villiers.

He rubbed his face and cleared his throat. "This isn't about me, though I'm glad I haven't made you ashamed. Truly." His smile was no longer stiff. "As for your question... I'm not sure either. This isn't exactly an ordinary situation, especially now you're here and in hiding from a prince." She and Mother hadn't broken any laws and yet they were hunted by a member of the royal family. Did that mean they no longer owed Albion their allegiance—that they were nationless and didn't need to follow that nation's rules? He raised a shoulder. "You aren't in Albion, anymore... Maybe you don't need anyone's permission."

Her brows shot up and he had to chuckle at her surprise. "You're sounding like a republican, brother."

"There are worse things to be." A corrupt royal, for example. He shook away the thought of that man. "But, if you do feel you need someone else's permission, well..." He stroked a stray lock of her hair that wafted in the breeze. "Billy is a good man. Intelligent, kind, thoughtful... maybe the bravest man I know and the most forgiving. I'd be proud to call him brother-in-law, whatever his title or profession."

Exhaling, she leant into his touch and closed her eyes as though she'd been carrying around her worries as a lead weight. "And I"—she looked up at him and took his hand, a pull at the corner of her mouth—"wouldn't mind having a pirate queen for a sister-in-law."

His mouth dropped open before he caught himself. Damn her for disarming him with her sisterly sweetness. He clamped his lips together and pulled away with an exhale. "It isn't like that."

Is arched an eyebrow at him.

"It *was*, yes, but we're just friends now."

Eyebrow still raised, she looked back towards the bonfire he and Vee had stood beside. "Strange. The way you two were talking earlier didn't look like *just friends.*"

Double-damn her. He crossed his arms, though it would make a poor shield against his shrewd sister. "She wanted"—he cleared his throat—"a run through the forest at Calan Mai."

Is laughed. "You mean, sex?"

A breath burst out of him. He blinked at her and shook his head. "Well, yes, that is what I meant. Gods, you really have grown up, haven't you?"

"That's what happens to little sisters." Again, the impish look, all glinting and bright. "But no changing the subject. We were talking about Lady Vice."

He didn't even bother to suppress the sigh—Is could read

him far too well no matter how controlled he was. "She wants *that* and nothing more." Hearing his sister say *sex* was one thing, but saying it back to her was quite another.

"And you do? Want more, that is."

He clenched his jaw against the ache in his chest. So much more. He nodded, fingers grazing the edge of the abalone shell.

"Of course you do. You still have that shell, don't you?"

Exhaling with a groan, he pulled his hand from his pocket. So easily read, such traitorous hands.

"Well, the way she looks at you..." She cleared her throat, overly delicate with the gesture as though it were for his benefit. "That isn't the way ladies look at the men they're sizing up at the feast table before they light the bonfires at Calan Mai."

Because she was suddenly the expert? He gave Is a flat look. "We're friends, that's how she sees me. And as for tonight? She's drunk and it's her birthday and she wants a warm body." Every word of it cut like steel.

"Well, *he's* a warm body." Looking somewhere over his shoulder, she tipped her head in the same direction.

He turned—Aedan walked past wearing an uncharacteristic glower, clutching not one but *two* bottles of rum. Oh, gods, what had happened to—?

"And a fine specimen of one, I must say."

"Is!"

She just shrugged and continued: "But unless I'm very much mistaken, she spurned his advances not five minutes before she sought you out."

"Have you been watching—?"

"Good gods, Knigh, what do you think young ladies spend

their time doing? I'm a people-watcher. And I watched you and her yesterday on the boat—those little touches where she tried to comfort you. I watched how you looked at her as I told our story. I watched her with that man tonight, turning him away, and instead coming after you." She raised her eyebrows at him like he was a schoolboy slow on the uptake. "They were not the actions of a woman looking for a roll in the forest. And she may well be drunk tonight, but I'd wager that was only to give her courage to do what she already wished to."

A chill prickled through him, setting the hairs at the nape of his neck on end.

If his sister was right...

His throat tightened. If she took after Aunt Tilda, she almost certainly was right.

Which meant he'd lost his chance. Vee's pride wouldn't allow her to offer herself to him again, and he couldn't blame her.

What an idiot he'd been.

Perhaps if he approached her... Or would her pride still make her decline the offer?

He clutched his head as a pounding ache started behind his eyes. "Bloody hells, I need to think about this when I'm not drunk. I don't even know where to begin."

"At least ask her what she meant," Is murmured, "what she wants."

"Oh, right." He snorted. "'Excuse me, Vee, I was just wondering—when you tried to kiss me the other night, did you mean you wanted to be with me or that you just wanted a quick screw in your tent?'"

Damnation. This was his sister, he shouldn't use such language. *Or* snap at her like that.

But she didn't blush, she only raised her brows at him. And she didn't betray any sign of hurt as her chin lifted. "I think you're afraid of finding out."

He stiffened, the headache's beat increasing in tempo. "Oh, really? And you're an expert now, are you?"

She smiled up at him, so sweet it might've warmed his heart if not for the fire and sharp sapphire glinting in her eyes. "Billy risked his life yesterday, attacking those pirates and keeping them from our door. You're lucky, though—you don't need to risk your life, only your heart." Her head tilted and her smile faded, the sharpness in her eyes along with it. "But risk you must, big brother. With the greatest gamble, comes the possibility of the greatest reward."

With a groan, he slumped and screwed his eyes shut. Wild Hunt damn it, she was right. "Spoken like a true poker player." He opened one eye and dared a glance at her.

Head tilted, she smirked back, frighteningly like a sabrecat with a bowl of cream. "So that's why you won't play cards with me anymore." She scoffed before bending in. "But seriously, you need to up the ante, not fold."

"Oh, gods, please save me from any more poker analogies." He huffed and raised his hands in defence. "Fine. Fine! I'll... do *something*." He shook his head but gathered her into a hug and kissed the top of her blonde head. "It's not like I have anything pressing to do like, oh, I don't know, find you a home that's safe from all my enemies."

She laughed and patted his chest. "I have every faith that you'll do both things successfully."

That made one of them. Because even if Vee forgave him for turning her down, his enemies had a long reach that covered all of Arawaké.

Plus, it wasn't only Is and Mother's short-term physical safety that was at stake. Their future happiness, his sister's potential marriage prospects—all of it was in question.

And all of it *his* responsibility.

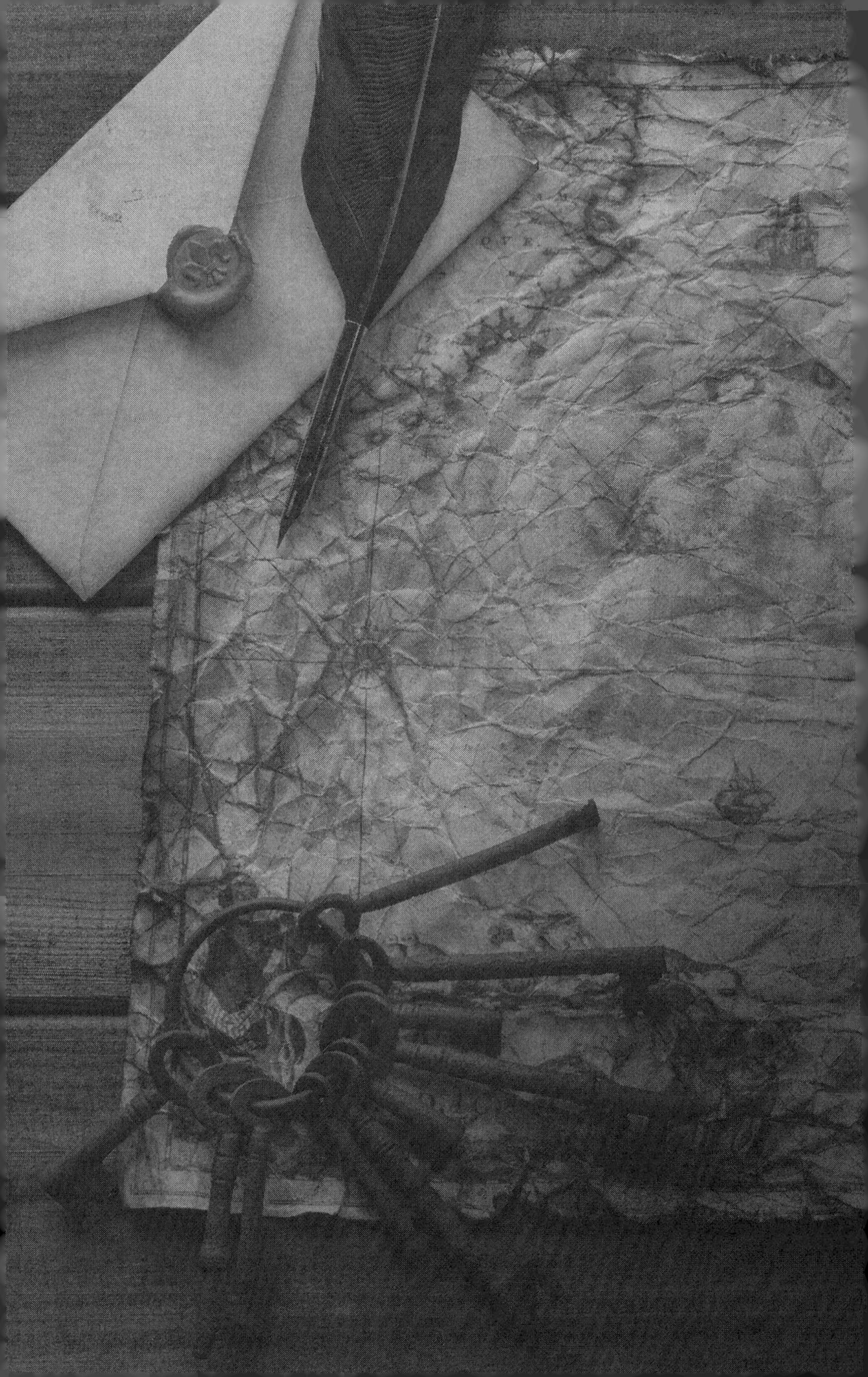

WORTH ASKING

Vice's head only mildly throbbed when she emerged from her tent the next morning—the sun already crept towards its zenith—*late* morning. After food and some fresh water from the nearby stream, even that throbbing ebbed away, which was a blessing considering what she needed to do today.

Her hands turned clammy. She wiped them on her shirt, scanning the camp sprawled across the beach and the fringes of the forest. Dozens and dozens of tents. Hammocks slung between palm trees. The scorched, ashy remains of last night's bonfires. All of that, but not a single sign of mid-brown hair streaked with white.

She found Perry, eyes rimmed red, nursing a cup of grog in the shade of her open-sided tent. Her sun-beaten skin had a distinctly ashen cast to it.

"Blimey, Perry," she said, ducking into the shade, "did you drink more than—?"

"Don't." Her friend raised one hand, eyes shut. "Just. Don't." She exhaled, inhaled, once, twice, before eventually peeling them open like it was a great effort and fixing Vice with a withering glare. "Where the hells were you half the night? While you were off gallivanting, I got roped into a drinking game with Clovis, Erec, and the lads from the *Firefly*. And because you weren't there, I didn't have anyone to make drink on my behalf and..." She shook her head, grimacing.

Vice raised an eyebrow. "So in all other things you try to keep me sensible, but somehow when it comes to drinking games, *I'm* the one who keeps *you* sensible?"

"I'm as shocked as you are. I think I might've kissed their captain." She screwed her face up. "On a dare, of course, but... I don't remember."

"Oh, *really?* I didn't have you down for a slice of him." Vice giggled. He was twice Perry's height for one thing and not much more than half her age. They'd make an interesting pair. "I wish I'd been there to see that."

"Which leads us back to my question—where *were* you?"

A groan edged Vice's exhalation. "It was... an interesting night. Have you seen Knigh?" Thumb rubbing over the drake pin, she glanced out from the tent. It was partially to search for him, but more to avoid Perry's look in the wake of that question. Even red-rimmed, her eyes saw too much, *said* too much.

"And why might you be looking for him, I wonder?" A tease lilted through her words.

"Have you?"

"I gave him directions to that pool you like so much. Said he needed a bit of space from his family. I understand his sister asks a lot of questions."

"I know someone else like that."

Perry chuckled, then sucked her teeth. "Now, who could you possibly mean? Oh well, I suppose we'll never know."

Vice couldn't help but give her a sidelong grin at that. Then, heart beating a little quicker, she asked, "Was he alone?" If Aedan or some of the others had also gone, she'd have to wait, but if it was only Knigh...

As though she understood the weight of that question, Perry's amusement faded with a slow blink. "Aye, and I can make sure it stays that way. Just him and you." Her eyebrows rose in query.

Tongue thick again, Vice could barely swallow. She certainly couldn't answer that unvoiced question. And her damn hands! She wiped them on her shirt again.

"So," Perry said. "You've made a decision, then?"

Her heart, her lungs—all out of control. If she couldn't give Perry this simple answer, how in the world was she going to tell Knigh everything she needed to?

So she swallowed and tamed her breaths to a sensible rhythm as she did when she focused to work her gift. "I have. And... it is worth it."

A tremor worked through Perry's lower lip before her mouth curved into a small smile. "Well done."

"Don't get too excited. He might not think the same." She lifted one shoulder and turned inland towards that pool she knew so well.

"He might not. But"—Perry tilted her head—"I think I know what his answer will be. And even if he doesn't, it's worth the asking, no?"

Another deep breath against the staccato beat of her heart. "It is."

"Then what the hells are you wasting time hanging around with me for?"

Vice laughed and it eased her heart and too-tight chest. She slung an arm around Perry, kissed the top of her head, and thanked her before setting off for the forest clearing with its waterfall.

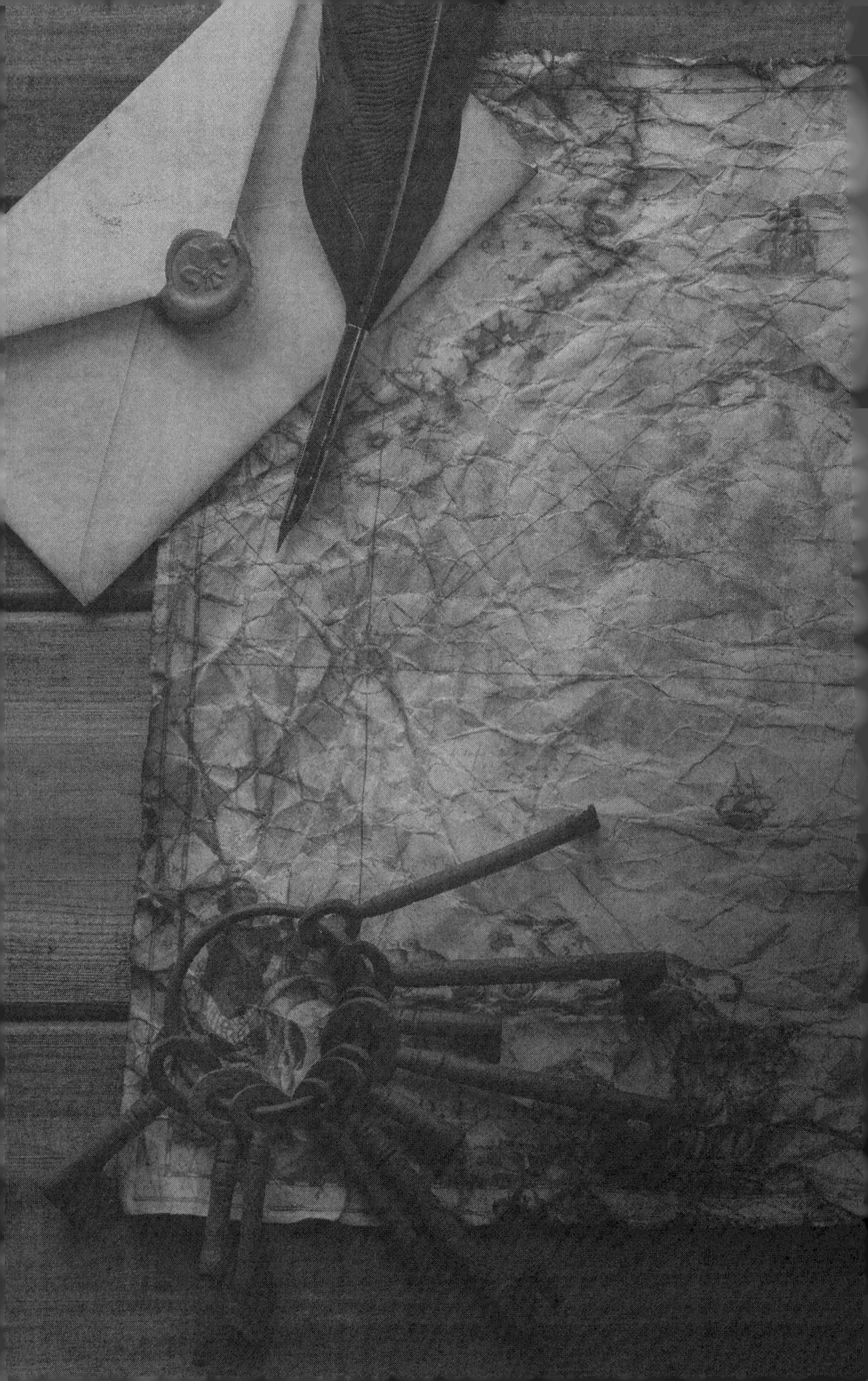

RISK

The forest was shady and damp as she hiked towards the same pool she'd swum in the very first time she'd come to Arawaké. Back then, she'd only just made friends with Perry, Saba, and Lizzy, but they'd taken her foraging for yuca. After, they'd shown her how to swing a sword until she'd been sweaty and trembling, and then they'd shown her the pool where they'd bathed and cooled off.

She smiled to herself, the thought easing her fluttering belly as she walked that same path, the waterfall's rush already audible. She rounded that familiar corner and...

There he was, in the water, half-turned away, entirely naked. The waterfall gushed down the dark rocks beyond, and above, the leafy canopy opened up to a brilliant blue sky.

Mouth dry, face hot, she stopped in her tracks. All the way here she'd focused so much on what she needed to tell him, she'd forgotten he would be bathing. Naked.

Very, very naked.

The broad expanse of his shoulders provided a perfect canvas for the black lines inked there. At this angle, a three-quarter view, his muscles cast a shadow over his spine. It curved between his shoulder blades and arched into the small of his back. She'd traced that line too long ago, running her fingers down the groove. Below it, the swell of his arse teased above the water's sparkling surface.

And those delicious back muscles of his *worked* as he lathered soap and scrubbed it across his chest and arms, one hand sliding to a shoulder, then behind his neck, leaving a trail of white suds in its wake.

They'd be slippery—*he'd* be slippery and clean-smelling and...

The edge of his jaw came into view as his head turned almost side-on.

Shit. But he didn't turn the rest of the way and look at her. Must not have seen. Was she meant to announce herself or just appear?

She wasn't one for protocol, but it would've been handy right now because her usual assurance had fled.

Coward.

She blinked and tried to remind her tongue how to work.

If nerves didn't have her palms sweating and stomach tight, it would've been funny. Almost four years ago, that first time here, she'd been in the water, not far from where he was now, and Fitz had stood here. She'd been naked, seen him walk around this very corner and stop mid-stride. Evered had still been alive then, though he'd refused to come ashore, not wanting to mix with *those filthy pirates*. She hadn't renamed herself Vice yet, just Avice. It wasn't just a different name, she'd been a different *person* then.

Hells, she'd been a different person *a year* ago.

In the pool, Knigh ran soap up one powerful arm, then the other, muscles rippling, tensing, easing in a complex symphony of movement.

Good gods, she wanted him. Yes, physically, as the tight coil of her thigh muscles reminded her. His was a beautiful body, capable of...

She blew out a shaking breath. Oh, she knew *exactly* what that devastating body was capable of.

But as frightening it was, she could admit there was so much more to her *want* than just the physical.

There were a million more facets to him, like each little ripple reflecting at a different angle on the pool's surface. His dry humour. His laughter, as rare and precious as any gemstone. His calm quiet, which was probably where his thoughtfulness came from.

Then there was the way he could admit when he was wrong and threw himself into making amends, no matter the cost to himself. Viscount or otherwise, Knigh Blackwood was noble in a way that had nothing to do with titles or bloodlines.

He'd saved her life more times than she could keep track of, and he'd thanked her when she'd saved his. He'd forgiven her cruelty and the lie of Avice Ferrers' murder.

But most of all, he had come for her.

He'd fought his way past storms and laws and iron and steel and a kraken and his own prince and admiral and even her prickly sea urchin armour. And he'd reached her even when she'd tried to make it impossible—even when it should have *been* impossible. He'd fought it all as though nothing would keep him from her.

I'll always come for you.

Maybe nothing *would* keep him from her.

Throat tight, pressure at the back of her eyes, she tried to find her voice and tell him all that.

She'd managed to *think* all those words, all she needed to do was open her mouth and say them. Even if his answer might be no. Because the chance it could be yes was worth the risk.

"Don't you know it's rude to stare?"

She froze. *Shit.*

He hadn't turned to face her, but he stood in exact profile to her, the straight line of his nose glistening with moisture.

She swallowed and worked her tongue around her mouth. "How did you know I was here?"

"I just knew." His lips curved and his eyebrow rose as he watched her sidelong. "Did you come for a swim or to take in the view?"

With a laugh, she put one hand on her hip and cocked her head. "Do the two have to be mutually exclusive?" This was safe. This she could do—silly, fun flirtation that didn't mean anything. Her tongue worked to say *these* words just fine.

At last he turned to face her, a smirk on his mouth as her gaze did the inevitable and trailed down...

Down his throat, his chiselled chest, the ripples of his muscled stomach, the hollow of his belly button...

Down the creases above his hips that pointed to the dark hair peeking just above the waterline.

The flash of his teeth dragged her attention upwards to find him grinning. "There's plenty of space for two and the water is *glorious*."

She *was* sweaty after her hike and the pool was deliciously cool on a hot day. They could talk while they swam. Besides, it didn't feel right for her to be fully clothed while he wore nothing—not level pegging, somehow.

She circled around to the water's edge and emerged from the leafy canopy's shade beside his pile of discarded clothes. Every step, he watched.

The back of her neck prickled as she unslung the bag from her shoulder and threw it next to his—even that simple action went under his scrutiny.

Surely he wasn't going to watch her the whole time.

She flicked him a glance as she unbuckled her belt. He stood about twelve feet away, the water lapping just below his belly button. The corner of his mouth might've risen a touch, it was hard to say, but his eyes didn't dart away as though ashamed that he'd been caught staring.

Her fingers closed around the hem of her shirt, and she raised an eyebrow, all cocky like her heart wasn't speeding, like her thighs weren't tense. "I thought you said it was rude to stare."

Now *both* corners of his mouth definitely rose, revealing his teeth in a wolfish grin. "Consider it payback."

Bastard. He was actually going to watch her undress without an ounce of shame. Yes, he'd seen her naked dozens of times, but this was different. Then it had been play—or at least she'd told herself that—and they'd tugged off each others' clothes to get to bare flesh, specifically to enjoy it.

Now? *This?*

This was something else entirely. This was undressing ready to swim rather than for sex, which somehow made his watching all the harder to withstand. Maybe because it still made her body react even though there was no promise of imminent fulfilment.

Worst of all, not only was she baring her flesh, but she was about to bare her feelings, her wishes, her desires for more than only the physical. And there was every chance he'd reject her. Again.

She squared her shoulders.

Joy. Pain. It was worth it. That's what she'd decided and she wasn't going to back away because of a little fear.

"You could *pretend* you're not staring," she muttered as she peeled off the shirt. Even with her view blocked by the fabric over her head, she could *feel* his heavy gaze on her, drinking her in, consuming her.

Goosebumps, tight chest, racing heart. Her body knew it, too.

She threw her shirt with his clothes, sighing as the air cooled her sweat-bathed skin.

Knigh, the bastard, trailed his attention down her body, just as she had his. At least that arrogant grin of his had disappeared, replaced by parted lips.

As she unbuttoned her breeches, his grey eyes, dark despite the light in the clearing, followed the movement of her fingers as if hypnotised and her core tightened in response. It could be his fingers on her, undressing her, touching her, toying with the edge of the waistband. She swallowed. Was he imagining the same?

She kicked off her boots, letting the front of her breeches fall open. He stared at the plane of her belly and the hint of dark hair now visible. His throat bobbed.

Bloody hells, considering she was meant to be declaring her desire for more than just his body, this had all grown very sexual very quickly.

It would be so easy to march into that water, stride right up to him, kiss him, and order him to take her that instant.

The way he watched her, he might not say no.

But this wasn't meant to be about that. She'd bathed in this pool with members of the crew dozens of times and in the sail bath rigged beside the ship a hundred more. It was always innocent, playful, just a matter of cleaning bodies. Foolishly, she'd thought this would be the same.

This *had* to be based on talking, not bodies, no matter how unbearable the ache of attraction between them. If he felt the same, wanted the same, they could do what the hells they wanted to each other later, but until then, until she'd said all she needed to say, and he said out loud a resounding *yes* to wanting to be with her, she would not touch him. She vowed it.

They needed to be on the same page. He needed to say *yes*. And she wouldn't touch him until then.

Vow or not, when she pushed her breeches down, he bit his lip and her blood simmered. Wild Hunt take her, he wasn't going to make this easy.

Closing her eyes to block out the sight of him, she stepped one foot out of her breeches and used the other to kick them away with the rest of their mingled clothes. That allowed her to take a few steadying breaths. When she walked down the gentle slope of pebbles and silty sand and into the water without needing to clench her hands against the desire to reach out for him.

The water at least did something to cool her burning skin.

He watched her the whole time, but as she waded in to her calves, her knees, her thighs, he mastered his expression, sliding on a *mostly* blank mask, and backed away to give her space. When the water reached her chest, she ducked into it up to her neck and sighed as it rinsed away the hot sweat.

He stood in deeper water, too, and mirrored her, sinking until only his head and neck and the tops of his shoulders were visible. "You know," he said with a lopsided smile, "I was just thinking about you. Perhaps I summoned you."

She snorted and shook her head. "I'm not one of those djinn they have in the east, you know."

Exactly *what* had he been thinking about her? Lords and ladies, what she wouldn't give to be a mindreader, just for a moment. It didn't feel safe to ask, so she submerged herself.

The world was blue and rippling, weightless. Simpler, somehow. It was easy to believe that if she held her breath long enough, she could just stay here and not have to deal with Knigh, with her feelings, with... anything.

But even if that were possible and not just an illusion cast by the water, it would be a coward's way out. And she was no coward.

So, she swept her hair from her face and surfaced.

A bar of soap awaited her, a foot away in his outstretched hand.

No touching. Easier said than done in this instance, but she'd meant it. She managed to slide the tan-coloured soap onto her other hand without the slightest contact against his skin.

Its scent touched her nostrils, deep and woody with a hint of sweetness, masculine and warm. So this was what he always smelled of, and now she was about to slather herself in it. She'd be marked with his scent for the rest of the day. Great. If he said no…

"This island," she said, voice wavering a touch as she lathered the soap between her hands, "is where I first made landfall in Arawaké." A safe subject to let her voice settle.

Coward.

"Really?" Eyebrows rising, he surveyed the clearing, the pool, the waterfall, as though seeing it anew.

"That…" She ran soap up her arms and swallowed, as if that would stop her heart from feeling like it was in her throat, beating frantically like a bird trying to fly free. "That isn't what I…" She shook her head. Damn it, she hadn't come here to talk about her first time on this island. "You know last night when you said you didn't want *just bodies* with me?"

A beat of silence, maybe he was taken aback by the abrupt change of subject, then he squinted and touched his chin. "Hmm, that *does* sound vaguely familiar." He cocked his head as if racking his brain.

She huffed and shot him a glare. "Now you're the one making a joke when I'm trying to be serious. *Really?*"

His mouth opened and closed, and the humour evaporated from his expression. "Oh, you were being serious? Sorry." He winced in that charming way of his, the same as when they'd met in deLacy's ballroom. The damp skin of his arm glistened across bulging muscles as he rubbed the back of his head. "And, about last night—I'm sorry, I think I misunderstood."

Letting him talk would be easier, might save her from explaining her feelings. But that was a coward's way out.

"No, *I* misunderstood." She shook her head. "I didn't make myself clear. So let me be clear now." A shiver trickled through her and those goosebumps came back in full force. "I meant what I said on the *Swallow*—it isn't just bodies between us. It can't be."

His wince deepened, all the more charming as it crinkled the skin around his eyes. "I thought you'd changed your mind about that, after... after everything that's happened."

"I have, about a few things." *About you.* "But not about that."

He remained silent.

Ba-DUM. Ba-DUM. Ba-DUM.

Despite the rush of the waterfall, it was a wonder he didn't ask about that thumping noise. Her heart, about ready to come crashing out of her chest.

"Not just bodies," she went on, "that's not what I want from you—*with* you."

He didn't move. Didn't talk. Not a hint of reaction showed in that gorgeous face.

She exhaled, clutching the soap to her chest and staring at a point in the water a foot in front of him. "I've been battling it for weeks, telling myself we should be *just friends* over and over, because I was too much of a coward to face my feelings, never mind to bare them to you or anyone else.

"And I told myself that you couldn't possibly want me, not when you must resent me for costing you your career, your home, your place in the world. You gave up your uniform, when that's the very thing that made you."

Now she said it out loud, it sounded insurmountable.

On the edge of her vision, he moved.

"You might not even want... You probably don't, in fact..." She was babbling, yes, but if she left too long a gap, he might speak and she needed to get it all out first. "But I want to be with you, Knigh. Not just physically, but..." She ran a hand across the surface of the water, the ripples dragging on her fingertips. *"More* than that. I don't know what it would look like, what it would be. I do know I have things I need to work on—the idea of other people's questions and comments frankly terrifies me... Dealing with those on top of dealing with my own emotions and the responsibility of considering and guarding yours..." Grimacing, she shook her head. "But... I'd like to find out what it might be. And I'll try to do better, to *be* better than I was on *The Morrigan*."

The words ran out, like the last trickle of water flowing off the deck and out the scuppers. All she could do was breathe. In and out and in again.

As she did, a horrible realisation crept through her, far, far colder than the water. He didn't want *just bodies* with her and she'd assumed that meant he wanted more—a relationship. But he might have meant the opposite. That same phrase could have been him saying he didn't want sex, only friendship.

And here she was, flesh, feelings, *everything* exposed, only just realising that interpretation now she'd made this stupid speech.

She sank in the water until it lapped at her jawline.

"But... " She swallowed, shook her head. "That's what *I* want, what *I* think... I don't know what *you* want."

Finally, now she'd purged the words from herself, she could look at him.

His face was no longer that near-blank mask, but the lines of his expression were subtle. The slightest crease between his eyebrows where they rose and drew together, just a touch. His jaw loose as though his lips were about to part. His pupils weren't blown wide with desire anymore as they had been when he'd watched her undress, but his gaze tethered her, searching as it moved across her face as though he might spot some sign there. Of a lie? Or the full depth of her truth, perhaps. Maybe something else.

She couldn't blame him for needing time to think about it. She had just dumped *a lot* of information on him, all jumbled and messy.

Urgh, why couldn't she explain these things with Perry's clear efficiency?

A long breath in, then he swallowed. "Vee." He shook his head and it sent a chill through her.

No. He was saying *no*. He didn't want her.

She bit her tongue against giving away any response. Of

course he had every right to say no. She owed it to him to listen to whatever he had to say.

"I..." He shook his head again and came closer, sending wavelets rippling across the pool's surface as he stopped within arm's reach. "What I want is not to hurt you."

What did *that* mean?

He huffed again, as though talking was difficult. "Because I do want you."

She held still, even though it was unbearable, even though she wanted to laugh or maybe cry. He was within arm's reach, but she'd sworn she wouldn't touch him. If he wanted her, maybe that meant she would get to soon. She barely breathed, waiting for him to go on.

"I want you so much it frightens me." His brow crinkled that bit deeper and she understood.

Wasn't she terrified herself? Oh, yes, she fully understood being afraid of this want. It was only when her chin touched the water that she realised she'd nodded.

He ran wet hands over his face. "And, Vee," he said, voice raw, "I've hurt you before, so that only adds to the fear. But last night, after I sent you away, Is told me that the greatest risks bring the greatest rewards, so... maybe all those reasons we've been telling ourselves we should be *just friends* don't matter. I think they *were* just excuses." The creases deepened further as he winced. "But I still come back to that—I don't want to hurt you."

I don't want to hurt you—he said each word with such gravity, like it was its own sentence.

But it wasn't an answer. It was a doubt.

She *had* sprung the question on him.

"I don't want to hurt you either." Her brow hurt with the intensity of the look she gave him back. She didn't have the perfect words, but perhaps that look could convey how much she meant all this. "Maybe that means we won't."

Except he was going to leave at some point. Pain was inevitable.

She exhaled and managed a slight smile. "Or maybe... Perry said something recently and it stuck with me. She said it better, but the gist is... Maybe it's impossible to be with someone and not get hurt in some way, eventually, but a relationship means you've decided that the joy is worth the pain."

The frown on his brow eased and his head tilted, thoughtful.

Another wave of goosebumps trickled across her skin, but she had to say it. "I've decided it is. That... the joy with you is worth the pain, however inevitable."

Her chest ached, because there was no sign on his face of *what* he was thinking.

Or maybe it ached because she was hollow. She'd carved these words out of herself and spread them out before him and now there was nothing left until he either stamped them into a bloody pulp, or gathered them up and scooped them back inside her.

Behind him, the waterfall gushed. A light offshoot trickled between the grey rock over his shoulder and sprayed into the pool several feet away.

That was the only sound—no reply from him.

"Knigh," she exhaled and rubbed her sore brow. "I've laid it all out. I've spelled out what I want, what I'm asking of you. It just remains for you to answer. Because much as I'm burning to kiss you"—under the surface, she ran her hands through the water between them—"to hold you, to take you right this second, I've sworn not to touch you until and unless you say *yes*." Her voice had thickened; her eyes stung. It wasn't so much the fear that he would say *no* that threatened to crack her voice or push out tears, it was...

It was saying all this. Being so open with her emotions. Laying herself so bare. Her throat, her insides, her *heart*—they were all raw.

His eyebrows flickered, and perhaps the side of his mouth lifted, though whether it was in a happy smile or a sad one, she couldn't have guessed. But the way he looked at her—it was tender, as though he saw how raw she was.

It gave her the strength to go on in spite of the rasp in her throat. "I don't want this to be like on the *Swallow*, or in the glow-worm cave. I don't want us to just give into a thing that's been bubbling away. We didn't make the decision to do anything more than screw in that cave, and at Yule we were rash and drunk and sad and longing. But this? I want *this* to be our choice. A decision made, not a desire given in to." She dragged in a lungful of air, despite the tightness of her chest. "So I need to know, Knigh. Do you want me? Do you want to *be* with me?"

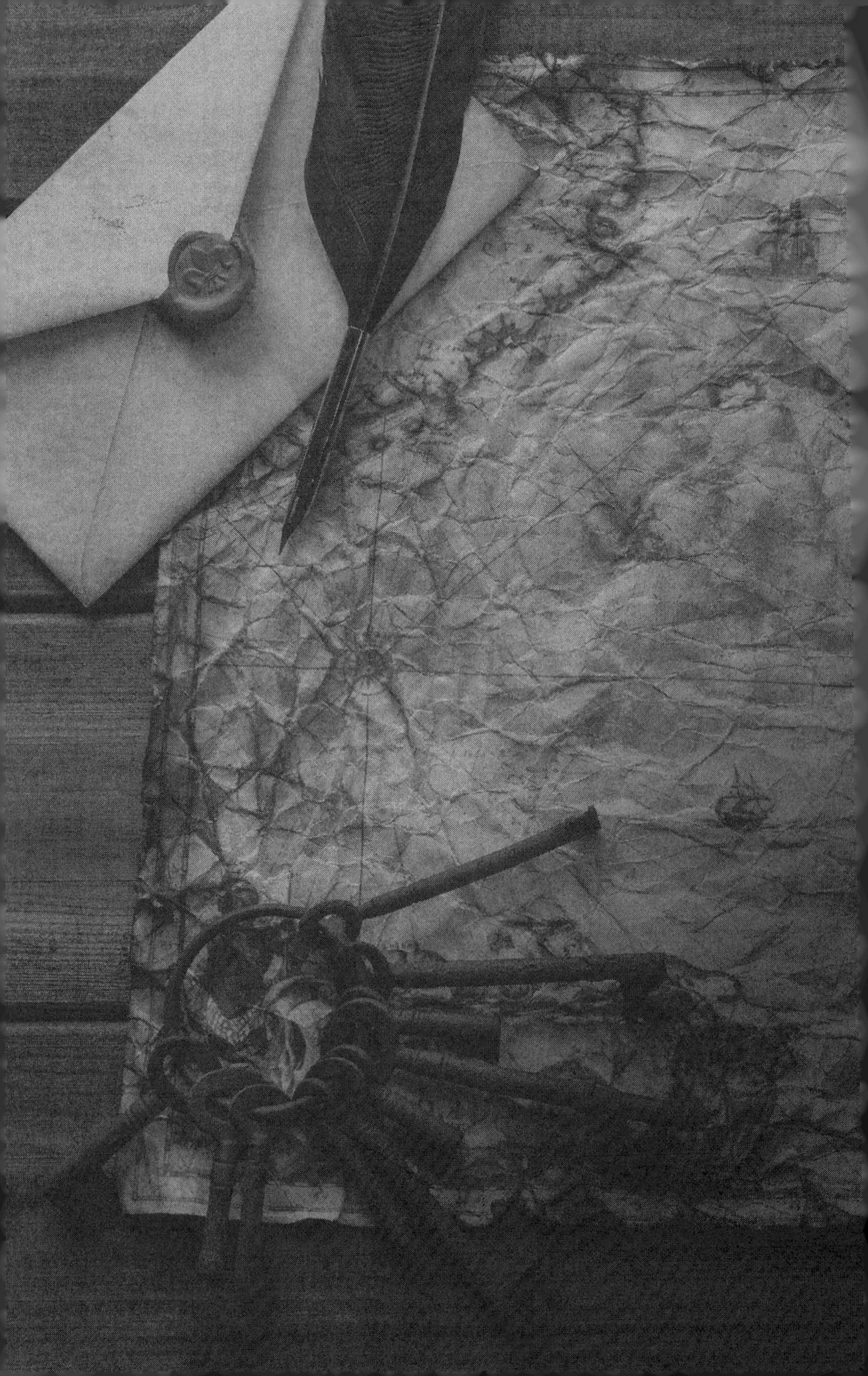

REWARD

A heartbeat passed. It might as well have been a century. But then a definite smile dawned on his mouth, and he came closer, barely more than a foot away.

As she held her breath, the rest of the clearing, the waterfall, whether the water was cool or the air hot—all of it faded until she only knew his every movement and response.

He exhaled what might've been a sigh of relief. Was that relief at her question or that fact she'd finished talking?

Would he please just *say* something?

His chin dipped, once, and she just stared at him, blinked, stared some more.

Wait. That... was that a nod?

That meant yes. That meant...

She let out the breath.

He wanted to be with her. He was taking up her offer to

explore what this was between them, to find out what they could be *together*.

Thank the gods she was in the water, because her knees gave out. "You do?"

His smile took on a wicked edge. Not cruel, but the same as she'd seen before when they were alone. Teasing. Eyes glinting. Rakish.

Her blood ran cold, then hot, then cold again, as though her body didn't know what to do with itself. What did he—?

"Do *I* want you?" He arched one eyebrow. "Now *there's* a question." And his voice? His voice had gone low, almost a purr.

"You... you nodded. I thought that was your answer. You..." She shook her head, throat too tight. He'd nodded and looked so close to saying yes. "I need to know you're sure," she rasped, "that you've decided."

"Oh, you'll have your answer. But I want to check I fully understand your question. That I'm not mistaken." He edged that bit closer and his hand rose from the water, glistening droplets falling from it. "So, you're asking whether I want you mentally"—her lungs stopped working as his thumb brushed down her temple, contact at last, warm and longed-for, a bright light in her awareness—"emotionally"—his hand lowered and he ran the backs of his knuckles from her collar bone to a spot right above her heart, where the swell of her breast began—"and physically?" His hand turned so the palm was over her heart and then slid back up that same path.

It was fire. *He* was fire and he'd set her ablaze.

For all the loaded looks and the lack of clothing, this was the first time they'd touched in this clearing, and it had her trembling like a fawn. She could barely exhale through it. She certainly couldn't speak, only nod to confirm it was what she was asking, what she needed him to answer.

On his face, the wickedness flickered, disappeared, and in its place was a warmth that had shone when they'd been reunited on the *Venatrix*. Inside her chest, something bloomed, as bright and warm as he was. That nod *had* been his answer. So what was this?

A second later, that glint returned, sparking and so very wicked. Damned.

His head cocked. "And you've sworn not to touch me until and unless I say my answer in the affirmative?"

Somehow this was a trap. Still, she swallowed, nodded.

"But this is allowed?" His eyebrows rose, echoing the question as he feathered his fingertips along her collarbone.

She nodded again, that apparently the only movement she could manage. At least the trembling had stopped.

He pulled his hand away. The cold inched in where he no longer was and she almost stumbled forward, as if invisible strings tied her to his fingers.

"Do you consent to me touching you?"

Didn't her response give it away? Her chin touched the water, once, twice.

He inclined his head, suddenly serious. "You can stop me at any time. A word and I'll stop."

"I know," she breathed. Before he'd said it, she'd known. He held the reins of whatever was happening right now, but only because she allowed it. She could back away or tell him no and that would be an end to it. They'd always played with power, teasing it from each other, granting it. Back and forth, back and forth, like ebb and flow tides.

But never stealing it. Never demanding it. Not like Fitz.

This was part of their pattern. Not knowing what he was doing had her off balance, but now she tethered it on a long mooring line to their play, she could ride the swell and wouldn't be washed away on his tide.

After watching her a long while, his seriousness vanished as suddenly as it had appeared. "Do I," he said, all wicked and glinting once more, "want to talk to you for hours on end?" The warmth edged into his eyes as he held her gaze and planed his fingers along the top of her shoulder. "Do I want to share the world with you?" The seductive purr vanished in that sentence, settling into something lower and thicker, something artless.

That hollow in her chest wasn't just full, it overflowed. Because he was posing these questions, but the way he asked them, the way he looked at her as he spoke—the answer to each was *yes*. It was unmistakable, as obvious as that streak of white hair. He just wanted to take his time saying it aloud.

Although waiting was sweet torture, she could do it.

"Do I want to touch you here?" His other hand joined in below the water, sliding up her arm. "Do I want to touch you *here?*" Just one fingertip, that was all it took, circling the spot where shoulder blended into neck, to tug the air from her lungs and streak a shiver through her. "Right where it makes you squirm because you enjoy it *so much* but it's also just that little bit ticklish?"

He knew her. That's what he was saying without saying.

How had he come to know her so well? It must've

happened somewhere between the enmity and the desire, the betrayal and the cruelty. They had spent a great deal of time together. In that time, he'd seen her at her most raw. And he was so observant, so vigilant—of course he'd noted every detail.

"Do I want to breathe your name in your ear"—he ran a fingertip down the edge of her ear, torturously light, and smiled as it reached her earring—"and kiss you here?" He forged a line downwards, grazing a sensitive spot that had her thighs tightening.

As if he could read the reaction on her face and had to hold back, he bit his lip. A long moment later, he cocked his head with a lazy smile. "Do I want to kiss you in the hollow of your neck"—his thumb slid there—"right where there's a drop of water that's glistening and just begging me to suck it from your skin?" He brought his thumb away with a glittering droplet on the tip, and, never taking his eyes from hers, he licked it off.

A sigh that was almost a moan fell from her lips at the sight of that pink tongue laving the pad of his thumb. She knew all too well what that tongue could do. Every inch of her flesh rose in goosebumps, lifting the hairs on the back of her neck.

Why had she made that bloody vow? Even worse, she'd told him about it. He'd given his answer, even if he hadn't said it out loud, but… She clenched her hands at her sides. She couldn't touch him. She *wouldn't*.

"Hmm." He narrowed his eyes as if contemplating her reaction. "Now, do I want to touch you here?" The back of his knuckles grazed down her breast and across her nipple bringing it to a tight peak. Then, smile broadening as he watched that response, he turned his hand over and ran his thumb over that same, sensitive tip.

She didn't just tremble now, she quaked as he drew slow circles around her nipple. This man... *This man.* To think she'd once expected some inexperience, perhaps even a level of innocence from him. She'd known he'd be good, but... straightforward. Not such a damn tease.

"Do I," he went on and she could only watch his lips and hope he'd put them upon her soon, "want to take this into my mouth and suck on it while I stare you straight in the eye and smile before biting, just a little?" He pinched and it shot right to her core, bright and searing, tugging a sound from her chest.

He ducked his head like he was about to tell her a secret. "I think you want me to," he whispered. The water let him press the pad of his thumb hard against her nipple but still glide across it in a slick circle.

She had to bite her tongue against the word quivering there. *Please.*

That would be begging. She didn't beg, but good gods, she might for him. But no. No *please*. Especially as saying that word would only let the others come spilling out after. *Please kiss me. Bite me. Take me. Harder. Faster. Now. Now. Now.*

"Do I want to cup this breast"—he did it as he spoke, attention now on the other, even as his thumb kept circling—"and knead it and pinch just here"—the nipple, leaving her tight and throbbing—"in that way I know makes you wet?"

Begging or not, she'd have got down on her knees right then and there if she hadn't been up to her neck in water. If he would just—

"Do I want to trail further south"—his fingers traced down over her ribs to her waist—"and touch every part of you"—her hips and belly—"explore every inch I can get my hands on until you scream my name?"

Breath held, she strained as his path continued lower, lower. He stopped on the edge of that dark hair, so close and yet...

She huffed in frustration.

He grinned, wolfish and wicked and wanton, and leant so close that if she turned her head, she'd kiss his temple. "And," he said, the word warm in her ear, "do I want to bury myself inside you and make you fall apart in my arms over and over and *over* again?"

If not for the water holding her weight, she'd have fallen at that question, that promise.

With a ragged rise and fall of his chest, he pulled back enough to meet her gaze. The grin was gone and he wore no mask. All that remained was him, grey eyes earnest as they flashed in the watery light, mouth now curving in a smile that was gentle and real, done toying with her.

There had never in all the world and every second of its history been a more beautiful sight than his face lit up at that moment.

It was an answer. Clear and bright and wondrous.

He wanted the same thing she did. He too thought the pain was worth enduring for the joy.

His throat constricted as he swallowed. "Yes, Vee," he said, voice rough, "I want all of it. I want all of you."

And he kissed her.

Her lips tingled as they pressed against his, because just touching wasn't enough—she wanted to be a part of him, for him to be a part of her, melded at every possible point of contact. Their tongues collided, slid together and apart and together again. Her hands were in his hair and her feet weren't on the stony floor of the pool anymore, though she had no recollection of telling any part of herself to move. But then, her body wasn't entirely her own around him.

His arms slid around her until there was no space between them, and nothing except the sea had ever felt so right.

At last. *At last.* They fit flush together and this time it had been a decision, not some war of attrition waged by their mutual desire.

The relief sent the world off-kilter, dizzying. Or perhaps it set the world right and it had been off-kilter up until now.

The hard planes of his chest against her breasts. The strength of his arms encircling her. His powerful thighs keeping them both upright. His body was as solid and reassuring as any harbour wall.

Apparently the touches around his endless, torturous questions hadn't been enough, because Knigh's hands planed over her shoulders, her back, her backside as though he was reminding himself of her exact form.

All she could do was cling to him and kiss back, slipping her tongue against his, running it over the roof of his mouth, retreating and letting his sweep into her mouth. Nothing had ever been sweeter than the taste of him—fruity and fresh like the pineapple he'd eaten from her hand.

He stiffened against her belly, which only made the throbbing at her core all the more insistent, the want—the *need* burning all the hotter. It was a wonder the pool sloshing around them didn't hiss and sizzle into steam.

At last, shivering, she cupped his cheeks and broke away, just far enough to get her breath back. Pressing her forehead to his, eyes still closed, she panted. His chest heaved against hers, too. "Knigh." She swallowed and looked into his grey eyes. "I've missed you."

Goosebumps speckled their way across his broad shoulders. "I'm here," he said, so simple, so raw, his voice a low rumble that filled her body.

When she wrapped her legs around him, bringing herself against his cock, he squeezed her with a groan that might've been her name. A shudder rippled through her from head to toe at the sound, at the touch.

Once her muscles were her own to command again, she clung to his shoulders and ground against his length, circling her hips, the friction turning heat to flame. She had to bite back a low cry at the delicious feel of his hardness right against her entrance and her sensitive bundle of nerves.

He wasn't unaffected. The column of his neck corded, rigid, and he swore. He panted, then seemed to realise he was losing control of the situation and grabbed her hips, easing the pressure.

Half a smile on his mouth, he shook his head as if to tell her off. One hand slid down her belly, his movement sending water rippling across her breasts and back—light sensation dancing across her skin in sublime contrast with the firm journey of his fingers, lower, lower.

Her breath caught when they glided between her legs and right across her centre. But not inside. He only stopped there, the light pressure teasing, unbearable.

Nostrils flaring, she exhaled through her nose, skin too hot, too tight, like her body couldn't contain all this sensation, all this aching need.

His teeth flashed in a grin, amused at her frustration. "And did you miss this?" He pressed the slightest bit harder, threatening to enter.

A whimper was all the answer she could give.

It was all he needed—his grin broadened as he plunged inside. "I can tell you did." His voice was hoarse, though, and when he'd said the words, he had to bite his lip. A sound still escaped from deep in his throat. "I've missed you, too. The feel of you."

Other hand kneading her arse, he took up a long, slow thrust with first one finger, then two. His touch drove through her, insistent, irresistible, stoking that fire within to a pleasure that was almost unbearable. Her back arched, out of her control, but she wanted more. She wanted *him* inside her, thicker, longer, driving harder, bringing him closer to her like nothing else could. She opened her mouth to say so, but…

His thumb joined in, keeping time with those languorous thrusts by circling her pearl, and the words died on her lips as she drowned in his consuming touch.

"And I missed the taste of you," he murmured, chest heaving, "but I'll have that later." The promise blazed through her, sinful and delicious. "For now, I want to watch you come undone for me."

And watch he did, eyes hooded, utterly riveted, like she was the most wondrous sight he'd ever beheld.

Crowned by his reverent gaze, she felt every bit the Pirate Queen.

He slung an arm under her backside and lifted her higher. Even with that manoeuvre, he didn't drop a single beat of his torturous rhythm. He lowered his head, eyes still on hers, and closed his mouth around her nipple, right where he'd touched and teased her earlier. Only then did he increase his pace inside her.

The fire he stoked was beyond fever, beyond sense, beyond... *beyond*.

But he kept her there, hovering right on the edge of explosion into nothingness, his speed and pressure just shy of exactly what she needed. And he damn well knew it.

She tried to talk, to tell him, to curse him, but it just came out as another whimper.

His eyes crinkled and glinted up at her like he was smiling —*smirking*, more like, and he sucked, then flicked his tongue over that tight tip. She bucked, tension twitching through every muscle, utterly beyond her control.

"Please," she gasped.

Pillaging her breasts with his mouth, keeping that smouldering look on her, he played her harder, deeper, faster, building the flames higher, higher, higher.

He was a tease. He was a bastard. He was damned. He was...

Then he inched his head back and grazed his teeth across her oversensitive nipple, releasing it, and smiled.

All thought vanished.

There was only darkness and sparks like what was left behind after a powder keg exploded.

Then the trembling of her body, each muscle taut, and her cries that filled the clearing. Her body eased as he held her, fingers still driving, still stroking, albeit slower now.

And his eyes on her, bright, happy.

When she'd returned to Nassau after that terrible trip to Albion and the awful ocean crossing, it had struck her, hard and comforting at once—*home*. She was home.

This was the same.

Chest full, she pulled him close and kissed him. Kissed him for all the times she couldn't. For all the times she'd snapped. For all the times she'd been cruel. For all the times he'd shown her the broken parts of himself. For all the times she'd only been able to offer a touch to comfort him. For so many missed opportunities and misunderstandings and misused moments.

He returned those kisses as if ravenous for her—for *all* of her as he'd said before—before finally pulling away a hair's breadth.

She sighed against his lips, the sound laced with a whimper for the insistent touch he maintained inside and upon her, that kept her simmering on the edge of another orgasm. Her veins felt bright and hot, crackling almost, like when she dug deep into the wellspring.

Body shuddering as he built her pleasure again, she nuzzled against his bearded jaw, letting her gestures say what she could not. This was different. This was whole, not broken like the last time, on the *Swallow*. This was *them* and yet new.

Because she *felt*. She felt for him something that was uncharted territory.

A smile on the edge of his mouth, he grazed his nose across hers like he knew, like he felt the same.

The knot that had been tied in her for a long, long while eased. Still there, but looser. And it made her tremble against him.

And that trembling only built as he kept driving and circling, circling and driving, in a silent, irresistible demand.

The stubble on his neck, below the trimmed beard, grazed when she whispered his name and kissed his throat, like he was some god who needed to be appeased with prayers from her lips.

And maybe it was that additional sensation, or the loosening knot, or just that she was oversensitive after climaxing once... Maybe all of it together made her peak rise from the ashes of the last one. She came for him, hard and fast, crying out his name while he burned her to sublime nothingness.

Barely able to breathe, she clung to him and blinked to new awareness. He'd torn her apart and pulled her back together twice now, holding off on his own pleasure, and she ached to bring him to that edge and send him spiralling over.

She could do it with her mouth and tongue, she enjoyed the way his hips bucked when she did that. But this time, this first time in far, far too long, she wanted it to be face to face where she could put her mouth on his and see every sweet, aching expression he made.

Threading her fingers through his hair, she kissed him and

pulled his hand away. She couldn't help but shudder as he left her suddenly empty. But it would only be temporary.

It barely took a few strokes to bring him to full attention and she smiled into the kiss as her touches drew a low moan from his mouth vibrating into hers. He held her hips with both hands now, and as she stroked and explored him, running her thumb over the tip, his grip grew tighter.

How he hadn't died from anticipation was beyond her. It pulsed in her—raw need to have him beyond close, beyond the boundaries of her skin, to have him, to claim him utterly, and *she'd* already reached that peak of pleasure.

And she needed it because it wasn't only about the pleasure. It was about him and it was about her and this new thing between them. It was about sealing that with their bodies. About celebrating it. About their flesh saying what their tongues were too clumsy for.

With her thighs she pulled herself over him, letting the water hold her weight so she waited half an inch away, unbearably close.

His chest heaved like he was barely holding himself together. Somehow, that grip on her hips remained the same, not pulling her onto him like his lust-darkened eyes said he wanted.

Even as a pirate, Knigh Blackwood was a man of control.

That thought making her smile, she nodded and placed his solid tip at her entrance.

Apart from those ragged breaths, he still didn't move. His eyes, though. They scorched like molten steel.

"Now," she commanded, voice husky.

One more rise and fall of that solid chest and he pulled. Not fast, but not as slowly as he'd done their first time—maybe the waiting had been too much even for his control.

And hers wasn't fairing much better. She'd wrestled power from him with that order, but as he slid into her, shivers threaded through every inch of her body, stealing her breath clean away.

Oh, Lords, she'd forgotten how it felt, how he filled her, just how much of him there was. He wasn't even done yet.

Inches later, he was. They paused there, sharing air and a long look. This—*this* was the closeness she'd craved and the time afterwards when they'd talk and tomorrow when they'd wake together. All of it. All of him.

And all of him was there in eyes that smouldered as though he'd banked what would otherwise be a roaring flame. Such burning potential.

It sent another shiver through her.

She planted a single, sweet kiss on his mouth and smiled before giving her next order: "Don't hold back."

Before he could respond, she looped her arms behind his neck and used that and her thighs as leverage to ride the full length of him.

His lips parted as surprise flashed in the depths of his grey eyes. Then his fingers twitched against her hips and he dragged her onto him, adding depth to the rhythm she'd set.

She stole his mouth in a deep, entwining kiss. Their wet bodies slipped against each other as she rode him as slowly as she could bear, making each stroke long and deliberate until he shook under her touch.

She whispered against his lips. "I said, don't hold back."

Maybe that was the permission he'd been waiting for or needing, because the moment she finished the sentence, he turned that delving kiss back on her and he *surged*. Water rushed against her back and it took a second to realise they were moving. He strode through the pool, one hand coming up to cup her head, to tug her hair, angling her until he found the exact position he needed to thoroughly and completely plunder her mouth.

In the face of that onslaught, she couldn't breathe, couldn't *think*, could only continue pounding herself onto him again and again.

A side branch of the waterfall sprayed over them, cool and slick for a second, bringing her back to herself. Then solid stone was at her back, and he drove her into it, each stroke long and hard, building pressure at her very centre.

This. This. This.

They were utterly one. She didn't know if she was crying out or he was, didn't care. All that mattered was this, was him, was them.

Focus solidified the planes of his face. Droplets of water glistened on his skin, in his hair, a rivulet running down his temple, his cheek, and disappearing into his cropped beard. He'd never looked so wild, so beautiful, so alive.

With her wedged between him and the waterfall's sheer rock face, he released her hip and the back of her head and grabbed her wrists. A second later, he had them above her head, wrapped in the fingers of one hand, rasping against the worn-smooth stone.

She couldn't move beyond tilting her hips for the sweetest friction, the deepest access, but she did that, and she granted him that power over her.

Push and pull, ebb and flow. She surrendered to his tide. For now.

One hand freed, he palmed her breast, circled her nipple, cupped her face as he kissed and drove and kissed and drove, and every fibre of her body became nothing more than throbbing, writhing, raw pleasure a hair's breadth from shattering.

He drew out, plunged in, again, again, again, the movement more urgent, more demanding. The grip on her wrist squeezed, and his neck corded as tightly as an anchor cable. Still more tension rose in every part of his body. He was close. So close.

And she watched his build with greedy eyes even as the relentless pace of him drove cries from her open mouth, even as her head spun.

She wanted, needed to see it, the moment when pleasure wrung him out.

His brows were tight together, each breath tore through him like a raging animal, and his eyes had turned from molten steel to a wildfire, utterly frenetic, utterly consuming, and entirely fixed upon her.

That wildness sent her hurtling over the edge like the river above rushing into these falls, and she fell apart into shimmering pieces of bright joy.

It was only sheer determination that forced her eyes open, even as the orgasm's ending still ripped through her. Just as she managed to focus, his eyes rolled, then squeezed shut. He shuddered with a harsh cry and finished deep inside her, pulsing with completion. No mask, no holding back, just his parted lips and that crease of tension between his brows that finally gave into slackening relief and wonder.

Sublime.

And so near. No more keeping him at arm's length. No more resisting his allure. No more pushing him away. He was closer than close, a part of her.

Tremors still ran through her as he released her wrists, their chests crushing together. Loose-limbed, she barely registered where her hands landed, but she buried her face in the crook between his neck and shoulder and breathed him in—sweet and woody, spiced with cinnamon, and so warm, so *him*.

She kissed his shoulder, his throat, the hollow at its base, and murmured, "Knigh." As though that were a tether to the real world they'd temporarily left while they'd been lost in each other.

Hands running up and around her shoulders, he grazed his lips over that spot below her ear and left it tingling.

When he pulled back, all the restraint he'd used to bank his burning desire had vanished. His grey eyes were clear, bright. His flushed face was at ease, unmasked, with just a lazy smile tugging on his mouth.

She'd told him not to hold back and, good gods, he hadn't. All those other times, they had been just a fraction of him—Knigh restrained. With something close to a laugh, she stroked his cheek. He truly had given all of himself, just as she'd asked.

Such responsibility. She shivered. She had to work to be ready for it, worthy of it.

"Your hand." He frowned, capturing her fingers. A red graze

marred the back. He glanced at the stone above her head, where he'd held her wrists. "Sorry, I didn't..."

"It's fine." She shrugged. "Barely more than a carpet burn."

"The perils of sex. Who knew it was such a dangerous sport?" He arched an eyebrow. "Maybe we shouldn't do it anymore. I can't have—"

"Don't even joke about that," she growled. "I've only just got you back."

He chuckled and kissed her knuckles. "You have. But I'm not sure you want questions about this interesting injury. Allow me." He covered the scrape with his palm as that gold glow warmed the air between them.

Sunshine. Pure, bright sunshine on her skin, as pleasurable as lying on the grass, loose-limbed with daylight on closed eyelids. Another tremor tensed her around him, making her gasp, dizzying for an instant. A low sound rose from his throat, whether from her tightness or because he felt that same pleasure, she couldn't say.

However, there was more to his gift than that, and she dragged herself back, gritting her teeth ready for the pain...

But it never came.

When he removed his hand, the red mark had gone and she frowned from the smooth skin to him. "It... didn't hurt." Quite the opposite—that pleasure had been...

His wet shoulders gleamed as they rose and fell. "No, for such a small injury, it usually doesn't." He ran a thumb over her tanned skin as though checking his work. There wasn't so much as a scar—no pallor or redness. Nothing.

"Have you ever healed someone during sex?"

His brows shot up. "Of course not. If I'm healing someone, it's usually pretty serious."

"But not always." She flexed her healed knuckles, before sliding her fingers behind his neck and into his thick hair. If a mild dose of his gift had that effect in the aftermath, what could it do *during?*

Eyes narrowed, he gave her a thoughtful look as though he was wondering the same thing. He gave her another kiss before withdrawing from her, the emptiness eased by the fact it wouldn't be for long. Knowing Knigh, knowing *them*, they'd do this all over again before leaving the clearing.

He backed away from the rock, one hand keeping her against him, and walked to shallower water.

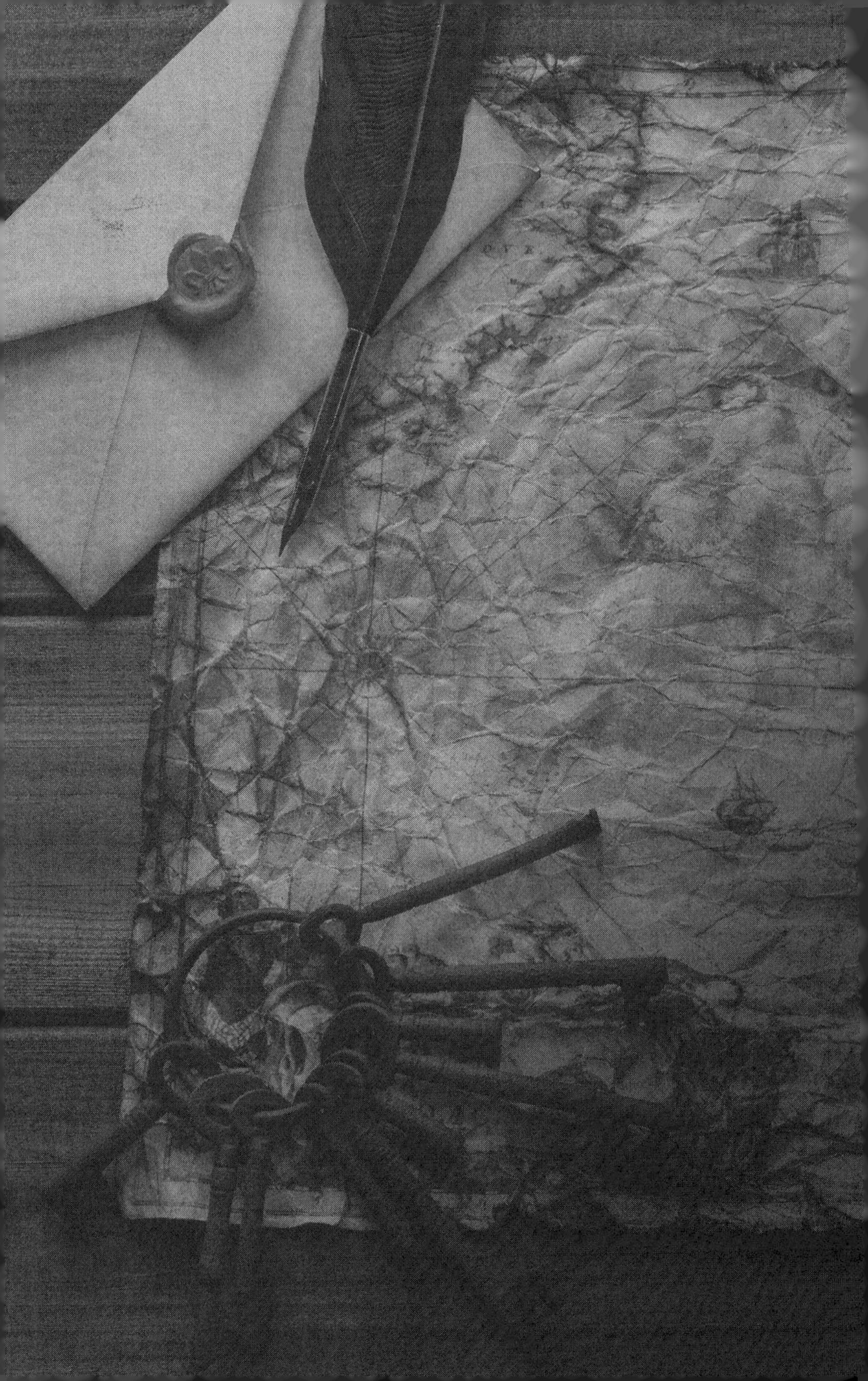

ONE THING AT A TIME

With the water rippling in their wake, Knigh marvelled at the reassuring weight of her in his arms. She was here. She was his. And she'd asked for him with an honesty, a rawness that still shook him.

So he'd given himself to her entirely.

When she'd told him not to hold back, it had so disarmed him that it had taken every ounce of willpower not to spill inside her right then and there. But he'd mastered himself and at her second command, he'd unleashed for her.

All the times he'd rolled over in the night and reached out to find the bunk empty. All the desperation and fear when Vane had taken her and Mercia had held her. Every wild want, every aching need, every moment that he'd longed to hold her, to kiss her, to take her...

He'd let it all free. And the moment it had ended him,

surging with irresistible, blinding intensity, he'd thought he might die from it.

Nothing in his life had been more powerful.

It had left him light-headed, and even now, the world on the edge of his vision spun slowly.

As he waded through the water she kissed his throat, his neck, his shoulders and chest, little crackling marks on his flesh, on his soul. A brand that said he was hers.

He was, gladly.

The water sheeted from them as they emerged from the pool, her legs still wrapped around his middle until he deposited her on the sandy silt and flopped beside her.

She stretched out on the sloping beach, long-limbed, all lithe muscle and tantalising curves. Every inch of her glistened with moisture like she was some fae creature sparkling in the night. He couldn't resist running his hand across her tanned skin, gathering those glittering droplets of water, planing them up her belly, her sternum, to the hollow of her throat where they formed a little pool. She watched his progress and he could tell from how shallow her breaths were that she was holding still for him.

Muscles slack for once, he dipped his finger into that little pool of water and smiled.

She gave him a sidelong look and grinned. "Tired out already?"

"No." He flicked the water from his finger in her face, making her yelp. "It's just the world's still spinning."

"Tell me about it." She wiped the water from her cheek before closing her eyes.

So he wasn't the only one this affected. With what *might* have been a smug smile, he rolled onto his back and gathered her to his side, then planted a kiss to her brow.

"Let's give the world a moment to right itself." Though it felt pretty damn right already, with the full length of her body against him, her arm around his waist, her head on his chest, and now her fingers tracing idle patterns on his belly. Speaking of the world... "I wonder what the others will think."

When her face angled towards him, it wore a wince. "About that... Would you mind if we don't tell them straight away?"

"Vee." He lifted his eyebrows in mock affront. "Are you ashamed of me?"

She scoffed, the movement pressing her breasts against the side of his ribcage. "Don't be ridiculous." She draped her thigh over his as though staking a claim. "I just..." The wrinkle forming between her brow was raw, vulnerable, like it had been earlier when she'd spilled her feelings. "This is... a lot. Even now, my heart is..." She placed a hand over his and tapped a too-fast beat. "I need to get used to it, and it'll be easier if I'm not also having to deal with everyone else's reactions. I want to deal with—"

"With one thing at a time."

Her body eased with an exhale, like she'd been holding it. "That's it exactly."

It made total sense. This was uncharted territory. They needed to discover what they were and what they could be.

It felt right, yes, but that didn't mean it was pure joy every second. She knew him at his best and his worst and yet she was still here. It was thrilling and bright in his chest. But also perhaps a little frightening.

He'd never... felt like this about anyone. He'd had crushes and lovers, but nothing with this intensity. He hadn't lied when he'd told Vee he'd never been in love.

His heartbeat stuttered.

He wasn't foolish enough to think this would be easy for her. She'd spent years living behind the walls she'd built after Evered's death, telling herself the spectacular lie that she didn't feel the *soft emotions* as she'd called them back on *The Morrigan*.

Plus, she might've claimed her relationship with FitzRoy had been purely physical, but it had lasted a couple of years and he'd been there when Evered had died. In his own way, he'd helped her move past it. He could acknowledge that, even if the thought of the man made Knigh's fingers itch to throttle him. The relationship must've meant something. His *betrayal* must've meant something.

She still watched him, that crease there, and he gave her a reassuring smile, squeezing with the arm looped around her back.

Of course she needed time to adjust without pressure from the rest of the crew. Perhaps their friends most of all. Wynn and Effie would start planning their wedding the instant they knew. Perry would be all knowing looks and questions that were well-meaning but risked pushing Vee more than she was ready for. Lizzy would grill him the next time they worked together. She'd probably make some excuse about needing help to take an inventory of her herbs and poultices, but the instant she had him alone, it would turn into a full-on interrogation.

As for Saba, that was a reaction he couldn't predict. A few days ago, there would've been no doubt. He'd have said she'd be happy for Vee and would tease him. But last night she'd acted strangely. With how physical the pirates tended to be compared to the stiff aristocratic society he'd grown up in, and the way the genders mixed with ease unlike all-male naval life, he struggled to know quite where the lines between friendship and flirtation were. But the way she'd touched his chest and angled her head up to him. That might've crossed the line.

Then there was Aedan...

But they weren't here. Vee was. He took her fingers, still resting on his chest, and pulled them to his lips. "That makes perfect sense. Take all the time you need." Having her, having *this* was what mattered. He squeezed her closer again and grazed his lips over her brow as she went back to tracing those lazy spirals across his chest, his ribs, his belly.

There was still a stiffness in her shoulders, as though she carried a weight. Perhaps this was all too serious, too heavy.

"So." He let a grin cover his face, unguarded. "The secrecy definitely *isn't* because you're ashamed of me, then?"

She jolted and stared up at him, but narrowed her eyes on seeing his expression. "You're joking, right?"

He shrugged one shoulder, easing the grin into a smirk. "Of course I am—how could you be ashamed of this?" Eyebrow raised, he indicated his body spread on the sand, half under her.

Long before he'd told her it was rude to stare, he'd felt her watching him. Even when he'd still been a pirate hunter, the enemy, she'd never hidden that she liked what she saw, especially not today. And when he'd turned and her gaze had roved across him, he'd loved every damn second of it, imagining it was her hands and mouth exploring, caressing his flesh, not just a look.

She snorted, and he shook with barely suppressed laughter.

The whites showed around her irises as she shook her head. "Wow." She hooked her leg over further and rested her hands on his chest until she sat straddling him. Frustratingly, she held her weight on her knees, keeping herself inches above his cock, now twitching to life. "Have you got even more arrogant?"

"If I have, it's your fault." His hands needed no instruction from his brain to find their way to her knees, her thighs. One finger swirled its way along the lines of her tattoo, starting on her thigh and trailing up to the side of her hip.

"How do you figure that one out?"

"You're the one who's been working so hard to make me believe in myself more, you didn't think that would come without any side effects, did you?" His smirk eased as he let it show just how much he appreciated her help, her belief in him. But that was too serious and he was meant to be lightening the mood, so after a few seconds, he let the smirk return in full force. "Well, that and the way you've been looking at me for weeks."

Expression narrowing in calculation, she pursed her lips. "Oh really? How does a look bring out *this*?"

He raised his chin, cocky, before yanking her hips down.

The flash of her eyes said she hadn't been expecting it, and she put up no resistance, so she came down on him, her slick centre resting over his length. "Having the Pirate Queen stare at you like she wants to devour you would be enough to drive any man to the height of conceit." He tried to say it all light and teasing, but he'd expected her thighs to tense and stop her from dropping onto him so easily, and that warm line of her brought a rough edge to his voice.

"Devour you, eh?" She arched an eyebrow and gave a wolfish grin. "Now you mention it..."

She slid backwards, peppering kisses and long laves of her tongue down his body, only stopping to suck his nipple and flick her tongue over it, sending pleasure crackling through him. He clutched a handful of sand when she finally took him in her mouth. The sight of her lips around his cock was almost enough to destroy him, but he gritted his teeth and held on for dear life.

Some time later, when he'd pulled her away and pressed her onto her back to finally get his own taste of her—even sweeter than he remembered—and after he'd knelt between her legs and pulled her onto him in the sand and had taken her far more gently than earlier... After all that, they swam and played in the water, washing off the silty sand and the sex, but unable to resist touching. A kiss on the cheek or shoulder. Clambering onto his shoulders and demanding he carry her through the pool. Tugging her hand until she was in his arms again. Fingertips brushing as they floated on their backs, staring at the sky and talking then falling silent.

And even later than that, stomachs rumbling despite eating the supplies they'd brought in their bags, they gathered themselves and dressed, and worked through the forest, foraging for fruit as they went. They talked a lot, laughed a lot, kissed more times than he could say, and somehow wound up making love once more, against a cinnamon tree this time as they lost themselves in each other and the spicy scent of its crushed bark.

Eventually, the sounds of work and voices threaded through the forest as they approached camp, his arm around her shoulders, hers around his waist. He couldn't help but sigh and pull Vee a little closer because those sounds meant one thing. Their blissful afternoon was over. Even the sun agreed, low in the sky, sinking into evening.

Once they reached the edge of the trees, they'd have to pretend they were nothing more than friends. He'd have to bite back the desire to crow from the main top that he was hers. Still, he could pull her in for one more kiss, and she'd already said she'd sneak into his tent tonight, since she was better at—

Ahead, something rustled.

Vee yanked out of his hold as if zapped by one of her own lightning bolts.

Shoulders sinking, he folded his arms as if that would make up for the lack of her in them.

Ahead, Saba rounded the corner, arms full of firewood. She stopped mid-stride, eyebrows flashing in surprise before a smile eased into place. But the expression stiffened as she watched them both.

"Saba," Vee said with too bright a smile, "been busy, huh? Let me help." She ducked into the undergrowth and started gathering twigs and branches.

Tilting her head, Saba threw him a questioning look.

"I'd best get back to my mother and sister." He inclined his head. "See you both later."

"Aye." Vee looked up as he passed and held eye contact a moment longer than necessary.

"See you later, Knigh," Saba piped up, something feline in the curve of her mouth as she watched him from below her thick, dark lashes.

He nodded again and strode to the beach camp, suppressing a wince.

"Where have you two been all day?" Saba's voice drifted in his wake.

"Oh, I think he'd gone swimming and I was, you know, around, foraging and so on," Vee replied. "We just bumped into each other on the way..."

He was too far away to hear the rest, but he'd caught the edge of something in Saba's tone. The way she'd looked at him as he'd left, the way she'd touched him last night. That had to be flirtation. Not for the first time, either.

And then there was that strange dare she'd thrown at Vee back on Hewanorra, something challenging in it.

His straight back sank a touch. Something said that wasn't the last time Saba would flirt with him either. So far, he'd managed to put her off politely, but if she didn't get the picture that he wasn't interested, and he couldn't put her off by explaining he was with Vee...

He raked a hand through his hair, wincing. Things were going to get awkward if he couldn't find a way of turning her down that left no doubt of his lack of interest while also being gentle enough to not harm their friendship.

Ahead, Billy sat with Mother and Is beneath the canvas shelter they were using as a kind of parlour. He sighed and squared his shoulders. Now he had to face his sister and hope their secret wasn't written all over his face in that language she seemed to understand too well.

At least it would only be secret for a while. Just until Vee got used to the idea.

His heart dipped a beat. He and Vee. Actually together. And in something real, something that wasn't *just bodies*, perhaps even something serious.

He didn't even try to suppress the beaming smile that spread across his face as he approached the makeshift parlour. He'd have to come up with some excuse when his sister inevitably asked, but it would be worth it—there were precious few reasons in life to smile like this and he would make the most of this one.

Even if he couldn't crow it from the main top quite yet.

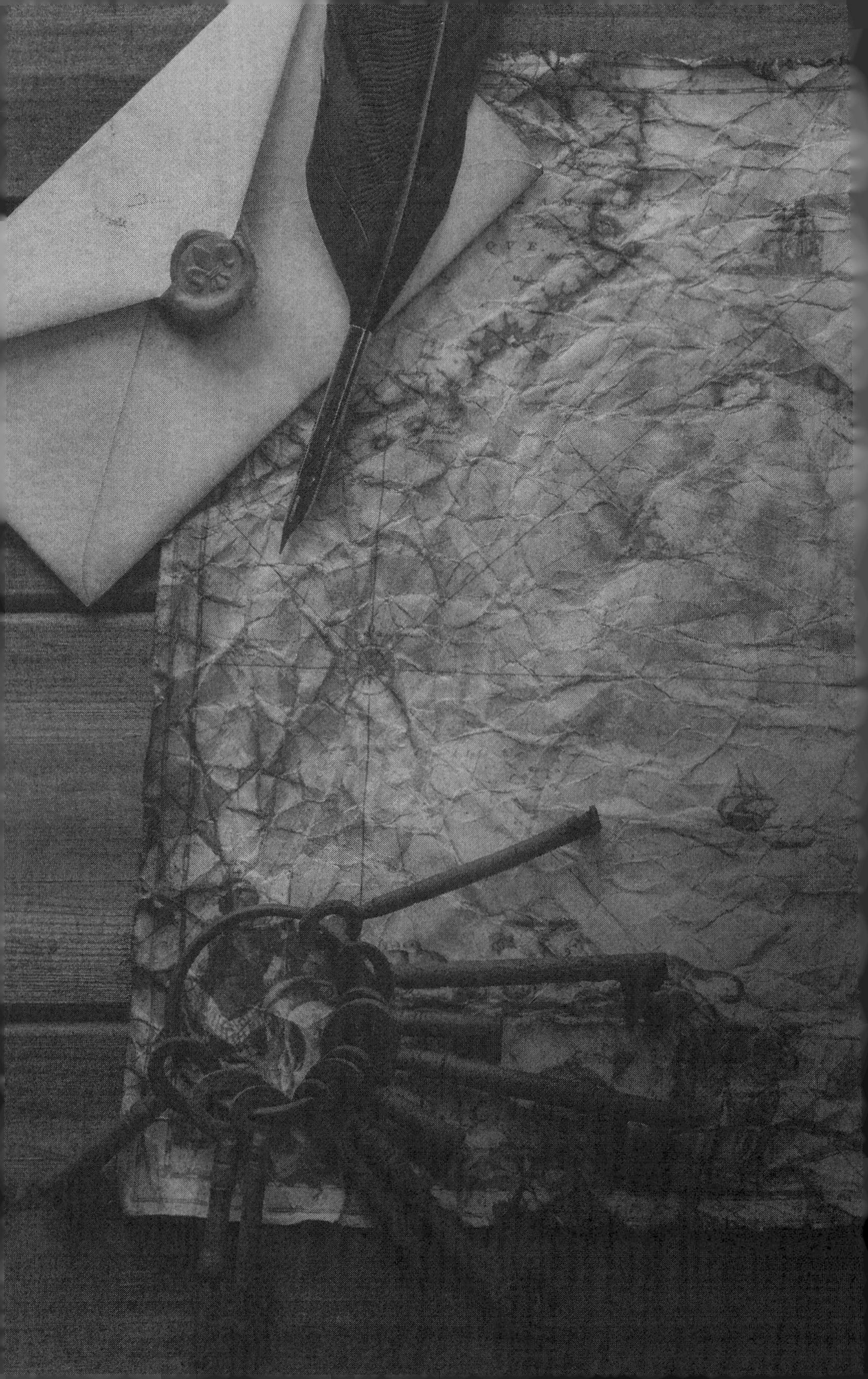

LADY ISABEL VILLIERS

Over the next four days as the repairs to the *Swallow* took shape, Vice took every opportunity to sneak away with Knigh between their duties, which included looking after Barnacle and the kittens as well as working on the Copper Drake. One morning, they hiked to a small, secluded beach with a coral reef not far from shore. Another day, they returned to their pool.

Although their relationship was a secret, Perry knew. It was almost impossible to keep anything from her when she seemed to understand the situation at a glance. That first time, when Vice had emerged from the forest at Saba's side with an armful of wood, she'd given her a look and raised her eyebrows in question. Vice had nodded and Perry had beamed.

Perhaps she'd learned from prodding too quickly on *The Morrigan*, because she didn't ask anything else, leaving Vice and Knigh to their sneaking.

Once the *Swallow* was ready to set sail again and they'd broken camp, Vice stood shoulder-to-shoulder with him on the beach, the backs of their knuckles brushing as if it was just an accident. As boats carried the last equipment and pirates back to their respective ships, Billy explained that Knigh's family would be safe at his home for now and threw Lady Villiers a winning smile.

Knigh's mother nodded, before her gaze passed to Vice. It set her teeth on edge.

Lady Villiers hadn't mentioned anything about Avice Ferrers, had barely said more than a dozen words to Vice at all, but she kept *looking*. Did she see the resemblance to the little girl she'd known? The changed eye colour tended to throw most people off, since it was usually a constant, but she still had the same pointed chin and dark hair, and although her eyes were a different colour, they were still that same shape. Knigh hadn't recognised her, but maybe his mother would the more she stared.

Billy went on, promising Lady Villiers she and her daughter would be well looked after.

"Thank you." Knigh squeezed his shoulder. "I find myself even deeper in your debt."

"Not in the slightest. I'm only glad I can help." With Billy's open smile and round eyes, Vice believed it.

"We're ready, Captain," Lyr piped up behind him. It had only been months since Knigh had pulled him from the night sea, but Vice was sure he'd grown taller in that short time. He threw her and Knigh shy glances and a sketched bow, whether it was out of habit or because Knigh was technically still a viscount, she couldn't say.

"Good. Right." Billy's brows drew together. "Where's Lady Isabel?"

Knigh didn't even need to search, he nodded up the beach's gentle slope. "Getting tips from troublemakers by the look of it."

Ah, yes, a flash of blonde hair below a dainty blue hat, sheltered from the sun at the edge of the forest. Is nodded, deep in conversation with Wynn and Effie.

Vice touched the small of his back. "I'll fetch her." At least that would free her from his mother's looks.

Wynn spotted her and waved before she and Effie hugged Isabel farewell. It seemed Knigh wasn't the only Villiers sibling who didn't mind befriending pirates.

Before Vice reached them, Isabel left the sisters and approached. Once those blue eyes were on her, a prickle traced over the back of her neck.

"Lady Isabel," she said with a stiff smile, "I'm sorry to steal you away but—"

"We're ready to leave. Yes, I gathered." Isabel smiled in return, apparently at ease, but her head cocked in a way that was anything but easy. "Can you believe this is the first time I've caught you alone?"

"*Is* it?" Vice forced a ripple of laughter through her words as though she hadn't realised until now. As though she hadn't avoided the young lady and her mother the whole time they'd shared this camp.

She turned to start for the boat where Knigh, Billy, and

Lady Villiers waited, but Isabel's feet remained planted in the sand.

"So you're the woman my brother couldn't get out of his head."

Vice stopped, swallowed, then raised her brows at Isabel as though she didn't even *know* her brother. Oh, gods. What had Knigh *said?*

Isabel's sky blue eyes scrutinised her, sharp in that they seemed to miss nothing, and sharp in that if Vice made a wrong move, they might cut deeply. "He told me about you when he visited at the end of last year. Couldn't keep his hands off that little shell you gave him. He was consumed by the thought of your trial and sentencing. It was like a ghost visited us, rather than my brother."

Now Vice's brows rose in true surprise. Knigh had told his family about her, even when they'd been enemies? But... no, she shook her head. That was before he knew she was Avice Ferrers —he couldn't have told them that. Her breathing eased.

"He said you weren't what he'd expected. I see what he means." Those too-sharp eyes narrowed. "Not so much notorious as..." A crease dipped between her brows. "Hmm. In another life you might've been like me, I think."

Like me. She meant *a Lady* with a capital *L*. Every hair on the back of Vice's neck strained to attention. It was fine. Isabel was fishing; she knew nothing for sure. Picking up on her accent wasn't that big a deal, not when everyone called her *Lady* Vice. It wasn't that great a leap to wonder if she had some aristocracy in her past.

She cleared her throat and seized the conversation's reins:

"Your mother's waiting." She tried to channel Knigh at his most controlled as she said it, but it came out too light. Pushing back her shoulders, she started towards the boat, letting Isabel follow or not. She did. Better.

"She is, but I'm more interested in my brother. What are your intentions towards him?"

A laugh burst out of Vice. "My intentions? Like I'm some flirtatious earl and he's an innocent debutante and *you're* the elder brother?"

Isabel chuckled softly, and her eyes shone with amusement, but something harder still glittered in their depths.

Despite the laughter still lingering on her lips, Vice shuddered. Isabel was as bad as Perry, *seeing* everything.

Urgh, Isabel might even be worse, though Vice had never thought it possible—at least Perry *said* the things she thought, asked awkward questions right away. Isabel just calculated quietly, as if storing all that knowledge up, then probed for more. What the hells was she planning to do with it?

"One thing my brother said about you did stump me," she said, as though she didn't need an answer to her earlier question. As though she'd worked it out. Which would be impressive, considering Vice wasn't entirely sure of her intentions towards Knigh herself. "When he visited, he seemed sure Lady Avice Ferrers was dead and Lady Vice was her murderer."

Somehow Vice's legs still moved, carrying her closer to Knigh and Billy and Lady Villiers where she'd be safe from these questions, since Isabel only seemed to want to ask them in private.

But Isabel had said those names in the same sentence. Too

close. Far too close. She managed to pull her shoulders into a shrug, though she couldn't say *What of it?*

"And yet by the time he wrote to me," Isabel went on, "he claimed it was all a misunderstanding and you hadn't killed her." Vice didn't dare look, but she could see enough in the periphery of her vision to know those clear blue eyes cut into her. "What I don't understand is, how one 'misunderstands' that someone murdered a person. Either you killed her or you didn't." Her slender fingers closed on Vice's forearm. "Or did you use your fae charm on him?"

The grip wasn't strong—Isabel was a true lady in that regard, but that, coupled with her final question, made Vice stop and turn. Isabel looked up at her, delicate brows drawn together, fine jaw tight.

Vice exhaled when she saw it. "You're worried for him." This sharpness, it was all to protect her brother, ensure he was safe and not being manipulated by the notorious Pirate Queen. She exhaled, managing to keep it this side of a laugh. Isabel didn't know Knigh was fae-touched and so was immune to fae charm.

"Can you blame me?"

"Not at all. But I can assure you that I didn't murder Lady Avice Ferrers. Nor did I or have I ever used fae charm on your brother, and I never will." She inclined her head, punctuating the statement with finality.

Isabel's shoulders sank as she exhaled. "Good." With that, she resumed her sedate pace.

Thank the gods they were only ten feet from Knigh and the

boat that would carry her away. Vice huffed a sigh, the back of her neck settling.

"Although," Isabel said, sliding her a sidelong look, "if Lady Avice isn't dead, where on earth has she been all these years?"

Vice's face tingled, but then they were in the group, Knigh gathering Isabel into a hug and kissing the top of her head before lifting her into the boat. She sat beside her mother, and as she arranged her skirts, she gave Vice a smile, the glittering sharp edges at bay. "Thank you for your reassurances, madam." She nodded once, then the smile turned narrow. "I'm glad we could have a chat. It's been most enlightening."

Sickly smile plastered on her face, Vice inclined her head again. Enlightening? What the hells did that mean? Damn it, this supposedly innocent girl had seen something, *knew* something. It was a good thing she was about to sail away to Billy's home where she couldn't uncover anything else with nothing more than a look and some unanswered questions.

Billy hopped over the gunwale, his grin as bright as ever, glad to be getting back to his ship and the wide sea. "Madam." With a wink, he half-bowed to Vice and took a seat beside Isabel.

Predictable. Vice arched an eyebrow at him, then at Isabel and it was a triumph to see the latter shift uncomfortably. At least she'd managed to turn the tables before they parted ways.

In a flurry, Billy's men surrounded the boat, with Vice and Knigh at the stern, and pushed her into the next wave. Isabel scowled and kept fidgeting with her skirts.

"Good luck with married life, Mrs Hopper," Vice called by

way of parting shot as the wave lifted the vessel and its oars dipped into the surf.

Billy's mouth dropped open before they were carried away, but Vice only laughed and waved.

There was clear attraction between Isabel and Billy, which only made it all the more amusing that she and Lady Villiers were going to live in his house, posing as his wife and mother-in-law to keep them safe from Mercia and any other prying eyes. Between Billy and Isabel and her and Knigh, the *Swallow* was fast becoming the ship of fake marriages.

As they started towards the *Venatrix's* boat, Knigh glanced at the retreating forms of Billy and his family. He brushed her elbow. "Imagine if they knew who you really were."

She twitched away, the horror of it jolting through her afresh. "They can never know."

He huffed a laugh, a frown etched between his brows as he shook his head and grazed her arm. "I was only joking."

"Jokes are meant to be funny." Heart beating too fast, shoulders stiff, she pulled away again. "And stop touching me in front of everyone. That's a secret too, remember?"

"Of course I bloody remember." The way his shoulders sank speared through her irritation. "I want to tell everyone I see, shout it from every mast, maybe even paint it across my face, but I say nothing. I've told no one. Because I respect that you need time."

Her shoulders sank, the tension deflating. "I'm sorry. Your sister..."

His eyebrows rose and he made a soft sound of understanding. "Asking awkward questions, was she?"

"How did you know?"

"She does that." He gave a rueful smile as they reached the boat. The kittens were in a basket to stop them getting too curious about the water. Barnacle sat at the bow, apparently grateful for the respite. "I hope she didn't push you too much."

"Nothing I can't handle." She'd tackled tougher folk than Isabel Villiers. "She's only trying to keep you safe."

"*I'm* meant to protect her."

"It always cuts both ways." Before she looped to the opposite side of the boat, she grabbed his hand and squeezed, the gesture shielded from view by their bodies.

Smile bright, he winked as he took a spot beside Erec at the gunwale and they pushed the boat into deeper water.

Back to the surf, back to the sea, back to that constant roll of the *Venatrix's* deck. But she was returning changed. She would set foot on that deck part of something. Just as she was part of the crew, she was now part of something bigger than herself. A partnership. Knigh and her. She and him.

Like the sea lapping at her thighs, it was welcome. It was right.

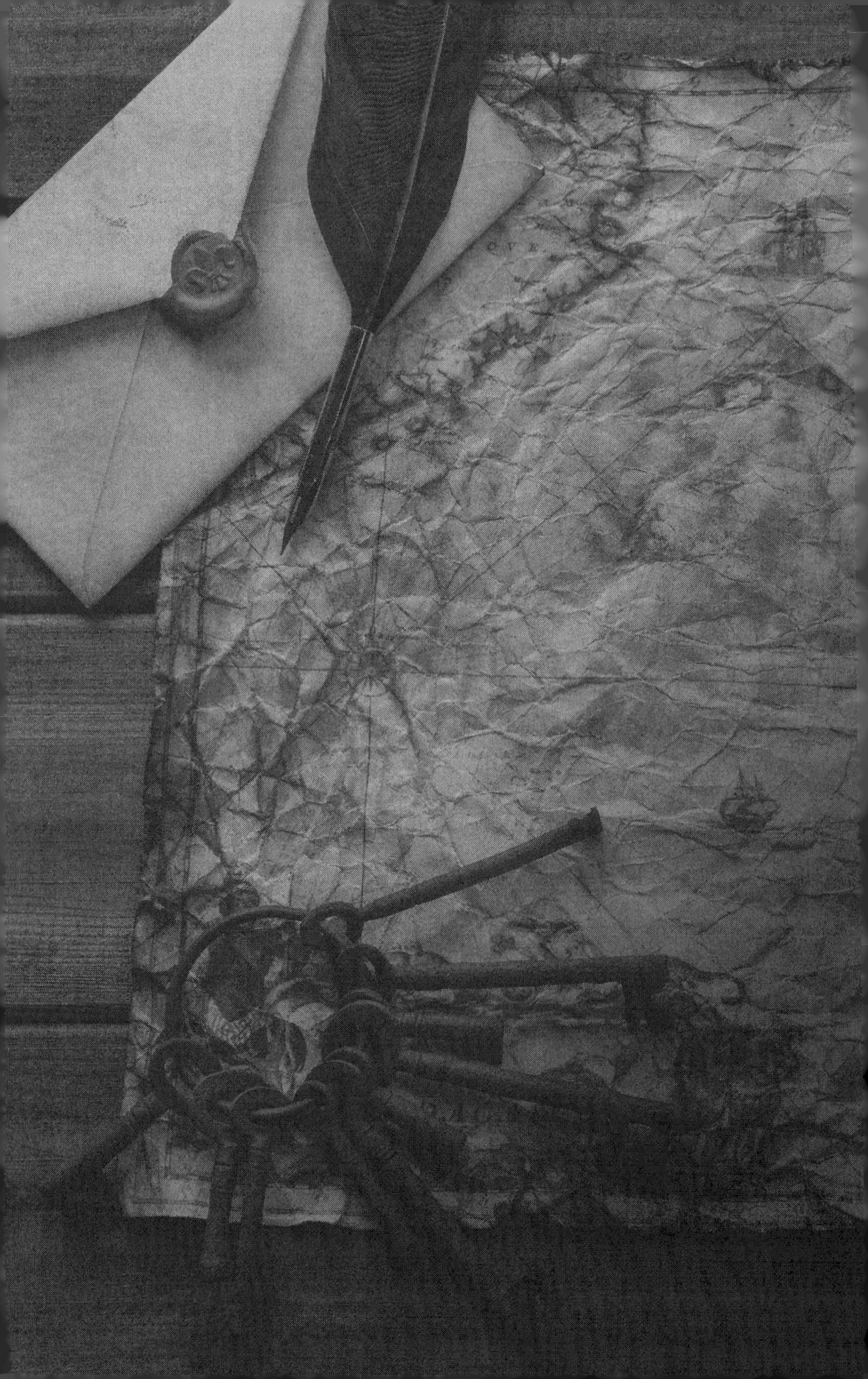

RECONNAISSANCE

They escorted the *Swallow* most of the way to Billy's home before splitting off and leaving her in busier seas. The *Firefly* and *Sea Witch* ventured north, while the *Venatrix* set sail for Ayay to claim Mercia's map.

The closer they got to the island, the less Vee laughed, the tighter her shoulders became. Knigh frowned, watching her over their work on the Copper Drake. He'd expected her to grow bolder and more excited as the prospect of Mercia's map became more real, but no.

Here in her cabin, which had been split off from Perry's, they'd spent the days since leaving his family working on the last third of the book. Admittedly, the sessions often dissolved into them *working on* each other since this place was their scrap of privacy. Although there was always the risk of someone walking in.

But it hadn't happened yet, and something about the risk

sent a thrill through him every time, whether it was that element of danger or just the fact that their secret would be out. So far Aedan hadn't realised, even though he shared a cabin with Knigh. He'd been on watch most nights, so that had been a stroke of luck disguising the fact Knigh hadn't slept in his own berth. But that wouldn't last forever.

"Don't you know it's rude to stare?" Vee's gaze slid from the page to him, a smirk tracing her lips.

"I never did listen properly in etiquette lessons." He raised his palms and lifted one shoulder, though there was nothing apologetic in his grin.

"And here I was thinking young Knighton had been such a star student." The smirk spread, glinting in her deep teal eyes, but an edge of tension lined her neck.

"What's wr—?"

The door swung open and Effie's face appeared, her warm brown cheeks flushed red. She huffed as though she'd run the full length of the ship. "It's show time." With a grin, she wriggled her fingers in the air and slipped away down the corridor.

Ayay.

Vee took a deep breath before rising. "Stay here. Please."

He suppressed a sigh. It was a well-worn conversation. She wanted to keep him away from Mercia. He shook his head. "I'm not letting you go face him without me."

"If all goes to plan, no one will be facing him. That's the point of sneaking."

It wasn't much of a plan so far. Everything rested on their reconnaissance.

They would land on the north side of the island, where their masts wouldn't be visible from the port on the south coast. Their usual boarding party would then cut across the land and stop at a vantage point to observe the lay of the land, whether or not the *Sovereign* was in dry dock, guard movements, any sign of Mercia and where he was staying. It was all information they needed before they could form a plan to get his map.

Knigh inclined his head. "And you won't be sneaking without me, either."

She opened her mouth to argue, but he held out a hand and stood. "Would you let me leave you behind if the tables were turned?"

Her face darkened in a glower. It was all the answer he needed.

"Exactly. Now save your breath and let's go."

They pulled into the small cliff-lined bay and set anchor. The cliffs plunged directly into the water to left and right, but ahead a sliver of beach sat squeezed between grey cliff and teal sea and Aedan explained it was only visible at low tide. Above, steps had been hewn into the rock, hidden amongst the craggy stones. A perfect smuggler's cove.

Perry watched them sling bags and weapons on their shoulders, her lips pursed, brows knotted. As they loaded into the ship's boat, she hugged them each in turn: Aedan, Saba, Wynn, Effie, Lizzy, and Knigh.

"Remember," she said as she squeezed Vee last, "I've rubbed off on you now. That means *sensible*." She eyed him over Vee's shoulder as if saying *Keep her sensible*.

Might as well tell the tides to stop. But he'd try. With a rueful smile, he gave a small shrug.

"No promises," Vee said and kissed Perry's brow before hopping over the gunwale. "Not if it comes down to sensible or successful."

As the boat lowered from the davits, the last thing Knigh saw was Perry's shoulders sinking.

They rowed to that tiny beach, Vee's gift helping them make light work of it, and hauled the boat into a cave where it would be safe from the rising tide. If for some reason Vee couldn't use her magic, they wouldn't be able to leave until the next low tide this evening. And if they missed it, they'd be stuck here overnight, potentially with Mercia's forces scouring the island.

Starting up the hewn steps, Knigh shivered.

By the time they reached the top of the stairs, even Knigh's legs were burning. Looking back, the *Venatrix* bobbed at anchor in the bay, her sails stowed, pirate flag hidden as though she might be nothing more than a simple merchant vessel. But what reason did a merchant vessel have to be in this secluded bay, when Port Ayay lay on the opposite side of the island? With a little luck, no one would see them to ask that awkward question.

They paused to drink from their canteens before setting off south. The hike was easy, following a faint trail through the forest, the ground blessedly level now they'd crested the cliffs.

After perhaps a couple of hours in the damp green shade, their glimpses of sun through the canopy grew brighter and harsher as it rose towards midday, and the ground tilted away, running downhill. Twenty minutes later and light shafted ahead as the trees thinned.

They crept to the edge of the forest, heads cocked, ears straining. Beyond their party, there were only the usual forest sounds—breeze on leaves, birdsong, squawks, the chirrup and buzz of insects.

No one nearby.

Below, between the shrub-scattered hillside and the sea, spread a town, its broad streets angling towards bustling docks. The usual towers and terrace buildings lined the streets, their timber and stucco facades painted in bright shades of turquoise, yellow, and pink.

Knigh pursed his lips as he drew his spyglass. Even without that magnification, the flashes of red were all too clear.

The place crawled with marines. Not on alert, just wandering from tavern to tavern.

And beyond the streets, the docks provided berths to far too many ships flying the Albionic flag. At least a dozen, maybe as many as twenty.

"Bollocks," Vee muttered.

"My sentiments exactly."

As he scanned the forest of masts, one set stood above the rest—the *Sovereign's*. Even with her sails stowed, he knew the configuration well enough to recognise her. She bobbed at the end of the longest jetty where the water would be deepest. The docks were so busy, civilian vessels sat crowded around her. Carpenters worked on deck, sawing planks and hauling them below decks.

"Well, the *Sovereign* isn't in dry dock." He pointed her out to the others. "Looks like they're strengthening her to take on heavier guns. Or more of them."

To his right, Aedan snorted. "Because she didn't have enough firepower already."

"Apparently not. And the fact they're doing it here means Mercia's paying it himself. For his own ends." Not commissioned by the Navy. Yet again, he was using naval resources for his own ends.

At his side, Vee made a low noise in her throat, almost a growl. "Question is, is Mercia staying on board or is he holed up in one of the inns?"

There was no sign of that shock of red hair on deck or his—

The sheen of peacock blue silk—not Navy uniform—caught the sun as someone emerged from the doors. Someone with mid-brown hair and a lordly swagger. Knigh's chest tightened.

"George," he breathed.

His brother reached into his breast pocket and looked down at his hand—checking his pocket watch, perhaps—then paused to speak to one of the officers. The officer summoned a much shorter lad, one of the servants who hurried over and stopped for a few moments, before crossing the gangway, trotting along the jetty, and disappearing behind the seafront buildings. Meanwhile, George strolled up to the poop deck and plopped on a chair fetched by another servant. He sat back, legs crossed at the ankle, arms folded. That pose and the way he'd checked his watch—he had the air of someone waiting.

"Mercia's still on board." Knigh forced the spyglass from his face. Staring at George wasn't going to make him see sense and walk away from the Duke. "I wager he's just been in there talking to him. And now he's waiting... Hmm... to go for lunch, perhaps."

Eyes narrowed at the town below, Saba put her hands on her hips. "So what's our plan?"

With a sigh, Vee tucked her spyglass away. "If he's quartered on the *Sovereign*, I know where the map is."

Knigh's brows knotted together before he realised why. *I know where the map is.*

I not *we.*

"And," she went on, "I like the way those civilian ships are crowded around her, shoulder-to-shoulder, practically. I'll climb in while the sun is high and hot—no one's going to want to be out in that, especially when I clear the clouds. And they won't be expecting any trouble with so many of their own around. Plus, those marines are practically on holiday, waiting for the carpenters to do their work."

Ignoring the sinking sensation in his belly, Knigh raised his eyebrows at her. "And while you're doing that, what will we be doing?"

"Keeping watch from here." She surveyed the rest of the group, skipping past him. "That clearing where we refilled our canteens"—she jerked her chin back the way they'd come—"that's our rendezvous point once I'm done. You can hide behind the rocks there."

"You're not seriously going in there alone."

"Keep watch?" Saba spluttered at the same time. Her expression darkened. "And what are we meant to do from up here if there's trouble?"

Vee exhaled through her nose. "First, I can be stealthier on my own. Second, if anything happens, you can go and get help or light a fire to distract them or shoot a pistol in the air to warn me." She shrugged, flinging her hands up. "I'm sure you can think of something. But all seven of us wandering into town and sneaking aboard the *Sovereign?* That isn't happening."

Much as it made Knigh's teeth grind, she had a point. Maybe they couldn't all sneak together, but... "I'm coming with you."

"You're not." He'd never heard her voice so flat before. A muscle ticked in her jaw. "You're not boarding that ship."

This again. "I don't have to board. I can create a distraction while you—"

"No. You can't. I refuse to lead you anywhere near Mercia or the *Sovereign*."

Because of last time. Despite the warm air, a chill crept across his flesh and Aedan's presence at his side was a sudden weight. A hot flush of shame chased away that chill.

His berserking. His failing. Thrown right in his face.

"Huh." It was Effie or Wynn who made the noise. "Was that a hummingbird?"

"A hummingbird?" the other replied. "Really?"

"I do love a hummingbird," Saba muttered. There was a shuffle as they edged away, conversation too bright.

He swallowed, throat easing enough to talk, though it still burned. "Because you think I'll berserk again. You don't trust me."

Shoulders sinking, she exhaled. "No. Gods, no, not that at

all." She came a step closer. "I want to keep you safe—physically and mentally. I feel..." She shook her head and looked away. "I should never have put you in that position. I was a poor leader that day and I won't do it again. It was *my* failing, not yours." Her throat bobbed.

Her failing? *He* was the one who'd lost control. *She* hadn't almost cut off Aedan's arm. "Vee, I..." The others had backed away, but they were still within sight, so he just gripped her elbow, lightly but enough to get her to look at him. "I want you to trust me. To rely on me." Like she relied on herself. "Not coddle me or push me away." His chest was too tight to go on.

She only frowned back, breaths rushing into the space between them. Eventually she blinked, eyes staying closed a beat longer than normal, and shook her head as if shaking off the silence. "I need to go." She pressed his spyglass into his hand, letting her fingers trace over his as she gave the slightest smile. "Keep an eye on me," she said, raising her voice and glancing at the others. "Signal, distract them, get help—do any of that from up here. But don't come after me."

With a nod and a squeeze of his hand, she turned and strode from the forest.

Every muscle bellowed at him to follow. Or to stop her. Anything but stay here.

But she'd made up her mind. And he could berserk if there was a threat and too many reminders of Mercia. Yet somehow she was the one who'd feel guilty about it. That look on her face—she'd clearly beaten herself up about last time.

Gripping the spyglass, he ran his other hand over his face as though that might rub away these thoughts, the complicated emotions running between him and her.

"I can't believe you let her go," Saba hissed from his side as the others drew level.

"Let her?" Knigh snorted. "You know her better than that. No one *lets* Vee do anything."

Heart heavy, he watched her amble down the hillside until the shrubs and long grass swallowed her up.

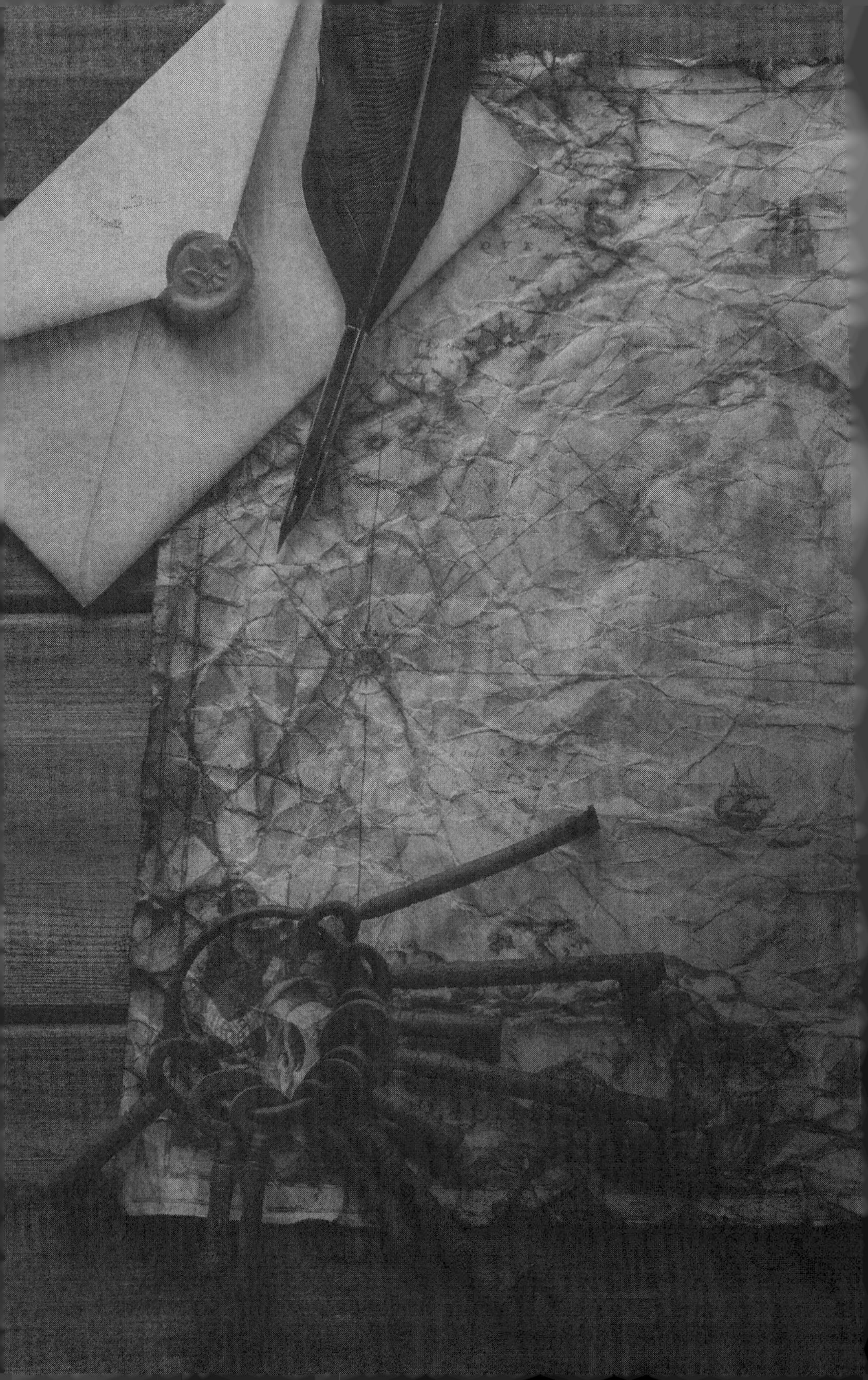

THE MAP

She would *not* risk his life. That was out of the question. Head bowed, Vice trudged through the streets on the edge of town. With her hat pulled low, she circled around to the docks.

As they'd noted from above, the marines she passed were largely idle—chatting and joking, drinking. Even though it was only noon, half a dozen spilled from the tavern ahead. Without missing a step, she skirted around them. Men on leave with nothing to do while they waited for their ships to be upgraded.

With a little luck that would mean fewer people guarding the *Sovereign* and no need for the others to interfere. If they stayed up on the hill, they'd be safe. *He'd* be safe.

That look on his face, flickers of hurt at his brow, tightening his lips—it had cut her and here it was again in her head.

He hadn't mentioned it, but when he'd practically begged

her to rely on him, she could hear it in his voice. *Let me help you, don't run off like you did in Redland.*

Well, this wasn't running off. Then, she hadn't even thought of asking for help. This wasn't the same at all.

She'd brought a team along and put them on lookout. Hells, she'd *considered* asking them to come and keep watch in the town itself. But then Knigh's expression as he'd spotted George—no, that had sealed the decision. He had to stay away.

She couldn't focus on getting Mercia's map if she was worrying about him.

And she couldn't have his death on her hands.

Not like Evered's.

Her stomach turned, curdling against the sweet air coming in off the sea as she reached the wharves.

Ayay was one of the smaller ports, ideal for lying low and shifting loot thanks to its lack of military presence. *Usually.*

Lips pursed, she strolled along the seafront, glancing at the ships and notice boards, looking for all the world like a merchant sailor seeking new work. A couple of sailors made lewd comments, but she just threw back replies that left them blushing in her wake. One merchant quartermaster offered her a job, which she pretended she'd mull over.

No one seemed ruffled by the *Sovereign's* presence, even though this wasn't a naval port. Mercia had chosen the place well, away from the Navy's prying eyes. Apparently, he too was lying low.

His Royal Slyness, indeed.

When she reached the *Sovereign's* jetty, she turned and strode up it as though she had as much right to be there as the handful of sailors working on the smaller ships. With the noon heat, most sailors and workers had disappeared for lunch or a nap, ready to return once it was cooler. Those who remained were quiet, pausing often to wipe sweat from their brows, movements lethargic.

Even the *Sovereign's* guard had depleted, leaving only a pair of marines stationed either side of the warship's gangway. George no longer sat on the poop deck—either he'd grown fed up of waiting or Mercia had emerged and they'd gone for lunch.

Thanks to the hat shading her face, the sentries wouldn't see her examining the merchant barque beside the *Sovereign*, scanning the deck for crew. No one there. Perfect.

She aimed for its gangway, shoulders back, gait leisurely, as though she was just strolling back to her berth to see out the noon heat with a nap. No one so much as glanced her way as she boarded and crossed the deck to the far side.

A moment later, her hat was in her bag and she hung off the barque's port rail, climbing aft.

By the time she reached the stern, her arms weren't the slightest bit sore or shaking. This was *far* easier then when she'd clambered along the *Venatrix* to break into Knigh's cabin last year. It had to be the exercises he'd shown her on the *Swallow* and the extra ones he'd added since she'd returned to the crew. He'd coiled up rope and made her use it to add extra weight as she did various squats, lunges, press-ups, and even pull-ups on the doorframe that left her fingers stiff and aching. She'd sworn at him, especially while doing the last of those exercises, but his punishing regime had done the trick.

A quick check around the corner—no faces up at the *Sovereign's* rail, no one in sight. So far, so good.

The main body of the *Sovereign's* hull rose several feet away—well out of her reach, even if she gripped with one hand and swung across, even if she found secure purchase for her toes and leapt. But only three feet of air separated the barque's stern from the *Sovereign's* port quarter gallery. A feature unique to larger warships, the quarter gallery jutted from the hull's smooth lines on the topmost decks, adding space to both sides of the officers' quarters that was usually used for storage and latrines. It was doubly to her advantage today, bringing the warship closer *and* providing a row of glinting sash windows that would allow her easy access.

One hand fastened to the barque, she swung, reached, and grabbed the nearest windowsill. The manoeuvre left her out of breath and strained her arms as each took her full, moving weight for a few seconds, but she was now, technically, aboard the *Sovereign*.

Another step closer to Mercia's map.

With a fierce grin, she slid open the window and crept inside, away from anyone who might see from the dock or poop deck above. She landed without a sound and paused in the narrow room that housed Mercia's toilet. Even princes had to piss, and this allowed his to drop into the sea as they sailed on by. She closed the window, before padding to the door and pressing her ear to it.

The sea outside and below. Gulls, too. No footsteps. Not even the sound of working anymore—the sun was too hot with not a cloud in the sky, thanks to her gift.

She counted to thirty.

Still nothing.

She couldn't wait too long—Mercia and George might have only left to have lunch or attend a meeting. Who knew when they'd be back?

Cocked pistol in hand, just in case, she crept out.

Just Mercia's ornate but tasteful furniture. She exhaled. The gods were on her side today.

Circling past his map table, she made for the desk positioned at the centre of the stern windows, facing the door. Behind it stood a padded chair silhouetted against the glaring sun outside. In one corner sat the armchair she'd occupied the last time she'd been here and the shelves full of the books he'd made recommendations from.

She rubbed her fingers together. There were books on magic he'd mentioned that she hadn't got around to reading before leaving his hospitality.

In for a penny...

If she took too many, he'd spot the gaps on the shelf instantly, but just a couple wouldn't stand out until he looked more closely. She snatched two and shoved them in her bag before returning to the desk.

She couldn't pick locks like Aedan did, but a quick stab, jiggle, and wrench of her stiletto's blade and she'd opened the desk drawer where Mercia kept the map.

It wasn't pretty—a dark scar mangled one edge of the keyhole—but it was efficient. Besides, Mercia would notice his precious map missing soon enough. During her time as his prisoner, he'd consulted the thing most evenings after dinner

—opening it, examining it, before refolding and returning it to the drawer, the whole thing compulsive. To let her see where he kept it, he must've been utterly confident she'd remain his property.

Well, he *had* taught her how to better use her gift, how to seize the wellspring—he thought he'd found himself a pet sea witch. In his mind, she was nothing more than another ship added to his fleet or another embroidered silk suit in his collection.

More fool him.

She smiled to herself and pulled the drawer open.

A familiar folded sheet of vellum waited inside, foxed and yellowed, edges a little tatty. Overall, it was in remarkably good condition considering its age.

Heart leaping, she exhaled with relief. There had been a chance he'd moved the map now she knew its location. But, no, Mercia was that full of hubris, it would never enter his mind that she'd dare come back here, that *anyone* would have the audacity to break into the Royal Navy's flagship.

Maybe no one else would be that bold. But a nickname like the Pirate Queen wasn't awarded to the faint hearted.

And now the map was hers.

With shaking hands, she unfolded it to reveal the outlines of islands she knew well. But the way the map had been drawn was... off. Islands weren't quite in the correct places—it placed the islands north of Hewanorra in a perfectly straight line, but in reality they formed an arc, bracketing the eastern end of the Arawakéan Sea. And sizes weren't to scale—Redland, for instance, had been drawn far larger than neighbouring Hewanorra when in reality it was smaller.

And yet, despite such obvious mistakes, the shape of Hewanorra was perfectly mapped, its coves and curving coastline exactly where they should be. Perhaps it was to make it difficult or even impossible to simply transcribe information from this map to another after catching a glimpse of it.

Then to the west... Whole islands were missing, the mainland, too, like someone had erased portions.

"What the...?"

Another puzzle. Bloody Drake.

She shook her head. Of course there would be—

Footsteps. Voices. In the corridor, growing louder. Coming closer.

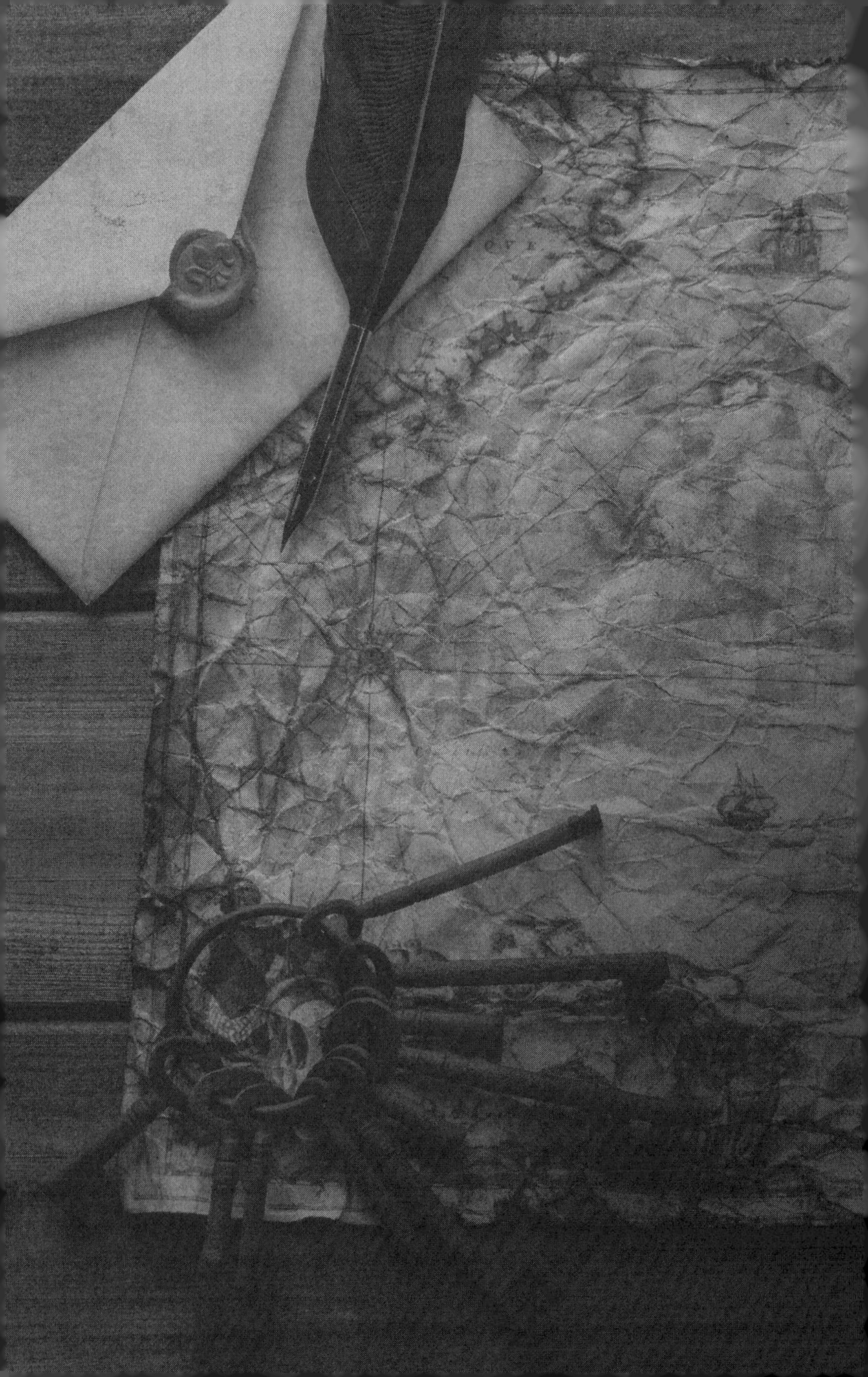

HIS ROYAL SLYNESS

Her pulse thudded in double time.

Options.

The map table stood between her and the port quarter gallery—her exit. If she ran, she'd make noise and still might not make it out before whoever it was entered.

She could fit in the desk footwell and hide until they left. But if they came around this side of the desk, they'd spot the damaged lock and probably her.

Behind the armchair would be a similarly bad hiding place.

The door to the store room in the starboard quarter gallery was nothing more than a rectangular groove in the oak panelled bulkhead. But it was close.

"I've told you, George," a familiar voice said just the other side of the double doors leading to the dining cabin, "I won't be long."

Shit. That was Mercia. Not just a servant coming to clean and leave.

Four paces took her to that near-hidden door, and as she pushed it open and slipped inside, the footsteps halted. She clicked the door shut, just as the double doors swung open.

Biting her lip, she pressed her forehead to the solid oak and forced her breaths slow and quiet, despite her thundering heart.

"You always say you won't be long." George huffed as their steps clipped into the room. "And when you use my name, that's when I know you're lying."

Behind her, sash windows mirrored those she'd entered through, but they'd squeaked as they'd opened and closed. No doubt these would do the same and Mercia would hear before she managed to climb out.

"Darling—"

"Good gods, *darling* is even worse. You're going to be hours, then, aren't you?"

She winced. *Hours?* Bollocks. Please, Lords and Ladies, say that was an exaggeration.

The steps stopped, now muffled by the rug. Papers rustled.

Fingers grazing down the oak, she crouched and put her eye to the keyhole. She could see up to the shoulders of Mercia's Navy blue uniform. He stood over the table, rifling through maps and charts. George had his back to her, mid-brown hair and peacock-blue silk jacket gleaming, one hand on his hip.

"This intelligence could change everything," Mercia muttered as he hauled a map from the pile and smoothed it over the table. She caught a glimpse of his face, drawn in concentration as he bent low, pencil poised, before George stepped in the way, movements stiff.

George's shoulders rose and fell as he huffed again. "I'm sure it could have waited until after lunch."

So Knigh had been right.

"Hmm." Mercia straightened, arms folding. He twiddled the pencil.

"That's *it?*" George leant over the table. "This grand *intelligence* and that's all it added to your bloody map? Oh, and don't tell me—you're now going to stand and stare at it for an hour." Throwing his hands in the air, he backed off. "Sometimes I understand you like I never thought it was possible to understand another person. And then..."

He shook his head and marched back to the double doors. As he swung them open, he muttered something. The only word Vice caught was *obsessed*. Then he was gone, slamming the door in his wake.

The pencil stopped moving. "George," Mercia sighed.

Go after him. Go after him. Then she could make good her escape. Her eyes ached where she stared so hard at Mercia's folded arms.

But he only sighed again and tapped that pencil on the table.

With a silent exhale, she rested her forehead on the oak door. He wasn't going anywhere. And if that intelligence he'd received related to Drake's map or something else in his desk...

Grimacing, she peered out again. He stood over the map

table and stayed there for several minutes, forcing her to shift from crouching to sitting to ease her aching legs.

Footsteps. Was he leaving? She jerked upright, returning to the keyhole.

But, no, Mercia paced, arms still folded, fingers tapping on his bicep.

She bit back a groan. She didn't have time to waste sitting here, not with the *Venatrix* waiting in that bay. Naval ships could easily go on patrol and spot her.

Hopefully Knigh and the others would be smart and return to the boat even if she didn't return. They could make use of the low tide to access the beach and escape, and she'd find her own way off the island if Mercia stayed here too long.

He veered from his pacing course and flopped into the armchair, bringing his face into view. Eyebrows knotted into a deep frown, he steepled his fingers and stared right at her.

Every hair on the back of her neck strained to attention. It was only the chair's angle pointing him in her direction, and he wouldn't be able to see her through the keyhole from there. He didn't even give any reaction to suggest he had spotted her. Still, it felt unnervingly like he was looking right *at* her. Right *through* her.

Exhaling through his nose, he reached to the small table beside him and poured a tumbler of honey-toned whisky from the decanter there.

He wasn't going anywhere soon.

Shit.

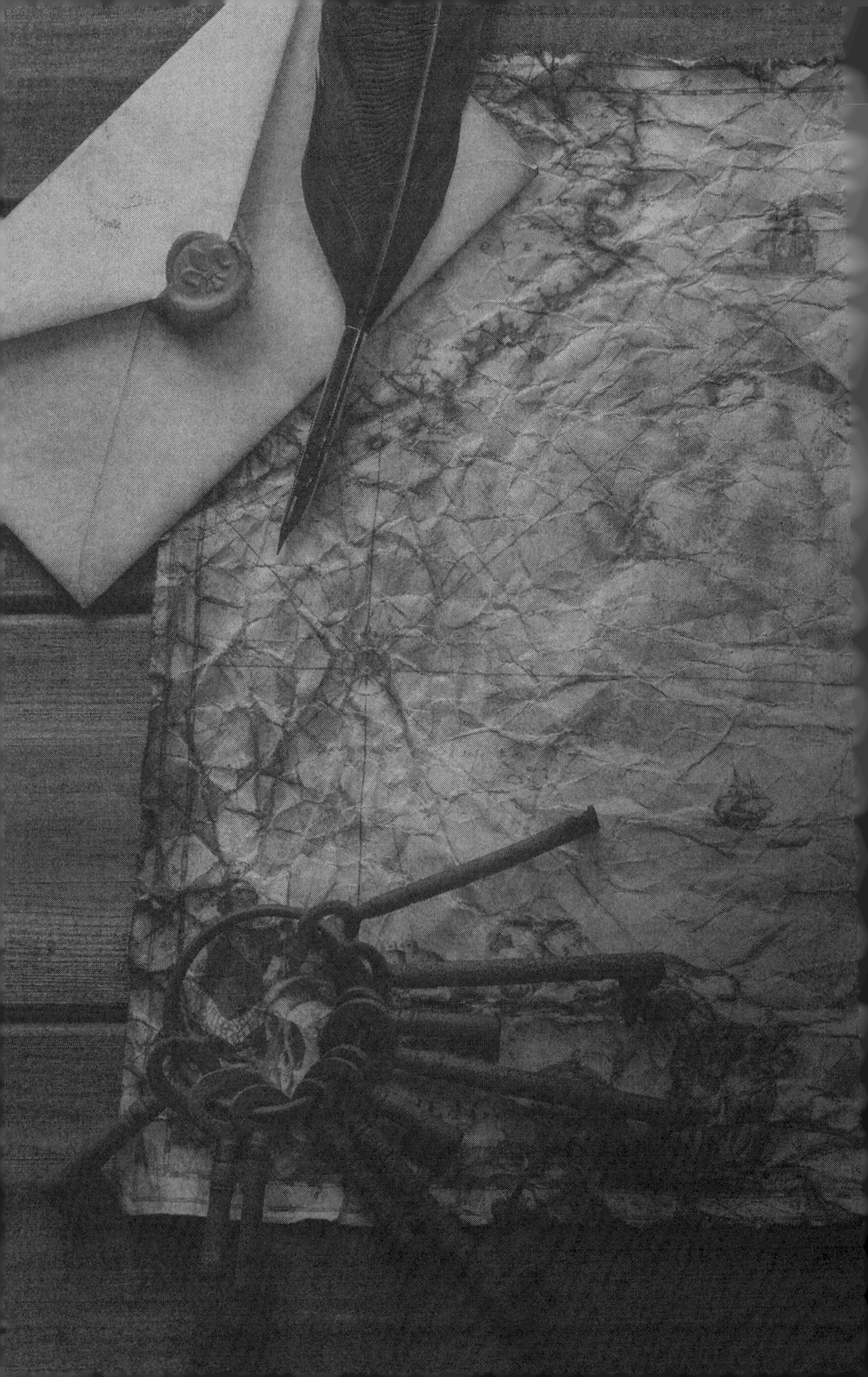

THE REVEAL

An age passed with just the occasional click of Mercia's glass on the table and the constant sigh of the sea outside. He'd finally finished the whisky but had made no move to stand, let alone leave.

Vice sat against the door, opposite the window. She could try it and just hope it opened quietly. If it made a noise, she'd have to jump into the water and use her gift to carry herself away as quickly as possible. But Mercia would raise the alarm. How quickly would his men have their rifles ready and—

Shouts from outside. A rush of running footsteps on the deck above.

She sat up.

Crack.

A gunshot.

Her lungs froze. Her heart stopped.

Who were they firing at? Surely the others hadn't come after her. Please, gods, say they hadn't.

Knigh *had* looked mutinous at her order to stay. Eyes shut, she doubled over and forced her breaths slow and even and quiet. Her ears strained as she tried to decipher the story in the sounds outside.

More shouts. More of those swift footsteps. A set coming closer—on this deck—at a sprint.

The double doors banged open, and she scrambled back to the keyhole.

Mercia was on his feet, George stood in the doorway, panting.

"It's Knigh." He ran both hands through his hair. "He's here."

She had to shove her knuckles into her mouth to keep quiet as the world dipped. No. No. No. He couldn't... He wouldn't...

He had, hadn't he?

He'd come for her. Just like he always did. Except this time...

Ice held her in its grip, goosebumps chasing across her skin.

"They have orders to bring him in alive." Mercia tugged his sleeve straight and crossed the floor to George.

"Yes, I'm sure they do, but someone still damn well shot at him." George's voice shook, and when Mercia reached as if to comfort him, he backed away. "Mercy, please—"

"Of course." He gripped George's shoulder, knuckles paling with the tension. "He's your brother. Come." He ran from the cabin, George on his heels. A moment later, bellowed orders drifted back through the corridor: "I said *alive!*"

Oh, Knigh, what have you done?

She stared at the doors closing in George and Mercia's wake.

Knigh had revealed himself. Deliberately. That had to be it. He'd watched through the spyglass, seen Mercia returning to the ship, and realised what that meant for her. And he'd come down the hill, striding into town, and used himself as... as bait. As a distraction. As...

They'd shot at him.

Had they hit?

Pain. Dull, but pain nonetheless—the physical kind. Easier to deal with than the mental agony that had engulfed her like a tidal wave.

That pain cut through the thoughts, the horror, the shock. She blinked, eyes stinging. She was biting her knuckles and when she pulled them away, teeth marks indented her tanned skin.

A deep breath. Another. Another.

If he'd done something this idiotic, he'd done it to allow her to escape. And if she stayed here, he'd have done this idiotic thing for nothing.

Wild Hunt, when she got her hands on him, she would wring his damn neck.

She rose on shaking legs. After a quick peek through the keyhole to confirm the cabin was empty, she strode out, crossed the rich carpet, and entered the latrine.

Bright sunshine, midafternoon. A breeze and a squeak when she opened the window.

That gunshot.

No, no. She couldn't think about that. Couldn't wonder if they'd...

Pain. Sharp, in her palms this time as she clenched her hands to fists and let the nails dig in.

She had the map. That was what they'd come here for. This would all be pointless if she didn't escape with the damn thing.

Knigh's sacrifice would be...

No. Not sacrifice.

He wasn't. He couldn't be. They'd missed.

His *risk*. That was all.

Limbs jerky and stiff, she clambered out the window and climbed back the way she'd come.

What have you done?

She would've got away. He should've known that. It wasn't worth him risking his...

Gasps tore through her by the time she blinked and found herself halfway along the merchant barque's port side. Then she was on deck, striding for the gangway, a squat man staring after her, asking where she'd come from. She just pulled her hat from the bag over her shoulder and shoved it on as she crossed to the jetty.

Towards the wharves, half a dozen marines raced away to the left, their red uniforms a streak against the sailor's drab clothing.

They were running. That meant he wasn't... No, no one lay collapsed on the ground. No blood. That was something.

Just keep walking. Keep breathing.

Head ducked to keep her eyes shaded, she stared after those red uniforms until they disappeared up a busy street. He'd gone that way. She could go after him, could...

But if she somehow found him, she'd only risk leading the marines to his location.

Her pace was steady, calm, just another sailor turning off the jetty, but her pulse thundered in her ears, at her throat, louder and more chaotic than any storm, even one out of her control.

A distraction. He'd turned himself into a distraction for her. Maybe she could do the same for him.

Gunpowder. A barrel of that and a flame. That was all she needed. But... no, people didn't just leave barrels of gunpowder unattended.

Good gods, she was clutching at straws. Gunpowder was a stupid idea.

And if she centred too big a distraction on herself, it would only undo Knigh's work.

She shivered as she strode along the wharves, putting distance between herself and that street the marines had turned down.

Hands clenched, she threw out a desperate thread of her gift. Waves rose, rocking the docked vessels, knocking them against the jetties and each other with solid thuds. Wind gusted, tugging on loose canvas and lines, rattling lanterns against masts.

Sailors swore and exclaimed, then rushed to secure lines and sails that threatened to fly loose.

She could take it further, raise a storm, but with this clear sky, she'd need to stop and use the wellspring. And a storm from nowhere would only alert Mercia to her presence.

On any other day, she'd have done it.

But she had to complete the plan and get away with the map, otherwise Knigh's stupid, *stupid* risk would've been for nothing.

So, face frozen, mind foggy, she strode through the town, up the hill, and into the damp forest.

Knigh had come for her. Had put himself in danger. Was still in danger. And she'd walked away.

What have you done?

If she gave Saba the map, told her to get to the *Venatrix*, she could go back for him. But short of searching the whole town... And, again, that stomach-turning risk she'd lead the Navy to him.

No, she couldn't go searching. She would have to wait.

Time must've passed, though it could've been a minute or forever with leaves and tree trunks going by, green shadows all around, soft soil underfoot. Eventually, the narrow animal track opened up to the clearing where they'd arranged to rendezvous, with great boulders marking the edge of the burbling stream.

Another day she might've shouted at the others for letting Knigh go, but when they poked their heads around from behind the rocks, she just nodded. Their faces were already tight, and when she explained what had happened in staccato sentences, Saba paled, Wynn and Effie's mouths dropped open, Lizzy's eyebrows creased together, and Aedan's jaw rippled. He squared his shoulders and looked back the way she'd come, as though he'd march into town and haul Knigh out himself.

Vice managed a grim smile at that impulse. But if anyone was going after Knigh, it would be her.

So she handed over the map and sent them back to the boat with strict instructions to take the low tide when it came, even if she hadn't returned. She would find a way back, if they'd already gone. Somehow.

"What will you do?" Saba tucked the map into her bag, lips pursed.

"Wait."

Aedan's brows rose, that muscle in his jaw feathering again. "And if he doesn't come?"

She swallowed past the tightness in her throat. "He'll come." Her tone didn't invite any further questions.

Before they left, she took back her rifle as well as Knigh's, which he'd left with Aedan. She also borrowed Aedan's rifle, powder flask, shot, and four more pistols. Just in case.

Throat dry, she watched as they disappeared along the trail, heading for the submerged beach. Once they were out of sight, she crouched by the stream and splashed her face, the chilly water making her gasp. It broke through the half-numb daze that had shrouded her since that gunshot.

Action. Preparation.

She nodded and prowled the rocks until she found the right spot—hidden from the trail leading from town, with three escape routes between the boulders and a broad, flat stone of knee height.

Her muscles eased as she settled into the familiar work of loading the borrowed flintlocks. Powder. Shot wrapped in cloth. Ram it down. Ramrod back in place beneath the barrel. More powder, finely ground, into the flash pan, ready to flare when the flint sparked against the frizzen.

If Knigh arrived with enemies at his heels, she just needed to cock the gun and pull the trigger.

And if somehow they'd made him talk or followed her tracks up here, well, she'd be ready for that too.

Her hand stuttered in its movement, missing the ramrod's slot under the barrel. If they made him talk... There was only one way they might do that.

No. Mercia wouldn't hurt him, not with George there.

Inhale. Exhale.

She slid the ramrod home and moved to the next gun.

Three rifles. Six pistols. All lined up on the flat rock within arm's reach, her fae-worked rifle closest. Still no movement on the trail save for the breeze in the branches and occasional call and rustle of birds.

The sun no longer glared overhead, sinking into late afternoon.

She clenched and unclenched her hands, staring at that trail until her eyes burned. *Come on, Knigh.*

Inhale. Exhale.

Forcing her shoulders down and back, she checked every pre-loaded cartridge for her fae-worked rifle. The metal casings were cold against her fingertips but familiar and solid.

Familiar like Knigh. Solid like him.

She squeezed her eyes shut and those thoughts from her head. Back to work.

Every gun was loaded, every cartridge double-checked, sabre and daggers at her belt, another blade in her boot.

And still no sign of him.

Clouds crept across the deep blue sky and shadows gathered in the east when a rustle sounded along the trail. Something louder, larger than the small creatures she'd heard all afternoon. Not something, but *someone*. Had to be.

Heart hammering, Vice levelled her rifle.

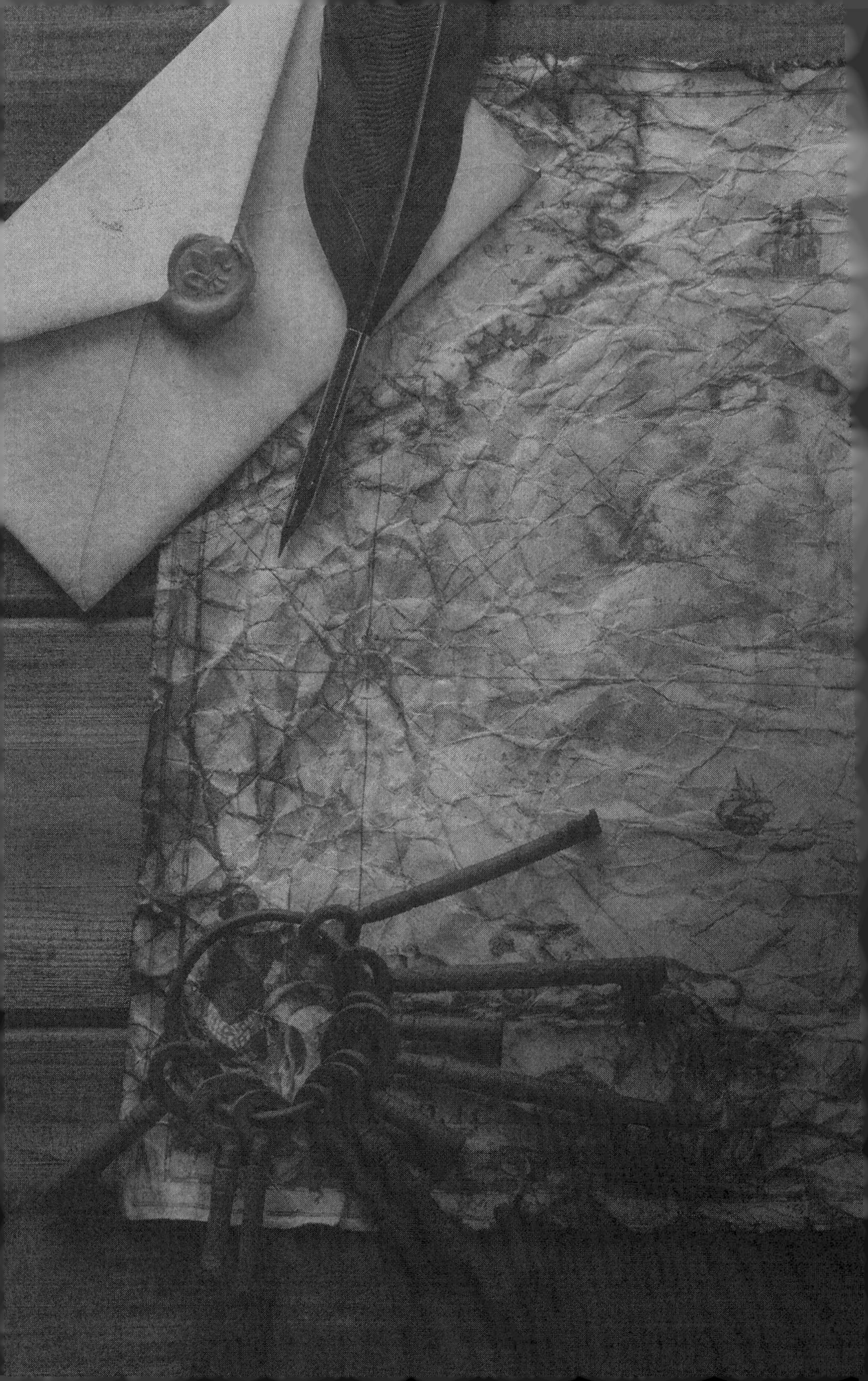

DOWN THE WELL

Knigh's legs burned as he sprinted through streets and alleyways, sweat stinging his eyes. His heart pumped, his legs and arms too. One corner, then the next, and into the courtyard with washing drying on lines overhead. He aimed for the well that squatted at one end and, without missing a beat, planted a hand on its stone edge and leapt in.

The air rushed from his lungs as he swung over and grabbed the lip running around the inside. Arm muscles taut, he hung on the inside of the well, out of sight of anyone who passed. Just as he'd planned.

It was easy to find footholds between the rough stones, taking some of the weight from his arms as he slowed his breaths. If he could keep quiet, they'd run straight through the courtyard and he'd be able to emerge and make his escape.

He'd spent time in Port Ayay during his naval days—it was

a good place to get intelligence on pirates, since the Navy left the port alone.

Mercia's presence here was confirmation the *Sovereign's* refit was off the books. He was using naval ships and crews for his own ends. Without the Copper Drake, he had no hope of finding Drake's treasure, so what *were* those ends?

He huffed a sigh and pressed his forehead to the cool, damp rock.

Footsteps slapped across the paved courtyard and sprinted straight past.

Grinning to himself, he counted to twenty. Their steps had faded to nothing by the time he poked his head up, confirmed the courtyard was empty save for the flapping sheets above, and climbed from his hiding place.

Vee had pointed out his lack of skill when it came to stealth, but that didn't mean he couldn't be sneaky in other ways. Especially not when he knew the lay of the land as he knew Port Ayay.

Before he left the courtyard, he shoved his waistcoat into his bag and pulled out his hat. Slightly crumpled, but it would hide his fae mark as he strode out into the streets and made for the market square.

The stalls were packing away, since it was late afternoon. The cart he'd spotted earlier still sat at the edge of the square, now loaded with timber and sacks of produce beneath a loose canvas cover. Its owner, a wiry middle-aged man with coppery hair and skin, chatted and laughed with a man who looked so similar, they must've been brothers. They were deep in conversation, so it took no effort for Knigh to slip beneath that canvas cover and hunker down between the sacks, surrounded by the resinous scent of wood. The broad-shouldered sabrecat that pulled the cart didn't so much as sniff the air.

Now to wait.

With the market stalls shutting up, it wasn't long before the cart began rocking and set off. One hand on his pistol, he watched through a gap between canvas and timber as the square trundled away without the slightest glimpse of a marine's red jacket.

Once the cart ambled past the town limits, he exhaled and loosened his grip on the gun. He was safe.

But was Vee?

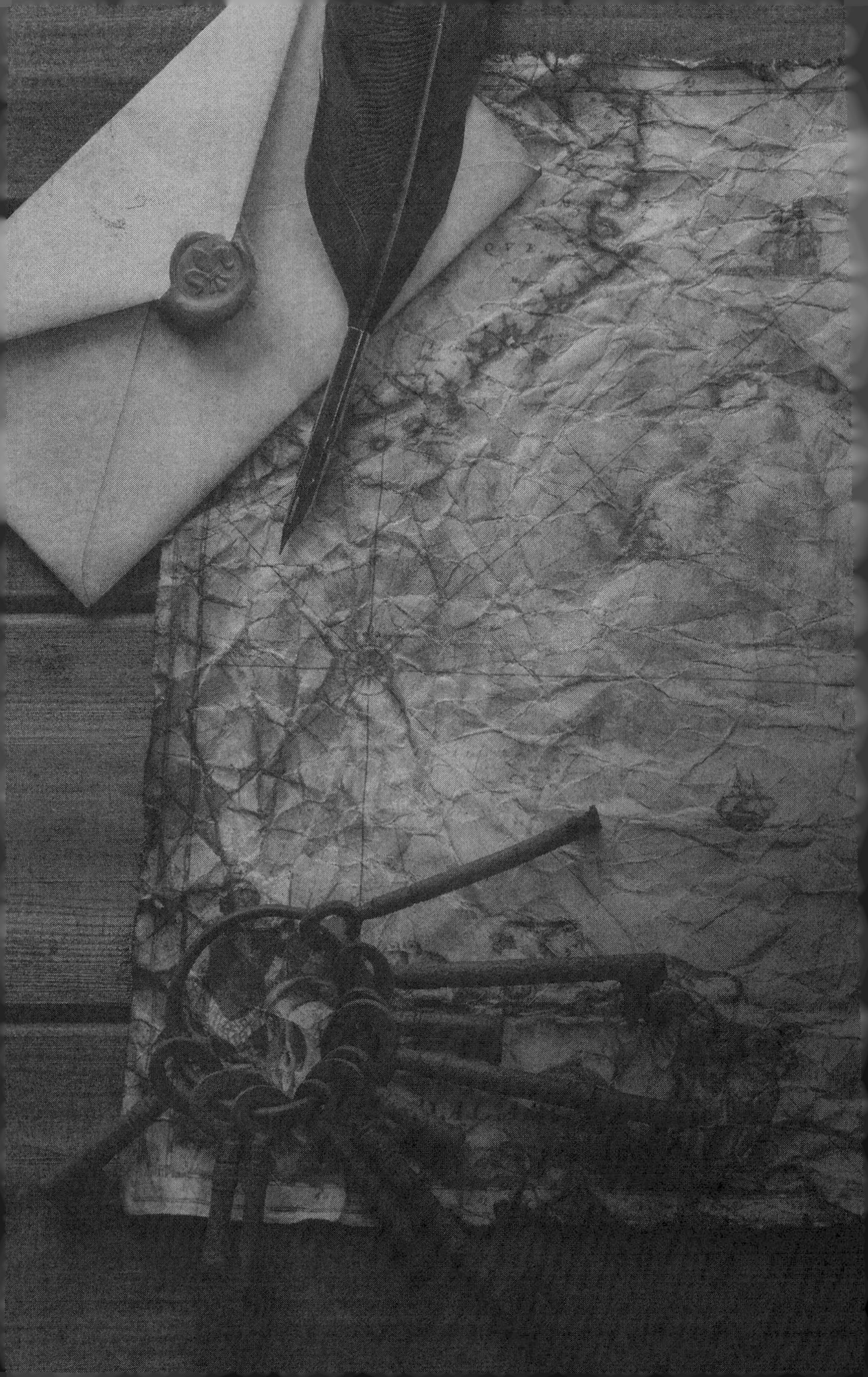

WEAPONRY & ARMOUR

Was she safe? Had she got away? The questions circled, his constant companions as he crept through the forest.

He'd jumped off the cart as it had turned towards the farms occupying the other end of the island. The scrub had provided him with cover as he'd hurried to the trees, but he needn't have worried about hiding—except for the cart disappearing along the road, there wasn't a soul nearby. Mercia must've decided he was more likely to escape on a ship—perhaps he thought the *Venatrix* was docked there in disguise and was now searching all the vessels at dock, just as he had once done in Port Royal, searching for Vee.

Was she safe? Had she got away?

Teeth gritted, he forged on.

The clearing was quiet and empty when he reached it, his

pistol drawn. Ears straining for any sound, muscles primed, he approached the boulders.

A low moan, then movement.

Knigh held his breath, raised his pistol.

Lips parted, eyebrows peaked together, Vee emerged from the rocks and the sight of her made him sag.

Safe. Alive. No sign of blood or injury.

Her rifle hung limp in her grip as she ran across the clearing and flung herself into his arms.

Safe. Alive. She was. He was.

He squeezed and inhaled her rain and vanilla scent, nuzzling into that crook between neck and shoulder where the rest of the world ceased to exist.

Her chest pressed against his as she clung to him. Then she was out of his embrace, shaking him in a steel grip. "What the hells, Knigh?" The creases between her brows scoured deeper. "How did you get away? What did you do? Did they…?" She took a step back, hand running over his arm, his chest, eyes skimming over the rest of him.

It was the same inspection he'd done of her on numerous occasions—checking for injuries.

"No." He holstered his pistol and gripped her shoulders, making her meet his gaze. "They shot but missed." He explained about the courtyard, the well, the cart, and she listened, muscles solid, eyes churning in a silent storm.

"I told you to stay here," she said once he'd finished. "I *told* you."

"And if I'd done that, you'd still be on the *Sovereign,* and they'd have found you by now."

Her frown hadn't faded in the slightest. Nostrils flaring, she turned and made for the boulders.

"You know I'm right," he said, following. He stopped in his tracks when he spotted an arsenal of guns lined up, ready to shoot. "Expecting company?"

She said nothing, didn't even look at him as she started gathering the pistols. Her hands shook. With rage or fear?

He bit back a sigh and shouldered his rifle and what looked like Aedan's before taking two of the extra pistols.

"I led him to his death," she finally bit out, still not looking at him as she slung her rifle across her body. "Evered. And Evans, too. But... I can't... I can't lead you. I can't keep you safe." She scrubbed her face. "In Redland I didn't ask for your help and you ended up outnumbered. On Hewanorra, I didn't even realise there was danger in that cave, and I thought..." A shudder rippled through her. "When the floor fell away, I thought..." Eyes closing for a moment, she shook her head. "And today, I left you at the top of a hill, thinking it would keep you safe, and still you had to flee for your life. Whatever I do, you end up in danger."

That's what was eating at her. Leadership. Risk. Fear. The terrifying spectre of failure, of letting down the ones who followed you. He'd been trained for it, had faced those demons within the safe framework of the Navy and its rules and procedures. She had none of that.

Did she believe leadership meant keeping everyone safe? Risking nothing?

With a fingertip, he lifted her chin. "This life is dangerous. It's the nature of what we do. That isn't your fault."

She scowled like she didn't want that to be true. He couldn't blame her.

He let that compassion show in a gentle smile as he pushed hair back from her face. "You say you can't lead me, that you were a poor leader the day we boarded the *Sovereign*." She'd apologised for it. He'd forgiven her. And yet it still bothered her. "Well, let me tell you some things about leadership, about captaincy. A captain doesn't do it all themselves. And a captain doesn't take their people into danger lightly, but at times they must ask them to face the possibility of death."

Her frown tightened.

"The responsibility of a leader is to balance risk and reward," he went on, words coming to him from captains he'd sailed under as a boy, "duty and danger, and judge how and when and who must face those things. You shy away from that, only risking yourself." He closed his hand on her shoulder, squeezed. Her frown lessened a touch. "Vee, I see so much in you. How incredible you are now, loved by your crew, bold, clever, determined. And how great you *could* be—such overwhelming potential. But"—he raised his brows and gave a slight shake—"you'll never become the captain I know is inside if you can't find that balance."

That tight frown loosened, faded. Her chest rose and fell as she looked left and right as though searching for an answer. She shook her head. "We'd better get going, if we're going to catch the tide."

Shoulders sinking, he exhaled. Conversation over, apparently. "If only we had a sea witch who could shift the tide. Oh, wait, we do." He arched an eyebrow at her.

But she didn't laugh, just narrowed her eyes as she tightened the strap of her bag. "I told them to leave without us if we weren't there by the time the tide fell. I didn't want them stuck here, if..." She shrugged and strode between the boulders. *If* she hadn't returned because she was waiting for or rescuing him. Shaking his head, he followed.

They made good time through the forest, partially because Vee marched at a punishing speed, stiff and silent.

Stewing. Still angry at him, either for risking himself or because what he'd said about leadership was correct. It had been a couple of hours, long enough for her to think about it, cool off perhaps. Except she wasn't going to cool off if she kept it all bottled up and didn't *talk*.

Besides, they weren't far from the cliff top now and this was their last chance before they joined the others. He cleared his throat. "Are you going to stop being angry at me any time soon, or should I stay in my own berth tonight?"

Ahead, her shoulders squared. "I'm not angry," she snapped.

"Yes, and you're doing an excellent job of looking *not angry*." He lengthened his strides, getting as close as he could without stepping on her heels. The trail was so narrow they couldn't walk side-by-side. "Look, I know we're not enemies anymore and we are... whatever *this* is, but you're still allowed to get angry at me sometimes, you're still—"

"I said I'm not angry." She whirled on her heels and although her brows were drawn together, there was no fiery temper in those eyes. "I'm confused, all right? I don't know what to... What you said about leaders, it made perfect sense.

And yet…" She shook her head. "I can't risk you, Knigh. I can't put you in danger."

The anguish on her face cut clean through him. Not as deeply as her words in Redland, though. "And yet," he murmured, "you think what happens to you doesn't matter." She blinked, swaying backwards. "That's what you said in Redland, and I told you then, it matters to me. But you ask me to risk you all the damn time. You need to extend me that same respect."

She exhaled, expression loosening, deflating. Her chin dipped and she rubbed her brow. "I do. But…" She shook her head again. "I can't face it. What if something…" She folded her arms, fingers biting into her biceps.

Holding back. Wall up.

He edged closer, ran his hands up her arms to her shoulders. Her muscles were solid. "Vee, I need you to trust me. Both to do what needs to be done and to talk to me. You can do that, you know. Like you did in the pool. Tell me what you're feeling, what's raging behind those stormy eyes of yours. I've never seen them so dark." He ran a thumb across her cheekbone, underlining her dark gaze. "I can see you're holding back. Is that what this stewing silence has been, you pushing me away?"

Her hands fell to her sides as she nodded. "I… yes. It's my first instinct—to push away when… when everything inside is too much." She bowed her head, shoulders sagging. "I'm trying, but… the reminder helps. Thank you."

His heart warmed to see the wall crumble away, to hear the fractured sentences where she pushed and tried to find the right words. He brushed his lips against her brow. "It's what I'm here for. And I know this doesn't come naturally for you, but you're doing so well. I'm proud of you."

She pulled back, eyes wide. Had anyone ever told her that before? The way she looked up at him, he'd guess no. She took a step closer, hands fisting in his shirt as his arms closed around her. As if encouraging herself, she nodded. "I... I feel safe with you, Knigh."

He couldn't help but smile at that, the warmth in his heart spreading through his chest, his arms, to his fingertips, which traced lazy spirals on the small of her back.

"And yet," she went on, "also like I'm in *such* danger." The pulse at her throat leapt. "I've never felt like this before. When you're not near, I think of you. And when you are, my eyes seek you out. I don't mean to, but they're not under my control—the damn things want to drink you up *all the time.*" She scoffed, and it brushed his lips, leaving them tingling, but he held back. However much he ached to kiss her, he had to let her speak. "Your smile. Your eyes, which I used to think were colourless, but that somehow reflect any shade they're near. That ridiculous shock of white hair." A grin flickered as she pushed the hat off his head and ran her fingers through the streak, tickling sensation through his scalp.

But more important than the delicious feel of her touching him was that flash of a grin because of what it said. She was relaxing into this. Talking about her feelings, letting the words come out, humour supporting the emotions she was expressing rather than blocking them, making them safe.

He pressed into her hand, silently asking her to go on. His

throat was so tight, he wouldn't have been able to voice the request if he tried.

"The way," she said, voice hoarse as though the effort had worn it out, "you shut other people out, but let me see." Her gaze roved over his face, as gentle and pleasurable as a light breeze on a hot day. It stole his breath. "Your expressions. Your feelings play out on your face in this subtle way that makes me feel special because I spot it."

Her chest heaved like she was still marching through the forest. Unmistakable fear flashed in her eyes as they widened.

"How I feel about you," she murmured, barely more than a whisper, "it doesn't feel safe."

Smiling, heart full, he squeezed her close and bent until his lips were only an inch from hers. "Don't tell me the great Lady Vice is afraid." He closed that inch and kissed her, then murmured in her ear, "Coward."

She shivered, perhaps at the warm brush of that word, but then with a huff, she pulled away, glaring. "I hate you."

But she let him pull her back into his arms and looped hers around his waist.

"I know you do." He grinned, head cocked. "Show me how much."

Eyes narrowed, she pouted, but tiptoed to his lips, pressing the length of her body against him. Hips and breasts and belly and thighs and... His hands planed up her back, savouring every inch of her.

The scowl should've warned him, but when she bit his lip, he still jumped. Heat streaked through him, tension plucking low in his belly and driving a groan against her mouth. Her mouth quirked against his, and he knew it was a smile.

Then she was a foot away, smirking, her reddened mouth and ragged breaths the only evidence she'd been kissing him a second earlier. "Tick-tock, Knigh," she said with a mocking lilt. "We need to get going."

Tick-tock. Yes, they had got distracted, hadn't they? He blinked, rubbing the back of his head.

Tutting, she turned and continued along the trail. "Report to my cabin tonight and I'll show you exactly how much I hate you."

He retrieved his hat from where it had fallen and marched after her, biting his lip at the seductive promise in that voice.

Tonight couldn't come soon enough.

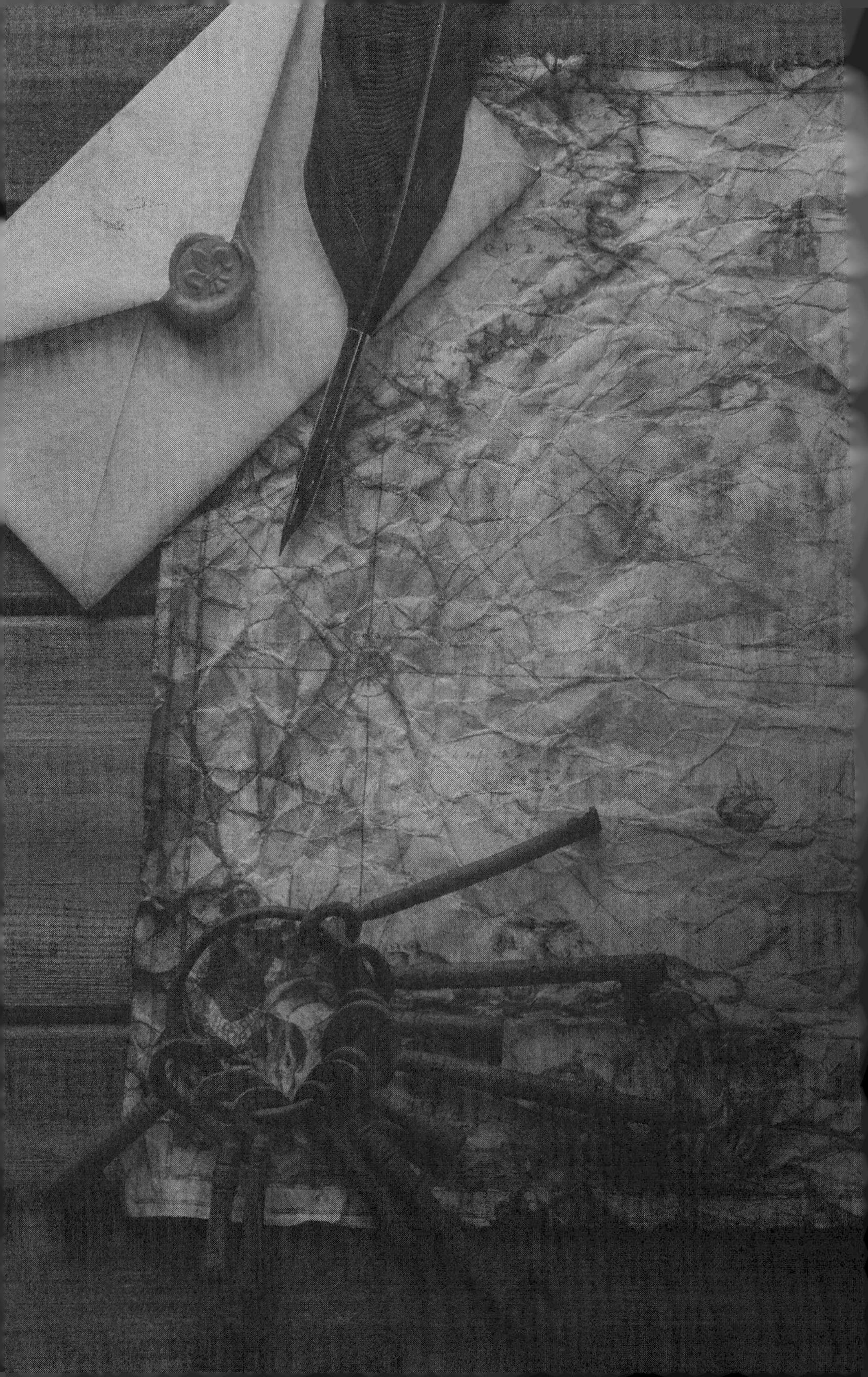

BLOODY SUPPLIES

"Bloody supplies," Vice huffed, pulling her hat lower to shield her eyes from the bright sun. She leant on his arm as they strolled along the streets of Ocamaniro. Despite taking ginger, willow bark, and honey from Lizzy's chest and making a tea from it, a fuzzy headache still throbbed.

Knigh squeezed her gloved hand. "Hmm, yes, because your headache is the supplies' fault. Nothing to do with the fact you didn't come to bed last night."

She grunted and nudged him. At least the ginger had done the trick and she didn't feel queasy from lack of sleep anymore. After they'd gathered the supplies Perry had requested, he'd suggested they take a walk to help her headache. It was no better.

"I must be losing my touch," he murmured, ducking closer, "if I can't tempt you to bed."

"Hmm, because twice on the desk wasn't enough?"

He raised an eyebrow. "There's such a thing as *enough?*"

"I'm sure you can tempt me back later."

"Oh, yes, just you wait until *later.*" His smile turned wicked, making her belly flip like only he could. "The things I have planned..."

"You have a plan, eh?"

"I always have a plan." With that cocky glint in his eye, she believed it.

She quizzed him about his plan as they continued along a quieter street at the edge of town, but he gave nothing away except for tantalising hints, and the conversation instead turned to the map and what she'd found out about Drake and his treasure. Knigh grumbled about her staying up all night with another man and she swatted him for his mock jealousy.

Yesterday, they'd reached the others and the boat just as the tide had revealed a thin strip of beach. They crossed to the *Venatrix* without any trouble and set sail at once. She'd gone straight to Perry's cabin with Knigh and the map and transferred that line from the blank paper, using the key symbol to ensure they aligned correctly.

The line from the cave plotted a course south, but with the strange way the map had been drawn, what was a straight line on the map, passing all those islands, would be a curved course in reality.

There were even islands on the map that appeared on none of their charts.

Knigh had agreed—it would make following the course challenging, and it meant the information from the map couldn't be readily copied to a chart. That had to be the point.

So Vice had stayed up all night with the Copper Drake, translating more, and searching through what they'd translated so far, until she'd found what appeared to be a set of instructions relating to the purple path. Those, together with the map and the course drawn on it, would take them to the next location. Not that the instructions *said* where they were leading, they only implied that if they followed the directions, they'd find something that would lead to *a treasure greater than gold and gems.*

But Perry being Perry, all sensible and cautious, had insisted they stop here for supplies first, since they didn't know what would await them.

So, yes, *bloody supplies.*

As they rounded a corner, the conversation turned to the past as it had started to do recently.

"I can't get a clear picture of Evered." A slight frown stiffened Knigh's brow as he glanced ahead. "Perry has talked about him a little, but everyone else says they didn't really know him." He looked at her sidelong, eyes gentle. "Am I allowed to ask what he was like?"

The back of her neck prickled, just a little. She gritted her teeth against all the words that wanted to come—the denial, the sharp jibes that would push Knigh away, telling him to mind his own damn business. They were instinctive. And on this occasion they were wrong.

She breathed past it, let the words go unsaid.

Once they'd withered on her tongue, she nodded. "They weren't being evasive, it's just none of them got the chance to know him. All the time he was on board *The Morrigan*, he refused to leave our cabin." Her mouth twisted, echoing the twisting discomfort in her gut. Admitting the truth, what he'd been like, how wrong she'd been. It wasn't only speaking ill of the dead, it was owning up to her own stupidity, her childish mistake.

But Knigh raised his brows a little and nodded—no judgement, only curiosity and surprise.

She could do this. She could explain some of it, at least. Rolling her shoulders, she squeezed Knigh's arm—warm and solid, a living anchor. "He was charming and lovely when we met." Enough to catch the attention of a girl who'd been shut away all her life. "And he didn't judge me for what I read or the fact I liked to write stories and wanted to do that with my life."

"You write stories?"

"Used to. Back then."

His head tilted and he smiled as if seeing her anew. "You never told me that. And you certainly didn't show it off to me when we visited your family—not like your Drake pin."

She laughed, his humour loosening the tension coiled in her muscles. "Well, young ladies aren't meant to write about wild adventures, are they? So when he said I could still do that as his wife..." She exhaled and shook her head. "It seemed like the answer—*he* seemed like the answer to the impossible problem I had of how I could live in that world." Where ladies were wives, mothers, their husband's possessions, defined by their relationships with others, never by what they did, never by their own achievements.

A flicker of a frown crossed Knigh's face. "Only *seemed*?"

Of course Knigh the Vigilant would notice her phrasing. "As

we fled, things changed. *He* changed." They crossed a busy intersection, and she took the excuse to pause and steel herself. "You aren't meant to speak ill of the dead, but... He took over my money, controlled it, but was bad with it. He gave it all to Fitz for the crossing, didn't stop to think we'd need money once we reached Arawaké, didn't even negotiate."

Knigh steered them away from people bustling along the street, keeping their conversation safe from prying ears. "And FitzRoy's deal was heavily biased towards—hmm, let me guess —*himself?*"

"Heh, that's Fitz. And when he threatened to kick us off the ship, Evered still wouldn't act, wouldn't work, thought it beneath him." Of course he did, as an aristocrat in Albionic society, his world had taught him exactly that. "I had to climb the shrouds to prove we weren't just dead weight. Fitz was *not* expecting me to succeed."

"I wish I'd been there to see his face." Knigh's hand closed over the back of hers, thumb stroking through the thin fabric of her gloves. "And to see you conquer the shrouds."

His warmth—not just of his hand and arm, but of his words and his look—it all seeped into her, kept her armour at bay. As they turned a corner, she caught her reflection in a shop window and blinked when it was her, Vice rather than Avice in a gown too pretty for a pirate ship, with eyes too desperate.

When she blinked again, it was both of them, Avice superimposed over Vice, staring back. Gods, she *had* been young, hadn't she? Cheeks still slightly rounded, expression open, eyes bright and wide and ready to see the world. Far, far too young.

"For all I thought I was married and thus a grown-up

woman, I was barely more than a girl. But I was the one who had to save us, because he would do nothing."

Mouth skewing to one side, she snorted. "He didn't even think women should enjoy sex. And I didn't with him—not once." The weight of Evered's judgement, the memory of his too-tight grip dragged away her sardonic smirk. This time when she exhaled, it was a heavy sigh for that girl who'd been so wrong. "I trusted myself to him in so many ways and… and when I even *tried* to solve any of it myself, he got so angry."

And his death had saved her from it. It was wrong to even think it, but there it was. Bald and dark and horribly true.

She clenched her teeth against the pressure at the back of her eyes. "I shouldn't have taken him away from the world he knew. I'm sure he wouldn't have changed, wouldn't have done that if I hadn't—"

"No." Knigh's jaw feathered as he shook his head. "No. His actions are *not* your responsibility. He did those things." He ducked closer, stopped her looking away, eyes almost gold in the sunlight bouncing off the shop windows. "What was it you said to me? '*He* did all that, not you. How is any of that your fault?'"

Her mouth dropped open. Using her own words against her—the ones she'd *drilled* into him about his father's failings. And if she'd been so adamant that he had to accept them, didn't that mean *she* had to do the same?

She swallowed past the blockage in her throat. "I… I'd never thought of it that way before."

"Of course not." His smile wasn't one of triumph at being

right, but small and sad. "You turned inward and looked for an explanation in yourself. I think perhaps we all do."

They cut across a small square without any more words.

If Knigh wasn't responsible for his father's actions, did that mean she wasn't responsible for Evered's? One couldn't be true and the other false, no matter how she shifted the pieces.

Either both were true or both were false. And there was no way she could condemn Knigh for what his father had done.

But she'd led Evered across the sea. She'd—

"So," Knigh murmured, something in his tone hesitant, "he was... well, he treated you poorly, but you still protected his memory, grieved, mourned him." His eyes narrowed like he was trying to reconcile those facts.

A chill traced down her back, despite the sun approaching noon. Mourning. Sorrow. Grief. Those *soft emotions* she'd denied having. And here Knigh was expecting her to talk about them.

No. Not expecting. *Asking*. Like his teasing touch at the waterfall, she could stop this at any time. It was her choice.

Back off. Or lean in.

Steeling herself, she pulled closer and let his warmth chase away that chill.

"I mourned it all." That confession forced her to pause and catch her breath. "Not just that he'd died, but that the whole thing didn't work out. I think I mourned the fact he wasn't what he'd seemed, the fact I'd been so stupid to love him, the fact I'd pulled my life apart for something that was so utterly wrong." Old guilt slithered through her gut. "And maybe he wouldn't have been like that if we'd stayed in Albion."

He tilted his head close enough that she could've kissed him. "Not your responsibility, remember?"

She grumbled. "Maybe."

"I'll take *maybe* for now." He brushed his lips over her temple. Another benefit of this walk—the fact they didn't have to hide their relationship. Talking about all this was one challenge, dealing with the crew's questions was quite another. "Was that when Lady Vice came along, immune to *soft emotions*?"

"Are you going to use *all* my own words against me today?"

"Only the ones I think you need to hear afresh."

"*Urgh.* You're insufferable when you're right."

His brows shot up, no doubt because she'd admitted he was right, but he quickly mastered it and instead grinned. "You're welcome."

Rolling her eyes, she shrugged. "Despite the way he was, his death did…" It had broken her. The shock, the horror, the sorrow. Her whole world had broken on that deck with his body. "Sad just felt hopeless, helpless, *weak*. Anger, though? That felt strong. Like something I could build upon."

With a thoughtful frown, he nodded. "I'm glad you survived it. Built something new. Though I also appreciate the… *existing materials* you used from Avice Ferrers." He winced. "I might've flogged that metaphor a bit too hard."

Again, that humour eased through her and she chuckled, planting a kiss on his cheek. "Just a touch."

Lips pursed, he gave her a sidelong look. "You were meant to humour me." They turned right. "I'm sure Perry will appreciate my extended metaphor."

Sure enough, just ahead stood Perry, peering up at something on a wall, one hand keeping the tricorne hat on her head.

"*Ha*, I'm sure she won't." They steered towards her. "Hey, Perry, can you settle an argument for us?"

Gasping, Perry spun on her heel, eyes wide. She blinked at them, face paling several shades despite her tanned skin.

That wasn't the only surprise. "What's wrong?"

"Vee," Knigh said, voice low, "the posters."

Perry turned back to the stretch of wall she'd been examining and when Vice followed her line of sight, the hairs on the back of her neck leapt to attention.

Wanted posters. With a sketch of her own face staring back. That wasn't anything new, but Knigh's right beside it? *That* chilled her to the bone.

And the reward below in bold, black text... *Twenty thousand guineas.*

Each.

That was an obscene amount of money. Enough to tempt anyone, even other pirates, even allies... They'd been sticking to friendly ports where they had allies, like Kayracou and Ocamaniro, figuring they'd be safe, but this?

This made her previous bounty look like pocket change. And these posters must've been from *before* they'd stolen Mercia's map. It would be even higher now.

She clutched Knigh's arm, fingers aching. Last year, she'd have crowed at such a high reward for her capture. It was a sign of success and fame—or infamy. It gave her bragging rights across the pirate world.

But to see such a sum against Knigh's name?

It was a lead weight in her belly. Heavy. Cold. Numb. How could she keep him safe with so much money massed against him?

"It mentions the capture of the *Venatrix*," he said, all matter-of-fact as though it wasn't a threat against his life and freedom, "so it's recent. And Governor deLacy is named, too—she's personally contributed to the sum on your head."

"How nice of her." The words came out with no intonation or thought. Those bold, black letters seared into her eyes. *Twenty thousand guineas for the capture of Knigh Blackwood, formerly Knighton Villiers.*

Blinking, she shook off the fog. "Knigh." She tugged on his arm, pulling his attention from the poster. "You need to get back to the ship. Quickly. Stay out of sight. With that much money on offer, you're not safe here."

As though their words had woken her from shock, Perry turned to them. She'd gone even paler, almost as grey as the streaks in her blonde hair. "Not just him." Her eyes shot to Vice, the whites visible all around her green irises. *"Both* of you."

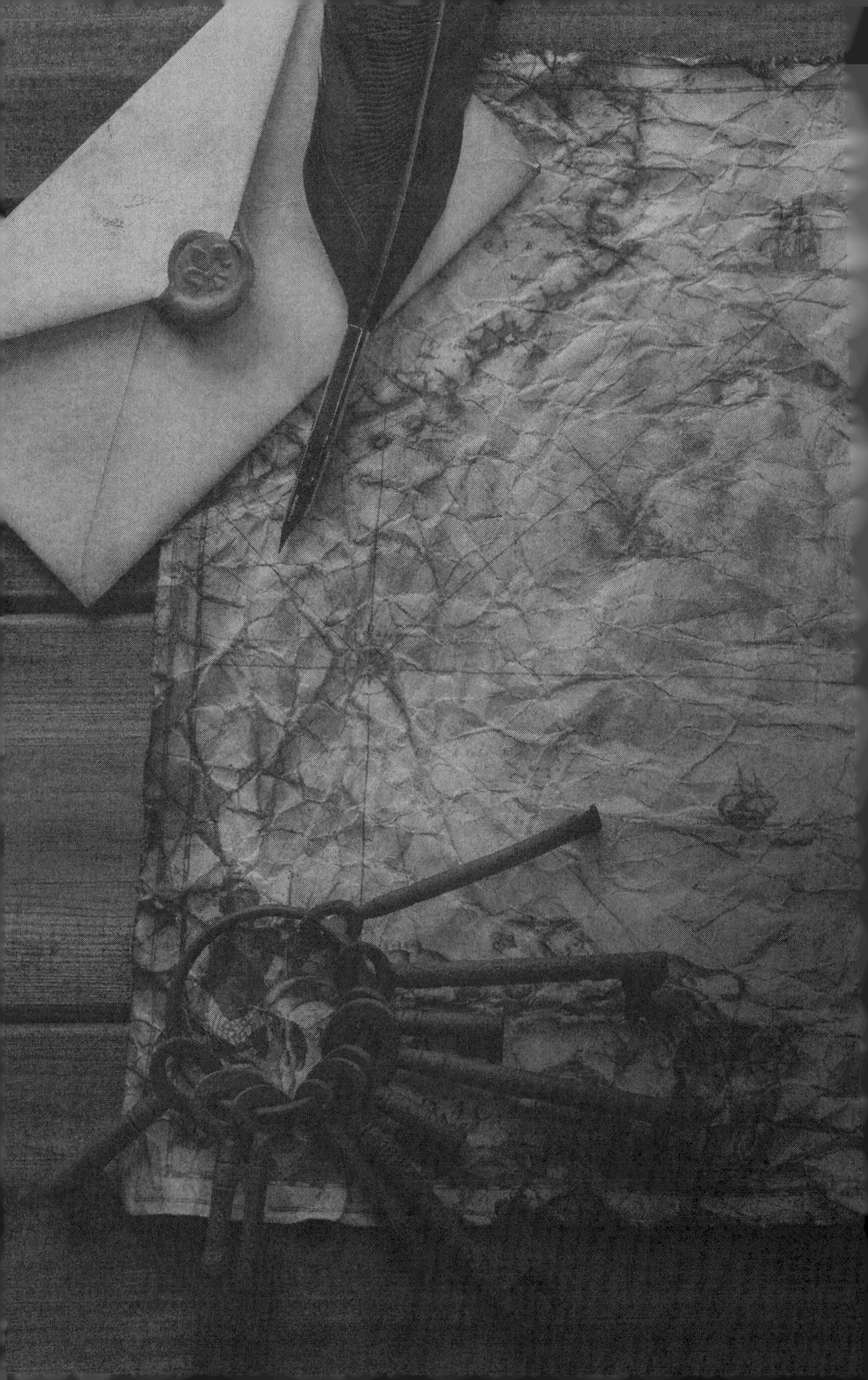

LIVE LIKE THIS

The world was sea and sky and ship, pitching as they crested one wave then another. Wind tugged at his hair and the wheel at his grip. At his side, Vee was warm and bright, eyes alert and flicking between their course ahead, the Copper Drake translation, and Mercia's map.

He could live like this. Forever. Even if they never found Drake's treasure.

"'Fly south with the butterfly,'" Vee said over the breeze, pointing at the translation, holding the flapping pages open. "Of course, Karukera—that looks kind of like a butterfly on maps, wouldn't you say?"

The dense green vegetation of that island lay beyond the waves and he found himself nodding, grinning. "I think you're right." He checked the compass and adjusted their course from south-southeast to due south. "And after that?"

"'Clear the crumbs.'" Her face screwed up as though re-reading the sentence would reveal what it meant.

"The little islets past Karukera, before you reach Guaticabon."

"Ah, *crumbs*. I see." Shaking her head, she held down the edges of the map and peered at it.

The Copper Drake had whole passages of nonsense. *Fly south with the butterfly. Clear the crumbs.* It didn't read like a set of instructions, but when they'd found reference to *purple*, they'd looked more closely and realised it was related to *the purple path*. And now here they were, following the apparent nonsense. To treasure? Or to traps? Or yet another clue?

Vee didn't seem to care which, as long as it was progress. She worked with feverish determination, eyes always fixed ahead, never to the past.

Except she *had* started to open up about her history. A little, which was a *lot* by her standards.

He had to clench his fists when he thought about Evered. Much as she'd tried to take responsibility for her late husband's actions and didn't want to speak ill of the dead, she'd revealed enough of the truth. Evered hadn't been worthy of her and had done nothing to even *try* to become worthy.

There were things she'd left out, he was sure, but he'd read between the lines. The way her jaw had clenched after she said he'd got angry, that meant *aggressive*, perhaps also *abusive*, whether physically or emotionally or both, he couldn't say. But it was enough. Enough to make his knuckles pale as he gripped the ship's wheel.

No wonder she was so sure everyone would let her down.

They leave, they die, or they let you down. That's what she'd said in Redland. The words were spelled out on his heart in little cracks. He didn't want to prove her right. Ever.

Her father had let her down. Evered, of course. And even her older sister—she'd mentioned before how Kat had left to marry. Which might not have been so bad if not for the fact it left young Avice with their father's full attention and no buffer.

And yet...

He found himself smiling. Because she stood at his side, intent on the map.

Passionate and clever. Funny and affectionate. Sharp as a blade. Wild as a wave. And as determined as the sea carving rock over centuries.

Yes, she had flaws, and yes, that past had left scars on her, but she'd stood back up and she hadn't just survived. She'd made a life and she'd *thrived*.

Strong enough to survive. Strong enough to adapt. Even when it was difficult—the way she'd spoken about Evered yesterday would've been unthinkable a few months ago.

It filled his heart, as warm and bright as a summer's day.

She glanced at him, attention snagging. "What're you looking at?"

He didn't bother to suppress the smile easing into place. Let her see it. Let her see it all. "Just you."

A flicker of surprise on her brows, her parted lips. Gods, he loved surprising her. For a second, it erased all those pretences she wore so readily—the tough façade, the distancing humour, the barbed tongue—leaving only her.

It took everything in him to keep his hands on the wheel,

squeezing, rather than tilting her chin up until their lips met. She swayed closer as though she felt it too.

But Clovis's deep bass rose in the opening lines of a shanty and within seconds, dozens more voices joined in as they worked.

Right. They were on deck in front of the whole crew and *this* was a secret. Somehow Aedan had swallowed the lies and excuses for Knigh's empty berth, but he wouldn't if they kept looking at each other like this. Steeling himself, he forced his attention back on course. "Where next, Pirate Queen?"

Following the coded instructions, they continued south for a day and a night, passing islands large and small, until they reached *the giantess's paps*, as the Copper Drake called them. Vee raised one eyebrow from the book to the twin mountains of Hewanorra. "*'Giantess's paps'*? Really?"

Saba squinted at them. "Hmm, no, I don't see it."

Lizzy screwed up her face and cocked her head. "No one's boobs are really symmetrical, y'know. But... they *are* pointy, I'll give you that."

Still, that had to be what the book referred to, and as the island they'd visited not so long ago passed to port, Knigh steered the *Venatrix* southwest. The only instruction left on the list was to maintain course until they reached the *snapping turtle*.

The rest of that day and the next, nothing but sea. Vee's frown grew deeper, her fidgeting more twitchy. Further south, out of view, was the mainland but here—

Her fingers tangled in his shirt, though her eyes were fixed ahead. "Land."

Sure enough, a deeper darkness on the rolling sea, dead ahead. He strained towards it and a moment later, the ship picked up speed with Vee leaning into her gift, as impatient as he was to see whether this was their *snapping turtle*.

Minute by minute the spot of land grew larger, clearer. A broad slant of forest rose from the surf, a larger island beyond it. At one end a bluff pointed northwest, its cliffs a warm, buttery yellow. The shape though... He didn't have to squint to see it—that broad slant could've been a great shell emerging from the sea, the bluff was a head.

The whole island looked like a snapping turtle basking in the sun.

"Do you see it?" Vee's voice came out breathless as she clutched his shoulder.

He took one hand from the wheel and squeezed her fingers. Excitement practically sparked off her. "I do."

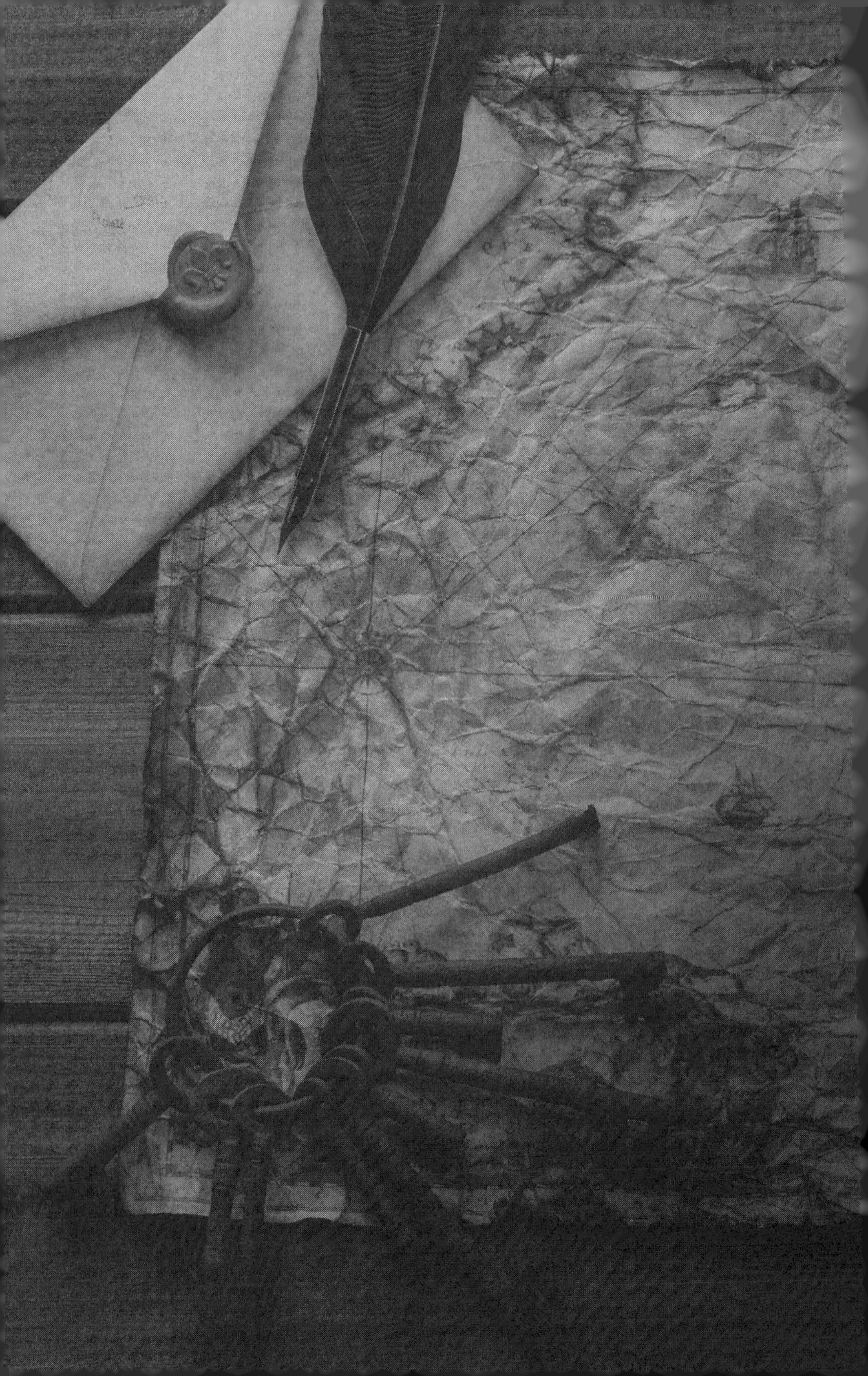

FLYING SOUTH

Halfway up the slope of the turtle's back, a tiered temple rose from the scrubby vegetation, its stones a dark, unforgiving grey. It sent a jolt of recognition through Knigh. Sure enough when he and Vee checked the Copper Drake, they found a sketch of it around halfway through. That had to be their destination, but what would they find there?

Supplies on their backs, rope over their shoulders, Knigh, Vee, and the rest of their party started up the slope towards the temple. It was much smaller than others he'd seen and Vee confirmed this was nowhere near as large as the place where she'd found the cipher key.

The land was sand and rock, the leaves a yellowy spring green, rather than the rich, dark growth of Hewanorra's rainforests.

Behind, the larger island was carved into terraces, as farms on the mainland often were. Stones that might've once been houses littered the overgrown terraces. The *Venatrix* was the only vessel anchored nearby, and no trickles of smoke broke the clear sky—no signs of current habitation.

The thorny trees and shrubs did little to stop the sun pounding on their backs and heads. Cicadas and other insects buzzed and hummed, forming a strange, arid song that ran counterpoint to the sea hushing against the cliff and beach. The dry air coated their tongues, and even though it wasn't a long walk, they had to stop and sip from their canteens.

As they approached the temple, Saba's lips grew more pursed, her frown tighter. Wynn and Effie came up on either side of her and rubbed her back, offering brief nods of acknowledgement. When Vee had described that other temple, Saba had listened rapt, her shoulders sinking to hear of sacred spaces defaced by Drake.

Vee paused at the entrance, wiping sweat from her brow as she peered up at the three tiers. The door stood open, its shade all the more inviting since the spindly trees offered little respite from the fierce sun. She looked at Saba in silent question.

"It's fine," Saba said. "You're not the one who used this place to hide your treasure. Come." She placed a hand on the small of Vee's back and they entered side by side.

When he followed, Knigh had to blink his way into the sudden darkness. He took in a long breath of cool air and rubbed his eyes. The shadows resolved themselves into one chamber that covered most of the temple's interior. The square room stretched perhaps forty feet across and twenty up, with a pair of huge, stone doors ahead.

Aedan lit a lamp, revealing that every surface had been painted or carved or both. Knigh craned his neck to take it all in. Above and to all sides, wide-faced figures, some kneeling, many with headdresses, stared back in black and russet and yellow ochre. Lines spiralled from them, dizzying and intricate and beautiful, like a dance he didn't know the steps to.

Vee and Saba explored the chamber, the former's shoulders tight and square. Wynn and Effie kept near the doors, often glancing outside.

"No sign of any traps," Vee said at last, words echoing in the empty space. *Traps, traps... traps.*

"Except that one." Brows raised, Saba nodded to the double doors.

Knigh edged closer, careful not to step any further than Saba did as he couldn't detect any clue to where the trapped area began or how it might trigger. "Fake doors?"

"Oh, no, the doors are real." Her hands landed on her hips. At her side, Vee craned her neck to look from bottom to top of those great doors, which stood some fifteen feet high. Knigh did the same, alert for any hint of mechanism, tripwire, pulley, or cog. There were only the paintings, the carvings, covering the doors and wall.

"But," Saba continued, "if you open them without taking the correct countermeasures..." She winced, dark eyes scanning the lintel above. She lifted one hand, then slapped it into the other, making Aedan jump as the chamber amplified the clap. Its aftershock still echoed as she went on, "My mother's shown me. It's a way of stopping tombs being desecrated by those who don't belong." Her mouth twisted with irony.

"Too late for that," Vee murmured and threw an apologetic smile to her friend.

Shaking her head, Saba sighed. "These islands, these temples—they are my history and the history of my neighbours, but... but Drake is too. I'm as much Albionic as I am Arawakéan. It's just..." She exhaled through her nose, something warring in her frown and the tight lines of her mouth. "Why couldn't he make his own place? Why did he have to claim and write over places that weren't his?"

Knigh blinked, the only sign of surprise he allowed. Saba and Vee had both mentioned that Saba's father had been an Albionic sailor with whom her mother had had a brief affair. The Arawakéan Union had a different approach to illegitimacy and marriage from Albion's. But with her terracotta complexion and dark, dark hair, it was easy to forget that half her blood was Albionic, and he'd never stopped to think what that might mean to her.

Vee squeezed her shoulder. "Because men like him think everything is theirs for the taking."

He blinked again. Vee saying something negative about Drake? That was a first. From the books in her old cabin on *The Morrigan*, her obsession with him and his treasure, and the way she usually spoke about him, she always seemed to hold Drake up as a hero.

And beneath that comment... it wasn't only Drake she was speaking of. FitzRoy? Her father? Her husband, too?

Saba patted Vee's hand, which was still on her shoulder, then cocked her head at the doors. "Lucky for us, this mechanism looks quite simple. Makes sense, with it only being a small temple. The larger centres tend to have more complex systems."

In spite of his control, Knigh's mouth dropped open for a moment. "You can see the trap?"

Saba grinned at him before her attention returned to the lintel above the doors, "I can probably see a lot of things on these walls that you just think are swirly shapes."

Knigh squinted at the walls and doors. There were a lot of circles, spirals, dots, and wavy lines. So they all meant something to Saba—something he couldn't hope to understand.

"But, yes," Saba went on, "I can see the trap. And how to get past it."

Thank the gods for that, because there weren't any sections of the Copper Drake they'd translated so far that related to these doors.

Vee's eyes sparked with excitement as she clapped Saba on the back. "I should've known you would. So"—she raised her brows—"how do I get it open?"

"*You* don't." Saba snorted. "At least, not on your own."

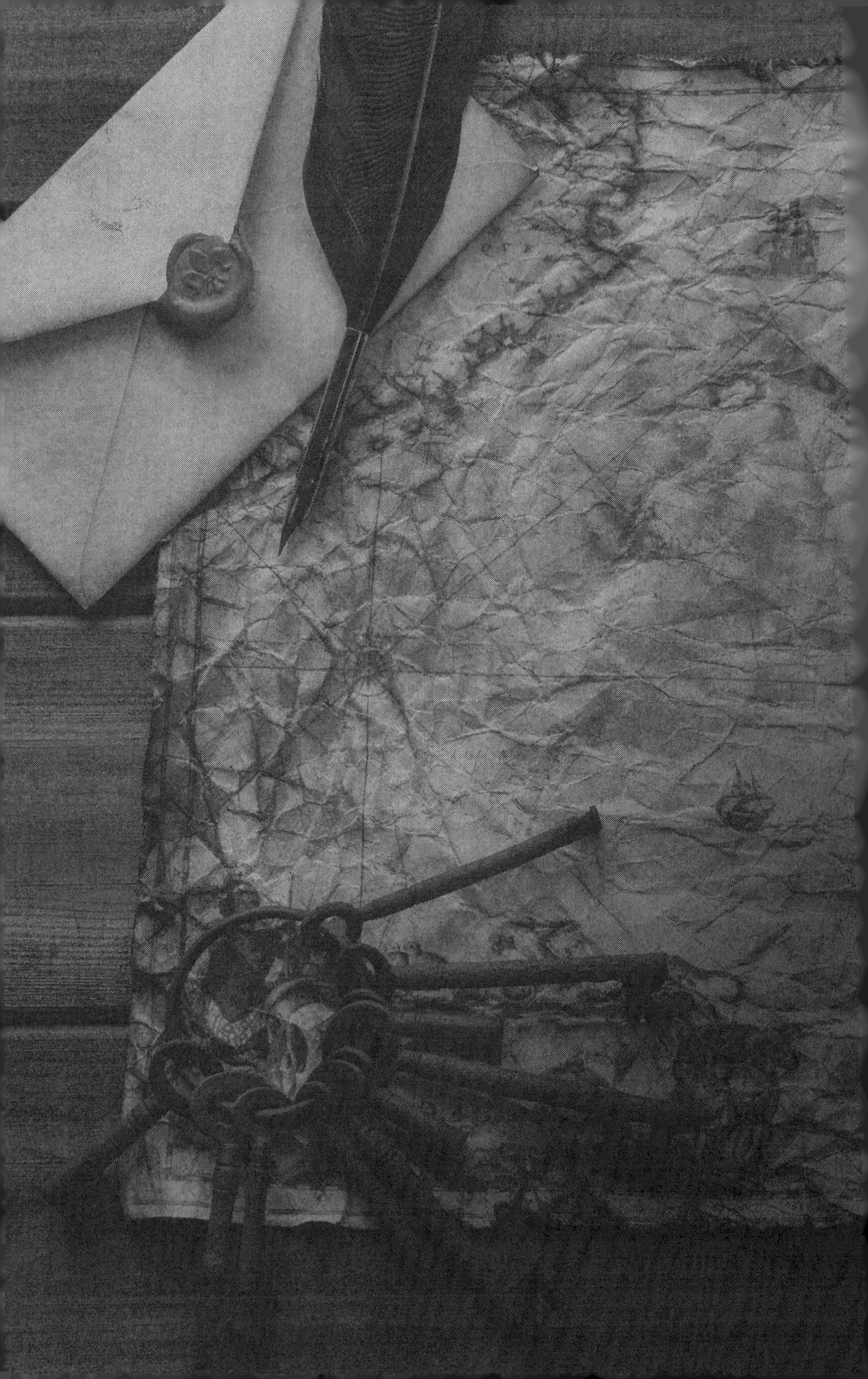

IRON & STONE

Vice barely bit back a groan as she eyed the double doors looming above. "Not on my own. Of course." The world wasn't letting her do anything on her own lately. She cocked her head at Saba.

Neck craned, her friend's dark eyes fixed on a point high on the wall. "It requires two people working at exactly the same time."

Over Saba's head, Knigh gave her a look. *Me and you.* That's what it said. A team.

Equal parts warmth and twisting dread worked their way through her. What if she failed him? What if he got hurt because of her? What if they triggered the trap and—

"You see that stone there"—Saba pointed—"with the three dots?"

Vice pressed close to Saba, following her extended arm in

line with the lintel, around three feet left from the doors. "Ah, yes. Below the serpent's head?"

"That's the one. The central dot is actually a metal ring disguised amongst the carvings—see, it's mounted at the top? That bit just catching the light."

The glint and shadow—yes, she was right. A metal loop embedded in the wall secured the top of the ring, almost like a door knocker but thicker, sturdier.

"Pull out the loop and the matching one on the other side." Saba pointed again and, sure enough, another stone with three dots mirrored this one to the right of the doors. "And it stops the mechanism, allowing us to open the door. On the other side, there should be a crank to reset the trap, but it isn't primed until the doors close."

"And what *is* the trap exactly?" A small frown tightened Knigh's brow as he looked along the lintel as though he might be able to work it out.

"Rocks. Falling. *Splat*. That whole lintel will come down and the stones above—you see those seams? They're separate from the rest of the wall."

Seams hidden amongst the carvings. Wild Hunt, the sections of rock were huge. There'd be no surviving that. Vice's mouth went dry as a cold knot tightened in her belly.

"Splat indeed," Knigh murmured, tanned face paling a shade.

Eyes narrowing, Saba tilted her head from one side to the other like she was weighing up possibilities. "Probably a bank of sand above, too, ready to flood into this chamber and bury anyone else with the defilers." She flashed a bright smile from Vice to Knigh. "Lucky I'm here, right?"

Laughter only a little forced, Vice slung an arm around her shoulder and squeezed. "Always." Which took them to the awkward question. "Are you sure it's all right for us to open this, though? I don't mean the trap. I mean... What Drake did—are we making it worse?"

With a heavy sigh, Saba slipped her arm around Vice's waist and squeezed back. Her shoulders bobbed. "It's already done, was done two hundred years ago and the evidence remains."

Vice promised to remove any trace of him that she could, then they'd send a message to the mainland, who would be able to send priestesses to reconsecrate the temple.

They directed Aedan, Lizzy, Wynn, and Effie to wait outside, just in case. Vice would climb up one side, Knigh the other, with Saba coordinating them from the ground. It also meant she'd be the first to see inside the chamber beyond, which was only right.

It sounded easy enough.

Weapons piled on the floor to make her as light as possible, Vice stood before the sheer wall. Easy. *Right*.

She exchanged a look with Knigh and the flash of his eyebrows said he was thinking the same.

The carvings were uneven and shallow for the most part—not exactly prime candidates for hand and foot holds. She'd spent a childhood climbing trees and getting in trouble for it, and for almost four years she'd scaled shrouds, masts, and hulls. She could do this.

The stone was cool and rough under her fingertips as she reached to the first handhold—a broad palm frond. Her toe found a spot wedged in the horizontal bands of the trunk. That was a good start.

"Try the palm trees," she called to Knigh. "The trunk's got a surprisingly good toe hold." Then she was reaching up, leg muscles propelling her to the next hold—a bright red bird, wings outstretched. And the next—a swirling, stylised cloud with lightning forking from it. Maybe that was a sign. Muscles warming, she grinned and pressed her toes into the next indent and the next.

By the time she reached the ring, sweat slithered between her shoulder blades, and her hands and forearms ached. Climbing a sheer face was different from trees or masts or ropes—this was all finger strength and holding her torso tight and straight, so she didn't fall backwards off the wall. Her stomach and back were solid, the same as when she held her body straight for press-ups or those awful planks Knigh made her hold for minutes on end.

He was a sadistic bastard. As was whoever had designed this.

Huffing, she clung to the grinning mouth of a figure beside the metal ring. He was a little lower, perhaps because he weighed more, but in a single surge that strained muscle against shirt, he reached for the same grinning mouth and pulled level. His teeth flashed as he smiled over at her, triumph in his eyes.

Hells, was that *excitement?*

The man who until recently had thought Drake's treasure

nothing more than a wild story, a legend to tempt foolish pirates, was excited at the prospect of getting through these doors and another step closer to that treasure.

Her heart leapt. What would it be? *Treasure greater than gold and gems.* She'd always dreamed it would be a chest or a room full of riches, but perhaps it was something else entirely.

Something they could sell to get Saba her home. Something that could get Knigh and his family a new place in the world—a place that was safe. No sweat dripped into her eyes, but they stung all the same.

Maybe it would even be something that would allow her to go back for Mama. She couldn't face her, but she might be able to do it anonymously, send someone else, or—

"Ready?" Saba called from below.

"Aye," Knigh called.

"And me." Vice pulled an empty pouch from her pocket.

"Hold the rings," Saba directed.

Even with the leather pouch shielding her skin, the iron was too hot, like she'd reached too close to a fire on a chilly night. Sickness tugged on her belly, tightened her throat. How had she ever thought it was only rock? But the carved design was so dizzying, so busy, it was easy to miss such a detail. Her right arm shook, holding her upright, but she didn't dare put any weight on the ring yet.

"Take the strain."

She extended the ring until it was at right-angles to the wall and tightened her shoulder and bicep muscles against it. The hold in the wall must've been tight, because it didn't slide even a quarter of an inch, despite the pressure on it.

"On three, I want you to start pulling, slow and steady. Report to each other how far out you are, inch-by-inch. Got it?"

"My arm's bloody killing," Vice huffed, "get on with it." Not to mention the heat and her rolling stomach.

Knigh's laugh was half-grunt. "Got it."

"One. Two."

Inhale.

"Three."

Across her shoulders and up her arm, every muscle tensed. With a grating groan, the pin holding the ring in place moved.

"Half an inch here," she called to Knigh.

"Aye... An inch now."

Attention fixed on his own pin, he couldn't see her, but she nodded anyway. "Approaching two."

The grating sound built and something rumbled through the rock and into her fingertips still holding that grinning mouth.

Every hair on the back of her neck strained to attention. Her right arm shook and shook.

"Almost on three," Knigh called and glanced over.

His eyes were sure, his jaw set.

She nodded back, swallowed, and kept pulling. He was sure of her. They could do this. Together.

"Three and a half," she called.

"Any idea how long this thing is, Saba? Four."

"Not a clue." Saba was out of sight, but the shrug sounded in her voice.

"Thanks." Vice didn't have the breath to laugh. "Five."

Something clicked behind the stone.

"And a half." The strain came through in Knigh's voice, a certain tightness that said he heard the click, too.

"Nearly at—"

Then the ring and six-inch pin were in her hand and not in the wall, yanking at her hold. She gasped her shock, fingers screaming—those of her left hand at the grotesque wrongness of iron, and her right at the clawed grip in that grinning mouth.

Tick-tick-tick, like broken clockwork. A whirr thrummed through her fingers and toes, moving behind the rock, up and to left and right.

Click. Click. Thunk.

A soft hiss of sand from above the lintel turned her insides to stone.

Too much like the hiss of sand and clack of rock just before Evans had fallen. It came in dreams on the bad nights, now here it was in reality.

But there was no clack. And no more movement.

Just silence.

Her arms and calves shook, but the wall was still. The rock above, too.

"I think we've done it," Knigh panted.

"We have," Saba called. "You can drop the rings, you know."

Gladly. The thing weighed on Vice, heavy and wrong. When it clanged to the floor, the relief was a palpable wave across her skin.

Muscles trembling, hands shaking, she climbed down. The last few feet she jumped and landed, staggering as her calves groaned at being on solid ground.

As Saba started forward to push the doors open, Vice grabbed her arm, albeit with a weakened grip. "Are you sure it's safe?" It was Saba's right to go first, to see this first, but at the same time, if the trap triggered…

"I'm sure." Saba patted her hand and strode to the doors, shoulders square, a bright smile on her face. Vice ghosted on her heels, muscles aching but still on alert. Her hands clenched against the urge to pull her friend away and throw herself against the doors.

Please, gods, if I've ever done anything that's pleased you, now is the time to smile on me. Keep Saba safe and I'll never bother you again.

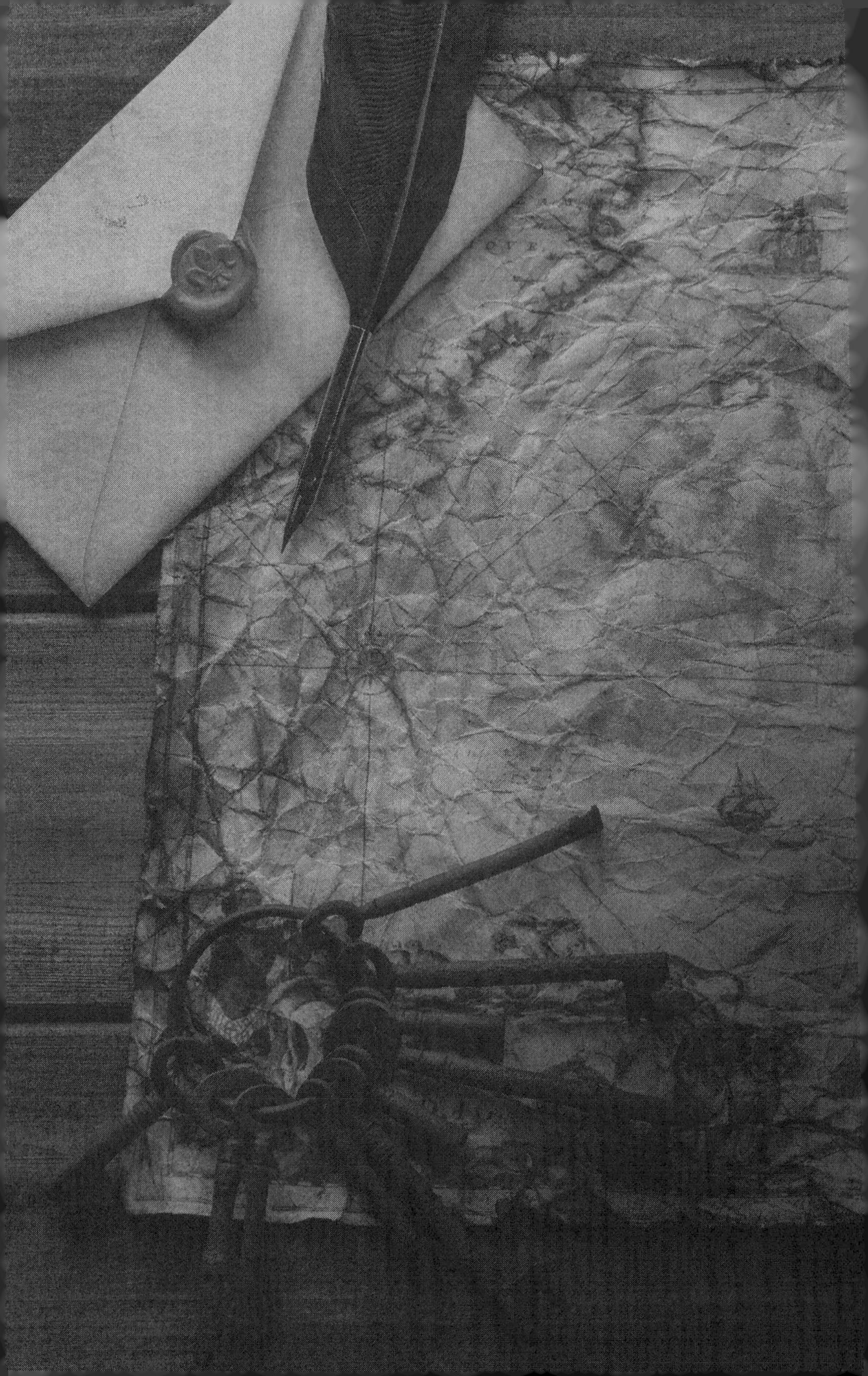

THE TREASURE

Vice held her breath. The hairs on the back of her neck remained flat. They sometimes rose in fear, yes, but her fae instincts always warned her even if she didn't understand the danger at the time.

Saba pushed, and the doors swung open. No movement above. No sound other than the soft scrape of the stone doors in their tracks.

Vice almost staggered after her. Knigh followed with the lantern and called to the others, "You can come back now. It's safe."

The room beyond was far smaller, perhaps a third the size of the main chamber with a lower ceiling, all covered in more carved and painted designs. Dead ahead, an alcove bit into the wall.

And inside that, a chest.

Heart pounding, Vice blinked. A chest. Dark, reddish wood

with steel bands over the lid and around the sides. That had to contain the next clue. Another step closer to Drake's treasure. It sparked through her, as bright and electrifying as the lightning she conjured with her gift.

But. She huffed a sigh. Perry would tell her to be sensible now. To check. To be sure. And she owed that to her friends and to all the effort and sacrifices that had gone into reaching this point—Evans' life included.

So she rolled back her aching shoulders and told them to keep back. Between her and Saba, they checked the floor and walls for false panels or tripwires or any other clever, vicious traps. But there was nothing in the room and nothing on the chest or in its alcove.

"I think we're safe." Saba gave a hopeful smile.

"Famous last words," Lizzy muttered, folding her arms. But she flashed a grin and didn't back away as Aedan inspected the lock on the chest.

"Looks quite simple." He shrugged. "Nothing dodgy going on, either—no poisoned barbs or anything like that."

They all looked at her, eyebrows raised.

Knigh cocked his head. "Well?"

Her decision. And her responsibility.

She nodded to Aedan. "Do it. But if anyone feels the slightest shift of the floor or rocks or the chest starts doing anything strange, you run all the way out of here and don't look back. Don't stay behind to help, don't pause to grab anything. You run and save yourselves, right?"

Knigh's mouth flattened and he shifted his weight as though he wanted to insert himself between her and the alcove. As the others nodded, he only looked away. He would stop and help her. And that was the problem. That was what she couldn't be responsible for.

As Aedan crouched and began work on the lock, Vice sidled between Knigh and the chest. Just in case. If anything happened, she might have an instant to shove him towards the doors and away.

But a minute later, Aedan stood back and dusted off his hands. "All ready to open."

Everyone turned to her. Saba gestured to the chest as if to say *after you*.

Vice shook her head. "But it's—"

"You led us here." Saba took another step back. "You found the cipher key and snuck onto Mercia's ship and endured living with him all those weeks. You've earned the right to open this and see what our next clue is."

It was no use arguing, not when Saba's shoulders and face were set like that, so she bowed her head. "Thank you."

The wood was smooth under her fingers. The chamber fell silent—the waves and insects outside weren't even audible from in here. She took a steadying breath against the excitement leaping through her veins and lifted the lid.

Before it was even fully open, golden light reflected onto her arms, splashed with green, blue, red.

Then it was open and...

Gold. So much gold.

And gems—rubies, emeralds, sapphires, and exquisite turquoise cabochons as bright as shallow seas.

She blinked at the dazzling light.

"Shit," Lizzy gasped.

"That's... that's treasure," Wynn whispered.

"*The* treasure," Effie added.

No, it... *Treasure greater than gold...* This wasn't greater than gold, it simply *was* gold. Lots of it, yes, but...

Aedan crowed, the sound echoing off the walls, soon joined by Saba and Lizzy. The sisters broke into laughter and squeals and might've grabbed each other in hugs, but Vice couldn't take her eyes off the velvet-lined chest.

Full of treasure, but... This wasn't Drake's treasure. This couldn't be the end point. There had to be—

"You did it." Knigh's hand closed over her shoulder and gave a little shake. "You bloody did it." He huffed a laugh and picked up one of the coins, holding it up to the light. "Vee, this is..." He waved it a few inches from her nose and laughed again.

She smiled, but only because it was impossible not to when he laughed. It wasn't for the contents of the chest. Unless... What if there was something hidden beneath the coins?

Hand digging into the cool metal, she swept left and right, dug as deep as she could, the coins and gems reaching her elbow before her fingertips found the bottom of the chest. But she found nothing else.

No, no, no. This wasn't—

"Vee?" Still holding her shoulder, he tucked in close beside her as the others continued their celebrations—laughing and running around the room, grabbing each other in hugs. "What's wrong?"

"I don't... This can't..." The warmth of his touch helped her push past the silence blocking her throat, but channelling her churning thoughts into sentences was impossible.

This was a great sum of money, yes, enough to make them all rich, but... It couldn't be *the* treasure. This couldn't be the end.

Saba called something about going outside to find branches to help carry it out before she and the others disappeared.

"Vee," Knigh said, "this is victory. Look at it—*look*." He came up right behind her, chest against her back. "Look at what you've done." His words tickled her ear, dispelling the shock and confusion that dammed her words. "You've made your crew rich. Every single one of them. You did what a hundred others failed at—what *Fitz-bloody-Roy* failed at."

Gleaming, glittering gold. Flickering, flashing gems. All in a chest so big, they would struggle to carry it out of here.

"You found Drake's treasure."

Had she?

Could this be it? It was a vast sum—she couldn't even guess the amount, but it was *enough*.

The day they'd left Portsmouth, she'd set out to beat Fitz to the thing he'd pursued for so long. Had she achieved that in mere months?

This much gold—it should've felt like victory, but...

Shaking her head, shaking away the circling thoughts, she turned her back on the chest and blinked up at him. "What was the point of the rest of the Copper Drake? We haven't finished deciphering it yet."

"Misdirection? For all we know, the rest could be his favourite recipes."

She exhaled through her nose, throwing him a dark look.

"Vee, look"—he scoffed—"I didn't even believe in this treasure, but here it is." His expression softened as he pushed hair back from her face. "Maybe you've been so absorbed with the chase, it's hard to believe you've actually achieved it. When I passed my lieutenant's exam, I still had dreams about it for months after. I'd wake up the day of the test, always with some catastrophe, like sleeping in or not being able to find my way to the examination room. Every time I woke, I had to go and re-read the letter saying 'full numbers' before I'd accept that passing was the reality and not just another dream."

It seemed hard to believe Knigh had ever doubted any part of his life at sea or in the Navy, but here he was with those earnest eyes. And despite the cocky arrogance he displayed at times, he'd always held that vulnerability inside, believing his judgement wasn't sound.

She tugged on the front of his shirt. It was believable that he'd had those dreams, but...

"It might take a while for it to sink in," he went on. "And I'm not saying you have to crow it from the top of the mainmast or display quite their level of exuberance"—he nodded towards the doors—"but maybe try to enjoy it?"

"There are other treasures in life than gold."

He cocked his head, frowning in confusion.

"You said that to me after we found the first clue. I'm telling you, this isn't Drake's treasure. It's something *greater than gold and gems*. You and the Copper Drake agree on that."

Lips twisting to one side, he rubbed his jaw. He opened his mouth as if to speak, but the others reappeared carrying two straight branches, and talk turned to fashioning a litter so they could carry the chest.

In stewing silence, Vice checked the room for any more evidence of Drake or secret doors—there were none. There had to be something she was missing. Something in the book or the map or...

But she helped lift the chest, taking one handle on her shoulder, with Knigh at her side holding the other, while Aedan, Saba, and Lizzy took the back.

She would help carry this thing to the boat and row back to the *Venatrix*. She might even smile when they reached the crew and revealed their find.

This was not Drake's treasure and nothing in the world would convince her.

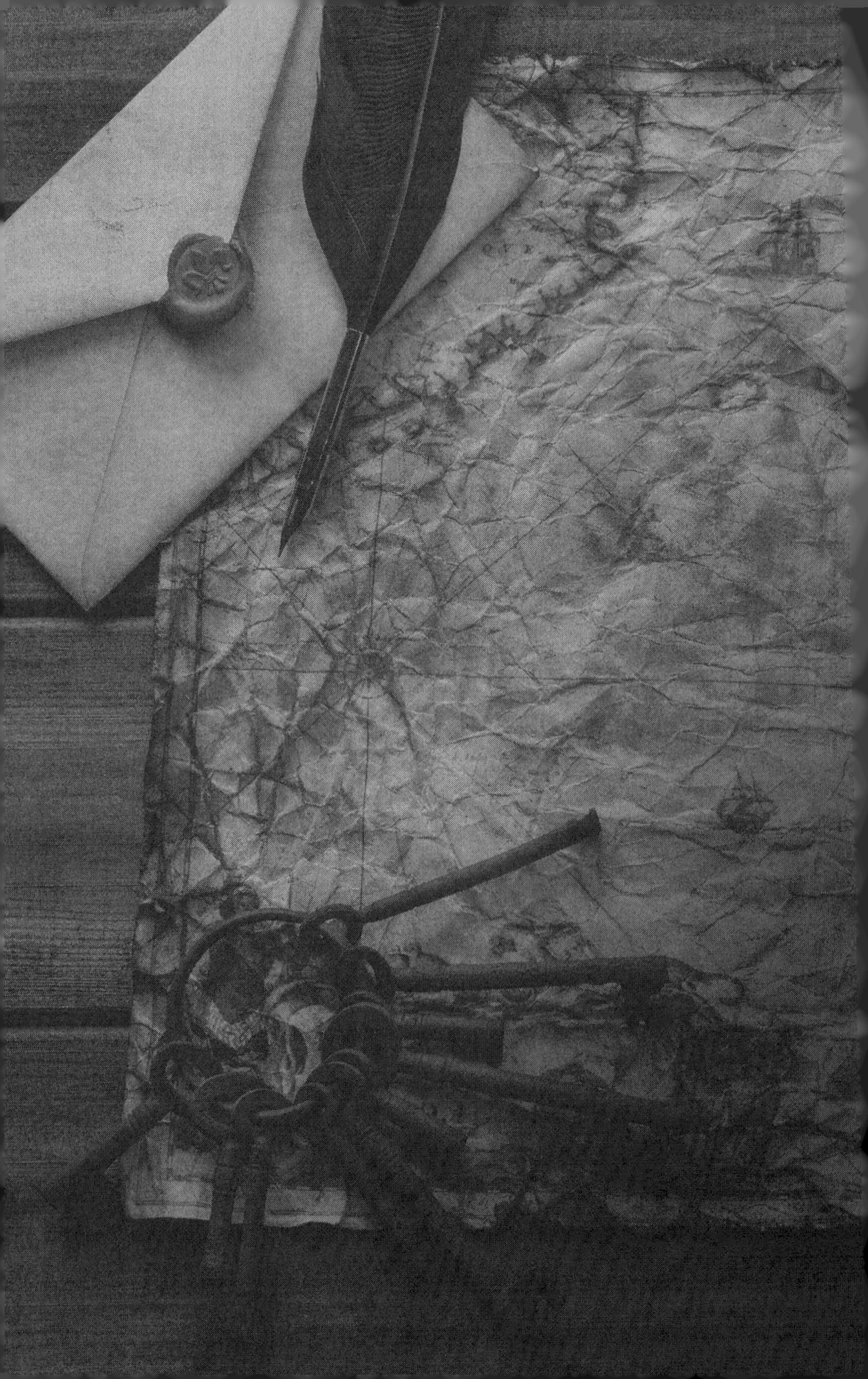

HONEY

That night they set up tents and lit bonfires on the neighbouring island. Perry had promised they'd leave tomorrow, secure their treasure, but tonight the crew would celebrate. Thick smoke tainted every breath, even here in Vice's tent, as she sat on the floor with the Copper Drake and its translations around her.

There had to be some clue, some way the gold and gems would point them to the real treasure. She'd read through the sections she and Knigh had translated, but there was nothing concrete, only little hints. *Treasure greater than gold and gems.* There had to be something in the last part of the book.

Knigh was off with the others, getting ready to celebrate. Maybe he'd play his guitar for them. Somehow he actually believed this was the treasure and didn't believe her when she swore it wasn't.

Scowling, she bent over the cipher key and the Copper

Drake and worked, letter-by-letter. First she deciphered into the Latium notebook, then she translated the words into Albionic and copied them into that notebook. It usually went much quicker when she and Knigh worked together, but...

"Vice?"

She blinked up from her work as Lizzy appeared at the tent flap.

"Blackwood said you'd be here." Lizzy's auburn brows pulled together as she scanned the papers and notebooks strewn around the tent. "You know we're only here one night, right?"

Vice rubbed her eyes. "Hence the lack of furniture." Her back and shoulders ached both from climbing the wall and from hunching over, but this work needed doing. She needed proof this wasn't *the* treasure and some idea of where to go next. So far, she'd managed to decipher two paragraphs. Good gods, how long had that taken?

When she looked up, Lizzy was still there.

"Right." Shaking her head, Lizzy shrugged. "Look, did you go through my medicine chest? Erec saw you with a cup of something sweet the other day."

"A cup of..." Vice blinked from Lizzy to the paltry two paragraphs and back again. "Oh, yes. I just made a little brew." She rolled her shoulders with a groan. "Had a headache and was feeling a bit queasy from lack of sleep."

Lizzy's mouth flattened. "What did you take?"

What did it matter? Still, maybe it was best to make the most of an opportunity to straighten her back. She cracked her neck, first left then right. "Just what you've given me before.

Ginger for the sickness. Willow bark for the headache. And honey to counteract the bitterness."

"Honey. Just to make your drink sweet." Lizzy snorted, but with her brows tight together, that was the only sign of amusement. "And did you notice it was the last of the jar?"

Lizzy was pissed off at her because she'd made her own tea and hadn't come and bothered her with something as petty as a headache. Face screwed up, Vice cocked her head. "There was a bit left."

"A bare scraping—nothing I could use." Lizzy stomped in, hands on hips. "Not enough to treat a cut on Clovis's arm and stop it getting infected."

Vice winced—he *had* looked a little ashen this morning as they'd anchored. An infection could be dangerous, deadly even with a small wound. But Clovis wasn't going to die, not when they had a fae-touched healer on board. "So ask Knigh to heal it."

"Aye, I already did and it's done." And yet she didn't look happy about the fact—quite the opposite with her hazel eyes flashing in the lamplight. "But if I'd had the honey, it would've been fine on its own and we wouldn't have needed Blackwood to step in."

Sighing, Vice sat back. She didn't have time for this—she had pages and pages more of this damn book to decipher. "If Knigh healed Clovis, I don't see what the issue is."

"What if he hadn't been able to? What if we had no healer? Do you have any idea how rare they are?" Lizzy bared her teeth in a bitter smile. "Rarer than sea witches. We're lucky to have him, aye, but I won't have the lad burning through his magic on injuries that don't need it when at *any* moment we might need every scrap of energy he has."

Vice bit her tongue against a reply. However careful they were, accidents happened at sea. A ship was full of dangers even outside of battle.

Perhaps Lizzy saw her words had sunk in, because her frown eased by a hair's breadth. "And I won't have us relying on his gift for cases that don't warrant it. I'd have told you all this if you'd just come to me. I'd have given you cinnamon to sweeten your drink, which would've worked with the ginger to help your stomach. And if I *had* given you honey, I'd have known to get more." She gave a sharp shake of her head. "But you didn't come to me, did you?" That easing had vanished—Lizzy was all sharp angles and glinting edges now. "You just helped yourself, because Vice knows best and must do everything for herself."

Vice's fingers tightened around her pencil. "I was trying to make your life easier. I—"

"I'm the ship's physic, and that medicine chest and the crew's health are *my* responsibility, but you just came along and pissed all over that." Again, that bitter smile as she shook her head. "You might as well have pissed all over me for all you value what I do." Every movement stiff, she turned and strode out, kicking sand in her wake.

"Ah, shit," Vice muttered and scrubbed her face. That sharpness wasn't just anger, it was *hurt*. "I'm sorry," she called through the open tent flap to Lizzy's rigid back.

She gave no reaction.

When Knigh came the other way, he frowned and spoke to

her, maybe asking what was wrong, but she just lifted a hand, shook her head, and continued out of sight.

You might as well have pissed all over me. The words twisted in her gut, as sharp as broken glass. Lizzy was straight-talking, but she'd never had a go at Vice in almost four years of working together—of being *friends*. Along with Saba and Perry, Lizzy was one of the first crew members to speak to her when she'd joined *The Morrigan*. And much as that glass scratched its way through her, Lizzy had only said those words because *she* was angry and hurt—because Vice had hurt her.

It was just as Perry had said back on the *Respair*. Leadership. Valuing the crew's individual skills.

"Bollocks." For all she'd tried, she hadn't grown. She was no better than when she'd lost the vote for captaincy.

Knigh arrived at the tent flap, one eyebrow raised. Even the sight of him wasn't enough to soothe her. He cocked his head, examining the jumble of pages and books on the floor. "What was that about?"

"Proof that I'd still make a poor choice for captain." She pushed the words out, their truth bitter on her tongue.

"Oof," he huffed. "It sounds like you need to get away from" —he waved his hand over the tent floor—"*this*. Stop stewing over the treasure and whatever that was with Lizzy, and come and *relax*."

She frowned from him to the papers. As slow-going as it was, she could decipher at least another page tonight, if she kept at it.

"Saba's made palm wine," he said, a coaxing lilt in his voice.

"We can work on this together tomorrow, but right now *we have treasure to celebrate.*"

Her head jerked back. "That's what I—"

"I know. After the *Covadonga* when I was agonising about berserking, you persuaded me to celebrate with those words."

"I didn't know you listened so closely to me back then." A half-smile tugged at the corner of her mouth.

"I always listened far too closely to you," he said, voice low and private. He held out a hand. "No matter the trouble it got me into. Now, how about you listen to me?"

She laughed and it unknotted her shoulders. Perhaps he was right. She was making such slow progress, she wouldn't achieve much tonight, and tomorrow they could work on it together. "Fine." She let him pull her up and planted a quick kiss on his mouth while they were hidden in the tent.

A small furrow formed between his brows, but warmth lit his eyes. "What was that for?"

"Do I need to have a reason?"

He looped an arm around her waist, drawing her close. "I suppose not." His words tickled her lips before he lowered his head and gave her a longer, deeper kiss that echoed right through to her toes and fingertips. "Later," he promised against her ear and backed away to the tent flap.

But as she followed, the clues were a tether at the nape of her neck, and she found herself giving a lingering look over her shoulder as though *they* had promised her 'later.'

Out on the sand, the music hadn't started yet, but three fires burned high and teeth flashed in wonky, drunken smiles. Erec was hard at work, raking embers and roasting fish and wild turkey over them. There was much clinking of cups and hoots of celebration, hugging of friends and sudden laughs as though they remembered what they now had in their possession. There was no sign of Lizzy.

Wynn and Effie approached as Knigh pressed a drink into her hand and gestured at their surroundings as if to say *you did this.*

With a frown she couldn't shift, she sipped her drink and watched her crew—her friends celebrate.

"Gold," they said, again and again. That word was everywhere, on each pair of lips, curling around every tongue.

But it was only gold. And Drake had said *treasure greater than gold and gems.*

By the time Aedan called Knigh over to play, Vice's shoulders had knotted up again and her hands itched. This was wrong. They were celebrating and *they* were wrong. They hadn't found the treasure. It was still out there somewhere.

As Knigh sat tuning his guitar, Saba sauntered towards him and each step crept down Vice's back. It was truly a saunter, like a sabrecat sizing up prey. She stopped close to Knigh—too close—and dropped her hip, smiling up at him as she said something. Her teeth gleamed in the firelight, and that same firelight painted her skin and hair gold, caressing the lines of her face, rendering her even more beautiful.

Knigh cocked his head, spoke back, smiled a touch. Was he really oblivious to her flirtation?

With a laugh, Saba tossed her hair and smoothed her hand over his shoulder. Her brows rose in question.

Fingers aching, Vice wrung the life out of her cup. She had

hurt Lizzy. Proved how crap a captain she'd make. Found this damn chest that was *not* Drake's treasure. And now Saba was arching her back and flirting with Knigh mere feet away.

Tempting as it was to stride over and plant a kiss on him so Saba would see he was already spoken for, it would raise too many questions, too many comments.

Besides, she owed Saba better than that. Damn it, why had she ever given her blessing?

Scowling, she grabbed another drink.

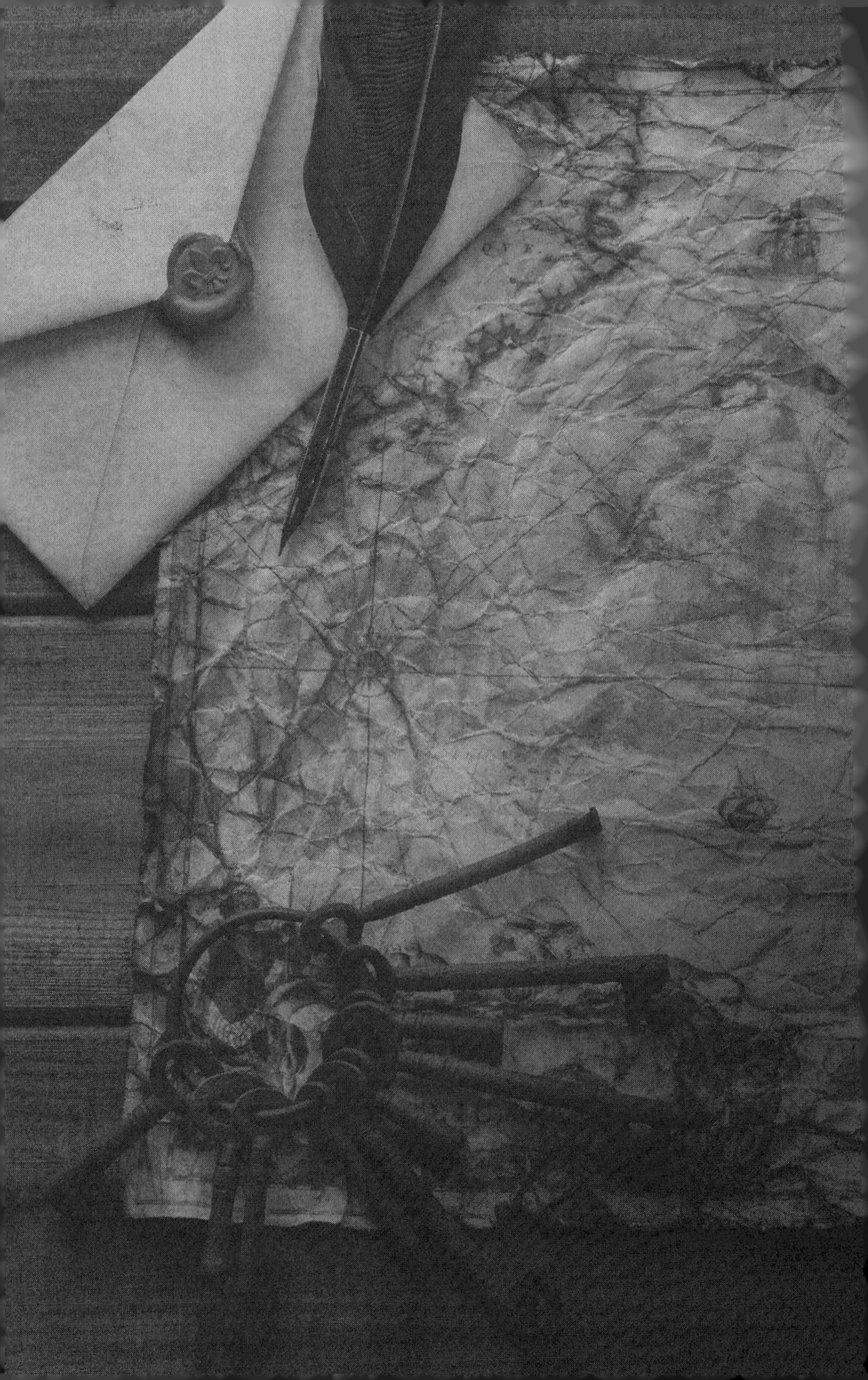

EVERYONE LEAVES

Knigh frowned at the tuning pegs, not because the guitar was being difficult—even though she didn't know about instruments Vee had chosen well—but because...

He sighed. *Vee.* That was the problem.

She'd holed herself up in that tent all day and persuading her to emerge had felt like a victory. But she just stood there drinking, surrounded by chatter and laughter. He'd barely been able to rouse the slightest scrap of conversation from her.

Over the past couple of weeks, she'd opened up so much, but now she'd grown more distant than Albion's shores, utterly absorbed with the treasure.

Obsessed, even. Was that why she couldn't accept the chest? Because then the search was over?

He winced. All those days they'd worked together on the Copper Drake, he'd enjoyed her company, enjoyed *her*, but he hadn't realised how much it had consumed her. There had to be signs he'd missed, too absorbed in them, too grateful for how much she'd soothed his anger and self-blame.

Maybe music would help. She loved to fling herself into it and dance the night away, and he loved to see her rhythmic abandon.

"So you're going to serenade us?"

Knigh blinked up from the guitar to find Saba standing barely inches from his knee, a smile on her face.

He cocked his head, letting the guitar rest on his thigh. "Hoping I can tempt someone to dance."

Her eyebrows flickered in surprise before she laughed and came closer. "Blackwood," she murmured, touching his shoulder, "if you wanted me to dance so badly, you only had to ask."

The smile froze on his face. Damnation. That wasn't what he'd meant. At *all*.

And the touch alone could've been that friendly piratical familiarity he was still trying to get used to, but with those words and the low, private tone of her voice?

That was flirtation.

He should've known. Should've put a stop to it earlier—back in Hewanorra's mud bath, back at Vee's birthday party, back over days and days and days with those little pats on the back and excuses to work beside him.

But he'd convinced himself it was innocent. Wanted it to be innocent. Because he didn't want to damage his friendship with Saba and…

Because Vee wanted to keep their relationship secret.

So he bit his tongue. What else could he say to let Saba down gently but thoroughly?

She looked up at him, head tilting in expectation.

Past her, Vee stood alone, draining her drink then topping it up. She must've seen what was happening. Any time she wanted to step in would've been mighty helpful.

But, no, she gulped down another cup of rum, eyebrows still tight together as her gaze flicked towards the tents. Towards the Copper Drake and notes strewn over her bedroll.

His heart clenched. "She just can't leave it alone."

Saba took a step back and followed his line of sight. "Vice?"

He blinked and shook his head—he hadn't intended to say it out loud. But Saba knew her, perhaps she would understand. "She's so obsessed with the treasure, she can't accept we've found it." Or was he giving her too little credit? There was still the rest of the Copper Drake that they hadn't deciphered, never mind used.

Saba pursed her lips and looked from him to Vee and back again. "And you're worried for her."

"Aren't you?"

"Hmm." Her shoulders sank as she exhaled. "Maybe. But give her a few days and she'll—"

"Blackwood." Vee appeared at Saba's elbow. "Sorry to pull you away from your adoring fans." She threw Saba a tight smile.

He leapt to his feet, unable to keep from grinning at her because she was giving him a path out. She was about to tell Saba he was taken.

"Of course." He gave her an encouraging nod as his heart

thudded in his chest. "You go right ahead."

She raised her drink, the gesture a little unsteady—how many of those had she had? "I'm sure Saba is as excited for your performance as I am, but I need to borrow you a moment."

He nodded again, eyebrows rising to coax her. But she said nothing more. His heart sank with his shoulders. That was it.

Saba inclined her head and shooed them off before going to chat with Aedan.

As soon as they started towards her tent, Vee's brows dropped into a scowl. "Saba wants you," she muttered.

"So I'd realised." He clenched his hands at his side to stop them reaching for her. Not in front of the crew. Never in front of the bloody crew. "You know what would keep her away?"

Vee raised an eyebrow. "Tell her you have syphilis?"

"Wow. That took a dark turn. I meant, tell her about *us*."

Her step faltered and made sure no one was nearby before shooting him a look that was all tense lines and dark-glinting eyes. "Except then it wouldn't be a secret."

"That's kind of what I was getting at."

She stopped in her tracks and spun to face him. "You agreed to keep it quiet," she hissed and cast another glance over her shoulder. "Don't tell me you've changed your mind now."

"Vee." He forced his arms rigid at his side, although his hands wanted nothing more than to take her shoulders and remind her he was on her side. She was so good at comforting with a touch—right now, it would've been helpful to do the same in return.

But not in front of the crew.

He took a long breath then blew it out. Again. "I don't think you understand just how proud I am to be with you. How *happy*." His throat was full, like pieces of his heart were coming out with each word. Perhaps this was dangerous, baring himself again, especially when she was so agitated and yet there was something intoxicating about speaking when he'd been closed for so long. "I want to shout it from the top of every mast on the *Venatrix,* and then I want to find a dozen more ships and shout it from each of their masts, too. I want the world to know I'm with you, that I chose you and you, somehow, chose me. That we're a partnership, a team, a..." He shook his head. "That we're something beautiful."

She'd gone very still, staring at him, the rise and fall of her chest the only movement.

"But," he went on into that silence, "I've kept it in because I understand you need time. I respect that. Only, now I'm starting to think you want to keep it secret forever."

Her throat constricted as she swallowed. "Not forever." A flicker of tension went through her mouth, her jaw. "When you leave, you can tell whoever you want."

When you leave. He blinked. "Sorry, pardon? What? Leave? Where am I—?"

"Once we have Drake's treasure, you'll have a home and life with your mother and sister."

He could only open and close his mouth at the leap in conversation.

Her expression softened as she raised a shoulder, the apparently casual gesture at odds with the tight edges of her smile. "I understand. But I'm in this for life"—she glanced towards the sea sighing on the shore, moonlight glittering on its black surface, and the *Venatrix* at anchor beyond—"I don't want to settle down on land." She exhaled, looking at an area at the centre of his chest. "I know it's selfish," she said, barely above a whisper, "but at least if the relationship is secret, it might hurt less when you go."

"*When I...?*" Squeezing his eyes shut, he shook his head and raked both hands through his hair, as though that might make this all make sense. No use, he needed more time to muddle through, especially after drinking a few cups of rum. "Come here." Damn the rest of the crew. He grabbed her hand and pulled her into his tent, away from the raucous celebrations near the bonfires.

Arms folded, she stood in the doorway like she might bolt.

"Sit." His mouth dropped open when she obeyed, crossing her legs on one end of his bedroll. He sank down next to her and pinched the bridge of his nose, elbow leaning on his knee. "So you think that when we get Drake's treasure, I'm going to bugger off to live with my mother and Is in some expensive house. Yes?"

"I've told you, I understand. You don't need to stay in this life—you didn't choose it. You're not going to be here forever, same as Saba." A laugh laced her words as if to say she didn't take this seriously, but her eyes glinted over bright in the dim light seeping through the canvas.

"Well, I *don't* understand." He took her hand and covered it with his own, letting his calluses press against hers. Her skin was chilly—the sea breeze was stiff tonight and she hadn't danced yet to ward off the cold. "When did I say I wanted that life?"

Her nostrils flared, but she remained quiet.

"Never. Because I don't. And when have I ever said I wanted to leave?"

Lips pressing together, her chest rose and fell in deep breaths as though she was mid-battle. She was holding back. There was something she didn't want to say. Something she *needed* to.

"Wasn't it enough that I took you from the gibbet? That I walked away from the Navy? That we fought our way to you on the *Sovereign*?" His voice shook, but he let it, and he let the force of emotion sweeping through his body show. Gods only knew what emotions they were exactly.

Want. Need. Desperation. Raw and messy and begging him to tidy them up and hide them away.

But no regret, though. Not an ounce.

Her lower lip wavered, but an instant later, it tightened. Still holding back.

Please. He almost said it, but instead went on with his questions, unable to stop now he'd torn his chest open: "I told you I'd always come for you and haven't I proved it? Why are you still convinced I'm going somewhere? Why won't you let yourself rely on me? Why do you think I'm going to leave?"

"Because everyone does."

Everyone leaves. Everyone, including him, apparently. It drove a lance through his chest. He'd worked so hard since arresting her, but she still saw him like that. He huffed, tugging on her arm. "What does that mean?"

"They leave or let you down, eventually."

And the lance twisted. Not deliberately, not like the cruel

things she'd said on the *Swallow* or the *Respair*, designed to push him away. No, this was a simple fact.

"I know I let you down, but—"

"It's not about that." Lips pressed together, she tugged on her hand, but he didn't release her. Her eyes flashed when she realised he wasn't going to let her slip from his grasp.

Just like he wasn't going to let her slip out of this conversation by twisting back into generalities like *everyone leaves*.

Her chest had stopped that deep rise and fall as though complete stillness was the only way to hold on to the words pushing against her fortified walls.

"Then what *is* it about, Vee? Because your father was a controlling arse?" She twitched, trying to pull away again, but he only squeezed her hand tighter. "Because Evered died, leaving you alone?"

She trembled now.

"Why can't you accept that some people can be relied on?" *That I can be relied on—or that I'll die trying?* "That not everyone leaves, that not everyone will let you—?"

"Because I let her down!" It burst out of her, so sudden it eased his grip enough that she could pull her hand away. She buried it in her lap and refused to meet his gaze.

He could only stare at her, swallow, then blink. "I don't... Who?"

"I—no." She shook her head, hair falling around her face in a dark curtain. "I meant, I let him down. I let Evered down. I should've been a better wife."

A lie. That wasn't—

Then she was on her feet and he shot up, too, ready to stop her fleeing.

"Vee, please. I know you don't believe that." And she'd said *her*. That didn't feel like a mistake.

But she'd retreated behind her walls and wouldn't look at him. Perhaps he—

"Blackwood," Aedan called from outside. "Where the hells are you? We've got sweet, sweet music to make."

"Gods damn it, Aedan." *Timing*.

Vee gave him a stiff smile. "I'm tired and, more importantly, I'm terrible company, so I'm going to bed. But playing guitar lights you up." She bent closer, smile softening to something earnest. "Go and play, have fun, distract your hands for a while."

Shadows gathered beneath her eyes. It was true, she hadn't slept well in days. He pursed his lips, unable to get an answer over his tongue. Not when it wanted to ask who she really thought she'd let down.

He'd pushed and she'd exploded, but if she wasn't ready to talk about it perhaps it was unfair of him to prod further. Perhaps doubly unfair with alcohol involved. Still there was a crack now, and giving her time might break it wider.

He sighed and raised his eyebrows. "Is that what you really want?"

"I love hearing you play, and I can listen from my tent as I fall asleep." She kissed his cheek before pulling him to his feet the tent flap.

"Sleep well, Pirate Queen," he called as he left the tent, but she'd already disappeared inside.

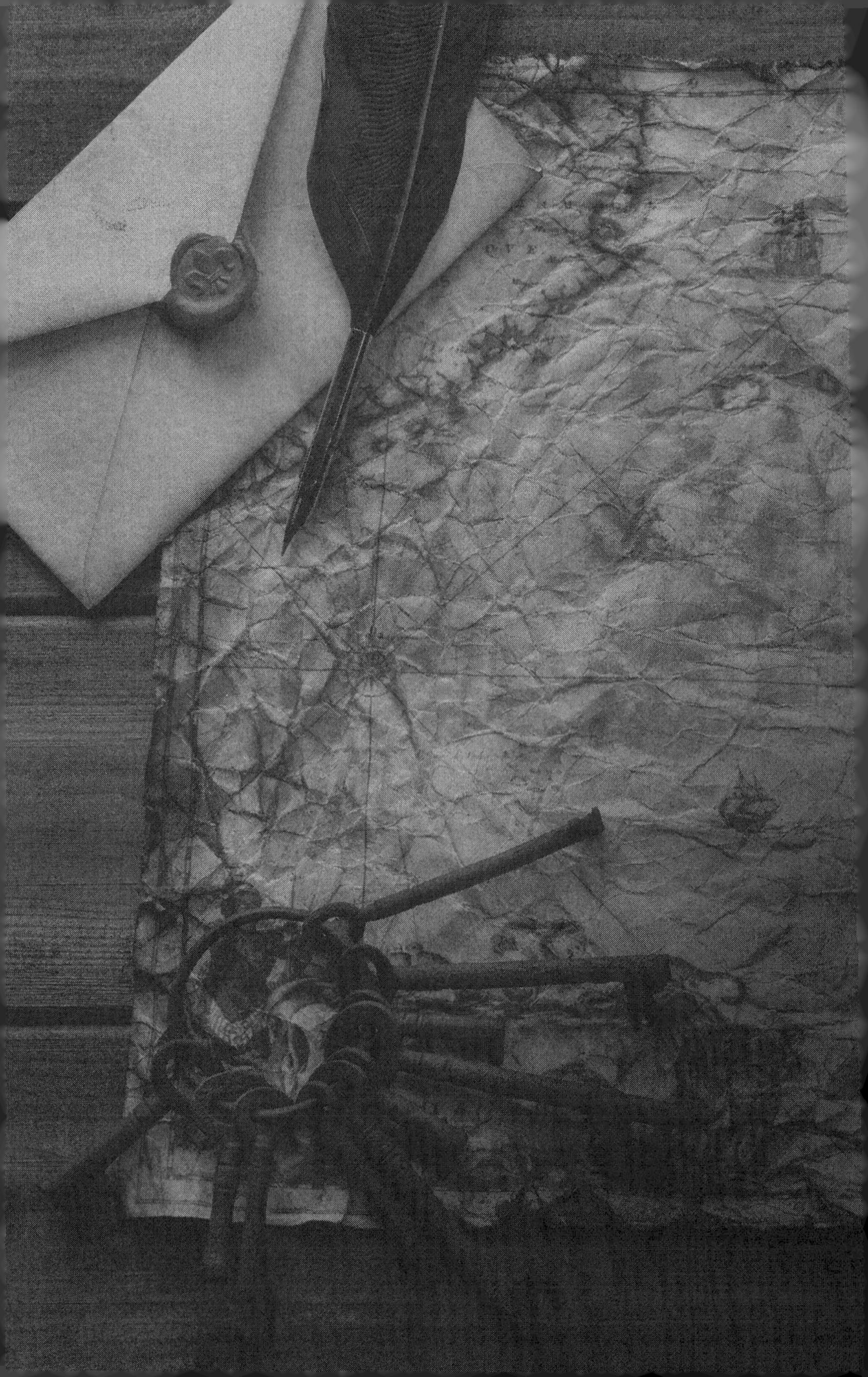

THE CHEST

Vice went to her tent and did not go to sleep. Instead, she pored over clues and deciphered more of the Copper Drake until the letters spun on the page.

Anything to avoid thinking about the fact she'd come so close to spilling her guts to Knigh. Apart from Mama, no one knew about that promise. No one knew that she hadn't fulfilled it. That she'd failed.

She'd tried to skip past it, but Knigh was no fool—he'd heard it. *I let her down.*

Stomach twisting, she rubbed her eyes and pushed her shoulders back until they popped.

He'd been a sentence away from knowing what she'd done —or rather, what she hadn't.

With a groan, she cracked her neck left and right. Treasure. Clues. She was focusing on that, not her stupid outburst. Mama and that broken promise needed to return to their hiding place, deep, deep, deep beneath everything else.

She'd worked past drunkenness and tiredness, and now her vision was only blurred from staring at the notes forming a messy circle around her, like a paper faerie ring. There was plenty of obscure text that could be coded clues or just details of Drake's travels. None of it seemed to relate to these islands or the chest.

She would explore this larger island at first light tomorrow, although she'd swept through the temple and hadn't found any more signs of Drake.

Which left the chest and the so-called treasure itself.

It was all coins and jewels, but there could be a clue in there. Maybe the number of rubies indicated a page in the book. A closer look at the coins might reveal something strange in their designs.

She bolted upright, eyes straining wide. Why hadn't she thought of that sooner? It was so obvious! Of course the not-treasure would be a clue. Maybe even one designed to put greedy treasure hunters off the scent. If they were only interested in gold, that would keep the true treasure safe.

Whatever the hells it was.

Those tantalising hints in the text... *Treasure greater than gold and gems*, and tonight as she'd skimmed through the translation, she'd spotted something that had slipped her notice over the weeks of looking at a handful of pages at a time. Throughout the book, one word came up over and over.

Sanctuary.

One sentence in particular stood out: *Sea witches will find sanctuary here.* Did it mean that literally, or was this another coded instruction?

Either way, *sanctuary* suggested a place, not a thing. Could Drake's treasure be a location? A palace? A library full of information, like the famed lost Library of Eskendereya?

Her blood thrummed, waking her aching limbs, clearing her tired eyes.

She sprung to her feet and snatched the books and notes, cramming them into a bag. Lantern in one hand, she hurried through camp, the distant song of some drunken crewmate reaching her on the wind.

The bonfires had died down now, one only embers. From the shapes silhouetted against the remaining flames, most people had gone to sleep, though the sky was still dark as ink, only interrupted by speckled stars, and not yet invaded by light from the east. As she picked her way around guy lines, snores rose from several tents and grunts and moans from others. What unusual pairings had tonight's drink and celebrations tossed together? It was something she would normally have placed bets on with Wynn and Effie, but...

Not tonight.

She squeezed the strap of her bag and slipped into the large tent Perry used as her command centre. The sides were down, closed up for the night, and Vice slipped inside, careful to keep her lantern away from the canvas.

Next to the kittens' enclosure, gleamed the chest.

"Right, you," she muttered, fixing it with a steely glare, "you're going to give up your secrets tonight. You understand?"

She dumped her bag beside it and threw open the lid.

The gold winked at her in the lamplight, mocking.

Snorting, she shook her head. "Yes, yes, gold is pretty and all, but I've got *real* treasure to find."

She sank onto the rug inside the kittens' enclosure, scooped out a handful of coins, and got to work.

Her eyes were bleeding. Had to be. There was no other way they could be hurting this much. But when she rubbed them, no blood came away.

She huffed and scooped the last of the sapphires to one side. Jetsam batted the gem experimentally, pupils widening at the flash of light it reflected.

"Leave that alone, you." Vice grabbed Jetsam and plopped the silver tabby kitten near a mouse toy she'd sewn from scraps. The kitten's bum-wiggle and pounce said that was a *much* better toy than the sapphire.

Vice massaged her forehead. She'd counted the coins and each different type of gem, but no configuration of the numbers pointed her to a page, paragraph, line, or word in the Copper Drake that was any help.

There had to be something she was missing. Some vital piece of information, some little clue that seemed insignificant but was in fact pivotal.

She scanned the stacked coins, the rubies, emeralds, and sapphires, all glittering and glinting. Light seeped through the canvas, not bright enough that she could douse the lamp, but a sure herald of sunrise.

And she was no closer to an answer.

Half-groaning, half-sighing, she flopped back onto the rug. Maybe there was no answer to be had. Was this it? Were these stacks of gold and jewels the great, final treasure of Ser Francis Drake that had been protected by traps, puzzles, an encoded book, and an elaborate journey that criss-crossed Arawaké?

Had they really done it? Had she achieved the thing FitzRoy had pursued for so long?

And if so, what next?

She swallowed and rubbed her throat, which was tight, strangled by the questions and the possibilities. She'd meant what she said to Knigh earlier: she was in this for life. She would sail the rest of her days, as a captain if she ever achieved it or as Perry's first mate if she didn't. Either way, the sea was home.

And after the talking-to Lizzy had given her earlier, captaincy was still far beyond her reach. She should've just asked for the medicine, rather than helping herself to the chest. It stood to reason Lizzy needed to keep track of stock. The chart inside the lid must've been a record. With the letters and tallies, Vice hadn't understood, but it could be a...

"Shit!" She shot upright. Inside the lid. Inside the chest.

The contents of the chest might not be a clue, but *the chest* could be.

She scrambled to her knees and bent over it. She'd already examined the exterior for marks, but *inside?*

The blue velvet lining was in remarkably good condition

considering it was a couple of centuries old. Aside from the pile on the sides and bottom being crushed from the weight of its contents, there were no discernible marks, even when she brought the lantern close.

"Beneath the velvet then." With a quick flick of her dagger, she cut one corner of velvet from the base. The rest gave way when she tugged and she smiled at the *riiiiip*.

Nothing there.

More rips as she took out all four sides.

Nothing there either.

That left only the lid.

Lined with deep blue velvet, its silky pile glistened in the lamplight.

Last chance. Could be nothing.

Although, if she was going to write something inside a chest, she'd write it in the lid, which could be angled for access and would be visible even when the chest was full.

Please, gods, say Drake thought the same.

Her blade flashed golden light from the lantern and burgeoning day as she sliced the corner.

Another *riiiiip* and the last scrap of velvet was gone.

Goosebumps rose on her arms and chased down her back.

Something had been carved into the wood.

She dropped the dagger and grabbed her lantern. A rectangle scoured around the edge, its shape and size familiar.

"The map."

She exhaled a laugh, face tingling as she ran her finger around the indented rectangle. So the map could fit in here and then...

Eyes narrowed, she bent closer and angled the lamp, letting it highlight the carved lines. More shapes, raised, not quite clear, except...

Wait, was that a key?

She traced her fingertip over the shape. Yes, the tiny, raised shape of a key. Pulse spiking, she rifled through her papers and pulled out the map. If she tilted the pencil on its side, she could take a rubbing, like she'd once done on the old tombstones at her family estate. But—

"Sensible," she muttered, mimicking Perry's voice. She grabbed a scrap of paper she'd scribbled notes on, held it over a section of the lid, and took a rubbing.

The faint lines resolved into figures... A dragon. A mermaid. An oyster. Palm trees. Clouds. Waves. Strange, impossible sea monsters. Land.

"It *is* a clue." The gold and gems were a ruse, a red herring to throw off treasure hunters who didn't understand or believe that Drake's treasure was *greater than gold*.

A half-giggle, half-guffaw burst from her. She'd done it. She'd been right. There was still more to this adventure.

Hands trembling, she placed the map inside the carved rectangle and scraped her pencil across it. Those figures she'd already found fell into place between islands, all over the sea, and the outline of islands and land appeared in the gaps left on the original.

This was the complete map.

Chills raced through her as she held it to the light. The symbols... they had to link back to clues in the Copper Drake.

Just wait until everyone sees this.

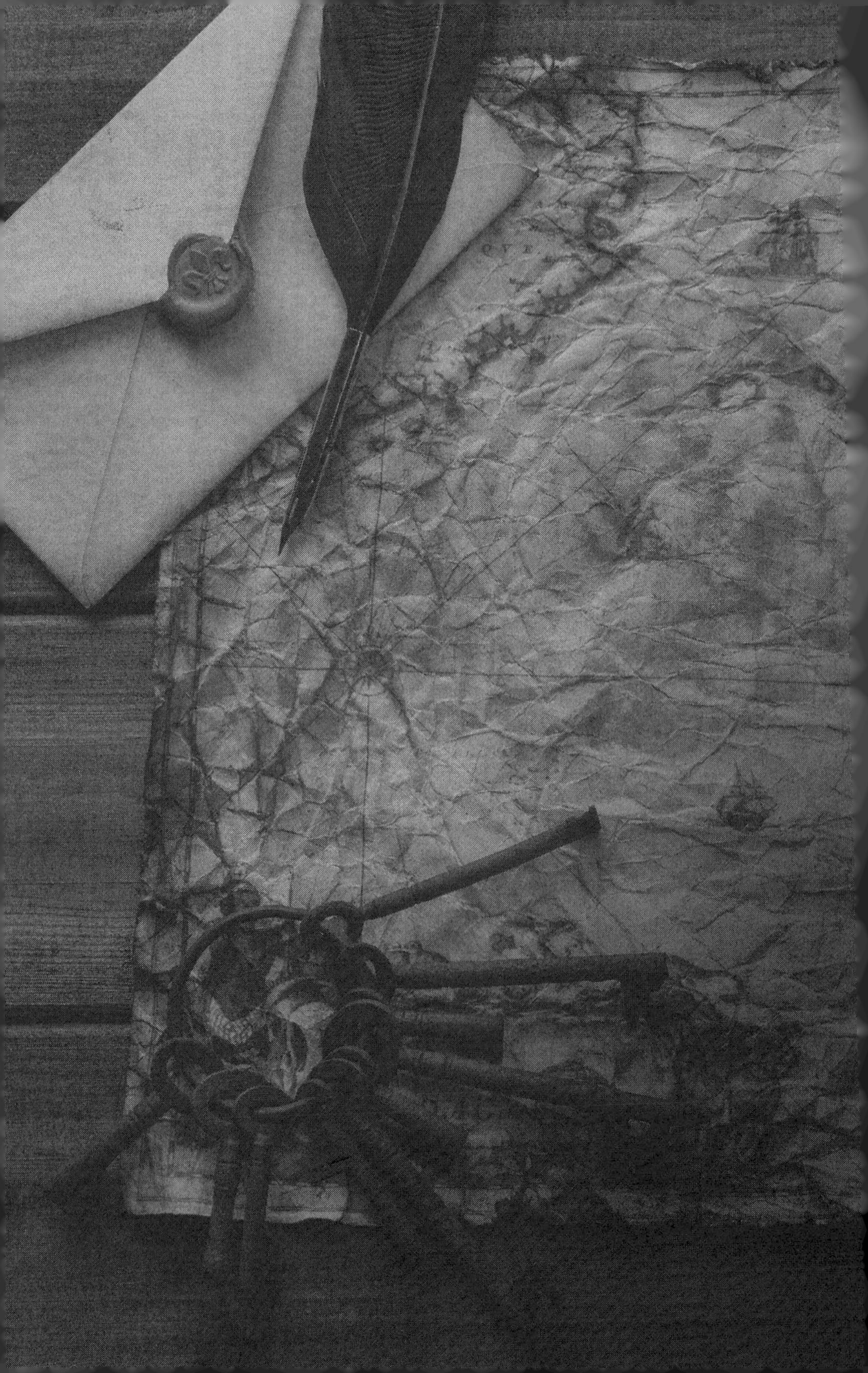

OBSESSION

By the time everyone was awake, the sun had fully risen in a sky that was mostly blue, save for a pale yellow hint of lingering sunrise. Awake might've been too strong a word for it—most looked more than half asleep, plus the bitter, fruity scent of brewing coffee laced the air, suggesting more help was needed.

But Vice didn't need any help to feel awake, despite not sleeping even an instant. She paced as her groggy crewmates gathered. When Knigh appeared, hair delightfully messy, head cocked in question, she grabbed him into a tight hug and might even have squealed in his ear. Just a little.

"You'll see." She grinned and kissed his cheek, even if the others could see.

"That's everyone." Perry raised her hands, silencing the grumbles.

Pulse thrumming loud and bright, Vice lifted her chin and

explained that she'd discovered a hidden addition to the map, one that included strange symbols that could point them to Drake's true treasure. Faces screwed up at the brightness shifted to frowns. Mouths dropped open. Murmurs rose. At her side, Knigh went from slack with sleepiness to upright and alert, like he'd jumped in cold water. Throughout her explanation, his eyes were wide upon her.

Perry covered her mouth, eyebrows disappearing behind her fringe. Wynn and Effie clutched at each other. Lizzy frowned, but one corner of her mouth twitched. Head tilted, Saba bit her lip.

"So, you see," Vice said, holding up the map and showing them the new lines, the symbols added, "there's *more* treasure." Never mind that she didn't know exactly what form it took, but if the gold and gems had been a red herring, then the final treasure had to be something truly incredible. A place, perhaps, but how could a place be a treasure? She had no idea, but finding out would be an adventure in itself.

She scanned the assembled crew—her friends, her family.

All silent.

Maybe it was too soon to tell them her theory that the treasure was a place—that could wait.

"We *have* treasure." At the front of the crowd, Luned, Perry's friend, lifted her chin, mouth flat. At once, Vice was back on the *Respair's* deck losing the vote for captaincy.

"Aye," someone else further back called, "we have what we wanted."

"Enough to retire," Luned added, nodding.

The nods rippled through the crowd, like the chill passing

down Vice's back. She resisted the urge to glance at Knigh or Perry. She would do this alone. She *would* persuade them.

"But this is..." She brandished the map. "This is a chance to find Drake's treasure—to find something greater. Something huge. Something..." She laughed. "To find *Drake's treasure*, that everyone thought lost or merely the stuff of legends. You find this, and *you'll* be a legend."

They muttered and murmured. One word rose above the hubbub.

Obsessed.

More nodding, more exchanged looks.

They thought she was obsessed. Not right, *obsessed.*

She exhaled, laced with a disbelieving laugh. "Don't you understand? That"—she pointed to the tent with the chest—"is a red herring, designed to fool the greedy so they don't continue on the path to the *true* treasure."

Lizzy's mouth twisted to one side. "Is it? Or is that"—she pointed at the map in Vice's hand—"the red herring, designed to keep anyone too greedy in thrall of the promise of more treasure?" Despite her harsh words yesterday, her expression softened as she lifted her eyebrows.

"Aye," Luned said, "we're not greedy. Not like those fools in the stories."

The stories where greed only led to misfortune.

More mutters. "Aye, there's always a curse in the coin."

"... trapped because they went back for just one more gem."

They didn't believe her. They didn't believe *in* her.

It sank inside, as cold and heavy as an anchor, dragging her down. She had proof—the additions to the map—but it still wasn't enough.

Even these clear lines in black and white weren't enough.

Just like the vote for captaincy when Luned had said, *You can't be trusted.*

They would forge into battle to save her from the *Sovereign*, but they wouldn't follow her.

Warmth at the small of her back cut through everything—a lifeline. When she blinked and looked up from the map, Knigh was close, hand on her. His chin dipped in the slightest nod, and his grey eyes were steadfast. Determined.

"Listen to you," he called over the pockets of conversation that had broken out, "suddenly you're the experts on Drake's treasure." He scoffed, everything about the set of his mouth brimming with scorn. "Vee has pored through each page of that book. She knows every inch of that map." He grabbed her hand and flapped that right along with the map. "If anyone in the world knows about Drake's treasure, it's her. And if she tells me this chest full of flashy metal and rock *isn't* it, I believe her."

Although his hand wasn't there anymore, the warmth remained at her back and bloomed across her skin, through her veins, her muscles, her fat and flesh, right to her heart.

"I'm just sorry," he said, pitched only for her, "that it took me a while to realise."

Her throat was too thick to talk, but she managed a nod as fresh debate broke out amongst the crew. Some called back to Knigh, saying he was just trying to get in her breeches. She almost laughed at that, and it eased the tightness inside.

If Knigh believed her, there was hope. The others might

take a while to come around—maybe once they'd secured the false treasure in Nassau and had drunk their way through town, they'd grow curious enough to follow her to the real thing.

And if they didn't, screw them. She'd use her cut of the gold to buy a boat and she and Knigh would follow the map alone, if they had to. That look he'd given her, steadfast, determined—he would follow her.

"Come on," he said, jerking his head towards the tents, "we'd better get reading that blasted book so we can work out what the hells all these symbols mean."

She laughed and bumped her shoulder into his. "Thank you."

He held her gaze and although they didn't touch, he leant so close his warmth reached her. He inclined his head once. "Any time."

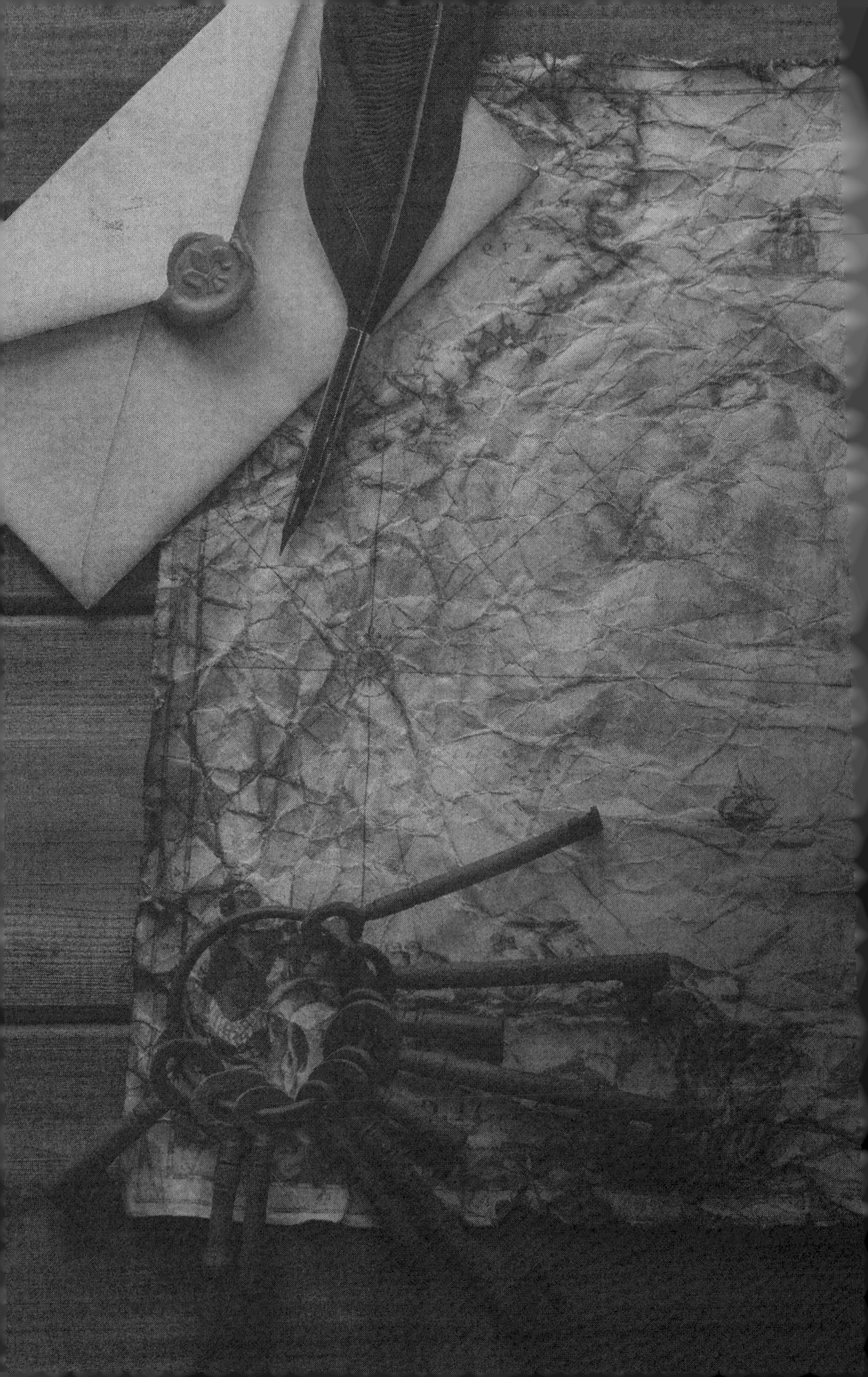

GLOW & SPARK

All the way to Nassau, Knigh was the one dragging Vice from her cabin to spar in the mornings, before settling down in her cabin to finish translating the Copper Drake. He made a copy of the map—to be on the safe side, he said—and she pinned it above her bunk.

Some days, she lay back and stared at it, following the lines of each symbol and land mass while he read to her from the Copper Drake's translation and the kittens bounded and hunted their ways across the table, the bunk, the floor, *everywhere*. If the treasure was a place, it was somewhere on that map.

Other days, she bent over the book and read and read and read until her neck burned and it hurt to blink. Her hunched position made her just another surface for the kittens to play on, leaving dozens of scratches from their little needle-sharp claws.

Most nights, she crept into her bunk long after Knigh had fallen asleep, but he woke and pulled her close and they ended up making love in the dark quiet beyond midnight. Losing herself in him was the only time her mind emptied of dragons and oyster shells and damn treasure maps.

Sometimes, they were too tired for anything other than sleep, which they did, entwined together with kittens tucked behind their knees and in the crooks of elbows, and Barnacle curled on her cushion by their feet.

They reached Nassau in record time, thanks to her gift pushing the ship along each day. Although they'd finished their translation, they still hadn't found the elusive clue that would tie the map to the book and reveal where to go next, and the crew still showed no desire to seek out the true treasure. They did, however, want to celebrate, and Perry had deemed Nassau the only town where Vice and Knigh would be safe from bounty hunters.

"Are you sure you won't come with us?" He stood at the door, hope in the raised lines of his eyebrows.

It tugged on Vice. How could it not? But…

She would be terrible company—*again*. Just like that night on the island. She hadn't been able to make conversation and drinking had only made her more miserable. And then she'd almost spilled her guts to Knigh about Mama. *I let her down.* He hadn't brought it up since, but almost telling him had brought it to the surface, leaving a raw edge inside.

Something to hide, something shameful.

And this treasure, this expanded map…

With an apologetic smile, she shook her head. "You go. Have fun. Enjoy yourself."

Shoulders sinking, he exhaled—not quite a sigh. But that hope didn't leave his face. "Perhaps I'll check in later. See if you change your mind."

Guaranteed not to happen. Still, she smiled and waved him off before settling down with one of the books she'd stolen from Mercia. Maybe something in here would spark an idea about the map and its symbols.

IT WAS hours later and full dark outside and even the kittens had all fallen asleep when a rap sounded at the door. *Knigh's* rap—the same rhythm she'd heard dozens of times.

"Since when do you knock?" she called, taking her feet off the table.

The door sprung open, bouncing back off the bulkhead, and Knigh strode in. Brow tight, lips pinched together, he slammed the door in his wake. "*That* man." His chest heaved, shoulders rising and falling as though it required his whole body to contain each breath as he paced the length of the cabin, fore to aft and back again.

Blinking, she closed her book and sat up. Much as Mercia opened all of Knigh's old wounds as well as plenty of fresh ones, there was only one person capable of filling Knigh with such pure irritation. "Let me guess. FitzRoy?"

His hands clenched at his sides as he exhaled through flaring nostrils. "Every time. Every bloody time." Fists shaking, he turned and executed another circuit of her cabin. "'How's Vice? Still treating you mean?' Prodding, prodding, prodding. That's what he does." His words descended into muttering growls.

Fitz really *did* get to him. And so easily.

Two possible reasons for that. One, lingering guilt from plotting with him to arrest her. Two, their history.

Actually, no, Fitz was entirely capable of infuriating anyone all on his own. He could be charming when he wanted to be, which had grown rarer and rarer over the years, but he could use that charm *against* people when he wished—turning himself into the ultimate irritant.

And with Knigh, Fitz had plenty of ammunition to strike right where it hurt.

"… of all the windbag…" Mutter, mutter, mutter. "… arrogant bloody cad…" Grumble, grumble, grumble.

It must've been mightily tempting to smack Fitz in the nose. Again. But Knigh had come to her instead. He'd removed himself from the situation rather than risk snapping.

A light kindled in her chest. Despite his fears about berserking, he was getting better. Maybe not as quickly as he liked, but he was moving in the right direction.

Perhaps she could help provide a distraction for his hands and… other parts.

Barely biting back a grin, she cleared her throat and approached. When he turned to pace aft, she stopped him with a palm against his chest.

Eyes locked with his, she sank to her knees and unbuckled

his belt. Her pulse spiked with the knowledge that she was about to wreak sweet havoc on him.

Chest and shoulders still heaving, he blinked at her, eyebrows squeezing together even more tightly. "What're you doing?"

"Distracting you," she said, untucking his shirt. He would know exactly what she meant by that and sure enough, the knot of his throat rose and fell. While she worked on the buttons, his cock twitched against the fabric of his breeches.

An answering twitch stirred in her body. He was already hungry for this. Though maybe not as hungry as she was for it. For him.

A new kind of tension etched its way across his face, eyebrows still together but less angry. Still just as intense, though.

Looking up at him from her knees, she didn't feel lesser or brought low as she had with Fitz. She... There weren't words. Not ones she could quite grasp. There was only a feeling—her body had always been far better at communicating than clumsy words.

Her chest was full and warm and that reached right to her fingertips and toes, like her heart wasn't just pumping around blood but also the pride she felt for him. He was working to master his anger and it wasn't in a way that made him that rigid man she'd met last year. He was becoming something else entirely. Something that took her breath away.

Exhaling what was almost a laugh, she lifted his shirt and planted a kiss on his muscled belly, right on the line of hair trailing down from his belly button, while her other hand kneaded his cock through his clothes.

His chest stilled. Tension thrummed in him, in the air.

She unleashed the grin she'd been holding back as he hardened under her touch, and when she let his breeches fall open, he sprang free, thick and long and ready for her attention.

Good gods, every bit of him was beautiful. And…

She paused there and glanced up at him. His eyes had gone dark, and he stood quite still, watching her.

Safe to say the distraction was working.

Holding eye contact, she kissed the tip, his flesh smooth and soft. His body tensed, but he made no sound, only stood there, rapt.

Oh, she would give him a show all right.

She let a smile play at the corner of her mouth, let her teeth show, just a little. As she opened her mouth and took him in, she didn't so much as blink.

His lips parted on a gasp and his eyebrows peaked together.

Beautiful.

And all hers.

Gripping his solid thighs, she took him as far as she could before adding one hand to reach the base. His fists remained gripped at his sides, but the hiss between his teeth when she flicked her tongue said anger was far, far from his mind.

Good. *Good.* She'd drive it and all thoughts of FitzRoy away. This was for them and no one else.

She built a deliberate rhythm, slow and deep, and it was a testament to his control that he held utterly still, not pushing or forcing himself any deeper, letting her hold absolute control.

He was trembling by the time he pulled out. She was still blinking at his absence when he tugged her upright.

"Enough," he rasped and yanked her shirt off.

The dark look in his eye, the roughness in his movements—it made everything inside her molten. She was going to push him onto the bed and ride him hard until they both tipped over the edge in quivering, panting joy.

And she couldn't bloody wait.

But when she smoothed her hands on his muscular chest, he shook his head and spun her around. "That wicked mouth of yours is going to get you in trouble."

Trouble. That word, the way he growled it, the way he'd somehow seized control of the situation, it drove the heat in her beyond molten.

With an unyielding grip, he propelled her to the dressing table and bent her over it, forcing a gasp from her lips. With lightning speed, he kept one hand on her back and pulled down her breeches.

Her skin was on fire and her reflection's cheeks had gone pink. She'd never let him take her over anything. It was a position she'd always hated—too powerless, too submissive.

But... but this wasn't powerless, this wasn't...

Gods damn it, this had her aching for him.

In the mirror, he surveyed her bared flesh before he met her eye. "I see you enjoyed that as much as I did."

She could only stare back at him, breaths heaving and

pressing her breasts into the dressing table. What the hells had got into him?

"Boots."

She half-laughed, brows raising. "Are you commanding me?"

No amusement on his face, only a challenging glint in his eye. "Are you arguing?"

Although her thundering pulse beat through every fibre, she didn't look away. She could stop this.

If she wanted.

She could order him onto that bed and ride him, just as she'd intended. A word and she'd have control back.

But then she'd never know where this would go. And the tight ache inside her demanded to know what Knigh had planned.

Although, it wouldn't do to hand over control *too* easily.

So she narrowed her eyes at him through the mirror, summoning an imperious look despite her position, and raised her foot. "You want them gone, you can take them off yourself."

A smirk flashed across his lips so quickly, she might've imagined it, but he bent and tugged off one boot, then the other. "I'm going to make you regret that."

The way he said it, a thoroughly indecent promise, had her biting her lip.

He shoved off his own boots and breeches and peeled away his shirt, hot and hard against her backside as he worked and kept her pinned. The anticipation had her gripping the edges of the dressing table. She didn't touch him, but she drank up the sight of his unyielding muscles, each part of his body as it was revealed, until her knees trembled so hard, she'd have fallen if she wasn't bent over this surface.

Then he slid against her, nudging her pearl with such sweet, wet pressure that she gasped and her knuckles whitened.

But the bastard did not enter.

Thick and hard, he kept gliding back and forth, teasing, merciless, building that coiling ache in her to something unbearable, something demanding and needy that had her whimpering. But when she arched her back to try and catch him, he only grinned in the mirror, eyes glinting. Wicked.

He bent and brushed his lips over her neck, her shoulder, her earlobe, sending shudders across her oversensitive flesh. "Do you want something?" he said, voice little more than heat in her ear and a rumble against her back.

The absolute bastard. He was going to make her beg, wasn't he? Or try to. She wouldn't give in—not entirely. She met his eye in the mirror and nodded, grinding against him, delicious pressure building in her core, throbbing through her being.

He bit down on her dagger earring and gave a gentle tug, the shock of it making her buck against him. Not that it gave her what she craved. The way he smirked, he knew it. "I'm going to need you to say it."

Gods, what new game was he playing?

And as long as he took her utterly and completely, did she care?

She swallowed and sucked in a burning breath. "I want you."

He smiled slowly and held her hips, pinning her in place so

she couldn't buck against him any more as he kept up those long strokes. She let out a frustrated grunt, but he didn't release her.

Instead, he raised his eyebrows. "To do what?"

"You know what I want you to do."

His teeth flashed, then he nibbled the sensitive spot between her neck and shoulder, making her gasp, turning her knees liquid. He straightened, towering above, dark gaze holding hers through the mirror. "I want to hear you say it."

Shit. She was done resisting. Done playing. She wanted him right this second and so what if he knew it? So what if he saw just how much she wanted—*needed* him?

"Take me," she panted. "I want you to take me."

At her words, his cock twitched, pulsing pleasure through her, and the amusement faded from his face, replaced by something hotter, wilder, something that watched with consuming intent, like a predator on the hunt.

So what if she begged? For a taste of that, she'd do anything.

"Please," she whispered.

His hands ran up her back, one going to her shoulder, the other into her hair, seizing a handful of it. He bent over her, hot and heavy at her back, never looking away.

"Who am I to deny my Queen?"

What game was this? Who had power? Because it didn't feel like she did and yet he called her queen and his every action was designed to tease her, please her, drive her exquisitely insane.

Using that hand in her hair, he turned her head and

claimed her mouth in a plundering kiss at the same moment he claimed her body, entering in one solid motion. Tongue stroking hers, he filled her utterly and she almost came undone just from that, moaning into his mouth.

She could barely contain her breaths, barely contain the pleasure that was now a teetering tower, ready to tumble down into darkness and take her with it.

She would go willingly.

He stroked into her, slow and hard, one hand still gripped in her hair, the other covering hers, holding it pinned to the dressing table. And still he kissed her like it would let him take her deeper, deeper, deeper.

Pressed against the table, she couldn't move, but then she wouldn't have stopped a single thing he was doing.

At last he broke that decimating kiss and stood upright, continuing that slow, driving motion into her.

The mirror shook with each stroke. The dressing table rattled. The room spun.

Her body trembled on the edge, the pleasure unbearable. Her limbs were no longer solid, maybe not even her own anymore.

"Come here," he murmured, voice softer than when he'd commanded her earlier. He pulled her upright, back against his solid chest.

Still inside her, tighter now, he drove at a different angle, hitting a spot that made spasms build between her thighs. She arched onto him, taking him fully, enhancing that glorious angle until tears built.

It was too much. Too much. She couldn't contain it all. It was going to consume her. *He* was going to consume her.

And he was welcome to.

His hands planed across her belly, up her ribs, palmed her breasts, wringing yet more pleasure from her. One thumb circled her peaked nipple while the other hand continued upward, pulling her arm with it until she was stretched out, fingers threaded through his thick hair.

And still that driving rhythm, achingly close to exactly what she needed.

Leaving her hand there, his glided over her skin on a downward trajectory and finally stopped at that bundle of nerves at the apex of her thighs that he knew how to play so well.

"Look at you," he murmured, consuming her in the mirror.

Her head hung back against his shoulder, eyes half closed. Her cheeks were flushed, her lips red and swollen from taking him in her mouth and then from that kiss. Her breasts bounced with his thrusts, which built in speed and ferocity.

"You are delicious." He kissed her shoulder, tongue laving her hot flesh. "Devastating." Then the side of her neck. "My Queen, my Captain, my ..." His breath caught, the first sign of quite how affected he was. That only tightened her, putting a teetering capstone on all he'd built inside.

She was too hot. This was too much. *He* was too much. The mirror was in danger of toppling over and she was in danger of losing herself in the reflection of his lust-darkened gaze.

He turned his mouth to her ear, breaths fanning against oversensitive skin. "Vee," he said, low and firm and hot, eyes locked with hers in the mirror, "I want you to come for me."

Maybe it was the command in his voice or the way he drove deeper at that instant or the steady, sure strum of his finger on her pearl, but her body arched and that tower of pleasure he'd built tumbled and she went headlong with it.

Falling, there was only bliss and him in the mirror, smiling as he watched it wreck her, as he smothered her cries, as she shook and shook and shook like the very world had come apart.

When her cries were done and she only panted against his palm, he loosened his grip. His devastating rhythm, though, that kept pounding into her, driving fresh pleasure with each stroke.

"Knigh," she whimpered on his skin. Gods knew why she said his name—it wasn't enough to convey quite what he'd done to her. She'd submitted, let him rule her, and had loved it—was still loving it.

She was his. Utterly.

But it didn't raise the hairs on the back of her neck in fear, it only built the waves inside.

With a moan, she took his finger into her mouth and ran her tongue against its length, just as she'd done to his cock earlier.

Hips bucking hard into her, he hissed. "Shit." His rhythm slowed a fraction, and as if sensing he'd almost yielded control to her, he pressed her back onto the dressing table until she was bent over it, hand braced on the surface, taking his entire length again, again, again.

Eyelids fluttering, she sucked his finger harder, the action barely keeping her moans in check as bliss thundered towards her in a towering wave.

"Do you want to come again, my Queen?" His voice came out ragged and breathless, jolting with each thrust.

She could only nod.

"I am your willing servant." He pulled his finger from her mouth and seized her hips as he pounded harder, faster and sent the wave crashing over her, drowning, obliterating, glorious.

Pleasure was all she knew and its name was Knigh Blackwood. Both it and he were hers and she never wanted that to end. Nothing but his fingers digging into her flesh, his thighs against the back of hers, and his cock inside her, filling her as no one else could.

Ruined. Completely. Those were the only words in her head as the wave sank away and he pulled from her.

Maybe ruined wasn't such a bad thing.

"Knigh," she whispered, her mouth and tongue the only parts capable of movement, "I can't—"

"You don't have to." He gathered her in his arms, strong yet gentle, and gave her a slow, thorough kiss. "I'm not finished with you yet"—he grinned—"but I think you need a moment."

She laughed and sank against him. More. Yes, she would always take more from him.

He doused the lamp and carried her to the bunk. By the time he eased her onto it, she'd caught her breath and was able to pull him close. Fingers tracing the lean lines of his back, she kissed him until she couldn't stand having him separate a moment longer. "Come back to me," she whispered against his lips.

"Always." His voice rumbled against her chest, making her

heart stutter, and he slid into her with deliberate, delicious slowness that had them both groaning.

But it didn't stay slow—within moments it had become hard and airless, her hips rolling with his, his thrusts driving her into the mattress. More, more, more. She would take whatever he gave; whatever his body demanded, hers would give. On and on in an endless cycle.

His each thrust pushed her towards another precipice, and the tension thrumming in his muscles said he was close.

Maybe she could help them both sail over that edge together in a blazing finish.

Panting, she tore her lips from his and used a fingernail to scratch a thin line of pain across her collarbone, little more than a graze. "Heal me." At the waterfall, it had lit up bright pleasure, perhaps this...

Arms wrapped around her, he blinked at the scrape, an uncertain smile flickering on his mouth. Scoffing, he shook his head. "You know I can't say no to you." Not missing a beat of his driving rhythm, he bent his mouth to her shoulder.

The golden glow of his magic lit up the bunk and then it lit up her body—not just the scratch but everywhere.

Her back arched out of her control, and his arms seized around her as he cried out against her skin.

She dropped over the edge, hard, let it take her, but fell into brightness, not darkness.

The warmth was all. Everywhere.

This was his gift. His power. And he was here, too, in her, around her, falling, falling, falling, as violet-blue energy crackled over their flesh, through their veins, and threaded through his golden glow, tingling, sparking, and there was no up or down, no her, no him, just sensation and explosion and their mingled magic on and on into infinity.

Then they were in her bunk, breathless, blinking at each other. His magic shone from their bodies, and little static sparks of hers raced across their flesh.

He drew a glowing fingertip up her arm, a tiny thread of lightning dancing between his skin and hers. It didn't hurt or even sting, just tickled pleasantly, like the threat of a sneeze. They both shivered.

A dazed smile on his lips, he traced their mingled magic in a spiral on her shoulder. "What just happened?"

"I... I have no idea." She'd never heard of anything like this. "But it was... is..." She shook her head.

As he sank onto his side and gathered her close, she turned inward to her gift. Around the wellspring, her lightning storm churned, violet-blue, but at the edges there was a golden light. "You're here," she murmured, "in my gift. It glows now."

His brows lifted and his eyes went distant for a few seconds. When he blinked back, a sweet smile bloomed on his mouth before he kissed her. "You're in mine too, crackling at the edges."

They both exhaled and sank into the bunk. He drew lazy circles on her skin, his glow and her lightning growing dimmer by the minute.

Her limbs were so heavy, she wouldn't have been surprised if she kept sinking and sinking through the bunk, through the deck and the hull, down to the sea floor. Whatever had happened, it had been intense, incredible, wondrous.

And all theirs.

She grinned and kissed his chest. "Did I succeed in distracting you then?"

His soft laugh rumbled through her. "A much better way to channel my energy than punching FitzRoy in the nose."

"Glad you think so."

He laughed again and kissed the top of her head. "I like this way of letting go."

He hadn't been the only one to let go. She'd yielded to him. Just enough. They'd shared power plenty of times, swapped it, but she'd never given it up so completely. And yet he hadn't abused it. She hadn't once felt like a possession; rather, he'd made her feel every inch the queen he called her. He'd called himself her willing servant, too, and he had indeed done everything for her enjoyment, even holding back his own climax until she'd had... enough that she'd lost count.

She nestled against him, letting her eyelids drift shut. "I do too."

Her arms were full and so was her heart. He was generous and thoughtful. Deliciously intense. Clever enough to keep her on her toes... No wonder he was the one who'd finally managed to catch her where other pirate hunters had failed.

She smiled in the darkness. Thinking about it didn't bring pain anymore. Yes, it had been awful and the aftermath too, but it had led here.

And here was somewhere she liked very much indeed.

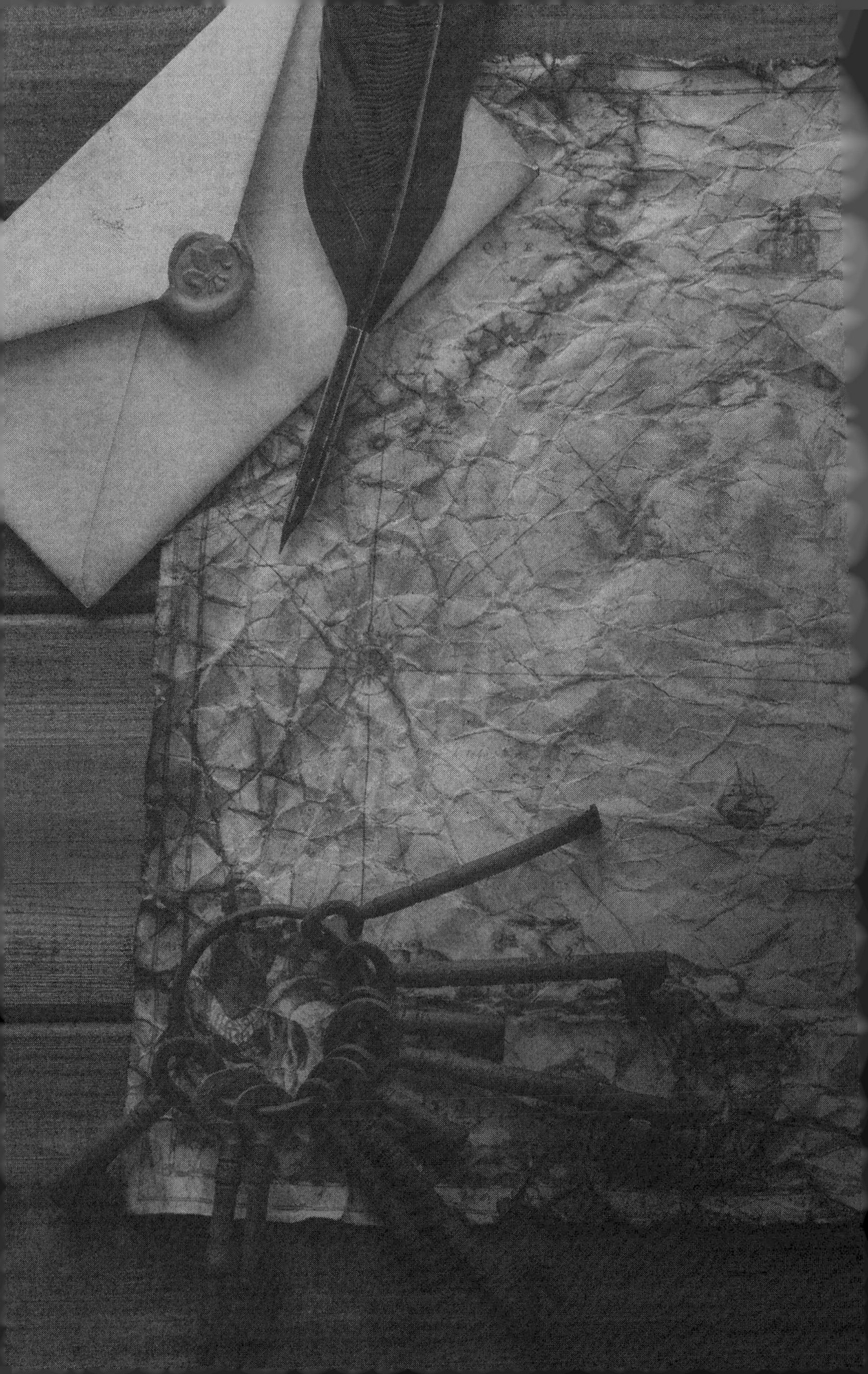

FAILED DISTRACTION

Knigh woke with a broad smile on his face and warm sun shafting through the stern window. That had been... He rubbed his face into the pillow. Last night, the way she'd distracted him, the way he'd let go—his anger converting from something dark and seething to something hot and bright and joyous...

And when he'd healed that tiny scratch on her shoulder...

His skin thrummed at the memory of that staggering pleasure, the warm glow, the flickering sparks. He'd never come so hard, surging not just from every part of his body, but from his entire *being*. And he'd never seen her lost in climax for so long, felt her so tight around him.

It had been everything.

He was undone. Completely. Utterly. Hopelessly... Hope*fully*. Willingly. Happily.

Although she'd initiated things as an attempt to distract him, it had been a much-needed distraction for her, too. And, sweet Lords, it had felt good to have her undivided attention.

"Well, *that* was quite something," he muttered. With a soft laugh, he reached out to gather Vee to him, but... the bunk was empty and cold, save from Anchor and Cable curled up together like a little ball of smoke and shadow.

He blinked, sat up. Barnacle sat on the dressing table opposite, wide green eyes on him as though she knew exactly what had happened there last night. To the stern, Vee was already working, brows knitted together as she bent over one of their notebooks.

His shoulders sank. So much for distracting her. Still obsessing over the treasure. If the crew wouldn't follow her clue, she wouldn't be able to pursue it. And what effect might that have on her? His throat clenched as he squeezed the blanket. He'd seen what obsession could do to a person, especially impotent obsession.

When he'd first started pirate hunting, he'd served with a captain who'd been determined to capture Bonny Steed. For all his years of work, he'd come close once or twice, but never caught him. By the time Knigh came aboard, he'd covered the bulkheads of his cabin with plans and sketches of Bonny Steed, of his ship, of the ways previous plans had gone wrong. He barely slept, instead he wrote in his ledger for hours and hours, night after night.

After his death, they'd discovered what he'd been writing: a summary of each encounter with Bonny Steed. Over and over and over again. The words were almost identical every time, but the handwriting dissolved into spidery scrawl, more and more illegible with each re-telling.

Absently stroking Anchor, he swallowed away the tightness in his throat. He wouldn't let that happen to Vee. There had to be some way—

"My co-captain," she muttered, frown deepening. She blinked, looked up, and her eyebrows rose, as though she was surprised to find him awake. "Did you ever hear anything about Drake sharing a captaincy?"

"And good morning to you too."

She waved a hand dismissively, returning to the book. "Did you?"

"Vee," he sighed. "If it's a fact about Drake that you don't know, I doubt anyone else does."

"Hmm." Without looking up, she grabbed a pencil and paper and scribbled furiously.

He watched her a long while, willing her to look up, step away from the desk. *Look up*. But she didn't. She continued working, twitching pages, jotting notes. The dark shadows under her eyes knotted his stomach.

When he slipped out, he passed the other cabins beneath the quarterdeck, including the one he shared with Aedan, and strode out on deck, just for a taste of fresh air, a touch of sunshine. Eyes closed, he leant against the door and raked his hands through his hair. They'd finally worked things out, were becoming something, and yet he couldn't shake it. He was about to lose her to this obsession. To a man two-hundred years dead.

"Now there's someone with the weight of the world on his

shoulders," Perry said, close-by. Blinking, he found her and Saba watching him, brows raised. "Just because they're broad shoulders, doesn't mean you need to carry it all alone."

Thank the gods for Perry.

With a sigh, he started fore and gestured for them to join him. The deck was quiet—most of the crew were on shore or sleeping off last night's celebrations. A few were probably *still* celebrating.

"It's Vice," Saba said, falling into step beside him, "isn't it?"

He stopped at the rail and leant back on it. They were a safe distance from the stern, so Vee wouldn't hear. That didn't make it much easier to speak of her, not with how badly it had gone when he and Perry had discussed her on the *Respair*.

Perry watched him, smile gentle, though her eyes glinted, like she knew exactly what was going on in the cabin next to hers. Had she seen it coming and that was why she'd asked the carpenter to reconfigure the room to give Vee her own space?

That look. She *had* to know. But to her credit, she hadn't asked, hadn't pushed. His chest warmed with gratitude. She was letting them come to her when they were ready.

"Of course it's Vee," he said at last. "She can't let it go. I mean, I'm sure she's right—the map, the book, all of it points to there being something more to discover. But..." He exhaled through his nose, the weight of what Vee might become was too much to bear, too much to say.

Eyebrows forming a deep valley, Saba bowed her head. "I had my concerns, but I thought she might've snapped out of it by now."

He gave a bitter laugh. Last night had been the closest he'd ever felt to another person, the most intense experience of his life, and the way she'd reacted, he was sure she felt the same. Even now, he turned inward to his magic and sparks of violet-blue energy laced his own golden glow, like she'd left a mark on him. On his soul.

And yet that wasn't enough to make her *snap out of it*.

Perry and Saba both watched him, heads cocked in question.

"Nothing keeps her distracted for long."

The flicker of a grin from Perry confirmed it. She knew.

"Try not to worry"—she patted his arm—"I'll have a word and we'll get her out of that cabin in no time." Smiling, she wandered aft and disappeared inside.

Saba shrugged. "Maybe." But she didn't look convinced as she turned and set to work.

Knigh busied himself checking lines and knots and generally tidying, though there was little for him to do. His former self would never have admitted it, but the *Venatrix* was as ship-shape as when she'd been a naval vessel. Every time there was movement from aft, he turned, only to find it was Saba or another crewmate working or a gull landing to search for scraps of food.

Eventually, Perry emerged. The flat set of her mouth said it all, but she huddled together with him and Saba anyway and shook her head.

Knigh gripped the rail. Even Perry had failed. She was always the safe bet when it came to Vee and yet... His stomach sank through his feet, through the deck, plummeting to the harbour floor.

"Fine," Saba huffed. "Give her some time and I'll go to her later." Eyes narrowed, she glanced aft. "I know something that will get through to her. She won't like it, but it will sure as hells get through."

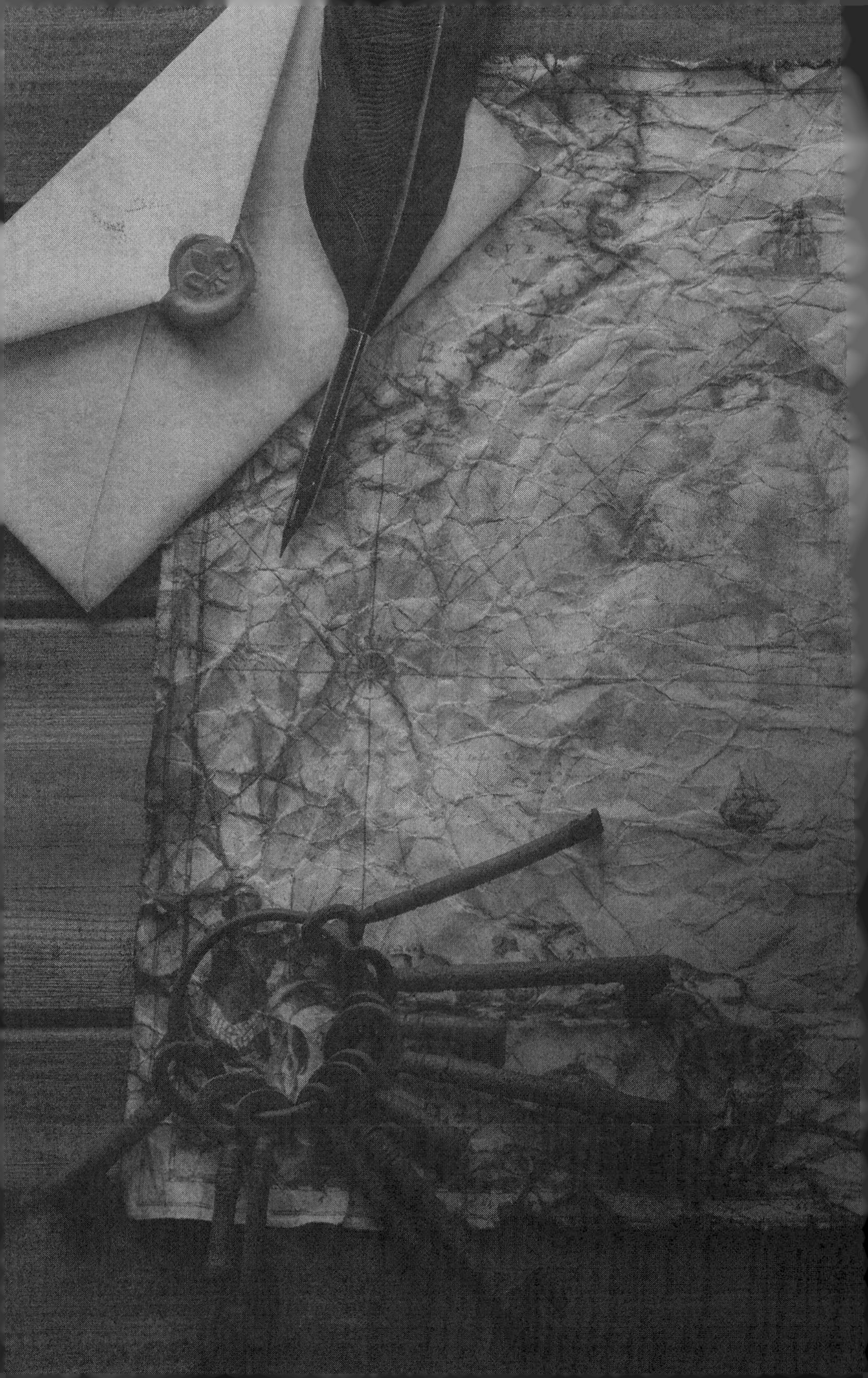

LOSING HERSELF

Drake had shared his captaincy. It said so right here. *My co-captain.* Vice traced her fingers over the ciphered words in the Copper Drake. It used that same phrase several times in the last section of the book and there was no other explanation. The great hero, Ser Francis Drake, had not led alone but with someone else. Someone he trusted. Someone who must've been as great as he was. Someone who'd been written out of history.

And she, a pirate, not a historian, had discovered it. She huffed a laugh, pulling a notebook across the table and shaking her head.

If a hero like him could share his captaincy, then—

A knock rapped at the door, and Saba poked her head in. Vice rubbed her eyes and huffed relief. It wasn't Lizzy come to give her another talking to. She'd tried to apologise to her on the journey to Nassau, but Lizzy always had someone else with her as though she was being deliberately evasive.

"That pleased to see me, huh?" Saba raised her brows, slipping in and closing the door behind her.

Vice scoffed and flipped the page. "Sorry, was thinking about something else."

"About that book?" Saba's voice was flat.

Ha, for once not, though she could see why Saba would think so. Still bent over the pages, she shrugged. "I'm popular today." She copied out the next word in the sentence—she was putting together all the paragraphs mentioning the co-captain to read in one go and show to Knigh. "Perry came in earlier."

This morning, she'd arrived asking about... *something*. Vice had been busy re-reading the sections about this co-captain. When they'd first seen the phrase in their translations, they'd assumed it was coded talk for something relating to the treasure, but in reading all the instances together, it seemed to be referring to an actual person. By the time she'd torn her attention from the book, Perry had disappeared.

"Can you look at me?" Saba huffed.

"I'm just—"

"Vice. Avice. Please."

She shuddered at the name. If Saba was using it, this had to be serious. She plopped the pen back in the inkwell and squared her shoulders. "I'm looking at you."

Brows low, Saba nodded and took the seat opposite. "All this"—her dark eyes roved over the table stacked with books, notes, pen, ink, pencils, and maps—"it's a bloody mess."

Fair point. It had been driving Knigh mad for days, but—

"And the fact you can't bring yourself to come out and celebrate with us means in there"—Saba tapped her own temple—"you're a mess too."

Vice bristled. "*What?*" She'd been working on her feelings, on expressing them, even the ones that felt dangerous. Sure, she wasn't perfect, but she was trying—she'd *grown*.

"You understand the treasure chest is enough to change all our lives, don't you?"

This again. She shrugged. "It's not the treasure."

"Maybe not *the* treasure, but it is still *a* treasure. It still means I can get that home I've dreamed of. It means Clovis can pay off his family's debts once and for all. It means Effie and Wynn could go back to Albion and force that arsehole cousin of theirs out of their business once and for all." She lifted one shoulder and wrestled with Cable, wincing as his claws dug in. "If they wanted to. And that's the point—they have the option now. It's given them a choice."

Saba was leaving. Oh yes, because she needed that reminder. And Wynn and Effie might too. She gritted her teeth against that fresh twist of pain and tried to comfort herself by watching Cable's little paws bat and kick.

Everyone leaves. She had to remember that, even if sometimes it felt like it might not be true. Sometimes, like last night...

Head cocked, Saba gave a deep sigh. "You've changed people's lives by pursuing Drake's treasure, do you get that?"

Did it matter when she hadn't even discovered the real thing?

"I understand you believe there's more to find," Saba went

on. "You've certainly convinced Blackwood and he's no fool. But"—she raised her hand, the palm pale, except for a red streak from Cable's claws—"the journey *might* be over. There might be nothing more. And you need to be able to find peace, satisfaction with what you *have* achieved."

Vice's lips pursed, tight like her shoulders. "That sounds a lot like settling."

"Gods damn it, Vice." Eyes shut, she pinched the bridge of her nose. "You're not going to make this easy, are you? Fine. I'm sorry to do this, but nothing else is getting through to you." Her hand landed on the table with a thud as her eyes flashed open. The kittens scattered, Cable and Jetsam bounding onto Vice's lap. "You know who else was always dissatisfied?" Saba raised her chin. "FitzRoy."

A gasp jerked through Vice's whole body, winning pinpricks from the kittens as they clung on. Saba thought she was like FitzRoy. No hot anger rose in her blood, only cold dread. It mattered less whether or not it was true—and it was *not*—but more that Saba could even entertain the idea. "*Him*? Really? Are you kidding me?"

Saba's lips pressed together as she returned a level gaze.

"You *actually* think that? The man who pulled us out of port before we'd fully restocked, before everyone had got their shore leave?"

"And you wouldn't have done that if you were captain?"

Jaw aching where she held it so tight, Vice shook her head hard. "Of course I bloody wouldn't! How dare you even..." Pain twisted in her chest, as sharp as the kittens' claws. "*How* can you even think that? The man who—"

"Locked himself in his cabin for days on end poring over hints in books? The man who emerged with dark rings under his eyes from lack of sleep? The man who lost himself in the pleasure of your body at night and had you translate anything Drake-related by day? That man?"

It was a trap. And Vice had walked right in.

A chill trickled over her skin, raising goosebumps. How long had she been shut away in here? Hadn't she been losing herself in Knigh's body night after night? And, yes, it was different, because she... she felt something for Knigh, where Fitz had only seen her as a possession. But the parallels...

She shuddered, pulling her arms into a tight fold around herself.

"Have you looked in a mirror lately?" Saba's voice softened, a faint crack in her words. "You look... I'm worried about you. I'm scared of what this is doing to you and what it might yet do."

To hear Saba so soft made Vice's eyes burn. This wasn't some manipulation to get through to her—this was truth. Her throat was too tight for words, so she only shook her head. It wouldn't come to that. She wouldn't become a traitor like Fitz. That wasn't her.

Saba's chair scraped closer and her hand squeezed around Vice's shoulder, warm. "There might be more treasure out there. But do we really need more? It's dangerous. You said yourself that boy with the Duke died in a trap."

Evans. She'd failed him. Yes, he'd been under Mercia's command, but *she* hadn't worked out the correct door to use before he'd chosen the wrong one. And it had cost him his life.

"But with what we have," Saba went on, tilting Vice's chin up until they were eye-to-eye, "after all these years of searching for hints and rumours, we can finally do whatever we want. And I always, *always* had faith that you'd deliver. Thank you, my friend."

It was unbearable. *Thank you.* Like she'd... like she'd changed Saba's life. And Clovis's. And Wynn and Effie's.

She swallowed, the pain in her chest easing because it was unable to withstand Saba's gentle smile, her loving words.

With a half-shrug, she cleared her throat. "Least I could do." She managed a tight smile, forcing the threat of tears away. Humour was safe, as always, but maybe, just maybe some of what Saba had said was right. Cable clambered up her shirt and sat on her shoulder, warm like Saba's hand had been.

Saba chuckled and ruffled her hair before sitting back. "You're something else, Vice. And I'm glad that storm brought you into my life so thoroughly." She grinned. "Now, even if we don't have *the* treasure, this is the furthest anyone's got in, what, two hundred years? That's worth a night out drinking, isn't it?"

Laughing, Vice rubbed her face. "Fine. Maybe I can celebrate this milestone along the way. After all, it *is* a pretty impressive haul."

"The stuff of legends. Plus"—Saba's grin broadened, a wicked glint in her eye—"guess who's here. Someone who'll be sick as a dog when he sees you."

Vice gasped, cheeks tight with a dawning smirk. "FitzRoy?"

"Fitz-bloody-Roy. And I cannot wait for you to rub his face in it."

"Right. That's persuaded me. Come on."

It took twenty minutes for Vice to ready herself. Saba brought a pitcher of water to wash with, and helped her pick an outfit and tame her hair. The oil from Redland cut a sweet scent through the room and left a beautiful gloss on her curls.

When Vice emerged onto the main deck, she blinked at the setting sun, golden and low in the sky, just edging out of sight. A spark flared in her chest, and when she turned Knigh was there. The slow smile spreading across his face was as dazzling as any sunset.

Maybe she *had* been a bit obsessed with Drake.

She gave him a rueful smile as she approached and he pushed off the rail. Perry grinned and winked, before making for the gangway. She called over her shoulder, "I'll see *you* at the pub!"

Knigh's gaze skimmed over her and that alone was enough to send a warm wave through her. He stood very still as though all too aware of Saba's presence. "Thought you were staying in your cabin," he said at last, one eyebrow rising.

"You know what they say," she said, lifting her chin, "work like a captain, play like a pirate."

He laughed. That true laugh that lit up his face and made him throw back his head. And she couldn't help but smile all the harder.

Saba had been right to use the spectre of Fitz to drag her out of that cabin. Even if this wasn't *the* treasure, it was worth celebrating.

And even more than that—these friends, this *family* were worth celebrating while she still had them.

"Ah, so she *is* alive," Aedan said from somewhere behind. As he drew level, he clapped her on the back so hard, she stumbled forward.

"Bloody hells!" She gave him a playful swat.

He only shrugged and grabbed Knigh's shoulder. "Come on, Blackwood, you promised me a gentlemen only evening."

"*Gentlemen only?*" Vice held her chin, mock-thoughtful. "You'll have to find some first."

"That's true." Aedan laughed and tugged on Knigh's shoulder again before crossing the gangway, Saba in his wake. "We'll catch up with you later and let you know how we get on with our hunt for some *gentlemen*."

"Come on, Vice," Effie called from the docks. She and Wynn stuck their tongues out at Aedan as he approached. When Saba drew level, they linked arms with her, and Wynn waggled her free hand as if to say she belonged there on the end of their little line.

"Sorry, I did promise," Knigh muttered as they crossed to the docks together.

"Oh, don't you worry, Blackwood," she murmured, eyeing him sidelong, "I owe you an apology for being so… absorbed recently. So, I'll be finding you later to give my full and unabridged apology."

His brows rose as he gave her a lingering look. "Oh, *really?*"

"Mmm-hmm." She nodded slowly. "I'm going to do some *long, hard* apologising."

And then their friends were pulling them apart, the so-called gentlemen turning west and the women east, with promises to meet up later, once they were all incredibly drunk.

The look Knigh gave Vice, all hot and dark—oh, yes, he'd *definitely* come and find her.

No matter what.

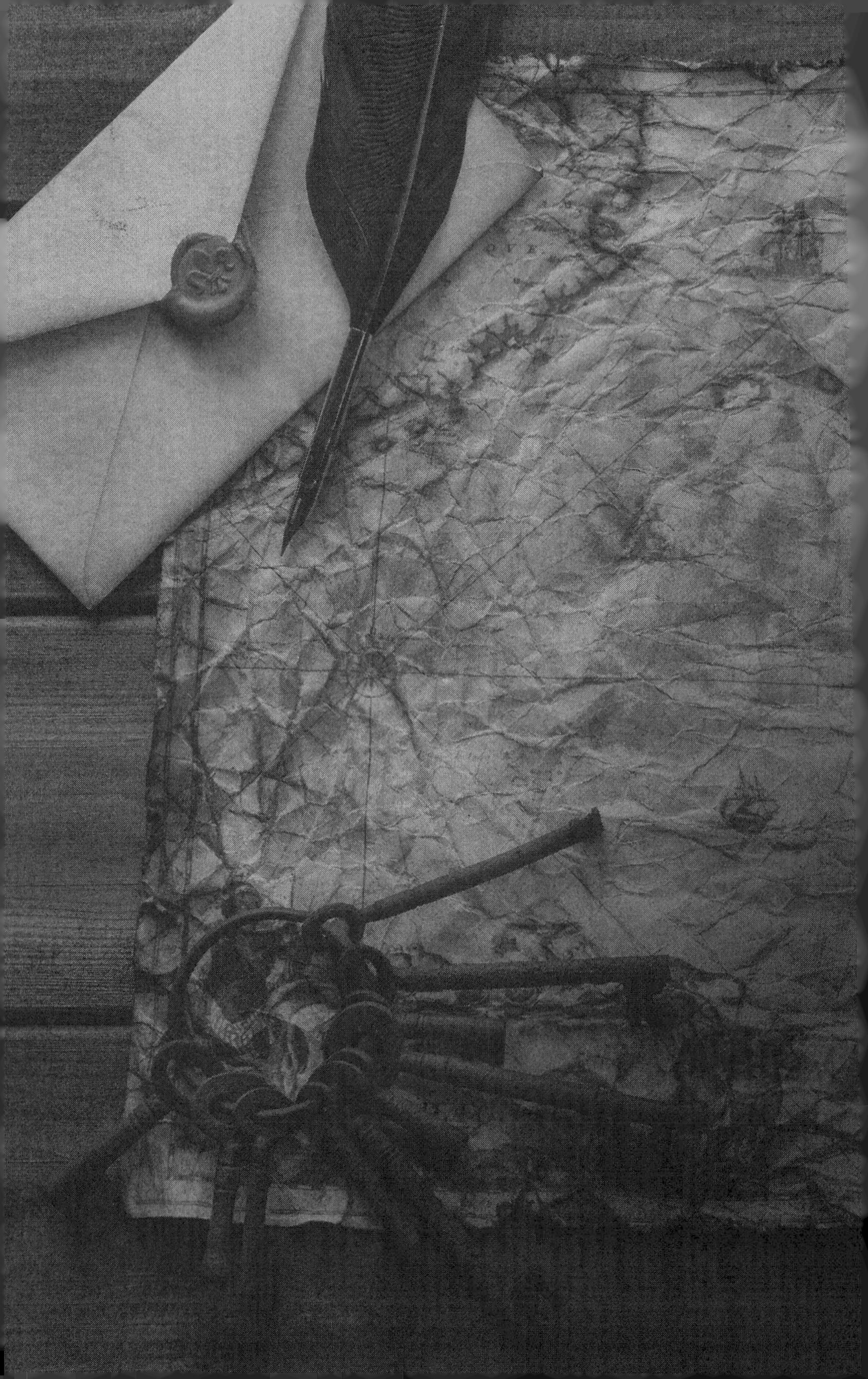

THE LAUGHING KRAKEN

The Laughing Kraken heaved with chatter and the scent of too many different perfumes and colognes in too small a space. Everyone was dressed—and scented—to show off their success and hard-fought-for wealth with fresh shirts, silk waistcoats, and so much gold braid, FitzRoy wouldn't have looked out of place in the slightest.

In sheer shirt and crimson waistcoat, with her dagger earring in one ear and one of Saba's feathered hoops in the other, Vice grinned to herself and took a gulp of spiced rum. Pirates on shore were a whole ostentation of peacocks and she was just as guilty of dressing to impress. The high seas were no place for clothes this fine, so she had to make the most of it when she could.

In one corner, a loud drinking game involved beating a tune on the table and chanting along. In another, one of the lads from the *Firefly* tried to start a song, but his words were slurred and he kept being thrown off-beat by the table-drumming, so Vice couldn't even hazard a guess at what song he was attempting.

She caught the eye of a woman with deep sea-teal hair at the same table. The newest member of the *Firefly's* crew. In fact, hadn't one of the lads said that was her name, Teal? Probably not her real one—it had to come from that hair colour, her fae-mark. Not that Vice was in a position to call out anyone on their name choices. Smiling, she raised her tankard to Teal and nodded. From what her friends on the *Firefly* had said, she was a sea witch, too, though only fae-touched, not fae-blooded.

Teal jerked her pointed chin towards the would-be singer on her table and her full lips twisted in what was part long-suffering grimace and part sardonic grin.

With a chuckle, Vice gave an exaggerated shrug.

At her side, Saba elbowed her. "Flirting with the new sea witch in town?"

"She *is* beautiful." But she wasn't Knigh. She hid what was probably a ridiculous smile behind her cup and angled her head as if evaluating. But inside, her chest warmed and she dipped into her gift for an instant—that golden glow of his still edged her own magic, like she was carrying a part of him. And earlier, when she'd emerged from her cabin, she'd been able to feel him before she'd seen him. What had they done last night? "But I'm not looking. This is just sea witch solidarity." There were precious few of them outside the Royal Navy.

Saba snorted and waved her drink, which sloshed over the edge of her tankard. "Sure it is. So, if not her..." She scanned the room, then pursed her lips at Vice. "Who've you got your eye on?"

No one. She could tell Saba now. But, in spite of the rum, her throat was too dry.

"We could always follow the others, if you're still looking."

Lizzy had taken the first opportunity tonight to slip away with Wynn and Effie, who'd sighed something about all the best-looking men preferring some new tavern near the docks. Perry had muttered something about wanting to check the veracity of their claims, for *reasons*, and hurried after them, promising to catch up with Saba and Vice later. Vice huffed into her drink. So much for celebrating together. Perry, she could understand. But considering Lizzy tended to prefer women... No, she was still avoiding her.

Barely able to swallow, Vice shook her head. Although they were keeping it a secret, she owed it to Saba to tell the truth. Hells, she owed it to Knigh—it would save them both from any more awkward attempts at flirtation. She grimaced into her cup. This whole thing was a mess with no simple way to clear it up.

Come on, you coward. She took a breath. "Actually—"

"Ah, I take back my offer," Saba said, eyes widening as a broad smile crossed her face. Another contingent of the *Firefly's* crew stood in the doorway, newly arrived. "I'm staying right here."

Vice ended her attempted sentence on a sigh. Maybe this wasn't the time.

One eyebrow raised, Saba watched over the rim of her cup as the group of men strode through the crowd. Her assessment lingered on one in particular. Tall, square-jawed, with deep ochre skin and piercing green eyes. Those green eyes swept the room, stopping on Saba where his brows rose in recognition and question.

Mm-hmm. So they'd already met, last night perhaps.

"*That's* why you've been watching the door all night." She gave Saba a sidelong look and a nudge. At least this bought her more time to work out how to broach the subject of Knigh. And he *was* striking. Had to be another new recruit, because she didn't recognise him, but the *Firefly's* captain chose his crew well, all friendly. He tolerated no ill-treatment of women, so Saba would be in good hands. "Can't fault your choice. Get over there before someone beats you to him."

"But what about—"

"Don't worry about me." She rose and waved Saba off. "I'll—"

The door remained open where the *Firefly's* men had entered and in that rectangle of darkness from outside stood an all-too-familiar figure. The gold braid of his black jacket gleamed as he surveyed the crowd.

FitzRoy.

Gaze settling on her, he nodded.

The grin that spread over her face was probably predatory, but apparently that didn't put him off, because when she indicated the now-empty seat beside her, he strolled over, navigating the crowd with ease.

Oh, breaking the news to him was going to be fun.

He eased into the chair and gave her a once-over. "Looking

well, Vice," he murmured, raising a finger for one of the tavern staff to come over.

She wasn't, not with those dark shadows under her eyes. Still, she let him buy her a drink when he asked.

Knees, shoulders, hands angled towards her, he asked how she'd been since they'd parted ways after escorting the *Swallow*, how Perry was, and Barnacle and the kittens. He expected to hear her captaincy announced any day, after her recent success. That was all he said about the treasure. No matter. She would lull him into a false sense of security, then raise it after the polite chit-chat.

All the while, his hazel eyes barely strayed from her, even when a scuffle broke out over the table-thumping drinking game.

She knew that look, had been on the receiving end of it enough times, so it was no surprise when his fingers brushed her cheek, pushing back a lock of hair, before trailing down to trace a line along her shoulder.

And she felt nothing. That in itself felt like a kind of victory—proof that it wasn't *just bodies*. If she only wanted sex, if that was all she got from Knigh, then FitzRoy, for all his faults, was more than capable of delivering pleasure. But, no, not the slightest spark of interest.

One eyebrow arched, she gave him a smile that was all sharp edges and warning shots. "I don't remember giving you permission to touch me, FitzRoy."

He pulled away, though his hand hovered in the air above her shoulder. "Does that mean I don't have it?"

"What do you think?"

"I think you're still far too bewitching," he murmured, glancing at her lips. "I think we could keep each other company tonight." He exhaled, and if she didn't know better, she'd have sworn there was a tinge of regret in the small wrinkle between his brows.

But this was FitzRoy and she damn well knew better.

"I think," he went on, voice softer, "I'd get on my knees and do anything you asked just for the chance to taste you one more time. It could be just tonight, just sex. However you want it. Not like the old days. I'd let you have the wheel. I'd be yours to command."

Despite the sharp edges she tried to maintain, her mouth had dropped open. Fitz wasn't only offering himself, but he was offering control.

Wonders would never cease.

"You're about a year too late."

He cocked his head, a smirk twitching at the corner of his sensuous mouth. "For sex?" The smirk faded. "I'm not asking for another chance at—at something more. Just bodies. Just tonight. Just a bit of fun."

There was no going back to that—not with him. Not with anyone. Especially not after last night.

There was only Knigh.

She hid her foolish smile by taking a long draught of rum, which unfurled warmth in her muscles. Once she'd told Fitz about the treasure, she'd go and find him. They could share secret glances and touches, let anticipation and the frisson of secrecy rise until they could take it no more. *Then* they'd sneak away back to the *Venatrix*.

"Oh!" The way Fitz said it like a revelation made her jolt upright. His hand dropped away from that space near her shoulder. "Someone already got here before me."

She tried to bite back a smile and failed. Knigh's restraint, she did *not* have. Her thumb rubbed over the smooth blade of her dagger earring.

FitzRoy's gaze followed the gesture and his lips parted. "Huh. *Him*? After what he did?"

"And yet you're propositioning me when you did almost exactly the same thing?"

With a long exhale, he sat back, eyes narrowing. "Hrm, true. Why 'almost'?"

She gave him a sugary smile laced with cyanide. "Because I was nothing but loyal to you for three years, and I warmed your bed most of that time. But you still did it."

"Loyal?" He scoffed, brows shooting up. "You call lusting after my captaincy *loyal*?"

Huffing, she rolled her eyes. "I didn't want *your* captaincy, Fitz. I wanted *my own* captaincy. You could've given me any ship we took and I'd've sailed her for you. Like I said, oh, I don't know, a million times? You'd have had your own fleet."

"Fine. Maybe it was different. But, still. *Him*?" His face screwed up like she'd slapped a rotting fish on the table. "He has an opinion on hitches, for gods' sakes!"

"Yes, he does." But she couldn't mock him for it. That day in FitzRoy's cabin when he'd explained gasket coil hitches were better than bight coil hitches, she had, but now? If she could go back to that day and whisper in her past self's ear…

Past her would laugh in her face and call her a damn liar.

Didn't matter if it was a foolish smile on her face. Didn't matter one bit, not when his warm gift still glowed alongside her own magic. Not when she'd share her bed and herself with him again tonight. Not when she'd explain to him about Drake's co-captaincy tomorrow and they'd look through the clues and work it out *together*.

Lifting her chin, she met FitzRoy's gaze and let all that show in the smile that made her cheeks ache.

He blinked and leant away. "What—what's that on your face? Are you...?" He examined her, a frown between his brows, then his mouth fell open. "Good gods. You're in love with him."

"Typical FitzRoy, sees actual human emotion in someone and jumps to the wrong conclusion." But her heart beat a little faster and the light in her chest bloomed a little brighter, a little warmer.

Love was taking it too far. She didn't...

But he'd proved he'd die for her—all those times he'd risked ridiculous odds. And she... yes, she would die for him.

"Wild hunt," she murmured, hands tightening around her tankard. "I actually would. *Huh.*"

Because anything in the world would be easier to face than the prospect of him no longer being in it.

She had to go and find him. Kiss him. Hold him. Hear his voice. Tell him... tell him something...

A little streak of excitement crackling through her, she gulped her drink. She'd finish this, mock Fitz about the treasure, and then she'd go after Knigh. Sod *gentlemen only*, she had to see him.

When she looked up, Fitz was just staring at her, brows raised in utter incredulity.

"Oh wipe that look off your face," she snapped. "Caring about hitches is more than you ever did. You were always more interested in wealth than your ship or crew."

His eyes narrowed as he cocked his head. "Unlike you?"

"I look after my crew." Maybe not perfectly but... she tried. She was trying. To do better, to be better, just like with her emotions. Still, she'd already surpassed Fitz. "I value them over gold."

"So, what, you're about to be made captain and suddenly you're the expert?"

Ah, the perfect chance. With a feline smirk, she leant back in her chair, slid her hands behind her head, and thudded her boots on the table. "I'm not just going to be a captain, Fitz, I'm going to be *the* captain to find Drake's treasure."

The skin around his eyes twitched. A strike. Perfect.

But he didn't storm and rage, he only leant closer, head tilting in curiosity. "What do you mean? I thought you had it."

For all his *many* failings, Fitz had pursued the treasure for years and, other than her, Knigh, and probably Mercia, he knew more than anyone else about it. She'd evaded his questions when they'd teamed up to save the *Swallow*, but maybe he had some scrap of information he'd kept quiet all this time. It could shed new light on the map and its symbols.

She checked no one was near before righting herself and leaning in. "That's just it," she whispered. "The gold, the gems? I don't think that *is* the treasure."

He didn't laugh or tell her she was mad for wanting more

than the chest's contents. No, instead his thumb traced over his lower lip, thoughtful. "Treasure greater than gold and gems."

The words jolted through her, raising the hairs on the back of her neck. She seized his wrist. "Where did you read that?"

He shook his head with a shrug, but didn't move to free himself from her grip. "Just something I heard a long, long time ago. It was part of what got me interested in Drake's treasure. After all, what would be greater than gold and gems? That was a mystery I had to solve."

Huh. All this time she'd thought he was only after riches, but—

Boom.

Even over the clamour of the tavern, she heard it. Cannon fire? But this was the middle of the night.

And yet she was already on her feet, FitzRoy a beat behind.

They exchanged glances and a handful of patrons in the tavern looked up, frowning.

"Was that...?"

He nodded. "I thought so, too."

They were the first people outside, squinting towards the fort then the distant sliver of docks visible between buildings. Saba arrived a moment later.

No sign of smoke rising, though it was dark. An accident, maybe? Or some drunken idiot playing a joke with deadly equipment.

"Bloody morons," Fitz muttered, "dicking around with gunpowder. Don't they—"

Boom!

This time, she caught the flash from a cannon's muzzle

near the harbour entrance, further out than any ships docked. Not an accident, then.

    A whistling *whoosh* ghosted through the air.

    Round shot. Coming this way.

    But before she could cry a warning, the ground shook.

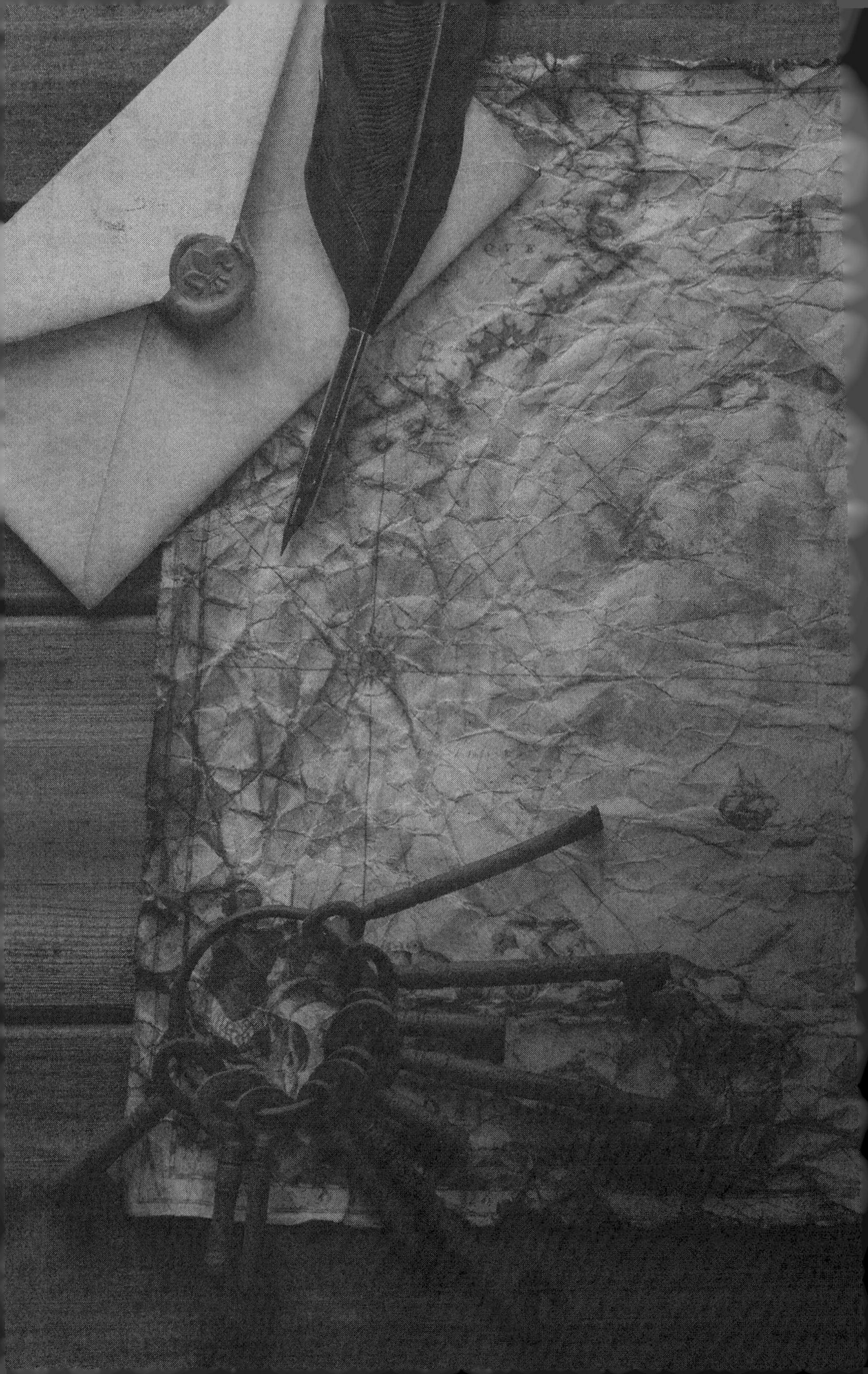

THE DEAD OF NIGHT

Shards of stucco and timber blasted the arm she'd raised to shield her face. Crashing and creaking, thunderous and close, but impossible to tell exactly how far because she couldn't even see her hand in front of her face. And the noise...

Loud and everywhere. Dust and debris rained down, blocking her throat and stinging her eyes. Over the pounding of her heart, voices rose in shouts of alarm, of fear, of dismay.

Ahead, someone screamed, the sound pure agony that stilled the blood in her veins.

Shit.

Shit, shit, shit.

Focus.

The cannon fire. That second shot must've struck a building on this street. Probably not the tavern, since she wasn't buried under it, but...

"Saba," she choked out, groping through the haze as she pulled her collar over her mouth and nose.

"Here." Nearby, just behind.

A few steps more and Vice's hand closed on something warm—a shoulder? "You all right?"

"Think so. Nothing hurts, so..."

"I'm safe, too," FitzRoy's disembodied voice said, "thanks for your concern."

She coughed a laugh and swatted in the direction of the sound but only swirled dust motes. "You get all the concern you deserve."

Boom. Boom. B-boom!

More shots—a volley of them all blending together and drowning out that agonised scream. On instinct, she pulled Saba close and hunched over her. But the shots didn't land here, didn't thunder through these buildings.

A bell rang. Another tower answered and another. The peals clanged a dissonant cacophony that blanketed the town in one message.

Nassau was under attack.

It rang through her, as harsh as the bellowing bells.

Knigh. Perry. All their crew—their *friends*. Barnacle, the kittens.

Waters. Vivienne. So, so many others who lived and worked here.

Coughing, Saba pulled out of her shielding hold. "The dust's clearing."

Sure enough, when Vice rubbed her streaming eyes and

blinked away the grit, she could see Saba's outline and just beyond that, a shadow that had to be Fitz.

The scream broke, then sounded again, quieter this time. It came from further down the street, perhaps one or two buildings away.

"Come on, we need to help." She half felt her way along, Saba and Fitz in her wake as more *booms* cracked the sky and shot *whooshed* overhead, making her duck. But it crashed further up the street or the next road over.

Breathing through her shirt, she followed that weakening scream until she stubbed her toe on something and stumbled with a curse at the dull pain.

When she looked up, she saw it.

Ahead, the ruin of half a house spilled its guts onto the road. Timber and crumbled stucco. A chair sprawled on its side. Splintered cupboards and what might've been a headboard.

"Good gods."

"Vice?" Saba's voice wavered. Her hand found Vice's and squeezed.

"It's fine," Vice lied. "We'll help and... and it'll all be fine." But her heart tolled in her chest, cold and aching.

Knigh. Perry. Their friends. Those other shots, had they...?

The screams died down to whimpers. Nearby, now.

She could do something to help this person. Focus on that. As she followed the sound, the air grew clearer, allowing her to pick through the debris.

Cries of shock came from behind—the tavern must've emptied out. More came from ahead, quieter, distant. *All* the taverns were emptying out as pirates and smugglers recognised the sounds of cannon fire and injury and... death.

Because the whimpers had stopped entirely.

She stepped over a fallen beam and narrowly missed a hand peeking out from a great pile of timbers. Her gut lurched and she crouched closer before her gaze even followed that slender arm to a crimson-smeared shoulder and a bare neck and above that, a still face. The eyes didn't blink despite the dust in the air, they only stared up, up, up into the night sky.

The cold engulfed her and a strangled sound made its way out of her throat.

This person—this woman was dead. She vaguely recognised her. Someone she'd passed in the street or who'd sat on the next table at a tavern. She didn't know her, but...

But she'd been killed in her own home, in the place where she should've been safe, in an attack out of nowhere in the dead of night.

Skin frigid, throat sore, Vice called into the ruins of the house for any more survivors, for anyone injured, but the only response was quiet and the distant *boom* of more cannon fire.

Think. Plan. Act.

There was nothing more to do here. Squaring her shoulders, she turned and picked back through the debris, Saba and FitzRoy following her in silence.

I need to find Knigh and Perry.

I need to check on Waters.

I need to get him—get everyone safe.

I need to stop this attack.

I need to free anyone who's trapped.

I need to get the injured to Knigh and Lizzy and anyone else who can help.

I need to...

It was a wave of needs—of things *she* had to do—towering so high, about to crash over her.

She couldn't do it all at once.

A crowd had built outside the Laughing Kraken, the tavern patrons, but also people who lived nearby in nightclothes or crumpled, thrown-on breeches and shirts, some buttons still undone. Hands raking through hair or over their mouths, they talked in knots, some shouting questions to each other, arguing about what was happening, what to do. Familiar grey hair stirred in the breeze, and Vice sagged when she saw it was Waters at the edge of the crowd, Vivienne's arm through his. *He* was safe, at least.

One of the lads from the *Firefly* spotted her, his eyes widening before he nudged another. It rippled through the crowd until roughly half of them looked at her in question.

As if she was the one to lead them, to tell them what to do. Maybe it was her fae charm or that she was well-known in the town, or maybe it was the stories. Whatever the reason, they looked to her.

But she had to find Knigh. And Perry. She...

If she failed them—her friends, the people of Nassau...

Those eyes, staring up, up, up.

If she failed them, there would be a lot more of those tonight.

She swallowed away the dust still coating her mouth and met gaze after gaze. This was their town. This was their home. And she would fight for it.

"I need to find out who that is and what they want." She used the voice that carried across deck when she gave orders.

Wild Hunt, it sounded sure, like she knew what she was doing, like she had a plan. But she only had the words tumbling from her lips and no clue what the next one would be or where her sentence was going.

"Check the damaged buildings. Help anyone who's injured or trapped."

Eyes, staring up, up, up.

Even as she shuddered, she caught Nell's attention. There *was* a plan, something that could help save lives. "You have a stone-built cellar, right?" Many buildings here were timber, and just like on a ship, they'd become a source of splintering shrapnel once struck by round shot. That, or they'd collapse like a house of cards, crushing everyone within.

Staring up, up, up.

She bit her tongue, let the pain blot out that image.

At least stone had a chance of withstanding a direct hit or two.

Nell nodded, her bronze skin gleaming in the streetlight. "Aye, two entrances, like most in town. Good for a sneaky getaway." She gave a grim smile.

"Then get everyone evacuated from their houses to tavern cellars." She caught the eye of a couple of sailors, barely more than kids. "If you're fast and brave, spread the word across town, get the other taverns doing the same."

They all stared back at her, ashen-faced. But she had nothing more for them. There was no cunning plan—not yet, not until she knew her friends were safe and exactly what they were up against.

And then: battle.

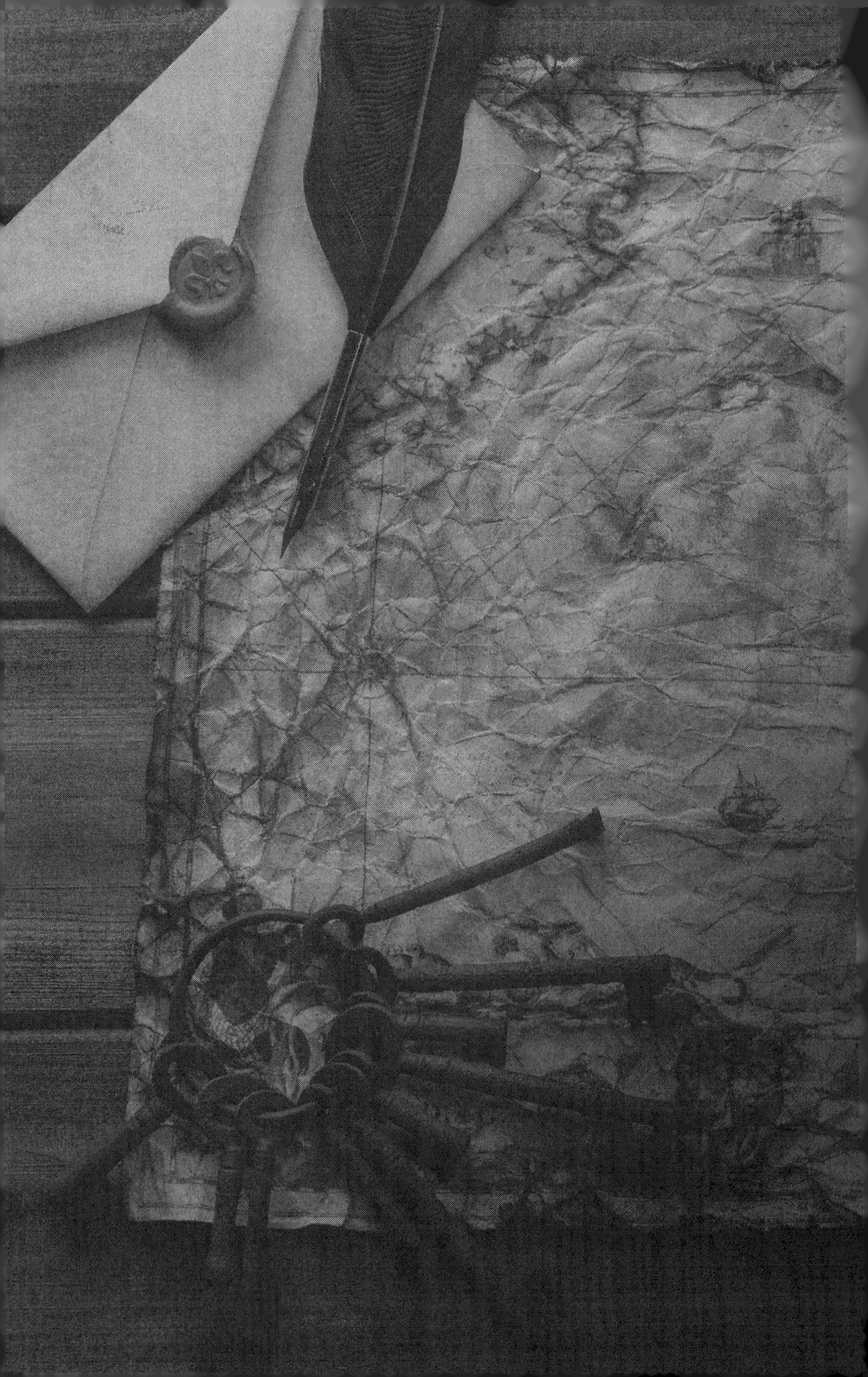

NEW MOON

When they hurried off to their tasks, Vice turned away, stomach churning. Saba remained in place, face slack.

"That was... something." Fitz nodded, a flash of a smile on his mouth before he glanced west. "I'm going to the fortress. I know the place, I can help the defences. They aren't even firing back yet." His brows drew together in a deep V as he huffed through his nose. "Where will you go?"

"I need to find the others." *I need to find Knigh. And Perry.*

Because if they were dead already...

Her heart tightened like someone held it in their fist.

Fitz arched his eyebrows. "Do you? Seems to me a sea witch would be pretty useful right about now."

She shot him a glare. "As always. Isn't that why you kept me in your crew so long?"

"This isn't about you and me. You can throw them off course, take them aback... Do *something*."

When did Fitz start being right? But she had to find her friends first. Make sure they didn't end up like...

Staring up, up, up.

"I need to get to the others. Besides, I can't do anything from here, we're too far away and I can't see what's going on."

His jaw twitched and he opened his mouth to reply, but then a contingent from the *Firefly* swarmed around them. Ollie, a short, slender man who was as quick as a whip, nodded to Vice. "We're heading to the *Firefly*. We'll give them a few gifts of our own."

Saba blinked, apparently waking from her shock. "Are you going along Brewery Lane?"

"Aye, we can go that way."

"I'll come with you." She raised her eyebrows at Vice. "I'll find Perry, Lizzy, Wynn, and Effie."

"Good thinking." Vice squeezed her shoulder. "I'll go after the 'gentlemen'. Meet back at the ship."

Lips flat, Saba nodded and hurried away with the *Firefly* crew.

"Come on then," she muttered to FitzRoy and they jogged west.

People huddled in doorways or stood in the road staring, and she and Fitz told them to get to the nearest tavern with a cellar. Crossing their path, pirate crews ran towards the docks, still in their finery. More than once, they had to double back, finding the road blocked by a fallen building. After that, they tried to stick to the wider streets.

All the way, the cannons continued their booming attack.

Where was Knigh? Was he safe? He and Aedan and the others had split off towards this side of town. There were half a dozen taverns they would probably work their way through. He could still be in one, helping the injured, or...

Her heart squeezed, skipping a beat in its swift rhythm.

Whoosh.

Overhead. Close.

Crash. Dust and stucco shards burst into the road feet away.

One arm shielding her face, she grabbed a handful of FitzRoy's jacket and veered right down an alley.

Whoever that was out in the harbour, they were completely bombarding the place.

Boom! B-b-b-boom!

Louder. Closer.

"That's the fort firing back." FitzRoy panted, tugging his arm from her death-grip. "Thank buggery for that."

Maybe that would put off the attackers.

Two more corners, then they reached the junction where one road led up to the fort, and the other would take her to the first of the taverns on her list. Over this side of town, most buildings were stone or stucco—marginally safer than timber.

"Smash them, Fitz." She clapped him on the shoulder.

"To smithereens." He flashed her a grin, but there were shadows around his eyes. He knew what all these fallen buildings meant—many more eyes staring up, up, up.

She shivered and pulled away. She couldn't save them all. She couldn't—

Rough cloth against her fingertips. When she blinked down, he was pressing a pouch into her hand.

"Almonds and cashews," he said. "Your favourites. I figure you might need the energy."

She snorted and hefted the pouch—more than a good handful. "And you just carry these around, in case you happen upon a sea witch who needs a snack?"

He shrugged, a coy smile at the corners of his mouth. "Force of habit."

"You're getting soft in your old age, Fitz. But"—she huffed and dropped the pouch in her pocket—"thank you."

He sketched a salute and turned up the road to the fort.

"Try not to die," she called when he was a few paces away.

"Didn't know you cared." He looked over his shoulder, brows raised.

"I don't." She threw him a cocky grin. The brash and bold Pirate Queen was better equipped to survive a night like this. She wouldn't get lost in the image of staring, blank eyes. She would save everyone she could and get the job done. So Vice leant into the role, hands on hips, chin raised. "But if you die tonight, I'll never get the joy of seeing the look on your face when I find the real treasure."

His laugh echoed off the houses and shops as he jogged away.

A little warmth trickled through her, as though laughter meant this wasn't real.

Clinging on to that, she ran to the Copper Flagon. No sign of Knigh or Aedan or any of the *Venatrix's* crew and the barkeep said there hadn't been all night. Maybe checking each individual tavern wasn't the best way. If she could get the lay of the land...

Over the road, a clock tower peeked above the other buildings. The perfect vantage point. She ran to it and up the staircase, thighs burning with step after step after step, until she finally emerged into the cool night. Up here there was no dust and she could catch her breath with lungfuls of blessed clear air.

She approached the north side of the tower and...

Beyond the parapet, dark holes pockmarked the town. Whole buildings were simply *gone*. The bells had stopped—everyone knew the danger now—but there were still screams. So many screams.

Men and women hurried through the streets below, some clutching weapons, others with bundles as though they'd gathered their valuables and didn't expect they'd ever get to return home. Some cradled their bundles with both arms and hunched over like they were precious—their babies. Others ushered children at their sides as they streamed towards the bright sign of the nearest tavern.

Above, the night sky was inky black and strewn with stars, except for one area with no light at all. That empty circle made her shudder.

A new moon.

Back in Albion, the Wild Hunt would be pounding through the land tonight, and although that was thousands of miles away, it still blocked her throat with terror for long seconds.

Her bones screamed to get inside and lock every door, close every curtain, lest they spot her and come to claim her as quarry for their hunt.

But that was Albion.

Here, beneath the new moon, beyond the town, the barest slip of starlight glimmered on the sea and it was so dark that even her fae-blooded sight struggled to pierce it from this distance. The attacking ships weren't so much visible as clear lines of hull and mast and sail, they were mere shadows on the sea where no light flickered. The same as that blank new moon in the sky.

And those shadows blotted out the whole entrance to the harbour. Dozens of vessels.

Their sides lit up with row upon row of yellow flashes as their cannons fired.

Bollocks. Dozens and dozens and dozens. A *fleet*.

BOOM!

Round shot whooshed past, left and right, and ear-splitting crashes opened fresh pockmarks in the town.

Her town.

Mouth open, she clutched her chest. So much. So much damage. And so many ships. With so many cannons.

She couldn't go after Knigh. Though her heart crashed against her chest in rebellion at the idea.

She had to stay here, use her gift now she could see the water, push these bastards away, smash their ships in her storm. Whatever it took. Whatever—

In the harbour, something white caught the scant light. She

squinted, leaning over the parapet as if that little extra distance might help.

Froth. It was froth. Not near the attacking vessels blockading the harbour entrance, but by the ships at anchor, where a few lanterns studded the darkness, so jolly and yellow they were sorely out of place on this night.

The light from one of those lanterns glistened on something red. Something long. Something that writhed and slithered.

A low moan tore from her throat before the word formed in her mind.

Kraken.

More tentacles broke from the water and wrapped around that boat with its jolly little lantern.

Fighting to breathe past the bile bubbling up in her throat, Vice reached for her gift—the sea coming to her a fraction before the sky... but both too late.

The boat was no more.

Just like that little fishing boat all those months ago when she'd been a prisoner.

Doubled over the parapet, she threw up again and again, until there was nothing but bitterness left.

Panting, she pressed her brow to the cool stone. The kraken was here. At her home dock.

And that meant Mercia was here too. The *Sovereign* had to be amongst the blockade. How did he have so many ships at his disposal to attack Nassau when he wasn't even assigned to pirate hunting?

Fine. She'd beaten the kraken once before. And she'd got the better of Mercia, too. She could do it again.

Another breath and she pushed herself upright and spat out the last remnants of vomit.

To smithereens.

She threw a cashew nut in her mouth and sank into her gift.

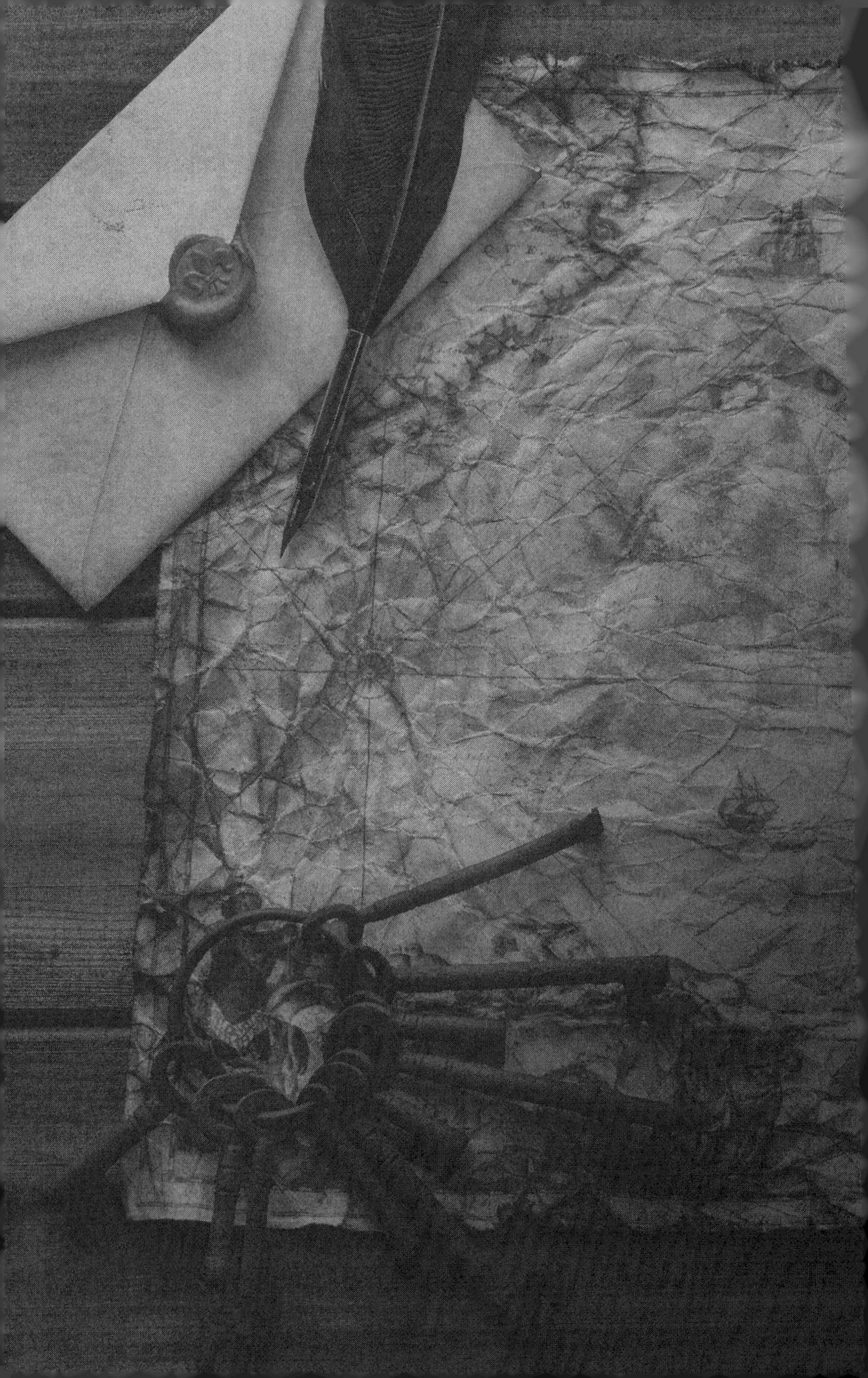

THE FORT

"Fire!" Knigh bellowed the word with every fibre of his being.

Cannon fire boomed through the fort, trembling in the stone, thrumming in his bones. The scent of sulphur and charcoal traced through the smoke that hazed across the battlements.

He nodded with approval as the gun crews set to work swabbing and reloading.

Out in the harbour, timber creaked and screams reached across the water. Too dark to tell the exact damage, but with that degree of noise and now a low splashing—one of the ships had to be sinking. "A direct hit." He flashed a fierce grin. "Keep it up, ladies and gents!"

But as he turned to the wall, his gaze snared on the town below.

Vee.

Where was she? And was she alive or…?

… Or *not*?

His throat closed and he had to grit his teeth to prevent any more reaction than that.

She had to be all right. Had to be. Anything else was inconceivable.

When the attack began, his first instinct had been to find her, to ensure she was safe, to heal her if she needed it, but…

But, no, duty first.

He'd been separated from Aedan and the others, caught either side of a fallen wall. Aedan had called through the debris and dust that he was going to find the others on Brewery Lane. Wynn and Effie had taken a shine to twins who worked at a tavern down there and he was sure that's where they'd be.

When Knigh had realised the fort wasn't firing on the attackers, duty had brought him here. And just as well, because no leader had shown up to direct the ragtag part-time garrison, which was largely made up of townsfolk and injured pirates who could no longer sail. He'd organised them and now they called their readiness for the next shot.

No change out on the water, except maybe… "Fire."

Another thunderous report shook the night.

He squinted at the attacking fleet dimly outlined by the pre-dawn light. The Albionic flag had been easy to pick out even in the near-dark of a new moon—a dragon against a white field. But not every ship flew it and although he couldn't make out the detail in the dim light, one thing was clear. Those other flags were black.

Pirates had banded with Mercia to attack Nassau.

They had to be assured of complete, obliterating victory to dare to attack their own. Any pirate who survived this battle would pursue these traitors to the ends of the earth. Could it be Vane and his cronies? He'd already pitted pirate against pirate and wanted to work with Mercia, but bombarding their haven was many strides beyond that.

More creaks and screams out on the water, a crack and crash. That had to be a mast falling. "You're—"

Boom. Out on the water, not here.

Whoosh. Coming this way.

"Incoming," he roared, ducking behind the hewn walls.

The floor shook. Stone shards blasted through the air, battering him, clattering to the ground. There was dust in his eyes, his mouth, down his throat, choking and thick.

But the ground didn't fall away and nothing else struck him.

Coughing, he scrubbed his cuff over his face and blinked away the grit. "Report."

But when he rose, he could see for himself—a hole in the battlements. One gun lay crumpled in the courtyard inside the walls, half its crew with it, bent bodies strewn amongst the rock.

"Fire when ready." He nodded reassurance to the remaining teams, even though his gut twisted. Men and women lost under his command. It was never easy to take, but for the sake of those left, he couldn't hesitate in his orders. "More powder and shot," he called below before turning to the gunners left standing upon the walkway, their crewmates below. "Guthrie, isn't it?"

The team leader tore her attention from the courtyard and her fallen comrades, one eye wide, a patch covering the other. "Aye." Her pale hair whipped in the wind.

"I can help them, but you need to supervise the other teams. Understand?"

She blinked from cannon to cannon. "Aye, Captain." It must've been force of habit, because he'd told them he was no captain. Not anymore. But whatever habit or reassurance she needed to cling onto was fine by him, as long as she did the job.

He ran, jumped to the steps leading down to the courtyard, and took the remaining stairs three at a time. The first person he reached, a dark-haired woman, was dead, her chest caved in by the gun. But the other three were only injured, one bleeding profusely from his head.

Knigh healed him first, threads of lightning still dancing on the fringes of his own magic. Vee. Did that mean she was alive? Would the mark of her magic upon his disappear if she wasn't?

"Please gods," he murmured, kneeling to help the next gunner.

When he'd helped the third, he shook out his tingling arms and inclined his head to Guthrie, who was doing a good job keeping the remaining guns loading, firing, reloading, again, again, again.

But now they—the only resistance in Nassau—had Mercia's attention, more of his ships would fire upon them and enough of those shots would land true.

"Get down to the docks and the town," he told the freshly healed gunners. "Spread the word to every crew you can—they need to attack, otherwise the fort will be lost and with it, the whole town. Understand?"

Faces drawn in grim lines, they nodded before running for the fort's open gates.

And in the gateway, black coat dusty, short hair caked with the stuff too, stood FitzRoy.

Knigh didn't have time for anger or for snide remarks, so he drew a long breath and returned to the battlements. "Keep it up, Guthrie," he called, circling around to the next bastion and its set of guns.

Footsteps slapped behind. "Blackwood."

"What do you want, FitzRoy? I'm busy." He paused to let a powder girl hurry past, her halo of curls bouncing as she ran.

"What's the status?"

"The status is"—without missing a step, Knigh gestured for a restock when he spotted a pile of round shot was low—"that I don't report to you. Never have. Never will."

"Which, ser?" one of the runners below called up.

"Stick to round. Chain's a waste of time—they're not moving." Not when they could sit there and fire on the town to their hearts' content.

FitzRoy drew level, swatting at his own sleeve in a doomed attempt to dust it off. The dawn seeping overhead revealed just how thick a coating of grime was all over his skin and clothes, as though he'd been buried and had resurfaced. "I came to help."

"Then man a gun." Knigh didn't even spare him a glance. "Fire!"

More shots rumbled through the floor, and a fresh report fired back. Thankfully, they whistled overhead.

"I know this fort. I can take over while you get to the ships."

Holding his face rigid, Knigh stopped. "And why would I do that?"

FitzRoy's arms folded and a little muscle in his jaw ticked. Typical, he finally gave the man a chance to speak and here he was delaying.

"*Why*, FitzRoy?"

"Because you probably have more experience of sailing in a fleet than anyone else in Nassau. And you know the Navy better than any of us, too." He said it quickly, like each word pained him and he wanted it over and done with.

He was an arse. But he was right.

That didn't mean it was going to be easy to say.

"And," FitzRoy's eyebrows rose, "it'll give you a chance to find Vice."

His heart stuttered, and dizziness tilted through him. "You've seen her?"

"Aye. She's looking for you." A bitter smile flickered on Fitz-Roy's mouth. "*Of course*, what else would she be doing?"

"So she's...?"

"Alive and uninjured last time I saw her."

Alive. *Alive*. It eased the tightness he'd been carrying in his chest since he'd heard that first shot back in the tavern. "Where?"

"On the corner by the Copper Flagon. That was maybe twenty minutes ago."

He had to get to her. And then he had to help coordinate the ships, make them work as a fleet.

Violet and pink streaks crept across the sky, catching on clouds that had formed so quickly, they had to be Vee's. He smiled and turned, a fierce pride in his chest.

Out in the harbour, the burgeoning dawn lit the masts of the attacking ships and their black flags. A white spear piercing a red heart.

Vane's flag.

FitzRoy followed his line of sight. "Son of a..."

Crack.

A rifle shot, somewhere to the east, in the town itself. Half a dozen more echoed up from the streets. Knigh's feet carried him towards the sound before he'd even told them to move. "They've landed a force."

"Shitting bastards," FitzRoy growled, keeping pace with him. "And with Vane on their side, they know the town just as well as we do."

They peered down into the streets, but the only sign of battle was another report of gunfire.

FitzRoy's fingers bit into his shoulder. "What are you still doing here?"

Knigh shook him off. "Fine." He took a step forward until they were nose-to-nose. "But I swear, if you betray us, I'll hunt you down and feed you to the kraken myself."

A smirk tugged at FitzRoy's mouth. "Ah, so you do have a touch of the monstrous about you after all. Congratulations, Blackwood, you just got a hundred percent more interesting."

"Don't make me regret this," Knigh growled, before turning and flying down the steps.

As he grabbed a sabre, rifle, and pistols from the courtyard armoury, he caught FitzRoy's voice bellowing from the walls: "Take down any boats you see coming in to land."

That was a good start, at least.

Hooking the rifle over his shoulder, Knigh slipped one hand into his pocket and squeezed the little abalone shell. "I'll always come for you."

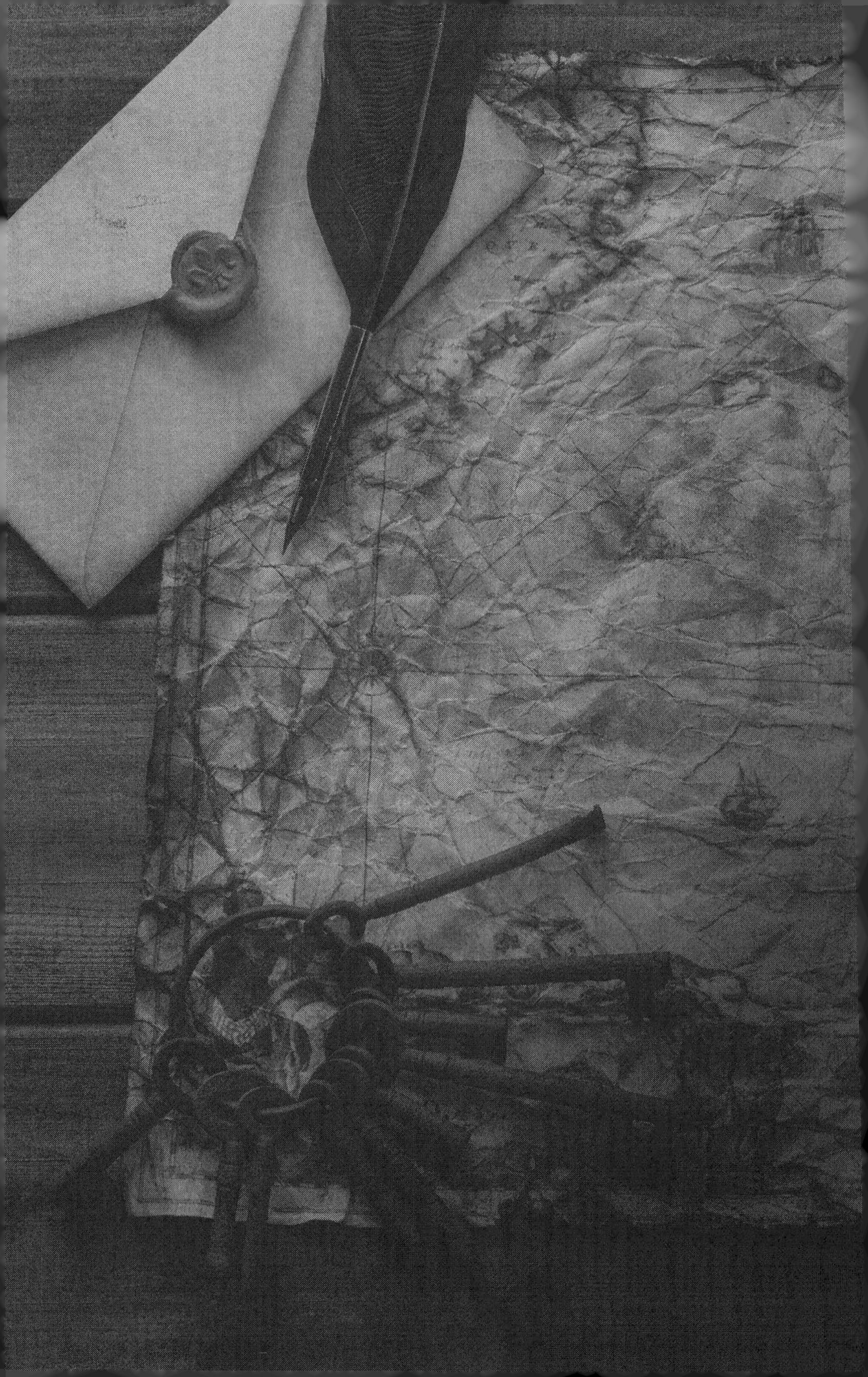

OPEN WOUNDS

Lightning and thunder and cloud churned inside, edged with a golden glow. As she hauled on that magic, let it crackle through her, she also let Knigh's golden warmth light up her veins. It had to mean he was alive. Had to.

In the world beyond, she channelled the wellspring's roaring energy into a localised storm, centred on the harbour and the attacking fleet.

Running along the northern end, Hog Island sheltered the harbour, and to the east, it linked to Nassau via a narrow sandbar that peeked out of the water at low tide. To enter or exit, a ship would need to pass between Fort Nassau and Hog Island, right where the attackers were gathered.

But a familiar wall made the sea there a blank space to her.

Mercia.

He was protecting his ships, holding them still in the water, stopping any current or wave she tried to use against them.

Their gifts were different, she'd known that, but that difference had never been so stark before.

She moved with the sea, in it, was part of it, mutable. She used its natural waves and forms and merely bent them to what she needed—stronger, smaller, larger, in this direction or that, but always things the ocean was naturally inclined to do.

Mercia carved it to his will. He could hold it as still and flat as a mirror or raise it in a great roaring wall of water, so Knigh had told her. His grip on the sea was rigid, solid, blocking it from outside influence, like a bottle around water. When she opened her eyes, she could see in, but she couldn't affect or even *feel* the area under his control.

And his beast, the kraken... She charted its movements through the harbour, or at least the absence of sea that marked where its great and terrible body passed.

Static coiled in her clouds, ready to strike lightning into the creature. But...

She'd done this once before and...

Pain! No! Please! That vast and ancient awareness... It had touched her mind, begged her to stop, shown her itself, its... *personhood.*

The turning of her stomach tore her from the wellspring, and if she'd had anything left to vomit up, she might've done so. She gasped for air, hands on the parapet, gift still holding on to her storm, still feeling the kraken pass through the water. It kept well below the surface like it knew those clouds were hers and what waited in their churning darkness.

But even if the kraken rose to the surface, could she unleash lightning upon it?

The searing pain that had brushed against her when she'd struck it before had been beyond horrific. To do that to another living creature was no quick death like a headshot from her rifle or pistol. That burning explosion of absolute agony—it was nothing short of torture.

And to knowingly do that to an intelligent being, albeit one as alien as the kraken? *That* would be the action of a monster.

Grimacing, she gripped the parapet and let its rough surface graze her fingertips. This tiny drop of pain was nothing to the ocean of torment lightning caused.

She couldn't do it.

Wouldn't.

She had a gift that could make her a monster, but that was not a path she would take.

Instead, she dropped crackling forks into the sea, mere feet from the attacking ships. A warning shot. Maybe it would frighten them into inaction or mutiny or even just slow their constant barrage of cannon fire.

Because if she couldn't hurt the kraken like that, she couldn't do it to a person either.

No sea. No lightning. Muscles aching, she gusted stormy winds at them, aiming for the few sails that remained unfurled, taking them aback. She cracked one mast, two, three. One took out a neighbouring ship as it fell.

But what were three toppled masts and one sinking ship when Mercia and Vane's combined fleet remained an entire forest of masts out in the harbour?

A flash of red near the docks caught her eye: the kraken

surfacing while she was distracted by the wind. Its glistening red tentacles wrapped around a small vessel at anchor.

"No." They had, at most, eighteen pirate ships, and they needed every single one of them.

To evacuate, whispered a dark corner of her mind.

No. It wouldn't come to that. She gritted her teeth and unleashed a bolt of lightning near the kraken. Another warning shot.

Releasing the small vessel, it streaked away, disappearing into Mercia's waters. But the damage was done. The boat's yards were all snapped and hanging loose. It, like half a dozen other ships in the harbour, wouldn't sail today.

Then she'd have to make sure they didn't need to evacuate.

She scrubbed her face before snacking on a handful of nuts. Although she was using the wellspring whenever she could, things like aiming her winds to take down those masts had required her eyes to be open and thus required her strength alone. Running out of energy would mean losing herself or losing her life.

Gunfire echoed through the streets below, and from the harbour, another barrage carved more pockmarks in the streets. The slanting light of sunrise cast the destruction in deeper shadows. Those open wounds covered almost half the town. She shivered, clutching herself as if each wound was in her flesh rather than in timber and stucco and stone. But this was her home on land. And these fallen buildings were home to hundreds more people whose only crime was to trade with pirates and smugglers.

Down in the harbour, fresh movement opened on the

waves—ships from the docks setting sail. The pirates were fighting back.

Her stomach shrivelled, threatening to send her snack back up.

If they stayed in place, they'd be safe from the cannons, at least. A jutting outcrop of land just east of the fort sheltered the docks enough to stop Mercia from pulverising Nassau's ships where they sat.

But if they sailed out to meet them, they would be destroyed. There were just too many ships in Mercia's fleet, and they all sat perfectly aligned to fire full broadsides. No matter how many of Nassau's vessels fired back, how many of Mercia and Vane's ships they took down, there would always be another ready to take its place.

It would never be enough. Didn't they understand that?

The knowledge was a ball of round shot in her gut—heavy and cold.

But the pirates sailed on.

Somehow, she had to work with the pirate crews below, even though they had no method of communication.

Being a captain is about trusting them to do their jobs. Urgh. Why did Perry always have to be so mercilessly right?

Cannon fire from the fleet and from the fort sounded again and again, punctuating every minute that passed.

Brow tight and aching, she leant on the parapet and gave herself to sea and sky.

From Mercia's wall to the sandbar at the harbour's eastern end, she held a decent expanse of water. But what could she do with it?

Above, her storm still trembled, lashing the attackers with wind and rain. She couldn't whip up waves in the area Mercia controlled, but she could make life on deck miserable. Cold, fumbling fingers made mistakes. Eyes full of rain missed their targets. It wasn't much, but it was something.

She sifted through the water. Rock and sand. Shallow. A flagship like the *Sovereign* couldn't come much further into the harbour without running aground. If she could wrestle control from Mercia, she might be able to use that. What else?

No sign of the kraken for now. The unmanned boat it had damaged drifted along, untethered, with no crew and no sails.

But she didn't need sails.

In the distance, a smile tugged on her mouth as she channeled a current beneath the little boat and dragged a thread of storm cloud over it. Each movement sapped her energy, but this was worth it.

A *fireship* was worth it.

Her lightning struck both masts with a *crack*. She squinted down at her handiwork and was greeted by the telltale flicker of orange and yellow. It was working. She hit the bowsprit, and that too lit up. If she struck the hull, she'd risk sinking the vessel and that wasn't her aim. Not when it could do so much more damage afloat.

With a little luck, it might even have a full magazine. A fireship's threat could scatter a formation, but that kind of explosion would blast a hole in the blockade.

It could grant the pirates an opening to counterattack.

That thought bright in her mind, she drifted cloud and mist across the water, hiding her boat, and pushed it towards

Mercia's fleet. They kept pummeling the town and the fort. One warship unfurled minimal sails, just enough to turn so it could take aim at the pirate vessels creeping out from the docks.

"Hmpf." She curled her fingers and brought cloud and mist in to shield the pirate ships, too, just while they got into position to attack. Once she'd carried her precious load to the fleet, she would snap that warship's mast like tinder.

Only once it was near the fleet did she unveil her gift, the low cloud dissipating to reveal the roaring red and gold of a boat aflame and mere yards from enemy lines. Her boat might stop once it hit the water Mercia controlled, but if she gave it enough momentum...

With a deep breath, she propelled her boat towards that blank wall. Arms, legs, back straining, she heaved.

Her knees trembled. Her eyes watered. Her teeth were going to break against each other.

It wasn't enough. It would lose momentum before it struck.

She dipped inside, into blackness and crackling energy edged with gold, and she took and took and took. She let it surge through her, pushing that current with such unnatural speed, it would've knocked anyone aboard the boat off their feet.

And then it was out of her reach and she fell to her knees, blinking at the sudden brightness.

She fancied she heard the shouts of dismay as her small boat darted into enemy territory, its roaring flame a match light against all those warships.

Small but mighty, it kept going, even through that blank water—Mercia must not have spotted it—and it had the nearest ships unfurling their sails, trying to turn in the packed waters.

Panicking.

With a grin, she swept in with a gust of wind and roared into those sails, forcing them against their own masts, taking three warships aback.

Just a little harder.

A splintering *crack* echoed across the water—the sound different from booming cannon fire. Then another and another, and one by one the masts of all three ships fell.

Half-laughing, half collapsing against the parapet, she let go of her gift and let her awareness fully settle in her body.

"Urgh." In her *aching* body. Every muscle burned, most quivered, too, and sweat slicked her forehead and the back of her neck. But she'd done it. She'd managed to open a chink in Mercia's formation. It could be enough to turn the battle.

She shoved a few almonds into her mouth, even though her throat was so dry she could barely swallow. But she needed the energy, so she chewed. With the second mouthful, she dragged herself to her knees and peered over the parapet.

Fire blossomed at one corner of Mercia's fleet, smoke blooming into the morning sky and merging with the remnants of her storm. But only four ships had caught and they were already drifting inexorably away from the rest of the fleet. Mercia's gift in action.

Yet more cannons boomed—this lot coming from half a dozen pirate ships who'd broken from the docks and had taken advantage of the cover from her clouds and mist to line themselves up for full broadsides. But the attacking force fired back mere seconds later. A yawning hole opened up on one of the pirate ships and it listed to one side. Sinking already.

"Bollocks," she hissed, head bowing.

Which brought her face to face with the town.

Or what was left of it.

Shadow and splinters and the broken open shells of stucco homes merged brown with black and flashes of turquoise and yellow paint. A chaos of timber and stone. Curtains flapped in the breeze, outside when they should've been in. What was...?

She blinked and stared and had to rearrange her brain before she understood.

Those pockmarks and dark wounds she'd measured earlier no longer covered almost half of the town. The cannons' devastation had spread like a plague until one caved-in building merged into the next into the next into the next. Only pockets of intact buildings remained amongst the debris.

Two thirds of the town was a wasteland.

Eyes burning, she gaped and turned south where the town climbed low hills. Or at least it once had.

Make that three quarters.

The shadowy holes on every block on every street dragged at her limbs like the kraken dragging a ship beneath the waves. Only the parapet kept her semi-upright, but that didn't stop her heart sinking, until she couldn't even feel its beat anymore.

This time the dark corner of her mind didn't whisper, it spoke with full voice, emboldened by the fact it was truth: they needed every ship ready to evacuate.

Nassau was lost.

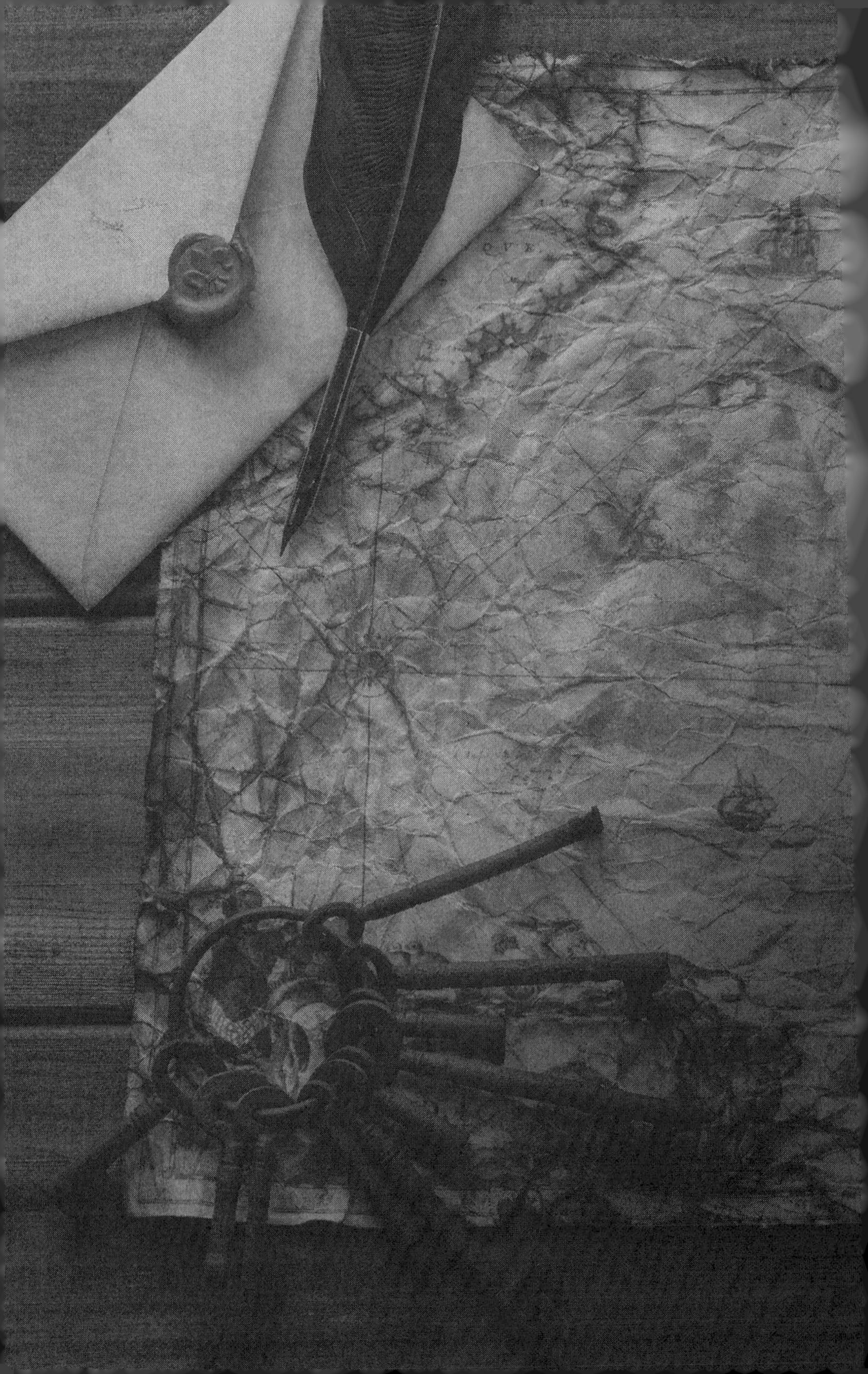

RED TENTACLES

Knigh loped along the ruined streets, pausing to fight, to heal, to search, to double back when he reached blocked roads. All the time, the sun rose higher and higher, spelling out the delay in reaching Vee.

The fights were short and brutal—pockets of marines trying to hold a line against townsfolk and pirates. From the small size of the detachments and the way they retreated so swiftly, it looked like the fort was doing its job and preventing more from landing.

His shoulders eased. This was a day for small mercies and he would take even the slightest relief wherever he could find it.

He passed one side-street, then the next, checking each one.

No sign of her yet, but he hadn't reached the Copper

Flagon. Not that there was any guarantee he'd find her, not when—

Ahead, a familiar figure crossed his path—tall, broad, cropped hair.

"Aedan."

Yes, it was him, now turning, eyes wide, shoulders sinking with a sigh. "Good gods," he huffed as Knigh closed the remaining feet between them, "you're safe."

A smile tightening his face, Knigh grabbed him in a brief embrace and clapped his solid shoulder. "I could say the same. After we got separated..." He shook his head. Anything could've happened in that time.

So many buildings lay scattered across the streets, decimated, it was a wonder anyone was still alive in this place. But he'd passed the messengers racing up and down every street, each one of them saying the same thing—*get to the taverns, you'll be safe in their cellars.* Wherever that message had come from, it had saved hundreds of lives.

Jaw tight, Aedan nodded. "I know. I feared..." He glanced back the way he'd come. "I was looking for you, actually. The order's to evacuate."

Knigh's heart dropped, but... The debris of ruined homes and businesses scattered across the streets. No. It was no surprise. "Have you seen Vee?" The evidence of her gift played out over the harbour—that localised storm lingering over the enemy fleet, Nassau's ships crossing the water with unnatural speed.

"She's the one who gave the order."

"What?" His gaze collided with Aedan's. "So she's already at the *Venatrix* clearing the escape route?"

Aedan's mouth skewed to one side as he looked away. "Not exactly. She's"—he wiggled his fingers in the air—"in the tower opposite the Copper Flagon. Best I can tell, she flagged someone down and got them to spread the message. We need to hold the docks, get everyone to the ships. Perry, Lizzy, Wynn, and Effie—others too—are already gathering folk from the furthest taverns and herding them down."

The Copper Flagon. So close. But when he craned in that direction, slumping buildings blocked his view. He scowled down the hill towards the harbour. "How the hells are we meant to escape when they've blocked the entrance? The instant we leave the docks, we're sitting ducks." For the guns *and* the kraken. He shuddered.

Aedan's hand landed on his shoulder and squeezed. "Not with a sea witch up a tower." He cleared his throat, eyebrows rising. "A sea witch with a plan."

Perhaps it was meant to be comforting, but the idea of Vee with a plan...

He shuddered harder.

That plan would involve her taking on all risk herself. Doing it all herself. That's why she was up a bloody tower ordering everyone else to safety. Wild Hunt, had the woman not learned a single—

A low moan fell from Aedan's lips as he took a step back.

Knigh scanned him, expecting to find blood on his shirt, but, no, he only stared down the hill. "Knigh," he breathed, gripping his sleeve.

Knigh followed his eyeline and it was like he and the world moved through treacle.

He knew. He *knew* what he was going to find when he turned.

Aedan's eyes were fixed on a point beyond the end of this street, out in the harbour. There was only one thing that could've made his skin so pale.

But Knigh's gaze trickled along the ruined street, across the glittering, shifting water, and...

Red tentacles hugged one of the smaller pirate vessels still in the docks. The flesh glistened and tensed, and a great round eye rose above the frothing water. Even from this distance, he could still see it clearly. Huge. Horrible. Inescapable.

The boat was never going to escape. In a heartbeat, it splintered, deck and rails splitting, hull crushing, masts falling like saplings, and the kraken disappeared beneath the waves.

"Shit." Aedan ran a hand over his mouth and shook his head, as though the creature's disappearance had unfrozen his body. "We—how the hells are we going to escape with that thing lurking around? We need every boat we can get our hands on if we're going to stand a chance of evacuating everybody, and it can just pick us off like fish in a barrel."

"You're... you're right." With a heavy glance towards the Copper Flagon, Knigh squared his shoulders. He couldn't go after her.

Not when yet another duty called.

"We need to deal with it or else none of us are getting out of here alive."

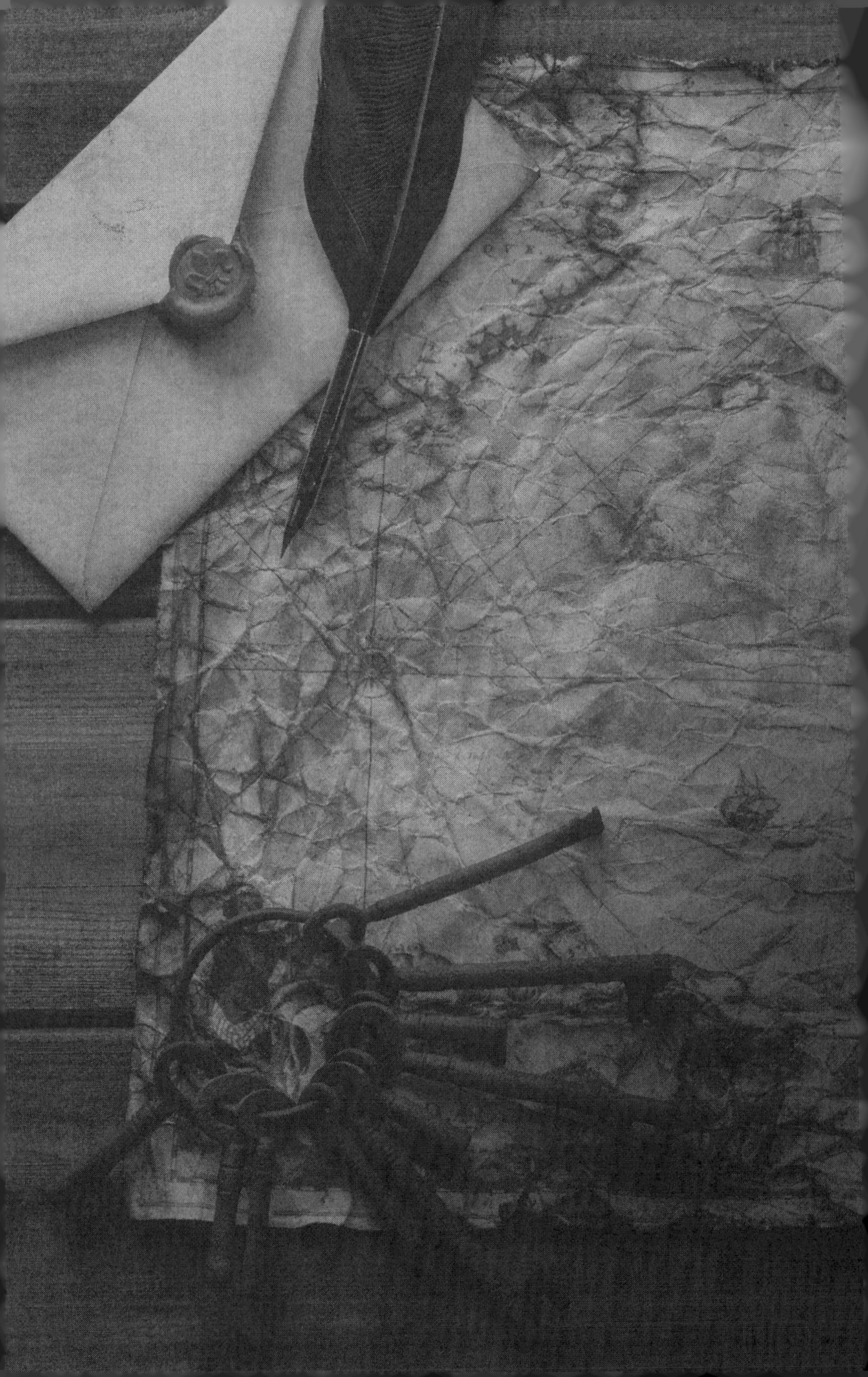

CREW

By the time they reached the waterfront, townsfolk were already filing onto the larger civilian vessels, but their eyes were wide and many hung back. They'd had a ringside seat to what the kraken had done to that vessel. But their town sat in ruins behind them, more round shot still raining down.

Here they were sandwiched between two horrors.

Wincing, Knigh nodded to a group of familiar faces. Saba, Clovis, and Erec hurried over. "No need to look *quite* so happy to see me," Saba said when she reached him, but her smile carried none of its usual spark and even her voice was hollow.

If he could blow up one of those horrors...

"We need explosives." He didn't bother to check their reactions, already scanning the vessels remaining at the docks. At the far end, near the shipwright's workshop were all the damaged boats and ships—well, those damaged *before* today's battle.

Clovis chuckled, a low rumble like distant thunder. It was almost comforting compared to the all-too-close boom of cannon fire. "Good to see you, too, my friend."

Head cocked, Knigh raised one shoulder. Amongst the damaged ships was a small sloop with a snapped bowsprit. Not exactly seaworthy, so she'd be of no help to the evacuation effort, but she floated and judging by her smooth lines and small size, she'd be manoeuvrable and quick. Especially with the help of a sea witch.

He peered back the way they'd come. Partway up the hill, the grey tower near the Copper Flagon was visible now, and at its top a lone figure.

Vee. His heart squeezed. He'd only been a couple of streets away when he'd bumped into Aedan. So close. And now so far.

The instant he'd dealt with the kraken, he would go to her.

"Aedan, Clovis, I need your help." With a long, burning breath, he tore his eyes away from Vee. "I think we can crew that thing at a pinch." He pointed out the damaged sloop. The jagged end of the bowsprit pointed out to the harbour, like a knife held in defence. And it *was* sharp... "Hmm." Maybe he didn't need explosives.

"What's your plan?"

"Dangerous." He didn't say it like Vee would've, with a flashy grin and plenty of swagger. No, it was matter of fact, grim, true. "But it's the only way I can see we're going to get rid of the kraken."

"Perry's going to love this," Aedan muttered. "Where the hells is she?"

Clovis gave a curt nod. "Erec." He turned to his partner, regret so strong in the downward lines of his mouth, it made Knigh look away with a belly full of guilt. "I must—"

"Then so must I."

Knigh opened his mouth to protest.

But Erec and Clovis only had eyes for each other, and clearly didn't give a damn about his argument. "I mean," Erec went on, chin lifted in determination, the movement so like Vee it made Knigh's heart ache, "you're not going on a suicide mission without me." He touched Clovis's chest, hand over his heart. "If you're dying today, then so am I."

A low sound came from Clovis's throat as he covered Erec's hand with his own. "I couldn't have said it better myself."

Saba cleared her throat as it looked like the pair were about to kiss. "And you're not going without me, either. That thing looks fit to make it out of dock, but it'll sail better with five hands than with four."

Folding his arms, Aedan cocked his head at Knigh. "Well I'm dying to hear this plan that's going to get us all killed."

There was no time to argue with Saba or Erec, and, really, Saba was right—despite its size, the sloop would be easier to handle with a crew of five. "Fine, I'll explain while we get that thing ready to sail. But, first, I need someone to take a spyglass and a message to Vee."

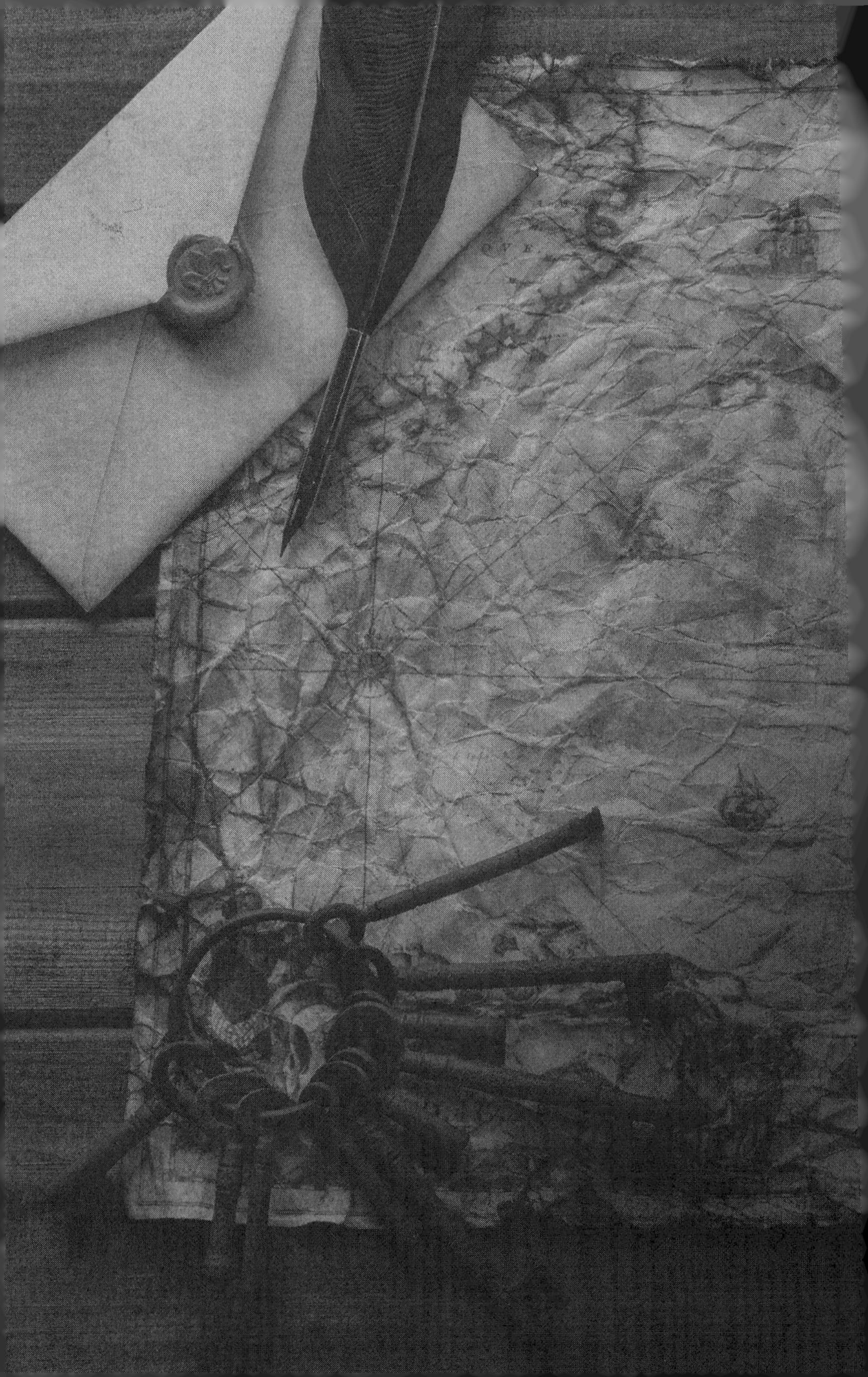

A MESSAGE

"Watch that boat and get it close to the kraken," the young woman, one of FitzRoy's crew, said, holding out a spyglass. Black braids hung over her shoulder, tied in a fat knot to keep them out of the way.

Vice stared at the spyglass, brass gleaming in the late morning sun. "Watch that…" She blinked at the little sloop the messenger had pointed out. The hairs on the back of her neck had been on end since this whole nightmare had begun, but now a chill crept through them.

Knigh had a plan. She didn't even know what it was, but it was enough that it involved him going anywhere near the kraken.

The messenger had arrived a few minutes ago, puffing from running all the way from the docks. She'd started by giving Vice a canteen of water and a bruised banana, both from Knigh. Had he told the woman to distract her with food and water before she delivered his message? Vice gritted her teeth. She'd wager her last gold piece that was exactly what he'd done.

"No." She shook her head and held the spyglass out. "Tell him I'm not doing it. Tell him *he's* not doing it." Whatever *it* was. "Get him to lure the kraken out and I'll take care of it." Lightning. She'd have to.

Pain! Hurt! No! Please!

She shuddered, grip tightening on the spyglass because the woman hadn't taken it back. If the choice was between lightning and this madness, she would have to become a monster.

"There isn't time." The messenger shook her head, eyebrows drawing together. "He said you had to do it as soon as you got the message. If I run back, I'll be quarter of an hour too late. He'll already have set sail."

Indeed, there was movement around the little boat as a small team worked to get it ready. That tall one—even from here, even without the spyglass, she knew it was Knigh. She should be the one readying that boat, the one risking herself. She should…

A leader doesn't do it all themselves.

But not this. Knigh, good gods, not this. Eyes burning, she stared down at his distant figure, now in the sloop, as if she could think it into his head and make him stop this madness. He kept working and one by one, the people with him climbed aboard. Clovis—his size easy to recognise. That meant the small figure at his side was Erec. The tall, tanned man next to Knigh—that was Aedan. And the small, dark-haired figure was Saba.

In one fell swoop she could lose them all.

"Are you going to do it? Because he said he *needs* you. He can't do this without you."

Throat blocked, she forced her attention away from the boat, away from her friends. *He needs you.* And what if she let him down? What if she failed them all? But there was no time to get a message back. There was no time at all. If she failed, she'd have to live with it. Assuming she survived.

At least if she helped him, she'd be able to push the boat off course if they tried to do anything too foolish.

She drew herself to her full height and nodded. "Fine."

THE TILLER TUGGED against Knigh's grip and the sails only filled with a desultory wind as Aedan finished coiling the mooring line. Out in the harbour, the kraken's red tentacles appeared between the waves, harassing a brigantine as it fired upon Mercia's fleet. Lightning struck the sea nearby, but not the kraken itself. A warning shot.

In one of their late night talks, she'd told him how the kraken had somehow communicated with her. It had shared its pain, had *spoken* into her mind. And she'd been left sickened. He couldn't ask her to do that again, not when she believed the creature was a *being* not a beast.

But it still needed dealing with. And he needed her help to do so.

"Come on, Vee," he muttered, leaning on the tiller and steering them to port. Too slow. They'd never make it in time to help the troubled boat, and then the kraken would disappear beneath the waves and they'd have to wait for another chance.

Sea spray dusted his skin, refreshing, and canvas flapped, pulling his gaze from the tentacle rising ahead. Overhead, their sails filled.

Bracing the sails with Clovis, Aedan threw Knigh a tight smile—he felt it too. With Vee's help, they clipped across the waves. Mist rose off the water and grey storm clouds drifted down to meet it, shielding them from view of Mercia's fleet. Saba and Erec readied the sloop's jolly boat in silence. He'd explained the plan and they hadn't argued or called it insane, but...

His grip tightened on the tiller and he adjusted course. Perhaps it *was* insane—a plan worthy of Vee, one Perry would shake her head at. But here they were, out of options.

They needed the kraken to remain at the surface, preferably *not* attacking their sloop. Meanwhile, they would speed towards it and drive that broken bowsprit into its fleshy body. Round shot bounced off its rubbery flesh, but the pointed bowsprit, with enough force behind it stood a chance. After, the jolly boat would be their escape.

It sounded simple. And yet...

Vee must've seen his adjustment and understood his aim, because the wind moved with them, carrying the boat inexorably towards the beast.

The brigantine had cleared the kraken's reach and now retreated to the shallow waters close to Hog Island. The red tentacles did not pursue. One disappeared beneath the waves, then the next.

"No," he groaned. But within seconds, the kraken was gone. "Find it!"

But even the kraken's telltale *V*-shaped wave was lost in waters chopped and fragmented by wind and the intersecting wakes from pirate ships criss-crossing, constantly on the move to try and avoid enemy fire.

A ripple to starboard. Was that—?

He pushed on the tiller, instinct saying *yes*.

Right where he'd seen that ripple, the sea exploded. Water gushed off mottled red flesh, rising, rising, rising as the kraken reared from the waves.

All its attention on them.

The blood stopped in Knigh's veins, but he still clung to that tiller, holding it steady against the waves radiating from that creature, pitching the little boat fore and aft.

Gods, it was so small. Ridiculous compared to the sheer size of that thing.

Just one of its pale suckers could've engulfed his head. A swipe of a tentacle would turn them to kindling.

Their only hope was to charge it at full speed and skewer it before it destroyed the boat.

Above, their sails faltered.

Damnation. This was exactly what he'd been afraid of—well, this and the damn sea monster. But... "No, Vee. Please. I need you to let me do this. It's the only way."

Boom. Boom. Boom! Nearby.

Gasping, Knigh dragged his eyes from the kraken, just as it twitched and twisted to starboard.

Cutting through the water, the *Venatrix* and *Firefly* in full sail, smoke rising from their guns.

B-b-boom! To port, this time.

The *Sea Witch* landed a volley on the kraken's fleshy body, which wobbled with each strike, though appeared uninjured. The creature turned to FitzRoy's ship now, reaching out with writhing tentacles. It had to be his first mate in charge, since the fort was still firing on the enemy fleet.

BOOM.

Between flinging tentacles, he caught a glimpse of black sails beyond the kraken. They had it surrounded.

Distracted.

It flailed between the attackers as another broadside thundered from the *Venatrix*, followed a split second later by the *Firefly*. It reached one way, then the next, as if unsure what to do.

And maybe it was confused. The first time anyone saw the kraken, they usually froze in terror. He'd seen it during his time on the *Sovereign*—the gaping mouths, the loaded cannons left unfired. It only required moments of inaction for the beast to strike and destroy.

Most people didn't survive to see it a second time.

So, of course, the kraken wasn't used to being attacked. Certainly not by four ships taking it in turns to unleash broadside after broadside.

The pirates circled, weaving in and out of the kraken's reach, firing again and again and again. The other vessel swept into view, gold paint on its hull naming it: *Ram*.

Knigh angled the tiller a fraction to port, adjusting for the kraken's new position. "Sails full as you can," he called to his crew over the barrage of cannon fire. "Let's end this."

Eyes fixed on the kraken, shoulders and arms in complete mastery of the tiller, he held their course. This was it. This was their chance. Just a bit more speed. "Come on, Vee," he murmured. "I need you."

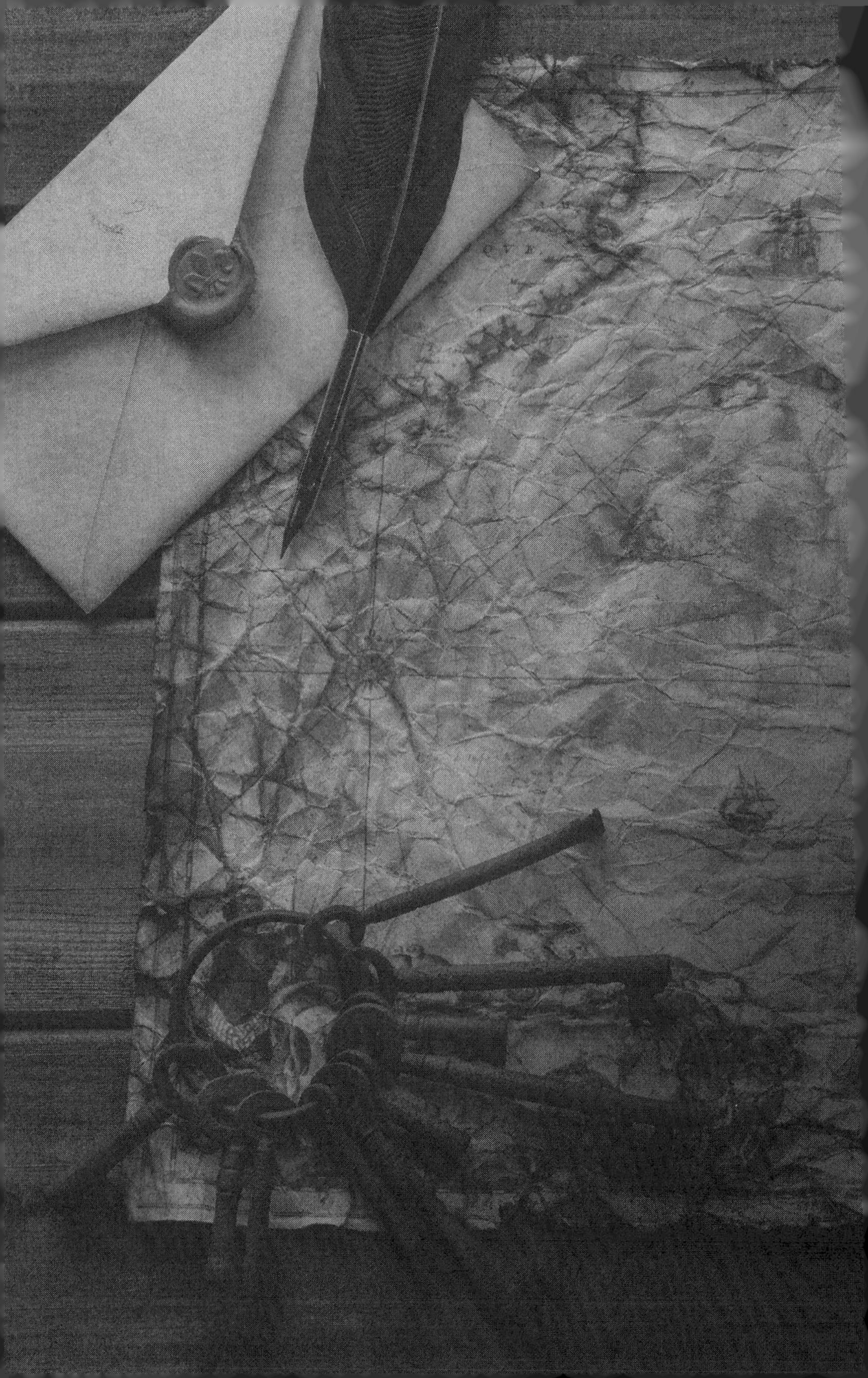

THROUGH THE SPYGLASS

Vice's stomach roiled as hard as her storm clouds. The spyglass trembled, making the image of that little boat quiver. He was sailing straight for the kraken. Straight for...

No, no, no. That wasn't... that wasn't in his message. That wasn't what she'd agreed to—not with them all on board.

She would pull them back to shore. Back to safety.

One corner of herself kept the veiling clouds and mist in place. Although she'd gobbled down the banana the messenger had brought, her muscles still throbbed as another part of her awareness helped the pirate ships evade the kraken's attacks, weaving them out of its path. Even her eyes ached from staring so intently at that one churning knot of battle, trying to keep up with every tentacle and each ship, and that damn boat.

Clenching her hand, she gathered the rest of her gift into

the space around the sloop and shifted the wind and the current.

But the little boat kept going. Its sails shifted, remaining full.

A fist gripped her innards in a grip as cold and hard as iron.

Knigh was fighting her.

The grip twisted.

They were sailing so close to the wind that if she changed the angle any further, she'd risk damaging the boat.

A tentacle crashed into the *Ram* and splintered her mizzenmast. Her hold on Knigh's boat loosened as she shoved the damaged ship away from another muscular tentacle.

With a *boom*, the *Venatrix* opened fire, drawing the kraken's attention. That was Perry, helping, flinging herself into bloody danger. Vice gritted her teeth. She'd spotted Perry's slight form and blonde hair when they'd first joined the battle. And she'd cursed her all the way. She was meant to be the sensible—

A splintering crash dragged a gasp through her throat, and she tracked the spyglass just in time to see a tentacle rake the *Ram's* side, opening a gaping hole barely above the waterline.

The *Sea Witch* fired, distracting the kraken before it could finish its destruction, but the *Ram* was damaged enough— they'd need to abandon ship.

And still Knigh had his sloop pointed at the kraken's fleshy body.

If she didn't help him... They were already out on the water and the kraken had seen them—the instant the other crews lost its attention, it would crush the sloop, together with him and their friends.

Whatever the plan, he needed her gift to execute it. That's why he'd asked for her help. He was relying on her. He'd asked her to use her skill to do the thing she did best.

He was being a good leader.

That iron fist worked its way up from her guts and closed around her throat. Pressure built behind her eyes.

"Gods damn you, Knigh." Her voice came out on a gasp as her vision blurred. "You're a better captain than I."

But he was relying on her to do better, to be better.

He was staking his life on it.

The kraken turned one great eye on his boat.

Tears brimming over, Vice closed her gift around that little boat and pushed.

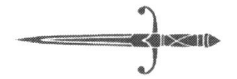

KNIGH CLUNG TO THE TILLER, despite every jangling instinct screeching at him to turn and flee from that knobbly red flesh, those huge round eyes. The wind swept his hair. It still lagged in their sails, hesitant to push them forward. Vee's hesitance.

They were going too slowly. If the kraken didn't crush the boat to kindling and they managed to reach it, their bowsprit would never pierce its body at this speed.

To one side, water gleamed and glistened, dripping from a tentacle that rose over the *Venatrix*. His jaw ached as he gritted his teeth and bent forward. *Come on. Faster. Faster. Please, Vee.*

She could do this. She could risk. She could *lead*.

Hair tickled his cheek. A breeze cooled the nape of his neck.

The wind—it had turned. It was with them. And the deck jolted under his feet as a current joined the effort.

The boat shot ahead.

Fifty feet from the bulbous body of the kraken.

Forty.

"Jolly boat ready," he bellowed, the cry snatched away by the wind.

Thirty. Saba and Erec nodded, ready to launch.

Twenty. It was like sailing at a cliff rising dead ahead, crimson and craggy, mottled with shades of orange and rust.

Ten. The salt tang of the sea, of the kraken, seared his nostrils, filled his mouth just as that wall of red flesh filled the world beyond their sails. "Brace!"

An instant later, they hit that red wall, sending a shudder through the deck. The kraken's skin indented around the bowsprit. It wasn't going to—

With a jerk, the flesh broke. As the point drove in, blue blood, dark and inky, welled around the wound and—

A shriek split his ears.

Or his head?

Agony speared through his gut, knocked him to his knees. Choking on each breath, he clutched his belly and stared down, expecting to see a blade jutting from—

No hands, just blue blood trickling into the sea and red skin and a tiny boat—

Just his hands on his belly. *His* hands. *His* shirt. For a second it had been...

Pain!

A vastness. An eternity. Crossing from Albion to Arawaké,

there would be weeks where the ocean was everything, from horizon to horizon to horizon. This thing, this place stretched far beyond that, was far greater.

Only it was... not a place, but a...

Three drums sounded a constant beat.

Ba-dum, ba-dum, ba-dum.

Not drums. *Hearts.*

The kraken?

Please, no! Not choice. Not—

Water sloshed in his face, cold. He spluttered, blinking. Aedan's grip was a vice on his arm. Groaning timber and snapping lines. His hand closed on a gunwale—somehow he was on the jolly boat, which still dangled from the davits. The sloop's deck sloped at a forty-five degree angle. All around, the sea frothed and roiled as the kraken's arms writhed and jerked.

He shook his head—no time to be dazed. No time at all.

Around him, Aedan, Erec, and Saba had turned different shades of green. Even Clovis's rich complexion was ashen. But they were all in the boat. All alive. All safe. The tightness in his chest eased, but his heart hammered, its rhythm much faster than the one he'd heard moments ago. Had that been the kraken's—?

The jolly boat lurched on its lines, dragging cries from their throats. The sloop's deck tilted, now almost vertical, her tiller dangling above, rudder in the air.

Below, the creature—the *being* sank, round eyes disappearing underwater as it pulled their bowsprit under.

The kraken was trying to escape beneath the waves.

And it was dragging them with it.

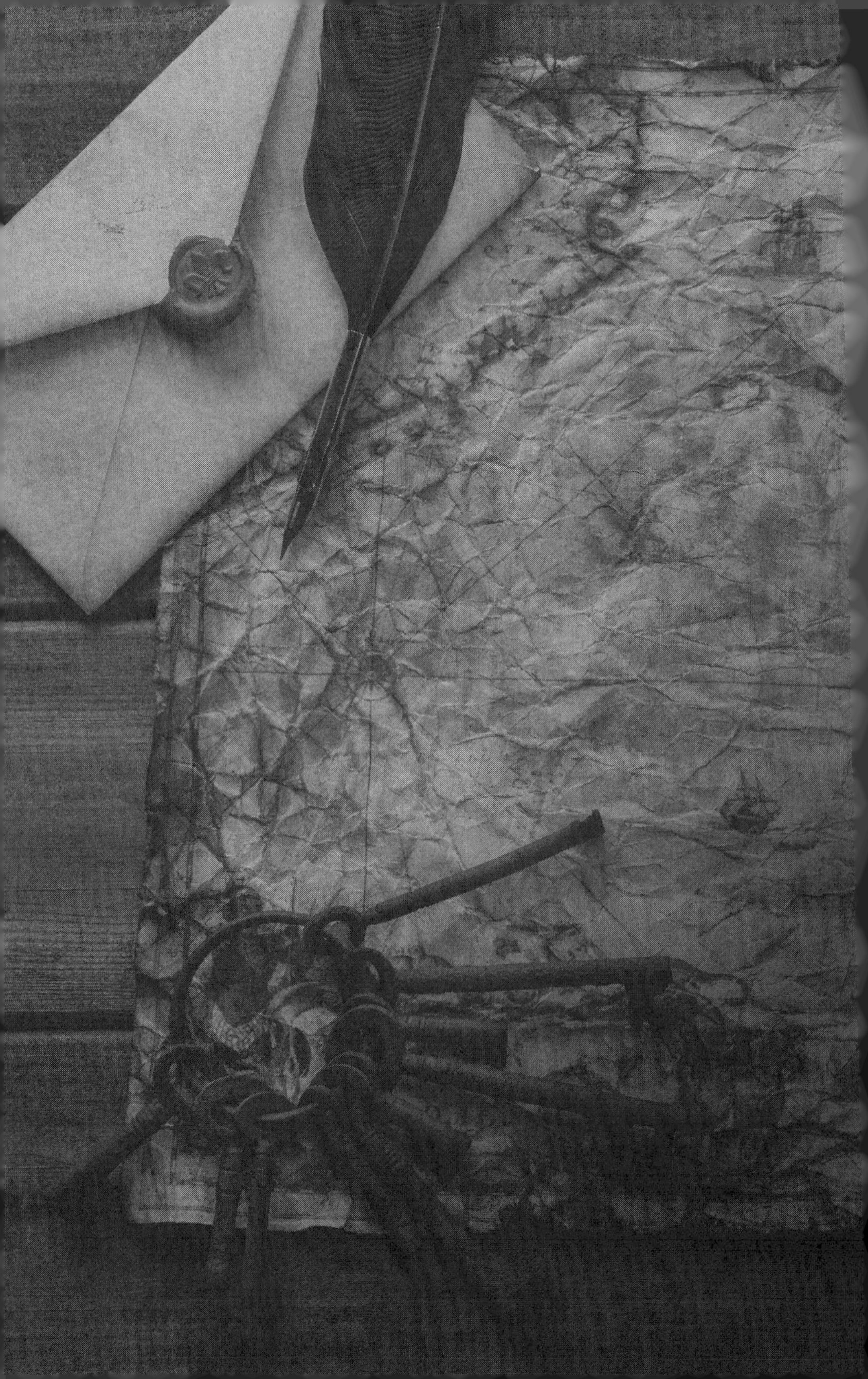

UNDERTOW

The jolly boat jolted through the air. The kraken twisted, sending them swinging wildly, but at least that meant that they hung over water rather than the sloop.

"Launch," Knigh rasped and grabbed the line holding their bow in place. In the corner of his eye, Clovis did the same at the stern. At Clovis's answering shout, he released and…

And the boat *should* have fallen into the water, davits squeaking. But they still dangled in place.

Shoulders knotted, Aedan peered over the gunwale. "We're stuck in the lines."

Damnation. All this tipping had them tangled. "Cut it." Knigh drew his dagger. "Cut every bit of line you can reach."

The boat tipped and bucked as they leapt into action—steel flashing as they sawed through damp rope. Wind flapped the sails and whipped against his face, as though it was trying to pull them away from the kraken.

He grabbed, sliced, sawed, cut, the hemp fraying so slowly it had to be mocking him.

And still the water below churned and thrashed.

They lurched, dropping a few feet, but it was only that the kraken sank deeper. They were still tangled with the sloop, and her bowsprit was still stuck in the kraken.

"Come on!" He had to get the crew to safety. He had to go to Vee. He couldn't die here. He *would not* leave things on such a hollow goodbye as that *see you later* they'd tossed over their shoulders at the docks. That couldn't be the end.

He gritted his teeth and sliced another line. Another. But—

A shadow passed over them, dulling the gleam of his dagger.

"Get your arses up here!"

Perry.

The end of a rope landed by his foot.

Gaping, he turned, blinked, blinked again. Four more lines, all stretching from the *Venatrix*. She sat right beside them, rocking in the rough waves, but here and solid and not damaged by the kraken.

"Grab the bloody lines, then!" Perry stood at the rail, practically doubled over it, her face red, eyes wide.

A breath blasted from him—something beyond a sigh of relief—and he did as he was told. Lords and Ladies, rough hemp had never felt so wonderful. "You heard your captain."

No sooner did they have hold of the lines than the boat dropped from under his feet and overturned. If not for Perry's impeccable timing, they would've been tipped into the harbour. With a splash, the kraken twisted and finally dislodged the sloop, a gout of blue blood coming from the wound. The great, red body heaved like a bellows and jetted away, leaving sloshing waves.

They scrambled up the lines to the *Venatrix's* deck, crewmates helping to haul them up. Nearby, the *Firefly* rescuing the last of the *Ram's* crew, while the *Sea Witch* stood guard. At the docks, the remaining ships sat heavy in the water, and the wharves were almost empty. The civilians were all aboard, ready to leave.

"Wild Hunt, you absolute bloody lunatics." Perry appeared at his side and wrenched him into a hug. A sting tingled his arm as she swatted him, mid-hug. "Never *ever* do anything like that again." She pulled back, eyes bright before she gave Aedan the same treatment. "I'd expect that sort of madness from Vice, not you."

"Speaking of whom..." Rubbing his chest, Knigh sought out the tower. It still stood. Thank the gods. Sunlight reflected off something at the top—the spyglass, perhaps. "I need to—"

"I know." She released Aedan and shouted an order to return to the docks, before saying at normal volume, "Get to her and then we can all get the hells out of here."

He sagged. Enough. He'd done enough. With the kraken gone, they could get Nassau's survivors to safety.

And he could go to Vee.

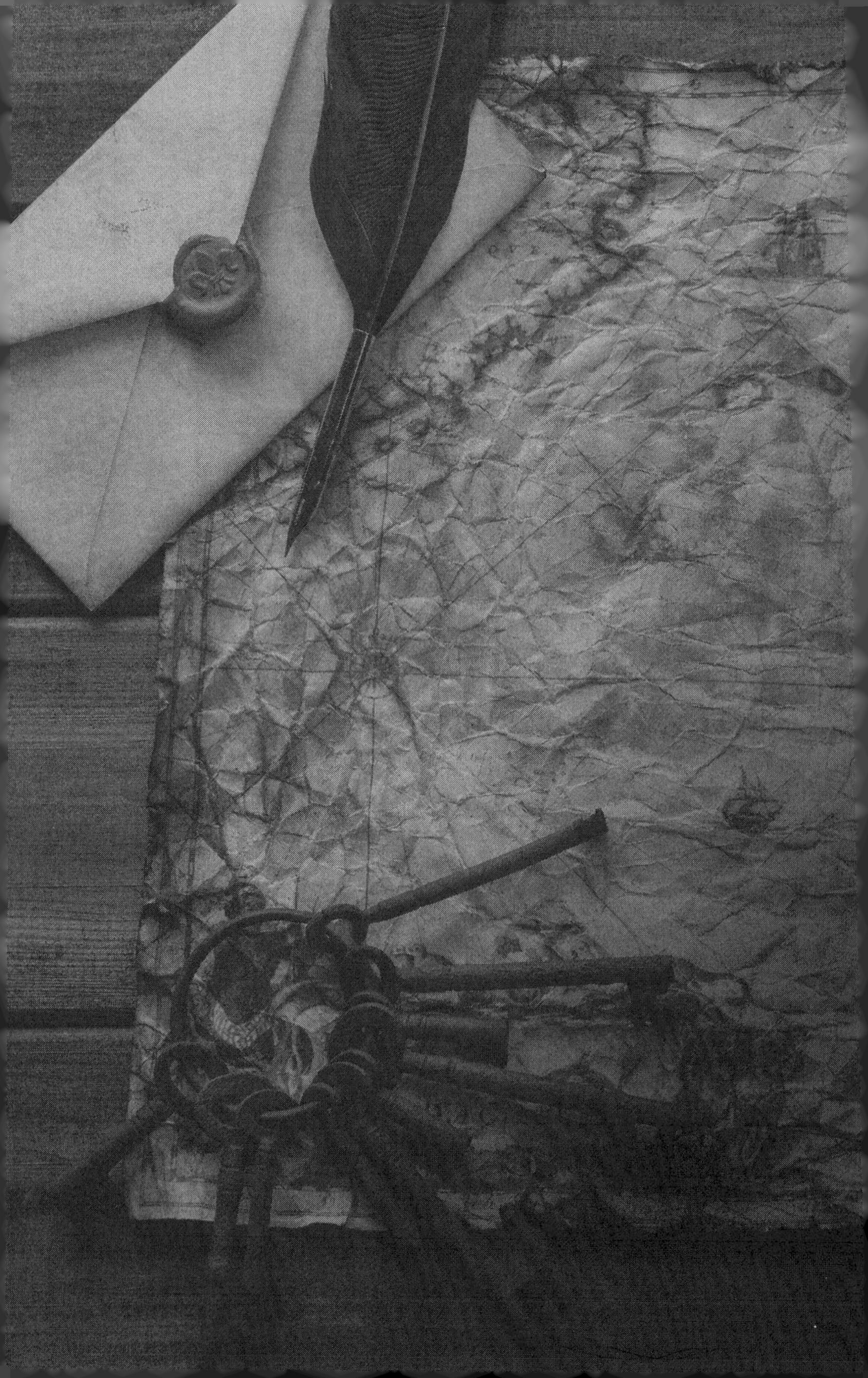

TIME TO GO

When familiar forms appeared on the *Venatrix's* deck, Knigh among them, Vice fell to her knees. Somehow, he'd survived that. Saba and Aedan and Clovis and Erec, too. They were alive and so was Perry, and they were all crossing the harbour without a tentacle in sight.

Thank every god. Thank the fair folk for her gift. And thank whatever twist of fate had created Knigh and brought him into her life.

Her hands shook too much to keep the spyglass to her eye, so she slipped it in her pocket and felt in the other for the pouch of snacks. It was empty. Only a trickle of water remained in her canteen. She dropped it on her tongue and swilled it around as best she could before attaching the canteen to her belt.

Out on the harbour, the *Venatrix* clipped across the waves towards the docks where the last trickle of evacuees boarded.

Past that, her low clouds veiled the water, but the attacking fleet still pounded the town and the harbour, hoping to get a lucky shot.

Someone had money to burn on round shot and powder.

The only return fire came from the *Sea Witch* and a couple of the larger pirate ships. Even the fort had fallen quiet—whoever had been manning it must've made their way to the waiting boats now.

Was she the only one left?

She scanned the sky above the docks for the signal that they were ready for her to open the escape route, but nothing yet.

Exhaling, she sat and leant against the parapet, ears alert for the hiss of a flare, and turned inward.

Her body was too tired to do much more with her gift—every muscle throbbed and trembled—but in here, the core of her magic still crackled bright, touched with Knigh's glow.

The storm over the enemy fleet thickened, rain lashing, wind whipping. Numb fingers. Wet fuses. Eyes blinded by the downpour.

She gave herself to it, making the most of energy that didn't come from her own body, that only passed through it, sizzling with raw power.

Gods knew how long she stayed that way, but when something brushed her face, gentle and warm, she jumped, and Lords, every inch of her ached.

But she inhaled cinnamon and soap and old, familiar leather, and she caught his hand and pressed it against her face.

"Knigh." She finally gathered the awareness of her body enough to lift her head.

His grey eyes, the worried furrow between his brows, the slow-dawning smile that had to mirror her own—it was the most perfect sight she'd ever seen.

"You're alive," she said. He said. Both together.

They laughed, a breathy, shared thing, and he bent his head closer as though he was about to rest his forehead against hers, but with a sharp inhale, he stopped and instead nodded.

"Barnacle and the babies are safe, too. I checked when Perry picked us up."

Thank the gods. She squeezed his arm, eyes burning at the fact they were fine and that he'd thought to look in on them.

"Oh, and here." He held out a dark slab of chocolate. "I raided your stash, too."

"We thought," Saba's voice rose behind him, and he edged to one side, revealing Aedan and the sisters, too, "you might need some energy to get down to the docks."

To the docks. Vice tried to hide the wince behind a stiff smile and held out her hand, letting Knigh help her to her feet. She didn't wobble too much—there was strength in her tired muscles yet. But she still shoved a piece of chocolate in her mouth and moaned as its bitter sweetness melted on her tongue.

Knigh exhaled a laugh, the worry between his brows easing. "The last people are boarding the vessels. It's time to go."

Wynn shielded her eyes from the sun and peered north. "One ship left."

"Chop, chop, Vice," Effie said, grinning.

The bitterness of the chocolate took over. She'd left out this part of her plan when she'd sent the message to evacuate. Chest tight, she met her friends' gazes one-by-one, finishing on the one who was far more than a friend. "I can't."

Knigh froze, all except for something flickering in his eyes. Slowly, the knot of his throat rose and fell. "What do you mean?"

"As soon as we go, he'll follow." She nodded east, grateful for the excuse to look away. "I need to raise the tide over the sandbar so you can all get away, but I also need to stop him coming after you, otherwise what's the point in all this?" She raised her brows at them. They'd seen the devastation—they knew. For all their efforts in the harbour, the fort, gathering people in the tavern cellars, there had to be more eyes staring up, up, up into the endless sky. If Mercia caught them at sea, all of that would be for nothing.

Saba bit her lip, rubbing a lock of hair between thumb and finger. Aedan's mouth flattened, but he looked away as though he couldn't bear to see the truth of what she said. Effie linked her arm through Wynn's. Both their expressions matched, brows peaking at the centre, eyes beseeching.

And Knigh?

His jaw twitched and below that, his neck had corded, like he was trying to hold back the tide with nothing more than self-control. "Then what's your plan?"

Now she'd met his gaze again, she couldn't look away. He was a delicious trap, one she'd run to again and again. "I'll stay here," she murmured, "work my magic, then once you're clear,

I'll draw in a huge wave to destroy their formations, throw them into chaos. Probably sink a few." She shrugged.

"What about the town?" Aedan asked. "Won't the wave destroy that, too?"

She snorted, a bitter edge to that not-quite laughter. "What town?" The tower was an island in the wasteland. Perhaps they hadn't realised the full extent of the destruction without this elevated view. She gestured, though Knigh didn't look.

He stood a little over a foot away, his eyes seeking and intent, like they held a million questions and the answers were on her face. It set her tired, aching heart throbbing.

The others gasped and groaned in mingled shock and horror, then fell silent.

Skin cold, bones cold, she shook her head. "Nassau has fallen."

No one argued.

Knigh's chin rose a fraction. "What about you?"

He wasn't arguing about the plan—at least not yet. It wasn't the comfort she might've expected.

"Get me a small boat, something easy to sail, like a pinnacle, and leave it at the end of the jetty where we moored the *Venatrix*. I'll keep that area and this tower clear of the wave. Head to Yuma and I'll meet you there once I've dealt with Mercia."

That muscle in his jaw ticked again. "And this is your plan?" His voice was so low, it could've frozen water. "Send us all away. Do it all yourself." That terrible stillness of his face broke as his eyebrows clashed together in a fierce frown. "Send *me* away."

She bit her lip. It wasn't like that. It was...

Fading shuffles and murmurs suggested the others had suddenly found something terribly interesting on the other side of the roof.

His shoulders sank once they'd moved out of earshot. That look he gave her—hurt, disappointed—gods, it cracked something inside her, burning at the back of her eyes. "You're trying to keep me out of the way, just like in Ayay."

"No." She closed the distance until her toes touched his and placed her hand over his heart. Her veins thrummed in time with the steady beat. His warmth seeped into her palm and up her arm, spreading and spreading until it filled her entire body.

Inside, her gift flickered, the gold a little brighter like a candle in a window welcoming him home.

It took a few breaths before she could form more words. "No, that isn't it *at all*. I'm asking you to lead them, to help me. You're the best person to do this. You know how to lead at sea, you know fleet formations and communication, and"—she tried to chuckle, but it stuck in her throat and threatened to break her voice—"and I trust you to stick around and keep everyone safe, rather than run off at the first sign of danger."

That terrible frowning disappointment had faded, but he still didn't say anything.

"Knigh, please." Her hands knotted in his shirt and she pushed everything into her eyes. The aching disbelief of that second cannon shot when she'd realised it was no prank, no drunken accident. The horror of that first fallen building and the screams. The dismay of not being able to save the woman in its ruins. Each thundering heartbeat as she had ran and ran, avoiding falling debris. Every desperate moment when all she'd wanted was to go and find him.

She let him see it all.

"I'm asking you—I'm *begging* you, please help me keep everyone alive."

Ba-DUM. Under her hand.

His brows rose, less in shock, more in horrible realisation as he shook his head.

He was going to say no.

Eyes squeezing shut, he exhaled. When his head bowed and his shoulders curled in, that was when she knew he understood.

He would lead them. He had to.

She needed him to. She was relying on him.

A soft sound in his throat, he opened his eyes and squared his shoulders, ready to take on that mantle. The corner of his mouth rose in the smile that meant he was going to make a joke in the midst of a decidedly un-funny situation, all in an attempt to put her at ease.

Gods damn it, she ached to kiss him.

He cocked his head. "I thought the Pirate Queen didn't beg."

She laughed, although the burning of her eyes threatened to turn it into a sob. "For my people, I make an exception." Her smile faded as she released his shirt and cupped his cheeks. His beard tickled her palms, such a sweet, soft sensation amongst all this chaos. "For *you*, I make the exception." She tiptoed up to him, body flush against his.

Her lips were a hair's breadth from his when he spoke. "But the others will see. Secrecy and—"

"I don't care."

Apparently he didn't either, because his arms came round and crushed her against his chest. Their mouths melted together in a kiss that said all the things she'd tried to push into her eyes earlier. Desperation and relief. How much it had ached to not know whether he was safe. A thread of fear for what might come.

But he was here now, as he reminded her with a stroke of his tongue. And he was solid, like his hand as it cupped the back of her head, angling her for better access.

Fierce pride burned through her as she threaded her fingers into his ridiculous, untameable hair. Pride that this man, brave and strong and sweet and smart, was hers and would lead Nassau's survivors to safety. Pride that she, for all her failings and monumental mistakes, could trust and rely on him to do this. Pride that they had become something that meant she could ask this without feeling a need to sharpen her claws and lash out. Something that meant he could accept without questioning himself and his readiness to take on the role.

A hiss sounded from the north.

It was a monumental feat to tear her lips from his, and when she did, they were both breathless. "You need to go."

He sighed at the arcing flare. "The signal. I know."

"Wow." That was Effie, who stared, mouth open. Wynn giggled behind her hand. Aedan's eyes were wide as he cocked his head at Knigh as though asking a question.

With a grimace, Vice had to steel herself to look at Saba—

after all, she'd given her blessing and hadn't told her friend what had been going on.

But Saba grinned, unsurprised. "At last."

Another barrage of cannon fire reminded them there was no time. So she hugged them each in turn. When she got to Saba, she whispered, "I'm sorry, I should've told—"

"I should've realised." Saba squeezed her. "You'd better not die, because you need to tell me *all* about it."

"Even if I do, I'll come back as a ghost just to tell you." Vice winked and turned to the last one. Knigh. Yes, they'd had that embrace and *that* kiss, but that hadn't been goodbye. It had been... something else. Something that felt like words in her throat, but ones she didn't know how to say.

So she flung her arms around his waist and tucked her head under his chin. For a second, he rubbed her shoulders and stroked her hair and for a second, it was perfect. But, *time*. "I'll see you later."

"You'd better." The words rumbled from his chest into hers.

"I'm wounded that you doubt me." With the Pirate Queen's cocky grin, she removed the dagger earring and pressed it into his hand. Black jet winked in the sun. "I'll come for it." *For you.* "I promise."

He held it over his chest and nodded, then they filed away down the stairs, one by one. Knigh was last, lingering for long moments and then he too was gone.

She was alone.

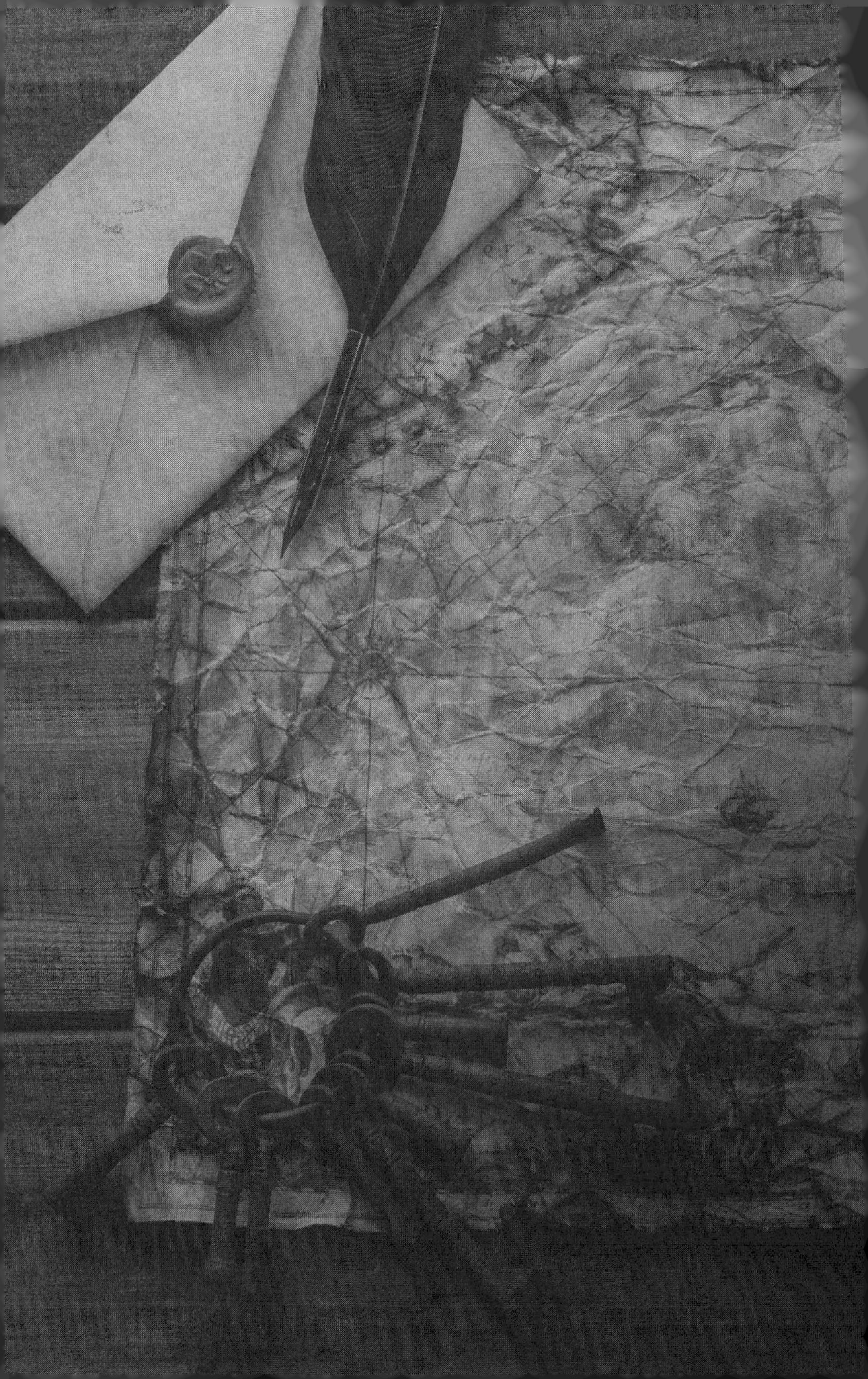

THE GREAT WAVE

The *Venatrix* was the last ship to leave the docks. The others already gathered at the eastern end of the harbour, waiting for her to open the way. Once they were clear, she'd be able to close her eyes and mine the wellspring without worrying about hitting their own ships with her tidal wave.

Part of her attention on the *Venatrix* and a few dawdling ships she herded eastwards, Vice felt along the edges of Mercia's wall. Perfectly straight and perfectly smooth, it cleaved through the harbour from north the south. Exhaling, she pushed her awareness further out into the open water and approached it from the other side. From the western point of Hog Island, it ran west-southwest, passing through Mermaid Rock before hitting Lucaya, the island Nassau occupied.

Or had once occupied. Her throat tightened.

But Nassau was its people and—

A *whoosh*. Getting louder. Closer. Coming this way.

Gasping, she blinked back from her gift.

Her hand sliced the air, summoning a cross wind before she even spotted the round shot. It came straight for her. Had they spotted her tower or was it just chance?

Teeth gritted, she pushed that wind harder, harder. The shot's path bent, but slowly.

With a crash, the roof shook, and stone burst from one corner.

Her heart thundered as she shielded her face and coughed away yet more dust, but the floor was still beneath her feet. It didn't tilt or tremble.

When the air cleared, one corner of the parapet was missing. Just a glancing blow. The tower's structure was untouched.

No time to waste, though.

The evacuating pirate fleet was gathered at the sandbar, ready.

She closed her eyes and sank.

In the darkness, she plunged her hand into the thunderous light, warm sparks illuminating her not-skin where she touched the motes of golden light that were Knigh's. Somewhere, far away on the outside, her other hand reached out over the parapet.

Mercia controlled a wedge of water at the harbour entrance, yes, but he didn't control the sea beyond it.

That was hers.

First, she coaxed the tide higher, drawing the swell to the sandbar that blocked the eastern end of the harbour for all but the smallest fishing boats. The water deepened, like a chest rising on a breath.

Movement threaded through her, through the sea. Vessels crossing. Just a few, just tiny indentations in the sea's surface. That had to be the smallest boats. A deeper breath, she lifted the sea higher. More movement, ploughing through the water now, larger gaps in the sea signalling that these were the ships.

Good, it was deep enough. She could hold that in place.

But she could only focus on so much, and her storm had collapsed as she'd poured herself into making the sandbar traversable.

The walls of Mercia's gift pressed in from the west. Now her clouds had gone, he'd spotted the pirate fleet escaping.

Maybe, on that far-off rooftop, she was grinning.

Here, in the wellspring, though, magic pounded through her. It could do more. *She* could do more.

It didn't matter that Mercia had seen or that he'd moved, because she had the tide in place and the people of Nassau were escaping, and now she would deal with him.

She reached north. The sea had no sense of distance that meant anything to human measurements, but it felt like she reached far. One hand drawing from the wellspring, her other pulled from that expanse of sea to the north.

Come. Come to me.

Each winter as a child, she'd built snowmen in the grounds of her family's estate. She'd always started with a snowball, packed between her gloved hands. Just one handful of snow tamped down. Another. Another. Until it was almost as big as her head and ready to go on the pristine lawn. *Then* began the fun part. She would roll it across that crisp snow, not giving a damn about her numb cheeks and frozen toes. Because as she rolled and rolled, she could see the ball she'd created pick up more snow and grow and grow and grow.

What she gathered from the north was not a ball, but it started as small as that handful of packed snow.

And it grew and grew and grew.

It didn't matter that Mercia had control of his wedge of water and held it out of her grasp. Not when she was going to bring in her own water, right on top of it.

On that far-off rooftop, she was definitely grinning.

All she had to do was think of this tower and the bobbing presence of her escape boat as two rocks. Her wave would crash around them, leaving them safe. She marked the two locations like pins in a map.

Then—

Movement.

To the east. Coming west.

A ship was going the wrong way.

The absence of water cutting through her awareness trembled. Firing. Whoever that was, they were firing.

Bollocks.

Others still moved east, crossing the sandbar. She couldn't drop that, they'd be run aground.

And north, her wave was building, building, inexorable. She couldn't drop that, not when Mercia's wall of control still advanced east, speeding up to chase the Nassau fleet. She needed her wave to stop him in his tracks.

It was all necessary. She'd had to keep hold of it all *and* turn that idiot around. Somehow.

She pushed deeper. Although she didn't really have a body here, she still thought of her presence as having a form, and it was up to its elbow in the wellspring. The usually comforting song rose like a choir approaching a crescendo. Faster, louder, higher in pitch.

North. Growing, growing, growing.

East. Still high.

The pins here and at the boat, they trembled, flickered. But they were still there.

Turn the hells around. With wind and current, she spun that straying ship on a point the size of a dinner plate and sent it east. It reached the sandbank just as the penultimate ship crossed and shot over.

In the distance, her shoulders sagged and her head pounded in time with her pulse. But she'd done it, she'd—

Something pushed back. Something in the north.

A wall that she could see through, but could not reach past.

Mercia.

So this is what it came to—sea witch against sea witch. Fae-blood against fae-blood.

Fine.

Her wave built, but it would just break against the area of sea under his control. It was no use just gathering more and more water, she had to loosen his grip.

His hold on the sea was inflexible, solid, like a bottle around water.

But bottles could be broken.

And hadn't there been an edge of concern in him when he'd seen her break the storm around the island with the key, like he feared she was stronger than he was?

They were about to find out.

Awareness blazing, she didn't just reach into the wellspring, she *dived*.

Everywhere shook. Everything roared. Her soul, her veins, her muscles and bones. Power burned through her as though it *wanted* this, wanted to be free, and she was its way out.

The wave kept building, she left that to its relentless rise, and instead she channeled all her raging power towards the rigid glass of Mercia's hold.

Shrieking. Whether it was the energy or her throat out in the world making that noise, she had no idea, but the sound split the air inside and out.

A crack opened.

A crack in Mercia's wall.

It trembled. Another fissure opened, radiating, its threads racing across the surface until they met the first.

Another. Another.

They traced crazed lines over every inch of his wall until—

It shattered.

And she tore through the space where it had been, roared across the sea, a behemoth of churning, thunderous water.

Hog Island was nothing, a mere pebble in the sand.

She—her wave swept across it, decimating.

Those shapes in the water. They had destroyed her home, the one place on land she loved.

Now she destroyed their fleet.

They scattered under her onslaught, though a faint shard of something resisted. Someone else's magic, stuck in her—

Vice. She was Vice. Not a wave, not—

A sharp gasp tore her throat. She blinked. The ships, her boat—gone.

There was only the wave, *her* wave. It filled the sky, roared across Nassau's rubble, and blasted salt air in her face.

No. This tower was a rock.

A rock.

But her mental map pin... it was gone.

With a cry, she pushed every ounce of herself into her gift, even as dread made her stomach plummet like a lead weight. Her muscles screamed. Her bones groaned. The wave had to part around the rock. Around this rock. Had to.

But its towering white mass rushed in, harder than a gunshot, and every way was down, and everywhere was airless, and she clawed and clawed and clawed for purchase, but there was only water, each drop of it out of her control.

Her head jolted. An instant of pain.

Then nothing.

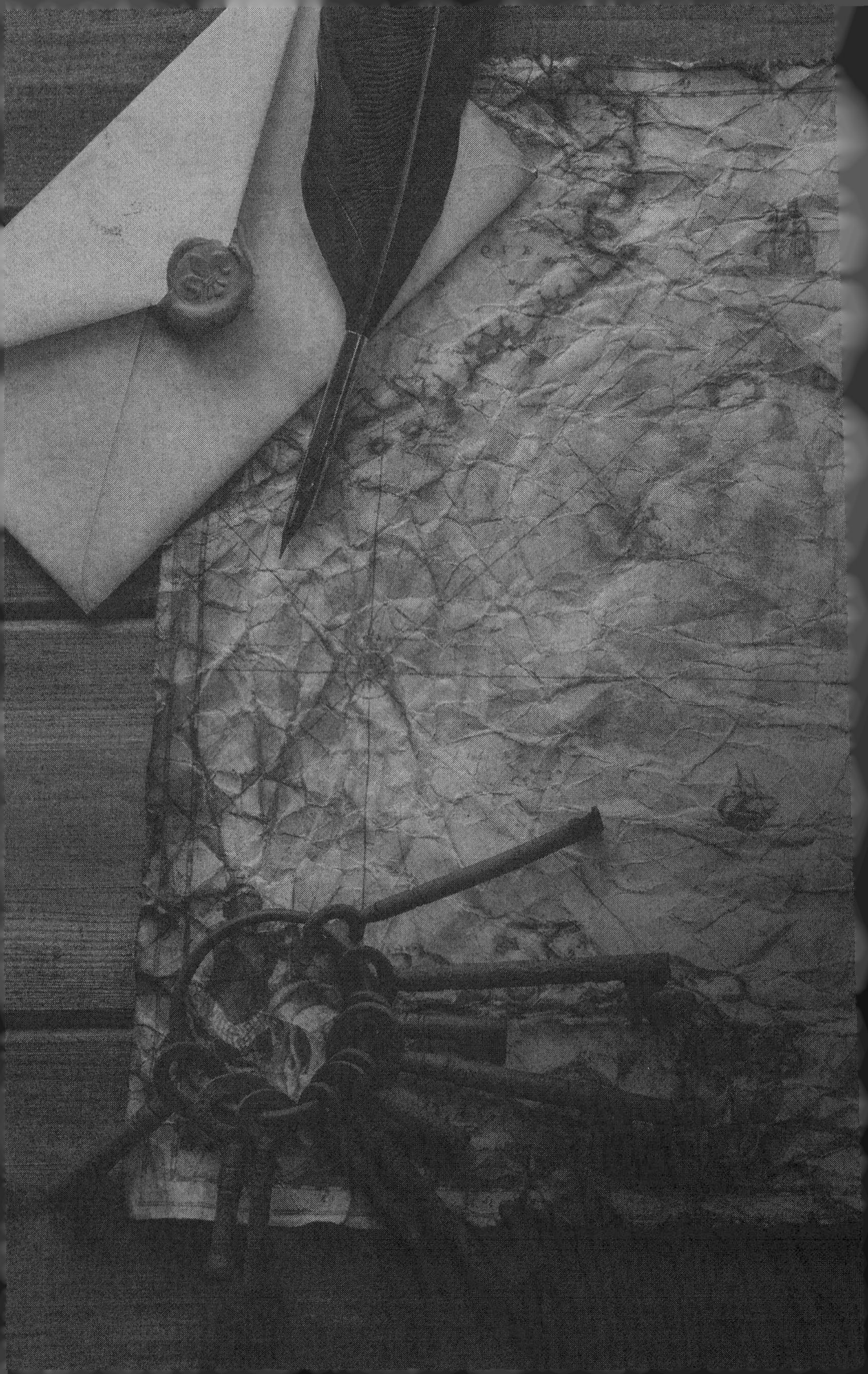

THE FOX

The gold light around his hands guttered, the usual warmth flickering cold for a moment. Knigh squeezed his eyes shut and pushed. Just a little more. Just enough. Beneath his hands, threads of flesh knitted together. The bleeding stopped. The skin smoothed.

He let go of his gift and exhaled, arms falling to his sides, as heavy as lead. His head buzzed like he was in a small room with too many people talking at once.

"Thank you." His patient, a green-eyed man from the *Firefly*, gaped at his arm where moments ago there had been a hastily bandaged gash from a flying splinter.

Words were too difficult. Too much energy. Knigh only nodded and heaved to his feet, fighting his aching muscles. He picked his way through the injured and newly homeless huddled beneath the canvas shelter covering half the *Firefly's* deck.

Wide stares followed him. A baby squalled, and children cried. Men and women sat in silence, cheeks glistening. Some folk smiled as he passed. More than a few whispered, *"The hero of Nassau."*

It curdled in his stomach. *Hero.* What a joke. The town was lost and many lives with it.

And he'd walked away from Vee.

Dread wrapped finger and thumb around his heart, and he had to turn his back on all those people staring at him with that terrible, hopeful light in their eyes. He stood at the rail and sucked in salt air.

Vessels at anchor clogged the glittering bay. Most of them had erected similar sheets of canvas over their decks to try and shelter more people, their numbers swollen by the surviving population of Nassau. He, Lizzy, and a few others, had rowed from ship to ship, healing wherever they could.

But his gift was…

He turned inward. The golden glow of his magic was little more than a single lamplight. Flickers of violet energy sparked along the edges, and he paused there, watching them flash and fade and light again.

Shivering, he emerged back into the outer world and touched his breast pocket. The line of her dagger earring pressed into his fingertips. *I'll come for it. I promise.*

"Come on, Vee," he muttered, scanning the pockets of open water visible between the fleet.

Somehow they'd all followed when he'd set a course avoiding naval patrols and the wave she'd been planning.

Although he'd once hunted their kind, they'd followed. He frowned.

Perhaps it was because of that stunt with the kraken. Perhaps because no one else had looked so sure, and square shoulders and a steady voice were an appealing combination when the world was crumbling.

Vee had said they would. She'd been right about that. Please, gods, say she was right about everything. He needed her to be.

He ground his teeth, eyes aching from staring across the glittering water. Where the hells was she? She should've been here by now.

Stopping had been a mistake. He needed distraction, he needed—

Leaving her had been a mistake.

And that was why he needed distraction.

Another finger joined the grip dread had around his heart.

Work. Busy. There was still much to do. Even if his gift was depleted he could—

When he turned, Lizzy stood in his path, arms folded. "When was the last time you ate?"

"I grabbed something from Vee's stash." Where was she? Where *was* she? Had she made it to the boat? Had she—?

"And you've been healing people ever since."

It was a battle to keep his face still, but it was one he'd been waging a long time. If he let any feeling show, it would all come and then he might break. "I don't need food. I need work."

"Fine," she sighed. "We have bandages and salves. If you see anything that looks"—she winced—"*iffy*, fetch me."

So he worked. He bandaged and fetched water. He applied salve to the lesser wounds until his fingers were stained yellow and reeked of herbs. He bent and lifted. He crossed the deck a dozen times. He fetched Lizzy for one particularly nasty cut that a middle-aged man had kept hidden beneath his jacket.

He did it all. And it still wasn't enough.

Where was she?

After nearly two hours, Lizzy's chest was depleted of bandages and almost every pot of salve and tincture bottle was close to empty. So they rowed back to the *Venatrix*, every *swash* of the oars dragging on his arms, heavy in his heart.

When he reached the deck, Perry stood waiting.

News? That had to mean—

He scanned the deck, pulse picking up from its exhausted toll. But no grin lit up. No glint of bright eyes that matched the sea. No shift of the wind or tug on the current that he could feel in the deck. Nothing. And the *Fox*, the little boat he'd readied for her—there was no sign of that, either.

Perhaps he'd missed something. She could be in her cabin. He raised his brows in question at Perry, not trusting his voice.

Gaze skittering away from his, she shook her head.

The sun had long passed its zenith and was sinking into late afternoon. Even if she was too tired to push hard with her gift, she should've been here hours ago.

Another finger of dread squeezed around his heart.

He sidled up to Perry and when she jerked her chin, they edged to the rail, as far as they could get from everyone else with the extra numbers on board. Hair a mess, eyes hollow, lips dry, she looked as haggard as he felt.

"I don't..." She kept her voice quiet, but it still cracked. She shook her head, frowning out over the water. The *Venatrix* was stationed at one end of the bay, with a clear view of the entrance. They'd be the first to see if any vessel approached. "There's been nothing, Knigh. How many hours have we been here?"

Despite the steely command he had over his squared shoulders, his arms at his sides, his straight back, a shiver ran through him. "Too many," he muttered. "Do you think...? What if Mercia...?"

Perry flinched as though she didn't want to entertain the possibility just as he couldn't stand to give it full voice. "No. She'd sooner..."

She'd sooner die.

Bile licked the back of his throat, because it was true. "We need to go back. Go and check. Go and—"

"She said to wait here." But Perry bit her lip, leaning over the rail and searching the bay.

"And what if she's injured?" His voice came out hoarse, tearing from his throat. "What if she's lying there, hurt, and she needs us and all we do is *wait*?"

Perry's chin trembled.

"Anything could've happened after we left, Perry. *Anything.*" He shook, his voice, his arms, even his breathing. He swallowed, grasping for control. It wasn't Perry's fault. None of this. He was the one who'd left her. Walking away had been the hardest thing he'd ever done. Worse because he'd sensed the distance grow. Apparently whatever had linked their magic also told him she was close. It had sung in his chest as he'd climbed the tower's stairs. *She's near. She's near. She's near.*

And even though leaving had felt wrong—*so wrong*—he'd told himself that it was right, that she could handle it, that it was her using her skill. And now...

Calm. Calm. Losing his mind wasn't going to help anyone.

A long breath. Another. Another. That was better. "I have no doubt of her ability, but a moment's bad luck could've wrecked her plans, and she isn't here."

Perry's lids fluttered shut and she bent her head. "Let's go."

They set a course for Nassau, with their sharpest eyes on the main top, alert for any sign of Mercia's fleet or the *Fox*. The *Sea Witch* accompanied them, just in case there was any danger, and Teal, the sea witch who'd recently joined the *Firefly's* crew, sped both ships along, cutting their travel time.

Knigh tried to keep busy, and when that failed he told himself that Vee was probably stuck on a sandbar, too exhausted to use her gift to free her boat. Or becalmed. Hells, they would probably find her still in that tower, passed out from expending too much energy.

He filled his pockets with snacks and stationed himself at the bow. Barnacle sat on his shoulder, tail draped around his neck, and watched the sea.

There was no sign of the *Fox*, though he stared so hard at the horizon for any sign of triangular sails, his eyes felt like they were bleeding. Barnacle's familiar weight was a small, warm comfort.

They sailed on and on. Teal's gift tugged on the ship, occasionally twitching through the deck, so different from Vee's.

Ahead, something broke up the light and shade of endlessly shifting waves. A dark shape.

But the watch hadn't shouted. He strained over the rail, knuckles white, dread's grip on his heart pausing. It could be Vee clinging to flotsam. It could be…

Closer. Closer.

Light glinted on the waves carrying the object and tipped it up, revealing a circular cross-section.

It was a section of mast. Probably a frigate's mainmast, judging by the size. And no survivor clung to it.

Barnacle's wet nose touched his cheek, and he absently lifted a hand and scratched under her chin.

More shapes bobbed on the water. Timbers lined with copper. Rope and canvas. An eagle figurehead. The remnants of warships.

There were bodies, too. A couple at first, but by the time the island of Lucaya came into view, they'd counted almost two dozen men, some in naval uniform, but most wore brown and faded black. Vane's fleet.

Still, fewer bodies than he might've expected for the amount of wreckage. Had some ships escaped and come back for survivors? Or had sharks and other sea creatures already eaten their fill? He grimaced and searched ahead.

The back of his neck prickled as he surveyed Hog Island through his spyglass. With a low yowl, Barnacle leapt from his shoulder and disappeared aft. Something was off. The island looked different. Almost black, rather than the usual deep green forest, lined with pale sand.

And the *smell*.

Knigh wrinkled his nose as they drew closer. The sea was a fresh scent, clear and clean and comforting after all these years of living with it. But this? This was brackish and mouldering and faintly sulphuric, like a stale corner in a dockyard.

They passed as close to the island as their shallow draught allowed. The trees were gone. That dark colour—it was seaweed, piled high. The crew fell silent, hands still working lines as their eyes flicked to a familiar place as they'd never seen it before. Tension thrummed across the deck.

Destroyed. Utterly destroyed.

Perhaps Hog Island had shielded the town from—

They rounded the western tip and swung towards Nassau.

Or what had once been Nassau.

Half-floating wrecks and entire trees choked the harbour. More dark seaweed lay strewn across the beach, littered with torn canvas, strips of timber, and flashes of orange from copper-sheathed hulls. To the south, most of the fort remained, but the closest bastion was missing its crenelated top, and...

And beyond that, there was not a single shape recognisable as a building. Rubble and wreckage stood where once had been taverns and shops and homes.

It had been bad when they'd left, but this?

Total annihilation.

As they halted, his stinging eyes shot to Vee's tower, but the great hulk of a grounded ship blocked his view.

Everything fixed on that point, he barely breathed. And he must've stood there a long while, because Perry came and touched his sleeve and told him they were ready to row to shore.

He didn't see who else was in the boat. He didn't remember taking the oars. He didn't know, see, or think anything other than the fact a grounded ship stood between him and Vee's tower.

In silence, they dragged their boat up the stinking beach. Seaweed tugged at his feet, but he tugged harder and refused to stumble. Half a dozen sea chests studded the leathery seaweed, some open, some broken. All empty.

With debris covering every surface, it was hard to tell where the beach ended and the town began, but Knigh trudged through it all, gaze swinging back and forth, back and forth, searching for the slightest sign of life. After the fighting, the running, the use of his gift, his muscles must've been tired, some corner of his mind knew that, but he didn't feel it. The only ache was the one in his chest.

He had to find Vee. That was the only thing.

The tower. He started up the slope it stood on, passing so much destruction, he became blind to it within minutes.

Sea birds screamed and wheeled into the sky at his approach. It was only when he almost trod on a dead octopus with peck marks on its knobbly skin that he understood they were feeding on the sea life that had been washed ashore.

He blinked and stepped over it. *The kraken.* That corner of his mind still capable of thought said it reminded him of the kraken. But he couldn't even bring himself to shudder in response.

Leg up and forward and down. The other. Again. Again. Onwards, up the hill. There were other sounds, other footsteps, the click of debris moving underfoot, raw voices shouting her name.

He only looked ahead at that wrecked ship.

Her masts were gone. A tangle of rope and seaweed lay strewn over her side. The lids from her gun ports had been ripped away and a jagged crack opened her hull from main deck to hold.

"The *Maelstrom*." It was only when Perry appeared at his side saying that that he realised he'd stopped. "Vane's ship. Poetic justice." He'd never heard her voice so low and vicious. Another day, it might've made him concerned for her, but today he liked it.

He tried to smile in approval, but it felt more like he'd bared his teeth. He strode on.

Close now. He was close. Heart thrumming against his ribs, he circled around the *Maelstrom* and...

And there was no tower. Not even a crumbling wall.

He stared at where it should've been. Blinked. A raised square of stones—that had been its base. He stumbled towards it, choking. The base of the staircase remained. Three steps. With a trembling hand, he touched the top one. He'd walked up here earlier today.

Today. Hours ago. And now...

It wasn't...

No. This wasn't...

He shook his head. They weren't the same steps. This was the wrong place. He'd miscalculated the location. This was a different tower, not the one he'd stood upon and said goodbye to Vee.

"No." But the word choked him. Just two letters but thick in his throat. He tried to say it again as hot panic rose, engulfing the numb coldness that had consumed him since he'd caught sight of Nassau's ruin.

"Maybe," Perry said from behind him, voice hollow, "this happened after she left."

That. That could be true.

"Vee," he bellowed. That word didn't choke him. He shouted it again. And again. If she was here, she had to hear it.

He ran. He called. He ran some more. He stumbled on rock and shattered timbers, lancing pain through his ankle, but it was nothing. It was nothing.

Nothing at all.

Not against the tearing agony in his chest.

He ran and ran. He shouted himself hoarse. But there was never any reply.

Sweat beaded his cold skin, slicked his palms as he shoved unruly hair from his face, as he found himself back at the sea. He'd worked off all that hot panic and slowly, his mind was emerging from the blank depths. Panting, he blinked at the posts jutting above the lapping waves. The remains of a jetty.

Frowning, he glanced left and right, then back the way he'd come. This was the jetty where he'd left the *Fox*. Perhaps there would be some evidence of Vee coming through here. It was a slim chance, but...

Seaweed. Stones. Sand. Timbers. Rope. Rotting fish, eyes pecked out by gulls. More and more of the same, but he picked his way through it.

Amongst a knot of seaweed, something glinted. Something gold. He toed the weed away revealing a plank with gold lettering.

Before he even registered the word, dread closed its cold fist around his heart. It knew before he did.

The gold paint spelled out *Fox*.

Vee's tower was destroyed. Her boat was destroyed. Her safety and her escape. Both gone.

He didn't know what happened next. The world and time were a blank space where the only thing he knew was that the ruins of Nassau were nothing compared to the ruin inside his chest. Inside his soul.

The sun was setting when Perry found him sitting on the beach, cradling the plank of wood from the *Fox's* hull.

She said no words, but the pallor of her face said she understood.

Vee was gone.

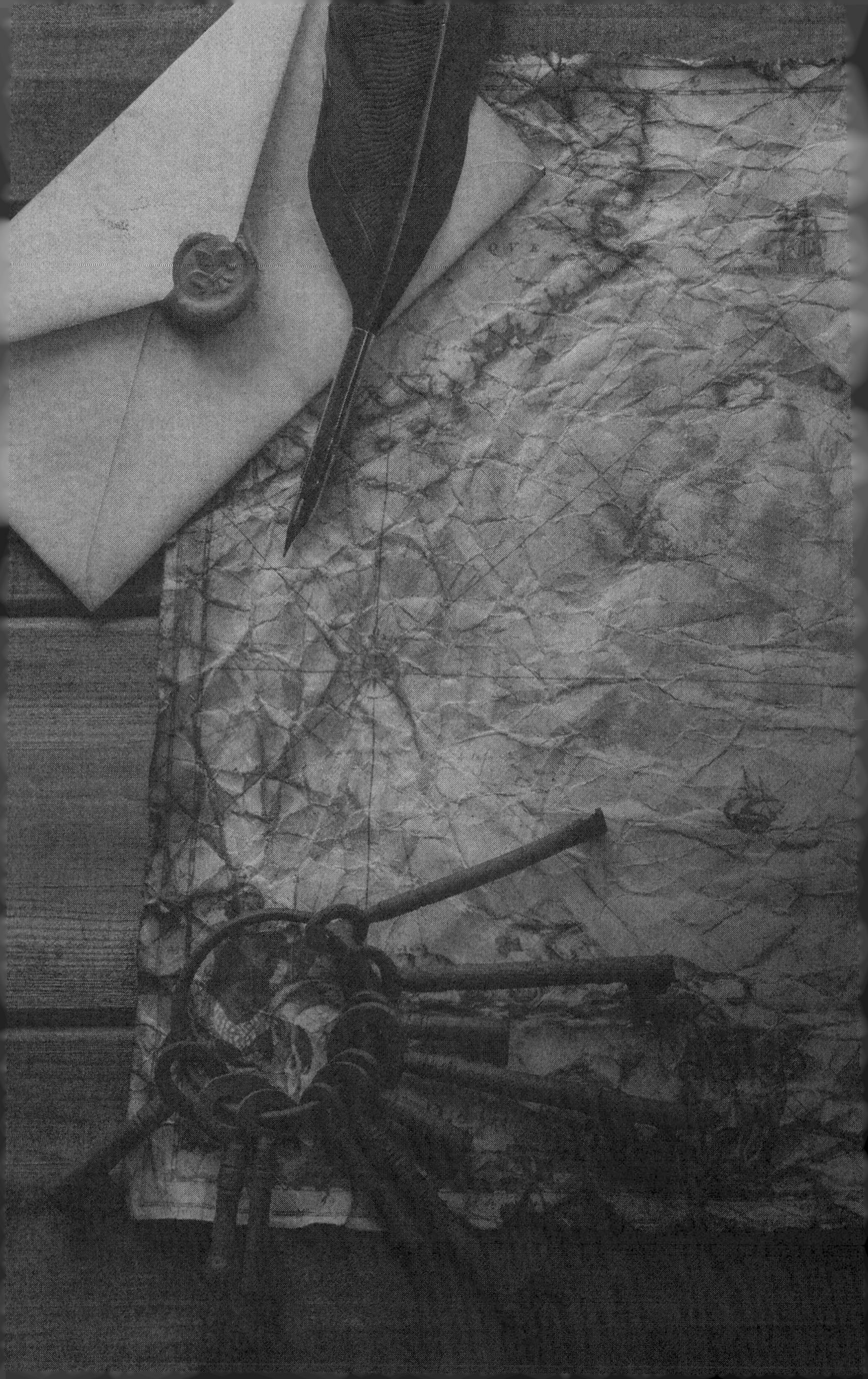

EPILOGUE

Thirsty. So thirsty.

The sea sighed nearby. Something hard pressed against her face, and—*urgh*, grit crunched between her teeth. She opened stinging eyes.

Sand. From the ends of her eyelashes, to... well, as far as her blurry vision could see. A smear of green up there. Flickering light down there.

Arms trembling, she pushed herself upright. Oh, Lords, *her head.* She clutched her throbbing temple and found a bump. Earlier... her head had snapped to one side and there'd been pain and...

The tower. The wave. The fall of Nassau. It all rushed in, making her head spin, so all she could do for long minutes was sit and breathe with her eyes screwed shut.

When she looked again, the green smear and flickering light made sense. A forest starting at the edge of the beach and rising inland to a rocky hill. The sea reflecting afternoon sunlight. Amongst the sand lay knotted rope and broken timbers. A square of canvas flapped in the breeze. Further along the sweeping beach, other flotsam stood out dark against the pale sand.

No people, though. None of the shapes looked like bodies or survivors. No beachcombers picked through the wreckage searching for valuables. She scratched a tickle at the back of her neck. The tide must've only just brought all this—and her—in or maybe no one had spotted the flotsam yet.

She groaned to her feet, muscles sore, body bruised and battered, but—she rolled her shoulders and circled her neck—no, no serious injuries. That was lucky.

When she turned inward, her gift still guttered, energy far too low to use. She brushed her not-fingers against the buttery glow of Knigh's magic where it edged her own. That had to mean he was safe.

Smiling, she opened her eyes and touched her chest. It was warm.

Now to find the nearest town. Gods knew what island this was, but they'd have boats in port, and with her skills, she'd be able to trade her way to...

Not to Nassau. Anything that had remained, she'd decimated. Nassau was no more.

She'd have to go to Yuma. With a little luck, Knigh, Perry, and the rest of the pirate fleet would still be at the rendezvous point. And even if they weren't, it wasn't as though people wouldn't notice a fleet of pirate vessels and civilian boats all travelling together. She'd find word of their location.

After wincing her way through a series of stretches that Knigh had shown her during his gruelling work-out routines, she could move a little more easily. The movements had the added benefit of revealing a number of items still upon her person, digging in as she assumed different positions. The canteen at her belt, empty. One dagger in her boot, another at her belt. The spyglass Knigh had sent her, dented. The pouch from the nuts Fitz had given her, also empty.

At one end of the beach, a stream scoured through the sand, so she made for that and followed it into the forest. Once she was past the brackish water near the beach, she splashed her face, filled her canteen, and drank deeply. The water was cool and drove away the gritty dryness in her mouth.

Lords and Ladies, water had never tasted sweeter.

It took a couple of hours to drag herself up the hill, but she managed it and along the way she found a grove of cocoplum shrubs. Their leathery oval leaves and dark purple fruit couldn't be mistaken for anything else, like poisonous manchineel, so she paused to fill her growling belly and empty pockets, and continued up the hill.

She was too tired and her head too heavy to dwell upon the battle. Or that wave or Mercia's ships.

Nassau's fleet had escaped. She'd felt them all go across the sandbar. She held on to that thought like it was a line helping her climb the hill until finally she emerged from the forest into late afternoon sunlight.

Shielding her eyes, she looked back and scoured the island. The green forest stretched on and on until it reached the glinting sea. No structures pierced the canopy. No clearings opened in it to accommodate any towns or villages. No vessels cut through the water.

Well, at least that meant she didn't have to walk back the way she'd come to reach civilisation. The island's towns had to be on the other side of this hill.

She turned on her heel and continued to the summit. By the time she reached it, sweat streamed down her face and her head pounded even harder than it had when she'd first woken up. But she would have proper food and medicine soon. She just had to…

At a rocky outcrop, she wiped the sweat from her eyes and blinked.

Forest. Rolling forest and then rolling sea.

No buildings. No vessels. Not even a trickle of smoke rising from a homestead.

No sign of humanity whatsoever.

She scoffed and shook her head. There had to be a little fishing village hidden in a cove. Exhaustion dragged on her limbs and head and dampened her gift, but she could still reach out and *feel*. Her awareness skimmed through the turquoise sea surrounding the island. There were no telltale absences of water to signal the presence of any boats. She reached out beyond the coastal waters. Still nothing. And when she blinked back to herself and turned in every direction, no sails broke the curving horizon.

Despite the beating sun, a cold pit opened in her stomach.

The island was uninhabited.

Now she was alone.

Vice & Knigh's adventures conclude in THROUGH DARK STORMS, available for pre-order now.
Read on for the author's note with behind the scenes details about *Under Black Skies* and bonus extras.

If you enjoyed *Under Black Skies*, please leave a review on Amazon and/or Goodreads.

AUTHOR NOTE

Caution: Here be Spoilers!
Read After *Under Black Skies*.

I know. I *know*.

Sorry... Please don't hurt me!

Trust me when I say:

1. It had to end there.

2. It isn't over.

3. It will be worth it.

And remember, in the author note for *Beneath Black Sails*, I promised a happily ever after for Vice and Knigh. I very much stand by that promise!

(In case you've missed any of my author notes, you can find them (together with some other bonuses, like playlists) here: https://www.claresager.com/bbssecret/)

As well as being *sliiiightly* evil, I had a lot of fun writing this book. In particular, I loved getting to reference a couple of favourite pop culture moments that have stayed with me for years.

You might've noticed Knigh's method for dealing with the kraken felt kind of... familiar. Yep, I was totally inspired by Disney's *The Little Mermaid*, which I might've watched EVERY DAY for about a year as a kid. That moment Eric skewers Ursula was so iconic, and when I was searching for a way to hurt the kraken (sorry, kraken!) other than lightning, it of course came to mind.

Then we have a less famous moment, but one that for me was much more emotionally resonant...

I **love** Bioware games. LOVE THEM. Mass Effect is my favourite video game franchise of all time (yes, even more than Baldur's Gate). When I first played Dragon Age Inquisition, there was a moment that stuck with me.

(Skip the next paragraph if you're worried about vague spoilers from a seven-year-old video game (at time of writing).)

Early on, your base Haven is attacked by the Big Bad (I said they'd be vague spoilers!) and realising they're the target, the main character, The Inquisitor, volunteers to stay behind and act as a distraction/face the Big Bad, buying time for everyone else to evacuate into the mountains. Seeing this puny mortal face the overwhelming force of the Big Bad's army (complete with flaming catapults) and then, injured, try and follow the trail of their friends into the blizzard was... I can't explain it, but it was a powerful moment for me. There's something in there that epitomises heroism, bravery, sacrifice, and, most importantly, **vulnerability**, as the Inquisitor stumbles through the cold, alone and unprepared for the elements. She only survives because her friends find her... but they only survive because she took that stand.

As soon as I played that scene, I knew I had to include a moment like that in one of my books some day, and as I planned the Battle of Nassau, I knew the time had come.

I hope you enjoyed it as much as I enjoyed writing it. And I also hope you enjoyed seeing Vice and Knigh **finally** come together properly. Of course, it isn't all resolved, yet, but... well, things are better than they were in BBS or ADT, right?!

Speaking of things getting better...

Sometimes our characters say the things we need to hear. Never has this been more true than when Vice tells Knigh in no uncertain terms that his father's actions weren't his fault.

Oof! Right in the feels, that one.

It was a hard scene to write (on a par with the final Knigh scene of this book ... broken Knigh breaks me), but an important one for Knigh as an individual, for them as a couple, and for me. Maybe it was important for you, too.

I see you.

As the dedication for this book says:

To everyone who's ever blamed themselves for someone else's decisions, someone else's actions.

There's something in us, especially as children, that looks for understanding. Why did X happen? Because if we know why, we can maybe, *hopefully,* stop it happening again.

And when we can't find an obvious answer, we look for the less obvious answer ... and often we turn inside for that answer. What did I do that made X happen? What did I do wrong that made this person do this thing?

That is how we form misbeliefs. *I am not good/pretty/smart/strong enough. That's why they did this. If I can* *only be the perfect daughter/son/student/sibling/friend/football player, the perfect **everything**, then it won't happen again.*

And those misbeliefs stick with us. They inform our decisions, our behaviours, the way we interpret the world ... everything.

That's why it's hard to shift. That's why sometimes you need to break before you can come back together in a new form. That's what I've been putting Vice and Knigh through.

That's sometimes what we need to go through.

I know there will be some of you that this resonates with. Maybe the first time Vice and Knigh bonded over 'disappointing fathers' you bonded with them, too. Maybe Knigh's fears about not knowing who to trust and his unwillingness to trust himself and his own judgement were a kick in the feels. Maybe those words Vice clings to felt horribly familiar: *everyone leaves. They leave or let you down or die.*

I cannot wait to share the final part of Vice and Knigh's story with you. I have such plans for them in *Through Dark Storms*. (Insert evil laughter here.)

But in the meantime, I'm going to wish you all the best and remind you that you can get your free copy of *Across Dark Seas* (in case you missed it) **and** the short story *Hissing Hellcats* (featuring Vice, Knigh, and Barnacle) right here: https://www.claresager.com/bbsback/

That gets you on my newsletter, which is also the best way to keep up to date on release details for *Through Dark Storms* and other cool things (like merch and maybe even book boxes ...).

Happy reading.

All the very best,

Clare Sager
    May 2021

Updated April 2022: Read on for your sneak peek of Through Dark Storms...

THROUGH DARK STORMS

SNEAK PEEK

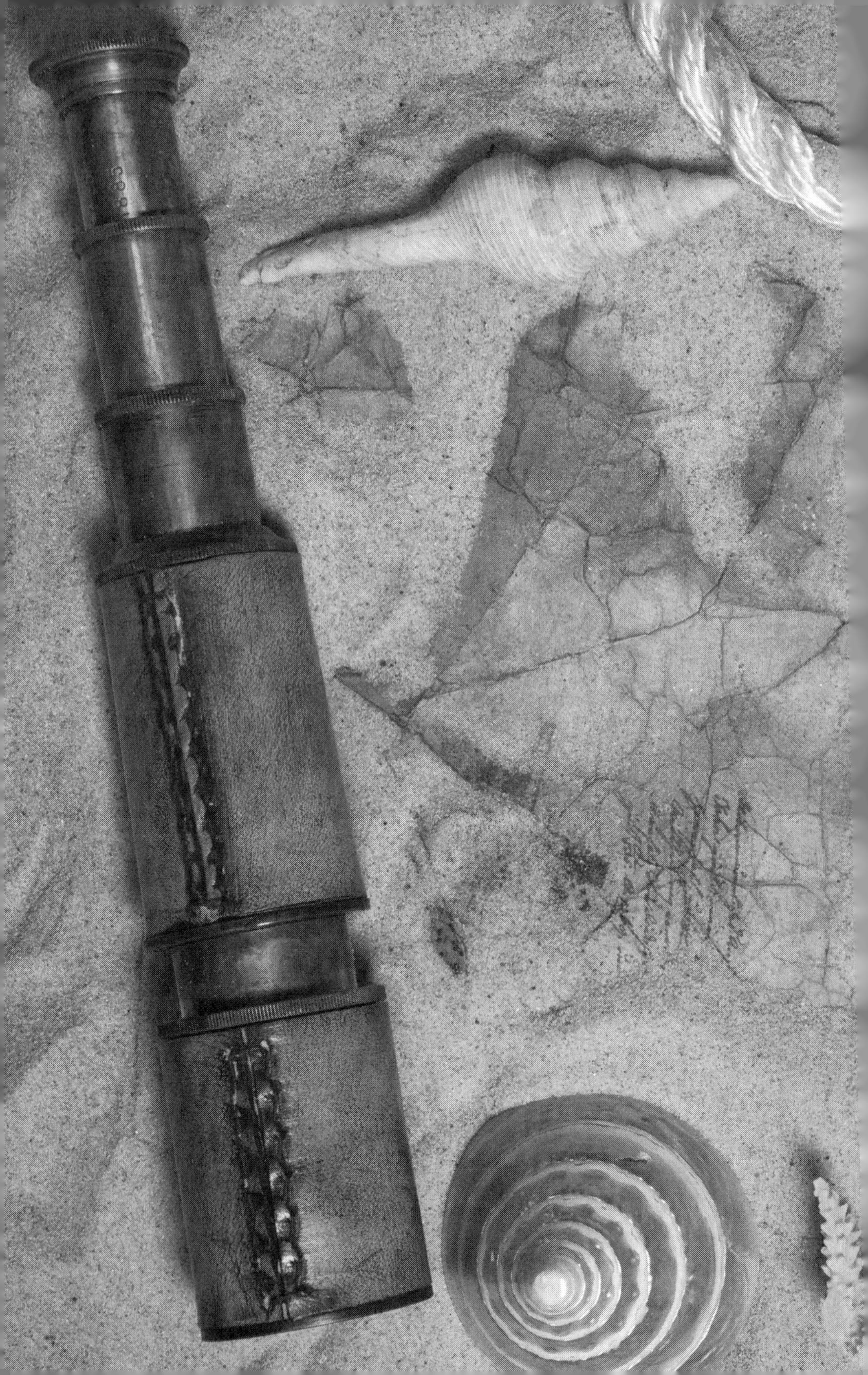

TO THE SEA WE RETURN

The sun glared down, flashing off the sea and adding to Knigh's headache. The pain was a constant companion now, thudding behind his eyes no matter how much water he drank or how many cups of willow bark tea Lizzy brewed for him.

The stark light bleached his crewmates' faces, making them squint even though their heads were bowed. It dazzled off the three white canvas forms lined up on the *Venatrix's* deck, carving them in brilliant white and deepest black shadow.

At Aedan's nod, Knigh joined him in lifting the first one. The weight wasn't much, but it dragged on his chest—another person he'd failed.

He had poured his gift into healing day after day, but this was one he couldn't save. The woman had succumbed to injuries and now here she was with two others, bound in hammocks and sewn in these neat parcels, ready for delivery into the sea's embrace.

The only comfort was that *she* wasn't among them.

Perry cleared her throat and a shift swept through the crew and townsfolk as they all straightened.

Jaw ratcheting tighter, Knigh raised his head. Perry stood close to the rail, facing her crew, lips folded.

A fae-touched person with pointed ears and pale blond hair stepped to her side. Knigh hadn't caught their name—there had been so many new names over the past week and most hadn't made it past the hammering headache—but they served on the *Fortune* and had a gift for sound. They took a deep breath and nodded to Perry.

The noon light cast her eyes in darkness, but they gleamed, betraying that she glanced this way before pressing her mouth into an even thinner line and crinkling the slip of paper in her hand.

The list of names.

The dead and the lost.

It was a week since the Battle of Nassau. A week since he—or *anyone*—had seen Vee.

A week of this constant hollow ache that had worked its way into his very bones. A week of missing her laugh and the glint in her eye that could mean she had a terrible, incredible idea or that she wanted him alone, or both. A week of missing the simple pleasure of her voice and the way she made him laugh. A week without that stretch she did every morning that trembled from her toes to the tips of her fingers and made him want to run his hands up her full length, kiss her, taste her, and gather her close to make love in the morning light.

A week without *her*.

A week was enough, Perry had said, and the council of pirate and town leaders had agreed. They made decisions about this refugee fleet—where to go, when, how to avoid the Navy's patrols. Today they'd decided to read the names of those who hadn't been seen since that terrible night, adding them to the dead to be mourned, even though there were no neat parcels for them. The fae-touched person at Perry's shoulder would ensure every ship in the gathered fleet could hear Perry's words and pay their own respects.

But not her name.

Over his dead body and banished soul would she read Vee's name.

His knuckles popped, and the canvas bit into his callused hands. It took a tug from Aedan to bring him back to the body and the ritual they'd gathered to perform. He straightened his back, squared his shoulders.

"From the sea we come." The words whispered across deck, thousands of voices murmuring at once, his own included, all bouncing back from the cliffs they'd anchored off.

In one heft, they sent the woman's body overboard. *I'm sorry I couldn't save you.* A splash, then she was gone.

They lifted the next body. This was one they'd found in the water, bloated and half-eaten, but someone had recognised the tattoo, and one of Nassau's tattooists, a woman from Hinomoto, had confirmed their identity. A pirate from one of the ships they'd lost in Nassau's harbour, sunk by the kraken.

Had someone found Vee and done this for her?

"On the sea, we live." He couldn't get the words out.

No, he would know. He turned inward. Violet light crackled along the edges of his buttery-yellow magic. Both were dim—he'd used his gift for so much healing this past week, it was no surprise. But they were both there. If she'd gone, he would know. Surely.

With a swing, he and Aedan sent the body overboard. *I'm sorry I left you.*

Perhaps he was a fool for hoping. Perhaps the flicker of lightning inside him was the only thing left of Vee.

That was what Perry thought. He could even pinpoint the moment she'd lost hope.

Not lost hope—given it up.

Yesterday, they'd spotted a makeshift camp on an isolated beach, and his heart had soared as he'd rowed the jolly boat closer with Aedan, Clovis, and Erec. Saba and Lizzy clung to the gunwales, eyes fixed on the folded canvas and charred remains of a campfire, their oars forgotten. Effie and Wynn huddled together in wide-eyed silence, hands clasped. Perry gripped the tiller, knuckles white. None of them had said a word when news of a camp had come down from the watch. But the looks they'd shared had spelled out their hope. Was it Vee? Had they finally found her?

For the first time in days, Knigh had been able to move his face in something other than a tight mask or even tighter frown. And when he'd spotted the figurehead of a ship lost in Nassau's harbour planted in the camp, he'd almost choked on a laugh. It had to be her.

Fool.

All they'd found was a haze of flies and the corpse of one of the pirates who'd attacked Nassau. He was curled up, arms around his belly as though he'd died in pain. Nearby lay the pale core of a fruit with white flesh that even the flies left well alone.

The idiot had eaten a manchineel.

His was the last body lined up on deck. An attacker from Vane's fleet, but he deserved a burial all the same. That was duty. That was honour. Even in the Navy, they'd done as much for the enemy.

Duty. Honour. Navy. They didn't mean much anymore. Not when she was lost. They were just patterns his body knew how to follow. Empty comfort.

He hefted the last body, throat burning with the memory of the laugh—the stupid, hopeful laugh he'd given at the sight of that figurehead, like hope was trying to choke him. He bowed his head, body hollow, as though that laugh had carried the last part of him away.

"On the sea, we die." As the rest of the crowd spoke, his lips moved around the syllables, but no sound came out.

Just as they had for the others, he and Aedan sent the attacking pirate's body overboard. With a splash, the canvas disappeared beneath the waves. Sunlight glittered on the ripples and the bubbles popping to the surface, and then it was like he'd never been there.

Movement from the next ship, the *Sea Witch*, made him look up. Crew and townsfolk stood at the rail, FitzRoy to one side, alone. They had no bodies to bury today, but they threw something else into the water, and now he raised his head, he could see the same happening on the other vessels in the fleet.

Orange, pink, white, and red—petals and flowers drifted across the island's coastal waters in a hundred shades. Even that hot coral pink that often came at sunset and reminded him of the flush of Vee's cheeks. It was a painting, a symphony in colour for those lost.

His eyes burned, blurred, and he gripped the rail, holding his breath like that would let him hold on to control. Because if he lost it—if he let the tears come, they might never stop.

"To the sea, we return."

He couldn't say it. It felt too much like admitting defeat. Admitting that *she* had returned to her beloved sea.

Perry cleared her throat and rustling paper sheared through the silence. The names. The list.

"Alicia. Joan."

He clung to the rail, daring to take a breath. Not Vee. She wasn't on the list. She wasn't lost, just temporarily misplaced. They would find her. *He* would find her. He had to. He'd promised it.

I'll always come for you.

The names were a litany, on and on. They'd saved many that night, but they'd lost many, too.

"Donald. Demelza."

All that work and desperation, and they'd still failed all these lives. He hung his head and let the names crash over him like a wave on shore.

At last, Perry fell quiet. But it was a pregnant silence—they had not been dismissed yet. She drew a long breath like she would go on, like there was a name left that she hesitated to say.

No.

Dashing his eyes, he whirled to face her. Whether it was the speed of his movement or that she was expecting his objection, she finally met his gaze. The shadows under her eyes, the hollowness of her cheeks—she'd aged a decade in the past week, and it seemed half of that had been as she'd read those names.

But she was not going to add another one to the list.

Jaw so tight it felt like his head might explode, he shook his head.

Perry's lips flattened and her throat bobbed. Her gaze skimmed away to the paper, then back to him. She touched the arm of the blond person helping amplify her voice and took a step closer.

"Knigh," she whispered, reaching out like she would touch his arm too.

"No." He wanted to roar it, but somehow kept his voice quiet. Still, his fists knotted at his sides. Vee wasn't dead. That wasn't possible. The world without her was unthinkable.

Rage bubbled horribly close to the surface, hot and wild. He would burn the world before he'd accept she was gone.

But... No. He had to keep himself together, somehow; he couldn't lash out. Surrender to that terrible, beautiful, brutal mistress was not an option—it had already caused too much damage to Billy, to Aedan, to so many others, and to *himself*. One breath. *Two. Three.*

Perry folded her arms, brows drawing together. "We need to—"

"Don't you dare include her." The words scorched his throat, sizzled in the air. *Four. Five.*

Because if she was gone, that was his fault. And he'd borne a lot of things in his life, done more than his share of wrong and carried the guilt of it, but this? Losing Vee because he'd left her at the top of that tower? Unbearable. Unforgivable.

"But—"

"Perry." The breaths came too quickly to count, threatening to break him open. "Please."

Her eyes narrowed and passed over him, but her shoulders sank, and she returned to the fae-touched person. With a nod, she instructed them to resume broadcasting her words. "They are the lost of the Battle of Nassau, and we honour them. Friends, sisters, brothers, lovers, fathers, and mothers, sons and daughters, too, walk in the sun and know you carry our love until we see you again in the next place." She nodded as though acknowledging a friend across a room, and a watery gleam entered her eyes. "Until then."

The crew and townsfolk nodded back. A few raised cups and bottles. "Until then."

"I will see you in *this* place," Knigh muttered, head bowed, "not the next." He squeezed the pocket containing the small, hard shapes of Vee's dagger earring and the little abalone shell: talismans to bring her home. "Until then."

Now dismissed, the townsfolk retreated to the canvas awning set up on deck, and the crew returned to work.

Perry tugged on his sleeve as she passed.

And now for the dressing down.

"Blackwood, my cabin."

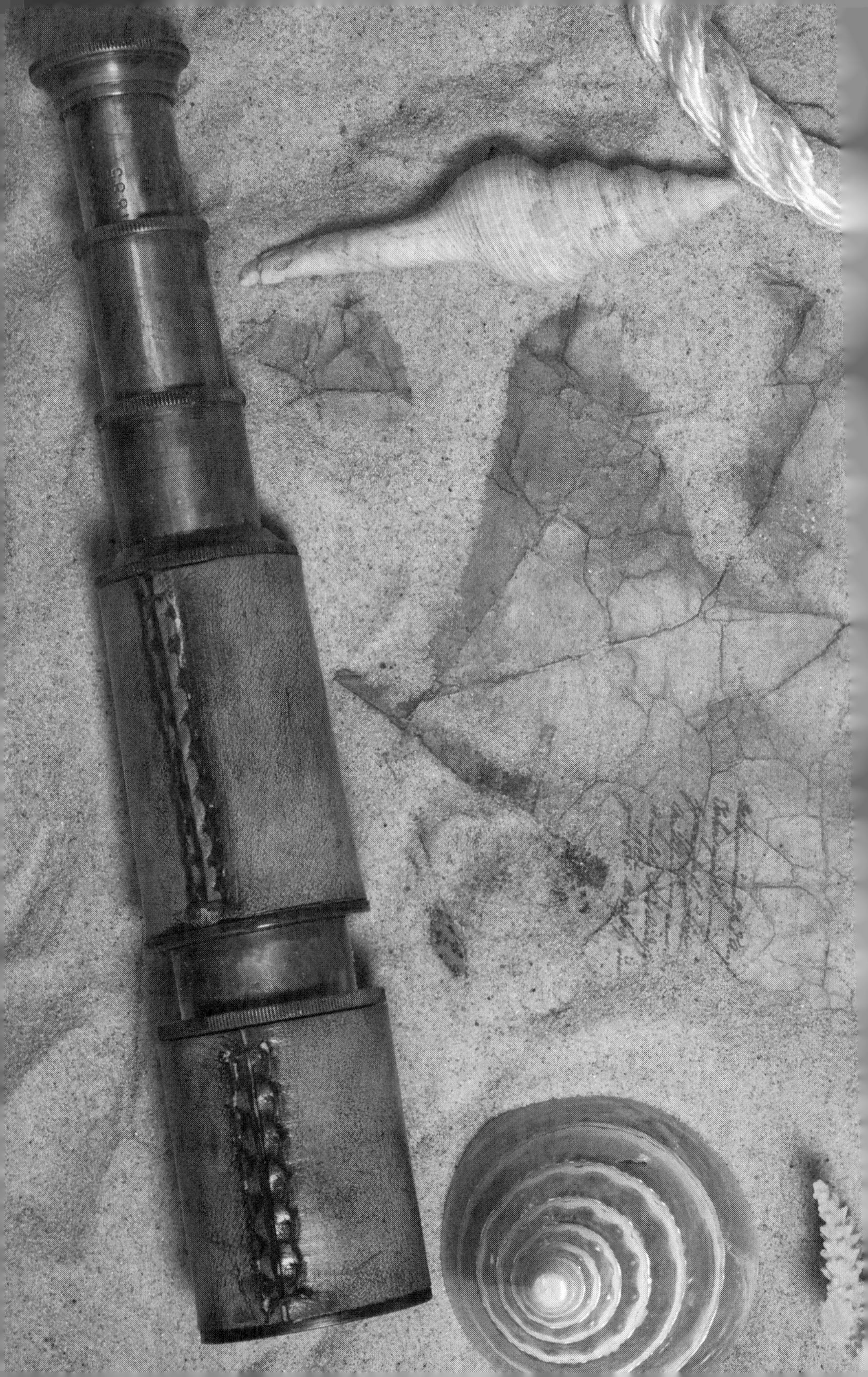

THE HERO OF NASSAU

Knigh kept his gaze on the deck, but he could *feel* their eyes on him. And although their voices were too soft to pick out the exact words, he'd heard them before—he knew what they were saying.

The hero of Nassau. He saved us.

It was enough to make him want to fling himself over the side, follow those bodies to Davy Jones' locker, and never have to hear such nonsense again. He was no hero. No saviour. He'd just done his job. The one who'd really saved them was gone.

The one time he glanced up, he met Waters' eye. The bookseller stood beneath the awning, mouth twisting in a smile of apology—no, of pity.

Good gods, which was worse, the gratitude or the pity?

It was a relief to duck into the passageway running beneath the quarterdeck, away from too many grateful faces. He followed Perry into her cabin. It wasn't his first time being reprimanded by his captain, and he'd take it as he always did, with back straight and face still. He shouldn't have questioned her in front of everyone, but he couldn't let her add Vee to the dead.

He stood to attention, despite the hollowness in his bones that groaned about how easy it would be to sink into his bunk, pull the covers over his head, and disappear from the world.

Perry stood, hands on hips, silhouetted against the stern windows. "What was that?"

"I'm sorry, Captain, I shouldn't have questioned you."

"Good gods, Knigh." She huffed, eyes shutting as she shook her head. "I don't give a damn that you questioned me. I'm talking about the fact you looked about ready to swing for me—or anyone else who strayed too close, for that matter."

Anger. The enemy inside that he just couldn't shake. Had it been that obvious? His shoulders slumped. This wasn't a military dressing down from his captain—it was something far more personal from his friend. "I didn't... I wasn't angry at you."

"Let me guess. You're angry at yourself?"

So transparent. Maybe only to Perry, though—she had a way of seeing people, even the things they tried to keep hidden. Infuriating woman.

Vee would've seen it, too. She knew him well enough.

Throat tight, he crossed his empty arms to buy time until he thought he might manage to speak. "I should never have let her stay."

There it was, the words as raw as his throat.

Perry snorted, though the grim lines of her lowered brows

and tense jaw held no amusement. "You think anyone lets Vice do anything?"

"Then I should've stayed. I should've carried her out of there—tied her up, if necessary." Why hadn't he done that? *Why?* "I should've done *anything* other than let her stay alone."

"Knigh, we all..." Perry took his arms and gave him a shake, eyes beseeching. "We're all grie—*worried*, but it isn't your fault, you know. You have to stop beating yourself up about it."

He didn't deserve this kindness. Not any of it.

He backed away, pulling out of her grasp until a chair hit the backs of his legs and he sank into it. Covering his face, he hid from the gratitude, the pity, the compassion from *everyone*.

"I can't, Perry." His voice came out ragged, pulling from somewhere deep inside, from a truth he couldn't fend off. With a sigh, he dropped his hands. "I'm sorry. I know you must be... You miss her. But it isn't just that. Do you not understand? There's no escaping it. I'm going to regret this for the rest of my life because I think..." It was as though a grip closed around his throat, but he'd started now and it couldn't be stopped.

"I think she might be dead," he whispered like that might make it less true, "and if she is, I'll never get to tell her how I... how I..."

Eyebrows shooting up, Perry sucked in a breath, the picture of realisation. "Oh, Knigh." She crouched beside him, laying her hand over his.

"I love her." It was the first sure sentence he'd managed since the truth had started bubbling to the surface. "I love her. And I let her stay in all that." A tiny figure at the top of that tower. Alone against an entire fleet. What had he been thinking? How had he let her talk him into leaving? "And now I'll never be able to tell her or hold her or..." *Talk to her. Listen to her. Walk with her. Work with her. Laugh with her. Touch her. Kiss her.* He shook his head. "Or *anything*."

Perry looked up at him, brow screwed up in confusion. "You mean you hadn't told her?"

"No, I... I've felt this way for a while, but I only just realised what it was."

Her palm slapped against her face. "Oh, Lords, *how*? I— bloody hells, *I* realised *months* ago."

In different circumstances he might've laughed—at her, at himself, but...

He shot her a frown, and she lowered her hand. "I'm sorry, Knigh. I... I just... Good gods, for intelligent people, you two can be so dense."

"You're not wrong." He rubbed his forehead, the ache still drumming away. "I know it's been long enough. I know the chances are slim." *And getting slimmer by the day.* "And I'm sorry that this might make it harder for you. But do you understand why I can't give up? Not yet."

"We'll keep looking. If anyone can survive that, it's Vice." She cracked a lopsided grin, but it didn't meet her eyes. "She's stubborn enough to tell death to bugger off—she's got too much to do."

He exhaled the ghost of a laugh. He could almost hear Vee saying those words.

"I think we need a drink." Perry rose and fetched glasses and a bottle of spiced rum from her stash. She paused at the cabinet and gave him a level look, tension around her eyes. He wasn't the only one suffering: she was bowed by Vee's absence, too. "And you can still feel her"—she pointed the bottle at his chest—"there?"

He closed his eyes and sank inside. His power glowed a little brighter than earlier, and around the gold, threads of violet flashed.

"I do." He placed his hand over his heart, trying to trap the feeling there so he'd remember when despair raised its head.

Even if the despair was right, he couldn't give in to it. Not yet. He could pretend there was hope a little longer. "I do."

ACKNOWLEDGMENTS

They say it takes a village to raise a child... Well, it also takes a village to create a book. I absolutely did not do this alone!

Some particular thanks are owed to my author wife, Las McMaster, for keeping me going with her epic cheerleading and whipping my words into shape... to my books and booze buddy, Carissa Broadbent, for her support, advice, and belief in me... to my Romantic Fantasy Shelf admin friends Jessica, Lea, and Miranda (and Catharine—you make the list twice!) for being awesome human beings with integrity, smarts, and compassion... to GLORF (Beth, Catharine, and Jen) for their unwavering support, friendship, and for putting up with my pages long posts where I think out loud and sometimes realise I had the answer all along!

Massive thanks to my beta readers, Alicia Rae, Clare D (AKA 'Chat Clare'), Mariëlle, Rachel, and Ellie for putting up with my un-proofread words. No one should be subjected to that, but they valiantly ventured in and helped identify the wheat from the chaff of my early draft.

Huge thanks to my wonderful ARC readers for down-loading and reading early copies and leaving honest reviews right from the start. There are so many who wouldn't take a chance on these books without seeing your thoughts. <3

In particular, thanks to Karolina Z for suggesting the ship names, Seahorse and Undine, and to Clare D (again!) for helping name the kittens (a very important task)!

Thanks also to Deranged Doctor Design for the epic covers to this series. I can't wait to share the cover of Through Dark Storms!

Special thanks to my mum, mother-in-law, and sister for their love and support... and for reading these books and loving them, but not talking to me about the steamy parts. (OMG.)

The biggest thanks of all, as always, goes to my gentleman, R, for embracing me for all my—ahem—quirks, flaws, and anti-social tendencies... for making me laugh every day... for getting me through the year of a bajillion lockdowns... and for all-round being awesome. Here's to another 15 years. <3

ALSO BY CLARE SAGER – SET IN THE SABREVERSE

Beneath Black Sails – Piracy, magic, and betrayal all tied up in a steamy romantic fantasy bow. Complete series.

Book 0 – *Across Dark Seas* – Free Book

Book 1 – *Beneath Black Sails*

Book 2 – *Against Dark Tides*

Book 3 – *Under Black Skies*

Book 4 – *Through Dark Storms*

Bound by a Fae Bargain – Steamy fantasy romance stories where you can learn more about the elusive fae.

Stolen Threadwitch Bride

These Gentle Wolves – Available in Flirting With Darkness, a fantasy romance & paranormal romance anthology

---

The Prince & the Thief – Quin cons from the rich to give to the poor. Fantasy adventure with darker themes and steamy romance.

Book 0 – *The Thief's Gambit*

Book 1 – *The Prince & the Thief* – Forthcoming, join the newsletter crew to be the first to know when it's released.

ABOUT THE AUTHOR

Clare Sager writes fantasy adventures full of action, intrigue, and romance. She lives in Nottingham, Robin Hood country, so it's no surprise she writes about characters who don't always play by the rules.

You can find her online home at www.claresager.com or connect with her on social media at the links below or by email at clare@claresager.com.

instagram.com/claresager
tiktok.com/@claresager
bookbub.com/authors/clare-sager
facebook.com/claresagerauthor
amazon.com/author/claresager
twitter.com/ClareSAuthor